Sword of Honor

Boundary's Fall
by Bret Funk

Path of Glory
Sword of Honor

Sword of Honor

Book Two of Boundary's Fall

by
Bret Funk

Tyrannosaurus Press
New Orleans, Louisiana
www.TyrannosaurusPress.com

SWORD OF HONOR
Book Two of Boundary's Fall

First Printing 2003. Printed and bound in the United States of America. All rights reserved. No part of this book may be reproduced in any form or by any means, electronic or mechanical – except by reviewers who may quote passages in reviews to be printed in magazines, newspapers, or on the web – without permission in writing from the publisher.

This book is printed on acid free paper.

ISBN: 0-9718819-0-1
LCCN: 2003091804

Cover art by Nesandra Oswald

For information contact:
Tyrannosaurus Press
PO Box 15061
New Orleans, Louisiana 70175-5061
www.TyrannosaurusPress.com

Praise for *Path of Glory*
Book One of Boundary's Fall

"A memorable tale that belongs in most fantasy collections."
- Library Journal

"An entertaining epic and a deftly written saga of hope, determination, and courage."
- Midwest Book Review

"Epic fantasy in the tradition of *The Lord of the Rings* and the *Shannara* series."
- Baryon Magazine

"A good start to what should be a great career..."
- Scifantastic Magazine

"A captivating tale in which you follow Jeran and his close friends on their journey from boys, to men, and ultimately to leaders of men."
- SFRevu

"*Path of Glory* makes the classic fantasy approachable for every reader."
- Weedhopper Press

"This will certainly be a series to follow!"
- Quantum Muse

"A fine and thrilling fantasy novel."
- Myshelf.com

To my mother, who taught me about honor, duty and sacrifice. Without her love, I would never have had the courage to embark upon this journey.

For your constant support and encouragement, and for other kindnesses too numerous to mention, I am eternally grateful.

I love you, Mom

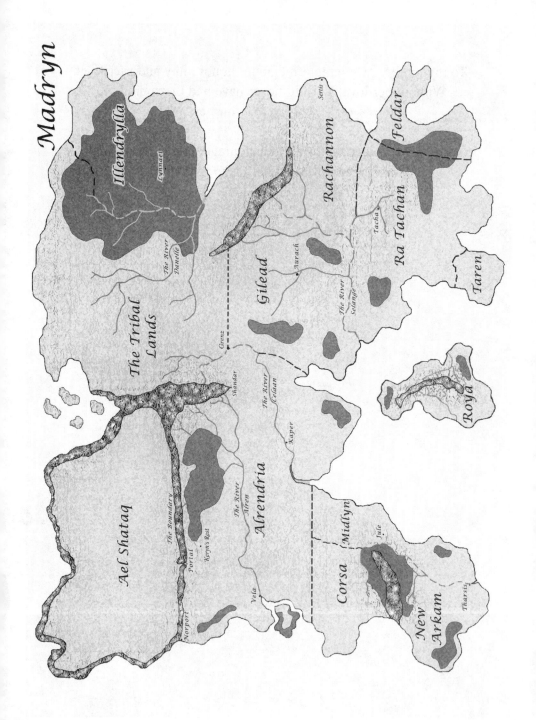

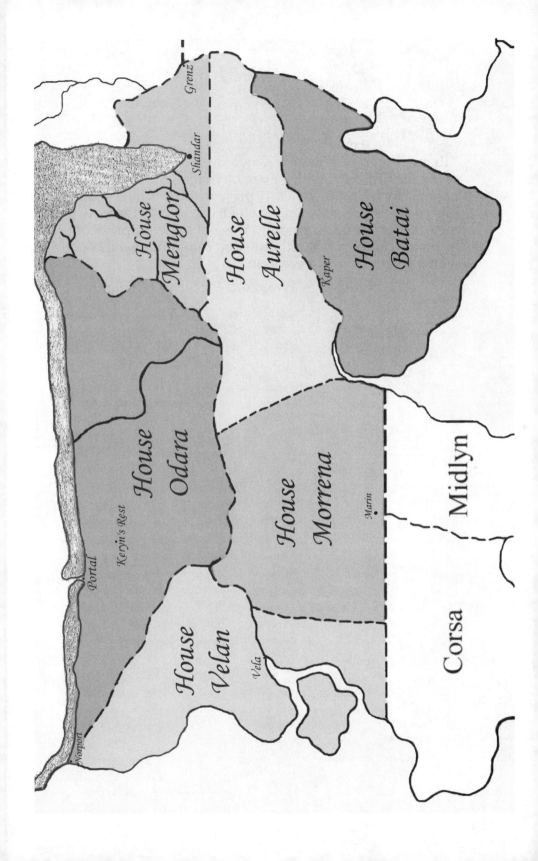

"To me, honor is a sword. A sword is forged to defend one's life. To defend the lives of others. So it is with honor. Honor protects us. It protects others. If a man understands honor, it can be wielded with deadly accuracy. If it is not understood, if it is not wielded properly, honor can hurt not only the innocent, but also those who would use it as a weapon."

– BattleMage Tyre, Lord-Protector of Shandar

Remembrance

Whack! The blow caught the young boy across the face, nearly knocking him from his feet. He staggered, but caught himself, and used the momentum to pull away from his assailant. His heart pounding in fear, he started to half run, half stagger down the stone-paved alley.

"Come back, freak!" cried the bully, and the sound of footfalls followed the boy.

The boy turned onto a larger avenue, sprinting until it opened into a market square. A few people were visible, setting up their stalls and wagons, and relief flooded through him; perhaps someone would notice his plight and offer help. To his great dismay, no one did. Other than the curious, startled stares he received as he darted past, he was ignored.

Cursing between gasps of air, the boy scolded himself. Had he waited a little while longer before leaving his room, the streets would have been crowded enough for him to escape.

He risked a look behind, then wished he had not. The three bullies who had cornered him in the alley were gaining ground. Swallowing hard, the boy ducked under a wagon and darted across the center of the square. A vendor screamed when one of the bullies plowed into her cart, spilling melons across the market.

The boy did not dare turn to look. Instead, he darted down another alley, turning left at the first crossing. Left again, then right, never looking back and praying his blind flight would be enough to lose his pursuers. Already his lungs burned from the exertion, and he knew he could not keep up the pace for long. He had to find a place to hide soon. If he slowed, the bullies would catch him, and he was not strong enough to stop one of them, let alone all three.

He turned another corner, and was surprised to find himself in another square. The plaza, this one full of people, offered safety, but the boy hesitated, afraid to step into the open. The stores across the plaza beckoned, but the square was open to the light, and he felt more comfortable in the shadows.

The rapidly approaching footfalls forced him to move. Suppressing a shudder, the boy ran into the open, praying to the Five Gods that he make it across the market unnoticed. He dodged between two moving carts, and the horses drawing them came to an abrupt stop. Angry cries followed his passage, and the boy called out apologies, tears streaming down his face.

When he reached the north side of the market, the boy tripped and tumbled behind a wagon, scraping his knees. He stopped himself from crying out and huddled behind the cart, panting heavily. Slowly, brushing the hair away from his eyes, he turned and eased his way upward, peering out over the top of the wagon.

Across the square the three bullies were fanning out, searching for him. The boy ducked down lower, until only his eyes poked out from behind the wagon. Whenever one of the boys looked his way, he crouched behind the large, ripe melons.

"What are you doing, boy?" came a cry from behind. "Hands off my wares! Turn around!" Silencing a frightened gasp, the boy slowly turned, keeping his head bent low.

A hand pulled him away from the wagon. "What's one as young as you doing out alone this early?" asked a kind, womanly voice. "Not a thief, are you?" The boy shook his head frantically. "Then you've nothing to fear, child. No need to hang your head." A hand cupped the boy's chin and lifted it slowly. He fought for a moment, then met the vendor's gaze.

She was an unremarkable woman, of average height and thinly built. Her hair was a rich brown and her eyes were kind, though they widened in fear when she looked upon him. The vendor stepped back, withdrawing her hand as if she had touched fire, and drew in a hissing breath. "Wh… Wha… What are–?" She was unable to finish.

The woman's reaction drew attention, and soon several more sets of eyes were on the boy, though everyone kept a discreet distance. The boy backed away from the people, from their whispered comments and terrified stares. As he stepped from the wagon, he lost its protection, and one of his pursuers spotted him.

"There he is!" came the triumphant cry. The boy turned toward the sound, and he saw the bullies start in his direction. One of them waved a large stick menacingly. Fear welling within him, the boy pushed through the throng of people, dashing toward the safety of yet another alley.

He ran blindly, oblivious to the carts he upset and the people he bumped into. The havoc he wreaked slowed his pursuers, but also left a trail easy for them to follow. Arms reached out to stop him, and he flailed wildly, biting down on a finger that happened to touch near his mouth. He heard a muffled cry, but neither glanced back nor called out an apology. Finally free of the market, he entered the more comfortable shadows of an alleyway.

Away from the crowded market, his footfalls echoed painfully loud, but he dared not slow. Turning at every opportunity, he hoped against hope that he would outdistance his pursuers before his pitifully weak body failed him yet again.

After only a short sprint, his breath came in quick, ragged gasps. Bright, white lights flashed before his eyes, forcing him to drop his gaze to the road before him. He turned down a dark alley, unaware of the dead end until his head contacted the hard, white stone.

The boy crashed to the ground, pain pounding through his head. Dizzy, he dragged himself to his knees, knowing his luck had run out. He saw a few discarded boxes to his left. Slowly, he crawled toward them, hiding behind their wooden frames. Settling against the wall, he put a hand to his near-fevered brow, comforted by the touch of his cool, clammy fingertips.

Footfalls reached his ears, and the boy ducked down, trying to keep out of sight while simultaneously watching the entrance to the alley. He hoped it was a Guardsman. Or a beggar. Anyone but the bullies. He muttered another quick prayer to the Five Gods, though he had long since stopped believing in them.

Once again his prayers were not answered. The three young men appeared, walking slowly and deliberately toward him, their eyes searching the shadows. All three were now armed with makeshift cudgels. "–must be around here," said one of them. "He couldna run fast."

The boy's eyes darted to the ground, and he saw a small piece of wood, much smaller than the clubs the others carried. He grabbed at it anyway, knowing every advantage he could gain might be the difference between life and death. "I saw him turn down this alley," the second boy said. "I'm sure of it."

The leader waved irritably. "Quiet!" he hissed. "If he's here, we'll never find him with you two making so much noise. Spread out." The three boys fanned out and continued down the alley, their eyes filled with hate.

The boy cringed in the shadows, certain he would be found. He drew his knees to his chest, gripped the small chunk of wood tightly in his hand, and lowered his head, trying to stifle his sobs. He willed himself to silence, hoping by some miracle that the three would not notice him.

After several tense moments, two of the boys turned toward each other. One shrugged. "I guess he turned down the next street," the other said. "Let's go back."

The larger boy cuffed his friend on the shoulder. "We'll go back when I'm ready!" He walked to the end of the alley, stopping several hands from the boy's hiding place, and peered into the shadows. The boy felt angry eyes pass over him, and he waited for the bully's excited cry.

Finally, after what seemed an eternity, the bully turned and started back toward his two friends. "Let's go," he said. "We'll take care of that freak some other time." The boy let out a silent sigh; relief flooded through him. He lowered his hand to the ground, and felt the coarse fur of a rat beneath his fingers. The rat squealed in fright and scuttled away, and the boy jerked his hand up, the stick he had held clattering to the ground.

Three sets of eyes turned toward him. The lead bully leaned forward, and a wicked smile played across his face. "There he is!" he said happily. "I knew this was where he was hiding." He advanced, urging his friends to follow. "Come on out, freak!"

The boy climbed to a crouch, stepping forward only slightly. He reached for his stick, gripped it so hard that his knuckles turned white. "Leave me alone," he said weakly. "I did nothing to you." Tears threatened to fall, but he blinked them back.

"You're a monster," said the bully, "and Lord Peitr says all monsters should be destroyed." He swung his club back and forth.

"I'm not a monster," the boy insisted, almost hysterically. He had heard those words before, on many occasions, but their sting never lessened. "I'm just different."

"You *are* different, freak," agreed the bully. "That's what makes you a monster. Don't fight us, and it won't be so bad. I give you my word." The bully took another step forward; his friends were a half-step behind.

The boy moved away, but his back smacked into the wall. His breathing was again quick, but now anger had replaced fear. His whole life he had been called names. Freak. Monster. All for things over which he had no control. His free hand tightened into a fist.

"If you fight," the bully reminded him, "this'll be more painful."

"Maybe," the boy hissed. "But it might be more painful for you as well." His eyes burning with the fires of his hate, the boy charged, swinging his stick wildly.

It slammed into the bully's shoulder with a loud crack, and he fell back, his eyes widening in surprise. The boy tried to force his way past, but the bully recovered quickly. Eyes narrowing to thin slits, he swung his own club in retaliation.

The blow knocked the boy to the ground. His stick flew from his hand, clattering across the stone-paved alley. He scrambled back to his feet and lunged at the leader, ducking under the larger boy's swing and darting between his legs. One of the other bullies made a grab for him, but missed, and the boy sprinted down the alley, hope surging through him.

A sharp blow to the head dropped him to the ground again. Bright lights flashed before his eyes. The third bully stood over him, laughing.

Crouching down, the bully grabbed the boy's shirt and hauled him to his feet. His hands scrabbled over the ground desperately, searching for something to use as a weapon, and one closed on a chunk of stone, rounded on one side and jagged on the other. With a grim smile, the boy swung the rock with all his might.

The stone smacked into the bully's head, and a loud, pained scream resounded through the alleyway. Released from the bully's grasp, the boy dropped to the ground a third time; the jarring impact knocked the wind from his body. The bully landed at his side, blood flowing in a river from his temple.

The bully's pitiful cries brought a feeling of power and wild exhilaration to the boy. He tried to flee, but rough hands seized him, and he was thrown against the wall, his head smashing into hard stone. Blackness surged over him, but he remained conscious. He stood, wobbling slightly, and watched as the two remaining bullies approached.

One bully, quivering with suppressed rage, picked up a stone and threw it. It hit next to the boy's shoulder, driving chips of stone into his cheek. "You made a big mistake, freak," said the leader. Snarling, he ran forward, his fist drawing back to punch.

The boy ducked the swing, and the bully's fist smashed into the wall. He screamed in pain, and the boy felt a surge of joy. He had to restrain himself from laughing. When the bully's second punch caught him in the midriff, his smile faded. Doubled over in pain, he gasped for breath.

The other bully joined his friend, their blows falling rhythmically. His strength gone, the boy collapsed, and for a time, the two bullies took turns, one holding him up while the other punched. Before long, the boy could hardly feel the pain. He knew he was going to die, and his only thought was to wish that he had been able to hurt more than just the one.

One particularly nasty blow knocked him from his captor's grasp, and the boy fell to the ground, landing amidst slime-covered refuse. Spitting out blood, he pushed himself to a seated position and leaned back against the corner of the wall. Through swollen and tearing eyes, he glared at his assailants, and they watched him with amusement, enjoying their sport.

Anger rushed through the boy in a torrent. His eyes glowed with hatred, and his body filled with power. He tried to scream, but the sound came out as a gurgle; more blood and spittle ran down his face.

"Look at the monster now!" cried the leader joyfully. "Let's put him out of his misery." With a shared laugh, the two started forward.

The boy's face flushed with warmth. Suddenly, his pain was distant. He still felt it, even more than he had a moment before, but it was far away, inconsequential. The alley lit up, and he saw details he had never before noticed. The smell of blood and fear surrounded him, and a dirty, unwashed odor emanated from the bullies. He raised a hand at their approach, as if to ward them off.

"He's still trying to fight!" laughed the second bully, running forward. An unseen force threw him backward. He crashed into a pile of broken, rusty tools that lined one side of the alley. Standing, he looked at his partner and asked, confused, "What did he hit me with?" The other boy shrugged, and they both advanced again.

Fire erupted behind them, and the bullies turned, jumping back when they saw another stack of boxes go up in flames. They exchanged shocked glances, and the leader licked his lips nervously. "The monster's a Mage!" he said finally, his hand trembling. "Lord Peitr says that Magi are the worst kind of monsters. He says they'll enslave us all."

The bully stooped to pick up a large rock. "He's weak now, and confused. We should finish him off before he can harm others with his powers." The other boy nodded again and picked up his own rock. In unison, they screamed, "Die Mage!" and snarling in rage, they drew back their arms.

"Enough!" said a voice from out of nowhere, full of command and radiating power. Both bullies whirled, shocked expressions on their faces. Their stones clattered unused to the ground. A man stood behind them, dressed in the dark grey robes of the Magi. He was of average height, with piercing blue eyes, thick brown hair streaked with grey at the temples, and a matching, close-cropped beard. The Mage stared at the ruffians with both anger and resigned sadness.

"Leave him be," the Mage said, lowering his voice. "The boy has done you no harm, and he's a menace to no one."

"But he's a monster, Lord Mage," stammered the leader. "Look at him!" When his reasoning gained no sympathy, he resorted to a different tactic. "He hurt Naykma!"

The Mage cast a cursory glance at the crumpled form on the cold, hard stone of the alley. Then he returned his piercing gaze to the bullies. "And what would Naykma have done to him, had he not defended himself? Likely much worse."

The Mage closed his eyes and took a slow, calming breath. "Yet if it is concern for your friend that spurs you to this dishonorable act, then perhaps I can help."

The Mage walked to the fallen boy and knelt beside him. He looked at Naykma for a moment, then lightly cupped his hands on the boy's head. Closing his eyes, he focused his Will. His talent for Healing was not strong, but he believed it would be sufficient to speed this young man's recovery.

After a moment, Naykma's eyelids flickered, and he let out a weak groan. The Mage stood up, brushed the dust off his robes, and looked at the others. "Your friend will have a headache," he told them, "but is otherwise well. I suggest that you help him to his feet and leave this place. Now." When the bullies made no movement, the Mage hardened his gaze. A small fireball formed above his hand. "I will not allow you to harm that child. Leave now, or fight me."

The leader swallowed his fear and glanced uncertainly at his companion, but the other boy was staring in awed silence at the Mage. Grabbing the other boy's shirt, the leader started toward Naykma, but his eyes never left the Mage. Together, the two bullies dragged their now-conscious friend to his feet and backed slowly out of the alley.

When they reached the cross-street, the leader yelled, "It won't be long before you and your kind are taken care of, Mage! Lord Peitr says so!" Their footfalls faded in the distance.

The Mage sighed, but offered no reply. Instead, he turned his attention to the boy who crouched in the corner of the alley. At the Mage's approach, the boy's eyes widened in fear, and he pushed back with his feet, as if he hoped to push himself through the wall.

"I will not harm you, my boy," the Mage said gently, dropping to his knees. "I give you my word." Extending his hand slowly, the Mage cupped it over the boy's cheek and focused his Will, once again using his limited abilities to heal.

The boy shuddered; a tingling warmth flowed through him. When the Mage removed his hand, the boy reached up and touched an eye that was no longer swollen. His bruises were smaller, too. They barely caused him pain. "I'm not skilled enough to remove your injuries entirely," the Mage said with a sad smile, "but you should heal in a day or two."

"Thank you, Lord Mage," the boy stammered, fighting back tears.

"You're quite welcome," the Mage replied politely. He rose, once more carefully brushing the dust from his robes. "Stand up, my boy," he said, "so I can have a look at you." As the boy struggled to his feet, the Mage asked, "Why were they chasing you?"

Once on his feet, trying not to look as dizzy as he felt, the boy answered, "They were chasing me because I'm a freak. A monster."

The Mage's laugh brought spots of color to the boy's cheeks. "A monster? I think not. You're different than most, my boy, in more ways than one, but you're no monster. It's best not to let others convince you otherwise."

The boy nodded at the Mage's words, and the old man looked him up and down. The boy was twelve winters old at most, very young to be able to use his Gift, and thin, almost emaciated, though poor diet was likely at fault for that. His white, almost alabaster skin looked as if it had never been touched by the sun.

The Mage crouched down to look at the boy's face. His hair was white, too, so white it made his skin dark in comparison, but it was the boy's eyes that held the Mage's interest. They were red, a deep red like the coals at the center of a fire. They blazed, as do many of the Gifted's eyes, shining with their own radiance.

The Mage looked deep into those eyes, lost in thought. Sensing that the child was growing nervous, he attempted to relieve the tension. "Did you know that you have the Gift?" The boy's blank expression was answer enough, even without his tentative head shake. The Mage smiled. "That you could use magic?" he prompted. "Did you know that?"

Understanding dawned in the boy's eyes, and he shook his head more emphatically. "Magic? Not me, sir. Though I thank you for what—" The boy cut off in mid-sentence and swallowed hard. "You didn't set fire to those boxes, did you?" The Mage's smile broadened, and he shook his head. The boy started to tremble. "You mean, it was… That I …."

The Mage laughed. "Yes, you have the Gift. With training, you could be a Mage." The Mage rose from his crouch and gestured for the boy to follow. "Have you a family?"

The boy shook his head. "Never knew my father, sir. My mother died last winter. My brothers and sisters are all gone, dead or taken in by someone else. I've been taking care of myself."

The Mage looked at the boy, dressed in tattered rags, with unkempt, dirty hair. "Yes, I can see that." As they walked down the alleyway, the Mage scratched his beard. "You could come with me, if you'd like. I can take you to the Mage Academy, and there you can train your Gift. You'll have a place to live. Food to eat. In several winters' time, you might even become a Mage yourself."

The Mage paused for a moment to let his words sink in. "If you're not interested, I can take you to a place where you might find work. Perhaps as a stableboy. I know some people in the city."

The boy looked into the older man's eyes. "*I* could be a Mage?"

The Mage nodded. "If you're so inclined. Are you?" The boy nodded eagerly, and the Mage's smile broadened. "It's settled then." They walked a few more steps before laughter once again echoed down the alley.

"Have you a name, my boy?" the brown bearded Mage asked. "I can't go around calling you 'my boy' for the rest of your life."

"Lorthas, sir."

"Lorthas," repeated the Mage. "That's a fine name. You may call me Aemon. Once we get to the Mage Academy, I'll introduce–" The Mage stopped when he realized that the boy was no longer next to him. Confused, he turned around.

Lorthas had stopped several paces back. His eyes were wide with shock, and his mouth hung open. At Aemon's confused expression, he fell to his knees and lowered his head in an overly respectful bow. "High Wizard!" he said in a quiet whisper, almost too low to be heard. "High Wizard Aemon. I'm not worthy of your attentions, Great One!"

Aemon rolled his eyes. "Stop that!" he said. "Stand up, Lorthas! Honestly, if I had known that being High Wizard would mean that people would be bowing and scraping to me for thousands of winters, I'd never have accepted." He reached out and pulled Lorthas to his feet. "Come on, my boy, we should be getting to the Academy."

Staring at Aemon with unhidden awe, the boy followed placidly. Together, they wove through the streets of Jule, past shops and markets, inns and houses. As they walked, all eyes were on Aemon. Lorthas heard whispered greetings to the High Wizard, and more than one person dropped to his knees at the Mage's passage. Aemon accepted their praise, but Lorthas heard him mumbling under his breath. Hardly anyone paid notice to the boy at Aemon's side, and Lorthas found the lack of attention refreshing.

They left the market district behind and entered the center of the city. The grand palaces and vast estates, more magnificent than any of the buildings in the poorer sections of Jule, amazed Lorthas. He stared slack-jawed at everything, but nothing so much as the Mage at his side. He finally worked up the courage to ask, "Are all the stories about you true, High Wizard?"

Aemon laughed, a warm, rich laugh, and looked down at Lorthas. "My boy, I doubt if one in a hundred of the stories I hear about me are true. And please, don't call me High Wizard. My friends call me Aemon."

"But Aemon..." replied Lorthas, uncomfortable addressing the most famous person in Madryn by name, "you're the greatest Mage alive!"

"Greatest?" Aemon repeated. "Likely not. Just one of the oldest."

Lorthas frowned at Aemon's humility, but did not gainsay the great Mage. Instead, he imagined what it would be like when he himself could wield magic. "Once I master my powers," he said triumphantly, "once I'm a Mage like you, no one will treat me as they did today. I'll be respected and honored, maybe even feared! No bully will push me around then! If they do, I'll make them pay!"

Aemon frowned sadly. "You have a great many things to learn, Lorthas. It's true that men fear what they don't understand. What is different from them. Oftentimes, they react violently to those things. They strike out in anger and fear, forcing their will onto others. When they do this, they make others fear them, and the cycle continues.

"Magi are not immune to such feelings. Millennia ago, the Darklords controlled much of Alrendria, and still they were not satisfied. They feared the Orog, whom their magic could not affect. They feared the Elves and the Garun'ah. They feared each other. If they had not been stopped, they would have destroyed all of Madryn with their fear, and all who lived would have been their slaves."

Aemon put an arm around Lorthas' shoulders. "After the Darklords were vanquished, the Magi, even those of us who helped overthrow the Darklords, were feared. In time, the Kings of Alrendria created laws to prevent the Magi from ruling. Rather than dulling the fear, those laws keep fear of the Magi fresh. I had hoped that with the death of the last Darklord, all of humanity would come together in peace. Yet it has been thousands of winters, and the Magi are feared more than ever, especially in this part of Alrendria.

"Those bullies attacked because they hate you. Which makes you hate them. So you train very hard to become a Mage, and one day you attack back, to settle the score. That only confirms their fear of the Magi, whether you attack out of hatred or in self-defense. Thus the circle continues. Hatred and fear creating more hatred and fear.

"We Magi have a responsibility. We must strive at all times to use our Gift for the benefit of all. Sometimes it's difficult to do, other times impossible." Aemon smiled fondly. "But these are all things you will learn at the Academy. In time, the actions of these bullies will not seem as bad to you. You'll understand that their hatred stems from their fear, and their fear from their ignorance. At the Academy we will remove your ignorance, and then you'll find that there's nothing left to fear at all."

Aemon turned the corner and pulled Lorthas to a stop. "There," he said, pointing to the building in front of them, "is your new home."

Lorthas looked at the Mage Academy, his eyes wide in amazement. The building stretched high into the sky, its towers and minarets looking down over the city. He had seen those towers before, from a distance, but the brief glimpses he had from the market district had not prepared him for the building's majesty.

The main structure was immense, fully covering a block, and crafted from a light, rose-colored stone. Secondary buildings and apartments spread out to either side, each formed of a differently-colored stone. Windows of stained glass, each depicting a different scene, reflected the morning sunlight, and four towers reached into the sky. The towers were of lighter stone, the round columns stretching up from the corners of the building. On top of each tower flew two flags, the Rising Sun of Alrendria and the banner of the Magi. One tower, the tallest, flew the sigil of House Arkam, on whose land this Academy was built, and above the giant, oaken entranceway fluttered Aemon's banner, a golden eagle in a sky of blue, to signify that the High Wizard was in attendance.

A groan pulled Lorthas' gaze away from the Mage Academy. Aemon had fallen to his knees, a pained expression on his face. "No," he murmured. "It cannot be." Tears fell unabashed down his face.

Lorthas reached out, grasping the High Wizard's shoulder. "Aemon?" he asked tentatively, a note of concern in his voice. "Aemon, what's the matter?" When the Mage did not answer, Lorthas began to worry. He shook Aemon desperately. "High Wizard?"

Aemon suddenly recovered. "What? Oh Lorthas, I am well. Forgive me for startling you."

"What's the matter, High Wizard?" Lorthas asked, "Are you ill?"

Aemon shook his head, deciding not to chastise the boy for calling him High Wizard. "No, it's nothing like that. I just had a flash of Divining, that's all." At Lorthas' blank expression, Aemon forced a smile. "Divining is a Talent some Magi have. It allows them to see a piece of the future, and the results if a certain event is allowed to happen."

"What did you see?" Lorthas asked, already afraid of the answer.

Aemon shuddered as he remembered his vision. "Lord Peitr will march an army against Jule. He will declare war against Alrendria and will try to destroy the Mage Academy. He may already be marching here."

"Will you fight him?" Lorthas asked. "He could never stand against you! You're the great Aemon!"

"Your faith in my abilities is quite refreshing, Lorthas," Aemon said wryly. "But no, I will not fight. That is what I saw with the Divining. If the Magi stay to fight, we will be defeated. Peitr will conquer Alrendria, and the freedom we have enjoyed since the fall of the Darklords will be lost."

Lorthas swallowed. "What happens if you don't fight? Does Peitr lose? Will Alrendria remain free?"

"I don't know, Lorthas," Aemon said with a shrug. "Divining only shows what will happen if a certain action is taken. Sadly, it doesn't show the consequences of every path. If we abandon Jule to Peitr, he may yet win control of Alrendria. But if we stay and fight, he certainly will. I would take a chance for freedom over a certainty of slavery any day."

Lorthas trembled at Aemon's words, but he tried to hide his fear. Aemon put a reassuring hand on his shoulder. "Be calm, my boy. These things are rarely as bad as they seem. With a little help from the Five Gods, all will turn out well." Aemon looked at the Mage Academy, drinking in its beauty for what might be the last time. "Come, Lorthas. There's much to be done if we are to abandon the city before Peitr arrives."

Aemon started across the square, and Lorthas followed a step behind. Even though he would never have a chance to get to know his new home, he hated Peitr for destroying it. "Someday," Lorthas muttered under his breath. "Someday I'll make them pay for what they've done to the Magi. Once I learn how to control my Gift, no one will ever push me, or any other Mage, around again. This, I vow." Lorthas quickened his steps, hurrying to join Aemon as he entered the Academy.

Chapter 1

"Halt!" Lord Iban called, and the column reined in behind him, stopping in a small hollow carved out of the dark forest. "We will camp here tonight. Quellas! Varten! You're in charge of the mounts. See that they're well cared for. Nystra! Take half a score of Guardsmen and set up a perimeter."

Iban turned to Charylla, the Aelvin Princess, and bowed. "I mean no offense, Princess, but these last few winters, there have been few opportunities for field practice in Alrendria."

Charylla turned cool green eyes on the Guard Commander. Straight-backed in her saddle, her thin form outlined by a green silk riding dress, she seemed out of place on horseback. Nevertheless, she maneuvered her mount deftly, and the horse danced sideways, bringing her around to face Iban. "No offense is taken, Lord Iban. We, too, are using this meeting to train our soldiers."

Prince Luran rode past, looking even less comfortable in the saddle than his sister. Short for an Elf, Luran was broad and stocky, muscled more like a Human. "Besides," he said with a sneer, "if our warriors wanted to enter your camp, it would not matter if you had all your Guardsmen looking for them." He brought his horse to an ungraceful stop, nearly falling from the saddle. Embarrassed, he glared at Iban, then continued down the Path of Riches, signaling for his nephew, Treloran, to follow.

"It appears that I must once again apologize for my brother." Charylla's said, her angry gaze following the departing Elf. "He forgets his manners. There is no excuse for his behavior." A squad of Aelvin archers walked past, all but ignoring the Humans.

"No apologies are necessary, Princess," Iban assured her. "I've known others like him. Remind me, sometime, to tell you stories of Brell Morrena."

A horn's shrill note resounded through the dark trees of the Great Forest, and Jeran shivered at the sound. "Odara!" Iban called sharply. Jeran's eyes jerked up from the ground, and he fixed his gaze on the grey-bearded commander. "To me, Odara. We have things to discuss."

Jeran dismounted and walked toward Iban and Charylla, keeping his eyes averted. As he approached, Charylla said, "Lord Iban, there are things to which I must attend. If you will excuse me." Without waiting for a reply, she urged her horse away at a fast walk.

Jeran stopped next to Iban, and the Guard Commander jumped from his saddle, landing lightly at his side. With a gesture, he signaled to a pair of Guardsman, who came running. "Hand over your reins, Odara." He gave his own reins to one of the waiting warriors and headed toward the edge of the thick forest. Jeran followed, sighing deeply.

Iban sat on a fallen log, motioning for Jeran to join him. "What do you make of this?" he asked after a long pause.

Jeran frowned, considering the question. "Obviously, there are factions. The Emperor, and perhaps others, desire to open trade with Alrendria. Perhaps with all the Human lands. They do not want to remain apart from the world."

Two Aelvin archers, dressed in dark leathers, stepped out of the trees, walking past the Alrendrians on silent feet. Both Jeran and Iban started at their appearance, and followed them with their eyes. "How can they be so bloody quiet?" Iban muttered. "I should have heard something!" His lips pressed together in a tight frown, and he waved to Jeran. "Continue."

A flash of Reading, accompanied by a stabbing pain to his head, filled Jeran's vision. For an instant, instead of seeing the Alrendrian camp, he saw a long caravan, heavily laden with goods. Closing his eyes, Jeran forced the image away. "Luran hates Humans," he said. "He believes dealing with us is a mistake. He's angry with the Emperor for proposing these negotiations, and he's angry with his sister for supporting them."

Jeran thought about it a little more. "It would be a mistake to think he's alone in his feelings. Or even in the minority."

Iban nodded, absently scratching his beard. "And what of the princess and Treloran?"

"I have seen little of the princess' son. Outwardly he seems to share his uncle's beliefs, but there is more to him than unfounded hatred. Princess Charylla is the real mystery. She claims to see the merit in trade, yet she does not share the Emperor's faith in these negotiations. If we can win her to our cause, I suspect that we'll eventually find the Elves as allies."

Iban knew Jeran no longer spoke of trade, but he continued the charade. "Having Illendrylla as a trade partner would be a great boon to the economy." Another flash of Reading hit Jeran, and he squeezed his eyes shut. They popped open again when Iban asked, "How do you think we should proceed?"

"I doubt Luran would risk open confrontation, especially against the Emperor's wishes. However, the more Guardsmen we have patrolling the forests, the easier it would be to stage an incident. Keep our sentries to a minimum and instruct them to remain in pairs, in sight of the camp at all times. If we make no attempt to defend ourselves, the Elves will take it as a show of respect and trust.

"Besides," Jeran added, pointing to another troop of archers walking toward forest. They disappeared into the thick underbrush almost immediately. "If the Elves wanted to attack, I doubt a camp this small could survive, even if it were on full alert."

Lord Iban clapped Jeran lightly on the shoulder. "You see the situation well, Odara. That's precisely what I've decided to do, and for the same reasons. You'll make a formidable commander."

Facing the Path of Riches, Iban's gaze settled on Charylla and Luran, who, despite their calm appearance and quiet tones, were locked in heated argument. "I will continue to ignore Luran and try my best to foster trust between Princess Charylla and myself. I agree with you. She's the key to alliance with the Elves."

Jeran hissed in a gasp as the view before him changed yet again. Since entering the Great Forest, his Readings had grown steadily worse, and it seemed he could do nothing to stop them. He put his hands to his temples, pressing hard. "Is all well, Odara?" Iban asked, showing concern.

In a whisper, Jeran answered. "Yes, as well as can be expected." He met the Guard Commander's stern, and confused, gaze. "It's a problem with my Gift. A result of my lack of training. I've been working with Jes, but so far our attempts to solve the problem have been unsuccessful."

Iban pressed his lips together. "I cannot afford you weakened, Odara. Especially now. I suggest that you spend more time with the Lady Jessandra." Standing, he put a hand on Jeran's shoulder. "I'll send her to you." Iban walked into the camp, calling out orders to the Guardsmen.

Jeran put his head in his hands, breathing slow and deep. Though the Readings came more frequently, they were usually little more than brief flashes. At times, when image after image superimposed itself in his mind, it was all he could do to keep from crying out.

Worse, there was no telling what would set off a Reading. Sometimes touching an object triggered his Gift; other times they appeared in response to a sight of striking beauty or the retelling of an old story. And sometimes, the visions came upon him for no apparent reason, in response to some stimulus of which he was unaware.

Jes had been helping as best she could, but she claimed to have little experience teaching, and even less with Readings. Thus her recommendation had been for him to suppress the visions, though she was not quick to tell him how to go about it. She had, however reluctantly, agreed to continue his training, though she was furious for the danger in which he had placed himself while helping Dahr rescue the slaves.

"Lord Jeran! Lord Jeran!" came a call from Jeran's right. Smiling, he turned toward the sound. Mika, one of the slaves he had freed, was running toward him. The boy, twelve winters old, had his mother's brown hair, cut in an imitation of Jeran's style; but in all other respects he favored his father, a man who Jeran had never met. Tall for his age and growing fast, Mika's blue-green eyes held a maturity far beyond their winters.

"Good afternoon, Lord Jeran," Mika said politely, stopping in front of Jeran. He stood with his back straight, like a Guardsman, and met Jeran eye to eye. Two Aelvin archers walked past. One whispered to his companion, and the other smiled at the comment. They watched Mika out of the corner of their eyes.

"Good afternoon, Mika," Jeran replied, lightly rubbing his temples. The sun was still high in the afternoon sky, but the dense trees blocked most of the light, giving the forest a twilight feeling even early in the day. "Is there something I can do for you?"

"Lord Jeran, you told me it was my responsibility to care for the children." Jeran hid a smile at Mika's serious tone and nodded as solemnly as he could manage. "The other children are restless. They're scared and tired of sitting around with nothing to do. If they're not allowed to run around until we reach the Aelvin city, then they'll grow... annoying."

Mika cast a glance to either side, to make sure no one was listening. "I know, Lord Jeran, because of my sisters. Whenever they're not allowed to play, they get into all sorts of trouble, and they usually drag others into it as well." Mika's slight blush told Jeran who they dragged into trouble the most. "Causing trouble around the Elves doesn't seem to be a good idea."

Jeran grasped Mika's shoulder warmly. "I'm glad you brought this matter to my attention. You're quite right; trouble with the Elves is not something we desire. What do you suggest?"

Mika's blush deepened at the praise. "I suggested that we play in the forest, just along the edge of it, but every time we near the trees, Aelvin archers appear. Then I suggested that we play on the road, back away from the camp, but my mother and the others don't like us out of their sight. Lord Jeran, I know they're only children, but...." Mika trailed off, unable to find the right words.

Jeran scratched his chin thoughtfully, then waved to one of the Guardsmen. "Bystral, I want you to escort the children. They need some time to play, and I think it best if they do it someplace where they won't be under foot. Take them down the Path of Riches and watch them play, but don't let them go into the forest. You may take two of the women with you, but no more. I want the children to have time to themselves."

Bystral, a large man with thick blonde hair and a matching beard, frowned at Jeran's orders. He looked at Mika for a moment. "With all due respect, Lord Odara, I'm an Alrendrian Guardsman, not a nursemaid."

Jeran stood slowly, his eyes locked on the Guardsman's. "Guardsman," he said in a cold, emotionless tone, "you will follow the orders I give. If it soothes your pride, consider yourself an escort, not a nursemaid. I'm not asking you to play with the children, though you're welcome to if you desire, but I need you to ensure their safety. If you think this too taxing a duty, I'm sure I can talk Lord Iban into making it a permanent assignment."

Bystral's eyes flashed, but he quickly suppressed his anger. "Forgive me, Lord Odara. I spoke out of turn. There's no need to trouble the commander. If I can have a moment to gather some things?"

He turned to walk away, but Jeran grabbed his shoulder. In a calmer voice, he said, "My apologies, Guardsman, for losing my temper. This duty is not so difficult, and I promise it will only be this one time."

Bystral bowed and walked away, but the heat in his eyes had dimmed. Jeran turned to Mika. "Will that be sufficient, do you think?" At Mika's eager nod, Jeran smiled. "Good. Then gather the others, but be sure to keep everyone out of the forest."

Mika saluted Jeran like a Guardsman, then ran off to join the other children. Liseyl watched her son pass, then approached Jeran with a steaming cup. "Here," she said in a soothing, motherly voice. "Drink this. It will help with your head." With her chin, she pointed at Mika's retreating back. "I thank you for humoring him."

Jeran took the proffered cup. "Humoring him? He's doing exactly what I asked. So long as he keeps the children happy, it's one less thing for me to worry about. That's a fine son you have, Liseyl. A credit to you." Jeran sipped the bitter, herbal tea. "Is it that obvious?"

"That you have a headache?" Liseyl responded. "You don't hide it that well." A wry smile touched her lips. "You're a little better at pretending you're not about to fall from your saddle, but I think an observant person would notice." Jeran took another sip of tea, inhaling deeply.

"As to why you get the headaches...." she added after a moment's pause. "I don't think many have figured *that* out. Maybe not even the prince."

Jeran's eyes widened. "I don't know what you mean." He fell silent, unable to continue. Liseyl's expression told him that she would not believe his lies anyway.

"Lord Odara, you have nothing to fear from me. I know you have the Gift. Before the war, my parents helped smuggle the gifted out of Ra Tachan. I was only a little girl then, but I remember some of what the Magi could do. I watched you the night of the storm. How else could you have known where shelter was?"

Jeran's apparent anxiety forced her to continue. "No one else knows, my Lord; at least, none of the slaves do. I will never betray your secret, not for as long as I live. I owe you and Dahr a great debt. You gave me—you gave my children—their freedom. I just wanted you to know that you have my loyalty, Lord Odara, completely."

Jeran let out a sigh of relief. "Thank you," he said, drinking deeply, surprised to find his headache already fading. "Your son keeps me informed of the children, but what of the others? I did not expect to find myself in charge of twoscore people, and I'm afraid I know little about caring for them."

"They are frightened, my Lord. So am I. We're far from home, in a place known to us only in legend. Even the allies we have are strangers. The only person they fully trust is you. Dahr as well," she added hastily, "but he's no longer with us."

She offered Jeran a sympathetic smile. "The Elves have treated us well, though, and we expect to have a great story to tell when we return to the lands of men." Her calm assessment eased Jeran's worry. "They're tired, but they know that there'll be plenty of time to rest in the Aelvin city."

"For some," Jeran laughed. "For others, the real work begins when we reach Lynnaei." He drained his cup, hissing in a breath to cool the hot liquid. "Keep an eye on them for me, will you? Lord Iban has made it abundantly clear that you are my responsibility. If there's a problem, I expect you to tell me of it."

Liseyl bobbed her head. "Of course, Lord Odara."

"Please, call me Jeran."

Liseyl cocked her head to one side and smiled, glad that Jeran had recovered enough to remember his dislike of formality. "You're not like the other nobles, Jeran."

Jeran laughed again, this time louder. "I thank you for the compliment, my Lady. Tell me, what did you–"

Prince Martyn came running from the center of the camp, interrupting the conversation. "Jeran! There you are." The prince smiled his warmest smile, his teeth visible through the scraggily blonde beard he wore. "I've been looking all over for you. Some of the Guardsmen are setting up a practice ring. I thought you might like to spar." He looked at the cup in Jeran's hand. "Ah a drink! That's what I need." Martyn waved a dismissive hand toward Liseyl. "Find me something to drink."

Liseyl bobbed her head submissively, "At once, my Prince." She hurried into the camp.

Martyn sat down unceremoniously, his breath coming in quick gasps. He scratched his beard furiously. "No one ever said these things were so irritating. As soon as we reach Lynnaei, I'm going to shave it off!" Martyn took a few more deep breaths. "What say you?" he asked again. "A little practice before the evening meal?"

Jeran shook his head. "I think not. I'm not in the mood for swordplay. Besides," he added with a glint in his eye, "I thought you swore you'd never spar with me again."

Martyn rolled his eyes. "Not against me, you fool! The Elves! Guardsman Lisandaer actually managed to strike up a conversation with one of the Aelvin warriors. He seemed to think we might be able to talk a few of them into some friendly sparring."

Now it was Jeran's turn to roll his eyes. "That's all we need! You and the Guardsmen fighting with some hot-headed Elves. We'll likely end up at war!" Jeran laughed, and even Martyn smiled, though the joke was at his own expense.

"Not this time, Martyn," Jeran told him, shaking his head. "Especially without Dahr here to help keep you out of trouble." Seeing the hurt in the prince's eyes, he added, "Maybe tomorrow."

"Come on, Jeran," Martyn pleaded. "You're the best swordsman we have. None of the Elves would stand a chance!. If Katya were here–"

A new voice interrupted, and Martyn's sentence went unfinished. "Jeran will not be able to join you today, my Prince. He and I have matters to discuss."

Martyn looked at Jes. She wore a white riding dress, cut to accentuate her striking, well-curved figure. Silky black hair fell to the middle of her back, hanging in loose curls. Her blue eyes regarded the prince coolly.

The prince smiled, and feeling impish, he jokingly said, "Of course, Lady Jessandra. I know how important your time with Jeran is. The word among the Guard is that there may soon be a union between House Velan and House Odara."

Jes offered the prince a small smile and stepped toward Jeran. "You should not believe everything you hear, my Prince," she said, gently caressing Jeran's cheek, which instantly grew flushed. "Still, I have heard it said that there's an element of truth in every rumor." She let her hand slide down to Jeran's shoulder, where it remained.

Martyn's smile faded, and his gaze shifted from Jes to Jeran, back and forth. Licking his lips, he rose to his feet. "If you'll excuse me, there are things to which I must attend." In his haste to leave, the prince nearly tripped over his own feet.

Jes' laughter followed Martyn across the camp. "He bluffs well," she said, sitting beside Jeran, "but he does not know how to react when someone plays the game with him."

"The next time you decide to play his game," Jeran retorted, pursing his lips angrily, "find yourself a different game piece."

Musical laughter filled the forest. "Remember, Jeran, our courtship was your idea." Her voice was cool, but her blue eyes flashed with white-hot brilliance. "To provide us an excuse to spend time together. You can't be angry if I add to the illusion."

Jeran refused to answer. Instead, he looked away and asked, "Have you any word from Alrendria?"

"It is difficult here," Jes replied. "There are Magi around, though they take great pains to hide their identities. Under the circumstances, I felt a similar approach on my part prudent." Two brown squirrels ran by, not four hands distant. The animals stopped and looked at them, chittering wildly, then bounded off into the forest. "However, I had an opportunity to slip away this morning."

Jeran's eyes perked up. "What news then?"

"Mathis is in Gilead, meeting with King Tarien. The negotiations for the alliance are underway, and Mathis believes Martyn and Miriam will be betrothed as soon as we return from Lynnaei."

A stick cracked nearby, and Jes' eyes flicked to the noise, wary of an eavesdropper. Satisfied that they were alone, she continued. "There's been no word of the Durange, though none of the patrols sent by Lord Talbot have returned from the Boundary. He's preparing to send a larger force to look for Tylor's stronghold."

Jeran shook his head. "That's not wise. If Tylor does have a stronghold, he'll expect us to come looking for it. He likely already has a trap ready for any incoming force." Tapping a finger to his chin, Jeran frowned thought-fully. "If you have a chance to send a message, instruct Lord Talbot not to venture into the mountains of the Boundary. If he feels that he must, tell him to be cautious. Tell him it was I who said so."

"I've never known Gideon Talbot to be anything but cautious, but I will relay your message if I have a chance."

Jes' eyes darkened, and a frown marred her otherwise pristine features. Jeran discovered that he did not like it when Jes frowned. "I don't know why I'm telling you this," she added, "except I feel that I should. There was an altercation at the Mage Assembly."

Jeran's brow furrowed. "An altercation?"

Jes nodded, though it was quite a while before she spoke. "Yes. Aemon counseled the Magi–as he always does–to offer their aid to Alrendria. Some of the Isolationists, a radical group within the Assembly, insisted that we leave the affairs of Humans to Humans. The argument in the Assembly grew heated, and it ended with one of the radicals using his Gift against another Mage."

Shock and disappointment were evident on her face. "The offender was quickly subdued, and rather strictly punished, but the message behind the action is clear. There are those in the Assembly who feel very strongly against fighting alongside Alrendria. Some are willing to fight to prevent it. By the time the Assembly agrees to offer its aid, I fear it will be too late."

"That is dire news indeed," Jeran said, though his tone lacked conviction.

"You don't sound surprised. Or overly concerned."

"I'm not," Jeran answered with a shrug. "It's a problem for another day. We have more immediate concerns." Jes' gaze bored into his very soul, prompting him to add, "It may surprise you, but King Mathis never count-ed on the Magi. They've never factored strongly into any of his plans."

"Have things changed so much?" Jes asked, shaking her head sadly. "There was a time when no Alrendrian war was fought without the advice of the Magi."

She took a moment to compose herself. "No matter. As you say, this is a problem for another day. You are still having Readings?"

Jeran nodded. "They're coming more frequently, though they rarely last more than a moment."

"What do you see?"

"Sometimes nothing. Sometimes it's just a sound, or a fragrance, or a flash of light. At other times, the landscape changes around me. I see cara-vans, or Aelvin patrols, though they're dressed differently. A few times I saw Humans, and Garun'ah, and what I assume are Orog."

Jeran put a hand over his eyes, as if merely discussing the visions made them reappear. "The worst is when there are multiple visions overlaid on top of each other. Or when the visions last for more than an instant. Sometimes it's difficult to tell what's real and what's only in my mind."

Jes put a hand on his shoulder. The touch was light, but Jeran felt a warmth suffuse him. "We will fix this, Jeran," she said, her tone comforting. "We'll find a way." Standing, Jes looked around the camp. "There's too much noise here. Let's find a place back in the trees." Beckoning for Jeran to follow, she walked into the forest, making little more noise than the Elves.

Jeran stayed a few paces back, his eyes fastened on Jes. The light breeze that blew through the trees caught her raven black hair, blowing it out in billowing waves. Her dress clung to her body, and despite his best effort, Jeran's eyes were repeatedly drawn to the sway of her hips. When he looked at her, his heart raced, and he had to remind himself that she was not several winters his senior, as her appearance suggested. She was a powerful Mage, one who had been alive since before the Boundary was raised.

They stopped in a small, secluded clearing less than three hundred hands from the Path of Riches. Jes sat and motioned for Jeran to join her. Her gaze flicked suddenly to the left. "We mean your forest no harm," she called out. "Nor will we attempt to escape into the forest. We merely desire a little privacy." Jeran looked in the direction she spoke but saw nothing. Another moment passed, and Jes added, "I assure you, we need no chaperone."

There was a sudden movement at the edge of the clearing, and an Aelvin archer stepped from the trees, all but invisible before he moved. Jeran sucked in a whistling breath and looked at Jes in shock. The archer smiled slightly, offered Jes a respectful bow, and walked off to rejoin the main Aelvin force.

"Now that we're alone," Jes said, "clear your mind." She took several slow breaths, relaxing herself. "I want you to reach for your Gift, but as soon as you seize the slightest flow, I want you to let go. Is that understood?"

Jeran nodded and slowed his breathing, clearing his mind of thought. "Once you touch your Gift," Jes continued, "I will aid you in releasing it, but the more you seize, the harder it will be to let go. Remember what happened in Grenz. If you seize too much magic, I won't be able to stop it."

"If that's the case," Jeran asked, "then why do we risk this?"

"Because you need to be able to touch your Gift, if only slightly. A Mage can extend his perceptions even if he holds a tiny bit of magic. If you can touch your Gift, you will be free of the danger you put yourself in when freeing the slaves."

Jes inhaled deeply, continuing the mediation. "And learning marginal control might make it easier to control your visions." She did not sound convinced of the last, but Jeran was hopeful.

Jeran took another breath, then opened himself to magic. As always, he could feel the flows of energy around him, but every attempt he made to seize them failed. He knew what he had to do. If he surrendered, the magic would come to him on its own. Jes swore it was impossible, but Jeran knew it to be true.

The problem is, how can I surrender to only a small portion of magic? Jeran knew that was the key, if he could discover how to do it. Time passed, but every attempt Jeran made failed. Sweat soon beaded on his forehead, but Jes was relentless, forcing him to try again and again.

Panting after yet another failed attempt, he opened his eyes. "It's no use! I can't do it."

"Nonsense," came Jes' reply. "You almost had it that time. I could feel the magic ready to rush into you. All you have to do is make sure you take only a small part."

Jeran nodded and tried again. He imagined the flows as individual strands, and he tried to imagine himself surrendering to one of them. Suddenly, he felt his body tense as a small jolt of energy rushed into him. He gasped, reveling in the warm feeling that suffused him. "Good," Jes said. "Now release it. I will help."

It took all of Jeran's effort, with Jes aiding him, to release even that tiny amount of magic. Any more would have been impossible. "It is a step," Jes said at last. "Though a small one. Again." Once more, Jeran allowed a bit of magic to enter him, and again it took all his effort to force it away.

"I've never seen magic fight so hard before," Jes told him. "Even if you seize a small amount, the rest tries to follow it." Jeran did not argue with her; try though he might, she would never believe that he surrendered to the magic, instead of forcing the magic to surrender to him.

"Again," she ordered.

They continued well into the evening. When the sun neared the horizon, and the dim gloom of twilight fell over the forest, Jes finally said, "Good. I think you're getting better. This time, extend your perceptions, but only for a moment. Then bring them back and release the magic." She wiped sweat from her own brow. "I think we'll stop after that. We've made a lot of progress."

Jeran surrendered to his Gift again, reveling in the feeling. As he had done before, he extended his presence from his body. He could still see Jes sitting before him, but he could also see the land around him. He rose up, high above the trees, and looked out over the Great Forest, which stretched as far as he could see in every direction. Birds of prey sailed the air above, wheeling in lazy circles. Below, the white line of the Path of Riches snaked its way through the forest.

Jeran lowered to the ground and moved through the trees. A glow attracted his attention, pulsating from behind a nearby tree. Curious, he approached, and he realized that he was looking at an aura, yellow tinged with green, that belonged to an Aelvin archer. Looking around, Jeran saw other auras, all of a similar color. The Elves kept themselves so well concealed that he never would have noticed them without the benefit of his Gift.

He continued on, emerging on the Path of Riches. The children stood before him, running back and forth, playing some game. Bystral watched them, a small smile on his face. His aura was gold and white, infused with a reddish hue. Two women were with him. One stared at the Guardsman, her aura colored deep red, the other watched the children; streaks of blue and gold danced around her.

Bystral called out, "Children, it grows dark! We must return to camp!"

Amidst a chorus of lamentation, Jeran moved toward the Alrendrian camp. He looked at everything, knowing that he only had a moment or two before he had to return to his body. He passed by a small party of Elves that included Treloran and Charylla. The Aelvin nobles were talking in their own, fluid tongue, and though Jeran could not make out the words, he was fairly certain that the princess was chastising her son. If the expressions on their faces had not been evidence enough, the angry, blood red spikes flaring through Treloran's aura would have convinced him.

Suddenly, Charylla stopped speaking, and she turned toward Jeran. Frowning, she squinted, as if looking for something. Jeran sucked in a panicked breath and hurried away.

He was about to return to his body when he saw Martyn talking with some Guardsmen. He drew closer, smiling to himself as he listened to Martyn retelling the story of the time he, Jeran, and Dahr had wandered into the catacombs below the castle. It had taken them a full day to find their way out again.

Jeran was about to pull himself back to his body when he noticed a figure standing at the edge of the woods. This man was different than the others; his aura was muted, the colors harder to see. Jeran moved in to investigate.

As he neared, he realized that the figure's aura had the yellow and green shared by most Elves, but the colors were surrounded by a thin haze of black. As Jeran watched, the Aelvin archer lifted a bow from his shoulder and drew an arrow from the quiver on his back. Confused, Jeran turned, but the only thing he saw was Martyn.

Gasping, his body tensed, but he felt it only in the back of his mind, as if it were another person's body. Jeran quickly withdrew his perceptions, returning to his body. "The prince!" he yelled, jumping to his feet and leaving the clearing at a run. He did not have time to explain matters to Jes.

"Jeran! Wait! You have not released–" The rest of what Jes said was lost to him. He ran through the trees, praying to the Five Gods that he did not arrive too late.

Bursting onto the Path of Riches, Jeran knocked over an Elf and shouldered his way through a cluster of Guardsmen. He ignored the angry cries from behind, thinking only of reaching Martyn before it was too late. His tenuous hold on magic was breaking, but he paid it no heed.

Reaching the center of the camp, he spied Martyn, still standing amongst the Guardsmen, oblivious to the danger. He tried to call out a warning, but as he opened his mouth, his hold on magic slipped, and the flows rushed into him in a torrent. He choked on his words, and tensed. Pained flared throughout his body.

Ignoring the stabbing lances of pain that shot through his body, Jeran forced himself to run. He looked to the trees, to where he knew the archer was waiting, and saw the dying sunlight glint off the head of an arrow. The magic continued to pour into him, filling him, and he knew he had to find a way to release it or the consequences would be dire.

The arrowhead disappeared, and Jeran, his head pounding with the power of his magic, sprinted the last few hands and dove toward Martyn.

Everything happened at once. Jeran felt his hands grasp Martyn's shoulders. Pain seared through him, originating in his shoulder and spreading in waves through the rest of his body. The pressure inside his head released and he hit the ground. Jarred by the impact, he lost consciousness. Around him, the forest erupted in flames.

Chapter 2

Martyn spat dirt from his mouth, groaned, and drew himself to a sitting position. "Jeran!" he exclaimed. "What in the name of the Five Gods do you—" When he noticed the turmoil around him, his sentence cut off. To his left, a fire raged along the Path of Riches. Flames had engulfed several of the large trees, and the fire was spreading. He stared in stunned silence, waves of light and heat rolling over him.

Elves and Guardsmen were running everywhere; someone shouted, directing the Aelvin archers to a nearby stream, where they could fill buckets to quench the flames. Lord Iban stood atop a stump, yelling for the Guardsmen to help the Elves contain the fire. Pained screams came to the prince's ears, though he could not tell from which direction. To his left he saw some of Jeran's children, the freed slave children, staring wide-eyed. As he watched, Liseyl hurried over and ushered them away.

"This forest is full of surprises!" Martyn said sourly. "What do you make of it, Jeran? How do you think it started? And why did you knock me over like that?" When Jeran did not answer, Martyn craned his neck around.

Jeran had not yet risen. "Jeran?" Martyn called tentatively, reaching out. Something about the odd angle at which Jeran lay concerned the prince. He shook Jeran gently, and his fear grew when Jeran remained unresponsive. Scrambling to his knees, Martyn rolled Jeran over and for the first time noticed the arrow.

The shaft, midnight black and etched on the side with unrecognizable characters, was buried deep in Jeran's shoulder. Three feathers, also black, adorned the end. Jeran lay unmoving, his breathing short and shallow. Martyn inspected the wound; once certain it would not prove fatal, he sighed in relief.

He shook Jeran again, but his attempts to rouse his friend failed, and the prince's anxiety returned. Jeran's lips were blue, his skin pasty white. Martyn called for help, but his words barely carried over the tumult. He struggled to rise, to lift Jeran and carry him to someone who could offer aid. Slender fingers grasped his shoulders and pushed him to the ground.

"Leave him," commanded Charylla, Princess of the Elves. She looked at Martyn with piercing, dark green eyes that seemed to glow in the light of the fire.

"I need to find help," Martyn replied, trying to lift Jeran.

Charylla's hands forced him down again. "If you move him, he will die. The poison works fast. I can help, but you must do what I say. Without question!" Her tone was sharp, but Martyn thought he detected a hint of concern. As Charylla knelt, he scrambled aside, giving her room to work. With a deftness born of experience, she lifted the arrow and probed the wound beneath.

"Poison?" Martyn repeated in astonishment. "Who would fire a poisoned arrow at Jeran?" Charylla squeezed Jeran's shoulder, and thick dark blood oozed from the wound. A low, pained moan escaped Jeran's lips.

"There is not much time," Charylla said, her eyes never leaving her charge. "Have you a knife?" While Martyn fumbled at his waist for his belt knife, Charylla placed one hand on the inside of Jeran's shoulder and pressed with all her weight. Jeran groaned louder, and Martyn cast a worried look at his friend.

His eyes shifted to Charylla, and he offered his knife, hilt first. "Press down here," she said, taking the blade and pointing at Jeran's shoulder with the tip. "Press with all your weight. It will slow the spread of the poison." Martyn placed his hand over the Elf's and she quickly pulled hers out. "Hold him tightly," Charylla commanded, and Martyn leaned into Jeran. "Removing the arrow will cause great pain."

Martyn shouted to a passing Guardsman, a broad-shouldered, quick-tempered man named Bystral. At the prince's call he came running, his eyes shooting momentarily to Martyn before dropping to the ground. "Lord Odara?" he asked weakly.

The prince nodded. "Grab his legs, Guardsman. We need to remove the arrow, and the princess thinks it won't be a pleasant experience." Bystral swallowed, knelt at Jeran's feet, and placed two huge hands on Jeran's legs, just above the knee.

Charylla looked up. "Ready?" she asked, and Martyn nodded curtly. With swift, practiced motions, she sliced into Jeran's shoulder, once on either side of the wound. Jeran spasmed, his torso thrusting up with more force than Martyn had expected. "The poison makes the pain more acute," Charylla explained. "But you must hold him still!"

Martyn leaned down with all his weight, forcing Jeran to the ground. The princess made two more incisions, forming a cross around the shaft. Using the knife to pull back the skin, she reached into Jeran's shoulder with her long, thin fingers. Jeran thrashed beneath Martyn; even Bystral had trouble maintaining his grip.

Jeran screamed as the arrowhead pulled free. Martyn saw it in the light of the fire: polished steel, gleaming silver even though it was streaked with bright red blood. The back of the head curled around in two wicked-looking barbs. Charylla studied the shaft for a moment, then tossed it on the ground at her side.

She squeezed Jeran's shoulder, and dark blood seeped from the wound. Frowning, Charylla balled a thin hand into a fist and pounded it against Jeran's shoulder. Screams echoed through the camp, and Martyn winced at the sound. "What are you doing?" he demanded.

Charylla answered through thin, worried lips. "We must remove as much poison as we can. If his blood does not flow bright red, I will not be able to heal him, even with my Gift."

"You're a Mage?" Martyn asked incredulously.

"I am *Ael Maulle*," she replied, her eyes locked on Jeran. She pounded on his shoulder two more times and massaged his arm, coaxing blood from the wound. Despite her efforts, the blood remained dark.

"You!" she said, pointing at Bystral. "Hit him." Bystral moved to obey, bringing his fist down against Jeran's wound. Jeran jumped, but even Martyn could tell that the Guardsman had softened his blow. "Again," commanded Charylla. "This time, hit him with some strength!" The Guardsman hesitated for a moment, then brought his fist crashing down. Amidst a loud snap and the tearing of tissue, Jeran screamed in agony.

Squeezing the wound again, Charylla smiled slightly when Jeran's blood began to flow bright red. "Good," she muttered. "But we have not saved him yet." She placed her hands on Jeran–one on his forehead, the other above his heart. Her eyes grew distant, and Jeran started to shudder. Martyn did his best to hold him in place while whispering a prayer to the Five Gods.

After what seemed an eternity, Charylla straightened. "He will live," she said finally, and Martyn was relieved to see Jeran breathing even and regular. "We were almost too late," the Aelvin Princess added. "If I had been any slower...." She let the thought trail off.

Turning to Bystral, she said, "Carry him to his tent. Keep him warm and make sure there is water near. He will be thirsty when he wakes."

Standing, she brushed dirt from her white dress. "Someone must watch over him. If he seems in distress, send for me."

The Guardsman stood and bowed deeply before gently lifting Jeran off the ground. "I will watch him myself, Highness." Bystral said. With Jeran cradled in his arms, he turned and disappeared into the tents.

Martyn stood as well and ran a hand through his hair. "My thanks, Princess," he said graciously. "If not for you, my friend would have died."

"He may die yet, Prince Martyn," she replied honestly. "Though his chances for survival are greatly improved."

"Who would shoot at Jeran?" Martyn asked again, hoping the Aelvin Princess would be more forthcoming than before.

She stared at him for a moment, but the shouts of her countrymen distracted her. "I must make sure the situation is under control," she said suddenly. "Tell Lord Iban that I will meet with you to discuss this unfortunate event as soon as the fire is contained."

She started to walk away, then hesitated. "I must offer you my apologies, Prince Martyn, for this attack upon you. The arrow was not meant for Lord Odara. Had he not pushed you out of harm's way, it would have been you the arrow felled, and likely nothing I could have done to save you. You have my word. The assassin will be found." She hurried away, her long legs carrying her quickly toward the flames.

Martyn stared after her in shock, then cursed himself for a fool. *The arrow couldn't have been meant for Jeran!* He had only appeared at the last instant, with just enough time to push Martyn out of the way. The prince wiped a tear from his eye. He owed Jeran a debt he could never repay. He owed Jeran his life.

Taking a deep, steadying breath, Martyn looked around. The fire still burned, but the Elves had it contained. Guardsmen ran back and forth, some carrying buckets of water, others gathering gear and mounts and hustling them away from the flames.

In the distance, shouting orders and rallying the Alrendrians, stood Lord Iban, his short stocky form silhouetted in firelight. Martyn started in the direction of the Guard Commander, groaning at the ache in his side. A hand caught his shoulder before he had made it halfway across the camp. Martyn turned to see Jes, a frightened and concerned look on her face. "Where's Jeran?" she asked, her voice trembling.

Her fear surprised Martyn, and he felt his own stomach knot in response. *Jes is a Mage! The Magi aren't supposed to be afraid.* "He's in his tent," Martyn answered. "He's alive, but not well."

Blushing, the prince explained. "Jeran took an arrow meant for me. A poisoned arrow. If Princess Charylla had not been there, he would've died. She's a Mage!" Jes nodded once and turned away. Hiking her dress up, she sprinted in the direction of Jeran's tent.

"You're most welcome, my Lady," Martyn muttered sarcastically, jogging the remaining distance to Iban. The Guard Commander stood on a different stump than before, but he surveyed the scene with the same harsh, disapproving gaze. Soot streaked his face and beard, and his armor was dull and dirty.

"Lord Iban!" Martyn called, waving to get the older man's attention.

Iban jumped down, landing next to Martyn. "This is a fine mess!" he said sourly. "A bloody fine mess." He turned back to face the forest, where all but a handful of trees had been extinguished. "And do you think I could find Odara?" he asked, not waiting for the prince to answer. "No! That fool. He's probably out in the middle of those flames."

"I know where Jeran is, Lord Iban," Martyn said, and the grizzled Guard Commander swiveled his head to look at the prince. Martyn explained what had happened, starting with Jeran knocking him from his feet. As the story unfolded, Iban's frown grew deeper and deeper.

"An assassin? Here?" he repeated incredulously when Martyn was done. "An arrow meant for you?" Iban ran a hand over his mouth, scratching his salt-and-pepper beard. "I wonder if it was a mistake to bring you after all, my Prince. Odara is well?"

"Princess Charylla cleaned the poison from Jeran's body before it killed him. He's weak and tired, but she says he'll survive." Martyn chose to ignore Lord Iban's comment about his presence, which he knew stemmed from a desire to protect the Prince of Alrendria.

"Where is the princess now?" Iban asked, his eyes flashing.

"She's helping contain the fire. She told me that she would meet us in your tent as soon as the situation was under control."

"Is that so?" Iban stared at Martyn for a long time, lost deep in his own thoughts. "Then we had best go. I would be waiting for her when she arrives." Iban grabbed Martyn by the arm and turned him around, leading him toward the center of the camp. He yelled to a Guardsman, who ran over to join them. "Jolina," he said to the thin blonde, "triple the sentries, but instruct them not to enter the forest. Post two guards outside the prince's tent and two outside Lord Odara's. There has been an attempt on Martyn's life!"

The woman's eyes widened. She saluted Lord Iban fist-on-heart, then hurried off. Iban watched her retreating form for a moment, then ushered Martyn toward the tent.

Martyn pushed through the flap, Iban a step behind. The Guard Commander threw himself into his camp chair and looked at the papers arrayed on his makeshift desk. Martyn grabbed a stool from along the tent's wall and dragged it to the desk. He sat unceremoniously, rubbing his shoulder with one hand.

Iban did not speak. He sat stone still, his expression tight, his eyes brooding. Martyn tried striking up a conversation with the Guard Commander, but a warning glance convinced him that, for now, he should hold his tongue.

Not many moments later, the flap was pulled aside, and Princess Charylla appeared. "With your permission?" she asked, waiting for Iban's curt nod before entering the tent fully. Her son, Treloran, entered as well, his dark green leather armor smeared with ash. Luran, Charylla's brother, followed. The elder Elf wore a contemptuous scowl, which he aimed at Iban. A large, red welt circled his right eye.

In her hand, Charylla held the arrow. She placed it on the desk. "Do not touch the head," she warned. "There may yet be some poison on it, and the *Noedra Shamallyn* use only the most potent."

Lord Iban lifted the arrow by its feathers and traced a finger down the ebony shaft. He turned it, feeling the texture of the wood and the burnished, golden runes. Lifting it above his head, he leaned in until the barbed head was only a finger's distance from his eyes and spun the shaft again, frowning. Slowly, deliberately, he lowered the arrow, returning it to the desk. *"Noedra Shamallyn?"* he repeated in a cold voice. Those two words were the only sound he made.

"It means 'Shadow of the Night' or 'Night's Darkest Shadow,' " Charylla explained. "They are outlaws and assassins, hunted throughout all of Illendrylla." The princess waited, and after a long pause, Iban signaled for her to take a seat. Bowing her head, she waited while Treloran walked to the side of the tent and retrieved three stools, which he carried to his mother. She sat, inclining her head to her son, and Treloran followed her lead. Luran looked disdainfully at his stool, then pushed it away. Crossing his arms over his chest, he stared at Lord Iban angrily.

"They are a small society," Charylla continued. "One which has its start nearly a thousand winters ago. It was the *Noedra Shamallyn* who allied themselves with the Darklord. They betrayed the Empire and tried to kill the Emperor, my beloved grandfather." Charylla's voice caught when she mentioned the Emperor, dispelling her calm, emotionless demeanor.

"Even during the MageWar," she said, recovering quickly, "the *Noedra Shamallyn* were few in numbers, for those of Illendrylla knew the folly of dealing with a demon like Lorthas. The traitors became creatures of the night, masters of stealth and deception. Guards were posted at the Emperor's bed throughout the war for fear that *Noedra Shamallyn* would find a way to slip into the heart of Lynnaei.

"Many hid their allegiance to Lorthas, retaining their positions in the Empire and doing their best to sabotage our efforts to aid Aemon. Others met with the Darklord himself. Some became his private guards and others his personal assassins. Still others combed the forests, looking for plants and mushrooms from which to make deadly poisons."

"The assassins, or *Noedra Synissti*, were the most feared of the *Noedra Shamallyn*. It is said that the Children of the Night only take a single arrow when they stalk a target, for they never miss. If a *Noedra Synissti* fails in his assignment, it means his death, either by his own hands or by the hands of his brothers." Charylla shifted her gaze to Martyn. "To the best of my knowledge, this is the first time one has failed."

Martyn shivered, knowing full well that, if not for Jeran, he would now be dead. Charylla turned back to Lord Iban. "After the MageWar, a few *Noedra Shamallyn* were banished through the Portal, but most were executed. Some escaped. They hid deep in the Great Forest, until none could remember their faces. To this day they are hunted, but we have yet to eliminate their society completely."

"An interesting story," Lord Iban said, his face betraying nothing. "Yet why would these assassins wish to kill the Prince of Alrendria? I know alliance between our Races is not supported by all." Iban's eyes flicked toward Luran, and the short Elf scowled, but said nothing. "But I cannot see the wisdom in attacking Prince Martyn."

"The *Noedra Shamallyn* have always desired strife in Illendrylla. If your prince had been killed, would you have believed me if I told you that my people had nothing to do with it? The death of the Alrendrian Prince would likely have led to war. At the very least, it would have ended our talks of trade and fostered animosity between your land and ours."

Lord Iban nodded. "Where is the assassin now?"

Charylla's lips turned down in an angry frown. "Unfortunately, he died. His remains were dragged from the trees moments before I came to your tent. Little remains, but my warriors are scouring the forest for others." The princess' gaze hardened, and her dark eyes flashed in the dim light of the tent. "I have made it clear that all will share the assassin's fate if any harm befalls Prince Martyn."

Lord Iban dipped his head in thanks. "I would appreciate it if you'd allow one of my Guardsmen, Willym, to inspect the assassin's remains and the area of the forest where he was found. There are few in Alrendria more skilled at tracking than he."

"Why were you so near when Jeran was struck by the arrow?" Martyn suddenly asked. "I was across the camp from the Elves, yet you were at my side almost immediately!"

The Aelvin Princess eyed him coolly. "Lord Odara came barreling out of the forest behind us just before the attack. He crashed into Luran, knocking him to the ground." Luran scowled, and Martyn looked at the Elf's bruised eye with a new understanding. He had to hide his smile.

Charylla turned a cold glare on the Aelvin warrior. "Luran's temper almost got the better of him, but I convinced him to let the matter drop. Yet something about your friend's haste worried me. I followed, and as he neared you, I saw the archer at the edge of the woods. I called out a warning, but it was not heard.

"The archer loosed his arrow just as Lord Odara dove at you. When you both fell, I was not sure which of you had been hit. I would have been there sooner, but when the forest erupted in flames, the resulting chaos made navigating the camp difficult."

Martyn scratched his thin blonde beard, but before he could speak, Iban stood. "This night has been full of tragedy," he said, "but I appreciate your honesty." Crossing the room, he offered an arm. "Please, Princess, walk with me. We should be seen together, so our peoples know there is no bad blood."

Charylla smiled slightly and took the commander's hand. "As you will, Lord Iban. Luran, take Treloran and scour the forest. Make sure there are no further surprises! Until we reach Lynnaei, the safety of the Humans is on your honor." Luran bowed stiffly, his eyes flashing murderously as he exited the tent. Treloran followed, his expression blank.

Martyn stood. "I will go to Jeran," he told Iban, who grunted an acknowledgment. The prince darted away before the Guard Commander could change his mind.

The fires had been extinguished, and the camp had resumed a more sedate appearance. Smoke still clung to the air, and Martyn breathed shallowly, not caring for the stink. He wove deftly through the tents, looking for Jeran. He was stopped only once, by Rafel Batai.

"Cousin," the corpulent man called in greeting. Rafel wore loose robes of purple silk that made him appear fatter than he really was. Numerous gold chains, each garishly bejeweled, circled his neck; and rings adorned nearly all his fingers. The light of the fires reflected off the jewelry, flickering across the pasty white skin of his face.

"Such a terrible thing," he said, shaking his head with feigned sadness. "I hope Lord Odara recovers. It would be such a waste were anything to happen to him." No true sadness reached Rafel's voice; it was as if he were rehearsing a speech. "I knew we never should have trusted these Elves. From the start I told Geffram that we needed more Guardsmen. Maybe now he'll listen to my concerns."

Rafel's expression grew indignant. "In fact, I think I'll insist that he provide me with my own guard! None of us are safe in this–"

"The Guardsmen are Iban's concern," Martyn said, cutting Rafel off. "I suggest that you leave such matters to him."

Rafel's eyes widened. "Of course, cousin," he replied, his tone careful and calculating. "Whatever you think wisest."

Martyn ignored the subservient tone. "Excuse me, *cousin*," he stated. "I wish to check on Jeran's condition."

"Of course. Of course." Rafel turned so Martyn could slip past, but the prince felt the fat man's eyes on his back as he hurried through the camp.

A commotion, the sounds of a struggle, caught the prince's ears, and Martyn ran the last fifty hands to Jeran's tent. An army of children surrounded it, many struggling to enter. Three Guardsmen, aided by a few of the women Jeran had freed, were trying to hold them back, but the adults were nearly overwhelmed. Some of the children were crying; their sobs echoed through the darkness.

A small blonde girl darted past the nearest guards, making a beeline for the tent. Martyn rushed in and grabbed her, scooping her off her feet. "What goes on here?" he demanded, his voice even. Though he tried, he could not hide his smile.

The children froze, and one, a small boy, whispered, "It's the prince!" The others gasped, and several of the older ones dropped to their knees. With a flourished bow, Martyn released the girl, setting her gently upon the ground. She scrunched her face up and looked at him angrily, then cast her eyes toward Jeran's tent, but she did not try to force past him again.

"What goes on here?" Martyn repeated, his eyes shifting between the children and the Guardsmen. The three Guardsmen blushed, embarrassed that they had not been able to subdue little children.

A boy stepped forward, showing more bravery than the Alrendrian Guard. He was little more than twelve winters old, with bright blue-green eyes and dark brown hair. Martyn recognized him: Liseyl's son, the boy Jeran had put in charge of the other children. "Mika!" Martyn said, remembering the boy's name. "Explain this."

Mika swallowed his fear and took another step forward. "We heard Lord Jeran was hurt," he said, taking a deep, fortifying breath. At first, his voice trembled, but as he continued, the words began to flow more smoothly. "Hurt bad. The children were afraid, and they wanted to see him. We came to the tents, but the Guardsmen wouldn't let us in, nor tell us what happened.

"The children panicked! I tried to stop them, but they wouldn't listen. They're just afraid, Prince Martyn. For Lord Jeran." Mika's entire face flushed red; the effort of speaking to the prince taxed his strength.

Martyn offered the children a warm smile. "Lord Jeran," he answered, trying not to laugh at the title, "will be fine. He was struck by an arrow meant for me." A murmur arose from the children, and even the Guardsmen cast furtive glances between each other. "His injury is serious, but not mortal. What he needs is rest. If you are concerned for his health, you should give him peace."

Martyn felt a tug on his shirt. He looked into the little girl's sky blue eyes. "Yes, little one?"

"Wanna see Lord Jeran," the girl said politely, blinking innocently.

"How will we know if anything happens to him?" Mika asked.

"You can see him in the morning, if you'd like," Martyn told them. "But tonight he needs sleep. I'll remain at his side until he wakes, to make sure his condition does not worsen. Will that suffice?" Mika nodded slowly, and other children accepted his decision.

"Then off with you!" Martyn said, and the children filed away, escorted by the women. Martyn smiled wryly when he passed the Guardsmen, shaking his head in feigned disappointment.

Jeran's tent was spartan, adorned with only a simple cot, two stools, and a small pile of gear. Jeran lay with his hands crossed over his chest, his shoulder bandaged in clean, white dressings. He was sleeping soundly, though perspiration beaded his brow. Bystral sat beside him, his uniform stained with blood and ashes.

As the prince entered, the Guardsmen looked up. His eyes were sunken, his face haggard, and he wiped one hand across his head, leaving streaks of black soot. Martyn, drawing up the other stool, sat opposite the Guardsman. "Has he been left in peace?" Martyn asked quietly, scared by Jeran's pallid skin and weak breathing.

Bystral was slow to answer. "The Lady Jessandra was here," he said weakly. "She dressed his wound and mopped his brow. She even tried to get him to drink, but he would not stir. She said she would return."

Martyn nodded. "You are excused, Guardsman."

Bystral's head snapped up. "With your permission, Prince Martyn," he managed, "I'd prefer to stay."

"Guardsman?" Martyn prompted, wanting an explanation.

Bystral swallowed and licked his lips nervously. His spoke barely above a whisper, and Martyn had to strain to hear. "He dressed me down today," the Guardsman said. "Made me look a fool in front of a child." Bystral closed his eyes, and a pained expression ghosted over his face.

Martyn cocked his head to the side, confused, but before he could speak, Bystral continued. "No matter that he was right, I resented his words. I wished him ill!" Bystral raised his head, and Martyn was surprised to see tears in the burly Guardsman's eyes. "Never before have the Gods answered my prayers. Why they chose today to start, I'll never know."

The prince rubbed a hand over his mouth, choosing his words carefully. "The arrow was meant for me, Guardsman. If not for Lord Odara, I'd be on that cot, except I'd have a burial shroud draped over me. Jeran did his duty. As I know you would."

His words did not have the desired effect; the Guardsman still looked ashamed. Martyn tried again. "Though you resented his orders, did you follow them?" Bystral nodded.

Martyn allowed another pause. "Then you're no more at fault for his injury than I! In fact, if not for you, he would have died from the poison. The Aelvin Princess told me as much." At that, Bystral looked up; a measure of pride had returned to his eyes.

Reaching over the cot, Martyn put a comforting hand on the Guardsman's shoulder. "Go clean up," he said. "Then return if you wish. You may keep vigil with me tonight."

Bystral stood, but before he left, he leaned over the cot and whispered, barely loud enough for Martyn to hear, "I am your man, Lord Odara, from this day forward." Martyn felt the oath behind the statement. Bowing to the prince, the Guardsman slipped from the tent.

When he was at last alone, Martyn allowed his forced calm to dissolve. "You will be well, Jeran," he said, more a plea than a statement. "I have but two true friends in all the world, and one of them is gone, wandering the Tribal Lands. I could not bear to lose you, too." He put a hand on Jeran's good shoulder and bowed his head, praying to the Five Gods, asking them to return his friend unharmed.

How long he sat there, he did not know, but after a while he felt a gust of wind. Opening his eyes, he craned his neck around, not surprised to see Jes behind him, holding the flap aside with one hand, a steaming bucket of water in the other. She nodded to him, but said nothing as she crossed the tent. Kneeling at Jeran's side, she removed the bandages and exposed the raw wound underneath.

Martyn winced at the bloody cut, crusted with dried blood and ringed with pale bluish flesh. Jes squeezed the wound until a thin trickle of red appeared, then took a cloth from the bucket and daubed it away. Her eyes were sunken and her hair disheveled, the first time Martyn had seen it anything but perfectly coifed; her normally alabaster skin was almost completely colorless. From the way she looked at Jeran, Martyn suspected that Jes shared his concerns.

"There are herbs in the water," she said at last, "which will leach out any remaining poison. Thank the Gods the Elf was there, and that she was *Ael Maulle*, or we would have lost him. Even now I'm not so sure he'll live, though she believes his recovery is assured."

"I will stay with him," Martyn promised. "If his condition worsens, I'll send for you."

Jes pursed her lips. "Send for the Elf first," she told him. "Then send for me. She has more skill at this than I." Holding up a roll of bandages, she had Martyn hold Jeran's arm while she dressed the wound.

Standing, Jes gathered her things, but hesitated before leaving. Her eyes rested on Jeran, but her thoughts were far away. "He will live," Martyn assured her. "It would take more than an assassin's arrow, even a poisoned one, to kill Jeran."

"He had better live, Prince Martyn," Jes answered simply as she ducked out of the tent.

Jeran stirred, the first movement he had made since Martyn had entered the tent. His head moved back and forth, and his mouth worked silently. Martyn put a hand on Jeran's shoulder. "Peace, my friend. I will guard your sleep as you guard my life."

Bystral returned, dressed in a clean doublet and hose. He no longer wore armor, but he still carried a sword at his hip. Silently, he took a seat opposite the prince, and together, they began the night's long vigil.

Chapter 3

Jeran opened his eyes to near-blinding light. He yawned, stretching his arms, and was surprised by the flaring pain. Then, it came back to him. He remembered the arrow…the magic…the forest exploding…the pain. Wincing, he looked at his shoulder, amazed to see no wound.

Sitting up, another wave of pain shot through his arm, and he groaned. He was in his tent, though he did not remember being brought there. A bright light shone through the tent flap, obscuring the view. Jeran looked around, concerned that neither Jes nor Martyn were with him. He had expected at least one of them to be at his side when he woke.

Dropping his legs to the floor, he stood, flushing when he saw that he was naked. Rubbing his eyes with his good hand, he offered a belated prayer to the Five Gods that it had been Martyn, and not Jes, who had removed his garments.

Jeran did not see his sword, but his clothes were in a neat pile beside his cot. He dressed hurriedly, gently massaging his shoulder. "Martyn?" he called out tentatively, but received no response.

Shielding his eyes, he stepped from the tent. "Martyn?" he called again. "Jes?" His call broke off short when he realized that he was not in the Great Forest. A long, bare corridor, lit by rows of torches, had replaced the trees. It stretched out before him, its end lost in the distance.

Gasping, Jeran jumped back into his tent. "What's going on?" he demanded of no one in particular. "Am I awake?" He felt awake. He looked around his tent again, noting several details he had missed before. Not only was his sword missing, but so was his gear, including the large leather saddle and the great Odaran banner King Mathis had gifted him. The two stools he kept in his tent were gone, too, and the floor pulsed with a strange, white glow.

Jeran closed his eyes tightly and rubbed his temples, but when he opened them, nothing had changed. Curious, he stepped out of his tent and walked toward the strange, dark grey wall, a hand extended before him. The stone was cool to the touch, but it, too, pulsed with a dim white light.

After a quick inspection, Jeran grabbed a torch and brought it to eye level. The flames flickered, but neither cast heat nor crackled with the sound of burning wood. Licking his lips nervously, he turned back toward his tent.

It was gone.

An oaken door stood in its place, lined with steel studs and dark iron hinges. Jeran pulled on the door, but it would not open. Steeling himself, he lunged against the door, hitting it with his good shoulder. The impact passed through him, and he grunted as the pain flared down his left side. His efforts were fruitless; the door did not budge. It hardly shuddered in its frame.

Reluctantly, Jeran began the long walk down the featureless hall. His footfalls were muffled; the sound barely reached his ears. For what seemed an eternity he walked, his eyes shifting uneasily from one side of the hall to another. It continued on ahead of him, the torches spaced evenly. "What is this place?" Jeran asked, happy to hear a noise other than his own muted footsteps.

He continued, his fear growing as fast as his curiosity. In the far distance, a break in the light, a darkened hollow appeared, and Jeran found himself running toward it, hoping against hope to find something that would tell him where he was.

When he arrived, he saw another hall branching off the first. It, too, stretched into the distance, its featureless grey walls an exact match for the corridor in which he now stood. Jeran crouched, considering his options. In the end, he decided to continue down the hall from which he had come.

That he had made the right choice became evident not long after the crosshall disappeared. Doors, similar to the ones that had replaced the tent, appeared each side of the hall. Excited, Jeran tried the first door, but it was locked. The second was similarly sealed, as was the third. He continued down the hall, trying each door, praying each time that the next would be unlocked.

At long last, he reached the end of the hall, with only two doors remaining. Jeran turned to the door on his right, twisting the handle and pushing on the oaken panel. It did not open. Wearily, he turned around and walked across the hall, reaching out to the last door, not relishing the long walk back to the crosshall. Before his hand touched the door, it swung open, and light poured out from the chamber beyond.

Squinting, Jeran peered into the room, but saw nothing except bright whiteness. He leaned forward and took a small step, but it helped little. All he saw were blurry shapes and dim silhouettes. Holding onto the door handle, lest it try to disappear, Jeran stepped into the room, wary of attack.

As soon as he crossed the threshold, the light dimmed, and he could see better. The chamber was large, with a high ceiling. The wall stones were lighter than those in the hall, though they glowed with the same faint light. Countless tapestries, ancient and slightly faded, hung on the walls. They depicted a variety of scenes, from glorious battles and wondrous feats of magic to serene landscapes and portraits of noble heroes. Several had men and women engaged in acts of love. Jeran's cheeks burned when he looked upon those, and he quickly averted his eyes.

Lanterns hung between the tapestries; the light from their flickering flames cast shadows over the pictures, making them appear like real, living things rather than captured scenes. In the center of the chamber hung a brilliant, crystal chandelier. The light reflected off many-faceted crystals, sending sparkles around the room.

The floor beneath Jeran's feet was carpeted, the fabric a good weave colored with alternating red and gold diamonds, but the chamber was sparsely furnished. Two large chairs sat across the room, one to either side of a grand stone hearth. Ornate bottles, each a different shade of blown glass, lined the mantle, and above the fireplace hung a massive shield, black with a white diamond. A fire crackled in the hearth, the flames glowing red and yellow. Jeran could feel the warmth from across the room.

"Ah, there you are," came a quiet voice. Jeran jumped at the sound, his eyes searching for the speaker. A silhouetted shape sat in one of the chairs. Jeran could have sworn it had not been there a moment before. "Come," the voice beckoned. "Join me by the fire. Warm your bones."

"Who are you?" Jeran called, straining to make out the stranger's features. "What is this place?"

"Come and join me," the voice called back, the whispered words carrying through the chamber without weakening. "I will answer all your questions, and give you many more to ask."

Hesitantly, Jeran started across the room, each step carefully placed, but as he drew nearer, it became no easier to determine the identity of the man in the chair. "You have nothing to fear from me, Jeran," the man said. "I mean you no harm, and could not harm you even were it my desire."

Jeran froze in his tracks. "How do you know my name?"

The man laughed, and the sound was warm and friendly. "I told you, young one, that I will answer your questions once you've joined me by the fire." He pointed a shadowy finger at the chair across from him.

Jeran crossed the remainder of the room and sat, his eyes blinking at the sudden flare of light. The room brightened around the stranger, and his features became visible. The man was reed thin, almost sickly in appearance. Bones, prominently visible beneath his exposed flesh, were covered with thin muscles and pronounced tendons. Robes of thin, white wool, pristine in appearance, covered his gaunt frame. His skin was pale, so pale it made the robes seem dark; not a blemish marred his milk-white flesh.

His face was narrow, the bones angular and pronounced. Long white hair hung in curls down his back. Blood red lips, virtually the only color on his body, twisted up in a wry grin. His eyes were red, the same color as the coals in the hearth. They burned with their own heat.

Despite his efforts to remain calm, Jeran pushed back in his seat. "Lorthas," he said, the word a whisper. Jeran's mouth was dry, so dry he was surprised he could utter the words. "The Darklord!"

Lorthas dipped his head in acknowledgment. "Greetings, Jeran Odara, grandson of my one-time teacher, Aemon." Despite his frail appearance, the Darklord had a strength about him. He held himself with confidence and assurance, and smiled almost warmly down his beak-like nose.

"What do you want, Darklord?" Jeran hissed, his own courage surprising him.

"Why, I only wish to help you, Jeran. To guide you."

"Lies!" Jeran spat. "All you speak are lies, Darklord! I need no help from you. You're a monster!" Jeran started to rise, feeling no shame in his desire to run. Lorthas waved his finger, and Jeran felt himself rooted in place. Whether from fear or magic, he could not tell.

Lorthas sighed sadly. "Monster... Freak... Demon... Traitor. I have been called all those things and a thousand more." Lorthas shook his head, a disappointed movement. "Once those words angered me. Once I would have burned you to a cinder where you sat, if I could. But I am not the same as I once was. I will not hold your words against you, for you know no others. In the long centuries since my imprisonment, Madryn has heard naught but that I was evil. How can I blame the ignorant for their fear?"

Jeran forced himself to his feet. "I will not listen to your lies, Darklord. I am leaving this place."

Lorthas pressed his palms together, the tip of each bony white finger pressed against its opposite, and touched them to his brow, as if he were praying. "Of course, little one, you may leave if you wish," he said quietly, almost resignedly. "But where will you go?"

Jeran looked toward the door, only half surprised to find it no longer there. Featureless white stone stood in its place, barring the only escape. Defeated, Jeran sank back into his chair and repeated, "What do you want of me, Darklord?"

Lorthas lifted his eyes. "I told you, Jeran. I wish to help you."

"Why should I believe you?" Jeran demanded. His courage returned, if only slightly. "Why should I listen to your lies?"

"How do you know my words for lies, young one? Have you not heard that there are at least two truths to every event, and likely as many truths as there were eyes to see it? Have you not been told how time perverts history? That history is rewritten by the victorious?"

Jeran looked less certain now; he remembered Tanar's words clearly, knew that the old Mage agreed with the Darklord. Swallowing the thick saliva that had worked its way into his mouth, he struggled to find the right words. Lorthas offered him a pleasant smile. "I've been wronged by history, young one. Don't I deserve the chance to tell my story before you pass judgment ?"

A silence ensued. Jeran stared at Lorthas, trying to hide the fear that made his heart pound so ferociously in his chest. "How could I possibly know if your words were true?"

"You desire truth?" inquired Lorthas, nodding. "Then I shall give you truth." He reached to his right, to a small table topped with two long-stemmed glasses and a bottle of blood red wine. Neither had been there a moment ago.

Lorthas took the bottle and raised it to eye level, examining it closely. Uncorking it, he filled their glasses halfway. He took one for himself and offered the other to Jeran. "Call me Lorthas. Darklord is so formal." His smile was icy.

Jeran looked at the glass suspiciously. "You fear poison?" Lorthas asked. "I've told you twice before that I can offer you no harm in this place. If I could, there are easier ways for me to dispose of you than poison." He drank a small sip from Jeran's glass, as if to show Jeran that the wine was not dangerous. When the Darklord extended the glass a second time, Jeran reluctantly took it.

Lorthas turned toward the fire, silent for a moment. When he faced Jeran again, the flames reflected in his eyes. "You think that I've escaped the Boundary." He said the words as a statement, not a question. "You fear it," he added, a small smile splitting his lips, "as I imagine nearly every creature on your side of the Boundary fears it. When last I was free, I made the whole of Madryn tremble."

Lorthas' smile changed, and Jeran thought he detected a hint of sadness. "But that was long ago," the Darklord told him, "and I am not the same as once I was." He sipped his wine. Jeran did the same, surprised by the refreshingly sweet taste. "Truth," said Lorthas suddenly. "I am still encased in *Ael Shataq*, my prison, and unless a way can be found to tear down the Boundary, I will likely be there for centuries more."

"Truth," the Darklord continued. "The Boundary is weaker than before, and I can, in a limited sense, view your world again. But I can not enter it. Yet."

Jeran furrowed his brow in confusion. "If you cannot enter Madryn," he asked, "then where am I? How did I get here?"

Lorthas laughed, and again the sound was friendly. "To be honest, I don't know where you are. But you are asleep, and you are weakened, or else I would not have been able to bring you here."

Jeran looked at the white-haired wizard skeptically. "This is a dream?"

Lorthas pursed his lips in thought, then bobbed his head. "In a sense," he said ambiguously, then laughed. "You desired truth, so I will not be cryptic. You dream, but it is my dream you see.

"It is a Talent of mine, to see into the dreams of men. I can affect things," he explained, motioning to the walls. "The walls...the doors...the wine." Lorthas met Jeran's eyes squarely. "But I can cause no harm. Yes, I can make the person fear, I can learn some of what they think, of what they desire, but I can do no lasting physical harm."

"Truth," Lorthas said again, as if emphasizing that his words were not lies. "Even in your current state you can leave here at your will, all you have to do is wish it. I was only able to find you because you shine in the Twilight World, almost as bright as I, myself, shine."

He looked at Jeran appraisingly. "Only a handful of the Gifted are as powerful as we."

Jeran sipped his wine to hide his fear. "What do you want of me, Dark–" At Lorthas' wagging finger, Jeran corrected himself. "–Lorthas."

Lorthas spread his hands, palms up, as if in supplication. "I wish only to tell my story," he said. "Events from my point of view. I am not the monster history has made me." Jeran looked at him warily, but he pretended not to notice.

"You will have power in Madryn," Lorthas continued. "You are from an honorable family with a noble heritage. What harm can it do to listen to my tale? You know some Magi, I am sure of it. You can ask them their side of the story as well. All I ask is that you listen. Is that too much?"

Jeran did not answer for a long time. He remembered Tanar's lectures, his constant reminders of how time has a way of changing history. The old Mage had often told him to be cautious of how he interpreted the tales told by others, because they would be biased by the prejudices of the teller, and all the tellers before him.

That Lorthas' words would be biased, he had no doubt, and despite the kind words and demeanor, Jeran did not trust him. But would not the Magi's memories be similarly biased by their hatreds and fears? Could there be any harm in listening to Lorthas' version of events? Perhaps with both sides of the story, Jeran could piece together the truth.

"I will listen to your words," he said at last, feigning more confidence than he felt. The room began to waver around him, and the sudden blurriness made Jeran dizzy.

"Excellent," Lorthas said with a smile. "Though I see you are waking now. Fear not, Jeran, I will seek out your dreams some other night. I will tell you my tale, and let you judge for yourself whether history has done me justice." The Darklord faded from his vision, and the world around Jeran faded to black.

The darkness lasted only a moment, then light returned. Jeran found himself lying in a warm, green garden. Flowers and trees grew all around him. He knew he must still be sleeping, for the trees of the Great Forest were darker and thicker than the thin grove around him.

Above, birds sang sweet melodies. Larks, sparrows, and jays darted from branch to branch. Squirrels and rabbits ran across the ground, chittering to each other. Jeran stretched, barely noticing the pain in his arm. He sat up, and a warm breeze blew through his hair. To his right ran a thin stream, the water babbling as it tumbled over the smooth stones in its bed.

Jeran leaned over and grabbed a handful of the cool water, splashing it against his face. The water ran in thin rivulets down his neck and into his shirt, and Jeran shivered with pleasure at the feeling. He lowered his mouth to the water and drank, finding the taste even sweeter than the Darklord's wine.

"I sat face to face with the Darklord!" he said, amazed, "and I lived!"

"That's no small accomplishment!" said a voice in front of him. "Yet in truth, you were not ready to face the likes of him."

Jeran opened his eyes, a knot of fear growing in his gut. A man sat across from him, another stranger. This one was tall, nearly Dahr's height, and broad of shoulder. By all appearances, he was Human. His black hair was shoulder length, and it hung straight. His eyes were the blue of the sky, and his gaze seemed to take in everything. He wore a brown shirt and breeches tied at the waist with a belt of rope. A sword was sheathed across his back, and he held a book in his hand; his thumb marked his place.

"Who are you?" Jeran asked.

"A friend," said the man. "A guide."

Jeran forced a laugh. "That's what the Darklord said."

"There are many guides in this world, Jeran. It's up to you to decide whose counsel to heed and whose to disregard. No one, not even your truest friend or wisest guide, can make *that* decision for you." The man smiled, and Jeran felt calm spread through him. He did not know why, but he trusted this man, believed him without question.

"Where am I?" he asked.

The man looked around. "You are still in the Twilight World, though this place is more of my design than yours." He grabbed a handful of loose, black soil and squeezed the dirt through his fingers, watching as it fell back to the ground. "This is the way I like to remember the world."

Jeran laughed again. "Are you a ghost then, that you must remember the way the world was?" Suddenly, Jeran's suspicions returned. "Or are you a Mage," he called in a sterner voice, "that you have watched the centuries pass and can remember ages long gone?"

"Perhaps I'm a little of both," the man said simply, his smile still broad. "And a little more."

Jeran stood, looking up at the blue, cloudless sky. "If you're a guide," he said after a moment of reflection, "then what advice do you offer?"

"The Darklord will find your dreams again," the man said, dipping his fingers in the stream. "Were I you, I'd stay away from him. He will tell a different version of history, and it will confuse you and cause you pain."

"You warn me that the Darklord will lie? If that's the best you have to offer, then perhaps I should look for a different guide."

The man laughed, taking Jeran's comment for jest rather than insult. "Oh, no doubt the tale he spins will contain truth, at least the truth as he sees it. But his truths may be different than yours, as all people's truths are different from real truth.

"Only the Gods know what's really true," the man concluded, though he paused at the last and ran a finger down the line of his jaw. "Sometimes I'm not too sure of them, either."

"Should I fear the Darklord? He claims he cannot hurt me here."

"You would be wise to fear Lorthas," the stranger replied, "but he told you true. He has no powers in the Twilight World that you, too, do not possess."

Jeran frowned, but before he could ask another question, a great, bellowing voice reverberated through the air. "Brother?" it called. "Where are you hiding? It is time to hunt!"

The stranger offered Jeran a weary smile. "It seems that I'll have no time to read today. I'd like to stay and answer your questions, Jeran, but my brother gets agitated if I delay his hunts too long. We will meet again. If you wish it, perhaps I will offer you more counsel then."

The world blurred slightly, and the man smiled. "Besides, it seems you are about to wake." Before Jeran could reply, the world faded to black.

Jeran noticed the pain in his shoulder before anything else. It had faded to a dull throb while he talked to the stranger, but now it returned in full force. Groaning, he opened his eyes, surprised to see faces hovering above him. Martyn was there, as was the Guardsman, Bystral. Jes stood to one side, her bright blue eyes boring into him.

He struggled to sit up, but Martyn pushed him back onto the cot. Jeran was surprised at how easily he yielded to the prince's touch. "Rest," the prince commanded. "You're not yet well. The poison has been leached from your body, but you still suffer from some of its effects."

"Poison?" Jeran asked weakly, turning to look at the wound. The throbbing was worse than a moment before, but Jeran could see nothing. The wound was bound with thick, white bandages; not even a hint of blood showed through.

Martyn nodded. "Poison," he repeated, and told Jeran what had happened since he lost consciousness. He listened in astonishment as Martyn explained about the fire, Charylla's appearance, and the *Noedra Shamallyn*, nervously licking dry, cracked lips. Bystral knelt beside him, holding a cup to Jeran's mouth. He drank greedily, relishing the feel of the cool water as it ran down his throat.

Jeran turned his head toward the Guardsman. "It seems that I owe you my life. You have my thanks."

Bystral smiled weakly, but said only, "I am your man, Lord Odara. My sword and my life are yours."

The intensity with which the Guardsman spoke surprised Jeran, but he did not gainsay him. Instead, he turned to Martyn. "I can't see what advantage these *Noedra Shamallyn* could hope to gain by killing you. Unrest in Alrendria would certainly not aid them here." The Aelvin words were alien to him, but Jeran felt the evil in the name even as they rolled off his tongue. He had dark suspicions as to the attack's motivation, but he dared not voice them aloud.

A new voice spoke from the tent flap. "The Shadows of the Night serve the Darklord," Charylla said, appraising Jeran from across the tent. "Though he is forever imprisoned in *Ael Shataq,* anything that leads toward peace between the Three Races is a threat to him. Trade with Alrendria is far from military alliance, but it is a step toward lasting peace. These traitors to the Empire will stop at nothing to destroy what we try to build."

The Aelvin Princess knelt at Jeran's side. "I will inspect your injury," she said matter-of-factly, not even pretending to ask his permission. She unwound the dressing from his arm and examined the wound. The cross cut into his arm had blackened at the edges; the tissue looked dead and dry. The skin beneath was pink, though, and the wound appeared to be healing, though it would leave a scar.

Charylla squeezed Jeran's shoulder, and he fought not to cry out. A thin trickle of bright red blood flowed from the wound, and Charylla smiled faintly as she daubed it away. "The poison is gone," she said triumphantly, "and you will heal in time." Green eyes met Jeran's blue. "If you wish it, I can heal this for you, and you will not have a scar."

Jeran considered her offer. His mistrust of magic had lessened over the last season, but he was still uncomfortable with people wielding it around him. He cast a quick glance at Jes, but the black-haired Mage ignored his unspoken question. To the princess, he said, "I'd be honored, Highness."

Charylla placed her hands on the wound and closed her eyes. Jeran thought he felt something, a vibration originating from within the Aelvin woman. Suddenly, he felt a tingle spread through his shoulder, suffusing his entire arm. He sucked in a breath, and heard Bystral mutter, "A miracle." Martyn watched the Healing in awe.

The feeling lasted for several moments, and was gone as suddenly as it had appeared. Charylla drew a slow breath, then said, "It is done. You will be weak for a day or two, but it will heal without scarring." She removed her hands, and Jeran looked at his arm. The mass of blackened tissue was gone; a faint cross of pink flesh had replaced it.

Jeran stretched his arm over his head, surprised to discover that he had full range of motion. "I thank you, Princess," he said, and she bowed in acknowledgment. He went to stand, but memories of his dream came back to him. Peeking under the covers, he was only half surprised to find himself unclothed. His cheeks flushed red, and he drew the blanket tightly around him. "Do you think the assassins will make another attempt?" he asked to hide his embarrassment.

Charylla pretended not to notice, but Martyn's eyes were laughing. "I do not know for certain," she said at last. "The *Noedra Synissti* have never before failed, and this must wound their pride greatly. Prince Martyn may yet be in some danger."

At the Alrendrians' worried expressions, she added, "We are aware of their interest now, which will make them more cautious. Perhaps they will try to find a different way to foment dissent between our peoples."

"Either way," Jeran stated, "we must be wary."

Charylla agreed. "I have already warned Luran that the safety of the Alrendrians is on his honor. We will arrive in Lynnaei without incident, Lord Odara."

"I'm happy to hear that," he said, casting his eyes about the tent. "If you'll excuse me, I wish to dress and walk the camp. It would be best if I were seen outside, whole and unharmed. If any damage to our negotiations was done by the assassin's arrow, perhaps we can undo it with quick action."

"You are wise beyond your winters, Lord Odara," Charylla said graciously. "Lord Iban suggested much the same to me yesterday." Her eyes darted to the blankets, and the hint of a smile twisted up the corners of her mouth. "I will give you your privacy." Standing, she walked silently out of the tent.

Jes left too, but the stony, cold gaze she cast in Jeran's direction informed him that they had much to discuss. He did not look forward to that discussion.

"You look exhausted, Guardsman," Jeran said to Bystral. "Go and rest. I will prevail upon Lord Iban to halt our travels one day, that I might recover my strength." Jeran reached out and clasped Bystral by the shoulder. "And again, thank you."

Bystral saluted fist-on-heart, then left the tent. With only Martyn remaining, Jeran stood and grabbed his clothes. He dressed hurriedly, eager to be out of the confines of the tent and back in the open air. Once dressed, he grabbed his sword, sheathing the shining blade at his side.

Martyn watched him with an amused expression, but when Jeran's eyes met his, the smile disappeared. "I owe you thanks, Jeran," he said solemnly. "You saved my life. I don't know where you came from, or how you knew of the assassin, but you were there nonetheless. You've always been my shield. You and Dahr. I often resented it, resented that you were given freedom, and I was coddled like an infant."

Jeran listened in stunned silence. "But no longer," Martyn assured him. "I see my father's wisdom now, and my own childishness. I'm grateful to you. And ashamed of myself."

Jeran laughed and drew Martyn into a great bear hug. "You fool!" he said jovially. "You don't have to be ashamed! In your place, I'd have felt the same. I saved your life, true, but I would have done the same for anyone in the party, including foul-tempered Elorn." Jeran pushed Martyn away and held his head up proudly, speaking with a feigned haughtiness. "Don't let my legendary heroism swell your head, my Prince."

"Don't let *your* overwhelming arrogance allow you to overestimate your worth, Odara," the prince warned in a cool tone, hiding his mirth. "Else you may find yourself Lord of the Kitchens!" Both laughed.

Together they left the tent, and Jeran was instantly mobbed by children. "Lord Jeran! Lord Jeran!" they called, hugging him tightly.

Jeran laughed as they came, and knelt, hugging each to his chest and tossing the smallest into the air, despite the pain to his shoulder. "It's good to see you again!" he said, laughing all the more.

Mika approached, always the leader, and the others fell silent. "We heard you were shot," he said. "That you were near death. Even the Guardsmen and Lord Iban were worried."

Jeran smiled and clasped Mika's shoulder; with his other hand, he tousled the hair of Mika's sister, Ryanda. "I am well!" he said, lifting his arms and spinning around, daring them to find any wounds. "I was shot with an arrow in service of the prince. It's a risk we all face when we swear our loyalty to another. But the wound was not fatal, as you can plainly see."

He picked up Ryanda and looked her in the eyes. "In fact, it's hardly more than a scratch!" The little blonde girl smiled back and pulled Jeran into an embrace.

"I am glad you are well, Human," said a cold voice. Luran stood on the far side of the children, his eyes boring into Jeran with intense hatred. "Making you pay for your insult will be all the more rewarding." He strode forward boldly, without a care for the children he was about to trample. They parted before him, scrambling to get out of his way.

"What's the meaning of this?" Martyn said defiantly. He stepped between Jeran and Luran, but the Elf hardly slowed. Quick and graceful, he slipped around the prince, stopping face to face with Jeran.

Luran looked Jeran up and down, sneering in disgust. "You knock me to the ground like a sack of oats," he said coldly, "and offer no apologies. You consort with the Wildmen, yet believe we will allow it to go unpunished. Your crimes are numerous, Human," –Luran almost spat the word– "and it is time you paid for them."

He looked at Ryanda, wide-eyed and nearly crying. "Or would you rather hide your honor behind this child?"

Meeting Luran's gaze levelly, he set Ryanda on the ground and bade her join her brother. "I meant no disrespect, Luran. Truth be told, I don't even remember coming upon you yesterday. Doubtless, it happened in my rush to save Prince Martyn."

"Lies!" Luran hissed, drawing a hand's length of steel from his scabbard. "Will you face me, Human, or will you make me cut you down here?"

"Such a cowardly act will surely restore your honor," Martyn muttered.

Luran sneered, but did not deign to look upon the prince; his eyes remained locked on Jeran. "Draw your blade, Human. This is your last warning."

"Luran, you go too far!" All heads swiveled toward the new voice. Charylla stood a few paces away, Treloran beside her. Even the hot-tempered Aelvin Prince seemed embarrassed by his uncle. "Lord Odara thought only about the welfare of his prince. He meant no dishonor, nor would you have acted any differently had it been Treloran at whom the arrow was aimed."

"He insults my honor!" Luran replied. "He insults me!" His gaze went from Charylla to Treloran, but when he received no help from his nephew, his eyes grew stormy. "He insults us all with his mere presence, yet you ignore it. *I* will ignore it no longer." He drew his blade, the morning light shining on the Aelvin-forged steel.

"You cannot kill him." Charylla said sternly. "He and all his companions are under Grandfather's protection."

"Then I will blood him," quipped Luran. "That will suffice to restore my honor." He spat at Jeran's feet. "And it will give this child reason to think. He will not dishonor me again."

"You are a fool, Luran," Charylla said coldly. "You have always been a fool. You will destroy all hopes of peace. All of this," –she gestured at the Alrendrian camp– "will be for naught. Do Grandfather's wishes mean nothing to you?"

"Grandfather is old," Luran replied. "His thoughts are no longer clear. Whenever the Empire has dealt with Humans, it has spelled disaster."

"Old or not, while Grandfather lives, he is emperor. Will you defy him in this?"

"The laws are clear. I have the right to demand my honor cleansed."

"I forbid this, Luran," Charylla said, her cold, dispassionate facade nearly breaking. "I will not allow you to–"

"That will not be necessary, Princess Charylla," Jeran said mildly. "If your brother wishes to teach me a lesson, then I'll gladly learn from his instruction. If his sword skill matches his manners," he added with a smile, "then the lesson will be short indeed."

Luran's face turned red with rage. "You accept my challenge?" he said through clenched teeth, his voice a near growl.

Jeran nodded. "Prepare the practice ring," Martyn called out to the nearest Guardsmen. "Prince Luran wishes to settle a matter of honor with Lord Odara." The Guardsmen hurried to carry out the command, but their laughter and jests drifted to Luran on the wind.

Silently, his face drawn so tight it looked as if it were about to break, he turned and headed to where the Guardsmen were forming a ring on the Path of Riches. Jeran sighed deeply, but offered Charylla a respectful bow before following.

Chapter 4

Jeran only made it three steps before Charylla stopped him. "You do not have to do this, Lord Odara," she said, though her eyes betrayed her. "I can stop my brother." At her side, Treloran scowled, but it was impossible to say at what.

"If it were that simple, my Lady," Jeran said, shaking his head, "I would take your offer. But Prince Luran will not be satisfied without a fight." He smiled. It was meant to be reassuring. "Besides, I have held a sword before. I promise, I won't hurt your brother if it can be avoided."

Charylla frowned. "Luran is *Ael Chatorra*, one of our best warriors. You will not find him an easy competitor, or a merciful one." She looked Jeran up and down. "You are just a boy, even in Human terms, and you have not yet recovered from a grievous wound. Now is not the time for heroics."

"My uncle has a prickly honor," Treloran added in a quiet voice. "If by chance you prove to be a better swordsman," –his tone made it clear that he thought such an event an impossibility– "he will not take it kindly should you use your skill to keep him at bay."

The Aelvin Prince's words surprised Jeran, not what he said so much as the mere fact that he said it. These were perhaps the first words Jeran had heard from him, definitely the first Treloran had spoken to a Human.

Jeran turned his gaze on the young Elf. "Nevertheless, I will not harm him if it can be avoided." Breathing deeply, relishing the cool morning air, he told Charylla. "I see no way out of this. If you stop the fight, Luran's anger will grow, but it will be shared between the two of us. If I fight him and lose, he will have a shallow victory, his pride will not be soothed, and his anger will grow. If I win, his anger will still grow, but perhaps he will be wary enough not to challenge me again."

With a sigh, Jeran shrugged his shoulders. "Given the options, I'd prefer to buy myself some small respite."

"As you will, Lord Odara," Charylla replied, sizing him up once more. "But this time, I will not heal your injuries."

"Nor would I expect you to, Princess. Though if the Gods are with me, there will be few enough to heal."

Charylla bowed her head and departed. Treloran remained but a moment longer, his green eyes unreadable. Then, without a word of parting, he turned and walked away. Martyn stepped around Jeran. "She's right, you know. You're in no condition to fight."

"My left shoulder was injured," Jeran reminded him. "Not my right."

"You're weak," Martyn said sternly. "I don't want you weaker."

Jeran laughed quietly, kneeling to grab a handful of dry dirt. He rubbed it into his hands to dry the sweat. "Normally, you're the one looking for the fight, my Prince."

Martyn returned the laugh, but his eyes remained serious. "And you're normally the one counseling me against it."

"You never listen to me."

"That doesn't mean you have to be as foolish as I."

Jeran shook his head, and his smile broadened. "There's no way out of this, Martyn. I wish there were. I want this fight no more than the rest of you, but the choice has been made."

Martyn stood in silence for what seemed an eternity. When he spoke, the words came out slowly. "Then best we get on with it."

They walked through the camp, past tents of cream-colored canvas, past Guardsmen tending horses and servants mending clothes. Alynna waved at them, her blonde hair blowing in the wind, and Utari's eyes followed them silently as they wended their way toward the practice ring. The forest surrounded them, broad branches and thick leaves arching high above, shading the Path of Riches from the bright light of morning. Birds twittered and sang in the branches.

The Guardsmen they passed called greetings, wishing Jeran well. "We'll cheer for you, Lord Odara!" called one, a skinny man with a hooked nose named Raeghit. The servants they passed watched as well, but only a few dared speak. Liseyl approached, offering Jeran a drink of cool, clean water, which he accepted thirstily. "We will pray for you," she whispered, backing away, her lips pressed together in worry.

They approached the ring of Guardsmen and Elves, and Lord Iban appeared, dressed in full armor. The Guard Commander scanned the crowd, his eyes burning with anger. When his gaze settled on Jeran and Martyn, his frown deepened and he stormed toward them, his armor rattling. "This is foolishness, Odara!" he growled, low enough that no one else could hear. "We're not here to fight Elves; we're here to befriend them."

Jeran had expected Iban's anger. "No," he agreed, "we're not here to fight Elves. But we will find no friend in Luran, even if I let him cut me down for his 'wounded honor.' " Jeran met the Guard Commander eye to eye. "The princess was ready to command Luran to forego this fight, and though he would have obeyed, it would have made us an enemy for life. Luran must have supporters throughout Illendrylla. He's the Emperor's grandson! This way, no matter the outcome, the matter is settled, and we are no worse off than we began."

Iban harrumphed, but some of the heat in his eyes died. "It seems to me you're right, though I hate to admit it." He appraised Jeran, looked him up and down, his anger replaced with concern. "You're up to this?" he asked. "That was a serious wound you took."

Jeran laughed. "It doesn't seem as if I have a choice."

Iban's head bobbed up and down. "We rarely do, Odara. We rarely do."

The ring of soldiers parted at their approach. Luran already stood in the center, his sword unsheathed. The Elf had removed his shirt, and the muscles on his hairless chest rippled as he danced from stance to stance. Jeran stepped into the ring and spun slowly, not surprised to find most of the camp in attendance, Human and Elf alike. They formed a ring sixty hands across and four rows deep, pressing in from all sides to get a better view. Mika waved from the shoulders of one Guardsman; a handful of other children had earned similar vantage points.

Charylla and Treloran stood in the front ranks. Though the youth looked eager for the fight, Charylla's expression was sad. Iban took a place beside Jes, opposite the Aelvin royalty. His face was unreadable, but Jes gazed upon the proceedings with obvious disappointment. Jeran winced when he saw her dark expression, not sure whether she was upset with the whole situation, or just with him.

With a resigned sigh, Jeran unlaced the ties on his shirt and removed it, tossing the garment to Martyn. He drew his sword, and the sound of steel rasping on leather silenced the crowd. Suddenly, all was quiet. The forest was still; even the birds stopped their singing.

Charylla appealed to her brother one last time. "Luran," she all but pleaded, "I ask you as your sister, not your princess, to set aside this folly. The Human meant no disrespect. He was only protecting his prince."

Luran sneered. "I have made my challenge and he has accepted. I will brook no interference from you, Sister. Honor will be served."

Charylla stepped back, scowling darkly, but Treloran moved forward, taking a place beside his uncle. With one hand, he grasped the Elf's shoulder, with the other, the hilt of Luran's sword. "You offer challenge?"

Luran nodded. "The Human has slighted my honor. I will see him humbled."

"What do you pledge," Treloran asked, "should your claim be forfeit?"

Luran's eyes flashed again; his hard, angular face pinched even more. He sneered at Jeran and spat on the ground. "Should Valia, in Her wisdom, find my claim unjust, I will yield my sword to the Human." Luran lifted the blade high, so all could see.

The sword was of shining steel, inscribed on the side with Aelvin symbols. Its hilt, forged in the shape of a tree, glittered gold. The trunk formed a handle and the broad, golden branches, capped with leaves of burnished gold, fanned out above to protect the hand. "This blade was crafted during the Great Rebellion to fight those who spurned the Empire's protection. It was blessed by *Ael Maulle*, so the blade would never dull, and was carried by Emperor Llwellyn himself into battle on the Anvil, where vile treachery cost him his life."

He aimed a cold glare at Jeran. "Should my claim prove false, the Human will have this sword." Quieter, so that none but Treloran and Jeran could hear, he added, "The Goddess is with me, and I will be victorious. Do not worry, Human, you will get to feel my sword even though I will defeat you." His grin was malicious.

Treloran frowned at his uncle's words, but said nothing. He turned and crossed the circle to Jeran, placing one hand on Jeran's shoulder, careful to avoid his injury. The other hand, he put on the hilt of Jeran's blade. "You accept this challenge to your honor?"

"Yes," came Jeran's quiet reply.

"And what do you pledge, should your honor prove false?"

For a long moment, as Jeran considered the question, he did not move. Reluctantly, he reached into his shirt and withdrew the wolf's head medallion. "I pledge this," he said in a voice barely above a whisper. "It is the symbol of House Odara, crafted for my father as a wedding gift. I was told it, too, has been blessed by Magi, but whatever power it contains has been lost to time." Sadly, he pulled the chain over his head and offered it to Treloran. "It is all that remains of my family."

Treloran regarded both the pendant and Jeran silently. With a stiff jerk of his head, he accepted the medallion and stepped away. Centering himself between the two combatants, he spoke in a voice that carried to everyone present. "The challenge has been made and accepted. The first to yield loses; truth and honor go with the victor. Should one fall to the other's blade, then both your lives are forfeit. May Valia steer the hand of the righteous, and protect the misguided from harm."

The Aelvin Prince returned to his place on the edge of the circle, leaving Jeran gaping at his words. *If Luran dies, I'll be killed, too. If Luran wins, I lose my father's medallion!* When he had entered the ring, he had thought to let the Elf score a few weak blows, and then yield, giving Luran back his honor. But now that meant giving up the last remembrance he had of his uncle, his only tie to both Aryn and Alic Odara.

Luran did not leave him much time to consider his options. As soon as Treloran was clear of the ring, the Elf leapt forward, his sword flashing in the sunlight. Jeran ducked the swing and stepped to the side, trying to size up his opponent. Again Luran swung viciously, and Jeran stepped back to dodge the blow. The Elf snarled, and his sword flew again. A third time Jeran stepped out of the way. He had not yet moved his own blade, not even in defense.

Luran circled, his sword thrusting out periodically in quick stabs or violent slashes. Jeran kept Luran on his right, circling backward, refusing to meet the Elf's blade with his own. Luran's temper flared, and he lunged, his blade whistling through the air. Jeran twisted to the side, and the Elf's sword hit the ground, clanging as it contacted the smooth stone.

Luran recovered quickly and scuttled back, wary of a return attack, but Jeran did not lift his blade. Trembling with rage, Luran attacked again, his sword a blur of silvered steel. One, two, three quick slashes, but Jeran dodged them all, his blade never leaving his side. "Fight me, coward!" Luran demanded, his voice a howl. He ran toward Jeran, his sword swinging in a wide arc.

Jeran ducked aside, and Luran's blade whistled above his head. As the Elf rushed past, Jeran extended a foot, and Luran tumbled face first onto the Path of Riches. Gravel scuttled across the stone, clicking and clacking.

Jeran waited patiently for Luran to regain his footing. Blood, mixed with dirt, streaked the Elf's chest. "A coward's trick," he called out, loud enough for all to hear. "The Human is afraid to meet me blade for blade. He is craven, as are all Humans."

Lord Iban's voice thundered across the circle, not quite mocking. "The surest way to avoid a blade is not to be there when it falls," he called out to the Guardsmen in a lecturing tone. "Lord Odara teaches a valuable lesson, Guardsmen! Best you remember that, and learn from his example." Luran glared at the Guard Commander, but said nothing else. He started circling again, muttering 'coward' low enough so only Jeran could hear.

Luran was only half right. Jeran *was* afraid to cross blades with the Elf, but not because he feared him. He was weak–Charylla had not lied–and once they fought blade to blade, what little strength he had would quickly disappear. His only chance lay in enraging the Aelvin Lord, and hoping that anger forced Luran to make mistakes.

Jeran smiled, but said nothing, and Luran approached again, more cautiously. He feinted to the right, then shifted his attack to the left. Jeran was not caught unaware, and he spun away from the blow. When Luran's sword hit the ground, Jeran stepped on top of it, trapping the Elf's blade. "Do you yield?" he asked quietly.

Luran snarled and swung his free hand. The blow was lightning fast, and Jeran did not have time to dodge. The Elf's fist slammed into his injured shoulder and a wave of pain radiated down his arm. Jeran stumbled back, hissing in a breath, and Luran was on him in an instant. Their blades met for the first time, and Jeran forced the pain to the back of his mind.

Luran attacked without remorse, his blade moving so quickly the eye could not follow. His movements were graceful; Jeran had to use all his skill to keep the Elf at bay. Their blades whirled, and the sound of clanging metal rang through the forest and down the Path of Riches. They moved as if dancing, and even Jes could not keep her face even. She watched with growing fascination, as did all assembled.

Jeran, backing away, slipped on some loose gravel. He dropped to one knee, and Luran pressed the advantage. He tried to deflect the blade, but was not quick enough. The tip of Luran's blade cut a shallow gash down his injured arm, and a lance of pain shot through Jeran.

Their blades hit the ground together, and Luran was momentarily exposed. Grasping the hilt of his sword in both hands, Jeran rammed it into the Elf's midriff, sending his opponent staggering backward, gasping for air. Jeran stood, pushing back a wave of dizziness, but Luran recovered more quickly. Smiling in triumph, he swung his blade in a wide arc, hoping to catch Jeran full force with the flat of his sword. At the last possible instant, Jeran ducked under the swing, rising up to catch the Elf's sword from behind. With a flick of his own sword, Jeran knocked Luran's from his hand. The blade slid across the ground, scraping the gravel.

"Do you yield now?" Jeran hoped the answer would be yes, but knew otherwise. Luran did not disappoint him. The Elf dove to the ground, rolled across the ring, and retrieved his blade. He stood, blade in hand, and ran toward Jeran, screaming defiantly.

Jeran pushed Luran's blade aside and stepped into him, shoving with his shoulder. The Elf flew backward, smashing into the wall of people around the ring. Amidst thuds of armor and cries of surprise, two Elves and a Guardsman fell, with Luran landing on top of them. While the four untangled themselves, Jeran caught his breath. He was panting hard and knew he could not last much longer. He had one, maybe two more chances to stop Luran, or he would be too weak to continue.

Luran finally escaped the knot of fallen warriors and stepped back into the ring. "End this now," Jeran said. "I don't want to hurt you."

At Jeran's words, Luran went wild. He spat blood and saliva on the stones at his feet. "I *will* end this now, Human!" he replied. "But I will end it with your blood." Screaming, he hurtled across the ring.

Jeran sighed, and ran to meet the charge. Their blades collided with a thunderous clang, and then they were past each other. Luran turned slowly, his hand ringing from the blow, but Jeran pivoted easily, using all of his self-control to hide his pain. Yet again, the Elf raised his sword and started forward, shambling across the field. Jeran met Luran's weak assault, flicking his wrist in a circle. The Elf's blade flew into the air, and Jeran used the opportunity to smash his elbow hard into Luran's jaw. The Elf stumbled, dropping to his knees.

Sucking in a pained breath, determined not to fall, Jeran caught Luran's sword by the hilt with his left hand, nearly dropping it as pain raced up and down his side. He lowered both blades to Luran's neck, one on each side. "Do you yield?" he asked for the final time.

It was Treloran who spoke, not Luran. "He does not have to," the Aelvin Prince replied. "You hold his weapon to his neck. The Goddess has spoken. Honor has been served."

"Honor has been served," repeated the Elves around the circle.

Jeran stepped back, his breath coming in short, ragged gasps. Luran struggled to his feet, and Jeran stepped forward, offering the Aelvin blade, hilt first. Luran's eyes flashed angrily, but he made no comment.

"The blade is yours, Human," came Treloran's sullen voice. "It was my uncle's pledge to you, should his claim of dishonor prove false." He lifted the medallion by the chain and waited for Jeran to lower his head before returning it to its place around his neck.

When they were close, he whispered, low enough that only Jeran could here. "To refuse the blade would be a worse insult to my uncle's honor than he claimed you gave before. Were I you, I would accept."

The Aelvin Prince stepped back, and Jeran licked his lips, uncertain how to proceed. Finally, he stepped toward Luran again, offering his own blade to the Aelvin warrior. "A gift of friendship, Prince Luran," he said, holding the hilt of his own sword toward the Elf. "Forged by King Mathis' master smith. It's one of the best blades in all Alrendria."

Luran glared at the sword with disgust. Turning on his heels, he stomped off, pushing his way through the throng. "My brother is a fool," Charylla said, stepping forward. "You were more courteous than he would have been. He should have accepted your token in good faith, but I will accept it in his stead, and offer my friendship in place of his."

Jeran cast his eyes about, but could find no one to offer him advice. Finally, he handed his sword to the princess' waiting hand. "I accept your friendship, my Lady," he said formally, bowing low.

She returned the bow, then handed the blade to a waiting Aelvin warrior. "I told you that I would not heal your wounds. If you wish it, I will break my word."

Jeran looked at his arm. Bright red blood ran down it in a tiny stream. "I would not wish to make you renege on your promises," Jeran replied solemnly. "It's only a scratch. I believe that bandages will suffice."

Charylla, nodding, waved to one of her servants. "Find dressings for Lord Odara's wounds," she commanded. "And ointment to ease his pain." She looked Jeran up and down. "Perhaps some wine? My Lord looks quite parched." The Elf departed at a run, without speaking a word.

"I thank you, Princess," Jeran laughed. "I am indeed thirsty."

"If you will excuse me, Lord Odara, I wish to speak to my brother."

Jeran inclined his head, and Charylla left at a stately pace. At her departure, others approached–Lord Iban and Martyn, Jes and Mika, a handful of Guardsmen. All congratulated Jeran on his great victory.

Martyn took the sword from Jeran's grip and lifted the blade high. "It's exquisite," he remarked, looking at the cut of the blade. He tested the edge with his finger, yelping when the slightest touch cause a thin line of red to form.

Jes and Iban each offered their congratulations, then quietly stole away. Iban looked pleased, but Jes' cool gaze made Jeran suspect that he would face another of her lectures when next they were alone. The Guardsmen praised his sword skill and claimed they were glad Jeran would fight on their side, if ever they faced battle.

Mika stared at Jeran wide-eyed. "It was like a story," he said raptly. "You fought as bravely as Jolam Strongarm, or King Makan!"

Jeran laughed at Mika's praise and thanked everyone for their compliments. He managed to escape only when the Aelvin servant returned, burdened with both medicines and wine.

After allowing the Elf to clean and dress his wound, Jeran drank greedily from the glass of pale, white wine. The taste was bitter, but it felt wonderful as it settled in his stomach.

The ointment eased his pain, and Jeran thanked the Elf for her kindness. The woman merely bowed her head and walked away; she had not spoken a word throughout all her ministrations. As she retreated across the camp, Jeran furrowed his brow at the strangeness of Elves.

Cool fingers brushed his still-bare shoulder, and Jeran jerked. Spinning around, his hand reaching reflexively for his sword, he stopped only when he realized it was Alynna. She had pulled her hair up in an elaborate bun, and her blue eyes danced with delight at Jeran's expression. A sky blue riding dress, cut low in the front, clung to her every curve.

Red lips pulled up into a beautiful smile. "Do I frighten you so terribly, Jeran?" she asked in a breathless whisper, her lips pouted. "All I wished was to congratulate you on your victory. The Elf was a fearsome fighter."

"Lady Alynna," Jeran replied, returning her smile, "I tell you truly, you frighten me more than Luran ever could." She blushed at his comment, her laughter sounding like the ringing of a tiny bell. A finger ran down Jeran's arm, causing his hair to stand on end. "Was there something else, Alynna?"

She shook herself, as if she had not been listening. "What? Oh no. Just my congratulations. Forgive me, Jeran," she said, smiling demurely. "I was thinking of something. Perhaps you will consent to dine with me tonight? I've been so very lonely since leaving Kaper."

Jeran looked left and right nervously, but again, no one was around to aid him. "I've already promised to share my meal with Lady Jessandra," he said, wondering if he had spoken too hastily.

Alynna allowed her gaze to roam over his body. "A pity," she said. "Perhaps tomorrow?"

Jeran stepped away, bending to pick up his shirt. As he laced it, he bowed respectfully and offered a noncommittal, "We shall see."

Alynna watched him dress, and Jeran felt his cheeks burning. Once his shirt was fully tied, she returned his bow with a polite nod and walked off, hips swaying suggestively.

Jeran fled from the camp before anyone else could waylay him. Passing Lord Iban, he asked the commander if they could rest a day, to allow him to regain his strength. Lord Iban considered his request, then nodded. "I don't like to delay, but the last two days have been harrowing, and I think it would do us good to rest a night. I'll speak to the princess." Jeran thanked him and continued out of the camp.

Weaving through the thick trees of the Great Forest, Jeran left the noise of the camp behind. He passed many trees, some that stood only a few hands higher than he did and others that climbed high into the sky. The trunks of these giant trees were so large that Jeran could not circle them with his hands. He sat at the base of one, on the rounded knob of a root, and stared at the tiny patches of blue visible through the canopy.

He found himself thinking of Dahr. They had been apart only a handful of days, and yet this was the longest they had been separated since meeting on the bank of the stream by Keryn's Rest. Over the winters, Jeran had come to rely on Dahr's calming presence and unyielding loyalty.

Now Dahr was off searching for his people, and Jeran hoped he was welcomed by them. Dahr had been little more than an oddity in Kaper: the King's personal Garun'ah. Maybe among the Tribesmen, he would find the peace that had so long eluded him.

Still, Jeran would have given much to see his friend's smiling face. Or even Katya's, the Guardsman to whom Dahr had taken a liking. The two had become nearly as inseparable as Jeran and Dahr themselves. She cared for him greatly, Jeran knew; that Dahr was enamored of her was more than an understatement.

He wished them both well, knowing they would be better off exploring the vast Tribal Lands than cooped up in Lynnaei. Dahr wanted to be in the open. He *needed* to be in the open. Going to Lynnaei would have only been exchanging one prison for another. Dahr was better off.

But am I better off without Dahr? I'm not so sure. True, he still had Martyn, but though he loved the prince like a brother, they had never been as close. Martyn did not understand Jeran's dislike for the nobility, his unwillingness to accept his role as First Seat of House Odara.

Leaning back against the tree, Jeran closed his eyes and let the cool breeze pass over him. He breathed slowly and deeply, allowing muscles knotted during the fight with Luran to relax.

Jeran did not want to be a lord. He did not want to rule people's lives. And their deaths. Uncle Aryn had raised him as a commoner, not a nobleman. In Keryn's Rest, not Portal. His uncle had always claimed that he wanted peace for his nephew, not the life of a Guardsman's son, but Jeran was no longer sure. Many noblemen did not value their vassals' lives. They plotted and schemed against each other and against the King, vying for more power for their House, more honor to their Family.

In the end, the nobles always had more, the commoners less. Most were not mistreated, but neither were they treated well. Jeran suspected that his uncle had raised him as he had, so that when Jeran's time to rule came, he would understand the needs of the people and respect their desires.

Perhaps Uncle Aryn had been right to do so, but he had done his job too well. Jeran did not feel the equal of these lords and ladies. He felt like a usurper, a thief, someone had stolen his way into the castle one night and taken someone else's title. Someone else's duties. "What do I know of being a lord?" he asked, his hand sliding over the hilt of his new sword. "It should be somebody else's honor."

"Somebody else's honor?" Jes asked, stepping from the trees. "Or somebody else's responsibility?"

Jeran's eyes snapped open at her first word. "Maybe both," he admitted reluctantly. "I never asked for any of this."

"You could have refused," came Jes' quick reply.

"Perhaps," he answered, though he did not sound convinced. "Perhaps not. But I did not refuse, and now I am stuck."

"Truly spoken." Jes sat beneath the tree, gently settling her weight on another root. She eyed him coolly, and Jeran tensed, ready for her lecture. Instead, Jes simply said, "You risked much today." After a brief hesitation, she added, "And yesterday, much more."

"Each time," Jeran answered warily, "I didn't feel I had a choice."

Jes nodded thoughtfully. "I will not tell you of the risks. You knew them already and still chose as you did. In the end, things worked out the way you wanted them to, so I have no reason to complain." To Jeran, she looked as if she wanted to complain.

Jeran did not want to tell her. He did not know how she would react. He was not even sure how *he* felt about it, but there was no one else he could trust. "I dreamed last night."

Her gaze did not waver. "I presume this was not an ordinary dream."

Jeran shook his head. "It was in a place called the Twilight World."

Jes' eyes narrowed suspiciously. Her gaze bored into him. "The Twilight World," she repeated. "Where did you hear that name?"

"From two people. Two different people. From two different dreams. Once from a stranger, dressed in brown and with straight black hair, as tall as Dahr, but not quite as broad. He pulled me from the first dream."

Jes nodded. "And the first person of whom you dreamed."

"Lorthas," Jeran replied. "The Darklord."

This did evoke a response. Jes hissed in a breath. "Lorthas!" she said in a tight whisper. "He's free then? The Boundary has fallen?" Jeran discovered that he did not like hearing fear in Jes' voice.

"No," Jeran answered, though he did not believe Jes expected him to. "He claims he can only see Madryn from the Twilight World, and only found me because my Gift is so strong. He says he's still trapped behind the Boundary, and will be for a long time, unless one of his Magi finds a way to bring down the wall. I believed him."

"The Darklord speaks lies like a bard sings songs," Jes replied.

Jeran did not take the bait. "He claimed his words were truth, but that's not why I believe. His words *sounded* true. I know little of the Twilight World, but I believe I would know had he lied to me."

Jes was dumbfounded. "Anything he said was true, had to be. That's the way the Twilight World works, though I have only been there a handful of times. Entering the Twilight World is not a talent I possess. Aemon has taken me there, on occasion, and he explained the rules; at least, he explained the ones he knew. If a person says something is true, then he must speak truth, but if he makes no such claim, he can still lie."

Jeran nodded, trying to remember the conversation. *How many things did the Darklord say were true*, he wondered, *and how many did he just say?*

"What did he want?" Jes asked, interrupting Jeran's thoughts.

"He wanted to tell me his story." Jeran answered levelly. "He claims that time has judged him poorly, that his tale has been twisted by the victorious. He wants me to listen, to question, and to pass my own judgment. Nothing more."

"Nothing more?" Jes barked. "What more is there? You did not agree, of course." Jeran blushed, and Jes' eyes widened in surprise. "You agreed? You are more a fool than I thought! You fall into a fire and escape unburned, then run eagerly back to the flames. Any child knows better than that!"

Jeran refused to let himself grow angry. "Tanar told me that time changes history, that people are biased by their own beliefs. The Darklord told me truthfully that he could bring me no harm in the Twilight World, and asked only that I listen to his version of history, that I may better understand why he did what he did. Is that so wrong?"

Jes only shook her head. "He will hurt you."

"He cannot. He said as much."

"And what of this other stranger?" Jes asked coolly. "What did he have to tell you?"

Jeran frowned. "He said I was not yet ready to meet the Darklord, and that I was fortunate to have escaped unscathed. He told me to be wary."

Jes snorted. "Would that you had listened to the advice of your unknown counselor." Jeran lowered his eyes, and Jes softened her tone. "It is not that your idea lacks merit, Jeran," she admitted. "But the Darklord is dangerous. Even the truths he tells will be twisted with lies."

"He said you Magi would feel that way," Jeran told her. "He said you would not want your version of history corrupted by the truth. Lorthas said I should question his tale, ask you and the other Magi what happened. Get your opinions as well as his." Jeran shrugged. "At the time, it seemed a reasonable request."

Jes reached over and put a comforting hand on Jeran's shoulder. "What's done is done," she stated. "Besides, if Lorthas can visit your dreams, there's little you could do about it. He could pull you into the Twilight World whenever he wanted. Promise me that you'll share everything he tells you."

Jeran nodded. "Good," Jes said with a note of finality. Then she smiled. "I was going to give you a break today, but seeing as you had enough energy to humiliate the leader of the Aelvin Armies, you are probably strong enough to practice seizing magic. At least for a little while."

Jeran's mouth hung open in astonishment. "Luran is the leader of the Aelvin Armies?"

"Maybe not after today," Jes laughed. "Charylla was most disappointed in him, both his manners and his sword skill. You likely made yourself a powerful enemy. I'd watch that one, Jeran, were I you."

Jeran shook his head in disbelief. He cupped a hand over his forehead, trying to ward off the headache he felt forming.

"Are you ready to begin?" Jes asked. Without waiting for an answer, she said, "Good. Then clear your mind."

Chapter 5

Jeran dismounted and handed his reins to a waiting Guardsman. They had traveled late into the evening, as they had for the last ten days, using every bit of daylight. Tomorrow, Charylla had told them, they would reach Lynnaei, and Jeran had no cause to doubt the Aelvin Princess' words.

They raised their tents on the road, lighting their cookfires on the small circle of grass cut into the Great Forest. Wood was plentiful in the forest, as was game, and the Alrendrians had feasted well since joining the Elves. The Elves brought meat every night–turkey and pheasant, deer and boar– but they did not allow the Alrendrians to hunt on their own.

Lord Iban had Jeran raise his tent, then called for a meeting. Their discussion was brief. The Guard Commander outlined what he hoped to accomplish in Lynnaei. It was a speech Jeran had heard many times; he could have spoken it back to Iban verbatim.

Not that the old warrior could be blamed. Their destination lay less than a day away, and then their real mission began. Iban did not look forward to sitting through the negotiations while Jeran did the important work; he would have preferred to meet with the Emperor. Jeran chuckled as he left the Guard Commander's tent. Given the choice, he would gladly switch places with Iban.

By the time he located his belongings, his own tent had been raised. Three of the older children and two of the women were carrying his things into the tent. Bystral supervised the work. "I told you this isn't necessary," Jeran scolded, ignoring the Guardsman's salute. "I can care for myself!"

The Guardsman lifted his hands in supplication. "I had nothing to do with this, Lord Odara. The children insisted, and I've done nothing but watch." Bystral smiled, and Jeran knew that though the Guardsman had not encouraged their behavior, he had in no way tried to stop it.

Since Jeran's injury, Bystral had never been far from him. Jeran often saw the burly Guardsman skulking in the shadows near his tent. *How someone so large thinks he can escape notice is anyone's guess,* Jeran said to himself, smirking. Though not quite as tall, Bystral was as broad as Dahr and nearly as strong. His father was a blacksmith for the Family Inaerion, in House Aurelle, and though Bystral had not taken on his father's trade, he had inherited the man's size.

Jeran also knew which of the children was to blame. "Mika!" he called sharply, and the boy scampered from his tent. He saluted, fist-on-heart, and brushed a strand of brown hair away from his eyes. "I told you that you are not my servant!" Jeran spoke in as authoritative a voice as he could manage. "You do not need to do these chores for me." Louder, so all could hear, he added, "None of you do."

"Lord Jeran," Mika replied, "the other nobles have servants to fetch them things and care for them. You're nobler than all the others, so you deserve servants more than they do!" He said it so matter-of-factly that Jeran could hardly keep from laughing. The other children nodded their heads in agreement.

Jeran refused to yield. "I did not set you free so you could enslave yourselves to me!"

"Begging your pardon, my Lord," said Jan, one of the women helping Mika. "You are not forcing us to do this work, we are volunteering. We aren't your slaves; we're your subjects. You saved our lives, and we wish to repay the debt as best we can."

Jeran shook his head. "I appreciate your gratitude, but all of this..." he said, waving his hand at the children, who were still carrying things back and forth, "is unnecessary. I don't need your loyalty. Or your obedience."

"They are yours regardless," Jan told him, and her tone brooked no argument. "My Lord," she began again, this time in a hushed tone, nearly a whisper. "It makes us feel better to work. All of us. It's as if we're part of your party, and not pitiful wretches surviving on your charity. Please, allow us some measure of dignity!" Her voice was pleading.

Not knowing what else to do, Jeran sighed. "If it means so much to you, I won't force you to stop." Jan smiled, then resumed her work. The others ignored him completely, leaving only after every piece of his gear was placed as he liked it.

Once they were gone, Jeran sat on his cot for a long time, wondering what he would do with the slaves once they returned to Alrendria. He supposed King Mathis could—and would at his request—find them places at the castle. *But would they serve the King as willingly as they serve me?* They were not Alrendrians, not a single one of them; their loyalties might belong to someone other than Mathis.

It was a problem for another day, he decided at last, grabbing his sword and walking from his tent. He ignored the calls of Guardsmen and nobles alike as he crossed the camp and entered the shadowy recesses of the Great Forest. Only after all the sounds of the camp—the neighing horses; laughing, boisterous people; and the clanging of metal as the Guardsmen cleaned their arms and armor—had disappeared did he stop walking.

The trees of the Great Forest loomed above him, higher with each day's travel. The tops of the tallest could not be seen; they were obscured by the thick canopy of leaves. In the forest, midday was only marginally brighter than dusk, and night was black as pitch. The sun could be seen only from the Path of Riches, and then only when it reached its zenith.

Jeran eventually found a clearing large enough for him to practice in. Laying his blade on the ground, he stretched his arm. "I know you're there," he said, hazarding a guess. "I'm no threat to your forest. I wish only for a little privacy and a place to practice." The silence stretched out interminably, and after a moment, he began to think he had been wrong.

Suddenly, the underbrush before him parted, and a figure emerged, a longbow slung over her shoulder. She was tall, less than a hand shorter than Jeran, and thin, with slanted green eyes and angular features. She wore dark green leathers that blended in with the foliage. A thin sword hung at her hip, but she looked more comfortable with the bow than the blade. Once fully in the clearing, she bowed her head.

"I don't know what your orders are," Jeran admitted. "Honestly, I mean no threat to you or your forest, and I will return to the camp before the sun has fully set. If you are to guard me, then you are welcome to watch me practice. Or you can spar with me, if you prefer."

The Elf's green eyes dropped to the sword on the ground, then returned to Jeran's face. "I watched you battle Luran," she said in a lilting, accented voice. "If he could not beat you, then you would not find me a challenge." Her accent was thick, her voice nasal, but she pronounced each word with care and precision, and her tone was musical and light.

Jeran was stunned. In all their time with the Elves, he had heard none but Charylla, Treloran, and Luran speak–except to each other. Even then, their words were often whispers. He said as much to the archer before him.

"Prince Luran, the *Hohe Chatorra*, instructed us not to fraternize with your Guardsmen," she explained, her expression impassive. "He does not wish for us to form friendships with you Humans. I would not have spoken to you either, since you are noble born–*Ael Chatorra* are not to speak in front of *Ael Alluya*, unless spoken to first–but I have seen your servants speak to you, even words which obviously displease you."

"The Guardsmen and my...servants," –the word was still strange on his tongue– "often say things I don't agree with, yet that doesn't mean their words are not true." Jeran thought of Rafel and the manner in which he treated his servants; he thought of Brell Morrena's casual disregard of the Alrendrian Guardsmen as anything more than hired swords. "Though many Humans are not as...forgiving...as I."

A new question came to mind, and Jeran asked it. "Why doesn't Luran want us to form friendships with you Elves? Forming bonds between our peoples is the very reason we're having these negotiations."

The Elf did not immediately answer. Her eyes were distant, and her lips pressed into a thin line. "He did not give a reason," she finally stated, "only a command. He is *Hohe Chatorra*. It is not my place to question his orders." Jeran stared at her, until her cheeks turned a shade pinker. "Luran has no love of Humans. That much should be plain to you by now."

Jeran smiled and nodded. Lifting his sword from the ground, he unsheathed the blade and raised it to eye level. The Elf considered his unspoken offer, then shook her head. "I would not test my blade against yours. I will watch." She sat on a fallen tree, folded her hands across her lap, and stared at Jeran expectantly.

Jeran looked at the blade, which felt alien in his hand. The hilt of the sword was molded in the shape of a tree. The roots formed a rounded ball at the bottom of the hilt, the trunk shaped the grip, and the thickly leafed branches acted as the cross-piece, protecting his wrist and hand from injury. The hilt was burnished gold, but the blade was shining silver steel. Aelvin runes were inscribed on each side.

Jeran swung the blade to test its balance, and it hummed through the air. He started slowly, moving from one stance to the next, sparring with an invisible opponent. The blade whirled and dipped, singing its own song, and Jeran danced to its music. Faster and faster he moved, until all thoughts fled and he was one with his sword.

Still faster, flowing from one stance to another. The trees spun around him, dark brown streaks in the fading light of day. Sweat beaded on his head, then ran down his face in tiny rivulets, but Jeran refused to stop. He allowed all the anger, all the tension, to drain out of him as he twirled his new weapon. The sword felt as if it had been made for him! Its balance, its length. No longer did the weapon feel like a stranger. It was a part of him.

With a cry, he focused on one of the trees, nearly five hands in diameter, and brought the sword slashing toward it. He stumbled, thinking for a moment he had missed completely, then heard the tree groan. It fell to the ground with a crash, and Jeran stared at his sword in awe. He had sliced cleanly through the tree without so much as smudging the blade.

Panting, he wiped the sweat from his brow. The archer stood. "I thought you meant my forest no harm."

Jeran blushed. "I guess I got carried away," he said in apology, sheathing the Aelvin sword.

"Others will grow. That is the way of the forest." The archer shrugged and started toward the trees. Looking back over her shoulder, she said, "A warning to you, if you choose to heed it. Luran does not like to be humiliated. I have had friends die for doing much less to his pride than you. Whatever hatred Luran feels for Humans, you can be assured it burns twice as hot for you." Without waiting for a reply, she disappeared into the rapidly darkening forest.

Jeran stared silently into the forest long after the Elf had disappeared. Sighing to himself, he began the long walk back to the Alrendrian camp.

The Reading, so strong it dropped him to his knees, caught Jeran by surprise. Around him, the forest burned. The crackle of flames echoed in his ear. The pain in his head was excruciating. Smoke filled his nostrils, his lungs, and he lowered his head to the ground, coughing weakly. Waves of heat rolled over his body. Rolling onto his back, he stared up, his eyes squinting at the bright fire.

The flames roared, creating a pillar that reached higher than the forest around him. The smoke was thick, dark and oily, but occasionally it thinned enough that he could see stars above, though only dimly. All around him the forest burned, and the flames crawled closer with every passing moment.

The pain in his head was unbearable, and he squeezed his hands against his temples, trying to force the vision away. The heat continued to rise, until it felt as if he were roasting alive. He tried to crawl away, but there was no escape; fire burned in every direction. He wanted to scream, but could not find his voice. He tried to tell himself it was not real, that he could walk through these flames and not be singed, but his body told him different. Real or imaginary, he would not be able to pass.

Jeran curled up on the ground, wrapped his arms around his knees, and wept. The vision passed as quickly as it begun, and Jeran once again found himself in darkness. He lay there for a long time. Finally, he stumbled to his feet and worked his way back to the camp.

He ate in silence, then retreated to the edge of the wood, where he tried to build a fire. But each time he struck the flint with his dagger, his hands began to shake, and he opted instead to sit in darkness. Though spring had long since begun, this far north the temperature plummeted after dark. Before long, Jeran's breath was coming in small, white clouds.

The cold did not affect him. In fact, he barely noticed it. Keryn's Rest had not been much warmer than this, situated as it was so near to the Boundary, and he had grown up playing in snow and swimming in icy mountain streams. The chill of the Great Forest was much more to his liking than the temperatures in Kaper, where he often found himself stifled.

Tomorrow they would reach Lynnaei, and the real mission would begin. Tomorrow, he would meet the Emperor. Those thoughts did not frighten him as much now as they had earlier. Sword practice had burned away most of his nervousness; the Reading had burned away the rest. He stared silently into the woods, lost deep in thought.

How long he sat alone in the dark he could not say. When Liseyl placed her hand on his shoulder, he whirled, surprised to find the camp dark, the only fires burning those of the sentries.

Liseyl jumped at his sudden movement, spilling the tea she carried. "Forgive me, my Lord. I didn't mean to startle you."

Jeran forced a smile. "It's my fault," he admitted, accepting the steaming cup and waving toward a nearby rock. "Please, have a seat."

She sat next to him, and they stared at each other. Using the dim light drifting from the camp, Jeran studied her. Liseyl looked a great deal better than when they had first met. Her cheeks were not as hollow, nor were her eyes so haunted and dim. Her brown hair was pulled back in a tight braid, her cheeks rosy from the evening's chill.

Though she wore a thick, dark cloak, Liseyl brought her knees to her chest and wrapped her arms around them for warmth. Jeran offered his coat to the shivering woman. "My Lord, I cannot!" she said forcefully. "You'll freeze!"

"I'll be fine," Jeran promised. "It's not cold enough to freeze out here. Besides, the chill doesn't bother me." She eyed him strangely, but did not protest when he laid the warm wool around her shoulders.

Jeran breathed deeply, filling his lungs with the cool night air. After a few moments, he asked, "Is there something you wanted?"

When Liseyl turned toward him, he could see the concern in her eyes. "Is there something wrong, my Lord?"

Jeran's brow furrowed. "What do you mean?"

"You've been distant these last few days, and getting worse the nearer we draw to the city. The children have been asking about you. Yesterday, Mika saluted, but you walked past without saying a word." Liseyl hesitated, then added, "Today you seemed a little better. Then you went into the forest. You haven't spoken a word since!"

Jeran opened his mouth to speak, and Liseyl hurried to finish. "I know it isn't common for nobles to spend their time with commoners. Nor is it my place to tell you that you're acting strangely. Yet you seem to be not yourself, and I worried that something was wrong." She waited close-mouthed, as if expecting chastisement.

Jeran considered her words. After a while, he barked a laugh. "There are a great many things wrong," he admitted, keeping his voice calm and quiet, "but they don't excuse my behavior." He looked at Liseyl sharply, deciding whether or not to trust her. In the end, it seemed he had no choice. "You already know most of my secrets. I see no harm in sharing the rest with you."

"Lord Odara, I don't–"

Jeran cut her off. "You know I have the Gift of magic, though I am no Mage. I also have another Talent. I see visions. Sometimes they are over-powering."

Liseyl pressed her lips together. "You see things that are going to happen?"

"Things that have already happened," Jeran corrected, shaking his head. "If they're strong enough to leave their mark on a place." Memories of the fire came back to him, and he shuddered. He caught the scent of woodsmoke in the air, and could not tell if it were real or imagined. "Sights, sounds, smells. Sometimes I can't tell what's real. The visions come at will, and I have no control over them. They're what cause my headaches."

"Is that why you sometimes look dizzy?" Liseyl asked. "Why you sometimes slump in the saddle?"

Jeran nodded. "Tonight," he found it difficult to continue. "Tonight I was in the forest, and suddenly it was burning. I knew it was only a vision, but it felt so real! It was almost as if I were burning, too, the pain was so bad." Jeran's description broke off; his voice caught.

"How terrible!" Liseyl said, rubbing him lightly on the back. "All will be well, Lord Odara."

Jeran instantly stiffened, and his eyes sought Liseyl's. "Stop calling me, Lord Odara!" he snapped harshly, instantly regretting his anger. Blushing, he lowered his voice. "My name is Jeran."

"You are so odd!" Liseyl said. Surprised by her own words, she clapped a hand to her mouth. Her cheeks turned red, and she fumbled to apologize. "Please forgive me, my Lor–Jeran. That did not sound like it was meant. You are unlike any nobleman I've ever met. Are all Alrendrians like you?" Her eyes went toward the camp. Before he could reply, she answered her own question. "My experiences tell me no."

"My secret is simple," Jeran said, a smile once again brightening his features. "I was raised a commoner, in a small village just south of the Boundary. My uncle thought it wise to raise me apart from other nobles, so I didn't develop their bad habits." His serious tone made Liseyl smile, too.

They both fell silent, and Jeran periodically sipped his tea. An owl hooted, and the sound echoed through the forest. "What did you do before you were captured by the slavers?" Jeran asked.

Liseyl was slow to answer. "My husband was a merchant in Rachannon. One of the best. He could sell a fur coat in the jungles of Feldar, or talk a Royan into parting with his sailboat." She smiled at the memories her words resurrected. "But he could not manage our estates to save his life. I kept the records, cared for our lands, and made sure the servants did what they were supposed to."

"How were you captured?"

"My husband had done business with the slaver, Gral, on several occasions. When he–"

Jeran's head whirled to face her. "You husband was a slave trader?"

Liseyl shook her head violently. "No!" she insisted. "Byron was no slaver." Though her words were harsh, they lacked conviction, and at Jeran's cold stare, she explained. "My husband was a merchant. But sometimes, when money was scarce, or trade bad, he dealt with the slavers."

She looked at Jeran pleadingly. "If you're a merchant in Rachannon you have to, else you're not trusted. Byron didn't like to, I swear it, and if I'd known how the slaves were treated, I'd never have allowed it. I swear, Jeran, that's the truth!"

She grasped his shoulder; the hand which, only a few short moments ago, had comforted him now grasped him desperately, begging for forgiveness. "Byron always sought a good home, with a kind and just Master, for the slaves he sold. As many as we could, we kept ourselves, and freed into our service." Her eyes were heavy with tears. "It was either deal with the slavers or watch our estates dwindle, our children go hungry. My Byron was a good man, Jeran. I swear he was."

Jeran put a comforting hand on her shoulder. "Peace, Liseyl. I spoke out of anger, and I beg your forgiveness. I will not judge you or your husband, nor will I speak of this to anyone, so long as you swear to me now that you'll never deal in the trade of slaves again." He looked at her, his features even, waiting for her answer.

She looked deep into his eyes and nodded. "I swear it, my Lord." She smiled warmly, and Jeran returned the gesture in kind. "Thank you."

A thought occurred to Jeran, and he tapped his lip thoughtfully. "I wouldn't mention this to Dahr," he said in warning.

Liseyl took a deep breath. "Then he *is* an escaped slave," she said, not needing Jeran's nod to confirm her suspicions. "I thought so from the instant he crawled into the wagon to save us."

Jeran closed his eyes, silently begging Dahr's forgiveness for betraying his secret. "Dahr was captured very young. His parents were murdered by the same slaver who captured you."

Liseyl gasped; her hand went to her mouth. "He was not treated well," Jeran added, shaking his head sadly. "If Dahr discovered that you and your husband had dealt with Gral in the past...." Jeran cut off abruptly and lightened his tone. "I don't mean to frighten you. Dahr would do nothing to harm you or your children, but he would never trust you again."

Liseyl nodded, but she did not look completely relieved. Jeran's expression became puzzled. "If you traded with the slavers," he asked, probing, "why were you taken as slaves?"

Liseyl's face fell, and she did not immediately respond. Jeran waited patiently, giving her the time she needed to deal with the memories. "I don't know exactly," she said at last. "One night, Gral came to our estates. He and Byron went off alone. I heard yelling, but couldn't make out what was said. When they returned, Gral was yelling obscenities. He called for his horse and led his caravan away, the whole time yelling that we'd be sorry."

Liseyl's hands went to her face, and she started to sob. Jeran tried to comfort her. "I'm sorry, Liseyl. I never should have asked. It's all in the past now. Please—"

"No," she said, sniffing back her tears, "I'm glad you wanted to know. Someone needs to know our story. That night, my husband awoke to a noise strange noise outside our manor house. He thought it might be a bear and went to investigate. He never believed Gral meant to make good on his threats.

"He was gone so long, I should have known something was wrong, but at the time I thought nothing of it. When the door to our bedroom burst open, there wasn't even time enough to scream before they grabbed me.

"They destroyed everything, trying to make it look like a Garun'ah raid, dropping bits of boiled leather, beads, and feathers around our grounds." Liseyl barked a short laugh. "The Tribesmen have not raided into Tachan lands in over two hundred winters, so I doubt their ploy would have worked. Not that it mattered.

"They took our cattle, stole our money, and set fire to our house and fields. The servants who weren't taken as slaves were murdered before our very eyes. My husband they beat unconscious. He only woke once, and then only long enough to...to beg my...."

Liseyl drew Jeran's coat tightly around her. "They threw us in their wagons and headed north. We were in there for days, with only what little food and water they gave us for nourishment. If Dahr and you had not come along, we would have surely died. Or...." she trailed off, not wanting to think about a fate worse than death.

"It's all over now," Jeran promised, squeezing her shoulder. "You need never fear Gral again, not so long as you stay with me and Prince Martyn. There is a place in Kaper for a woman of your talents. I guarantee it. Your children will be well cared for." She looked at him, tears in her eyes and a grateful smile on her face.

Jeran smiled in return. "It's late, Liseyl, and the night is chill. Seek your tent." He stood, offering Liseyl his hand. She grasped it and climbed to her feet, shrugging off his warm coat and handing it back to him. Offering his arm, he escorted her to the camp. Bidding her goodnight, Jeran threaded his way through the encampment to his own tent, rolled himself in his blankets, and tried to sleep himself.

It was a restless sleep at best. As the night wore on, some of Jeran's nervousness returned. The sun was rising before he knew it, and regretfully, he yawned, stretched, and rose. Mika and a handful of the children were in his tent at the first sign of movement, scarcely before he had finished dressing, accompanied by Jan. They began to pack up his things without a word, and at Jeran's curious glance, Mika said, "Lord Iban wants to be underway early!"

Jeran nodded and patted Mika on the head, ruffling the boy's hair. Grabbing his saddle, Jeran went to his horse, which was tied with the others along the edge of the forest. He brushed the tall, black stallion and offered the beast a handful of oats. Other Guardsmen joined him, each saddling their own mounts and leading the horses into formation. When the servants began hitching the pack horses to the wagons, Jeran climbed into the saddle and walked the proud animal over to Lord Iban.

"Are you ready, Odara?" the Guard Commander asked. He wore his best armor, and from the looks of it, he had spent most of the night polishing the silver plate. Jeran nodded, and Iban said, "Good. Ride beside the prince."

Iban pulled on the reins and urged his horse forward, where it joined Charylla, Treloran, and Jes. The two Elves rode in the center, flanked by Jes and Iban. Behind them rode Jeran and Martyn. The rest of the company, Human and Elf, fanned out behind them. When all were in position, Iban gave the signal, and the column started down the Path of Riches.

The day dawned cool, but the sun shone bright overhead, and patches of blue could be seen through the broken canopy. They rode in silence, and Jeran took the opportunity to look at the forest and drink in its beauty.

The Path of Riches cut a curving route through the trees, twisting back and forth for no apparent reason. To either side, bright green grass extended for a distance of nearly a hundred hands. The edge of the grass was a straight line, with the forest rising dark and impenetrable beyond. Though Jeran had seen no sign of gardeners, it seemed that great care was taken to maintain the distance between the trees and the road.

Jeran had thought the forest thick before, but as they neared Lynnaei it became ever denser, with more dark shrubs near the ground, many with long, thin thorns. Taking great care, one could thread his way through the brambles unharmed, but only at a crawl; the dense forest would be impossible to navigate on horseback.

The strategic advantage was apparent. An army's speed would be reduced to nothing should they try to sneak to Lynnaei through the Great Forest. They would have to go on foot and forage for food; it would be impossible to get wagons past the trees. Moreover, the advancing army would be easy targets for Elves. The only safe route of attack would be the Path of Riches, at most a distance of four hundred hands across. Even a small Aelvin force could hold off an army under those conditions.

Trees of every type lined the edge of the forest, growing taller than any in Alrendria. Pines, firs, and spruce were visible, though not in abundance. There were also oaks, cedars, dogwoods, and hundreds of other varieties, some of which Jeran had seen before, but many that were new to him.

The underbrush was thick, and thorned plants were the most plentiful. Still, Jeran saw herbs and berry bushes growing among the others. Birds sang in the branches above, while squirrels and other creatures darted from one tree to the next.

Jeran would have felt at peace if not for the brief flashes of Reading that interrupted his musings. Usually, they were not distinct enough to make out images, but they came frequently and unexpectedly. After a while, Jeran had a throbbing headache.

Once, after they had been traveling for a while, Martyn look around and said, "A lot of trees here." Jeran looked at him wryly, but the prince merely smiled, shrugged, and turned his eyes back to the road.

Though they had been traveling through Illendrylla for nearly twenty days, it occurred to Jeran that they had never seen an Elf other than those in the party. Their travels had not led them through any villages or cities that he could recall, nor did any other roads branch off the Path of Riches. They had passed game trails and other, slightly larger paths, perhaps designed to transport goods, but most ended abruptly, cut off by a thick line of trees while still in sight of the Path of Riches.

"Why haven't we passed any villages?" Jeran asked. "Or seen any Elves other Elves?" It seemed odd that no other settlements would line the one main road through Illendrylla, even if it had not been used in over three hundred winters.

Martyn shrugged again. "The Elves are a private people, or at least, that's what the records say." The prince looked at Charylla and Treloran. "Nothing I've seen leads me to disbelieve those accounts. They probably don't want their villages too close to the Path of Riches for fear of Humans and Garun'ah disrupting their lives."

The prince laughed. "Though if they can hide their homes half as well as they hide themselves, we could be walking through a town square right now and never even know it!" Jeran laughed too, nodding. The Elves had proven quite adept at stealth.

The Path of Riches had meandered over small hills for the last few days, but now the party began to descend more steeply. They rounded a bend, entering a wide valley. The trees obscured much of their view; the forest, if such a thing were possible, was even thicker here. Jeran doubted that even a single soldier could move between the trees without hacking out a path. Little light penetrated the canopy, even directly above the Path of Riches. Fresh, bright green leaves covered the trees, and wildflowers dotted the roadside.

They reached the bottom of the valley and walked along its base for a time. Ahead, the Path of Riches turned abruptly. When they reached the bend, they began to climb again, up a steep and winding path. After traveling a short distance, dark shadows covered them. Puzzled, Jeran looked up and let out a gasp.

He waved to Martyn, but the prince ignored him. He, too, had gone wide-eyed at the sight. Ahead stood a line of trees larger than any they had seen before. They towered over the forest, stretching more than two thousand hands high. Their massive branches intertwined, and their thick leaves formed an impenetrable barrier. From behind, Jeran heard his astonishment echoed by the Guardsmen. Alynna staggered in her saddle, and Rafel had to offer an arm to steady her.

At their startled gasps, Charylla turned her head, an amused smile plastered on her thin lips. "Yes," she said in a cool tone. "Lynnaei truly is a breathtaking sight."

Jeran and Martyn exchanged confused glances, then spurred their horses to catch up to the Elves, who had once again started forward. The nearer they drew to the giant trees, the more magnificent they appeared. Each was at least a hundred hands in diameter–some many times larger–with tough, thick bark, colored dark brown. The branches grew together so tightly that only pinholes of light penetrated. Enormous vines, some only a hand or two around, others nearly as wide as a horse, wrapped around the trees, tying them together. Thorns, imposing, razor sharp blades, laced the vines, protruding at every angle. Some were taller than Jeran.

The Path of Riches led to the base of one tree. Huge stone statues, giant Elves dressed in robes, their arms raised toward the heavens, guarded either side. Finally, Jeran understood what he was looking at. He shook Martyn to get his attention. "Those trees," he said, not quite believing. "That's Lynnaei!"

Martyn wrinkled his nose and stared at the trees for a long time, then shook his head. "Those are just trees. Amazing, yes, but just trees!"

Musical laughter drifted back to them. Charylla craned her neck around and said, "Trust your friend, Prince Martyn, and look again."

He did as told, and his expression changed when he saw the trees for what they truly were. "The walls of Old Kaper couldn't be any better fortification than this. Look there," he exclaimed, pointing to a mesh of thick vines hanging above the tree to which they were heading. "That's a living portcullis. And there!" –he raised his hand– "I swear I saw an archer up there!"

Jeran thought about all the trails that had ended in thick trees. They had been looking at Aelvin villages this whole journey and had not even recognized them. "The perfect camouflage," he whispered. Behind them, the others were gasping and staring in awe as word spread among the delegation. Hundreds of hands pointed toward the trees, and the excited whispers of Guardsmen and servants alike echoed through the forest. Even Lord Iban looked surprised; he kept scrubbing his mouth with his hand. Of the entire party, only Jes seemed unfazed.

Charylla turned around to address the Alrendrians. "I welcome you, on behalf of Emperor Alwellyn el'e Llwellyn, to the shining city of Lynnaei. May you find comfort beneath her branches and fruit from her vines." Wheeling her horse around, she passed through a hole in the great tree.

Treloran started to follow, but he paused to turn cold eyes toward Prince Martyn. "There has been no bloodshed in Lynnaei since the time of the MageWar." His voice was heavy with accusation, and his eyes flicked toward the Guardsmen. "I trust you will keep your Humans in line and make sure the Peace of Lynnaei is preserved?"

At Treloran's words, a Reading, the strongest yet, came upon Jeran, staggering him. The trees were suddenly burning, and night replaced day, though the flames cast even more light than the sun. An army of Elves and Garun'ah laid siege to Lynnaei. Fire flew from the hands of Human Magi, dressed in black robes and nearly disappearing in the shadows. Screams echoed from above, and archers fell from the wall. Warriors from both sides were impaled on spikes, or lying on the ground, broken and bloody. Many sported burns, and more than a few moaned in pain.

The pain was unbearable, and Jeran shied away from the flames, pulling his horse's reins tight. The animal fought him, neighing and stamping; it saw only the road in front and the Alrendrians approaching from behind.

Jes was with him in an instant, her cool hand on his temple. She took the reins from his hand and led him through the archway, cut through the heart of a living tree. Jeran shut his eyes to the vision, but could still hear the sounds of battle, still smell the blood, sweat, fear, and flames.

Once they were inside, the vision left as suddenly as it had began. Jeran shuddered and drew in a slow, sobbing breath. Jes mopped his forehead with a rag. He opened his eyes to see Martyn and Lord Iban staring at him with concern. Charylla and Treloran were watching, too. The Aelvin Prince's eyes were suspicious; the princess' wary.

Taking the reins from Jes, Jeran straightened. "Forgive me, but the beauty of your city overwhelmed me for a moment." Charylla's lips pursed together tightly. She urged her horse forward without comment, but her eyes said that she did not believe Jeran's lie.

Once past the wall, the forest thinned considerably. The huge trees were still plentiful, many even larger than those which formed the wall; but they were spaced farther apart, and sparse underbrush, interspersed with beautiful flowers, filled the ground between them. There were no signs of civilization, no buildings or farms, only occasional patches of dark soil lined with rows of growing vegetables. Elves, dressed in drab brown robes, tended the gardens; their eyes never once rose to view the procession.

It was not until Jeran looked up that he understood. The trees were not merely trees, they were the foundations of buildings. Huge rooms sat suspended from gigantic branches, structures that rivaled the largest palaces of Kaper were built into the trees themselves, often disappearing into the foliage high above. Branches, as wide as streets, were tied together, joining the forest into a single, giant structure, suspended high above the ground.

Where the branches were not thick enough for roads, bridges made of wood and rope spanned the distances. A vast network connected each tree to its neighbors. Elves walked the bridges and the branches with ease. Though some stared down at the Human delegation, most continued on without sparing a glance.

Squinting, Jeran saw more bridges higher up, a second level to the city almost invisible from the ground. Jeran pointed it out to Martyn saying, "I bet there are more levels, even higher. These trees must be at least two thousand hands high!" Martyn could only nod dumbly; he bent his head back as far as it would go and stared into the heavens.

Every branch was meticulously trimmed, producing a beautiful effect. As they watched, Aelvin workers darted from tree to tree, trimming branches, plucking dead leaves, and in some cases bending the branches themselves into shapes.

Children ran on some of the bridges, and others deftly climbed the great trees. A few scampered to the ground and cautiously approached. They kept their distance, but looked at the Humans with curiosity. Jeran noticed immediately that the young Elves were different than their parents. They were inquisitive and innocent, and lacked the cautious mistrust Jeran had come to expect from the Elves with which he traveled.

Jeran called out greetings to the children, bidding them to approach. His comments earned him odd looks from not only Treloran, but from

Martyn as well. Most of the Elves scampered away when he spoke, but one small child managed to raise her hand in greeting before she was whisked away by the older children.

Charylla led them through streets constructed of glistening white stone, a stark contrast to the dark wood of the forest. Every stone was laid with exacting precision; each one seemed to meld into the next. No weeds were visible, nor did Jeran see a single dead leaf. Every plant was spaced evenly with those around it, every shrub painstakingly pruned. Flowers grew in ordered rows, sometimes in beds of identical color, sometimes in fascinating patterns of alternating hue. Vines snaked up many of the trees, following specific patterns. Many of the vines had flowers of their own; they dotted the dark brown bark of the trees with spots of bright color.

Jeran reined to look at one bed of flowers growing near the edge of the road. They were a brilliant shade of violet, the color of a summer sky when the sun has just dipped below the horizon. He inhaled deeply, delighting in their sweet fragrance. While he stood there, several brown-robed workers appeared. They scanned the ground briefly, then began to dig. With great speed and efficiency, they removed the flowers and smoothed out the remaining grass, then disappeared as silently as they had appeared.

Confused, his heart nearly breaking at the destruction of such beauty, Jeran heeled his horse forward, returning quickly to the front of the column. He slowed as he approached Charylla and Treloran, and called out to get their attention. Treloran looked at him, his expression one of forced tolerance. "Why did they destroy that flowerbed?" he asked. "Those flowers were healthy and beautiful."

Treloran spared a quick glance back, then returned his attention to Jeran. His words came slowly, and his tone was somewhat patronizing, as if he were speaking to a small child. "They were not planned," was all he said, as if that should be answer enough.

Jeran did not press the Elf for information, though numerous questions sprang to mind. He followed along silently, still trying to view Lynnaei in all its splendor, but he no longer saw the city in quite the same way. Lost in his own thoughts, Jeran was unaware of the passage of time. He nearly walked his horse into Martyn when the column came to a sudden halt.

Looking at the prince, Jeran was surprised to see a look of amazement in Martyn's eyes. He laughed. "Surely you're used to the city by now!" In response, Martyn merely lifted his hand, pointing a finger. Jeran let his eyes follow, and his mouth dropped open in shock.

Ahead of them stood a vast mountain. Surrounded by trees, it seemed out of place. Formed of solid red-brown stone, the mountain was as large as Old Kaper; its flat top towering over the giant trees. Steps were carved in the rock, huge slabs of white marble climbing the hillside and ending in a broad, white-stoned plaza. A huge door, more than a hundred hands across, stood where the plaza joined the cliff face, and two giant statues, noble Aelvin warriors dressed in armor, stood guard before the entrance. Their swords were unsheathed, the blades alone twice as tall as Jeran.

The Emperor's Palace had been carved into the rock, cut into the very stone of the mountain. Vines of varying size sent snaking tentacles up the walls, and flowers blossomed around every window. Jeran closed his eyes. He could almost feel the power radiating from the structure.

Towers, each a different color, stretched into the sky, lining the outside of the plateau, ranging in shade from jade to emerald to deep forest green. Other towers–blues and reds and yellows–rose from the interior of the palace, but one tower eclipsed them all: A single column of bleached white climbing from the palace's center, its tip lost in the sky above, no more than a speck of darkness silhouetted in the light.

Charylla smiled. "Welcome to the Eternal Palace, home of the Emperor Alwellyn el'e Llwellyn." Her tone was regal and refined. She turned and led her horse up the broad marble stairs. Words failing them, the Alrendrians followed her dumbly toward the castle of the Elves.

Chapter 6

Dahr ran through the forest blindly, branches whipping his face. The trees streaked past, blurs of brown and green on the edge of his vision. Animals, frightened by his passage, fled before him. Deer, rabbits, and squirrels scattered at his approach; birds took to wing as he passed. He even startled a forest cat, gorging itself on a recent kill. It growled menacingly, but Dahr noticed it no more than the others.

"Monster!" came a cry from not far behind. "We *will* find you, monster! You can't run forever!" Wicked laughter echoed through the trees.

Dahr ignored the taunts as well, except to note their proximity, to tell how much closer his pursuers had drawn. They were gaining on him. No matter how fast he ran, he could not lose them. Already near exhaustion, he knew he would not be able to maintain his frantic pace much longer.

The forest was thinner here, not nearly as impassable as along the Danelle. The land rolled in gentle hills, and broad clearings interrupted the forest, allowing bright, warm sunlight to enter. Dahr found it easy to pick a path, though in his haste, he left a trail that even a child could follow.

Behind him, a stick snapped, and Dahr looked over his shoulder, afraid they had finally caught him. The forest was empty. Heaving a sigh of relief, he turned forward just in time to see the tree looming before him.

Ducking to the side, Dahr tried to change direction, but he was moving too fast. The thick, solid trunk slammed into his shoulder, knocking him from his feet. He fell, reaching out instinctively for the ground; when his shoulder contacted the hard-packed dirt, he rolled. His fast thinking spared him serious injury, but his momentum carried him over the crest of a hill, and he slid down the far side.

His hands scrambled across the ground, seeking a root or a rock, but there was nothing to grab. Tumbling end over end, he fell ever faster down the hill. His bruised shoulder struck another sapling, and his head smashed against more than a few rocks. Each impact sent a lance of pain through his body; bright lights flashed before his eyes, and the sounds of the forest dimmed.

At the bottom of the hill, he came to a stop. Breathing shallowly, he lay on his back in agony, one hand clapped over his eyes, the other squeezing his . Struggling for air, he drew himself to his feet, fighting off a wave of dizziness. Leaning against a nearby tree, he calmed himself.

"They're coming," whispered a strange, sibilant voice. Dahr tensed at the sound and looked around, his hand shielding his eyes. Almost immediately, he heard his pursuers crashing through the trees.

"I think he's down here!" called one voice. "I can see where he went down the hill." Louder, so he could be sure Dahr heard, the man yelled, "We're coming for you, freak! Stop running, and we'll make this quick. Even relatively painless! But if you flee, or even think about fighting...." The words trailed off, and Dahr thought he heard his pursuers laughing amongst themselves.

Turning, Dahr stumbled away from the voice. A broad, shallow stream, its bottom covered with smooth stones, snaked through the center of the valley. Dahr jumped in, wincing as the ice-cold water swirled around his knees. Trying not to splash, he waded downstream, hoping the maneuver would confuse his pursuers long enough for him to escape.

He half-ran, half-swam, letting the current pull him along, until his feet were numb from the cold and his arms started to shiver uncontrollably. Finally, when he could hear no more signs of pursuit, not even the echo of footfalls, he dragged himself from the stream and ran into the trees, looking for a place to hide.

He came upon a dense copse, well away from the water. Still shivering, he forced his way through the underbrush and crouched in the small hollow between the trees. Groaning, Dahr put his head in his hands, pressing his palms forcefully against his eyes. Exhausted, he collapsed, grunting when he landed on the hard, rocky soil. He rubbed his legs vigorously, eager for them to regain some warmth.

If only I can find Katya! Everything would be well were she with me. He had sent her off to scout this morning, to look for some sign of the Garun'ah. She had not been there when it happened, so he knew she was still safe, maybe even unaware of what had happened. When Dahr had fled, he had gone in the same direction as she had, so there was still a chance he would find her. Unless they found her first.

That dark thought took the last of his strength. *If they've hurt Katya....* If they had hurt Katya, or killed her, it would be his fault. She was all he had now. *If I lost her, too....*

Dahr curled up in a tight ball and wept.

"You are a disgrace, Half-man." said a heavily-accented voice. Dahr jumped at the sound, his head whirling around. Relief flooded through him when he saw the Tribesman, dressed in light brown leathers and with a long, curved blade at his side. The stranger watched Dahr warily, but with more than a hint of pity as well.

Dahr scrambled to his feet and walked toward the Tribesman. They were of a height, nearly fourteen hands tall, but the newcomer was half again as wide and thickly muscled. Jet-black hair, woven into a tight braid, hung halfway between his shoulders and waist. Almond-shaped eyes, nearly as dark as his hair, watched Dahr suspiciously. "Thank the Gods I found you!" Dahr said. "I've been searching for the Garun'ah."

The Tribesman stepped back and raised a hand, warning Dahr off. "What could you want of my people?" he asked, his eyes hardening.

"I come with news that the tribes must hear," Dahr answered. A wave of embarrassment washed over him, and his cheeks reddened. "I want to learn about my people, too," he added. "I'm Garun'ah!"

The Tribesman laughed harshly. "You are no Hunter."

The icy tone hurt. "I am," Dahr insisted. "Can't you see it? We look enough alike to be cousins! I have come to learn about my people."

The Tribesman spat on the ground. His eyes, now cold and angry, scanned Dahr from head to toe. "You have the body of a Tribesman," he acknowledged, his lips turned down distastefully, as if even that small admission pained him, "but you do not have the spirit. You have the mind of a Human. The soul of a coward."

Dahr tried to argue, but the Tribesman ignored him. "You have the mark of those taken by the Soul-Stealers," he said, gesturing with his chin. Dahr turned his head, surprised to see that his shirt had torn, exposing the condor brand of the Grondellans. "No child of Garun would have allowed himself to be marked by the Soul-Stealers."

"I was a child when it happened!" Dahr protested, but he knew his words would have no effect.

The Tribesman's lip curled up in a sneer. "Whether a cub at his mother's breast or a toothless old man, no Tribesman would allow himself to be taken. You do not have our blood."

Dahr tried to restrain his anger, but was only half successful. "I escaped!" he declared. "When I found the man who captured me, I attacked his camp. I freed his slaves and fired his wagons. I even released other Tribesmen who'd been captured!"

The Garun'ah considered Dahr's words. His expression relaxed a little, and his eyes softened. "You killed the Soul-Stealer?"

Dahr shrugged. "I defeated him in combat, but he crawled away before I could kill him." He saw that his words were not having the right effect. "His wounds were grievous! There is little chance he survived."

"You are not sure?" The Garun'ah frowned again, turning away. "You are no Tribesman. I begin to doubt that you are even Human."

Dahr rushed over and grabbed the Tribesman's arm. "None of this is important now," he said, a hint of desperation in his voice. "I'm being chased by other Humans. They intend to kill me. You must help me find my friend, a red-haired Human in dark leather armor."

The Tribesman growled and shoved Dahr, knocking him to the ground. "You are being hunted?" he spat derisively. "*We* are the Hunters, Half-man. The wolf does not run from his prey, he destroys it."

The Garun'ah moved toward the trees. He looked at Dahr one last time, his expression a mixture of revulsion and loathing. "Garun must have been drunk of *baqhat* the day he allowed you to be born. You shame us all, Half-man." With an animal-like growl, the Tribesman disappeared into the thick underbrush.

Dahr ran after him. "Wait!" he called as he burst from the grove, his eyes darting about frantically. The Tribesman was gone; not even a footprint remained to mark his passage. Dahr clenched his fists in anger, each indrawn breath hissed between his teeth, and bile rose in his throat.

An arrow thudded into the tree beside him. The shaft quivered, only a hand's distance from Dahr's head. "I missed!" a voice cried. Several others called in answer, and the sounds of people hurrying through the forest came once more to Dahr's ears. "Hold still, monster," called the voice. "It's easier to hit you that way!"

Panicking, Dahr looked left and right, but he heard footsteps approaching from every direction. Scanning the trees, he searched desperately for the archer, but saw nothing. He stepped forward, then hesitated, not sure which way to go. "This way...." whispered a voice to his right.

Dahr's eyes narrowed warily, but he turned right, expecting treachery. Behind him, his pursuers drew near; Dahr saw flashes of their shadowy forms in the distance. "This way," the voice repeated, more urgently, when the first figure appeared behind Dahr. The words drifted through the still, forest air, beckoning Dahr forward.

He ran, pushing heedlessly through the trees. The first rock struck him in his left thigh; the second scored a hit on his back. The third hit squarely on his head, and Dahr fell to the ground with a loud crash. He rolled to his back, stars flashing before his eyes. When his vision cleared, a figure stood above him, sword leveled at his chest.

"Why do you keep running, monster?" Jasova asked, his brown eyes staring at Dahr with even more hatred than the Tribesman's. The Alrendrian Guardsman gestured with his sword, and Dahr rose to a sitting position. As he did so, blonde-haired Nykeal stepped from the trees, slinging a bow over her shoulder.

"We've got him!" she called out, cupping a hand to her mouth. She lifted Dahr's chin with her gauntleted hand. "A fine catch, my Lord," she said, smiling adoringly at Jasova. "What do you plan to do with the beast? A rug, perhaps? Or will you mount his head on the wall?"

Jasova chuckled, but before he could answer, the others appeared. Broad-shouldered Wardel and olive-skinned Vyrina walked arm in arm from the trees, laughing when they saw Dahr on the ground. "A fine hunt," Wardel said to his companions. "Pity it had to end so soon."

They all laughed at that, and Dahr was dragged unwillingly to his feet. He glared at his one-time companions angrily. "Why are you doing this?" he demanded. "What have I done to you?"

"I can't speak for the others," Wardel announced, hitting Dahr with a vicious backhand, "but personally, I've hated you since you embarrassed me in front of the other Guardsmen." At Dahr's confused look, the brown-haired Guardsman sneered. "I know my mounts well! Yet you called me down in front of the others. In front of Lord Iban!" Wardel hit Dahr again, splitting his lip. Dahr tasted blood, and he felt a trickle of warm liquid on his chin. "I will make you wish you hadn't."

"I wanted to see the legendary Lynnaei," said Vyrina, a wistful smile dancing across her lips. "But I was ordered to join you. To follow you into this miserable, empty place."

"Jasova?" Dahr called out plaintively. "Nykeal? We fought together against the slavers! We're friends! How can you do this?"

"Friends?" Nykeal said, amused. "Why would I be friends with the King's Hound? A monster! A spy sent from the Tribal Lands." She grabbed Dahr by the collar and glared at him, though she had to crane her neck far back to stare into his eyes. "You disgust me!"

Dahr felt his anger growing, burning hot within him. "Jasova?" he asked again, almost afraid to hear what the other Guardsman had to say.

The tall man scratched his goatee for a moment, as if thinking about his answer. "It's really nothing personal, Dahr," he said at last. "I like you just as much as any other beast." Shrugging, he drew back his sword back. "But in the end, what does it matter if one more animal lives or dies?" With a laugh, he swung at Dahr's head.

Dahr ducked the swing and grabbed the Guardsman's arm. Shifting his weight, he threw Jasova over his shoulder, wrenching the blade free at the same time. The subcommander crashed into a tree and fell to the ground in a heap. Wardel, snarling, drew his blade and advanced, his eyes glaring daggers. Nykeal and Vyrina were slower, but they, too, drew their weapons and charged.

Growling, Dahr lunged at Wardel. He swung his sword and heard a crunch as the blade sank deep into the Guardsman's side. A spray of blood washed over him, and a cry of agony echoed in his ears. Howling with fury, Dahr rushed the other Guardsmen, bowling them over.

He turned, licked his lips, and considered killing them while they were disorganized. But Jasova was already on his feet, and the two women were struggling to rise, too, so Dahr once again ran into the trees. "At least I'm armed now!" he said to himself, wiping the blood off his face.

A shadowy form appeared before him, and Dahr came to a skidding halt. He raised his blade threateningly, but let out a grateful sigh when Katya stepped into the light. "Thank the Gods!" he said, recognizing her. "I was worried that something had happened to you."

"Dahr!" called the redheaded Guardsman, her voice concerned. "What are you doing so far from the camp?"

Lowering his sword, he hurried over to her. "Treachery!" he said. "After you left, the others attacked. I escaped, but have been running ever since. I hoped to find you. To warn you." A stick snapped, and Dahr whirled around in fear, but saw nothing. After a tense moment, he returned his eyes to Katya. "Hurry!" he said. "We have to go before they catch us."

"Peace, Dahr," Katya said softly, reaching out to him. "We have a moment or two." He went to her, and she took the blade from his hand as they embraced. Smiling, he leaned in to kiss her, and was stunned when a blow knocked him away.

He stumbled back, clutching the side of his head where Katya had slammed the hilt of the sword. "Katya?" he said in disbelief.

"Did you really think I'd give my affections to something like you?" she asked, laughing wickedly. She inspected the blade in her hand, looking closely at the blood. "Just being this close to you makes me want to bathe." She shrugged guiltily, and wrinkling her nose is distaste, added, "It's the smell that bothers me most of all."

Dahr could not catch his breath. He dropped to his knees, staring wide-eyed at the swordswoman. Words failed him. "But... But... Why?"

Katya laughed again, and the sound he once found so musical now echoed hollowly in his ears. "Why, to get close to Jeran, of course! I offered myself to him, you know, but he refused. It seems that Lord Odara actually considers you a friend." Furrowing her brow, she looked at Dahr disdainfully. "I can't imagine why."

Dahr shook his head, but Katya would not let him speak. "Once you're gone, Jeran would have no reason not to take me to his bed." An evil smile found its way to Katya's face. "Until then, I'll have to find other ways to entertain myself." Another figure stepped from the trees, and Dahr cried out when Elorn appeared. The dour Guardsman walked to Katya and drew her to him, kissing her full on the mouth.

"*No!*" Dahr howled, and the sound carried through the forest like the cry of a beast. Katya and Elorn turned toward him just as the other Guardsmen appeared behind. Jumping to his feet, Dahr rushed forward, his blood boiling. He swung a fist at Elorn, knocking the stocky man from his feet, and grabbed Katya. With little effort, he lifted her from the ground, squeezing so tightly that she groaned in pain. Screaming, no longer able to control his rage, Dahr sent her crashing into the other Guardsmen. All four tumbled to the ground in a tangled mass of limbs.

"Over here," whispered the voice. Dahr turned, confused, and saw a silhouetted shape in the distance, beckoning for him to come closer. "This way," the voice called again. "I can help." The figure stepped through a stand of thick pines and disappeared.

Dahr cast one final glance at Katya, and his heart rent when he saw her regain her feet, murder in her eyes. He ran toward the stranger, pushing through the thick, needle-covered branches.

And suddenly found himself in a stone room with high ceilings. Tapestries, separated by sconces, hung from the walls. A torch burned in each sconce, and a fire blazed across the hall, providing more than enough light. Around the fire sat two plush chairs, and the shadowy stranger was bent over the hearth, adding fuel. He straightened when Dahr appeared. "Join me, brother," he called warmly, waving for Dahr to come closer.

Slowly, Dahr crossed the room, staring at the stranger. Though the distance between them narrowed, the man's features became no more detailed. The man laughed. "Join me!" he repeated, urging Dahr forward. "You must be half frozen." Dahr was, and the heat of the flames felt good, even from across the room. Relaxing, Dahr quickened his pace.

"You are thirsty, too, yes?" the man asked, holding out a glass. "It's not the best vintage, but you'll find it palatable, I'm sure." The man pointed to one of the chairs. "Sit, Dahr. Make yourself comfortable."

Dahr took the glass and sat. As he settled into the chair, the room brightened, and the man before him suddenly became visible. He was tall and thin, with slightly sunken eyes and bony cheeks. Long, narrow fingers, capped at the end with sharp lengths of fingernail, reached for the other glass. The stranger wore robes of white that seemed dark in comparison to his skin, and long, white hair fell to his shoulders in loose curls. He drank deeply, his blood red eyes regarding Dahr over the brim of his glass.

Something about the stranger's appearance tickled Dahr's memory, and he felt like he should know the man. He was certain that they had never before met; he would have remembered a man with red eyes. "How do you know my name?" Dahr asked, taking a sip of the sweet red wine. He sighed as he swallowed, relaxing completely.

"I know much about you, Dahr," the man said amicably. "I told you, we are brothers, of a sort." He sat back in his chair, settling comfortably against the plush cushions, and thoughtfully tapped his lips. "I know of your abduction. Your time spent as a slave. I know of your seasons in Keryn's Rest. I know the story of your life." The stranger smiled. Thin red lips pulled back to expose narrow, slightly pointed teeth.

"The pain," the man added, nodding his head sadly, "The pain I know most of all. The fear and the worry. The feeling that you have no worth, that you live only in the shadow of a greater person. That you exist only because that person has offered you his protection." There was an edge to the voice now, tinged with the bitterness of old memories.

Dahr swallowed. "And what should I call you?"

The stranger cocked his head to the side. "Do you truly not recognize me?" he asked, not bothering to hide his disbelief. Dahr shook his head, and the man laughed. It was a cold sound, devoid of all human emotion.

"Forgive me, brother," the man said after he finally regained his composure. "I'm used to people knowing me at a glance." The cold smile returned. "I've been called many things throughout the long winters of my life, but my given name is Lorthas."

Dahr's eyes widened as the stories came back to him in a rush. The demon with white hair and red eyes, who had burned the world with his madness. The Darklord, who had tried to enslave Madryn. The monster who had betrayed his people and started a war that had lasted hundreds of winters. Without realizing it, Dahr pushed himself to the back of his chair, straining to maximize the distance between he and the Darklord.

Lorthas laughed at Dahr's antics. "Is something wrong, brother?" he asked with a note of genuine concern.

"Don't call me brother!" Dahr wailed, finding his voice at last. He struggled to hold back frightened tears. "We are not the same, Darklord! I'll never be like you!"

Lorthas hung his head sadly. "You do me an injustice, brother," he said in a quiet whisper. "Have I offered you any harm? Done anything but help you? I even led you out of that terrible dream."

"Dream?" Dahr repeated, the retort that had burned on his lips fading at the Darklord's words.

Lorthas nodded. "Yes, only a dream. A terrible dream, for sure, but very insightful." Lorthas looked around the room. "This is a dream, too, of a kind. Though one of my choosing. I tell you true, little brother, that I mean you no harm here. I wish only to talk."

"What could you have to say to me, Darklord?" Dahr asked, eyeing the Mage suspiciously. "And stop calling us brothers! We are not brothers!"

"Ah, but we are," Lorthas argued, waving his hand. An ghostly image appeared, a boy, about ten winters old, with scraggly white hair and flame red eyes. Dahr knew instantly that he looked upon Lorthas as a child.

From the shadows, voices whispered. "Monster!"

"Freak!"

"Demon-spawn!"

The epithets and names continued, whispered in a hundred different voices. "Your kind is not welcome here!" cried one. From every direction, the voices called curses and names–some directed at Lorthas, some at Dahr, and some that could be equally applied to both.

"You're nothing but the King's Hound!"

"White-haired ghoul!"

"Garun'ah animal!"

"Fire-eyed devil!"

The voices continued for a time, each remark more cruel than the last. When the last voice faded into nothingness, Lorthas stared at Dahr sympathetically. "You see," he said after a long silence. "We are not so different, you and I. Despised because we are different. Feared because of our Gifts. We are kindred spirits, Dahr. We are brothers!"

Dahr put his hands over his eyes. "What do you want of me?"

"To help you," Lorthas said. "To ease your suffering." The Darklord leaned forward and grasped Dahr's arm, pulling his hand away from his eyes. Dahr tried to resist, but Lorthas' frail appearance hid great strength. "In return, I ask only that you listen to me. History has judged me harshly, and that pains me. I want to tell my story, and leave you to decide for yourself whether I am a monster or a hero."

"Dahr," a voice echoed through the room. Dahr looked around, but saw nothing. Lorthas gave no indication that he had heard. Dahr shook his head, and tried to refuse the Darklord. "I don't want to hear your–"

"Dahr?" called the voice again, this time a little louder. For an instant, the room blurred, and Dahr grew dizzy. He put a hand on the arm of his chair to steady himself.

Lorthas patted him comfortingly. "This has been too much for you. I can see that now. Besides, you appear to be waking." The world blurred again, and as the room faded to black, Lorthas' final words echoed in Dahr's mind. "We will speak again, brother."

"Dahr?" Katya called, shaking him gently. When his eyes fluttered open, she hid a relieved sigh, and a smirk instantly replaced her worried frown. "I thought you were going to sleep all day," she quipped. "The others are up, breakfast will soon be ready, and last night you claimed that you wanted an early start. Have you changed your mind?"

Dahr struggled to rise. "No. I want to be underway before the sun is full up." He stretched, and was embarrassed when he realized he was only half dressed. Laughing, Katya playfully touched his cheek and stood. With an inviting smile, she pulled aside the flap and left the tent.

Dressing hurriedly, Dahr began the routine of taking down his tent and packing his gear. It took only a few moments, and he laughed to himself, remembering how laborious the process had seemed less than a season ago.

The others were waiting for him, their horses already saddled, as Dahr wolfed down the porridge Nykeal handed him. He thanked the blonde Guardsman between bites, and once finished, rinsed the bowl and packed it. He went to Jardelle, his huge black stallion, and after stroking the horse's cheek fondly, secured his gear, tightening the cinches with a series of deft pulls.

Reaching into his pack, Dahr measured out a large handful of oats and offered them to Jardelle. Whinnying gratefully, the stallion took the grain, chewing it contentedly.

Dahr climbed into the saddle and turned toward the others. "Are we ready?" he asked, earning himself a series of half-serious glares. Laughing aloud, Dahr led the way out of the camp, and his mind drifted back.

After separating from the Alrendrian delegation, Dahr had backtracked down the Path of Riches, but only until he found a side trail. On the journey from Grenz, they had seen only one Garun'ah, and him from a distance. Believing that their luck would be equally poor if they retraced their route, Dahr had decided to go north in search of his people.

An alternate path presented itself before they had traveled far. The narrow, twisting trail branched off the Path of Riches, disappearing into the thick trees of the Great Forest. No one had complained when Dahr turned his mount onto the trail, though Elorn had muttered something in a voice too low to be heard clearly. One stern look had silenced him, but for the rest of the day, Elorn's hateful glare had cut deep gashes in Dahr's back.

They had followed the trail north along the Danelle, and the forest served up sight after sight. Trees of countless varieties–firs and pines, maples and oaks–filled the landscape, taller by far than any in Alrendria. *This is thicker than the Darkwood!* Dahr thought, his memories drifting to the eerie woods where he and Jeran had hidden from the Durange. If not for the trail, they would have been forced to cut a path through the dense branches and thorny underbrush.

The terrain was hilly, though far from mountainous, and dotted with lakes and streams, all which flowed toward the larger Danelle. One day they had camped on the shore of a lake whose surface was as smooth as glass. The waters were as clear as crystal, yet so deep that Dahr could not reach bottom no matter how hard he tried.

Another afternoon, they had come across a clearing with a small pool of bubbling water in its center. Curious, Wardel had dipped his hand in the water, quickly pulling it back. "It's hot!" he had yelled, shaking his hand vigorously. The ground had started to tremble, and Dahr barely had enough time to pull the Guardsman away before a geyser of water erupted from the ground, spraying the Alrendrians with a warm mist.

After that, they had kept their distance, but had watched the geyser with fascination. Dahr, in particular, was awed by the phenomenon; it erupted with a regularity precise enough to mark time.

As the days passed, other wonders had presented themselves. A river whose bottom glittered with gold. One stretch of forest littered with beautiful crystals, some larger than Dahr's head. Wildflowers of all shapes and colors lined the trail. Game was plentiful, and they feasted each night on rabbit, pheasant, or duck. One evening, Vyrina brought down an elk with her bow, and Wardel cooked it on a huge spit that took two of them to turn. After that, they had eaten nothing but elk for half a score of days.

The farther the Alrendrians traveled north, the thinner the forest had become. Two days past, they had forded the Danelle, and according to the map Jeran had given him, their present course would soon lead out of the Great Forest. They had yet to see any sign of Garun'ah, and Dahr hoped that their luck would be better on the grasslands. The Tribesmen were nomads, and Dahr guessed that they would prefer the thinner forests and plains of northern Madryn to the dense trees through which he and his companions now pressed.

As they rode, Dahr studied his small party of Guardsmen. At the rear of the procession rode Jasova, tall and proud, eating a pear that he had plucked from a nearby tree. He sat in his saddle lazily, his eyes half closed, his free hand idly scratching a dark brown goatee. The lethargy was an act. Jasova was one of Iban's most trusted subcommanders, and his dark eyes missed very little.

To his left rode Nykeal. The Guardswoman wore her long blonde hair in a tightly woven braid to keep it from her eyes. An excellent archer, she had her bow slung over her shoulder, but could have it drawn and aimed in an instant. She watched Jasova with a smile; since the attack on the slavers' camp, the two had become virtually inseparable.

Wardel rode in front of Nykeal, and Vyrina beside him. At twenty-four winters, Wardel was the youngest Guardsman in their group. He was shorter than Jasova, but only by a finger's width, and half again as broad. The thickly muscled man, a farmer's son from Terrioc, a village within the domain of House Morrena, had joined the Guard at fifteen winters. At seventeen, he took an arrow for Jysin, First Seat of House Morrena, saving the nobleman's life. When Lord Iban found out, he had transferred Wardel to his command. Jysin was furious at the transfer, but since Iban was High Commander of the Alrendrian Guard, he could not refuse.

The third daughter of Iban's oldest brother, Vyrina was one of only a handful of the Family Iban to survive the Tachan War. At the war's end, she was sent to Kaper. Iban had raised her as a Guardsman, and it was no surprise that she had insisted on enlisting.

Vyrina was an excellent marksman, better even than Nykeal. She wore her hair short, like the male Guardsmen. Her eyes were chestnut brown, her face narrow and hard. She had distinguished herself in numerous exercises, but this journey was her first true mission as a Guardsman.

Directly behind Dahr rode Katya and Elorn. Elorn's short and stocky form hunched forward in the saddle, his eyes distant, a hand continually running through his short black hair. His face was a mixture of extremes: long hooked nose, prominent, bony cheeks, and an angular chin. Elorn had distinguished himself in Kaper, and had been selected by Joam Batai to be part of the castle's elite Guard.

Of all Dahr's charges, only Elorn seemed disappointed with his assignment. He kept to himself for the most part, but every now and then, his mutterings grew louder. Though polite to the other Guardsmen, and friendly with Katya, Elorn hated Dahr, and took few measures to hide it. Hoping to ease the tension between them, Dahr had tried to talk to the sour-faced Guardsman several times, but each attempt had been met with an icy glare. If Elorn even deigned to answer Dahr's inquiries, his replies were brief. Normally, he just walked away.

Dahr shifted his gaze to Katya, and he smiled involuntarily. The breeze stirred her hair, blowing the coppery curls out in gentle waves. Emerald green eyes watched the forest, but they were distant, as if she, too, were deep in thought. Dahr felt a rush of warmth as he stared at her perfect body.

Katya turned and, seeing Dahr watching, returned his smile in kind. Her expression made the world seem brighter. Embarrassed, Dahr returned his gaze to the trail.

Katya was one of the few people who accepted Dahr the way he was. She had never called him a monster, had never looked frightened or afraid when he approached. Few had made him feel so comfortable, so at peace, as she. Aside from Jeran, she was the most important person in his world.

Since they had met, Dahr's whole life had changed. He had been adopted in House Odara and given a name; he had impressed Lord Iban during the long journey to Illendrylla. A chance encounter had led to his discovery of the slaver who had murdered his parents, and Dahr had avenged their deaths, freeing scores of slaves in the process. He could now count Jasova, Nykeal, and Captain Bryn Corrine of the River Falcon among his friends, and likely Wardel and Vyrina, too.

Perhaps it was not all due directly to Katya, but it had all happened since she entered his life. She instilled in him a confidence, a belief in himself that he had never before known. She made Kaper seem like a home instead of a prison. She had made him happy, and Dahr loved her for it. More than he had loved anything in his life.

"If I could just tell her," he mumbled, but his confidence was not yet so great that he could share such things with her. That she liked him, he did not doubt. Yet he could not believe her feelings ran as strongly as his. Not Katya, who could have whatever, or whomever, she wanted.

"Dahr!" called Jasova in his deep baritone. "I see something." Dahr brought Jardelle to a stop and turned the huge horse around. The other Guardsmen had stopped, too, and Jasova nudged his mount to the edge of the forest. He leaned forward, squinting through the trees, and pointed with his left hand, the remains of the pear still clutched in his fist.

It took Dahr a while to find what the Guardsman saw: a mound, large and dark. Several crows sat on the mound, staring with black eyes at the Guardsmen. Dahr dismounted and looped his reins over a nearby branch. "Probably just a dead animal. But I'll take a look anyway. Katya?" The redhead dismounted and followed, handing her reins to Elorn.

They moved cautiously through the trees, trying to make as little noise as possible. The crows saw them coming and took to wing, cawing raucously. As soon as they neared, Dahr could tell that the mound was once a man. He grabbed a stick and used it to roll the figure over. Sightless eyes stared up at him.

"It's a Garun'ah!" Dahr called, loud enough that the others could hear. He knelt, and Katya dropped to her knees beside him. Gingerly, Dahr touched the Tribesman's head, tilting it back and forth. A series of scratches ran across the Tribesman's face.

"Look at this!" Katya exclaimed, pulling the Garun'ah's leathers aside. The broken shaft of an arrow protruded from the warrior's chest. Katya grabbed her belt knife and cut the corpse's flesh, wrinkling her nose at the smell. Pulling the arrow free, she held it out to Dahr.

He took it, spinning the shaft in his hand. It was steel, but pyramidal, not triangular like Alrendrian arrows, with four small barbs curving out from the edge. The shaft was of smoothed pine, inscribed up and down its length with unrecognizable symbols.

The other Guardsmen approached. Frowning, Dahr showed them the arrow. "Do any of you recognize these?" he asked, indicating the runes.

They each took a turn examining the arrow, but no one was immediately forthcoming. It was Elorn who finally spoke, which surprised Dahr more than what the Guardsman had to say. "My father once told me that the Garun'ah have no written language, that all their history is told by means of stories. Nor is this any Human writing I have ever seen. These could be magical runes, but I have never heard of the Magi using such. To the best of my knowledge, even the MageSmiths simply instilled magic into a weapon. They had no need of symbols."

Elorn looked at Dahr and frowned, as if he disliked offering his opinion. "This arrow is likely Aelvin, though I've never seen their writing before." The discussed other options, but in the end agreed that Elorn's explanation was the best.

"Before we left Kaper," Jasova said, drawing all eyes toward him. "I heard that the Elves and Garun'ah were fighting. Their races have warred on and off for centuries." He looked at the body again and frowned. "Though if this were the site of a battle, you'd think there'd be more signs of a fight. This body's only a couple days old."

"What do we do now?" Vyrina asked.

It was a long moment before Dahr realized she was asking him. He considered the question for a moment, then said. "We bury him. Then we continue on."

"Bury him!" Elorn huffed, snorting loudly.

"No," Dahr said, remembering the fight in the slaver's camp and how they had laid the fallen Tribesman to rest. "Not bury. Burn." His change of mind did not appease Elorn, whose frown grew even darker.

"And what if the Elves who killed him are still around?" Wardel asked.

Dahr shrugged. "We hope their grudge is with the Garun'ah, and not with us. Or we hope we're enough to discourage them from attacking."

"Or we hope we can defeat them," Katya added.

Dahr nodded. "Or we hope that we can defeat them."

Chapter 7

They followed Charylla up the broad, flat staircase, their horses' hooves clicking on each marble step. The pack animals and supply wagons were handed over to an army of silent, brown-robed Elves. They had gone east, along a different path, a broader, more gradual incline that disappeared around the side of the plateau.

The Emperor's Palace dominated the hill, so large it made Kaper Castle seem tiny. None of the giant trees grew around the vast mountain-castle, but flowers and shrubs, arranged with exacting precision, formed ornate patterns. One bed, each bulb placed with care, formed the image of a woman. Platinum blonde hair framed a perfect face; a knowing smile graced tulip lips. Arms outstretched, she gazed protectively at the forest below.

The massive trees circled the plateau, stretching thousands of hands into the air, but not even the tallest equaled the height of the palace. As the party climbed higher, the city became visible behind them. Jeran craned his neck, allowing himself another look at Lynnaei.

There were more levels to the city than could be seen from the ground. Intertwining, massive branches, some as broad as a city street, connected the lowest levels. Wagons, barely visible through the thick foliage, trundled slowly down the avenues, carrying goods from one tree to another.

Higher up, the paths narrowed, until the branches were only wide enough for two or three abreast. At this height, about two hundred hands, the first bridges appeared. Made of wood and rope, they spanned the distances between the Great Trees, swaying gently in the wind.

Wherever branch met trunk, the Elves had constructed a platform. Some were featureless, little more than stairways to adjacent levels, but most sported small buildings, broad open plazas, or bustling markets. A few were even more elaborate. Vast estates, enough to rival the manor houses of Alrendria's greatest nobility, spanned multiple levels, reaching out from their trees for hundreds of hands, in some cases nearly touching their neighbors. Giant braces and thick crossbeams, cleverly hidden behind a meshwork of leaves and vines, supported each level.

Open-aired pavilions were abundant in the upper levels, commanding spectacular views over the treetops. Elves boldly walked the bridges between trees, oblivious to their distance from the ground. From where the Alrendrians stood, they appeared as little more than black specks.

Jeran returned his gaze to the castle looming above him. The party was nearing the top of the hill, from which rose the reddish-brown stone of the Emperor's Palace. The last stair merged into a broad marble plaza, wide enough that the entire company could draw their horses abreast.

Charylla stepped down from her horse, handing the reins to a waiting servant. Smiling serenely, the Aelvin Princess stood before the palace's massive oaken doors. Treloran took his place at her left, his expression unreadable. Luran was nowhere to be found.

"We hope your stay in Lynnaei will be a memorable one," Charylla said. "From these negotiations, We hope that peace will be fostered between our Races, and that the Path of Riches will once again flow with goods!" The Alrendrians cheered the princess' words; even the Aelvin warriors joined in the applause.

"Our servants will care for your horses," Charylla added, clapping her hands. At the signal, more brown-robed Elves appeared, coming from every direction. "I promise you, they will be well cared for while under our protection." Charylla waited while the Alrendrians dismounted and gathered their things.

"The Emperor himself wishes to welcome you to Lynnaei! A feast is being prepared, and all are invited to attend. When the bells of the palace chime seven times, a servant will appear to lead you to the hall. Once there, the Emperor will greet you, and we can begin the process of bringing our peoples together." Again, the Alrendrians cheered.

"I know your journey has been long," Charylla continued, her eyes fastening on Prince Martyn. "Rooms have been prepared. If it pleases you, I will have my servants lead you to your chambers, where you will have ample time to rest and refresh yourselves."

Martyn exchanged a brief glance with Lord Iban, who ducked his head slightly. Turning to face Charylla, the prince answered in his most stately voice. "We are honored, Princess Charylla, by the efforts your people have made to make us welcome here."

"Your Guardsmen will be quartered in rooms on the lower level of the palace," Charylla said, ignoring Martyn's statement, "directly below your chambers. If you wish, some can be moved to adjoining chambers, but I assure you, your safety is guaranteed as long as you are our guest."

"I have complete faith in you, my Lady. It will not be necessary to find new rooms for my Guardsmen." Offering Martyn a cool smile, Charylla inclined her head in acknowledgment of the prince's trust. "Where will the rest of my people be staying?"

"All members of your party will be quartered on the eastern face of the castle, where the guest chambers are located. The Guardsmen will occupy the lowest floors, and the diplomats will be above them, with their servants housed in nearby chambers. Lord Iban and you will be given chambers near the top of the palace, so you may see Lynnaei in all its glory."

She clapped her hands again, and another wave of servants appeared. Each took a position next to one of the Alrendrians. In a voice loud enough to be heard by all, Charylla announced, "My servants will lead you to your rooms. Your things will be brought once the wagons have arrived at the palace." To Martyn, she added, "I have been long gone from Lynnaei, and there is much I must attend to before tonight. I ask your permission to leave, Prince Martyn."

"Of course, Princess," he responded. "You have been more than hospitable. Until tonight."

"Until tonight," she repeated, turning on her heels and striding toward the doors to the palace, which swung open silently at her approach.

Martyn watched her leave, then turned excited eyes on Jeran. "Can you believe this place?" he asked incredulously. "It's amazing! I can't wait to see the city! Do you think we have time to take a look–"

"My Prince," interrupted Iban. "There will be plenty of time for exploring the city in the days to come. I suggest we go to our rooms and prepare for tonight's reception. No doubt you will want to wash the dust from your body before meeting the Emperor."

Martyn blushed and nodded. "Of course, Lord Iban. My excitement got the better of me." His eyes flashed with mirth as he looked at Jeran. "Until tonight, Lord Odara." He said it formally, but with a laugh, then waved to the servant beside him, indicating that he was ready to go.

Lord Iban followed the prince, and Jeran bowed to the silent figure at his side. The brown-robed Elf did not speak, but began to walk toward the castle, following the others. The Guardsmen were led around the side of the palace, while the servants and freed slaves were gathered together in a separate group.

Some of the little ones looked at Jeran as he passed, mixed expressions of wonder and fear on their faces. He waved to them and smiled. "I'll see you this evening!" he said, hoping to reassure them. "Enjoy yourselves!" Then he was inside the palace, and the children disappeared behind a wall of red-brown stone.

The entry hall was vast, the ceiling eighty hands high. Statues of Elves–some in armor, others wearing robes–lined the chamber. Directly across from the door was an open hallway that disappeared into the castle's interior. Doors covered both sides of the hall, and two winding staircases, equidistant from the center, curled gracefully up to the level above.

The delegates entered the hall behind Jeran. Utari's cool eyes scanned the room, drinking in every detail, but her expression betrayed nothing. Alynna stared wide-eyed, her mouth slightly open. She walked to one of the statues, reaching out to caress the finely-carved stone. Rafel gave the room a cursory glance, then clapped his hands together and demanded to be shown his rooms. The brown-robed Elves led them to the left.

Jeran's Elf beckoned for him to follow. They started toward the prince and Lord Iban, who were climbing the staircase to the left, but Treloran appeared suddenly appeared, stepping out of the shadows. "My mother has asked me to show you to your chambers, Lord Odara."

Jeran regarded the Aelvin Prince curiously. "Very well," he said at last, taking his pack from the servant. Hoping to soften the young Elf's stony demeanor, he said, "Lord Odara is far too formal. You may call me Jeran."

Treloran grimaced. "This way, Lord Odara," he said, turning right.

Suddenly wary, Jeran hesitated. "We're not going with the others?"

Not bothering to slow his pace, Treloran answered, "At the Emperor's request, your rooms are removed from those of your countrymen. We could reach them by following the others, but this way will be shorter."

Reluctantly, Jeran followed Treloran up the winding staircase, sighing when the last of the delegates disappeared into the recesses of the castle. After they were gone, he focused his attention on not getting lost.

The palace was a maze of dim passageways and narrow steps. Treloran kept to a fast walk, giving Jeran little chance to orient himself to his new surroundings. They snaked through endless twisting halls, and Jeran knew he would never be able to find his way back without the aid of an Elf.

Several times they passed by windows carved through the rock of the mountain. Golden rays of sunlight streamed to the floor, providing ample illumination. Each window was higher than the last, with more of the Great Forest visible below. The Aelvin Prince never stopped moving, and Jeran had to run to catch him each time he paused to admire the view.

They passed only a handful of Elves during their travels, all dressed in brown robes. The servants, engrossed as they were in various chores, did not even look at them.

At long last, they climbed a final staircase, this one a long spiral stair lighted by flickering candles. At the top was a long, straight hallway, its floor covered with a thick layer of dust. They walked, and small clouds rose with every step. "This hall hasn't been used in a while," Jeran mused.

"This entire section of the palace has been empty for over three centuries," Treloran answered. "No Human since Prince Gregor of Alrendria has 'honored' us with their presence." Treloran's tone was cold. "These rooms," he added, with a sweep of his arm, "have been empty even longer. I do not know when last they were used."

The Aelvin Prince looked at the dusty floor with distaste. "I will have *Ael Namisa* clean this section of the palace." Without additional comment, he continued down the hall. Jeran followed a step behind, pausing only once, to examine the flickering globes that lined the hallway.

"Do you think we have a better chance than Prince Gregor?" he asked. "Of reopening the Path of Riches, that is?"

"Grandfather supports trading with you Humans, but he supported trade three centuries ago as well." Treloran fell silent, and for a moment,

Jeran thought he had received all the answer the Aelvin Prince was going to give. Treloran surprised him by adding, "But Mother appears to support trade, too, and she has much influence among *Ael Alluya*."

Quieter, so low that Jeran that had to strain to hear, Treloran muttered, "Though I doubt you Humans can offer us anything of value."

Jeran opened his mouth to respond, but Treloran suddenly stopped and turned the latch to a large, ornate door. It swung open on silent hinges. "These are your apartments," he said, gesturing toward the room. "We hope you find them satisfactory."

Bowing politely, Jeran thanked the Aelvin Prince. Treloran dipped his head quickly, then spun on his heels and left, nearly running in his eagerness to get away. Jeran was left alone in the dusty hallway.

Shrugging off the Elf's aloofness, Jeran stepped into his chambers. He managed all of two steps before shock froze him in place. Rubbing his eyes, mouth agape, he stared at the rooms that would be his for the next several seasons.

The door opened into a vast audience chamber. The walls, though fashioned of the same stone as the hall, were white. The room extended to his left and right so far that Jeran had to squint to make out details at the far ends. The walls were seamless and smooth, dotted with faded portraits of Elves and Humans. Lanterns hung next to every painting, their flickering flames lighting the chamber as bright as daylight.

The floor was of white stone, too, but an ornate rug, woven in an intricate pattern of gold and green, covered most of the cold rock. Three couches, large and covered with plush cushions, sat centered in the chamber. Chairs, carved from the wood of the Great Trees and polished until they shone, lined each wall. A low, matching table sat between the couches. Directly across from Jeran was a large stone hearth with wood in a bin to one side. Unlike the hall, the room was clean and free of dust, though Treloran had claimed that the chambers had not been visited in centuries.

Matching doors stood on either side of the hearth, and Jeran crossed through one. Entering a sitting room, he sighed in relief, feeling far more comfortable in the simpler, less audacious chamber.

The hearth opened on this side of the wall as well, but instead of couches, four cushioned chairs surrounded the fireplace. A blue and brown patterned rug lay on the floor; paintings depicting beautiful landscapes–mountains and waterfalls, lakes and oceans–hung on the walls. A book, its pages so faded that the words were unintelligible, sat open on a table.

Sunlight streamed through two windows, evenly spaced to either side of an oaken door. Another door stood to Jeran's left, and a third to his right. Jeran went right and entered a bedchamber. The bed was large, far larger than any bed he had seen before. Four wooden posts rose from the corners, supporting a canopy of beige material.

Dropping his pack, Jeran threw himself onto the bed. The mattress and pillows were soft, and he sighed as he reclined, his eyes rolling back into his head. The blankets, while old, were thick and warm, and it was all he could do not to wrap himself up in them and fall asleep.

Another fireplace, this one smaller, faced the bed, and a wardrobe sat against the side wall. A curtain obstructed the far wall, though two bright patches hinted at more windows.

Another doorway graced the side wall, and Jeran went through it. He entered a washroom with a large porcelain tub resting against one wall and a smaller basin, with a mirror, sitting alongside. The tub was raised, and a pile of wood, along with a striker, sat beneath it. A larger pile of wood filled one corner, and a privy pot sat in the other. Jeran was surprised to find it attached to the floor, with a dark hole descending into the recesses of the palace. The tub and washbasin had similar holes, he noticed, though they were equipped with stoppers.

Two golden cords dangled from the ceiling, one next to the tub, the other near the basin. Curious, Jeran pulled on one, and a thick stream of water poured into the tub, disappearing down the drain. Smiling with sudden understanding, Jeran resolved to explore the rest of his apartment before allowing himself the luxury of a bath.

He returned to the bedroom, and a breath of cool air billowed the curtain, raising the hairs on the back of his neck. He drew the drapes aside and found the oaken door ajar. Pulling it fully open, he stepped onto the balcony and filled his lungs with fresh air.

His apartments were near the top of the palace, far higher than the tops of the Great Trees, and Jeran looked down upon Lynnaei. Though the branches were thick with dark green leaves, he spotted several of the rope bridges that connected the buildings of the Aelvin city. Elves, so small they looked like insects, scurried back and forth.

Blue skies filled the heavens, and the sun—a brilliant, yellow orb—floated near its zenith. In the dark shadows of the Great Forest, the sun had become almost a stranger. Jeran stretched out his arms, drinking in the cool air and relishing the feel of sunlight on his skin. After a while, he walked down the balcony, passing the sitting room and stopping before a third door. Curious, Jeran pulled open the door and stepped inside.

He found himself in a library. Shelves, stretching from floor to ceiling, lined three of the four walls. A ladder, connected to a track that wound around the room, leaned against one wall. The shelves were broken in only two places: at the door leading into the sitting room and around a small fireplace. An intricately-crafted iron bin, filled with small logs, sat beside the fireplace.

Volumes, of every size and thickness, cluttered the shelves. Lamps were scattered about the room, offering adequate illumination. In the very center of the chamber sat a large, well-cushioned red chair. Small tables, covered with books, scrolls, and loose sheets of paper, flanked it; and an ornate silver lamp stood on a tall pole behind it. A series of small benches, many covered with open books, were scattered about the chamber.

Jeran circled the room slowly, randomly selecting books. There were adventure stories, war reports, trade tallies, children's tales, and complicated discussions of philosophy and magic–a nearly limitless selection! Most were written in the human language, though nearly as many held the flowing script of the Elves. Other titles were in an alphabet Jeran did not recognize, and he guessed they were Orog or Garun'ah in origin. Translations, all written in the same elegant hand, accompanied many of the texts.

"Lord Jeran?" came a call from the antechamber, and Jeran closed the book through which he was leafing. "Lord Jeran?" the voice called again, more urgently. Jeran opened the door and stepped into the sitting room.

"I'm in here, Mika," he called, hurrying toward the sound. Mika stood in the entry hall with Liseyl and his sisters, Ryanda and Eilean. Ryanda, the youngest, ran to Jeran when he appeared, throwing her arms about his legs and hugging him tightly.

Jeran smiled and gently stroked her hair. He looked at Liseyl, his gaze questioning. Before he could ask, she said, "The Elves told us you would be in rooms separated from the others, and that there were neighboring chambers for only a handful of your servants. I hope you're not angry, but I volunteered. The children will be happier near you." She flushed, lowering her eyes to the floor. "And I would feel safer, too. For all of us."

"Of course I'm not angry!" Jeran insisted. "But you're not my servant, Liseyl! It's not right for you to wait on me."

"Jeran," she replied. "If we're not your servants, than we're simply your responsibility. Perhaps the others would not mind. Perhaps! But it shames me to stand by while you feed and protect me and my children." Her eyes were pleading. "Do not make me beg this of you! Let me serve you in my own way."

"Peace, Liseyl," Jeran replied quickly. "If it means so much to you, I won't fight it. When we return from the Illendrylla, I'll swear my oath and become First Seat of House Odara. When I do, if you wish to come with me, you can run my House as you ran your husband's estates. Your talents go to waste as a mere valet."

Liseyl's cheeks turned even redder. "I'm honored, Lord Odara," she replied, her voice barely above a whisper.

"What of Mika? Ryanda and Eilean?" Jeran asked. "Wouldn't they prefer to stay with the other children?"

Liseyl started laughing. "Mika would rather be at your side," she responded, patting her son's head fondly, "even if you were facing the Darklord himself! As for my daughters... The other Alrendrians are but a few floors lower. It will not be difficult for them to join their friends."

Jeran shrugged, laughing. "It seems I'm out of arguments."

"It's settled then." Liseyl looked around the room. "It seems your apartments have already been cleaned, though the hallway could use a dusting. Is there anything you wish?"

"To be honest, a hot bath would be welcome. Perhaps you could start the fire under the tub? Pulling the cord fills it with water." Jeran flushed, reconsidering his instructions. "It's not that difficult, Liseyl. I'm sure I can manage without–"

"I will attend to it immediately, my Lord," she interrupted. "Is there anything more?"

"No," Jeran answered, shaking his head. "That will be all for now. I'm sure you, too, will want to wash up and rest before the feast."

Liseyl started to walk out of the room. "Perhaps you'd be kind enough to watch the children until I'm finished?"

"It would be my privilege." Jeran said, glad that he had something to do while Liseyl waited on him. He knelt on the carpet. "What do you think of the Aelvin city?" he asked the trio.

Ryanda was the first to speak. "The Elfs live in trees!" she exclaimed. She was young, four winters of age, with vibrant blue eyes and curly blonde hair. She beamed at Jeran, and he found her innocent excitement to be infectious.

Mika was Liseyl's middle child, twelve winters of age, though far older in both size and temperament. He often took a dominant position among his sisters, an attitude that had only been encouraged by Jeran's request that he 'lead' the children. Time among the slavers had hardened the boy, and he lacked the innocence that others his age took for granted. Ever serious, his blue-green eyes met Jeran's. "The city is well defended. It would take a large army to get past that wall of trees."

Jeran nodded, turning to Liseyl's eldest. Eilean, fair and blonde, was sixteen winters old and beginning to blossom. Her blue eyes were always sad, her lips forever puckered in the semblance of a pout. Her time in the cages had scarred her even more than her brother. She rarely spoke, and when she did, it was always in a whisper. Her eyes glistened with moisture. "The city is very beautiful," she said modestly, and Mika rolled his eyes.

"Would you like to see it from here?" Jeran asked them. "We're higher than the tallest tree, and there's a balcony. You can look out over all of Lynnaei, and see much of the Great Forest beyond!" Mika's head jerked up excitedly, and Ryanda started toward the door without waiting for Jeran. Eilean nodded sullenly and followed the others.

They stood together in relative silence for a long time, looking at the city and drinking in the cool, fresh air. Liseyl reappeared before long, informing Jeran that his bath was hot. "Return to your own chamber, Liseyl," Jeran ordered. "I'm sure you'll want to unpack and draw *yourself* a bath." Smiling, Liseyl bowed and ushered the children from the room.

When he heard the door click behind him, Jeran ran to the bath. Hastily removing his clothes, he climbed into the tub, and as the hot water flowed around him, he let out a deep sigh. Unable to move, he lay there for what seemed an eternity, drifting in a half-sleep, allowing the water to unknot muscles tight from the long journey.

The water eventually cooled, and Jeran reluctantly reached for the soap. After vigorously scrubbing his body, he submerged himself in the bath, staying under for as long as he could hold his breath. Standing, he rinsed himself with a spray of cold water, then stepped quickly from the bath, grabbing a towel.

Drying himself, he filled the washbasin halfway with water, then went to the bedroom for his razor. After a careful shave, he returned to his bed-chamber, dressed in a clean shirt and breeches, and stretched out on the bed. Sighing contentedly, he decided that he had ample time for a nap.

"Jeran?" called Martyn. "Liseyl said you were… By the Five Gods!" At the prince's excited cry, Jeran sprang from the bed. He found Martyn spinning slowly in the main hall, his expression one of utter disbelief. "Magnificent!" he said in awe. Finishing his circuit, he noticed Jeran for the first time. "I assume this is not the only room?"

Jeran laughed and showed Martyn his chambers, each room eliciting another exclamation from the prince. Relaxin in the sitting room after the tour, Martyn whined, "I thought *my* chambers were opulent, but these put them to shame! They're twice the size, better furnished, and even though you're only six levels higher, your view of the city is far superior!"

"Jealous, my Prince?" Jeran asked, laughing.

"You bet I am!" Martyn retorted, though his anger was feigned. "Explain to me why a lowly nobleman, one who has not even officially attained his rank, is given apartments better than those of his sworn prince?" Martyn's eyes flashed.

"These are the private apartments of High Wizard Aemon," Princess Charylla said from the doorway. "Grandfather thought Lord Odara might enjoy staying in his grandfather's rooms." She glided into the chamber, bowing formally. "Forgive my intrusion, Lord Odara, but the Emperor would like to see you." Her eyes shifted right. "You as well, Prince Martyn."

Martyn stood, nervously smoothing his shirt. "The Emperor wishes to meet with us *now*?" His voice trembled slightly. "I thought we were to meet him tonight!"

The Aelvin Princess smiled. "Many will try to gain Grandfather's ear tonight, and he feared the opportunity for conversation might be limited. Thus, he thought it wise to meet with you before the feast."

Martyn looked at the plain, grey woolens he wore. "I'm not dressed suitably to meet the Emperor," he stated. "If you'd allow me but a few moments to return to my apartments, I'd be happy to change–"

"That will not be necessary. Grandfather desires an informal meeting. Just a chance to exchange pleasantries before the tedium of tonight's festivities." Charylla's mouth pulled up in a tight smile. "Those were his exact words, Prince Martyn."

Cornered, Martyn could find no other excuse. "Very well, my Lady," he said, bowing. "Lead us to the Emperor."

Dipping her head in silent acknowledgement, Charylla turned and strode from the room, Jeran and Martyn following behind. Once in the hall they turned left, and Charylla led them down a long passageway with lamps evenly spaced down both sides. Doors appeared sporadically, as did adjoining hallways, but Charylla ignored them.

"What... What do you think the Emperor wants to say to us?" Martyn asked, his voice stammering slightly.

Before Jeran could answer, the princess' voice drifted back to them. "You have no reason to fear Grandfather, Prince Martyn. He means you no harm."

"And he is very old," Treloran added, appearing at the intersection ahead. "Should he try to attack, you will not find it hard to outpace him."

Charylla cast a stony glare at her son, but Martyn refused to take the bait. "Who wouldn't be afraid of meeting a legend?" he asked. "In Alrendria, Alwellyn the Eternal is more a myth than a reality. He's old enough to remember the Great Rebellion! Not to mention everything that's happened since!" The prince laughed suddenly. "When a character out of children's stories asks to meet you, it's quite a shock."

They continued on, the sound of their boots on the hard stone floor echoing loudly in the otherwise silent hall. The Elves took them up many flights of stairs, and their path led ever deeper into the heart of the palace.

Charylla set a slow, stately pace, and Jeran found it much easier to keep track of their direction than when he had followed Treloran. As they walked, he examined the palace's construction. The walls, smooth to the touch, arched gracefully, forming a half-circle above their heads.

To Jeran, the palace, though clean and well cared for, exuded an empty feeling. He asked about it, and Charylla replied, "This area was reserved for visitors of the other Races. After the last of the Orog died and the Garun'ah started warring with us, these halls were used only by Humans. When we closed *Ael Shende Ruhl*, no Humans were left, and we had no reason to maintain this section of the palace."

As they moved toward the interior of the palace, they began to encounter others. Brown-robed Elves hurried back and forth, their eyes ever downcast, and Aelvin warriors stood guard at the corridors, the lamplight reflecting off their bronze armor. Lamps lined every hall, and each lamp flickered with its own tiny flame. "It must take an army just to keep the lamps full of oil!" Jeran whispered, reaching toward a nearby lantern.

He withdrew his hand quickly, surprised that the flame carried no heat. Looking up, he saw Treloran and Charylla staring at him oddly, curious expressions on their faces. "The lanterns do not burn oil," Charylla explained. "They are fueled by magic. It takes only one *Ael Maulle* to illuminate the entire castle." Her lips twitched in a tight smile, which she hid by turning and continuing down the hall.

Jeran looked at the lanterns again, this time a bit more warily, and Martyn laughed. "I've never heard of a Mage who was nervous around magic!" he whispered, so low that only Jeran could hear.

Jeran sneered playfully. "I didn't know you were familiar with many Magi."

Martyn shrugged. "I know a lot of archers," he replied, "and they're not afraid of arrows."

"They would be, if the arrows were aimed at them!"

Laughing louder, Martyn nearly walked into Charylla, who had stopped in front of an ornate double door. The door was more than thirty hands wide and twice as high, crafted from dark oak, its hinges and handles gold, lovingly polished to a blinding gleam. A detailed figure, an Aelvin woman, nearly as high as the door, was carved across its center. The woman stood proudly, her arms folded, staring into the antechamber with a proud and mystical expression.

Huge lamps stood to either side of the doorway, lighting the entire hall. Charylla bowed before the door, dropping to one knee, and Treloran did the same. When they stood, the Aelvin Princess turned to face Jeran and Martyn, her expression one of reverence. "You stand before the Hall of the Goddess Valia," she said, her voice echoing through the halls. "Within sits Emperor Alwellyn, chosen by Valia Herself to reign until the time of her return. The Emperor sees with Valia's eyes. He speaks only the words of the Goddess."

She pushed on the doors, and they swung open effortlessly. Charylla disappeared into the darkness of the chamber, followed closely by her son. Martyn swallowed. "Are you ready?" he asked, with a sidelong glance at Jeran, embarrassed by his own nervousness.

Jeran smiled and clapped the prince on the shoulder. "What are you worried about?" he retorted, with a half-feigned quaver in his voice. "If you're lucky, this will be the only time you have to meet the Emperor. *I* have to spend the next few seasons with Him!"

Jeran's false fear eased Martyn's own worry. Sharing smiles, they walked into the Hall of Valia together.

Chapter 8

They entered Valia's Hall and were swallowed in darkness. The chamber sat at the heart of the palace, where no natural light could reach. Even after their eyes adjusted, it remained difficult to discern any of the room's details. Charylla and Treloran were visible only as silhouettes, dark outlines standing perfectly still before them.

Suddenly, two lanterns, one to either side, flared to life, their flames glowing yellow. More lanterns, one after another, brightened, forming a pathway twenty hands across down the center of the chamber. Beyond the lanterns, the room disappeared in shadow, the dim light unable to penetrate to the far distant walls. Above, the ceiling was black, darker than the darkest night.

"Approach," commanded a ghostly whisper, a whisper that echoed throughout the chamber. Charylla and Treloran started forward; as they moved, the lanterns began to wink out. Jeran and Martyn had no choice but to follow or become lost in the dark.

The rows of lanterns abruptly ended, and the Aelvin royalty stepped apart, forcing the Humans to stand between them. The two Elves said nothing, and both Jeran and Martyn had to fight their growing anxiety.

Suddenly, a shaft of sunlight appeared, beaming across the room through a window cut through the rear of the hall. The light fell across the dais, and Jeran gasped, averting his eyes from the sudden brightness. He was unable to decide which was more astonishing: the Emperor's throne or the simple fact that sunlight could find its way deep inside a mountain of solid rock.

Martyn lowered his gaze as well, whispering to Jeran from the corner of his mouth. "It's a good thing the Emperor desired an informal audience. I doubt we'd have survived a formal meeting." Jeran offered the prince a tight smile, but offered no reply.

The two Elves dropped to their knees when the light appeared, bowing low. Before them stood a raised platform of marble. Huge steps, each a slightly different shade, climbed to a summit dominated by a throne of gold, polished to a blinding intensity. Two ornately-carved pedestals flanked the throne, upon which sat twin multi-faceted crystals, more than five hands across. The sunlight reflected off the crystals, sending sparkles of color shimmering throughout the orbs.

The light was so bright that it was difficult to gaze upon the Emperor for more than an instant, and Jeran found himself wishing for the darkness to return. Heads lowered, eyes squinted, the two Alrendrians looked up at the figure on the throne. Though surrounded in light, the Aelvin Emperor appeared to them only in silhouette. Two striking, brilliant, emerald green eyes were the only discernible feature.

Jeran's chest tightened in a mixture of fear and awe, and Martyn's quick, shallow breathing indicated that he, too, shared Jeran's fear. Unable to speak, unsure of what to do or how to act, Jeran dropped to his knees, mimicking Charylla and Treloran. Martyn hesitated but an instant before following Jeran's example. They knelt in silence, waiting for the Emperor's instructions.

The throne room was utterly silent, the quiet oppressive. Not a whisper of noise could be heard, until it felt like the pounding of their hearts echoed loudly against the hall's distant walls. For what seemed an eternity, vibrant green eyes stared at them from the shadow atop the throne. Sweat beaded on Jeran's forehead. Beside him, Martyn trembled, though he tried his best to control it.

Finally, a firm, gravelly voice called out, "Rise, sons of Balan, and approach." The sound carried throughout the chamber, and the echoes of the command came back to them, barely diminished in volume. The voice was cold and emotionless, yet Jeran released a sigh, finding the harsh words more comforting than the silence.

Jeran pressed his eyes closed, drawing in a deep breath to steady himself. He rose slowly, and Martyn climbed to his feet as well. "Balan?" mouthed the prince, perplexed, as they started toward the dais.

Their footfalls echoed loudly, and Martyn winced at the sound. Treloran and Charylla closed in behind them, following the Humans up the marble staircase. Jeran's heart pounded ever faster as they neared the platform, though in fear or anticipation, he could not rightly say.

The top step opened onto a plateau of white marble. The sunlight reflecting from the throne, crystals–even the platform!–was nearly blinding. Jeran shielded his eyes until they had adjusted to the light, but even when he could finally bear to look upon the throne, the Emperor was still cloaked in shadow.

The Emperor moved, a shadowy arm slowly rose, and a narrow, gnarled finger pointed at Martyn. "You are the son of Mathis, King of Alrendria?" The Emperor's words thundered through the hall, vibrating the very stone of the mountain.

Martyn squared his chin and took a deep breath. The prince's hands still trembled, but his voice was firm, his reply to the Emperor delivered calmly and with great pride. "I am Martyn Batai, Prince of Alrendria, son of King Mathis. I am honored to be in Your presence, Emperor Alwellyn. It is my father's hope that these negotiations will bring our Races together." As an afterthought, he added, "I, too, desire unity between Illendrylla and Alrendria."

The Emperor's eyes flared an even brighter shade of green. He leaned forward, his bones crackling as he moved, his eyes boring into Martyn. "As do I, Prince of Alrendria. As do I." The Emperor fell silent again, his eyes measuring, calculating, staring intently at the prince as if they sought to see inside his soul. "Tell me," asked the Emperor, his inspection concluded. "What do you think of Our forests?"

Martyn had expected this question and answered immediately. "They are most beautiful, Emperor. In my life, I have seen nothing which compares to them. Lynnaei is a treasure beyond comparison. You must be most proud of your people, who put such love into the city's care."

"Indeed," replied the Emperor. "My people spend a great deal of time tending their gardens and trimming the trees of the Great Forest. Often to the exclusion of all else." Though his words were carefully chosen, there was the tiniest hint of anger in the ancient Elf's voice. "And Our people?" prompted the Emperor. "What does Your Highness think of them?"

"The Elves are a wise and noble race," answered the prince. "In what little time I've spent with them, I've developed a great respect, particularly for your family, Emperor." Martyn turned slightly, bowing his head respectfully to Charylla and Treloran. "Certainly, they are a tribute to your name."

The Emperor's rejoinder was delivered in a friendly tone. "For one so young, even in Human terms, you have the tongue of a trained diplomat. You will make a fine prince. I am honored that Alrendria has entrusted you to me, if only for a little while."

The Emperor's speech broke off, and a series of deep, wracking coughs, so powerful they shook his entire body, echoed across the chamber. The fit lasted several long, tense moments; when it finally passed, the old Elf breathed deeply, as if regaining his breath. "Know that you and your people are well come to Lynnaei," he continued, once confident he could speak without wheezing. "It is Our hope that, from these negotiations, a friendship will blossom between our Races."

The Emperor shifted his gaze to Jeran without allowing Martyn a chance to respond. His eyes now appraised Jeran as they had a moment ago appraised Martyn. Jeran's anxiety grew during the inspection; he desperately wanted to run. Using all of his will, he forced himself to stand firm against the Emperor's careful scrutiny.

"You do not look much like Aemon," the Emperor rasped.

Jeran waited, but nothing more was forthcoming. Swallowing back his fear, marginally annoyed that his identity was being questioned, he answered, "I am Jeran Odara, First seat of House Odara. I am the son of Alic Odara and High Wizard Aemon's daughter Illendre." He felt frozen in place by the Emperor's cold green eyes, but added, flushing slightly, "I am told by those who knew him that I favor my father."

Dry, raspy laughter drifted down from the throne. "You may not look like your grandfather," the Emperor admitted, "but you certainly sound like him." The ancient Elf's laughter continued until another series of coughs interrupted it. When he had regained his voice, he inquired, "What is your opinion of Illendrylla, Lord Odara?"

Jeran responded in as steady a voice as he could muster. "There is great beauty to your lands. The trees themselves seem blessed with an innate peacefulness. The Great Forest is majestic, and I have seen wonders beneath its branches I would never have believed, had my own eyes not beheld them. Your city has its own beauty, a quiet dignity stemming from its order."

Steeling himself for the Emperor's wrath, he shared the rest of his impression. "Yet I find Lynnaei forced and unnatural, and to me that mars its beauty. The Mage Yassik once wrote that, 'Beauty, honor, and truth are things of many facets. To be truly appreciated, they must be viewed on many levels, and from every angle.' To force your gardens and trees into any single pattern, rather than allowing them to find their own, destroys the very beauty you hope to create."

Jeran's cheeks burned red; his heart beat so fast it felt like it was about to burst, and his mouth was completely dry. Martyn stiffened at Jeran's harsh assessment, but Jeran ignored his friend's warning glance. He had started, and honor demanded that he finish. "It seems to me that your city has taken something pure and forced it into a pattern of its own design, hiding its inadequacies behind a facade of arrogance and control."

Charylla's features remained even, but her dark eyes stared at Jeran with interest. Treloran glared daggers at him, and the back of Jeran's neck tingled at the Aelvin Prince's angry glare. "Indeed?" came the Emperor's response, his tone even and measured, so much so that Jeran could not surmise his reaction. "I find myself most anxious to learn your opinion of Our people?"

Martyn's stern glare nearly matched Treloran's in intensity, but Jeran did his best to ignore the prince. He hesitated only an instant before saying, "My opinion of the Elves is the same as my opinion of their city."

Jeran's words seemed to have no effect on the Emperor, who leaned back in the chair, his thoughts unreadable. But Charylla regarded him coolly, as if seeing something in him she had not noticed before, and Treloran shook with barely-controlled rage. Martyn put his head in his hands and shook it back and forth slowly. He more than half expected to find himself facing the wrath of Alwellyn the Eternal, Emperor of the Elves.

Jeran held his breath and returned the Emperor's silent stare, waiting for his judgment. For an eternity they stood there, the Emperor unmoving above, and as time passed, Jeran grew more certain that he had made a mistake. The silence grew oppressive, and the darkness around them pressed in, constricting his chest. He shivered, but felt sweat running freely down his forehead. Though he felt like he was about to lose consciousness, he refused to take his eyes from the Emperor.

The ancient Elf began to laugh. A light chuckle at first, barely audible even in the suffocating silence of the chamber, but over time it grew louder, until deep, wheezing, uncontrollable laughs echoed through the hall. The laughter was not infectious–Charylla and Treloran still stared at him coldly–but Jeran felt relieved, as if a great weight had been lifted off him.

Leaning back in the throne, still struggling to regain his composure, the Emperor casually waved his hand in a sweeping gesture. At his movement, lanterns throughout the chamber flared to life, flooding the hall with light. The sunlight falling on the throne simultaneously dimmed, and for the first time, they could see the Emperor clearly.

He was ancient, and his appearance did not belie that fact. His hair, wispy and thin, the color of new fallen snow, fell to the level of his shoulders. His ears were slightly pointed, as were all Elves', but they drooped away from his head, as if they no longer had the strength to remain upright. His green eyes no longer glowed; they seemed cloudy and dull, sunk deep into the orbits.

The Emperor's body was reed thin, his arms bony and gaunt, his hands gnarled with age, closed permanently into half-claws. Snaking blue veins were clearly visible beneath too-white skin marred by the presence of dark brown splotches. Thick crow's feet extended from the corners of his eyes, and the rest of his heavily-lined face was tight and pinched. He wore a thin white robe and had a cape of gold draped over his shoulders.

The last echoes of laughter faded into the recesses of the cavernous room. Using his arms, the Aelvin Emperor struggled to rise. Groaning audibly as he settled his weight, he started forward, smiling at Jeran and Martyn with yellowed teeth. He was short for an Elf, only marginally taller than Martyn. Of all the Elves they had thus far encountered, only Luran was shorter.

As the Emperor neared, he chuckled again. "If I had any doubts," he said solemnly, "they are now gone. You are, without question, Aemon's kin."

He walked toward them with grace and dignity, placing each step carefully and never once faltering. His breathing was regular and even, and despite his aged appearance, he seemed to be in good health. His eyes were alert, and his gaze shifted among his four visitors, reading each of their faces. Those eyes radiated wisdom; countless winters of experience were evident in his bearing.

His smile broadened, and Jeran found himself returning the gesture gladly. The Emperor seemed different than the other Elves, though how was difficult to say. There was an openness to the old man lacking in many of his kin, a jovial spirit few Elves seemed to share.

Treloran could no longer contain his anger. Shaking with rage, he looked at the Emperor with a mixture of confusion and irritation. "Grandfather?" he called, his voice tight with the effort of maintaining control.

The Emperor's gaze shifted to Treloran, his expression thoughtful. "Grandfather," the young Elf repeated, "why do you indulge these Humans? Especially that one!" He leveled a finger at Jeran. "He has insulted our lands and our people with his words. He presumes to know more than us. He has the audacity to chastise us in our very home! Yet you honor him." Tears brimmed in the young Elf's eyes, and he fought desperately to keep them from falling. "They do not deserve to be in your presence."

The Emperor stared at his grandson for a long time, his eyes distant and searching. "You are wrong, Treloran. Jeran Odara has done none of these things. I asked for his opinion, and he gave me the truth with no regard to how I would react to his words. He shared his thoughts with me, whether they were right or wrong, and did not try to hide his feelings behind clever half-truths, as many of your cousins are wont to do. Would you rather that he lie? Tell Us only what We want to hear?"

Treloran flushed at the Emperor's chastisement, but said nothing in reply. Smiling, the Emperor reached out and placed a hand affectionately on the younger Elf's shoulder. "I can think of no greater honor than being told the truth, Treloran. The truth is rarely pleasant, nor is it often something we like to hear, but that makes it all the more important that we listen."

"Yes, Grandfather," came Treloran's muted response, but his eyes were no softer when he looked at Jeran.

The Emperor embraced the princess. "Granddaughter," he said in a voice full of love. "It is so very good to see you again. The halls of the palace wept while you were away." She smiled fondly as he stepped back and took her hand, touching it lightly to his lips.

"I am glad to be home, Grandfather," she replied, placing a kiss on his brow. "The days seem endless without your gentle wisdom to guide me."

The Emperor laughed at his granddaughter's praise. "You had best acquaint yourself with eternity, beloved," he countered. "I have far fewer winters ahead of me than behind."

"How will the world survive without you, Grandfather?" came her half-serious reply.

"Quite well, I assure you. It did well enough before I was born." He laughed even harder, until a wheezing cough forced him to stop. The Emperor released Charylla's hand and turned toward Martyn. "She flatters me shamelessly," he admitted. "Though in truth, I do little to discourage it." Charylla flushed, showing more emotion in the last few moments than during the entire trip through Illendrylla.

The Emperor extended a hand, and Martyn took it amicably, careful not to squeeze too hard. "Prince Martyn," smiled the Emperor. "Once again allow me to welcome you to Our home. A meeting between our Races is long overdue, through no fault of my own, I assure you."

"My father eagerly awaits the outcome of our negotiations," Martyn told the Emperor. "He hopes this will be the first of many such meetings with the Elves."

The Emperor released the prince's hand and scratched his chin absent-ly. "You know," he said at last, "I have met dozens of Alrendrian princes in my lifetime. The last was nearly..." The words trailed off, and the Emperor tapped his upper lip in thought. "...four centuries ago."

A frown suddenly covered the aged Elf's face, and his eyes grew sad. "Funny," he said, mostly to himself. "It did not seem so long ago."

Shaking away the heavy-heartedness brought on by time's passage, the Emperor continued his story. "When trade down the Path of Riches stopped, and my ambassadors were recalled to Lynnaei, Price Gregor trav-eled here at his father's request. He pleaded with me not to suspend trade with Alrendria. He said, truthfully, that closing *Ael Shende Ruhl* could only harm our Races. In that, he and I agreed, yet I could do nothing to help that young prince.

"I will tell you now, Prince Martyn, what I told Gregor those many winters ago. The words hold even more truth today. Though I am yet emperor, my commands do not carry the weight they once did. More than three centuries ago, I sided with Prince Gregor, insisting that goods contin-ue to flow down the Path of Riches. But my words were not heeded! Today I favor reopening trade, and though my family has consented to these talks, many would prefer to have no contact with Humans at all."

The Emperor's eyes flashed green, momentarily losing their dullness. "I tell you this as a warning, Prince Martyn: It is not me you need to con-vince. *Ael Alluya* rule Lynnaei now, and the Emperor is all but forgotten while they wait for me to die."

Treloran's mouth dropped open in surprise. "Grandfather!" Charylla exclaimed. "You know that is not true!"

"Is it not, beloved?" he asked. "Where once a whisper from me would have reopened trade with Alrendria, now must I argue endlessly with mer-chants and nobles alike, convincing them of the merits." The Emperor's eyes were stormy. Charylla refused to meet them; she preferred to keep her own gaze on the floor. "Once I would have led these negotiations, now I am supposed to be honored that you and Luran will speak in my place."

"But Grandfather–!" started Treloran. The old Elf cut him off.

"Even Luran, my own blood, now defies me. I have heard of his behav-ior, his 'challenge' against one who is a personal guest in Our lands." The Emperor's eyes sought his grandson's. "Even you, my most tempestuous heir, have more sense than Luran. Tell me, Treloran, how do you feel about your beloved uncle's dishonorable acts?" Treloran's eyes followed his mother's to the floor, leaving Jeran and Martyn staring at each other, embar-rassed to be witness to this heated exchange between the Aelvin nobility.

Charylla and Treloran both refused to speak, so the Emperor returned his attention to Jeran. "Though you have little of your grandfather's looks, you have his spirit. If your duties permit, I would request that you share some of your time with me."

The Emperor looked at his granddaughter from the corner of his eyes, but she still would not meet his gaze. "It seems my family believes that negotiating a trade agreement is too strenuous a task for me. Apparently, I am much the same as my father's crystals." He gestured to the giant spheres sitting to either side of the throne. "Imposing to look at. Nice enough to have around. But too fragile to move, lest you are caught by a stray breeze and your prized possession is shattered."

"Not fragile," came Charylla's tremulous response. "Valuable."

The Emperor grunted, but said nothing. His eyes locked with Jeran's, but it was Martyn who spoke. "If you wish Jeran's company, Emperor Alwellyn, I will see to it that he has no other duties. He is at your disposal."

"It seems," quipped Jeran, "that Alrendria does not consider me essential to the negotiations either. I'd be delighted to share my company with you, Emperor, for what it is worth." The Emperor smiled at the comment and bowed his head to Martyn in thanks. He opened his mouth to speak, but Treloran diverted his attention.

"You would waste your time with this Human?" the Aelvin Prince asked, his embarrassment forgotten. "You are better than he is, Grandfather. What could a Human, especially one little more than a child, say that would interest you?"

The Emperor leveled cold eyes on his grandson, and Treloran's eyes returned to the floor. "You have allowed your hatred–your uncle's hatred–to blind you to the truth. Humans are not our inferiors, no matter what Luran may say. They are a proud and honorable race, who live and learn more in their short lifetimes than we do in centuries. My father, Emperor Llwellyn, once told me, 'Their flames burn not so long as ours, but they burn ever so much brighter.' "

The Emperor reached out slowly and lifted Treloran's face, forcing the young Elf to look into his eyes. "He said this to me before he took our armies to the Anvil, and in the time of the Great Rebellion, his hatred of the other Races made Luran's pale in comparison."

The Emperor placed one hand on each of Treloran's shoulders. "These Humans can teach us much, Grandson. Much that you, in particular, could stand to learn." The Emperor fell silent, his expression thoughtful, considering. "Perhaps...." His eyes returned to Martyn, and another prolonged silence swept across the room.

"Perhaps," the Emperor repeated, "if it does not inconvenience the prince too much, he would be willing to companion you during his stay in Lynnaei. He will need a guide if he is to learn anything of our people, and maybe, if you are forced to spend time with the Humans, you will learn something of them as well." The Emperor looked at Martyn expectantly.

Martyn cleared his throat before answering. "It would be an honor, Emperor," he said slowly, though he, himself, was not convinced of the truthfulness of his words. "And I assure you, no inconvenience. It would be foolish of me not to take advantage of the opportunity we have to learn of each other. I'm curious to see what life in Lynnaei is like."

Treloran nearly trembled with the effort of containing his anger. In a quieter voice, Martyn added, "It appears your grandson does not share my enthusiasm."

Laughing, the Emperor replied, "My grandson does not have a choice in the matter." He turned to Treloran. "It is settled. For the duration of his stay, you are to act as escort to Prince Martyn. You will be his constant companion, and you will teach him the customs of our people. You may only leave him if he expressly wishes for you to do so. I beg of you not to dishonor Us in this manner."

Treloran eyes, full of anger, met the Emperor's. "It will be as you command," he said after a prolonged silence, bowing in supplication.

"Now I request that you leave me alone with the grandson of Aemon," the Emperor announced in a voice full of authority. "If I am to be nothing more than an ornament for these proceedings, then I wish to have nothing to do with them. Instead, I will share stories with Aemon's kin and relive my youth."

Charylla bowed formally to the Emperor, but her eyes were on Jeran, probing. "Until tonight, Grandfather," she said warmly, spinning silently on her heels and striding regally from the chamber.

Treloran bowed as well, but did not attempt to leave. Instead, he riveted his eyes on Martyn and waited; displeasure and anger warred with disgust to control his features. Martyn lowered his head reverently. "By your leave, Emperor Alwellyn." Offering Jeran a reassuring look, he, too, turned and walked away, Treloran following a step behind. As they neared the door to the chamber, the echo of Martyn's voice drifted back to them, "...find your way through these halls. It's worse than the hedge maze in..."

The Emperor waited until the last echo of their footsteps faded in the distance. He turned to Jeran, and the old Elf looked at his new charge with sad eyes. "You must forgive Treloran," he said sincerely, the love he had for his grandson obvious in his tone. "He is not as hateful as he seems. He has a proud spirit and a noble heart, but he is young and rebellious, and listens too often to the counsel of his uncle. He has found nothing to channel his energies into, so he lashes out at whatever displeases him, or more often, he lashes out at whatever would displease Luran. Though his words are poor, I assure you he means no disrespect."

Smiling broadly, Jeran replied, "No offense was taken, Emperor. We all of us are young at one time or another." He barely kept himself from laughing at the statement. In comparison to the long life spans of the Elves, Jeran was little more than an infant. Treloran, young as he appeared, was likely three times his own age. "I have made my fair share of mistakes."

Jeran's mind drifted back to his earlier statements, and he frowned. "Perhaps I spoke too harshly before. I wouldn't want you to think that I have any enmity toward you or your people."

The Emperor laughed again. Despite the weak coughs that interrupted the sound, it was friendly and comforting. "Do not entertain such an idea!" he insisted. "In my old age, I grow wearisome of people constantly hiding their true feelings in fear that I will find displeasure with their thoughts. It is refreshing to meet someone willing to speak his mind."

Sweeping his arm around, the Emperor turned away from Jeran and pointed a gnarled finger toward the rear of the chamber. "Walk with me, Lord Odara," he commanded. "There is something I would like to show you. Perhaps it will help you to understand my people."

Jeran followed the Emperor around the dais and toward the far side of the chamber. "Please, Emperor, call me Jeran."

"Ahhhh," hummed the Elf, tapping a finger to his lower lip. "Another one who dislikes formality. Whether you know it or not, you share much in common with Aemon." Jeran walked slowly to accommodate the elderly Elf, and the Emperor looked deep into his eyes, seeming to stare straight into Jeran's soul.

"I will call you Jeran," he said at last, nodding his head. "But only if you extend me the same courtesy." Jeran's eyes widened, and the Emperor chuckled. "I would have you call me Alwellyn, but I hear that name so infrequently I doubt I would answer to it. Most of those who yet visit me call me 'Grandfather.' Should it not trouble you, I ask that you address me so."

Flushing, Jeran replied, "I don't deserve such an honor...Grandfather." He said the word tentatively, enjoying the way it sounded as it rolled off his tongue.

"You deserve much more than you give yourself credit for," the Emperor returned. They walked along in silence for a few moments, the echo of Jeran's footsteps the only sound to be heard. As they neared the far side of the chamber, a door became visible.

"I sense that you are a Reader," the Emperor said suddenly, breaking the stillness. His words were offhand and casual, but Jeran's attention was instantly riveted.

"I have not met another Reader in...." The Elf trailed off, his face wrinkling in thought. "Oh, it must be nearly a thousand winters. It is amazing how fast the time goes by." A mournful glimmer in his eyes, the Emperor shook his head sadly.

"The Talent is quite rare," he added, then corrected himself. "At least, it is rare to possess the Talent as strongly as you and I do. Most Readers are lucky if they can sense vague impressions from an object, even if they *try* to read it." They stopped in front of a tiny door, hidden against the back wall, and the Emperor turned to face Jeran. "I hope you do not mind, but I took the liberty of suppressing your Readings since you entered Lynnaei. I found them most distracting."

"You can do that?" Jeran asked in amazement, his voice rising in pitch. He had noticed that the visions, which had been coming more frequently since he entered Illendrylla, had disappeared, but he had never connected their absence with his arrival in Lynnaei. "You can suppress my visions?" he repeated, full of excitement. "How?"

The Emperor's words finally registered completely. Calming himself, Jeran asked, "You're a Reader, too?"

"Indeed I am," the Emperor nodded. "Though I have often found the Talent more of an annoyance than anything else. Suddenly finding yourself reliving events that happened centuries ago, events you had not lived through to begin with...." The Emperor shook his head. "Most aggravating," he repeated, waving a hand irritably. "Especially when you reach my age. Sometimes, telling which memories are mine and which come from the things around me is more than difficult!

"I have found that the Talent is amplified, both in frequency and severity, when other Readers are nearby, especially when they do not have control over the visions. That is why I suppressed your natural abilities without asking your permission. In a place as ancient as Lynnaei, with the two of us in close proximity, we would never be certain if we were living in the present or the past. In time, the visions would likely have driven us mad." He chuckled at the last, though his words did not seem to be in jest.

Jeran reflected on what he had been told. "I know it's not the reason for our meetings, but would you teach me how to control the Talent? I promise I won't let it interfere with our discussions of Madryn."

The Emperor stopped walking and regarded Jeran with interest, his eyes once again glowing a brilliant green. He took Jeran's head between his bony hands and stared intently into his eyes. Jeran held his breath until the Emperor released his grip. "It has been a very long time since last I had an apprentice," the Elf whispered, "but if you wish it, I can teach you control of your Talent, and maybe a few other things as well."

He frowned thoughtfully, the skin on his face pulling tight. "We will have to discuss it with the Mage to whom you are already apprenticed," he added, "but I doubt she will resist allowing me to take over your training temporarily. Jes has never liked the pressures of teaching."

"You know Jes?" Jeran asked incredulously.

The Emperor wheezed a laugh. "Do not make the same mistake my family does," he cautioned. "I am old, but I am neither blind nor deaf, and my memory is not as bad as it sometimes may seem." Without another word he turned and gestured. The door before them opened on silent hinges.

Jeran stepped through the door into bright sunlight. They stood at the top of a long staircase cut into the red-brown rock of the palace. Below them spread a great park, surrounded on each side by walls of sheer rock. The park was open to the sky, a vast hollow in the center of the Emperor's Palace, and bright sunlight even now shined down upon it. Trees of all shapes and colors filled the depression, patches of wildflowers filling the gaps between. Bird song reached their ears, even though they stood well above the tallest tree. From the center of the park, a circular tower of ivory-white rose impossibly high, the top all but invisible. Only the tiniest glint of sunlight on the turret offered proof that the tower ever ended.

Jeran stared in awe. Raising a hand, he pointed a finger reverently at the structure. "What is that?" he asked in a stunned whisper.

The Emperor smiled again. "That is the Temple of the Five Gods."

"Can I see inside?"

The Emperor pursed his lips. "Perhaps someday I will take you to the top of the tower, to show you how the Gods view our world, but not today. Today, I wish to show you the Vale." He gestured at the park below them. "This is the garden of the Goddess Valia, and I believe it will help you understand my people." The Emperor laughed softly. "You know, you will be the first Human, other than your grandfather, to set foot in the Vale since before the MageWar!"

Jeran looked down upon the tops of the trees, the tallest several hundred hands below where they stood. "I am honored, Grandfather," he replied, shocked by the wondrous opportunities the Emperor had offered him.

The stairs wound down the side of the mountain, following the curvature of the rock. Jeran tried to keep his eyes focused on the steps; the walkway was narrow, barely wide enough for the two of them to walk abreast, and each glance over the side brought a spike of fear to his heart. Nevertheless, his eyes kept drifting to the park, the warmth and beauty of it too tempting a sight to ignore. Several times, he opened his mouth, a question on the tip of his tongue, but he could never find the right words. He did not wish to sound a fool.

Jeran's indecision was not lost on the Emperor. "You need never fear asking me a question, Jeran," he said when they were nearly halfway to the bottom. "There are few enough people still willing to talk to me. I cannot afford to offend those few who remain." When he realized that his words had not yet reassured, he added, "Your grandfather and I are very old friends. Until you convince me otherwise, I will treat you with the same respect with which I would treat him."

Jeran blushed in embarrassment. "My questions are somewhat personal," he said sheepishly.

The Emperor patted him lightly on the shoulder. "If they are too personal, I will not answer them."

Swallowing hard, Jeran asked, "Where is your wife, Grandfather?"

The Emperor's expression grew momentarily distant. He sniffed, and water pooled at the corner of his eyes. "She is with Valia," he said wistfully. At Jeran's perplexed look, he explained. "She died a long, long time ago. She is with the Goddess now."

Jeran nodded, his eyes sympathetic. "You had children?"

The Emperor nodded. "Many. But they, too, have been dead a long time."

"Charylla and Luran are your only remaining grandchildren then?"

The Emperor scratched his head, his look one of confusion. "Charylla and Luran, and Treloran, are all that remain of my direct bloodline," he replied. "But they are not my children's children."

Jeran stopped his descent and turned to face the old Elf. "I don't understand."

"My children died thousands of winters ago," the Emperor explained, his confused expression a match for Jeran's. "As did my wife. Charylla is the granddaughter of my granddaughter's granddaughter, with perhaps a few more generations in between. It's hard to remember so far back."

The old Elf chuckled wryly. "You make it sound as if we Elves are immortal!"

It was Jeran's turn to look puzzled. "Aren't you?"

"By the Gods no!" the Emperor laughed, letting out an explosive breath. "Do Humans really believe that?" At Jeran's blushing nod, the Emperor laughed harder, until his breath started wheezing and a violent fit of coughing forced him to stop.

Once he regained his breath, he explained. "It is true that we Elves have a lifespan longer than that of any other race, but we grow old and die like everyone else. An Elf is considered old when he reaches five hundred winters, and ancient if he survives seven centuries. Unless they are *Ael Maulle*, of course. The Gifted live longer than those not blessed with magic."

The Emperor's laughter returned, and Jeran shared a smile with the old man. "Excluding *Ael Maulle*, there are but a handful of Elves who were alive at the end of the MageWar," the ancient Elf explained. "And they are all near death."

The look on Jeran's face was skeptical. "But what of you?" he asked. "You've been alive since before the Great Rebellion."

"True," the Emperor nodded. "But your grandfather has been alive nearly as long, and Humans are not immortal either. I am an abnormality, just like he is. My extended life is a side effect of the Gift. I believe you Humans call it Slowing."

The Emperor started down the staircase again, and Jeran hurried to follow. "As with Humans, the Gifted live extended lives, generally as long as two millennia. For some of us, Slowing has an even greater effect. As to why I have been so...blessed...I would not even hazard a guess."

The Emperor shrugged his shoulders, laughing. After a brief pause, he asked, "What else do Humans believe of my people?" He sounded curious.

Jeran sifted through the legends he had heard about Elves. After discarding those stories he knew to be fiction, he shared the rest with the Emperor. "The Elves are renowned for their magical abilities, their skill at archery, and their incredible stealth. It is even said that an Elf can make himself invisible at will!" Jeran said that last with a smile, so the Emperor would know he did not believe that rumor.

"*Ael Maulle* spend a great many winters training their Gift," the Emperor explained. "It takes far longer to become one of their order than it does to be accepted as a Mage. So I can understand why they receive such high esteem in your folklore."

Smiling to himself, the Emperor leaned over and whispered, his voice conspiratorial, "I will tell you a secret, Jeran, if you promise that my words will never leave the Vale." The Emperor waited for Jeran to swear an oath of secrecy. "Your myths portray my people as incredible archers and unsurpassed in the ways of stealth. Do you want to know why they are so adept at those skills?"

Jeran nodded enthusiastically, and the Emperor paused dramatically before answering. "It's because your people were so good at killing us!"

At Jeran's horrified expression, the Emperor's laughter grew in volume. "During the Great Rebellion," he explained, "it quickly became obvious that both Humans and Garun'ah had little trouble defeating Aelvin troops in pitched battle. In single combat, the odds were more even, since many of our warriors considered warfare to be an art form and studied their craft as hard as any *Ael Maulle* studies magic. But even in single combat between equally-skilled opponents, the larger and stronger races almost invariably bested us Elves.

"The only way my people could compete during the Rebellion, and in all the wars that followed, was to learn to attack quickly from a distance and be gone before the enemy could rouse themselves to battle. So you see," the Emperor concluded, chuckling again, "our Race is no more mystical than yours. We are what we are because events have shaped us so."

The Emperor walked in silence after that, allowing Jeran to reflect on his words. It did not take them much longer to reach the bottom of the stairs, where a small clearing was quickly swallowed by the lush vegetation. "Welcome to the Vale," the Emperor said. "The Garden of the Goddess Valia."

Jeran stared in awe. Plants of all sizes grew from the dark, rich soil; small stalks reached tentatively toward the sky. The bushes and small shrubs did not look trimmed like the gardens of Lynnaei, but neither were they marred by any wild, unnatural growth. Flowers of all shapes and hues dotted the landscape, growing isolated and in small clusters along the sides of the snaking, stone-lined paths. Trees of every variety, some of which Jeran had never before seen, spread their branches above, their leaves interlacing to form a loving canopy. Through the tiny gaps, golden sunlight fell to the forested floor.

Birds flitted from tree to tree, their songs joining together in harmony. Several flew before Jeran, less than a hand away, drifting by on the warm air currents. Other animals–squirrels, rabbits, deer, and even a mountain cat–drank side by side at the small, twisting stream that flowed from a large, cracked rock. The animals looked up as they passed, but showed no fear nor made any attempt to flee into the underbrush.

They walked the Vale's many paths, and Jeran marveled at every new vista, every striking scene. Neither spoke. No words were necessary, and no description of the Emperor's could have enhanced Jeran's tour of Valia's Garden.

Eventually, the old Elf led Jeran to a large oak, as broad as the widest of the Great Trees he had seen in Lynnaei. The base of the Temple of the Five Gods was nearby; the smooth, ivory-colored stone rising to the heavens. They sat in the shade, and Jeran stared up in utter amazement, trying to visualize the top of the tower.

The Emperor looked at Jeran. "You feel at peace here?" he questioned, knowing Jeran would nod an affirmative. "You have felt this way before though, have you not?"

Jeran considered the Emperor's question. "Twice," he answered after giving the matter great thought. "The first time was in the mountains, when I first viewed the Anvil. Tanar, a friend of mine, told me it was a place where you could feel the magic within nature, one of the few places still untouched by the actions of the Four Races."

Jeran closed his eyes, remembering the mountains. "The second time was in the city of Shandar, when I explored a park very similar to this one." Jeran looked around once again. "Though it was not quite so lovely as the Vale."

The Emperor nodded and smiled warmly. "I know that park well. I helped Aemon design and build it. We modeled it after the Vale, but we could not do it justice." He opened his arms, making a gesture that encompassed everything around him. "Valia's Garden, like the park in Shandar, was created by magic, though unlike Shandar it was made long before even I was born. The Vale requires no tending. It is always in bloom and it is always beautiful. Many believe the Vale was crafted by Valia herself, as a model of what nature should be."

The Emperor closed his eyes, breathing deeply. "This is what my people strive so hard to recreate in the city of Lynnaei, and in all the forests of Illendrylla. But the beauty of the Vale is an ideal that will always be impossible to realize.

"Do not judge them too harshly, Jeran," the Emperor requested, his eyes sad. "Their ambitions are noble, and the forests as they are only serve to remind them of their failure."

Jeran nodded slowly. "I understand now, and apologize again for any disrespect."

The Emperor climbed to his feet, groaning audibly. "There is no need for your apologies. Your opinions are still valid, even if my people's eccentricities are somewhat justified." Brushing the dust from his robes, the ancient Elf signaled for Jeran to rise. "Come," he said. "It is time we started back. You must be tired from your long journey, and I wish to visit briefly with Jes before the celebration tonight. It has been much too long since last I saw her, and her smile alone will add seasons to my life.

"Besides," he added with a wink, "we have much to discuss if I am to take over your training." The Emperor led Jeran through the Vale, emerging from the trees near a small wooden door, inconspicuously placed in the wall of rock. "We will meet here tomorrow at first light. I am eager to hear all that you have to tell me."

Seeing Jeran stifle a yawn, the Emperor amended his statement. "Perhaps we should make it midday. Doubtless you will be up late tonight, and I forget that the young sometimes sleep past dawn." Smiling, Jeran held the door open while the Emperor walked into the palace. Taking a deep breath, Jeran gazed one last time upon the Vale before following the Emperor into the darkened halls.

Chapter 9

Hearing a soft knocking, Jeran opened the door. A brown-robed Elf stood outside, eyes downcast, waiting. "It is time?" he asked, and the Elf ducked his head. Stepped into the hall, Jeran followed the Elf toward the stairs.

The hall had been cleaned during his time with the Emperor. The finger's width of dust was gone, and the stone beneath had been washed and polished. The heatless flames of the lanterns, which before had flickered weakly, had been renewed. They cast a vibrant, yellow light across the corridor. Even the air felt fresher, as if the centuries of disuse had been scoured away during his visit to the Vale.

The servant halted at Liseyl's door, knocking softly. After a brief pause, the door swung open on silent hinges, and Liseyl appeared. She wore a gown of white, a gift from Princess Charylla. The Aelvin Princess had offered to clothe all of the freed slaves, for which Jeran had thanked her profusely.

Jeran was stunned. This was the first time he had seen Liseyl in anything other than makeshift outfits fashioned from the remains of the slavers' tents. The white silk clung to her body, accentuating curves which before had been concealed. Her hair she wore up, in an elaborate bun; thin, curly strands hung down on either side.

Jeran averted his eyes to stop himself from staring, his cheeks flushing red. Liseyl also blushed. "Should I take that as a compliment?" she giggled, lowering her eyes to hide her embarrassment. "Or do I look so terrible you have to turn away?"

"My Lady," Jeran said solemnly, offering his arm. "I was merely taken aback by your beauty. Tent canvas does not do you justice."

She blushed all the more at his praise, but took his arm, and in a serious tone, whispered, "Are you sure I'm invited?" The brown-robed Elf bowed and started toward the stairway again. The two Humans followed. "It's not common for servants to take part in a feast, unless they're serving the dishes, that is."

"I'm only repeating what I was told," Jeran shrugged, smiling. "The Emperor said that all the Alrendrians were invited, including those servants who could be spared from their duties."

Liseyl's eyes widened at the mention of the Emperor, as they had when Jeran had first given her the invitation. "What was he like?" she asked. "Anything like the stories?"

"I don't know many stories about the Emperor," Jeran admitted with a laugh, "but I'll tell you what I know. He's old, and tired, and I think he feels like he's outlived his usefulness. There's a sadness around his eyes that never goes away, even when he's laughing."

The Elf led down a winding staircase and through a series of interconnecting, nearly-identical halls. "But he's kind," Jeran continued. "And he cares a great deal for his people. More than anything, he wants these negotiations to foster trust and friendship between our races, if not a lasting alliance between Illendrylla and Alrendria."

Stopped before a large double door, the Aelvin servant signaled for them to wait. Walking to the door, he pulled on a cord, and a series of chimes echoed above. The door swung open, revealing a cavernous banquet hall. Some of the Alrendrians had already arrived, and stood, for the most part, in a small cluster at the center of the chamber. An equal number of Elves walked the room, and though a few exchanged pleasantries with the Humans, the majority kept their distance.

Two rows of tables ran the length of the hall, and at the far end, a larger table, with a giant, golden chair at its center, ran perpendicular to the others. Lanterns were spaced evenly along the smooth, red stone walls, their combined light as bright and warm as the midday sun. The floor was of grey tile, and a thin red carpet ran the length of the chamber, centered between the tables.

Martyn spotted them and headed over, calling out greetings. "Jeran!" he said, clapping his friend on the shoulder. "You look well. Your meeting with the Emperor must have gone better than you expected. And you, m'Lady," the prince added with a nod to Jeran's companion. "I don't believe we've had the—" His words trailed off.

Liseyl's cheeks flushed red again, and Martyn stammered an apology. "Liseyl," he said, laughing at his own expense. "I didn't recognize you." He bowed formally. "You look most lovely."

"Thank you, Prince Martyn," she replied, offering him a sincere smile. "It's amazing what a hot bath and a fresh change of clothes can do to your appearance. Might I say that our time in Lynnaei has had a positive effect on your appearance as well." Martyn stared at her in puzzlement.

Jeran laughed and ran a finger along the prince's now-smooth cheek. "I believe the Lady comments on your fresh, youthful appearance."

It was Martyn's turn to blush. Cupping a hand over his clean-shaven chin, he smirked. "You didn't like the beard?" he asked levelly, shifting his eyes from Jeran to Liseyl.

Hesitantly, Liseyl spoke. "It did not suit you, my Prince."

"It looked a little scraggily," Jeran added. "Maybe you should wait a few seasons before trying again."

"I'll give the advice of my subjects some thought," the prince promised, winking at Jeran. Utari appeared at the door and Martyn excused himself. "I must be the first to welcome each Alrendrian," he explained, bidding them farewell. "Princely duties and whatnot." Over his shoulder, he called back, "The Elf in the center of the room will tell you where to sit."

Jeran led Liseyl to the heart of the chamber, where an Aelvin seneschal stood, surrounded by a circle of Guardsmen. Under his breath, Jeran whispered, "For someone who claims she wants to be a servant, you sure need to practice how to behave among royalty."

Liseyl laughed loudly, drawing eyes in her direction. "It's hard to go from a rich merchant's wife to a young lord's servant," she admitted. "It's not something that can be done overnight. You'll have to expect some mistakes!" The smile she offered Jeran was warm and friendly. "But I will try harder, my Lord." They laughed even louder as they approached the Elf.

He was tall and thin, near the end of middle age. Wrinkles lined his face, and straight, white hair hung to his shoulders. His pale green eyes were alert, his ears slightly pointed. Fine robes, green and brown, covered a gaunt frame, and he carried a staff carved from the wood of a Great Tree.

He bowed formally as they approached, his eyes shifting uneasily among the Guardsmen. "My Lord," he said, heavy with accent. "I am Elierian, *Hohe Namisa* of the palace." He repeated his bow to Liseyl.

"Greetings," Jeran replied, inclining his head politely. "I am Jeran Odara, First Seat of House Odara. This is Liseyl–" he gestured to his right "–one of my servants."

Elierian withdrew a scroll from his robes and unrolled it, his eyes scanning the document. "Lord Odara," he said, rolling up the parchment and returning it to his robes. "Welcome to the Palace of the Emperor." Raeghit, one of the Guardsmen, let out a roaring laugh, and the Elf cringed at the unexpected sound. "You will sit at the Emperor's Table," he continued when he found his voice. "This side, second seat left of center.

"Lady Liseyl, you will sit at the servant's table." He gestured toward the far row of tables, where a small contingent of Alrendrian servants already congregated, huddled in a tight knot. Across the table sat a similar cluster of brown-robed Elves. Each group stared at the other nervously, but not a single word was exchanged. "There is no seating assigned," Elierian added, "but it appears you Humans favor the far side of the table, while my people prefer this side."

"With your permission?" Liseyl said to Jeran, waiting for his nod before joining her companions. With a few quick words, she convinced the other servants to take their places at the table and called out greetings to the Elves, asking them to join the Humans. A few of the more adventurous Elves approached the table; soon, with Liseyl's continued encouragement, the table was full, though conversation remained sparse.

Elierian let out a deep sigh, drawing Jeran's attention. "I was afraid my people would never take their places. *Ael Namisa* are not used to dining with the Emperor. They are not comfortable here." Another wave of laughter reverberated from the Guardsmen, and the old Elf tensed.

Jeran smiled knowingly. "It seems that you are not so comfortable yourself."

"It is not the Emperor who has my nerves on edge," Elierian explained. "As *Hohe Namisa,* the Voice of the Obedient, I am forced to deal with the Emperor and his family every day. There is little they can do that would surprise me."

A Guardsman walked by, and the Elf's eyes followed him until he was out of sight. "It is the soldiers," he whispered to Jeran. "And not just the Human ones. I am not comfortable around them, nor am I accustomed to them dining in the palace. At least, not in such great numbers."

Charylla walked by, heading toward the Emperor's Table. Elierian bowed as she passed. "I am an old Elf," he admitted. "Change is not easy for me. I serve as best I can."

"That's all your Emperor can ask," Jeran replied, his eyes shifting to the Alrendrian Guardsmen. "Would you feel more at ease if I convinced them to take their seats?"

"It would allow me a little room to breathe, Lord Odara," the Aelvin castellan replied. With a small smile, Elierian nodded to a group of archers standing opposite the Guardsmen. "Perhaps you could also convince *Ael Chatorra* to take their seats?" At Jeran's considering look, Elierian hastily added. "It truly is not necessary, my Lord. I can endure."

"No doubt you can," Jeran said as he joined the Guardsmen. He returned their greetings warmly, then locked eyes with Bystral. "Guardsman Bystral," he said authoritatively. "Is there a reason why you are clustered in the center of the room?" Looking around, Jeran noticed that the hall was rapidly filling. "Are you expecting an ambush?"

"No, Lord Odara," Bystral replied. "But there are Aelvin warriors at the table, and some of the Guardsmen felt uncomfortable with them around."

Jeran shook his head with exaggerated disappointment. Though he spoke to the burly Guardsmen, his eyes moved among all the Guardsmen. "Are we not here to foster friendship and understanding between Alrendrian and Illendrylla? Humans and Elves?"

"Yes, Lord Odara," came the sullen reply.

"Do you expect to form friendships with the Elves without speaking to them?"

"No, Lord Odara," the broad-shouldered Guardsman said, blushing. "But, Lord Odara," he protested, "the Elves weren't exactly friendly during our journey here."

"No," Jeran agreed, "they weren't. But they were under orders not to speak to us. I have a feeling those orders have been withdrawn. Likely you will find them more receptive now." Once again, his eyes shifted among all the Guardsmen. "This feast has been arranged to introduce us to Elves who hold positions similar to ours. Our servants sit with theirs. Our Guardsmen with their warriors.

"When we return to Kaper," he added, "the King will expect you to know the Elves. To understand them. If the Five Gods are willing, you will even consider some of them friends. But all of that is impossible if you don't *talk* to them."

Nervous, even frightened expressions passed over the Guardsmen's faces, and Jeran laughed. "Go!" he commanded. "You will find that they aren't so different, and that the stories we've heard since childhood are as much myth as fact."

"You have your orders, Guardsmen," Bystral snapped, ushering the other soldiers toward their tables. "I'll make sure the men take their seats, Lord Odara."

"Thank you," Jeran replied, starting toward his head table. All but the Emperor had arrived. Martyn sat opposite the emperor's golden chair, flanked by Jes and Iban. Charylla sat across from Jes, and Luran, scowling fiercely, faced the stony-eyed Iban. Utari and Rafel sat on the far side of Iban, Alynna to Jeran's left. Across the table, Treloran sat at his uncle's side, and Elves who Jeran did not recognize occupied the other seats.

"Jeran," Alynna purred at his approached, "it's good to see you again." Her eyes roved up and down his body, admiring the dark grey breeches and royal blue doublet, the color of House Odara. A small wolf was embroidered over his heart. "Your wardrobe suits you. You should dress like a lord more often."

"My thanks, Lady Alynna. I have never seen you more radiant." He smiled weakly, silently wishing that Utari, or even Rafel, had been seated next to him. Alynna wore a diaphanous red dress, the color of her House, and it clung tightly to her curves. Though high-necked, the dress was slit halfway up the right thigh, exposing a fair amount of smooth, white leg.

Predatory blue eyes fastened on Jeran. "You flatter me, Jeran. Perhaps after the ceremony, we might find some time together. We've not had much opportunity to talk since the journey began. There is much to be gained by a union...of our Houses. The prospect is simply tantalizing." Each word rolled off her tongue fluidly; despite the seemingly-innocent words, Jeran felt his cheeks redden.

He was spared having to answer by the arrival of the Emperor. A series of chimes rang in sequence, and the Elves stood. Hesitating only an instant, Martyn rose as well, followed by Jeran and the rest of the delegates. The remainder of the Alrendrians hurried to their feet.

Two doors opened at the rear of the hall, behind the Emperor's golden chair. The ancient Elf entered, taking slow, stately steps. Voluminous, pale green robes hung around his body, making him appear less frail than he actually was. A crown of woven vines, with forest green leaves and a sprinkling of snow white flowers, circled his head. Charylla went to meet him, bowing as she approached. He leaned forward to kiss her brow.

Taking her arm, they walked to the table, the Emperor's eyes wandering over the assembly. Standing before his chair, he smiled and called out in a noble voice, "I bid our friends from Alrendria welcome. I am glad I lived long enough to see our Races reunited in friendship. All of you have my permission to wander the palace and city freely. Should you wish it, guides will be made available to help you find your way around Lynnaei.

"I encourage you to see the wonders of our city and her people. We are nearly as curious as you, and though my people may at first be reticent, it is only because we Elves have as many myths about Humans as you have about us. Given time, I am sure we will find that our Races have more in common than any would believe." The Emperor raised his glass. "To friends," he toasted. "Both old and new!"

"To friends!" echoed the Alrendrians, raising their own glasses. The Elves sipped their drinks, though they did not repeat the toast.

"Now," commanded the Emperor, lowering himself into his chair, "be seated. Enjoy the bounty of Lynnaei." The sounds of sliding chairs filled the room as the Emperor's guests resumed their seats. An army of brown-robed servants appeared, carrying platters of steaming food and pitchers of iced wine. They glided through the banquet hall on silent feet, heaping generous portions onto the plates.

In the wake of the Emperor's speech, the silence throughout the chamber was palpable. The Humans stared at the Elves, and the Elves stared back, equally silent. Once food was available, many of the Alrendrians hid in their plates, using the meal as excuse not to talk.

The Emperor looked around, a wistful smile on his face. "Surely," he mused, "we can not have changed so much." All eyes swiveled toward the ancient Elf. "When last Humans dined here," he explained, "there was much conversation, and even a few tearful goodbyes.

"Now," he waved an arm to encompass the chamber, "we stare at each other like frightened animals, afraid to lower our guards, anticipating an attack at the first sign of weakness." The Emperor let out a resigned sigh.

It was Lord Iban who spoke. "Much has changed in Alrendria since last we dealt with the Elves. None alive, save the Magi, remember what an Elf looks like, and for the last two decades, the Magi have become nearly as reclusive as your people. This is all very strange to us."

Muted laughter came from the direction of the Guardsmen's table, and Iban smiled at the sound. "But Humans adapt even quicker than we live. It may take a little time, but once the novelty and mystique of your glorious city have faded, my people will become more bold."

Murmurs of conversation arose, quiet and sporadic. "You must be Lord Geffram Iban," the Emperor said confidently. "Tales of your prowess in battle and skill as a Guard Commander have reached me even in the deep recesses of Illendrylla."

Lord Iban bowed at the praise. "There was a time when I would have preferred to be remembered for other skills," he admitted, his icy eyes meeting the Emperor's cool gaze. "But I have long accepted what I am. Allow me, Highness, to introduce the rest of my company."

Iban waited for the Emperor's nod, then turning to the right, said, "At the end of the table sits Utari Hahna, of House Aurelle." She bowed to the Emperor. "Next to her, Rafel Batai, cousin to the King and representative of House Batai." Rafel, appearing even more corpulent in the presence of the slender Elves, smiled broadly. "I have been informed that you already met Prince Martyn and Jeran."

The Emperor nodded to Lord Iban and smiled at the young men. "Indeed I have. I found my conversations with them to be both informative and entertaining."

Iban cast a curious glance in their direction before continuing. "To the prince's left sits the Lady Jessandra Vela, newly raised First Seat of House Velan." Jes inclined her head to the Emperor, her blue eyes twinkling. "And at the end of the table is the Lady Alynna Morrena, who will represent the interests of House Morrena in our talks."

"I see what you are doing, Lord Iban," the Emperor interrupted, laughing weakly and waggling an admonishing finger, "but your trick will not work." Iban cocked his head to the side, a bewildered look on his face. "You fill your party with the most beautiful women in Alrendria, hoping that I will be distracted by their charms." Both Alynna and Jes blushed at the praise. Only Utari's expression remained aloof.

"I assure you," smiled the Emperor, "your stratagem would not have worked even if I were to take part in these negotiations. I am far too old to be enticed by such pleasures." His smile broadened, and the Alrendrians responded with polite laughter.

"You will not join us in the negotiations?" Iban asked, and even Jeran thought he sounded confused.

"My family has decided that negotiating a trade agreement would be too strenuous for me," the Emperor explained, his eyes growing dark. "I disagree, but it seems that the words of an old emperor are not as quickly heeded as the words of a younger one." The other Elves at the table were suddenly all looking in other directions; none was willing to meet their Emperor's ire.

His anger passing, the Emperor shrugged in defeat. "Luckily, Prince Martyn has graciously loaned me young Jeran Odara. He will companion me during your negotiations. I will tell him stories of his grandfather, and he will delight me with the happenings in Madryn." The Emperor smiled. "We seldom get news of the outside world here in Lynnaei. One must take advantage of the opportunities as they present themselves."

Luran's cold gaze shifted to Jeran, but he did not speak. Ignoring his grandson's cold glare, the Emperor continued. "And now it is my turn. You have all met my grandchildren; Charylla, Treloran, and Luran." He pointed to each in turn. Charylla smiled when her name was called, and Treloran bowed his head. Luran's expression, if possible, grew harsher.

"The others are my most trusted advisors. Nahrona and Nahrima." He gestured toward the Elves opposite Jeran and Alynna. The two were so close in appearance that it was impossible to tell them apart. Old, white haired, and wrinkled, both wore matching green robes, one with an oak leaf embroidered on the left breast, the other with a similar leaf on the right. They gazed upon the assembly with drooping, hazel green eyes.

"Next to Treloran sits Raithe, *Hohe Maulle*." Another aged Elf sat opposite Utari, this one so old and wrinkled that he made the twins seem young in comparison. "Raithe is the foremost of *Ael Maulle*, a position comparable to your High Wizard." The Elf dipped his head slowly, and for a moment, it did not seem like he would have the strength to raise it again.

"Raithe is the oldest living Elf," commented the Emperor, chuckling. "Other than me, of course. He was alive to see the foundation of Roya, over two millennia ago." Again, the Elf bowed his head, and the Emperor chuckled even more. "He used to talk all the time," the Emperor explained. "But in these, his final winters, he has resolved to speak only when he has something important to say."

Servants appeared to fill their glasses and set platters of steaming meat before them. The aroma made Jeran's mouth water, and he set upon his steak ravenously. Biting into the juicy, tender disk, he closed his eyes, savoring the rich blend of spices. Around them, more conversations had sprung up, especially from the Guardsmen's table, and laughter, from both the Humans and the Elves, drifted up to the Emperor's Table.

Luran scowled, his eyes burning with rage. "I have been informed of the orders you gave *Ael Chatorra*," the Emperor chided, "and have removed them." Green eyes flashing, the old Elf harrumphed angrily. " 'Do not speak to the Humans!' Do you *try* to find ways to displease me?"

The Emperor's question echoed down to the end of the table. He shook his head sadly. "You know I hope this meeting will bring our Races closer together, and still you find ways to oppose me."

"I am *Hohe Chatorra*!" Luran snapped. "It is my right to decide what orders to give our warriors."

"And *I* am Emperor of Illendrylla! Though you seem to forget that fact often enough." The Emperor schooled his features and slowed his breathing; he spoke in a frosty tone. "I have rescinded your order. It is my wish that our warriors befriend the Alrendrian Guardsmen."

Luran trembled with rage. "Nothing good has ever come from dealing with Humans. They are as bad as the Wildmen!" The Aelvin warrior clenched his napkin tightly, and his eyes shifted from the Emperor to Jeran. "They are honorless dogs, worthy of neither our time nor forbearance. Emperor Llwellyn was right. We should never have taken them from their mud huts and taught them to be civilized."

Luran's eyes wandered from one side of the table to the other, looking at each of the Alrendrians in turn. "They are not our equals," he spat. "Like all animals, they should serve. The gravest mistake our people ever made was freeing them from their chains."

The room was silent; all eyes had fallen on the head table. Even the servants, usually indifferent to their surroundings, had ceased their duties and were staring wide-eyed at Luran.

The Emperor's face hardened. "You have shamed yourself and you have shamed me, Luran," he hissed, the words inaudible to anyone seated beyond the table. Luran met the Emperor's cold stare with one of his own. "Your misplaced hatred and dubious sense of honor have already cost you my father's sword, the sword *Hohe Chatorra* has carried since before the Great Rebellion. Do not force me to strip you of your rank as well."

For a long, tense moment, Luran stood silently, then, with a snarl of rage, he pushed his chair back and strode from the hall. The Emperor shook his head sadly. "You must forgive my grandson," he said by way of an apology. "He has lost his way. Luran is a slave to his hatreds. I am not sure even Valia, in her wisdom, can bring him back to us now."

He closed his eyes, struggling to maintain his composure, and Charylla reached over to stroke his arm. Treloran, his own expression unreadable, stared thoughtfully at the Emperor.

"We are not unfamiliar with that kind of hatred," Martyn said, loud enough for all to hear. "There are plenty in Alrendria who feel as Luran, though their hatred is of the Elves. Or the Magi. Or anything different than they are." The prince stood, turning to address the assembly. "That is why we're here. Not for trade. Not for alliance. For understanding. Understanding and acceptance."

The silence stretched out for a long moment, until, slowly, the servants resumed their duties, and the guests renewed their interrupted discussions. Soon, the chamber buzzed with conversation. Satisfied, Martyn took his seat. "That was well spoken, Prince Martyn," Charylla said.

"I do, occasionally, have my moments," he replied with a smile.

"Occasionally," echoed Jeran. Martyn's head snapped to his left, and they both shared a laugh.

The situation salvaged, and the introductions completed, all settled down to enjoy the remainder of the meal. Small conversations broke out among those seated near each other. The Emperor discussed Alrendrian politics with Lord Iban and Martyn. Jes and Charylla spoke of the customs of the Elves. Treloran sat silently, looking pensive.

Jeran refrained from conversation. Instead, he listened half-heartedly to the talk around him. Lost in his own thoughts, he was startled when a voice called out to him. "House Odara is near the Boundary, is it not?" Jeran looked up into the smiling faces of the twin Elves, Nahrona and Nahrima. His eyes shifted from one to the other, but he had no idea which one had spoken.

Nodding, Jeran directed his answer to them both. "House Odara runs the length of the Boundary. I grew up in a village about eight days southeast of Portal. As a child, I used to wander the mountains with my uncle."

The aged Elves nodded slowly, their eyes distant. "I was there when it was raised, you know," one said matter-of-factly. Jeran leaned forward to hear the Elf's soft-spoken words. "A dreadful time, that was. So much death. So much pain." The Elf's eyes glistened with tears. The emotion in his voice was so poignant that Jeran felt his own heart rend.

Clearing his throat, the Elf continued. "We were young then, my brother and I. Just raised to *Ael Maulle*." He touched the golden leaf on his chest. Shaking his head at the memory, he laughed. "We were both so proud! So foolish! We were being sent to the front, to join Aemon's great army. Finally, after winters of training, we were considered skilled enough to add our Gift to the struggle against the Darklord."

"The MageWar had already lasted more than three centuries," said the other Elf, taking up the story where his brother left off. "Few places existed that remained unscarred by the fighting. Nature itself begged for an end to the hostilities."

"We traveled to the front on foot," said the first. "We could have used our Gift to take us there faster, but the Emperor commanded us to travel by land. To see for what we fought." The Elf's eyes grew distant and pained. "In all my life, I have never seen such suffering again. Villages–whole cities!–sacked and destroyed. Fields put to the torch. Forests uprooted and mountains gutted to provide the armies with their endless supplies. The dead far outnumbered the living."

"Such horrible things were done... By both sides, mind you!" the second Elf added, wagging a finger at Jeran. "The histories and stories may make it sound as if all the evils were committed by Lorthas and his armies, but only a fool would believe such nonsense."

"War is a dirty business," said the Elf across from Jeran. "Even the most honorable of men can succumb to his darker impulses. All of us did things we were not proud of during that time. Some just did more than others."

"That was the problem, you see," continued the other. Jeran's eyes jumped back and forth as the Elves told their story in tandem. "The histories would have you believe that Lorthas was on the verge of winning the war. That raising the Boundary was a last-ditch effort on the part of the Allied Races."

"But that was not the case."

"Heavens no! If the Boundary had not been raised, the MageWar could have stretched on indefinitely. The tides of battle had shifted many times over the winters."

"And would have continued to switch."

"But each time they did, greater measures had to be taken. Greater atrocities committed."

"That was the real problem, you see. We were in danger of becoming no better than the Darklord. All the ideals that were our war cries at the start of the MageWar had become little more than hollow words. Excuses to continue the fighting."

"If the war had been allowed to continue to its natural conclusion, all of Madryn would have suffered. Even if we had won, the results would have been but marginally different than if Lorthas had defeated us."

"Aemon knew this. He knew the generations-long conflict had hardened the people of Alrendria. Even the grandparents of the oldest living Human had known nothing of peace, until the word itself had lost almost all meaning."

"Aemon's thoughts were for *his* people, but the war had changed us all. Turned all of us into monsters, whether we choose to remember it that way or not. We enjoyed the evils we did, so long as we could pretend our crimes served justice. There are still nights I wake trembling, not from memories of things I saw, but from things I had to do in the name of peace."

"That was when Aemon proposed the Boundary." The Elf across from Jeran shared a knowing look with his brother. "It was a terrible notion. A barrier against magic! A prison entrapping Lorthas and his ShadowMagi. It went against everything we were taught as *Ael Maulle*. The Boundary is a crime against nature itself."

"But was it any more a crime against nature than the endless seasons of war we had visited upon our world?" asked the other. He nodded sagely. "Many thought so. At first, they fought against Aemon's idea, honestly believing that we would eventually win the war."

"Not the Emperor, though. He understood Aemon's fears from the start."

"He convinced us of the threat posed by prolonging the fight, and of the chance for salvation the Boundary offered."

"In time, Aemon and the Emperor convinced enough of us, and the plan was put into motion. A massive campaign was planned. For two winters our forces attacked, pushing Lorthas' troops into northern Alrendria."

"Even still, when Aemon announced that it was time for the Raising, he met resistance. Some had doubts about the plan. Others felt the advance could continue. They believed, or wanted to believe, that Lorthas and his armies could be shattered once and for all."

"They were deluding themselves, though, and most of us knew it. The day finally came. In the aftermath of a great battle, we learned that Lorthas had called the ShadowMagi north, to his stronghold, where he was amassing a great army. Aemon gave the order for the Boundary to be raised."

"It was an amazing feat," the Elf to Jeran's left exclaimed. "It took nearly every one with the Gift. Every Mage. Every *Tsha'ma*. Every *Ael Maulle*. The ground trembled for days afterward, and more than a few lost their lives."

"Not only during the Raising," the other interjected, "but after as well. Thousands died in the quakes and landslides that followed."

"Thousands more in the floods following the creation of the mountains."

"That was only on our side of the Boundary! We know little of what occurred within *Ael Shataq*. Similar things, no doubt."

"Plus whatever the Darklord did in his rage," the second commented.

The first nodded. "Lorthas was never known for his forgiveness, even before the MageWar." Both their eyes grew sad. In unison, they whispered, "The poor Orog."

At Jeran's questioning gaze, the Elf across from Jeran said, "You tell him, Nahrima. I am overcome." He lifted his napkin and dabbed it against eyes heavy with tears.

Nahrima did not look much better off. "That was the saddest part, you see," he explained. "The Orog did not have time to escape before we raised the Boundary. They were trapped on the far side, and Lorthas had no love for them. No love at all."

"Aemon was heartbroken," Nahrona added, "as were we all, when he gave the order."

"But if Lorthas had been allowed to march south, then everything we had strived for would have been for naught."

"After the Raising, many felt that the MageWar was finally over. The Alrendrian armies had only to mop up the remnants of the Arkam Imperium, and whatever small islands of support Lorthas had remaining."

"Without the aid of the Darklord, they fell easily."

"The tribes were decimated by the war, but so were the Drekka, and our Garun'ah allies dealt with the remnants of the Horde quickly."

"We Elves had a much longer battle ahead of us," Nahrima added. "The *Noedra Shamallyn* were well hidden. It took over a century to uncover the last of their cult and drive the survivors deep into the Great Forest."

"Everyone tried to remember what peace was like," Nahrona said. "And almost everyone did their best to forget the MageWar, thinking the danger was past."

"But not us!" exclaimed Nahrima.

"Not us," Nahrona agreed, shaking his head. "Like everyone else, we enjoyed this break in the warfare."

"But unlike our comrades, we knew this for what it was. Just a break in the hostilities."

"A temporary peace."

"The Boundary cannot last forever. What can be created by man can be destroyed."

"The Boundary goes against nature, and nature will find a way to compensate."

Nahrima smiled. "The Emperor's sudden interest in Alrendria. Your willingness to come to Illendrylla. That and many other events lead us to believe the peace is nearly over. That the war is about to begin again."

"And for some reason, we believe you are the key."

"We have enjoyed the peace," Nahrima admitted, and Nahrona nodded his agreement. "But should our suspicions be proved correct, we are ready to lend what aid we can. Know that we will support the Emperor, even if it incurs the wrath of his family."

Jeran stared wide-eyed at the twins. He looked around, fearing that they had said too much, and was surprised to find the room empty, save for him and the two Elves. How long they had been alone, he could not say, nor how he had not noticed the others leaving, or the silence that echoed from a chamber which had been full of noise when last he had noticed.

"He is speechless," Nahrima said to his brother.

"Absolutely dumbfounded," agreed Nahrona.

"Perhaps he desires a moral. Humans always were fond of morals."

"But there are so many!"

"Let me try." Nahrima turned to Jeran and said, "Remember what we told you of the MageWar? How even noble beings can commit atrocities if they believe their cause is just? Should war once again begin, there will be a time when you have to decide which is worse, surrendering to an evil or committing an evil to stop an evil." That said, the twins pushed themselves to their feet, and started to turn away from the table.

"Wait!" said Jeran, and the twins looked at him, matching smiles on their faces. "When that time comes, what do I choose? Do I surrender, or do I fight?"

Nahrima and Nahrona looked at each other for a long time, as if communicating silently. By the time they returned their attentions to Jeran, their smiles had faded.

"We do not know," Nahrima admitted, somewhat guiltily.

"We raised the Boundary so we would not have to make that decision."

"Think about our words, and when you are ready–"

"–seek us out. Perhaps together–"

They finished in unison. "We can find a solution."

They turned and left, leaving Jeran alone in the vast dining chamber. He sat there for a long time, pondering all he had been told, by not only the twins, but also by the Emperor. He was afraid of what was to come. He did not feel up to the task before him. *I'm not a great hero, like Aemon, or Emperor Alwellyn, or Jolam Strongarm. What chance do I have against the Darklord, Salos, or any of Lorthas' minions?*

"Is something the matter, my Lord?" asked Elierian, and Jeran jumped at the sound. The Elf stood behind him, looking decidedly more tired than when last Jeran had last laid eyes on him.

Jeran stood, groaning. "Nothing that will be solved by sitting here." He looked around the room, then asked. "Can someone lead me back to my chambers? I haven't yet familiarized myself with the palace."

"I will show you the way, my Lord, if it pleases you." At Jeran's nod, the Elf strode away, almost gliding across the smooth stone floor. Yawning, surprised by how tired he felt, Jeran followed.

To pass the time, Jeran asked a question that had plagued him since the start of the feast. "Elierian, why is it that you speak so openly, when the rest of the servants are always silent?"

"If you prefer, Lord Odara, I will keep my thoughts to myself."

"No!" Jeran said hastily. "I'm just curious as to why the other servants do *not* talk."

"It is not considered appropriate for *Ael Namisa* to talk to *Ael Alluya*," he explained. "At least, not unless they are spoken to first. But if none were to speak, then nothing would get done, for the Obedient know details that those of the ruling class need to run their households.

"Thus some *Ael Namisa* are given the title *Volche*. The *Volche Namisa*—Voices of the Obedient—relay to the other castes the desires and opinions of *Ael Namisa*." He offered Jeran a warm smile. "I am *Hohe Namisa*, the foremost of the Obedient here in Lynnaei. It is a position of much honor and responsibility, and I am granted privileges that others of my class are not allowed."

Jeran nodded, only half understanding the complex social network of the Elves. Elierian led him up a winding staircase, and the hallway suddenly appeared familiar. "Thank you, Elierian," Jeran said. "I can find my way from here."

The Elf bowed and turned around, descending the stairs silently. Jeran walked to his door and drew it open. Yawning again, he pulled the door closed behind him, longing for the warmth and comfort of his bed.

He had barely entered the sitting room when a seductive voice called out, "There you are! I was starting to worry that you'd never return." Jeran, startled, jumped, and his eyes scanned the room warily. Alynna was in his chambers, sprawled enticingly on one of the couches. Her dress lay at her feet; she wore only a thin, lacy shift that exposed an impressive amount of leg and bosom.

Jeran groaned audibly, and Alynna smiled. She rose gracefully from the divan and crossed the room, her hips swaying with every step. Her arms around Jeran, and she stepped in close, so that their lips were nearly brushing. "Welcome home, Lord Odara," she murmured. "I trust you weren't expecting much sleep tonight."

Chapter 10

Jeran tried to back away, but Alynna's grip was vise-like. "It's very late," he said, struggling to escape her grasp.

"I know," she pouted, locking her arms behind his back and drawing him closer. "You should have returned long ago. We've wasted half the night!"

She moved into him. Jeran felt the swell of her breast against his chest, the smooth skin of her leg touching his. Her blue eyes peered into his knowingly. He swallowed hard, and she pressed her lips against his.

He jerked his head back, breaking their embrace. "Alynna," he said, his breathing short and quick, "I cannot." She smelled of roses. The fragrance permeated the room, and he inhaled deeply. Part of him could not believe that he was turning down her offer.

She stepped away, her eyes glistening with tears, and her lower lip quivered. Her head lowered in shame, but the look she gave him was coquettish. "You do not find me pretty?" she asked, her voice quavering.

Jeran tried not to groan. "Alynna," he said carefully, "you're one of the most beautiful women in all of Kaper. Any man would be a fool not to want you."

"You are no fool," she replied accusingly.

"Some might disagree," Jeran returned, offering a tight smile. "But there are other reasons why this would not be wise."

"I would please you," she said, her feigned shyness fading. Her eyes roved up and down his body, hungry. "And you would certainly please me." She stepped toward him, smiling aggressively.

Jeran kept his distance. "I have no doubt but that you would please me, but I cannot."

"On a political level," Alynna added, "a union between our Houses would be very profitable. There are vast resources available in House Odara, and House Morrena has a strong Guard, as loyal to us as they are to Alrendria. Together, we'd possess a strength the other Houses could never match."

Jeran, suddenly wary, frowned. "What are you suggesting? Certainly you're not saying that we should–"

Alynna rolled her eyes dramatically, but she took another step in his direction. "Of course not, Jeran. I'm as loyal to Alrendria, and the King, as you. Besides, there'd be nothing to gain by overthrowing the Batai Family.

The King is a figure head, nothing more. He has only what power the Assembly of Houses gives him."

Jeran shook his head in denial, but Alynna seemed not to notice. She advanced, and Jeran was forced to retreat. A bead of sweat ran down his forehead. "I don't understand—"

"Trade!" Alynna interrupted, lecturing him as if he were a child. "Power is not about titles or Guardsmen. It's about money. If our Houses were allied, all land trade from the eastern nations to the western nations would have to pass through us. We could charge taxes on every wagonload of goods that passed through our lands, just like King Hasna has done in Midlyn."

She laughed; it was a gentle sound, like the tinkling of a bell. "We can even offer lower rates to the other Great Houses, if you think it wise." Locking her eyes with his, Alynna reached for Jeran's shirt.

He sidestepped, but found himself against the wall, backed into the corner. "Hasna's tax was a mistake," he said, shaking his head. "It's cost him a fortune! Few nations even deal with him, and virtually all trade to New Arkam arrives by ship. If we did what you suggest, the same would be true. The only people who'd benefit from this scheme are the traders of Roya."

"My uncle disagrees with you," Alynna replied. She caught Jeran nervously looking from side to side, and seemed to notice for the first time that he had run out of room. "He also said you'd never agree." Her eyes sparkled mischievously; the tip of her tongue ran across her upper lip. "I must admit, my purposes for proposing this…union…are as much personal as political."

She laughed, low and seductive. "I don't give up easily, Jeran. I promise, by tomorrow, you won't even remember why you thought this was a bad idea." She lunged at him, fast as lightning. Jeran tried duck under her arms, but his shoulder hit the wall, and he was left with no escape.

Alynna was on him in an instant. Her arms wrapped around him, one leg locked behind his, and she placed gentle kisses on his neck. He tried to fight her off, but she seemed to have more hands than he did, and greater dexterity as well. "Please," he pleaded, "I beg you to stop this."

She pulled back far enough to look into his eyes. "I like it when you beg," she admitted, "but you're not begging for the right things!" Her expression suddenly changed, became more suspicious, and her lips pressed together in an angry frown. "Is it that Velani tramp? Is that what you're worried about?"

Grasping at what he saw as a way out, Jeran eagerly nodded. "Jes is very dear to me," he said cautiously, hoping not to be forced into an outright lie. "I—" Alynna silenced him with a kiss.

"She's not worth your time!" Alynna said, pulling back; the mere thought of Jes made her sneer. "She may have some small measure of beauty, but it will fade soon enough. I don't care how young she looks, she acts like a greatmother! She's older than she appears, I assure you. Women know these things. If you stay with her, you'll find yourself married to a crone before you reach your thirtieth winter."

Seeing that he had sparked a nerve, Jeran pressed his advantage, hoping Alynna's anger would divert her mind from seduction. "There are qualities other than beauty to be appreciated in a woman," he said coolly.

Alynna laughed. "That may be true, but there are none she possesses that I do not have in equal amounts." Her eyes grew hungry again, and she let her anger pass. "Relax, Lord Odara," she murmured. "By morning, you will have forgotten all about her. That I promise, too."

Jeran tried to protest, but Alynna kissed him again. She fumbled with his shirt, trying to work the laces, and Jeran fought desperately to keep them secured. "I've never seen a man play so hard to get," Alynna chuckled, her eyes twinkling. "I find it most stimulating."

Hot lips pressed into Jeran's neck, biting playfully at his pulse. One hand slipped beneath his shirt, cool fingers probing; the other grabbed Jeran's and touched it to her. With each indrawn breath, he felt the swell of Alynna's breast press into his hand. Jeran's own breathing quickened, and his heart pounded in his chest.

No longer certain he had the will to stop her, Jeran wondered how long until he succumbed to Alynna's charms. Pulling back, he grabbed her arms and squeezed tightly, ready to make one last effort to push her away.

"Lord Odara?" came a frantic cry from the hall. "Lord Odara!"

Alynna backed away quickly, an angry frown on her face. In an instant she was at the couch; her red dress once more covered her milk-white skin. Hastily, Jeran tucked his shirt in and smoothed his hair. "In here," he called, grateful for the distraction.

Liseyl entered, her clothes disheveled, her hair disarrayed. Her eyes went instantly to Alynna, widening. "I do not mean to intrude, my Lord," she said, her breathing labored. She stepped back. "I won't bother you."

"What's the matter?" Jeran asked, afraid that, in her embarrassment, Liseyl would leave him alone again.

"It's Mika!" she said plaintively. "He's sick! Lord Odara, you must help him!" Her voice was pleading, and Jeran shared her concern.

"Of course," he replied, "of course." He directed an apologetic look at Alynna. "You must forgive me, my Lady. One of my servant's children is unwell. I need to tend to him."

Alynna bowed her head politely. "I understand, Jeran. The welfare of one's servants is quite important. I enjoyed our conversation, and I look forward to speaking with you again in the near future."

Liseyl headed toward the hall, looking back over her shoulder beseechingly. Alynna went to leave as well, but when she passed Jeran, she whispered, "You will be quite a challenge, but I'm not discouraged." The half-frightened expression on Jeran's face amused her; musical laughter followed her through the room. "Consider my offer," she added, a hungry look in her eye. "You will not regret it."

With that, she was out the door and down the hall. Jeran and Liseyl hurried to her chambers, and Jeran's anxiety grew with every passing moment. Her hand shaking, Liseyl fumbled with the latch to her chamber. Opening the door, she hurried in.

Jeran pushed past her, looking for Mika. He found the boy sound asleep in his room, not drenched in sweat, nor breathing shallow, nor in any discomfort. Perplexed, Jeran turned around, looking for Liseyl.

She was watching with a smile on her face. She had composed herself and smoothed her hair, but she was still shaking, though now from laughter, not fear. Cupping a hand to her mouth, she stifled a giggle. "I'm sorry, Jeran," she said at last, her voice low so as to not disturb the children. "It was the only thing I could think of. I didn't mean to worry you."

Jeran's forehead scrunched in confusion. Liseyl beckoned to him, and he closed the door to Mika's room, returning to the main chamber. Liseyl offered him a seat, which he took gladly. "I saw the Lady Alynna in the hall after the feast," Liseyl explained, "sneaking into your chambers. She did not notice me."

Liseyl shook her head. "That one is as aggressive as a tavern wench," she chuckled. "But much more dangerous. I took a guess at what she had planned, and from the look on your face when I walked in, she had nearly succeeded. I hope I didn't interfere with anything you wanted–"

"Certainly not!" Jeran exclaimed. "In fact, I'm glad you came along when you did. Alynna had left me no other options. I was either going to have to succumb to her advances or fight her off bodily! I only wish you had come along sooner."

"I had planned on intercepting you in the hallway," Liseyl admitted, her cheeks reddening in embarrassment, "but you were gone so long I fell asleep." Her smile returned impishly. "Lucky for you, I woke when I did."

"Lucky indeed!" Jeran agreed, and they shared a laugh. "I owe you a great debt."

She waved off his gratitude. "Not so great. You freed me from one type of slavery; I saved you from another. But *my* slavers are not coming back!" she added, her eyes dancing with mirth. "I suspect we have not seen the last of Alynna."

Jeran nodded. "She said as much before leaving my chambers." He knelt before Liseyl, laughing. "I never thought I'd have the need of a bodyguard, yet I find myself unequipped to handle some of the dangers life offers. Would you protect me from those things, my Lady?" He forced his voice to seriousness. "I would be eternally grateful."

Liseyl bowed formally, schooling her own expression. "It is a mighty responsibility you place on my shoulders, Lord Odara, but I will serve as best I can." They laughed again, and Jeran stood, starting toward the door. "I doubt she will be back again tonight," Liseyl said comfortingly, patting Jeran's shoulder. "If she does return, just scream. I'll be there in an instant."

Jeran laughed again and, bidding Liseyl goodnight, returned to his own chambers. Pulling the door closed behind him, he drew the bolt through the lock, ensuring that he would have no more interruptions. Overwhelmed with exhaustion, he climbed into his bed, wrapped himself in his blankets, and was instantly asleep.

His sleep was restless, troubled by strange and frightening dreams. In one, he was chased by a monster, a woman with eight arms, whose hands ended in sharp claws that reached for him. In another he was with Dahr, and they were hunted by some nameless pursuer. They ran blindly through the dark, not knowing where they were going, but knowing that it could not be as bad as what they would face if they stopped.

Other dreams were less frightening, though in almost all of them, Jeran was running from something. In some he ran through the twisting corridors of the palace; in others he wove through the thick underbrush and razor-sharp thorns of the Great Forest. In still other dreams he was back in Kaper, or Keryn's Rest, or the mountains of the Boundary; but now he was searching for something desperately, only he did not know what it was.

Throughout all these dreams Jeran felt a presence, an unknown entity watching him. No matter where he turned, or how well he hid, he could feel eyes on his back, laughing at his misfortunes. At first he dismissed the presence, believing it to be just another aspect of the dream. But though his dreams continued, ever changing, the presence remained, its quiet laughter echoing in his ears.

He woke with a start, drenched with sweat, the blankets moist with his perspiration. His breathing was fast and irregular, and he felt as if he had just finished a race, rather than a slumber. Memories of his dreams, and the omnipresent eyes that had watched his slumber, came flooding back.

His first thought was of the Darklord. *If Lorthas can enter my dreams, then is it not equally likely that he could watch them?* The thought sent a chill to the marrow of Jeran's bones.

He climbed from the bed, groaning, feeling completely unrested, and drew open the thick curtains. Warm sunshine immediately enveloped him. Opening the door, he stepped onto the balcony, taking deep breaths of the warm, midmorning air.

Stretching, he worked the knots from muscles still tense from his nightmares. A knocking forced him back inside. Reluctantly, he donned a robe and opened the door. Mika and his mother were waiting outside. "We thought you'd be up by now," Liseyl said. "I thought you'd like a bath before you went to the negotiations."

"I won't be attending the negotiations," Jeran said, standing aside so they could enter. "I'll be meeting with the Emperor." Jeran cupped a hand over his mouth, stifling a yawn. "But a hot bath would be most welcome."

Liseyl smiled and disappeared into the back. Several brown robed Elves entered on silent feet, carrying armloads of wood for the hearth bins.

Each bowed as they passed Jeran. At the mention of the Emperor, Mika's eyes brightened noticeably, and he hurried across the room. "Can I come with you?" he asked, his voice full of eagerness.

Jeran shook his head. "Not today. The Emperor and I have things we need to discuss. But I'll ask him if he would mind an audience with you in the near future. Maybe your sisters would like to meet him, too."

"What are we going to do while you're gone?" Mika asked sullenly.

Jeran laughed. "Whatever you wish." he replied. "Were I you, I'd talk your mother into taking you through the city. There's much to be seen here, and we're the first Humans in over three hundred winters to enter Lynnaei. It would be foolish to squander such an opportunity!"

Liseyl appeared at the door. "The fire's started. The bath should be warm shortly."

At his mother's appearance, Mika ran over to her. "Can we go into the city today, Mama?" he asked, trembling with excitement. "Jeran says we're the first Humans here in three hundred winters. We should see everything we can so we can tell everybody about it!"

Liseyl smiled at her son. "I'll talk to your sisters," she promised. "If they're as interested as you, then we shall." Mika ran out of the room, anxious to start coaxing his sisters into wanting to explore. Liseyl watched him run away, then looked at Jeran. "Would you like to break your fast before meeting with the Emperor?"

Jeran nodded, and Liseyl turned, asking one of the Aelvin servants if she would bring some bread and tea. To Jeran's surprise, the servant answered back in a lightly-accented voice. "They speak to you?" he asked incredulously.

Liseyl nodded. "*Ael Namisa* are not supposed to speak to *Ael Alluya*, their nobility," she said knowingly, as if it were common knowledge. "Unless spoken to, of course. They consider you and the other nobles part of the Ruling Class. Even still, they were tight-lipped around us, too, until we convinced them that we were servants. After that, it was all we could do to stop them long enough to ask a few questions of our own."

The last Elf passed Jeran, bowing submissively as she did so. "They're particularly impressed with you" Liseyl said, laughing at Jeran's surprise.

"Me?"

She nodded. "You're little more than a child to the Elves. Even in Human terms you're barely an adult! Yet you defeated their best warrior, the leader of the Aelvin Armies, in single combat, the day after receiving a grievous wound in defense of your prince!" Her eyes danced at his embarrassment. "*Ael Namisa* already consider you something of a legend."

Jeran groaned and put his head in his hands. "It's not that bad!" Liseyl insisted, laughing all the harder. Jeran ignored her and went to his bath. The water was not yet hot, but it was warm enough to suit his needs. He doused the fire beneath the tub and climbed in, luxuriating in the feel of the warm water. He closed his eyes and stretched tight muscles, working at a knot in his shoulders with one hand.

Once finished, he wrapped himself in his towel and returned to his bedchamber, where Liseyl had laid out an outfit for him. He dressed hurriedly and ate a quick meal of toast smothered in a sweet apple jelly and dark, bitter tea. Then he had Liseyl summon one of the Aelvin servants.

"I am to meet the Emperor in the Vale," Jeran stated. "Can you show me the way?"

The Elf smiled and, bowing her head, led Jeran through the twisting, labyrinthine corridors of the palace. Jeran paid close attention to their route, so that he could find his own way in the future. After a long hike, the Elf led him down a winding staircase and stopped. Bowing, she pointed at a small, oak door and walked away, disappearing down a nearby corridor.

Jeran opened the door, and the warm, natural smell of the Vale surrounded him. He stepped through, pulling the door shut behind him. Sunlight streamed down from above. It was not yet midday, but close enough that Jeran would not have to wait long for the Emperor's arrival.

Jeran wandered the twisting, white stone paths of the Vale. Squirrels chittered in the branches above, and birds sang merrily from their nests. Jeran inhaled deeply, allowing the sweet fragrances of the garden to flow into him, relaxing his muscles more completely than even his bath had managed.

The Tower of the Five Gods was visible through the trees, the enormous spire piercing the blue sky like a spear. Jeran kept the tower in front of him as much as possible, weaving down the Vale's shadowy paths. Before too long, he emerged in the tower's clearing. The Emperor was already there, sitting in the shade of the great oak.

The aged Elf sat cross-legged on the ground, his hands folded on his lap, his head tucked down. His breathing was slow and regular; his eyes were closed. Jeran thought him asleep, and he approached cautiously, not wanting to disturb the Emperor's nap. "Good morning, Jeran," the Emperor called in a dry, crackling voice. "I trust you enjoyed your evening."

"It was most informative, Grandfather," Jeran replied, hurrying to stand beside the Elf. "I had a long talk with Nahrona and Nahrima. It seems they have guessed the true purpose of our visit here."

"Ahhhh. The twins," the Emperor said with a fond nod. "They always were too smart for their own good." He opened his eyes, the green irises glowing with an inner fire. "They can be trusted," he assured Jeran. "The twins served me faithfully during the MageWar. And in all the winters since." Seeing the worried look in Jeran's eyes, the Emperor smiled. "I will speak with them, if you would like, though they know when to keep their opinions to themselves."

Jeran nodded. "Have you been here long, Grandfather?"

"Since sunrise," the Emperor responded. At Jeran's wide-eyed look, the Elf laughed. "I told you that I no longer sleep much." He looked around the Vale, his eyes distant. "There was a time when I was so busy governing Illendrylla that I could not spare a moment to sit and meditate among my trees. Now...." Sad, green eyes met Jeran's blue. "Now I have to look for excuses to leave this place.

"It is sad when the world no longer has a need for you," the Emperor told Jeran. "No man should live to see that day. I hope you do not."

"You haven't outlived your usefulness!" Jeran insisted. "You're Alwellyn the Eternal! You're a legend, Grandfather."

"It is kind of you to say so," the Emperor replied, gesturing for Jeran to sit. "But with the exception of a handful–me...Aemon...a few others–all the legends died long ago, like they were supposed to. In truth, the man rarely measures up to the myth. That is another lesson for you to remember."

Jeran sat across from the Emperor, in the hollow made by a curved root. Once he had settled comfortably on the soft dirt, the Emperor said, "Tell me what your king has learned of Lorthas, and what he intends to do about it."

"King Mathis knows little of the Darklord's plans," Jeran admitted, "and only slightly more about Tylor and Salos Durange. We're not even positive they're allies, though it's a reasonable assumption."

Jeran told the Emperor what little they knew of Tylor's plans. He spoke of the ships sailing the waters of Madryn, the ones that ran at the first sighting of another vessel, and of the assassination of Lobarin, Regent of Ra Tachan. King Mathis felt the crowning of Tiam Durange's youngest son was another step in Tylor's scheme.

He also talked about Salos, explaining that Salos was a Mage, and that he had never actually crossed the Boundary. Jeran knew everything, every scrap of information that the King and his agents had discovered, and he shared it all with the Emperor.

"How Lorthas fits into this is a mystery," Jeran admitted. "We believe the Darklord has strings tied to the Durange, that their actions are merely part of a larger design. But the Boundary, though weakening, is still impassable, and it will likely remain so for a long time to come."

"Even after all this time, I doubt Lorthas would give up his desire to control Madryn," the Emperor commented sagely. "While he certainly has a formidable force at his disposal within the confines of *Ael Shataq*, I am sure he would prefer to emerge from his prison to a world that was already under his thumb."

Jeran nodded. "Even if the Durange are unsuccessful, the chaos and death caused by another war, or series of wars, would weaken us, making it easier for Lorthas to conquer what little resistance remained."

"Everything the Darklord can do to form dissent between the nations of men–and between the three Races–serves his purposes," the Emperor added. "If war is coming, then we must use our time to bind the Races together."

They talked for a while longer, exchanging ideas, trying to find a pattern within the actions of the Durange. Finally, the Emperor raised his hand. "Enough!" he said. "We have talked of this enough today. Give me time to think on what you have told me."

Taking a deep breath, the Emperor focused his gaze on Jeran, and his eyes tightened noticeably. "Let us talk about magic," he said at last.

At Jeran's suddenly-wary visage, the Emperor laughed so hard that he started to choke. His wheezing coughs lasted so long that Jeran began to worry for the old Elf's health. Finally, his breathing under control, the Emperor said, "I have spoken to Jes, and she granted me permission to train you. She has already warned me about your strength."

The Emperor met Jeran's eyes levelly. "It has been a while since I have had an apprentice, but I am willing to offer you what instruction I can."

"I… It… It would be an honor, Grandfather," Jeran replied. "But you should not feel obligated. I do not want to inconvenience you."

"Nonsense," the Emperor laughed. "It is not as if you will be taking me away from more pressing duties. Besides, you could say I am motivated by self-preservation." Jeran's brow wrinkled in confusion, and the Emperor chuckled again. "I may be near death, but I do not wish to hasten my departure from this world. I have no desire to be burnt to a cinder because you accidentally seize the magic around you and do not know what to do with it."

He smiled at Jeran to show that he was joking, but Jeran took the comment seriously. "I don't want to be a threat to anyone."

"Then it is settled." Jeran could not argue with the Emperor's commanding tone. "Now close your eyes. And relax!" Jeran did as instructed, and the Emperor told him about magic. The speech was remarkably similar to those he had heard from Jes. "Magic is nothing more than energy," the Emperor began. "Limitless energy. And a Mage is little more than a conduit for that energy.

"Like a millwheel can capture the energy of a stream, a Mage can capture the energy of magic. The mill takes the energy of the water and uses it for some other purpose. To grind grain or cut wood, for example. A Mage transforms the flows of magic in the same way, harnessing the energy for his own purposes.

"Using magic is a skill like any other. And like any other skill, practice allows you to use magic more easily and with greater proficiency. Anyone can lift a sword or hold a hammer, but it takes much training to fight with expertise or forge a useful tool.

"There are three stages to learning control of magic. Each stage has its own threats, and its own rewards. The first step is seizing the flows of magic. Magic is formless energy. It does not wish to be trapped or constrained. The dangers at this stage are few, but so are the advantages. Among Humans, many go through their lives with the Gift, unaware that, with training, they could be a Mage.

"The second level of training deals with holding the flows of magic. Magic struggles against the prison a Mage creates for it, almost as if it had a life of its own. It takes a Mage's Will to hold the energy in check, to prevent the magic from using the Mage's own Gift as a release."

The Emperor's voice was cool and distant, as if he were reciting a litany he knew by heart. "This is the most dangerous phase of a Mage's training. A Mage at this stage is a threat to both himself and those around him. If he seizes magic but cannot control it, it will release itself, and the results are often disastrous.

"But this level, once conquered, is also the most rewarding. A Mage with his Will focused is at one with nature, and the world around him seems clearer. Once held, magic is at the Mage's control."

Jeran waited for the long pause he knew would come. Jes always thought it took him much longer to enter the meditation than it actually did. To his surprise, the Emperor did not stop his lecture. "The third phase in a Mage's training is learning how to use the energy of magic. This level of training continues throughout the Mage's lifetime, and is limited only by the Mage's imagination and his or her own specific abilities.

"You," the Emperor said to Jeran, "are hovering between the first two levels. With effort, you can seize the flows of magic around you. That will become easier with time and practice. However, Jes tells me that when you do seize magic, it is of a great volume, greater than most of your age and experience.

"The amount of magic a Mage can hold is usually proportional to the length of time he has trained his Gift. At the start of their training, most Magi can seize only the tiniest fraction of the magic around them. But just as some men are naturally stronger than others, some Magi are naturally more gifted, too. So it is with you.

"Your strength will increase with training, just like everyone else's," the Emperor assured him, "but you have an innate ability to seize magic, and that skill puts you in more danger than most Magi.

"Therefore, the first thing we must teach you is how *not* to seize magic. Once that is accomplished, I will show you how to release it before it runs wild. Then, and only then, will we begin to train your ability to hold magic.

"Are you ready to begin?" the Emperor asked, and Jeran nodded. "Then clear your mind. You know what you must do. As you did with Jes, try to seize only the tiniest flow of magic. I will guide you."

Jeran calmed himself, slowing his breathing. He emptied his mind of thought and reached out to the flows of magic around him. As usual, they shied away from him. The experience was not as annoying as it once had been. Steadying himself, he imagined the magic as tiny beams of energy, and allowed one of those beams to flow toward him, straining with the effort required to keep the rest away.

"Good," murmured the Emperor. "Now release it and do it again." Jeran complied with the Emperor's commands. They repeated the process over and over, until Jeran's body was slicked with sweat, and spots of light danced before his eyes.

"One last time," requested the Emperor, and Jeran struggled to obey. It was an effort to clear his mind, almost an effort to breathe. Visualizing the strands of energy, he opened himself to it. The magic quivered, on the verge of rushing toward him.

"Stop!" the Emperor commanded, his voice full of authority. "Tell me what you feel."

Jeran was slow to answer. "There is a tingling in my chest," he said, trying to put what he felt into words. "A lightness in my stomach."

"Remember this feeling well, Jeran," the Emperor said, his voice serious. "Recognizing this feeling could very well save your life." A tense silence filled the Vale; it pressed in on Jeran from all sides. "Hold yourself here," the Emperor continued, "on the verge of seizing magic, for as long as you can. When you can hold it no longer, release your will without seizing the flows."

Jeran did as he was told, dancing around the edge of magic for as long as he dared. He did his best to memorize the feeling, every nuance of the experience. When he finally released the flow and opened his eyes, he swayed with dizziness. The Emperor's thin hand steadied him.

The old Elf held out a cup of cool water, though where it had come from Jeran could only guess. He drank greedily as the Emperor concluded the lesson. "Remember that feeling! It is how you will feel every time you are about to seize magic. If you feel that tingling, that lightness in your chest, you must calm yourself and push the magic away. It is easier not to seize magic than it is to release it once held."

Jeran drained the cup, and the Emperor refilled it from a flask at his side. "You have great potential," he continued. "And thus you are in great danger until you learn control. For now, the wisest thing to do is run from your Gift. Do not attempt to seize magic, not even the smallest amount, unless Jes or I are around to guide you."

"What if I have no choice?" Jeran asked. "There have been times when I seized magic without even realizing it."

"We hopefully will not have to deal with such things," the Emperor replied, offering Jeran a thin smile. "Generally, such events as you have described only occur under duress. With a little luck, your stay in Lynnaei will be completely uneventful."

"Is there any way to–" Jeran started to ask, but a new voice, full of anger, interrupted.

"What," said Luran, his voice dripping with scorn, "is *that* doing here?"

The Emperor's eyes snapped up, making no effort to hide his agitation. "Jeran," he replied, emphasizing the name, "is here as my guest."

"This is Valia's Garden," began Luran. "His kind—"

The Emperor sprang to his feet, surprising Luran into silence. "*I* am the Goddess' voice in this world," he reminded his grandson. "Who I choose to bring to the Vale is my concern, not yours." The Emperor brushed dirt and leaves from his pale green robes. "Is there something you wanted," he asked, "or were you just concerned that you had not irritated me enough last night?"

Luran's eyes were cold, but his voice remained even. "There have been reports of skirmishes along the border. I wish to take a contingent of archers to the Danelle, to set up a regular patrol. It would not be wise to allow the Wildmen a foothold on this side of the river."

The Emperor was slow to respond. "If that is what you think best, Luran, I accept your judgment." After a short pause, he added, "I wish I could say I am sorry to see you leave. Perhaps you will take this time to reflect upon your actions. The Humans are not our enemies."

Luran's gaze remained icy at the rebuking. Sighing, the Emperor asked, "When will you leave?"

"In two day's time," came the reply. "There are some duties I must attend to before leaving. And I must find myself a replacement for the negotiations. Someone who can be trusted to put the needs of Illendrylla ahead of their own personal gain."

The Emperor nodded sadly. "I am sure your replacement will no doubt see things with the same perspective as you." The old Elf closed his eyes and banished his anger. When next he spoke, his tone was calmer, friendlier. "I wish you well, Luran. Keep me informed of what you find along the border. When you return, we will dine together."

Luran bowed to the Emperor, ignoring Jeran completely, then turned and strode quickly through the trees, eager to be away. The Emperor watched him leave, then looked at Jeran. "Again, I must ask you to forgive my grandson."

Jeran waved off the Emperor's apology, but the old Elf ignored him. "His hatred is not justified." An owl drifted in on silent wings, landing on a branch not far above the Emperor's head. He stared at the bird silently.

When he lowered his head, he had to wipe a tear from his eye. "Luran's—and Charylla's—parents were killed long ago in a Garun'ah raid. The far side of the Danelle has long been contested by our races. My people believe that all of the Great Forest belongs to us, while some of the tribes, including the Drekka and Tacha, claim that their lands extend to the river. The remains of the Drekka live to our north, and the Tacha Tribe holds dominion over the lands bordering the Danelle."

"Who's correct?" Jeran asked.

The Emperor shrugged. "It has been so long since the Great Rebellion that no records remain, and my own memory of the treaty is far from perfect."

Hiding a guilty grin, the Emperor continued his story. "When his parents were killed, Luran was even younger than Treloran. In a rage, he led a party of young Aelvin warriors across the river, intent on revenge. They were foolish, and did not take the necessary precautions. One morning, a large party of Tribesmen attacked them, and Luran's troops were ill-prepared to meet them.

"Luran does not know which tribe it was," the Emperor stated, "and to him, it does not matter. The survivors of his party limped back across the river, and since that day, he has hated everything not Aelvin. Human or Garun'ah, it is all the same to him.

"Losing my father's sword to you, and my chiding him last night at the feast, has only served to fuel his anger." The Emperor shook his head sadly. "There are times I wish I had better control over my tongue. After all these winters, I should have learned some small measure of temperance."

"I didn't want to take his sword," Jeran said solemnly. "Luran forced me into the fight, and Treloran warned me that refusing the sword would only incense his uncle more." Jeran rose to his feet. "I will return it to you, if you wish it."

The Emperor refused the offer with a shake of his head. "No, Jeran. You are more worthy of the blade than Luran. It is yours by right, and I would not ask you to give it back, even if I wanted it." Jeran yawned, and the Emperor looked at the sky. The sun had passed its zenith and was rapidly descending through the western sky. "We have worked hard enough today. Remember what I told you. Do not allow yourself to seize magic."

The old Elf led Jeran through the Vale at a stately pace. "I will think on your words tonight. Tomorrow, we will discuss the Darklord more, then continue with your lessons. I will also start teaching you how to control your Readings. The effort of suppressing your visions will grow quite tiresome if I do not."

The Emperor smiled and clapped a thin, bony arm around Jeran's shoulders. "Best you get a good night's rest. Tomorrow will be tiring."

When they reached the edge of the Vale, Jeran bid the Emperor goodnight. He retraced his steps through the corridors of the palace, intent on returning to his chambers and climbing into his bed. As tired as he felt, he could surely sleep through the night.

Chapter 11

"...Thus you can see why we must insist on a permanent Alrendrian presence in Illendrylla," Rafel intoned, ending his latest diatribe. He sat back in his chair, arms spread wide, as if there would be no further argument. Martyn sighed, glad that he would not have to listen to the corpulent nobleman's nasal monotone any longer. For a while, at least.

Rafel claimed it would be unfair to allow the Elves an embassy in Alrendria without giving Alrendrians equal access to the Aelvin lands. He adamantly insisted on an Alrendrian presence in Lynnaei, if not other areas of the Great Forest. The nobleman's true motives were transparent, though. The position of Ambassador to Illendrylla would be one of great esteem; he no doubt coveted it for himself.

The Aelvin delegates were of a different opinion. Though most did not voice their concerns as loudly as Prince Luran, who had expressed disgust at the very concept, there was nevertheless a general feeling of disinterest on the matter of the Alrendrian Embassy. The Elves did not relish the idea of Humans in their forest.

Martyn sighed again. The first day of negotiations had not yet concluded, and Rafel had already managed to turn the talks into little more than a pointless debate over trivialities. Luran had made his position known immediately, yet Rafel insisted on discussing this one item ceaselessly, even when there were a hundred others yet to be mentioned.

Martyn understood his cousin's position. As much as it galled him to admit it, he agreed that an Alrendrian presence in Lynnaei would be advantageous to both nations. But there was no point in butting heads with the Elves. Better to set aside the topic and return to it at a later date.

Rafel, however, was not so reasonable. Every time someone changed the subject, he found some way to relate it to an Alrendrian embassy. Martyn wanted to throttle him. *Not that it would do any good.* He knew that Rafel would belabor the issue until every Elf was against the idea, for the simple reason that he desired it. *That man knows no patience!*

The prince sat with his chin resting lightly on his hand. He tapped his upper lip with a finger, trying his best to look both interested and contemplative. In reality, he was fighting sleep. Concealing a yawn, he looked around the room.

The Humans sat on one side of the long, rectangular table; the Elves on the other. Lord Iban, as leader of the Alrendrian party, had the place of honor at the table's head. For once, the Guard Commander was not dressed in armor. Instead, he wore a doublet of golden yellow, the color of House Menglor, with the figure of a brown hunting hawk sewn into the back. The hawk was the sigil of the Family Iban.

Iban sat silently, as usual, with his hands folded on the edge of the table. He had rarely spoken during the day's negotiations, but when he had, his words instantly settled an argument or brought one of the Alrendrian delegates under control. His expression was unreadable, except for a slight tightening around the eyes when Rafel started talking again, telling the Elves of yet another reason why Alrendria should have an embassy in Lynnaei. Try though he might, Martyn could not understand why Iban refused to stop Rafel's ranting.

To Iban's left sat Utari, who wore a dress of sky blue silk, the color of House Aurelle. She sat her chair straight-backed, her proud features imposing. Tall, more than a hand taller than Martyn, with prominent cheekbones, Utari's ebony skin was smooth and unblemished, her long black hair pulled up in a tight bun. Golden chains encircled her throat and wrists. Dark brown eyes, serious and foreboding, stared at Rafel with unhidden anger. She, too, seemed eager for the negotiations to return to more important matters.

Rafel did not notice Utari's glare, and he took his time finishing his latest speech. Finally, he sat back, silently waiting for the Elves' response. He had worn his finest purple silks, his hands were bedecked with jewels, and a chain of finely-wrought gold hung loosely around his throat. A gaudy medallion dangled from the chain, and Rafel toyed with it, a smug expression on his plump face. Perhaps he had hoped to impress the Elves with his wealth, but to Martyn, he looked the part of a fool.

To the prince's right was Alynna, who watched the proceedings through half-sleepy eyes. She kept her gaze fastened on whomever was speaking, but had contributed little to the discussion. She had been the last to arrive, hurrying into the chamber, apologizing profusely. Even then she had looked haggard, as if she had not slept much, and her appearance had only worsened as the day progressed. Now, she looked to be having more trouble staying awake than Martyn.

Alynna wore a dress of blue, ringed with lace. Her hair was piled on her head elaborately, with twin curls framing a smooth, white face. Her lips, painted red, pressed together tightly, and her fingers tapped the edge of the table rhythmically. She caught Martyn staring at her and offered the prince a warm smile, which he politely returned.

Martyn let his eyes pass Alynna, focusing instead on Jes. Jes' dress was forest green, high-necked and conservative. Her hair hung loose; black curls fell well past her shoulder. Her eyes roamed the room, shifting from one person to the next, as if sizing them all up. When her eyes settled on

Rafel, they hardened, and face pinched angrily. She shook her head, almost imperceptibly, and her eyes moved onto Martyn.

When she saw the prince watching, her lips twitched, almost into a grin. Bowing her head politely, she shifted her gaze to Luran, who pushed his chair away from the table. Standing slowly, he leaned as far across the table as he could manage and looked directly into Rafel's eyes. "There will be *no* Humans in Lynnaei," he said coldly. "I will not have your Race polluting our ancient city. If this is the only thing you wish to discuss, then continuing these negotiations is pointless."

At the far end of the table, seated next to Lord Iban, sat two old Elves, virtually identical in appearance. Nahrona and Nahrima, they were called, though telling which was which was all but impossible. Each had hazel eyes and thin, white hair that fell just short of their shoulders.

The twins had hardly spoken, preferring to watch the proceedings in silence. Only twice had they shared their opinions; once to say they were glad to see Humans again after such a long time, and once to admit that they thought an Alrendrian Embassy would provide a unique opportunity to learn about their Human cousins. That had earned them a cold, angry glare from Luran, but neither of the Elves seemed affected by it.

Across from Martyn sat Treloran. Like the twins, he rarely spoke. The Aelvin Prince had spent most of the day staring into space, his features stern. It was almost as if he were not there. In fact, Martyn had only seen him move once. When Rafel first announced his desire to see an Alrendrian presence in Lynnaei, Treloran had offered his voice to his uncle's. Rising from his chair, he had made an impassioned plea, begging his mother not to allow such a thing. Charylla had silenced her son with a gesture, sending a suddenly sullen Treloran back into his chair. The silence that followed was broken by Luran's cruel chuckle; he was pleased that his nephew had taken his side.

Beside Treloran stood Luran, his eyes boring into Rafel's. He wore leather armor, the only delegate attired in such a manner. His appearance had earned him more than one scowl from the princess, but if anything, her displeasure only added to his delight. His black hair was slicked back, and his green eyes were filled with disdain for the Alrendrians.

Luran was every bit as stubborn as Rafel. Each time Rafel demanded something for Alrendria, Luran insisted that he would not allow it. For every long-winded argument Rafel made, Luran offered an even longer rebuttal. On the matter of the Alrendrian Embassy he was intractable.

Next to Luran sat a pale-haired Elf named Jaenaryn, chosen to represent the interests of the Aelvin merchants. With the possible exception of Charylla, Jaenaryn was the Elf most in favor of establishing trade with Humans. Of the delegates, he alone seemed to think vast fortunes could be made by selling Aelvin goods to Alrendria. He was not, however, convinced that the Elves would want Human wares, but if nothing else, he freely admitted that the Human lands had many resources that were less than abundant in Illendrylla.

Jaenaryn wore golden robes with a black scale, the insignia of the merchant class, embroidered above his left breast. With blue-green eyes and light hair, color far from prevalent among the Elves, he stood out at the table. Though not as outspoken as Luran, he, too, was not in favor of an Alrendrian embassy, though he had offered no explanation for his position. He sat with his lips pursed in thought, shaking his head at the Aelvin Prince, a look of disappointment on his face.

In the wake of Luran's pronouncement, an uncomfortable silence descended on the room. "Have you nothing to say, Human?" inquired Luran, breaking the silence. His lips twisted up in an evil grin, and he sneered derisively. "Though my sister may not agree with my opinions, she must at least give me credit for silencing your incessant ramblings!" His eyes shifted briefly to Utari. "I even think some of *your* countrymen welcome the respite."

The Elf's remarks infuriated Rafel. Mortified, his skin pale, he trembled with rage. He rose, shrugging off Utari's restraining hand, and met Luran's gaze eye to eye.

"That is enough!" Charylla called sternly from her place at the head of the table, opposite Iban. Much to Luran's dismay, the Emperor had given her the honor of leading the negotiations. Though the others could make pleas and voice opinions, the final decision on every matter would be hers. In robes of emerald green, her hair twisted in an elaborate coiffure atop her head, she was resplendent. Though she wore no face paint, she was the most beautiful woman at the table.

Rafel clutched the sides of the table angrily, his knuckles white from the exertion. Lord Iban met Rafel's eyes and shook his head warningly, but Rafel ignored him. "I don't think you understand," Rafel said to Luran, an edge in his tone. "As far as I'm concerned, this point is not negotiable. To better facilitate trade and communication between our two peoples, it is–"

"We have heard your arguments, Human," Luran responded heatedly. "And it is you who does not understand. There will be *no* Human presence in Lynnaei. There will be *no* Human presence in Illendrylla. You should count yourself lucky that you are even here today. If all goes well, you may return to your lands with some trinkets, and your memories of the greatest city in all of Madryn."

"You go too far!" Rafel yelled. "I will not stand for this. I will be accorded the respect I deserve."

"You are," Luran laughed. "More than you deserve. You are lucky I even waste my time with you. You have no power here. You have no authority, not even among the Humans."

Rafel sputtered, his anger so great he could not find words. "You... You cannot speak to me in–"

A fist slammed into the table, startling everyone. The sound was so sudden, so loud, that both Treloran and Alynna jumped. The other delegates turned their attention on Martyn, and Rafel fell silent, though his eyes burned with anger when he met the prince's angry glare. Luran's cold gaze shifted toward the prince as well, but Martyn ignored him; it was not his place to chastise the Elf.

He waited until the silence had stretched across the room. "Rafel, you have gone too far," Martyn said in the calmest voice he could manage. "You will apologize for your behavior. And since you cannot remember who my father put in charge of these negotiations, you will apologize to Lord Iban, too."

Rafel's eyes hardened, his anger now directed at Martyn. Swallowing down the bile rising in his throat, Rafel bowed stiffly. "As you command, Prince Martyn."

He turned to Iban. "My apologies, Geffram," he said, emphasizing Iban's common name. "I did not mean to speak out of turn. All know I want what's best for Alrendria."

Turning stiffly, Rafel faced the Aelvin Prince. He ducked his head in apology. "I regret my words, if they offered offense." Though delivered politely, Rafel's tone lacked all sincerity.

Luran smiled smugly, as if he had anticipated Rafel cowing to him. "You will accept his apology, Luran," came Charylla's stern rebuke, "and offer one of your own. I tire of apologizing in your behalf."

His sister's statement wiped the smile from his face. "My words were also hasty, Human," Luran said in a harsh whisper. "I am sure I did not mean all that was said." The smiles they shared were forced and phony.

"I think we have discussed enough today," Martyn announced, with a pointed look at Rafel. "I hate to break on such a sour note, but I grow weary of this pointless bickering. It's unlikely we'll accomplish more this afternoon, with tempers strained as they are. After an evening's rest, we'll be able to address these matters with fresh perspectives."

Martyn locked eyes with Rafel. "And with greater propriety."

The room remained silent for a long, tense moment. Finally, Charylla bowed her head. "The Prince of Alrendria speaks wisely," she told the assembly. "We have time enough. There is no need to rush. Let us adjourn for the day to collect our thoughts. Tomorrow, we shall set aside our personal feelings and continue these negotiations with more civility."

She stood, and the other Elves followed her example. "Luran," she said curtly, looking at her brother. "I wish to speak with you."

Before Luran could reply, the door to the chamber opened, and an Aelvin archer entered. He bowed to Luran, and met Charylla's eyes. "My apologies, Princess, but I have urgent news for *Hohe Chatorra*." He waited for Charylla's nod before crossing the room and whispering in Luran's ear. Luran's frown deepened.

By the time the archer stepped back, Luran's scowl encompassed his entire face. "My apologies, sister. A matter of some import requires my immediate attention. Though it pains me to disappoint you, we will have to talk another time." Without waiting for a response, Luran stormed from the room.

One by one the delegates left, some to return to the comforts of their chambers, others eager to be about their business in the city. "I am going to explore Lynnaei, my Prince," Alynna purred as she passed Martyn. "I would be delighted were you to join me."

"Perhaps next time, my Lady." Frowning demurely, Alynna walked away; Martyn allowed his eyes to follow her gently swaying hips.

Treloran stopped next to Martyn as well. "I wish to dine with my family," he said, and though it did not sound a request, Martyn knew the Elf was asking for his consent.

Martyn smiled at the Aelvin Prince. "I told you that you don't have to ask my permission every time you wish to leave my presence. I don't think the Emperor intended for you to share my every waking moment."

"Nevertheless, Grandfather's orders were clear, and I am not in a position to debate his meaning. I take my duties seriously."

"By all means then," Martyn answered, nodding his head and gesturing dramatically, "you have my permission to spend as much time with your family as you would like. As I told you be–"

"I will find you after the evening meal," Treloran interrupted. He started to walk away, but hesitated after several steps. "Thank you," he added belatedly, disappearing through the chamber's ornate oaken door.

Charylla bowed to Martyn. "I thank you for not taking my brother's comments to heart, Prince Martyn," she said. "He does not speak for all Elves."

"Nor does Rafel speak for all Humans," Martyn admitted. "I believe, as does my father, that there is much to be gained here for both our Races. I would not let the rantings of a single Human, or a single Elf, spoil all we are working toward."

"Perhaps Grandfather is right," said the Aelvin Princess. "In but a few short seasons, you Humans gain a wisdom that can elude my people for decades. Or longer."

Martyn flushed at the praise. "You compliment is most gracious, Princess, but there are many in Alrendria who would disagree with you as to the extent of my wisdom, and many more who make Rafel appear tolerant in comparison. If my meager abilities impress you, the credit must go to my father, who taught me all I know."

The princess laughed, the sound warm and friendly. "Prince Martyn, humility does not serve you. You seem better suited to the arrogance and confidence with which you usually grace us." At Martyn's hurt look, Charylla laughed all the more.

Placing a hand on Martyn's shoulder, she attempted to soothe him. "I meant no disrespect, and as proof, I offer a word of advice. We Elves consider humility a form of deference. If you lessen yourself in the eyes of my people, they will think you consider yourself inferior."

She frowned, tapping her lip seriously. "Modesty on your part will only serve the ends of those like Luran, who wish for us to fail in our attempt at friendship. Should you act humbly, he will use your actions to further his ends." She paused, her eyes distant. "The only Elf to whom you should defer is the Emperor. The rest of *Ael Alluya* you should treat as an equal."

Martyn stared at the princess, dumbfounded. "Why?" he finally managed to ask. "Why tell me this?"

She considered the question for a long time. "You have impressed me," she admitted at last. "You and the other Alrendrians. I find myself agreeing with Grandfather. There is more to you Humans than I anticipated."

Her eyes suddenly flashed, and her expression grew sterner. "I still believe Grandfather is keeping something from me. He was far too agreeable when we told him that he would take no part in the negotiations. His protestations lacked their usual vigor."

Swallowing nervously, Martyn waited while Charylla considered the Emperor's motives. "He is up to something," she said, eying Martyn suspiciously, "and I believe you Humans have something to do with it." She started for the door, pausing just before she left the chamber. "But I have not seen him this alive in winters."

She exited the chamber, leaving Martyn alone with Lord Iban, who still sat at the end of the table. The Guard Commander's eyes were fastened on Martyn, and he scratched his salt-and-pepper beard thoughtfully. Once the echoes of Charylla's footsteps had faded down the hall, he said, "You handled yourself well today."

Martyn blushed at Iban's praise, but said nothing, words failing him. Almost laughing, Iban waved for Martyn to join him. Hurriedly, Martyn crossed the room and sat on Iban's right. "You've learned much since leaving Kaper," the Guard Commander conceded. "You have put a rein on your temper and smoothed the barbs from your tongue. For the most part.

"You have a gift few possess, my Prince. The ability to lead is rare, even in those who style themselves as leaders. You still have much to learn, if you wish to use your gift to its fullest extent. I will teach you what I can, if you are interested."

Martyn frowned in confusion. When he spoke, his voice was weak; he was not sure how Iban would react. "Forgive me, Lord Iban," he said carefully. "But what could you, a Guard Commander, know of leading men? Other than in battle, that is."

Iban cocked his head to the side and stared at the prince for a long moment. After a tense silence, he started to laugh, a laugh that rolled from his belly outward. The force of the laughter shook him in his seat. It was the first time Martyn had ever seen the grizzled, old warrior laugh; the first time the Guard Commander had shown any emotion besides anger.

"Is it so different, my Prince?" he asked between roars. "Leading men in war and leading men in peace?"

Martyn started to shake his head, but Iban stalled him with a wave. Once he had his laughter under control, he explained. "Both require motivating your men. Both require loyalty and respect. Both require understand-ing the abilities of everyone under your command, so you can use them wisely. Without those things, a leader is useless, on the battlefield or off.

"I was not always a Guard Commander, you know. Before I devoted my life to the Guard, I was a nobleman and a pacifist." At Martyn's shocked expression, Iban nearly laughed again. "Prior to the Tachan War, the Family Iban was one of the most powerful in House Menglor, and I was my father's eldest son. I served as the Family's representative to Morrad, where House Menglor rules, for a long time, and for twenty seasons I was Alrendria's ambassador to Gilead, until my father's death brought me home."

Smiling, Iban drank a sip of the wine he had been given during the negotiations. "Some even credited me with reopening the old trade routes with Gilead, though in fact it was King Aavrid who suggested the arrange-ment. He anticipated trouble with Ra Tachan, and had hoped to foster a friend in Alrendria.

"Seven winters before the Tachan War, I became Head of the Family Iban. Our lands ran along the Celaan, from south of Grenz to the border of the Tribal Lands. They were fertile lands, and most of my people were farmers, though we had a few mines in the foothills of the Anvil. Our Guard was few and poorly trained, but it never bothered us. The Garun'ah had never caused a problem, and we did not feel the need for a large gar-rison, especially when Guardsmen were desperately needed elsewhere."

With a shrug, Iban took another long draught. "Back then, I did not believe in war; I thought it but a tool of the unenlightened. All my life I had solved problems without a sword, and I figured that words alone, if used properly, could settle any dispute." Iban swirled his glass, watching the red wine sail around the circumference. "The Durange taught me that war, too, is a form of diplomacy.

"When Ra Tachan started its fight with Gilead, I was one of the loudest voices against Alrendrian involvement. Alrendria had just finished its own war with Corsa, and I saw no reason to waste our lives on foreign soil." Iban drained his glass and poured himself a second. "As the Durange pushed north, Lord Fayrd begged me to send what troops I could spare. I had few enough that it likely wouldn't have made a difference, but I refused to send them nonetheless.

"After the Bull sacked Shandar, he knew that war with Alrendria was inevitable. On his return to Gilead, he burned and killed everything in his path." Emotion almost overcame Iban; his eyes were heavy, his face sad. "Only a few of us survived. Hundreds of my kin were slaughtered, and most of my vassals as well."

Martyn gasped, a hand reflexively covering his mouth. Offering a tight smile, Iban held up the bottle. Martyn nodded, and the Guard Commander poured him a drink. "To the Family Iban," he said, lifting his own glass, and Martyn drank with him.

"There, in the ruins of my Family's holdings," he continued, "I vowed revenge against the Durange. I knew how to use a sword. I had considered it an art form, and had spent many days practicing the blade, but I had never before used it to kill.

"That day, standing over the graves of my family, I renounced my right to rule, though I was not required to do so, and swore the oath of the Guardsman, vowing to give my life for Alrendria. I begged King Faldar to give me a command. He was reluctant, given my lack of military training, but my determination made him agree." Iban smiled, half wolfish, half sadly. "During the war, the only commander who won more battles was Alic Odara.

"After the war ended, King Mathis offered to restore my title and lands, but I refused. With the Odaras both gone–Alic dead and Aryn retired–there were none left to guard Alrendria from others like the Durange. For more than twenty winters I have served the King as High Commander of the Alrendrian Guard. I have used my sword on many occasions, but sometimes, I have used my wits instead. Even after all this time, I prefer talking my way out of a fight to actually fighting.

"You will make a formidable king, Prince Martyn," Iban admitted, eyeing Martyn up. "But there is still much about leadership you can learn. If you are interested in learning what I can teach, come to my chambers after dawn tomorrow." Without waiting for the prince to answer, Iban stood and walked away.

Martyn sat in the chamber for a long time, trying to absorb everything he had learned. He had trouble imagining the grizzled, old warrior as anything other than a Guardsman, yet his father trusted Lord Iban completely and often asked the commander's advice on nonmilitary matters. With little deliberation, he decided to learn whatever the High Commander was willing to teach.

Downing the remainder of his wine, Martyn stood, determined to find Jeran. Plenty of sunlight remained, and he wanted to explore Lynnaei. Martyn knew that if Jeran was not with the Emperor, he would be in his chambers. *There' so much to see in Lynnaei,* he thought, shaking his head sadly, *and I'm going to make Jeran enjoys it, even if it means beating some sense into him.*

The prince stepped into the hall and stared blankly at the featureless, red stone. Looking both left and right, he tried to remember which way he had to go to reach his chambers. He sighed loudly, embarrassed by his confusion. Kaper Castle was just as twisting as the Emperor's Palace, but Martyn had never had trouble finding his way around there. Guessing, he went left, striding confidently down the hall; it was not long before he realized he was lost.

He wandered aimlessly through the corridors for what seemed an eternity, hoping to come across someone, anyone who he could ask directions, but the halls remained empty, silent save for the sound of his own footfalls. Eventually, he found himself wishing for even Treloran's sour company.

Martyn turned a corner and found himself in a vast, open room, with giant doors against the side wall. The tension in his shoulder melted away as he recognized the palace's main entrance. He had gone the long way around, but he could find his chambers from here.

Climbing the twisting staircase two steps at a time, he hurried through the halls, calling greetings to the Guardsmen he passed. In but a few moments, he entered his chambers, and threw himself dramatically onto the bed. *Tomorrow*, he decided, *I'll wander the halls a little. Try to get a feel for the palace's layout.*

He changed into something more casual, more suitable for exploring the city, then hurried up to Jeran's chambers, eager to escape the red rock of the palace.

Pushing open the door to Jeran's apartments, he stepped inside. The size of the chamber still shocked him, and he had to fight down a spike of jealousy. That Jeran had been given rooms more opulent than his prince's, even if they *were* his grandfather's private rooms, grated at Martyn's pride. "Jeran?" he called out tentatively, looking around.

He found Jeran in the library, sleeping in the large, cushioned chair, a book open in his lap. A tray of food, still steaming, sat on the table next to him. Martyn looked around the room, shocked to see so many books in one place. The archives in Kaper were larger, of course, but these were private quarters. The only room in Kaper Castle with more than twenty volumes was the King's.

Martyn walked across the room, careful not to make noise. He lifted the book from Jeran's lap and examined it. *History of Alrendria*, written by some Elf in the winters before the MageWar. The book was in Aelvin, the flowing characters incomprehensible to the prince, but a translation was scrawled beneath every line in a flowing, Human hand. Additional notes were scratched in the margins, so many that it seemed like a second book had been written within the first.

"Jeran?" Martyn called again, somewhat louder than before, and Jeran stirred, his eyes opening halfway. "It's not yet evening!" Martyn protested. "Isn't it a bit early to retire?"

Jeran groaned, stretching. "I didn't sleep much last night. I had company." Martyn's eyes perked up at the statement, and he laughed while Jeran recounted the past night's events. Liseyl's timely rescue amused him even more than Alynna's persistence.

"It's a good thing you saved her from the slavers," Martyn quipped. "Else you'd now be caught in Alynna's web."

Jeran laughed. "Liseyl said much the same thing last night." He picked at the food on the tray next to him, then held it out to Martyn, who greedily snatched at a large piece of turkey.

"And where are your loyal servants today?" Martyn asked, dragging over a chair.

"Liseyl took the children into Lynnaei."

"Well, at least *she* has sense," the prince replied, gesturing toward the book. "There will be plenty of time to sit and read, Jeran, even after we return to Kaper. This is Lynnaei! Who knows how long we'll be here. I'm not going to let you lock yourself in these chambers. After we eat, you're coming with me."

Jeran held up his hands in surrender. "Very well, my Prince!" he said humbly, and Martyn laughed at his subservient tone. "I do not wish to offend you." They ate the rest of the meal in silence, and once finished, Jeran excused himself to change.

As Jeran was dressing, Martyn admitted to getting lost in the twisting halls of the palace. "Why do you suppose it's like that?" he asked, referring to the perpetually empty halls through which he had walked.

"I don't think it's as empty as it seems," Jeran replied. "It's just huge! The Emperor's Palace is bigger than all of Old Kaper, with passages carved throughout the entire mountain, and that's just above ground. The Elves have been carving rooms for over seven thousands winters. Who knows how far down the palace extends!"

Jeran poked his head out of the bedroom, waving his arm in the direction of the hall. "You must have noticed that this part of the palace is particularly empty." Martyn nodded. "The Emperor told me that this section was reserved for Human guests. Since the Path of Riches was closed, this entire face of the mountain has lain unused."

Jeran emerged from the bedroom, dressed in thin brown breeches and a light shirt. "Ready?" Martyn asked, and Jeran nodded. "Then let's go!" They headed toward the door.

"I envy you, Jeran." Martyn said suddenly, the admission a difficult one.

"Me?" Jeran replied, his eyes widening in surprise. "Why?"

"For one, you won't have to sit through endless days of boring negotiations. For another, you're spending your time with the Emperor of the Elves. The Emperor! He's just about the oldest living thing in all of Madryn!"

Now it was Jeran's turn to laugh. "It's not all fun and games, Martyn. The Emperor and I aren't going to spend our days sitting in his chambers, sipping wine and talking about winters past!" Jeran frowned, scratching his chin thoughtfully. "Still," he said in a serious tone. "I'm glad I won't have to listen to Rafel all day!"

Opening the door to his chamber, Jeran found himself face to face with Treloran. Smirking, he said to Martyn, "I believe you have a visitor." Confused, the prince leaned around the door and groaned when he saw the Aelvin Prince standing there.

Treloran wore brown leathers, and had a couple of bows slung over his shoulder. Inclining his head politely, his eyes remained focused on Jeran. "Actually," he said solemnly, "I came to see you. Though the prince's chambers were to be my next stop."

Jeran waved for Treloran to enter, gesturing toward a severely-cut, straight-backed chair. The Aelvin Prince took a seat; Jeran and Martyn sat opposite him. "What do you want?" Jeran asked suspiciously.

Treloran lost his smile, but it quickly returned. "Some of your Guardsmen were boasting about their archery skill at the banquet, and *Ael Chatorra* challenged them to a tournament." Treloran's smile broadened. "Your Guardsmen's confidence declined sharply after challenge was issued, but they accepted.

"The prince here," Treloran added, gesturing toward Martyn with his chin, "has mentioned that your bowmanship is exceeded only by your swordskill."

"I've used a bow before," Jeran answered carefully, a wry smile twisting up the corner of his lips.

"Then perhaps you would like to add your skills to those of your countrymen." Standing, Treloran started toward the door, his eyes glinting with anticipation. "If you are not up to the challenge, there is no dishonor in refusing, but if you are as good as they claim, then you have no need of false modesty."

Jeran made no immediate move to follow. "Jeran!" whispered Martyn. "This is a perfect opportunity! Remember what my father said? 'Get to know the Elves. They may be our allies one day.' "

The prince met Jeran's gaze levelly. "Besides, with Guardsman Vyrina gone, you're the best chance we have of beating the Elves in an archery contest, if the tales of their skill are even half true."

Jeran's eyes were unreadable as he considered the prince's words. "It's been a while since I used a bow," he said to Treloran, "but if you wish, I'll join in your contest." Jeran followed the Aelvin Prince out of his chambers and through the winding halls of the palace. They stopped before a large door, which Treloran held open for the two Humans. Stepping through, the three emerged into warm, bright sunshine.

Once outside, Treloran waved to a brown-robed Elf, calling out orders in Aelvin. The Elf bowed respectfully and disappeared, returning a few moments later with three horses in tow. Mounting, they followed the Aelvin Prince through Lynnaei.

Treloran set a quick pace, but it was not a short trip. To lighten the journey, Martyn tried to strike up conversations with his two companions, but his efforts were fruitless. Jeran was staring at the city, expressionlessly examining the neatly-ordered rows of flowers and trees. As Martyn watched, he frowned, though whether in thought or displeasure, the prince could not determine.

The Elf answered Martyn's questions curtly, all but ignoring the prince's personal inquiries. At one point, a female Elf, dressed in green leathers and carrying a bow across her shoulder, called out to Treloran. The Aelvin Prince raised his hand in greeting and called back an answer in the language of the Elves. Smiling, the archer climbed one of the staircases that wound around the Great Trees and disappeared into the city above.

"A friend of yours?" Martyn asked, and Treloran's face turned bright red. Martyn attempted an apology. "I meant no offense! You don't have to say anything. I was just curious–"

"It is of no matter, Hu–Prince Martyn," Treloran replied, clearing his throat. "I merely forgot that you were here. That archer, she was... That is, she is..."

Martyn, smiling roguishly, nodded. "Say no more. I think I understand."

"No!" Treloran said, a trifle too hastily. "That's not what I meant. She is my instructor, Leura. She is *Ael Chatorra*, charged with teaching me the ways of a warrior, the use of sword and bow, stealth and reconnaissance, strategy and tactics. She is a great warrior."

"And you have feelings for her," Martyn interjected. He cleared his throat nervously, afraid that he had gone too far.

Treloran shook his head vigorously, but his heart was not in it. His shoulders slumping, he leaned toward Martyn and said, "My every thought is of her. She fills my dreams! But I am the Emperor's kin. I will never be allowed to wed a common soldier. Do you know how much it galls to have your future decided for you?"

"I think that's the first thing you've said that I *do* understand," Martyn replied, and at the Elf's blank look, he laughed. "I, too, am not allowed to marry for love. My bride has been chosen for me, and even now awaits my return from Illendrylla." Martyn eyed Treloran appraisingly. "Perhaps we aren't so different after all."

"Perhaps," Treloran mumbled, his face resuming it customary impassivity. "You will not speak of this," he added, and though the statement was not a request, there was a hint of pleading behind it.

"Of course not," Martyn assured him. The stone path on which they traveled forked, splitting into two. Treloran led his horse down the path to the right, which, after only a short distance, opened up into a wide, grassy field. Ten Guardsmen stood in a group along one side of the field. Across from them were an equal number of Elves, all wearing armor similar to Treloran's.

Most of those gathered were stringing bows of smooth, polished wood or notching arrows, testing the resistance of their weapon. Treloran dismounted, handing his reins to a waiting servant, and when Jeran and Martyn stepped down from their mounts, eager hands instantly took their horses away.

The Elves bowed at Treloran's approach, and the Guardsmen hurried over to Jeran. "Glad we have you with us, Lord Odara!" called Raeghit, clapping Jeran on the shoulder.

"Wasn't so sure about this until you appeared, Jeran," added Quellas, a scrawny Guardsman with a pinched face and weaselly expression. He was one of Iban's finest archers.

Willym, the ranger, joined them too. "Seems that some of the boys had a bit too much to drink last night," he said. "Got it into their heads that we were better archers than the Elves." The older Guardsman let his eyes wander over to the Aelvin warriors, who were laughing quietly amongst themselves. "I have a feeling we're about to be taught a lesson."

"Not with Lord Odara here!" came one response. Jeran groaned.

A brown-robed Elf approached, carrying an Alrendrian longbow. Jeran muttered thanks as he accepted the weapon, but the servant walked away without a word. Hefting the bow in one hand, Jeran got a feel for its weight. Lightly, he traced a finger along the polished wooden shaft, then in one fluid motion strung the bow, pulling the string to test its tautness.

Jeran's Alrendrian bow was longer than the Aelvin ones, meant to shoot greater distances, but the shorter bows were far more accurate than their Alrendrian counterparts. In this contest, accuracy would make the difference.

Another servant appeared on the heels of the first, carrying a quiver of Aelvin arrows. Jeran sorted through them, to be sure the shafts were of the best quality. Of the entire quiver, he only separated out one arrow, and that because one of the feathers had fallen off.

Holding one steel-tipped arrow at eye level, Jeran inspected its construction. The tips were barbed and hooked to create maximum damage, the shafts dark brown, the metal dulled so that sunlight did not reflect off it, betraying the location of the archer. Jeran eyes shifted to the Elves, and he frowned. Spotting one of them in the shadowy recesses of the Great Forest would be an all but impossible task.

Treloran approached the Alrendrians, holding a square of parchment, on which were inscribed three concentric circles. "The rules are simple. Each archer shoots at his own target. If the arrow lands within the red circle, you continue to the next round. If your arrow lands in the yellow, you gain a second chance to hit the red. The blue circle is reserved for children, but if you wish it, we will allow it to count the same as the yellow." The Elf's smile was teasing, and the jibe was taken with good humor.

Jeran took the target from Treloran's hand. He held it up so the other Guardsmen could see. "Thank you," he replied, ducking his head to the Aelvin Prince, "but your handicap will not be necessary." Jeran handed the target back to the Elf. "Nor will I have any need of the yellow."

Several Guardsmen laughed, and quiet mutterings could be heard from the direction of the Elves. Treloran smiled, the first genuine smile Jeran had seen on his face, and bowing, he turned to the other contestants. "You heard the Human. The yellow disqualifies."

The archers lined up, the ten Guardsmen forming rank on Jeran's left, Treloran and his ten archers on his right. Treloran clapped his hands, and a group of Aelvin servants appeared, one for each archer. Grabbing a target, the Elves ran a two hundred hands across the field. Treloran twisted his head to look at Jeran. "Is that an appropriate distance for the first volley?"

Jeran squinted, peering across the field. "A little close for my taste, but this is your tournament." The Guardsmen laughed nervously at Jeran's statement, and each prepared to fire the first round.

"Prince Martyn," Treloran called, and Martyn turned to face the Elf. "We would be honored if you would signal the flight of the arrows. That is, of course," he added, "unless you wish to join the contest."

Martyn shook his head. "Neither my Guardsmen nor your archers would have any difficulty besting me. My skills lie elsewhere. But I will signal each volley." Treloran offered his thanks, and Martyn took his position at the far end of the row. When he was ready, he raised his hand, and twenty-two bows were simultaneously aimed. Taking a deep breath, Martyn cried, "Loose!" His hand fell, and more than a score of arrows lofted across the field.

A series of muffled thuds echoed back to them as the arrows struck the targets. The servants rushed across the field to retrieve the shots. Guardsman Varten was eliminated; his arrow had landed squarely in the blue ring.

The remaining twenty-one targets were moved another fifty hands back. When the last servant had returned, Martyn raised his hand a second time. "Loose!" he cried again, once everyone was ready. This time, four more Alrendrians were disqualified, but only one Elf was eliminated.

By the fifth volley, only Quellas and Jeran remained of the Alrendrians, but six of the Elves still stood in the line. The targets were now two thirds of the way across the field, and the circles had blurred together, until it was impossible to tell them apart. Martyn raised his arm again, allowing the archers a moment to prepare. Muttering a quick prayer that the Gods aid Jeran's aim, he let his hand drop.

More than half the remaining archers were eliminated, including Quellas, but both Jeran and Treloran still stood, neither of them showing the slightest bit of worry. They were joined by a third Elf, who was shaking his head and squinting at the targets, now at the far side of the field.

Once more Martyn raised his hand, and once more he allowed it to drop. Across the field, two solid hits were heard. The second Elf turned and walked away, knowing that his shot had gone wide. Seeing that Jeran was still in the contest, the Guardsmen let out a ragged cheer. "Jeran! Jeran!" Willym silenced them with a grim look.

Jeran turn to Treloran. "We have run out of field." He slung his bow over his shoulder, and bowed formally. "Thanks for the practice."

Treloran returned the bow, a friendly expression on his face. "The contest is not over, Lord Odara. In situations such as this, the remaining archers shoot at moving targets." Treloran gestured to his right and led Jeran to the side of the field, where a wooden machine was being unloaded from a large wagon. It looked something like a small catapult, with a crank and swinging arm, except that the arm swung sideways instead of overhead. A brown-robed Elf slid two wooden disks into the arm. Each disk was painted with the same red, yellow, and blue circles as the targets.

Treloran demonstrated how the machine worked, simultaneously explaining the rules. "The *trebuchier* sends the target disks into the sky. The archers stand at rest until the machine fires. Together, they shoot at the disks, and the archer who hits the most targets wins. In the case of a tie, more disks are added and the process is repeated."

Facing the machine, Treloran said, "We will start with three disks."

The servant bowed, loading a third disk into the machine. Jeran and Treloran took their places ten paces away, their backs toward the machine and their bows resting lightly on the ground. The Aelvin servant pulled the rope, and the arm of the machine swung out with a loud crack. Three disks hurtled into the sky, spinning furiously.

In a flash, both Jeran and Treloran had their bows drawn and arrows notched. Two arrows flew into the air, followed closely by a second pair. Two disks were knocked from the sky; the third soared into the distance. Servants ran across the field to retrieve the disks. They returned at a run, though one paused to pick something off the ground.

Both Jeran and Treloran had hit one target. Smiling, one of the servants held out his other hand, and a collective gasp escaped the crowd. The second volley had collided in midair, falling to the ground in a splintered heap.

Treloran turned to the Elf at the machine. "Five," he said, and the servant hurried to comply. Taking slow, deep breaths, the Aelvin Prince tried to focus, and Jeran did the same. The air was tense with excitement, so tense that no one spoke, nor made the quietest sound, lest they break the concentration of one of the archers.

Suddenly, in the midst of a deep, relaxing breath, Jeran felt a tingling in his chest. Recognizing the feeling, he stepped back, drawing in a nervous breath. Closing his eyes, he tried to will away the flows of magic that were forcing their way toward him. "Hold!" he called, turning to Treloran. "You truly are a master archer. I yield. You are the better marksman. If you'll excuse me." Jeran turned and walked away, stumbling in the direction of the horse.

A chorus of mutters went up from both the Elves and the Guardsman. Treloran followed after Jeran, pulling him around. "Is something wrong?" he asked, sounding concerned. "If something is the matter, we can postpone the contest until another time."

Jeran met the Elf's eyes. "If you wish another contest, I will gladly accept. But do not humble yourself on my account. Trust me in this: today, you would have emerged the better archer." Sucking in slow, deep breaths, Jeran ran to his horse and pulled himself into the saddle. Without so much as a goodbye, he galloped toward the palace.

Martyn watched, dumfounded, as Jeran disappeared. Muttering under their breath, the Guardsmen began to file away, calling out gentle jibes to the Aelvin archers. The Elves responded with jests of their own, and the two companies departed amidst much laughter. "It seems our soldiers are getting along quite well," Martyn said to Treloran, when they stood alone in the field.

The Elf nodded. "Perhaps Grandfather is right," he replied, his eyes still on the spot where Jeran's dwindling form had disappeared. "Your friend is odd, Prince Martyn. And formidable. I think I could like him."

Martyn smiled. "He has to be formidable. For the last seven winters, it's been his job to keep me out of trouble." Warm, genuine laughter drifted through the clearing.

After a moment's deliberation, Martyn asked, "What do Elves do for fun? I wish to see more of this city than the inside of the palace."

Treloran said nothing, so Martyn walked to his horse, accepting the reins from a brown-robed Elf. "Well?" he called. "There has to be *something* more exciting than standing in the middle of an empty field!" For a moment, Treloran stared at him wide eyed, then a wicked smile enveloped his face. He called for a servant to bring their horses.

Chapter 12

They rode in silence, Treloran leading Martyn down the winding stone paths of the city. Martyn scanned the trees, wondering if Lynnaei could really be called a city, or if there were another name for such a marvel. There were few buildings, only small stone structures that served as stables or smithies. Rope ladders and staircases led up into the branches of the Great Trees, where the homes and businesses of Lynnaei were located.

Few people used the roads. Most of the traffic was in the trees above, either on the interwoven branches or across the long rope bridges that spanned the distance between trees. Only a few bridges were visible through the thick mesh of branches, and from the ground, it looked like Lynnaei consisted of small tree houses. But Martyn had seen the city from Jeran's chambers. The Great Trees rose thousands of hands high, and Lynnaei had nearly a score of levels, each with its own series of structures.

The palace stood silhouetted on the northeastern horizon, the vast mountain looming above them, filling the sky. Treloran picked a path that kept the Emperor's Palace in front of them, and for a while, Martyn thought the Elf was leading him back there. Eventually, though, Treloran turned off the main thoroughfare and led Martyn west, into the heart of the city.

Martyn peered up at the trees, but he could see little through the thick leaves and dense web of branches and bridges. Sighing, he cast his eyes to the ground, which looked more like a garden than the base of a great city. Ordered rows of flowers, green and blue, lined the path; vines climbed the Great Trees, similarly flowered. Several brown-robed Elves busily dug at a patch of golden wildflowers growing amidst the roots of one tree.

Martyn asked Treloran about the flowers. "Green and blue are the colors of *Ael Chatorra*, the warrior class," the Aelvin Prince explained. "This is our section of the city, and the paths are lined with flowers of our colors." Pointing east, he added, "In that direction you will find the merchant's district. There, the paths are lined with yellow and red, the colors of *Ael Pieroci*."

Not long after, they passed a tree surrounded by alternating yellow and red flowers. It seemed out of place among the blue and green. Pointing to the tree, Martyn asked, "What about that one? Why haven't those flowers been pulled up?"

Treloran offered the prince a small smile and shook his head, as if the question did not deserve an answer. "Those flowers signify that this tree is a marketplace. You do not expect our warriors to cross half the city just to buy grain and cloth, do you?"

The Aelvin Prince laughed, and Martyn felt his cheeks turning pink. "Guard stations in other districts are ringed with blue and green flowers, so that, in times of trouble, our people know where to seek *Ael Chatorra.*"

The trip through Lynnaei was relaxing to Martyn. It seemed as if they were walking through a park, or an elaborate garden, rather than a city. There were none of the raucous noises one heard so often in Kaper, nor were there any unpleasant odors, like those which rose from the less reputable areas of Human cities. The paths were well lit, smelled of roses and lilacs, and it seemed like every blade of grass was grown with exacting precision.

The ground level of Lynnaei was virtually devoid of Elves. A few smiths labored in their workshops, pounding out arrowheads, swords, and other tools. Several others, dressed in thin, green woolens, tended the crops that grew in small plots between the Great Trees. Once, they passed a handful of brown-robed servants carrying baskets. At Treloran's approach, the Elves scurried to the side of the path, bowing low in homage to their prince. Treloran ignored them, his eyes fastened on the road ahead. Once past, the servants continued walking, resuming their duties without a word.

Martyn pulled his horse alongside Treloran's. "Why do you treat your servants so disrespectfully?"

Treloran's head snapped around, his slanted eyes wide in surprise. "I treat *my* servants disrespectfully?" he replied slowly, his voice confused and hurt.

"Not you personally," Martyn replied hastily, hoping he had not offended the Aelvin Prince. "But the Elves in general."

Treloran's face tightened, and Martyn worried that he had gone too far. "I am not sure what you mean," he said at last, his eyes suspicious.

Martyn scratched his chin, wondering how to continue. "Your servants are hard working, and better behaved than most. But you ignore them. Just now, some servants bowed to you, but you rode past without even noticing. You don't thank them when they perform a job well, and you do not reward them for their loyal service."

Martyn was not sure if he should continue his line of questioning. It seemed like he had made a little progress with Treloran, breaking through some of the armor the Aelvin Prince always wore, and Martyn did not want to jeopardize that by hurting his. Yet the entire reason for his being here was to learn about the Elves. He decided to press his luck. "You hardly even acknowledge their existence unless you need them for something."

Treloran reined in his horse, bringing the white mare to a sudden stop. Martyn stopped next to him, suddenly wishing he had kept his thoughts to himself. Treloran had a perplexed expression on his face, and his lips were pressed together in a thin, tight line, but his words were not angry. "You think *we* mistreat *our* servants?" he asked again, his voice disbelieving.

He stared at Martyn for a long moment, then shook his head in wonder. "Why should I reward *Ael Namisa* for doing what they are meant to do? I would not thank *Ael Chatorra* for fighting a battle, nor would I reward *Ael Maulle* for bringing the rains, or making the flowers bloom in winter."

Treloran shrugged his shoulders. "*Ael Namisa*–the Obedient–do the work they were born to do, just like any other Elf. Why should that earn them any special favors?"

"Forgive me, Treloran, but I still don't understand. You treat your servants like slaves." At Martyn's words, Treloran's expression instantly changed to outrage. "I don't mean to suggest that you're abusive!" Martyn added hastily. "Or that you hold them against their will! Not at all! I simply mean that you don't appear to appreciate the work they do."

Martyn shook his head, wondering why his tongue always got him into such trouble. "How does one become *Ael Namisa*?" he asked, slowly speaking the Aelvin word. "You say they are born into it. Does that mean rank is hereditary, like it is for the Human nobility?"

Treloran urged his horse to walk again, waving for Martyn to follow. Once they were on their way, the Aelvin Prince tried to explain. "Our rank is not hereditary, not in the same way as your nobility, and yet an Elf's position is known at the moment of his birth."

Treloran paused, his thin lips pursing in thought. "It is not easy to explain if you are not an Elf," he said by way of apology, "and I am not the best teacher you could have." Martyn suppressed the urge to comment. His mouth had earned him enough trouble today.

"When an Elf is born," Treloran explained, "the child is visited by *Ael Maulle*, the Gifted. Using their magic, *Ael Maulle* determine what path that the Goddess has chosen for the newborn Elf. The child is trained from birth so he can best perform the tasks Valia has set for him.

"Thus, a child born to *Ael Namisa*, what you would call a servant, may be raised a diplomat, a warrior, or a…" Treloran paused as he searched for the proper Human word. "Or a Mage."

"Every Elf has his future determined at birth?" Martyn asked, amazed.

Treloran nodded. "In winters long gone," he continued, "there were thousands of classes, one for every occupation. *Ael Gheronia* tended the land. *Ael Fleeha* fashioned arrows. These groups still exists, but many of the classes have joined together into six main castes. *Ael Maulle*, the Gifted, are our Magi." Treloran struggled for the words as he explained the structure of Aelvin society to Martyn. "*Ael Namisa*, the Obedient, are not only servants, but also farmers and laborers."

Several small parties of Elves passed them. Martyn noticed that most groups wore the same colors, or had identical insignia embroidered on their chests. Only a few mingled between classes. "*Ael Chatorra* are the warriors, *Ael Pieroci* the merchants, and *Ael Mireet*, which includes all craftsmen from smiths and fletchers to sculptors and weavers, are the artisans.

"*Ael Alluya* are the equivalent of the Human nobility," Treloran added. "They are charged with ruling the Aelvin Empire, making the laws, and determining the punishments when those laws are broken."

Martyn tried to hide his frown. The Aelvin Prince's tone made him feel as if he were a child who had not paid enough attention to his teachers. "Every Elf is assigned to one of the castes upon birth," Treloran said, ignoring Martyn's discomfort and continuing the lecture, "but how he serves his caste is left to the individual. *Ael Namisa* may serve, or they may join *Ael Gheronia* and tend the land. *Ael Mireet* may become smiths or carpenters, artists or singers. Each Elf can do what he wants, so long as it is in his caste.

"The only exceptions are the Emperor and his kin, who are members of two castes. At birth, they are still visited by *Ael Maulle*, but no matter what caste they are assigned, they are also *Ael Alluya*." Treloran look at Martyn closely, as if deciding whether or not to continue. "I was born *Ael Chatorra*. As was Luran. My mother is *Ael Maulle*, but we are all three *Ael Alluya*."

Finished, Treloran fell silent, and Martyn was left to ponder the Elf's words. "I can see the benefits of your ways," he admitted. "Finding how each Elf will best serve the Empire certainly has merit, but it doesn't explain your disrespect to *Ael Namisa*. You treat them as if they are inferior."

Treloran stopped his horse again, dismounting. He looked up at Martyn, his green eyes flashing. "Do you claim that you do not consider yourself better than your servants? I have watched you and the other Humans! You may speak to your servants more than we do, but if you are not issuing orders, you are berating them. I have never heard you inquire after their sleep as you do the nobles, nor have I heard you ask if they enjoyed their day. Their likes and dislikes are not important to you, so long as they perform their duties well."

Treloran became more animated; his arms swung wildly as he spoke. "Must you constantly praise your servants? If so, what does that say of them? That they will no longer perform their duties properly unless they are continuously reminded that their work has pleased?"

The Aelvin Prince started to lose the rein he had on his temper. His voice slowly rose in volume while he chastised Martyn. "Have you ever seen me chastise *Ael Namisa* in public? Has any Elf ever berated *Ael Namisa* in your presence, making them feel less than they are? Have we ever struck our servants, as I have seen your cousin, Rafel, do?"

Treloran fixed Martyn with a cold, stony gaze. "Do not presume to tell me how we mistreat *Ael Namisa*," he snapped. "At least we honor them for what they do instead of disdain them for what they are."

Martyn opened his mouth to retort, but Treloran forestalled him with a gesture. "Do not deny it, Prince Martyn. I have been forced to watch you Humans since your arrival and I have seen with my own eyes. You are not as bad as some. Perhaps Rafel Batai's and Alynna Morrena's behavior are not the norm, but it would be foolish to think no others in the Human lands behave as they.

"Your cousin is the worst. He treats his horse with more respect than he does his servants. They are berated when they perform their tasks properly and punished when they do not. Yet you claim *we* treat *Ael Namisa* as inferiors!" He let out a harsh laugh, shaking his head at the irony.

"Perhaps your words would have more meaning if they came from Lord Odara." Treloran's eyes bored into Martyn, making the prince uncomfortable. He shrank back from both the intensity of the Aelvin Prince's glare and the brutal honesty of his words. "Of all Humans, he is the only one I have met who treats his servants as equals." Treloran's breaths came quickly; the effort of keeping his anger in check was too much for the Aelvin Prince.

Martyn sneered, and a thousand razor-sharp retorts popped to the tip of his tongue, ready to be used in his people's defense. He opened his mouth, but closed it again before he spoke. There was a certain truth to the Elf's words. Martyn, too, had seen Rafel's poor treatment of his servants, punishing them severely for the most insignificant mistake. Alynna Morrena had once forbidden her servants to eat because one had dared speak to her rudely.

Nor was he innocent. Perhaps he was not as guilty as Rafel, but he had done nothing to stop his cousin's abuses, or soothe Alynna's temper. To a lesser degree, he was guilty of the same crimes as they. He closed his eyes and forced his anger away. Calmly, he said to Treloran, "Your words are true, Prince Treloran, no matter how much I wish they were not."

Treloran was taken aback. He had been expecting an angry riposte, and Martyn's casual acceptance threw him off guard. He pursed his lips in thought, studying the Human Prince warily. "I assure you," Martyn hastily added. "I meant no disrespect. Nor did I wish this to become a debate over the differing ideologies of our races. I was simply curious about your customs, and am trying my best to understand your people."

Martyn took a deep breath to help maintain his calm. "Humans have a great many shortcomings. Some have more than others. We are far from perfect." With a cold smile, he added, "Just like you Elves."

Treloran stood silent for a long time. Finally, in a voice that was almost as calm as Martyn's, he replied, "I, too, did not mean to offend. Sometimes my temper gets the better of me."

Martyn let out a barking laugh. "Sometimes?"

Treloran's eyes narrowed, but he chose not to retort. Instead, he turned toward the nearest tree. "We are here," he said simply. Martyn looked around, but saw nothing but trees in the dying light of evening. He dropped slowly from the saddle as two brown-robed Elves approached. With a silent bow, one of the servants took the reins from his hands and led the horse to a nearby stone building, where several other horses were tethered.

"There seems to be little excitement here," Martyn laughed. "Have we arrived early, or do you Elves truly like to sit in empty fields for fun?" A sudden movement caused Martyn to whirl about. Three Aelvin warriors, dressed in dark brown leather armor, stepped from behind the trunk of the Great Tree. They glanced in the direction of the princes, bowed formally when they recognized Treloran, and started down the white stone path.

Treloran smiled wickedly. "You are looking in the wrong direction, Prince of Alrendria," he said, pointing upward. Martyn followed the Elf's finger, but saw nothing except the tree's thick leaves. Puzzled, his gaze returned to the ground, and he noticed for the first time that something wrapped around the tree behind the Aelvin Prince. Taking a few steps forward, Martyn squinted his eyes in the growing shadows of evening, only half surprised to see a narrow wooden staircase spiraling up the trunk.

Swallowing, Martyn asked, "We're going up there?"

Treloran ducked his head in a nod. "Unless you would prefer to return to the palace," he replied, his tone slightly mocking.

Martyn shook his head sharply. "Not at all," he said, hoping he appeared more confident than he felt. "I wanted to see more of Aelvin life, and that is what I intend to do." Taking another deep breath to steady his nerves, he started toward the tree. "Are you coming?" he asked, taking the stairs two at a time.

The steps were solid, but Martyn nevertheless kept a tight grip on the handrail. Treloran followed behind, taking the steps slowly. The staircase opened onto a platform nearly a hundred hands above the ground, at a level just above the lowest branches. The limbs were so broad that a horse could have stood lengthwise on them with room to spare. Where the branches from separate trees met, sturdy vines secured the limbs, weaving the giant trees into a vast, interconnected web.

Martyn's eyes dropped to the floor and he studied the top of the branch. The upper side of the limb was flat, worn smooth by countless seasons of use. Smaller branches jutted out at odd angles from the large one, sometimes ending in a tiny platform, other times in an ornate arrangement of leaves and flowered vines.

Almost against his will, Martyn's gaze was drawn upward, and he gasped. "By the Gods...." he whispered. The thick leaves had concealed more than the prince had ever imagined.

Martyn had expected some tree houses, perhaps a few small observation platforms, but the truth was more than he could believe. Even from where he stood, on Lynnaei's lowest level, the grandeur of the city astonished him. *This,* he said to himself, *is the real city of Lynnaei.*

Elves bustled back and forth along the broad avenues; some had packs on their backs, others pulled heavy carts laden with wares. The staircase Martyn climbed opened onto a platform, then continued up the trunk, but other trees had buildings constructed around them. Huge structures with rooms both large and small, they projected out from the Great Trees in circles, supported by giant crossbeams and heavy vines. A clever meshwork of leaves and branches covered the bottoms of the platforms, hiding them. From the ground, most of Lynnaei was hidden from view.

Martyn's jaw dropped. "This is amazing!" he muttered.

"This?" Treloran replied, his brow furrowing. "This lower level is just where goods are transported back and forth," he laughed. "The branches here are thick enough to support great weights and wide enough for wagons. The chambers you see are just storage for the buildings above. For entertainment, we need to climb several more levels." Treloran gestured toward the branches above, then continued up the stairway.

"Higher?" Martyn said to himself sadly. He took a slow, deep breath before following the Aelvin Prince. They arrived at a second platform, similar to the first. The branches were thinner, though still broad enough for four or five people to walk abreast. Martyn walked slowly to the edge of the platform. Grabbing the rail tightly, he glanced nervously over the side. The broad branches and thick leaves of the lower level filled his vision. The ground was visible in patches seen through the gaps in the giant limbs.

Stepping back, he surveyed the second level, noticing that the buildings were marginally smaller than below. They fanned out gracefully from the tree trunks and were decorated with ornately-carved latticework. Vines and flowers dotted each building; a few had the blue and green of *Ael Chatorra*, but many were in combinations that the prince did not recognize.

Martyn walked around the platform, staring awestruck at the Aelvin city. He finally turned to face Treloran, who watched with a wry smile painted on his thin face. "This level," the Elf explained, "and several more we will encounter, are market levels. This is where the shops and craftsmen are located.

"You can identify a market by the red and gold flowers grown around it," Treloran explained, gesturing behind him. Sure enough, strands of yellow and gold flowers ringed the trunk on this level. Martyn turned around slowly. Several of the other trees in sight also had red and gold.

A series of shops, adorned not only with red and gold, but with flowers of other colors as well, stood atop each platform. "If you are looking for something in particular," Treloran continued, "you need only look at the windows." He identified a few of the stores for Martyn. "Dark red and dark blue for a blacksmith. Red-brown and white for a fletcher. Maroon and cyan for a carpenter.

"But you are not interested in crafts," Treloran said with a smirk. "You wanted entertainment, did you not? For that, we must climb higher." The Elf paused, his eyes flashing merrily. Fighting to hold back laughter, he asked, "Or would you prefer to shop? There is a masterful tailor around here. We could have some new clothes made for you."

Martyn rolled his eyes, but chose not to comment. "Very well," Treloran sighed, grimacing at Martyn's outfit. Shrugging his shoulders, he feigned a look of disappointment and continued up the staircase, disappearing around the far side of the tree. Steeling himself, Martyn mounted the stairs and ascended to the next level.

Treloran did not stop at the next level. He continued up the staircase, leaving Martyn no choice but to follow. The prince hurried to keep the Elf in sight, but paused on the landing to look out over the platform. The third level appeared much like the second; shops lined the platforms around each tree.

Sighing, Martyn continued up the staircase, noticing that the trunk of the tree was beginning to thin, and the branches, though still broad enough for several people to walk abreast, were not as wide as on the lowest levels.

They passed level after level, and Treloran stopped only long enough for Martyn to take a look around. As they climbed, the avenues grew less crowded. Fewer Elves traveled back and forth, and the branches thinned noticeably, allowing more of the city to be seen. When the limbs grew too thin to support the weight of pedestrians, bridges of rope and wood replaced them. Each level had its own platforms or buildings, but they were smaller and more spread out the higher one traveled.

The structures that did exist were larger and more elaborate than the ones below, adorned with windows of finely-blown glass and elaborately-carved designs. Trellised balconies extended from the far side of the houses, looking out over Lynnaei. Small chimney pipes, dark smoke rising from them in thin streams, extended from the roof of each structure.

The Elves on this level were dressed more casually than those below, and most carried themselves with the graceful, half-wary walk of a warrior. Only a handful of brown-robed Elves were visible, and each was intent on his task.

"This, and the next few levels, is where my people live," Treloran explained. "The buildings you see are homes. Specifically, the homes of *Ael Chatorra*. Most of them, at least. The residences of the other castes are also at this level, but are located in other sections of the city."

Martyn nodded, realizing for the first time how extensive Lynnaei actually was. He had been sorely mistaken in thinking that the Aelvin city was lacking in population. They had simply been out of sight. "Is this where we're going?" he asked, trying his best not to look too casual.

"No," Treloran said, shaking his head. "Unless you wish to find an inn, or stop by the home of an Aelvin warrior to see what is being made for supper." Treloran's smile was mocking, and Martyn returned the Elf's grin uneasily. He followed Treloran through several more levels of houses, each more elaborate than the ones below.

"The more powerful families and richer merchants own entire trees," Treloran explained. "Their manors stretch from the ground to the very top of the Great Trees, occupying multiple levels, and some have platforms that extend nearly halfway to the nearest tree."

He gestured to the small buildings around them. "*Ael Chatorra* do not have the riches of *Ael Alluya* or *Ael Pieroci*," he added, pointing down. "The homes on the lower levels belong to the common soldiers. "These more elaborate dwellings are owned by warriors of higher rank."

They continued their climb, and the width of the trunk began to decrease rapidly. After another five levels, the trunk was thin enough that Martyn could nearly get his arms around it. Above, a huge platform, nearly five hundred hands in diameter and supported by a series of crossbeams and braces, extended out from the tree.

Martyn let out a sigh of relief when they reached the platform and the staircase ended. A thin rope ladder took its place along the tree's trunk, climbing the last two hundred hands to the Great Tree's top. The tree up which Treloran had led them was the tallest for some distance, but not by much. Around them, the tops of other Great Trees could be seen, each capped with its own platform. Thin rope bridges spanned the distance between platforms, and Martyn goggled with amazement at the ease with which the Elves crossed the distances, seemingly oblivious to the height.

To the north stood the plateau that was the Emperor's Palace. The sun, which had been all but invisible since they left the archery range, cast golden rays against the red stone of the mountain. The top of the palace was higher than the platform on which Martyn stood, but the innumerable towers lining the plateau were more visible from here than from the ground.

The Great Forest spread out around them, as far as the eye could see. Martyn took a tentative step toward the edge of the platform, standing on his tiptoes to peer over the railing. Torches burned below, illuminating the lower levels. The ground was invisible, swallowed in the dark shadows. The prince stood agog, not sure if he would be able to see the ground even at midday.

Tables and chairs dotted the platform, many occupied by Aelvin warriors sipping drinks and talking merrily to their companions. Martyn looked at the little rope ladder that led up to the very top of the tree. Suppressing a nervous tremor, he grabbed the first rung, ready to show Treloran that he was not afraid.

The Elf's hand grabbed his shoulder, and Martyn craned his neck around. "If you really want to climb to the observation tower, Prince Martyn," he said, smiling jokingly, "we certainly can. But I am thirsty after our long walk, and would prefer a drink first."

The Elf laughed, the sound surprising Martyn. "Besides, I thought you wanted to see how we Elves enjoyed ourselves." Treloran cast his eyes up to the narrow platform. "Staring out into space is not how *Ael Chatorra* have fun."

Martyn stared at the Aelvin Prince for a long moment, then he, too, started to laugh. "After all your comments, you knew I'd assume we were going to the top of the tree! Why didn't you say something?"

Treloran spread his arms wide, his smile broadening. "You stopped at every other level, Prince Martyn," he replied seriously. "Why should I have assumed this level would be any different?"

Schooling his features, Martyn sourly grumbled, "I'm not sure I appreciate your sense of humor."

"Do you care where we sit?" Treloran asked, ignoring the prince's comment. When Martyn shook his head, the Elf led him to a table on the very edge of the platform. Sitting, they looked out over the forest below. Thousands of tiny lights were springing up throughout the city; the bridges and houses flickered with innumerable flames, until it appeared as if the very forest was on fire.

Around them, brown-robed Elves were lighting torches, spaced evenly along the railing. Each table had a lantern as well, its small flame lighting the table.

"Do you not worry about the flames?" he asked Treloran

"Fire is always a concern," the Elf admitted. "But it is not as much a threat as you might think. The trees themselves are quite resistant to flames. Only the homes and businesses are at great risk. But," he added, gesturing over the rail to the well-lighted walkways below, "many of the avenues are lighted by *Ael Maulle*. The flames they conjure cast light, but have no heat."

"Has there even been a fire?" Martyn asked. A servant stood next to the table, but said nothing, waiting for the two princes to notice her.

"Two," came Treloran's reply. "Once during the MageWar, and once long before. The fire during the MageWar was started by the *Noedra Shamallyn*. They hoped to cast Lynnaei into chaos, but the plan only served to bond Grandfather more tightly into the Alliance of the Four Races."

Treloran beckoned to the servant, who stepped closer. Leaning over, he whispered in the Elf's ear. She bobbed her head and ran toward the bar. While they waited for their drinks, Martyn scanned the platform. Nearly three score Elves sat at the various tables, usually in groups of three or four. A piper sat on the opposite side of the platform, playing a slow, sweet song.

A sudden breeze wafted over them, and Martyn shivered. "I find myself cold in your city, Treloran," he said with a smile. "Lynnaei is far colder than Kaper."

Treloran smiled back. "To be honest, I, too, am often cold."

The girl returned with two large glasses, filled halfway with a dark red liquid. Martyn lifted the short, wide glass and sniffed tentatively. The drink had a heavy aroma, and he coughed as he inhaled. Raising the glass to eye level, Martyn asked, "What do you call this?"

"*Brandei*," answered Treloran. "There is no finer drink in all of Madryn." The Aelvin Prince lifted the glass to his mouth and took a small sip. With a satisfied smile, he returned the glass to the table. Prepared for the worst, Martyn touched his own glass to his lips, taking the tiniest of sips. The thick red liquid burned down his throat, leaving behind a trail of fire that reached to his stomach. Martyn breathed deeply, hoping the cool air would somehow quench the burning.

Regaining his composure, Martyn met Treloran's green eyes, which were staring at him with delight. "This is a fine drink," he said. "Nearly as good as Alrendrian wine." He took another sip, this one longer than the last.

Despite the fire in his gut, Martyn found that he liked the taste of *brandei*. Treloran's pleased expression faded when the drink seemed to agree with the Alrendrian Prince. Laughing, Martyn said, "You can't win them all."

Treloran laughed as well, lifting his glass. "Perhaps not, Prince Martyn, but I do not have to enjoy losing." His face took on a serious expression, and he looked the prince up and down. "Perhaps Lord Odara is not the only formidable Alrendrian in your company."

Martyn lifted his own glass. "I'll drink to that!" Together, they downed their *brandei*, gulping the thick liquid thirstily.

Booming laughter interrupted the enjoyment of their drink. "Treloran!" called a voice behind Martyn. "I have not seen you down *brandei* like that in quite some time." Martyn craned his neck around to look at the speaker. A young Elf, not as tall as most but well muscled, stood behind them, dressed in dark green leather armor. His eyes had the customary slant of the Elves, but they were dark brown, not green. His hair was long and blonde, and he wore it pulled back behind his head.

A smile spread across Treloran's face. "Astalian!" he cried out jovially, rising from his chair and clapping the Elf on the shoulders. "It has been too long, my friend." Treloran's sour expression disappeared, and he seemed almost a new person, full of happiness and vitality. Martyn considered the changes in the Aelvin Prince he had witnessed this afternoon. If this were the true Treloran, then perhaps they could be friends after all.

The two Elves stared at each other for a long moment, seeming to forget Martyn's presence. "Astalian," Treloran finally said, pointing at Martyn, "This is Martyn Batai, Prince of Alrendria. He was one of the delegates sent to discuss reopening the Path of Riches." The Aelvin warrior folded his arms across his chest and looked at Treloran consideringly. "I have been showing him the city."

"And no doubt boring him to tears!" Astalian laughed. He turned to face Martyn. "You are the Prince of Alrendria?" he asked absently, his smile broad and warm. "Of course I knew that already, else I would have greeted my prince in our language, not yours." Laughing, he said, "You are well met, Child of Balan!"

Martyn stood, extending a hand to the Elf. Astalian stared him up and down. "Odd," he said at last. "You are shorter than I expected Humans to be." Martyn's cheeks burned red at the comment on his height. Noting the expression, Astalian raised his hands. "I meant no offense, Prince of Alrendria. We hear many stories about Humans, but you are the first I have ever seen."

The Elf gripped Martyn's arm, their wrists locking, and the prince realized that, despite Astalian's comments, the Elf's eyes were on a level with his own. "We, too, hear many stories," Martyn said. "About Elves, that is. I've found that only a handful are true." Smiling, he released Astalian's arm. "Call me Martyn."

"Martyn it is!" the Elf agreed amicably. "And I am Astalian, a simple warrior, hardly worthy enough to bask in the presence of such influential beings." He made no move to depart, though. Instead, his eyes scanned the table. "Ah, you drink *brandei*, Martyn? Does our drink suit you?"

Martyn nodded, and Astalian clapped him on the shoulder. "*Brandei* is the drink of a warrior!" he said. "Nothing will keep you warmer during the bitter winters!" Seating himself at their table, Astalian waved for a passing servant, "Bring three more glasses of *brandei*. No! Bring a bottle and another glass." The servant bowed his head subserviently, hurrying to the bar.

Martyn raised an eyebrow to Treloran, who shrugged. "Astalian is being modest, Prince Martyn," he said. "He is no mere warrior. He is *Sonate Chatorra*, one of our greatest warriors. Even my uncle listens to his counsel."

"You uncle listens to no one's counsel," Astalian scoffed. "Least of all mine." He smiled at the Aelvin Prince, but made no move to deny any of Treloran's claims.

The servant returned with the bottle of *brandei*. "My thanks, Yyrein," Astalian said to the brown-robed Elf, taking the bottle from his hands. He poured *brandei* into their glasses, filling each to the brim.

"My pleasure," the servant replied before disappearing.

Martyn looked back and forth between his companions. "I'm confused," he said to Treloran. "I thought you said members of the different castes did not socialize. Astalian seems to have no difficulty speaking to *Ael Namisa*." He smiled, glad he could finally return some of Treloran's earlier mocking. "And you," he added, "the Emperor's grandson, seem quite at ease with Astalian, a lowly Aelvin warrior." Martyn turned his gaze to Astalian. "Though an uncommon warrior, I grant you."

Treloran opened his mouth, but could not find the right words. Astalian stared at Martyn, then burst out in laughter. "No words Treloran?" he chided, clapping his hand on the table forcefully. "No witty response?" He had to force himself to stop laughing. "At least these Humans seem unafraid to speak their minds!"

To Martyn, the warrior said, "I will answer for my prince. First, there are no laws prohibiting the castes from associating with one another, just tradition. A tradition only *Ael Alluya* still adhere to."

Astalian's eyes danced merrily as he taunted the Aelvin Prince. "Second, Prince Treloran is not only *Ael Alluya*; he is *Ael Chatorra* as well. So not even *he* worries about sharing words or drink with lowly warriors." A smile danced across Astalian's face, and he winked. "In this case, Treloran has no choice. He is in the warrior's district, and I outrank him!" Warm laughter echoed across the platform.

Martyn found his mood much improved by Astalian's gaiety. Even Treloran shared in their laughter, and they all three drank deeply from their cups. Setting his empty glass back on the table, Astalian said, "You do not seem nearly as bad as the stories claim. If you are a fair representative of your Race, then I hope these talks of yours lead to friendship between our peoples."

He picked up the bottle and refilled their glasses. "Let us drink to friendship!" he called out loudly, lifting his glass. Several other tables returned the toast, lifting their glasses in salute. Laughing, Martyn raised his *brandei*, clinking the glass against Astalian's. After a brief hesitation, Treloran did the same.

Martyn downed the contents of his own cup. "May I ask a question, Astalian?" The *brandei* left another trail of fire down his throat, and Martyn struggled not to choke. Astalian was deep in his own cup, but he nodded and waved a hand, signaling for Martyn to speak. The prince struggled to find the right words: words that would not offend his Aelvin hosts. "You are more...expressive than the other Elves I've met. Why is that?"

Astalian laughed again, this time much harder. "I see you have been spending too much time with Treloran and the Imperial Family." He reached across the table and slapped the Aelvin Prince on the shoulder. Treloran smiled, but said nothing. "My people often confuse dignity and propriety with dourness and boredom. *Ael Alluya* are the most strict, even more rigid than *Ael Maulle*, and the Emperor's kin, excepting possibly the Emperor himself, put other *Ael Alluya* to shame!

"I have been trying to cure Treloran of this disease!" Astalian assured Martyn, whacking the Aelvin Prince on the shoulder a second time. Treloran winced at the blow, but again said nothing. Shrugging his shoulders, Astalian added, "Though only with marginal success."

Astalian finished his *brandei* and emptied the remainder of the bottle into his and Martyn's glasses. "In all seriousness, Prince Martyn, *Ael Namisa* are often aloof out of a false sense of humility, *Ael Maulle* out of a false sense of pride, and *Ael Alluya* out of a false sense of superiority."

The servant reappeared, and Astalian took the fresh bottle from his hands, popping the cork instantly. "*Ael Chatorra*, on the other hand," he said, taking a long swig from the bottle before setting it on the table, "are only solemn and aloof when we are ordered to be!"

The conversation drifted to other topics. Martyn enjoyed Astalian's company; he found the Elf's forthrightness refreshing. In time, even Treloran opened up, and Martyn discovered that the Aelvin Prince was a pleasant companion when he allowed his guard to drop.

The evening passed quickly, and night descended on Lynnaei. Every time Martyn set his glass on the table, Astalian feigned a wounded expression. "Prince of Alrendria," he slurred, "your glass is empty. Allow me to refill it!" In only a short while, the three of them were quite drunk.

Their revelry lasted well into the night. Astalian made it his duty to ensure that their cups remained full. They talked of a great many things, their conversations touching many topics. They spoke of the differences between their Races, and the similarities. They shared the legends and folklore they had heard, and laughed at the absurdity of every myth.

When darkness had long since enveloped the forest, and the only light came from the flickering lanterns and the thin sliver of moon above, their celebration was interrupted. A fist came slamming down onto the table, bouncing the glasses. An empty bottle of *brandei* crashed to the platform, shattering into tiny shards.

Martyn jumped, his head snapping up, his blurry eyes struggling to focus on Luran. The Elf glared at him with a look of distaste. Sneering, he turned his glare on his nephew, rumbling something in the flowing language of the Elves. Treloran shook his head, and finally raised a hand to silence his uncle.

"Uncle," he said pleasantly, with only a slight slur to the words. "There is a Human present. It is impolite to speak our language so he cannot understand."

Luran's eyes flashed with renewed anger. In a cold, hard voice, he said, "I do not care whether this thing can understand me or not! Why are you here? What do you hope to prove by spending time with *Ael*…" Luran paused, and fumbled for the translation. "…soldiers! And why do you insist on spending your time with this Human! You disappoint me, nephew."

Treloran cast his eyes to Astalian despondently. Taking the cue, the Aelvin warrior winked, grabbed the fullest bottle of *brandei*, and gestured to Martyn. "Come, Martyn," he said jovially. "Perhaps we should allow *Ael Alluya* a little privacy." Martyn stood, swaying slightly, and grabbed the side of the table for support. Treloran smiled at them gratefully before Luran pushed between them, blocking the Elf from Martyn's view.

Astalian led him across the platform, selecting a table closer to the piper. He filled their glasses to the top, then set the bottle on the table. "Miserable wretch," he said with a sidelong glance at Luran. "I do not know how such a loathsome creature could be descended from the Emperor."

The Aelvin warrior started to chuckle. "He is not much of a warrior, either!" he added. "I heard what your friend did to him on *Ael Shende Ruhl*!" Martyn snickered at the memory and lifted his glass, offering a toast to Jeran.

"He sends our archers across the Danelle repeatedly," Astalian confided to the prince, sending a sidelong glance in Luran's direction, "to gain vengeance against the Tribesmen. Hah!" The Elf's laugh was bitter and harsh. "He could kill every Garun'ah and his pride would not be healed."

Astalian looked at Martyn. "Luran's parents were killed in a Garun'ah raid," he explained. "As tragic as that is, we were at war! You cannot hold a grudge against an enemy for defending what he believes his!"

They sat in silence for a while, listening to the music of the piper. Martyn studied the woman appreciatively. Most of the Aelvin women Martyn had met wore thick robes that hid their figures. The piper, however, was dressed in an outfit more sheer and suggestive, though still tame by Alrendrian standards. She was thin, but not unattractively so, with well toned muscles and a flat stomach visible beneath the flowing garments.

Her legs were long and shapely, her hips amply curved, and her breasts small and perky, though Elves in general seemed less well endowed in that respect than Human women.

The piper's skin was smooth and white, with just a hint of color on the cheeks. Her slanted, emerald green eyes regarded him coolly. She kept her black hair short, and she had an air of exoticness that Martyn found most attractive.

Astalian watched Martyn for a moment, then patted him on the shoulder, nodding his agreement. He raised his glass and winked at the prince. Martyn smiled back, joining the Aelvin warrior in another drink.

The piper's song came to an end, and placing her instrument carefully in its case, she turned her green eyes on Martyn. "Is there something I can do for you, Human?" she asked in a cold voice.

Her voice was heavily accented, but clearly understandable. Martyn smiled and nodded, his head spinning from drink. "Yes," he answered, "but not right now," He looked around the platform. "And definitely not here!" Astalian burst out in loud laughter; he raised his cup to hide his smile. To the piper, Martyn flashed his best smile and said, "For an Elf, you're quite attractive."

The woman stepped down from the platform on which she had been sitting. She walked toward Martyn, hips swaying seductively with every step. Martyn could not take his eyes off her.

She stopped a pace in front of him and extended a delicate hand. Cupping it under his chin, she lifted his face so their eyes met. Martyn stared deep into twin emerald pools while the Aelvin woman lightly caressed his cheek with the back of her hand.

Smiling cruelly, the Elf backhanded him, knocking Martyn from his chair. Astalian's laughter followed him to the floor. Reeling from the unexpected blow, Martyn gingerly touched his already swelling lip. "You are not nearly as unattractive as I expected a Human to be either," she admitted, looking him up and down. "But nobody talks to me in such a manner."

She kicked him lightly in the ribs before walking away. Her words drifted back to him. "Your blatant advances and innuendo may work on Human trollops and weak-kneed *Ael Namisa*, but *Ael Chatorra* require more finesse."

Martyn slowly regained his feet. Astalian took one look at him and burst out laughing. Martyn rubbed his cheek and fell heavily into his chair, groaning. "You knew?" he asked Astalian, taking a deep swallow of *brandei*. The Elf nodded his head, still trying to get his laughter under control. "You could have warned me!"

Astalian shrugged. "It was funnier this way."

Martyn tried to look angry, but could not keep himself from laughing. "I owe you thanks, Astalian. I've had more fun tonight than in all the nights since entering Illendrylla!"

"Martyn, you are a warrior at heart," Astalian returned, bowing his head. "It is a pleasure to serve our Human guests. I only hope that, someday, you will return the favor." A loud crash echoed to them from the far side of the platform, interrupting Astalian's next statement.

Luran had swept the glasses from the table that he and Treloran shared. The older Elf spat out a curse, then stomped toward the stairway. Treloran stared after his uncle, then stood, walking pointedly across the platform. When he reached their table, he grabbed the bottle of *brandei*, draining it with a series of gulps. Smiling, Astalian called out, "*That* is the Treloran I remember!"

A noise behind Martyn made him crane his neck around. On the other side of the platform, a thick plank lay suspended between two tables. An Elf stood on either end of the plank, and they faced each other with quarterstaffs. Martyn watched, confused, as the Elves began to fight, balancing nimbly. Other warriors gathered around, cheering and calling out bets.

Intrigued, Martyn stood and crossed the platform, his eyes riveted on the duel.

One Elf struck out tentatively at his opponent, who stepped away from the blow. Lightning-fast, the second Elf thrust his staff forward, hitting a stunning blow into the first's midriff. With a grunt of pain, the Elf fell to one knee, but managed to maintain his place. He recovered quickly and bounced nimbly backward, toward the table. Breathing hard, he reappraised his opponent, then lunged forward again.

The second Elf smiled. He jumped high in the air, his staff spinning around his head. The first Elf ran forward, trying to catch the second on his way down, but he was too late. The Elf landed lightly on his feet, then used his staff to vault over his opponent. Planting one foot solidly on the plank, the Elf pivoted quickly, lashing out with his other leg.

The maneuver caught the first Elf by surprise. His legs were knocked from under him, and he landed on the plank with a loud thunk. Martyn winced at the sound. With a casual flick of his staff, the second Elf rolled the first off the plank, then raised his staff above his head in victory.

Astalian came up behind Martyn. "We call this jousting, though I believe the word means something different in your language." Martyn nodded his head. The games were a little different, but the idea was the same. "It is something *Ael Chatorra* do in training, but we also spar for fun."

Martyn smiled. "I'd like to try."

Astalian's eyes went wide, and he scratched his chin thoughtfully. "You are serious?" he asked, and at Martyn's eager nod, the Elf smiled anew. "Truly, you are a warrior!" He scratched the back of his head, thinking through the *brandei*-induced haze. "Very well," he grunted at last. "But if we are to do this, we will do it right."

Astalian clapped his hands loudly, and the assembled Elves turned to look at him. "The Prince of Alrendria wishes to joust with us!" he called, and a stunned silence descended over the crowd, followed by a chorus of drunken cheers.

Astalian raised his hand for silence. "We play teams of three. Prince Martyn, Prince Treloran, and I will challenge your three best. Arrange it!" With another cheer, the Elves burst into motion, moving tables and running to the side of the platform to gather more planks.

Martyn felt a hand on his shoulder. Treloran pulled him around roughly. The Aelvin Prince's cheeks were bright red, and he swayed on his feet. "Are you sure you want to do this, Human? Jousting can be dangerous."

Martyn pushed Treloran's hand off his shoulder. "If you don't want to join us, you don't have to. I, for one, am enjoying myself, and have no intention of stopping." Treloran spread his hands in surrender and led Martyn to a rack of staffs. Astalian joined them in selecting their weapons.

While they chose, Astalian explained the rules. "There will be three planks arranged next to each other, about one and a half paces apart. We will start on one side, our opponents on the other. You can move from one plank to another at your discretion, but you may not touch the floor, nor can you leave the planks and step onto the table. The object is to knock your opponents to the ground before you fall."

Martyn nodded, taking several slow, deep breaths to steady himself. Astalian slapped both of them on the shoulder, then led them toward the crowd. The tables and planks had been arranged, and a circle of lamps spread around them, providing enough light for them to see. The three planks were in a row, the farthest less than a hand from the edge of the platform. The tables were at a level with the rail.

Martyn climbed onto the center plank. Astalian took the one to his right, and Treloran climbed up on his left. Across from them stood three Aelvin warriors. The victor of the last joust was standing across from Astalian. With a smile, Astalian called out, "Begin!"

Martyn took a few steps forward, walking slowly so he could get a feel for balancing his weight on the plank. He swung the staff in his hands, squinting to get a better look at his opponent. With a sigh of recognition, he identified the piper; she had exchanged her gown for dark leathers. Her smile was wicked, and she bowed, calling out, "How pleasant to see you again, Human." Suddenly, she rushed forward, her staff swinging in the moonlight.

Raising his own staff in defense, Martyn noted that his companions had already engaged their opponents. Treloran was level with Martyn, but Astalian had rushed ahead, pushing his combatant nearly back onto his table. He kept him pinned down with a series of lightning-fast blows.

Martyn returned his attention to the Elf in front of him. She attacked forcefully, but he deflected each blow with ease. A look of surprise replaced her smile, and Martyn chuckled. "Were you expecting me to be easy prey? We Humans are full of surprises." She launched another attack, which he easily parried.

Spinning his staff in his hands, he swung low, hitting a glancing blow on the Elf's shin. She recoiled in pain, and Martyn's smile grew. He silently thanked Joam for forcing him to learn weapons other than sword and bow.

Risking a quick glance to the side, Martyn saw that Treloran was in trouble. The Aelvin Prince, more than a little drunk, was having trouble maintaining his balance on the narrow plank, and his opponent was using that fact to his advantage. Martyn sprang to his right, landing behind Astalian. Running forward, he jumped back to his own plank on the other side of the piper, pushing her off balance. She fell forward, rolling nimbly across the plank, trying not to fall.

Martyn swung his staff to the side, taking Treloran's opponent in the back. The Elf grunted in pain, dropping to his knees. Treloran took a step back, balancing himself. "That's allowed, isn't it?" Martyn asked, hoping he had not violated the rules.

Treloran nodded breathlessly, and Martyn squared his jaw, drawing back his staff to knock the Aelvin Prince's opponent off the plank. Martyn heard Astalian's warning just as he felt wood smack painfully into his back. The blow was not hard enough to knock him off the plank, but he stumbled forward, stunned.

He turned quickly, trying not to show how much the blow had hurt. The Aelvin woman smiled. "That was a warning," she said. "It is honorable to help your teammate, but you should never turn your back on an enemy." She swung her staff at his head.

Martyn ducked the blow, returning one of his own. The woman jumped over it easily, landing on the plank to his left. Astalian glanced behind him. "It's getting crowded over here!" he said, springing into the air and landing next to Martyn. His opponent wasted no time in following, his staff swinging wildly.

The female Elf took a step back, her staff swinging wide. At the last instant, Martyn blocked, flipped his staff, and trapped her weapon underneath his arm. Seizing the opportunity, he lunged forward and grabbed the Elf's hand, pulling her toward him. He kissed her full on the lips, then let her go, pushing her sideways so she would fall. "Thanks for the tip," he laughed. "I'll be sure to remember it."

Somehow, she managed to keep her balance, and pain exploded through Martyn's abdomen as her knee dug in sharply. Martyn landed on his back, pure luck keeping him on the plank. The Elf glowered at him. "That wasn't very smart," she said, taking a step forward, ready to finish him off.

Out of nowhere, a staff slammed into her side, knocking her off her feet and sending her crashing to the floor. Martyn looked up, still gasping for breath, surprised to see Treloran standing next to him. The Aelvin Prince smiled. "We are even now," he said, looking at the Aelvin warrior sprawled on the floor below.

"Now stop playing games and start jousting!" he demanded. "This isn't–" Treloran's jibe cut off when an Elf crashed into him from behind, sending the Aelvin Prince flying from the plank. Martyn stood, ignoring the pain in his chest, and faced his new opponent.

The Elf smiled, lashing out with a furious volley of blows. Martyn managed to parry them all, but had to jump to his right to avoid the onslaught. He caught a momentary glimpse over the edge of the platform, and his head spun as he stared down into the murky depths.

Turning away from the edge, he scuttled down the plank, his eyes never leaving his new opponent.

Astalian still stood, and was engaged in a furious exchange with the second opponent, though it looked like Martyn's teammate had the upper hand. The Elf next to Martyn abruptly sprang away, going to the aid of his companion. Martyn cried out, "Astalian! Behind you!" and the Elf pivoted sharply, springing backward. With a flick of his staff, Astalian caught the Elf in midair, flipping him over his head.

The Elf tumbled across the floor, crashing into some of the lamps, sending shards of glass and puddles of oil spraying everywhere. Martyn saw flames spring up from several of the puddles, spreading quickly across the well-polished wooden floor.

Martyn was about to cry out when he heard Treloran's voice. "Martyn! To your right!" He turned just in time to see the remaining Elf spring towards him, flying from one plank to the next, his staff swinging wildly over his head. Martyn tried to block the blow, but was too slow. The staff caught him squarely beneath the ribcage, sending another burst of pain through his chest and launching him off the platform.

He saw Treloran rushing toward him, arm outstretched. Then he dropped past the railing and was swallowed in darkness. The ground loomed far beneath him, black and impossibly distant, and Martyn felt a surge of panic. He felt a thud and saw a bright flash, then a wave of dizziness overwhelmed him and he struggled for consciousness.

His last thought as the platform faded from sight was to wonder how disappointed his father would be when he found out what had happened.

Chapter 13

Another day dawned hot. Dahr wiped sweat from his face, waving for the Guardsmen to join him. They walked their horses to the top of the hill, stopping just behind him. "Do you see anything?" Vyrina asked hopefully.

Dahr shook his head. "Just more plains and forest," he admitted. "Take a look for yourself." He dismounted, reaching in his pack for a water bottle. The Guardsmen spread out on the rise, peering across the vast plains of northern Madryn.

Nearly a score of days had passed since they stumbled across the dead Tribesman, and they had yet to see another living being. Dahr had led them more or less parallel to the Danelle, following the snaking river and its tributaries north. Around them, the forest had thinned, eventually giving way to open plains. Small groves still dotted the area close to the river.

Jasova knelt, grabbing a handful of rich, black dirt. "I don't understand," he said to the others. "The soil is good. Water is plentiful. The land teems with game. I can't imagine a better place to farm."

"The Garun'ah are not farmers," Katya reminded him. "They're nomads, traveling wherever game is most plentiful. If they aren't here," she said, looking around, "it means there are better places to find food."

"Perhaps there's another reason," Nykeal said, blushing when everyone turned their eyes on her. "There are many tribes of Garun'ah, and we don't know how they divide their lands. This could be disputed territory."

"Or an area near the border of two tribes," added Wardel. "Perhaps they keep their distance to prevent bloodshed."

"Or maybe this is not where the Tribesmen live," Elorn murmured in a sour voice. "Perhaps Dahr leads us in the wrong direction, away from the Garun'ah." He glared at Dahr for a moment before drinking thirstily from his water bottle. "Perhaps the tribes do not number many, and we waste our time scouring this barren land in search of them."

"I agree that we should have found something by now," Dahr told the Guardsman. "But if we press on, we're sure to find the Garun'ah eventually." Elorn grunted a reply, and Dahr shook his head sadly. "What would you have us do if not continue our search?"

"Turn back," Elorn replied sullenly. "Return to Alrendria. Go to Grenz and wait for the rest of the party to return from Illendrylla."

Dahr shook his head forcefully. "It will be a long time, perhaps seasons, before Lord Iban and the others return. I think our time is better spent searching for the Garun'ah than sitting in Grenz."

"If not Grenz, then Kaper!" Elorn snapped. "Allow us to resume our duties."

"No," Dahr replied adamantly. "We continue our search. We'll find the Garun'ah, Elorn. They're out here. I know it!" Elorn frowned, but said nothing more. Dahr used the silence to study the sweeping countryside.

To the east was the Danelle, a ribbon of blue twisting north through the rolling grasslands. Sunlight sparkled off the fast-moving water, sending flashes of light in their direction. In all other directions, the view was the same: rolling hills covered in knee-high, green grass and spotted with forest, some little more than groves, others larger, sprawling over vast distances.

Spring was well underway, and temperatures soared during the day. The Guardsmen had long since discarded their armor, preferring the comfort of cottons to the protection offered by stout leather. Even so, sweat ran freely down their faces as they surveyed the lands, looking for signs of the Garun'ah.

"Were I a Tribesman," Jasova said suddenly, "roaming the lands wherever food was most plentiful, I'd keep myself as far north as possible." The other Guardsmen eyed him curiously, but Dahr smiled in sudden understanding. "Winter comes quick to this part of Madryn," the subcommander continued. "I'd want to use the northlands during the warm months. That way, when winter came, I could lead my people south to warmer, more bountiful lands."

"I agree with Jasova," Dahr said, nodding. "We will continue on our present course, cutting back and forth to the north. Given enough time, we are bound to find some Garun'ah." Hopping into his saddle, Dahr waved, and the other Guardsmen mounted too. When they were ready, he urged Jardelle to a quick walk, leading the horse down the north side of the hill.

They rode in silence for much of the afternoon, each lost in his own thoughts. Dahr found himself wondering whether he was making a mistake. *Perhaps Elorn's right, and there are few Garun'ah to be found. We could spend seasons roaming these plains.*

Dahr kept his party away from the small forests and deep valleys. In those areas, their visibility was greatly reduced, and they were more exposed, easier targets for whoever had attacked the unfortunate Tribesman. Besides, atop the broad, flat hills they would be more likely to spot any nearby Garun'ah.

Though their path twisted and turned, zig-zagging across the plains, Dahr tried to keep the Danelle in sight at all times, using the river as a compass to mark their travels. The river had narrowed during the long trek north, but it was still broad and deep, with areas of fast moving current, dangerous to cross. Moreover, the river, and the narrow, trickling tributaries that flowed toward it, was often the only source of fresh water available.

The day, as all those before, passed uneventfully, and without any indication that they were nearer to finding their goal. Once, around midday, they came upon a vast herd of animals, nearly as broad as horses, though not as tall. The beasts seemed docile, and they all but ignored the Alrendrians, who cautiously picked a path through the herd. Nevertheless, Dahr and the Guardsmen stayed alert until the last of the large, muscular animals had disappeared behind them.

As evening approached, Dahr turned east, returning to the Danelle and wandering along the bank until he discovered a suitable clearing. He gave the order to halt, and the Guardsmen quickly dismounted. Each warrior erected his own tent, and the remainder of the duties were rotated, giving the Guardsman a turn at every task.

This was Dahr's day to care for the horses. After his tent was raised, he went to the line where they had been tethered. At his approach, their ears pricking up, and they craned their necks toward him, looking for a treat. He untied Jardelle from the line, and the other horses let out a displeased whuff, lowering their heads to graze on the tender grass.

He led Jardelle downstream, allowing the horse to drink its fill of cool river water. While Jardelle drank, Dahr brushed the animal fondly, scraping away sweat and dust, and massaged the horse's thick muscles. The powerful charger enjoyed the treatment, shifting his body so Dahr could scratch the places that itched the most. Once his horse had been properly cared for, he led him back to the line. One by one, he took the others to the river, repeating the process.

When he finally returned to the camp, Wardel and Elorn were gone, off hunting in a nearby thicket. Game was plentiful along the river, and even more so in the thick forests that lined it; it had been a rare night when they had not feasted on wild boar, roasted venison, or other delicious catches.

Katya had a small fire burning in the center of the ring of tents. It was the redhead's turn to cook, though she did not seem to relish the idea of spending the afternoon over the fire. Dahr, wiping the sweat from his own brow, sympathized.

Nykeal sat on a fallen log, mending a tear in her shirt. "Where's Jasova?" Dahr called out, scanning the camp for the dark-haired Guardsman.

"He's looking for Garun'ah," Nykeal replied, setting down her sewing. "When we climbed that last hill, he noticed that the Danelle narrows not too far upstream. He thought it might be shallow enough to ford. If so, he guessed the Tribesmen might cross the river there, if they ever travel to this area."

Dahr sat next to the blonde Guardswoman. "What do you think?" he asked. "What should we do?"

Nykeal shook her head. "It's not my place to say. I'm just a Guardsman."

"I'm asking for your advice, Nikki," Dahr said softly. "You need not fear sharing your thoughts with me." He waited, but nothing seemed to be forthcoming. "You agree with Elorn?" he prompted, half disbelieving. "You think we should turn back?"

"No!" she said hastily, her cheeks reddening. "That is, not completely. I don't think we should return to Kaper." She cleared her throat and tried to explain, starting tentatively. As she continued, her words gained confidence. "We are far from the nearest settlement. We have no friends and no reinforcements nearby. We don't know what to expect. We don't even know how many Tribesmen there are, or how they will receive us."

"If something goes wrong...." She turned away, allowing the silence to voice her concerns.

Dahr nodded in understanding. "Nothing's happened yet," he muttered. Against his will, a loud laugh bubbled up from deep inside. "We haven't even seen another living soul, Human or Tribesman!"

"But if we stumbled across trouble," Nykeal repeated. "If the Tribesmen, or Elves, or even another party of slavers attacked... I'm just worried that we'll find ourselves cut off, with no way to escape."

Steeling herself, she lifted her chin proudly. "I'm an Alrendrian Guardsman," she said with pride. "And you are my commander. I'll follow your orders, Dahr. Without question."

He patted her arm fondly. "I thank you for that, Nikki. I truly do." Smiling, he stood and walked down to the bank of the Danelle. Dropping to his knees, he cupped a double handful of water and splashed it against his face, shivering when the cold liquid ran into his shirt.

Jasova called out to him from behind, and Dahr stood, turning to face the Guardsman. "Come with me. You should see this." Dahr followed Jasova along the stream bank. The water was crystal clear, the sandy bottom visible from the bank. In some places, smooth stones lined the river bed, and the strong current rippled over the surface of the rocks.

They walked for some time without speaking, winding along the grassy riverbank. To their right, the Danelle narrowed, the bed growing increasingly rocky. At a flat basin, where a path led into the river, Jasova stopped. The crossing did not look deep, but the water moved quickly, roaring over the rocks that jutted above the surface.

Tracks lined the ground, going into and emerging from the river. They were not fresh, but neither were they very old. "How long?" Dahr asked.

Jasova scratched his goatee. "Two days at most. I'd guess a small party, four or five at most. Maybe a child or two." He shrugged his shoulders. "It might have been a family. But this isn't what I wanted you to see." Waving, he led Dahr to a thick stand of trees, the interior cloaked in shadow.

The tracks led into the trees, and Dahr looked at the Guardsman questioningly. "Best if you see for yourself," Jasova said, answering the unspoken question. Nodding, Dahr pushed his way through the thick trees.

He emerged in an open hollow and immediately noticed the signs of a struggle. Leaves were strewn everywhere; limbs were broken, some severed completely and others hanging limp. The ground was disturbed; footprints covered the clearing. Dahr knelt to examine the tracks. Some were made by men, others by animals. "There were more than five here," he said.

Jasova nodded. "If I had to guess, I'd say a family of Garun'ah crossed the Danelle at the ford. They came to this grove to find shelter and were ambushed." He knelt next to Dahr. "By the amount of destruction, the Garun'ah either put up a good fight, or they were greatly outnumbered."

The subcommander pointed to several large clumps of dirt. Blood, dried and congealed. "Perhaps the Garun'ah were captured. Perhaps they were killed." He held out a hand. In it he held an arrow, similar to the one they had found before, inscribed down the sides with Aelvin runes.

"If they were killed," Dahr asked, taking the arrow, "where are the bodies?"

The Guardsman shrugged. "Perhaps they escaped, or at least one of them did, returning later to care for the remains."

Dahr shook his head. "There were animals here," he said, pointing to the tracks. "Likely there was something here for them to feed on, or the tracks would not be so numerous." Jasova nodded, but said nothing. "Can you determine which race was the attacker and which the defender?"

Jasova shook his head. "It's difficult. Though there are some characteristics unique to each race, we are all much more alike than different. If I didn't know about the Garun'ah, I'd think you just a large Human."

Dahr laughed. "I know what you mean. I thought I was Human most of my life!"

"Still," Jasova added, "there's the arrow. My guess is that a party of Elves–We are not yet too far from Illendrylla!–crossed the river and surprised a family of Tribesmen. It would be consistent with what little knowledge we have." Jasova shrugged again. "But it could just as easily have been the Tribesmen who stumbled across the Elves."

Dahr scanned the trees warily. "Do you think the attackers are still around?"

"No way to be sure," Jasova admitted. "But even if they aren't, they must be less than two days distant. We run the risk of catching them."

"Should we turn back?" Dahr asked, seeking the Guardsman's advice.

"They could just as easily be south of us as north," Jasova replied, and a frown spread across Dahr's face. "Were I you," Jasova counseled, noticing Dahr's discomfort, "I'd continue on, perhaps leaving the river behind and looping to the west. When we reach the mountains, we could turn south. Start back toward Grenz. We'd almost have to stumble upon the Tribesmen before we reached Gilead."

Dahr nodded, considering the Guardsman's words. "I'll leave the decision to the group. We'll tell them what you found, and ask for their opinion. We'll cast votes, and whatever the majority decides, we will do."

Dahr stood, turning back toward the camp. Jasova followed behind. "A word, Dahr," he said, and Dahr waited for the Guardsman to catch up. "I understand what you're trying to do. Only a fool refuses to listen to the advice of his peers, and only a greater fool wishes to anger his own Guardsmen.

"But you're in command here, and it's a commander's duty to make the decisions, even if those decisions go against the desires of his troops." Jasova gave his words time to sink in. "Ask for everyone's advice. Listen to their words. But when the time comes, it should be you, and you alone, who determines our path."

Though just over thirty winters, Jasova was one of Lord Iban's most trusted subcommanders. "I thank you for your counsel," Dahr said at last, smiling at the Guardsman. "I have little enough experience with command. I welcome your advice, and ask that you continue to share your thoughts with me."

Jasova returned the smile. "All of us must have our first command," he said, laughing. "And you've already proven yourself a wiser man than I." At Dahr's questioning look, Jasova explained. "When I was young, I refused to listen to those with more experience. As a result, I had to learn everything the hard way."

They met Elorn and Wardel, carrying a large buck between them, on their return to the camp. Upon their arrival, Katya ordered them to carry the deer away from the river, skin it, and cut the meat from the carcass. The two Guardsmen staggered off, grumbling that they should not have to both catch and clean the beast.

Not long after the Guardsmen returned, Katya signaled that dinner was ready. As they ate, Dahr and Jasova recounted what they had discovered by the ford. After all had been explained, and the Guardsmen had exhausted their questions, Dahr stood. "I'd like your advice on what we should do. Do we turn back, or continue on in search of the Garun'ah?"

"I say turn back," Elorn said suddenly, surprising Dahr by being the first to speak. The dour Guardsman often sat silent, offering his opinion only when forced. "There's nothing out here but empty space. I don't understand why we were sent here at all."

Dahr answered carefully. "We're looking for the Garun'ah. When the Elves refused me entrance into Illendrylla, Lord Iban suggested that I find the Tribesmen. He hopes they can be convinced to reestablish trade with Alrendria as well." Though goods from the Tribal Lands still came to Grenz, they were not as abundant as they had once been.

"No," Elorn disagreed, shaking his head. "Trade may be the excuse you use, but you are here only because the Elves would not allow one of your Race into their lands. We are here," Elorn snarled, spitting on the ground, "because we were ordered to be."

"Lord Iban gave you an opportunity to refuse," Dahr reminded the prickly Guardsman, doing his best to keep his anger in check.

"Refuse Iban's commands?" Elorn repeated, laughing harshly. "Perhaps he gave us the option, but if any of us had chosen to remain, he would have questioned why." He cast a scathing glare at Dahr. "Unlike some, I do not ignore my commander's orders, but I have no wish to run around the Tribal Lands playing nursemaid to a tame Tribesman.

"However," he added hastily, before Dahr could speak, "that is not why I think we should turn back." He swept his arms in a wide arc. "There's nothing out here! You're wasting our time by leading us through this endless wasteland."

The Guardsmen were staring at Elorn, their expressions mixtures of surprise and disbelief. Katya and Jasova both appeared angry. "We could have been part of the greatest event in Alrendria since the MageWar!" Elorn continued, ignoring the warning glares from his companions. "Instead, we run in circles through an empty wilderness, looking for a bunch of animals."

Dahr's jaw tightened with each of Elorn's words. Anger swelled in his breast, and his hands slowly tightened into fists. "I am one of the animals you speak of, Guardsman," he growled through clenched teeth, "and I do not appreciate your words. You had better learn to control your tongue."

Elorn did not back away from Dahr's rigid tone. He stepped forward, staring into Dahr's eyes hatefully. "They should have sent you back to Grenz, or better yet, not allowed you on this mission at all. If not for you, we would all be seeing the fabled city of the Elves, the first Humans to walk its paths in over three hundred winters!"

He spat at Dahr's feet. "But we are forced to follow you instead," he snarled, his teeth clenched together as tightly as Dahr's. "What honor are we to win out here?"

Dahr's breaths came fast and short, hissing between his teeth. "You had a chance to refuse," he repeated. "Lord Iban and Lord Odara both told you it was your decision. Just because you chose poorly is no reason to take it out on me. I have done nothing to you."

"Lord Odara!" Elorn laughed spitefully. "Lord Odara is nothing more than a simple farmer, lucky enough to gain the King's favor. He doesn't deserve the honors he's received. And you!" he said, his voice dropping to a harsh whisper. "You've taken what I hold most dear and don't even realize it."

"What are you talking about?" Dahr asked, puzzled. "I've taken nothing from–" Elorn's eyes shifted left, and understanding dawned. "Katya?" Dahr asked incredulously. "You hate me because of Katya?"

Elorn's cheeks turned bright red. "She's perfect," he said in a voice full of adoration, the words were softly spoken. It was unlikely any but Dahr heard. "Yet she thinks nothing of me. I'm a great warrior from a powerful Family. I have wealth and power beyond your imagination. I can offer her everything, and yet she wants only you. She can have her pick of any man in Madryn, and she chooses a monster!"

Dahr's temper flared. With a growl, he reached out and grabbed Elorn by the shirt, pushing the short man back with all his might. Elorn tumbled over the fire, rolling across the ground. Regaining his feet, Elorn launched himself across the camp. "You don't deserve her!" he snarled, rushing toward Dahr, his fist swinging.

Dahr barely had time to bring up his arms before Elorn attacked. The Guardsman was short, but broad and powerfully muscled. The momentum knocked Dahr to the ground, and he grunted as Elorn landed atop him. Elorn swung his fist, landing a stunning blow to the side of Dahr's head. Lights flashed before his eyes, and he grappled with the Guardsman, no longer pulling his punches.

They rolled back and forth across the ground, the shouts of the other Guardsmen the only sounds Dahr heard. Hands were suddenly around them, many hands, pulling Elorn away and helping Dahr to his feet. Elorn struggled, trying to free himself from Jasova and Wardel's tight grips. Katya helped Dahr to his feet, her hand gingerly touching the red welt that throbbed below his left eye.

They stood there until Elorn ceased his struggles. When the dour Guardsman seemed to have himself under control, Dahr nodded to Jasova and Wardel, and they released his arms. As soon as he was free, Elorn launched himself at Dahr again, his eyes squinted in hatred. Dahr swung a fist, his blow lightning quick. The punch caught Elorn square in the gut, launching him into the air. He landed with a thud, wheezing through clenched teeth.

Slowly, he staggered to his feet and stumble forward. "That's enough, Guardsman!" Jasova shouted, and Elorn froze in his tracks. "What do you think you're doing?" the subcommander demanded. "Dahr is our commander, whether you like him or not. You disgrace yourself and the entire Alrendrian Guard with your actions!"

Jasova grabbed Elorn by the shoulder, spinning him around to face him. "If you want a fight, fight me. I guarantee that I'll not be as forgiving."

Elorn turned slowly, looking for support from his comrades, but they all stared at him with cold, hard expressions. Katya shook her head sadly, her eyes warning Elorn against another attack. Snarling, his hands clenched in rage, Elorn spun on his heels and stormed from the camp.

They watched him go in silence. After he disappeared into the dark shadows, Wardel turned toward the others. "Well," he said seriously, "I guess that's one vote to turn back."

Dahr stared open-mouthed at Wardel's comment, but the other Guardsmen laughed heartily. Katya smiled, once more touching her hand to Dahr's cheek. "Don't worry about Elorn," she said. "I'll speak to him."

"If Katya's words don't work," Jasova added, "I'll make sure his behavior improves." The bearded Guardsman looked Dahr up and down, reappraising him. "You're a more forgiving man than I, Dahr. Were I you, I'd be chasing Elorn across the Tribal Lands." The other Guardsmen nodded their agreement.

Dahr shrugged. "He already hates me. And he'll probably think twice about attacking again, now that he knows you won't support him. Seeking retribution would only anger him more, and though you may not believe it, I'd rather have Elorn as a friend than a foe!"

The Guardsmen laughed again, but Jasova nodded. "As I said. A better man than I."

Dahr looked at each of them in turn. "I still want to know your thoughts. Should we press on, or turn back to Grenz?"

"You know my thoughts already," answered Jasova. "I say press on. We're bound to find the Garun'ah if we circle their lands long enough."

"We're far from our allies," Nykeal added, restating her earlier concerns. "But as you said, nothing's happened yet. These lands are beautiful," she added, "and I'll cherish the memories for the rest of my life. How could I want to turn back when there's so much more we have yet to explore?"

"I'm eager to find the Garun'ah!" said Wardel. "I've never met one, except for you, Dahr, but I've heard stories about how the Tribesmen live. If only a fraction are true, we'll have tales to rival those of the Alrendrians in Illendrylla!"

Vyrina echoed Wardel's sentiments, adding, "If we go back to Grenz or Kaper, it'll just be guard and sentry duty for the lot of us." She met Dahr's eyes squarely. "I hate sentry duty," she admitted.

Katya smiled, her green eyes warm and inviting. "I go where you go, Hunter," she said, almost purring. "Even if you wanted to lead us into *Ael Shataq*, I'd stay at your side."

Dahr was nearly overwhelmed. "Th...Thank you," he stammered. "It's good to know that you support me in this. All of you." He took a deep breath, trying to get his welling emotions back under control.

Trying not to embarrass himself, he squared his shoulders and said, "We'll rise at first light. I won't turn back until I've found the Garun'ah." The Guardsmen saluted, and Dahr headed to his tent.

Dahr's sleep was restless, plagued by disturbing dreams. In many he was chased, not by all the Guardsmen, but just Elorn. Except that Elorn was a giant, towering over Dahr and carrying a bloody sword. In other dreams, it was Salos chasing him, and he was a child again, running for his life in the Darkwood. Throughout all his dreams, he felt eyes on him, as if he were being watched.

Suddenly, his surroundings blurred, and he found himself in a familiar chamber. "Greetings, little brother!" Lorthas said, beckoning him forward. "Come and join me by the fire."

Panicked, Dahr looked around, but the room was doorless. There was no way for him to escape. "Come, my friend," Lorthas beckoned, holding out a glass of wine. "There's nothing to fear here. You will find my company much more pleasant than the nightmares which have plagued your sleep."

"Why have you brought me here?" Dahr demanded, keeping his distance.

A tisking sound came from the far side of the room. "How sad," Lorthas said, shaking his head slowly. "I do you a service. I offer you an escape from your dreams, and you speak with such accusation in your voice. Is there no courtesy left in the world?"

"*You* expect courtesy?" Dahr scoffed. "You? The Darklord?"

"Ahhh, I see," said Lorthas. "An honorable person only has to be polite when dealing with other honorable people?" A mocking smile touched the Darklord's lips. "Is not how a person deals with his 'enemies' a better measure of honor? I am disappointed in you, little brother. Most disappointed."

"I am not your brother!" Dahr insisted, his voice nearly a growl. Reluctantly, not seeing any way out save by waking in the morning, he crossed the chamber and took a seat, but he refused the wine the Darklord offered. Hiding his fear, he glowered at Lorthas. "What do you want?"

The Darklord smiled. "To talk, little brother. I only wish to talk. Have you someplace else to be? Some other pressing engagement in the Twilight World?"

"I'd rather be anywhere than here with you," Dahr said, sounding more confident than he felt.

"Truly?" Lorthas asked, waving his hand casually. Behind him, a window materialized in the featureless stone. In it, Dahr saw himself running from a giant Elorn; the Guardsman's grim face split in a wide grin as he swung his sword. Dahr shuddered at the memory. "I thought not," Lorthas chuckled, allowing the window to vanish.

"You do me an injustice, Dahr," the Darklord added. "I have offered you no harm. Stay! We'll have a pleasant talk."

"It seems I have no choice," Dahr replied. "You can hold me here against my will, at least until I wake. Speak, Darklord. Tell your story."

"Not quite the response I was hoping for," the Darklord mused, "but I guess it will have to suffice." He set his glass upon the table and looked deep into Dahr's eyes. "I will tell you of my childhood," he said at last, and there was a note of hurt in his voice. "I think it is a story you will understand."

Lorthas pursed his lips, preparing himself. "I was born, approximately thirteen hundred winters before the Boundary was raised, to a flower seller in the city of Jule. I never knew my father; he was gone before my birth. My mother was a weak woman, beautiful in her own way, but sickly, with too romantic a heart. She offered herself to any man who caught her fancy, believing he would prove to be her one true love.

"In truth, most of her 'suitors' were very much like my father. They used her while they could, but left as soon as they discovered she was with child." Lorthas' eyes glinted. "Or after they got a good look at me."

Sighing, Lorthas sipped his wine. To Dahr's surprise, the Darklord seemed genuinely saddened by his tale. "By the time I was six, I had a handful of brothers and sisters. My mother did what she could, but was often ill and unable to work. Even as a child, it fell upon me to support my family.

"It was not easy, for reasons which are still quite apparent. My appearance is less than normal. I tried to sell flowers on the days when mother was too sick to work, but more people ran from me than looked at my wares."

Lorthas took a deep breath, allowed himself a moment to reflect on his past. "I was born prior to the Secession," he explained to Dahr. "Jule was in the heart of House Arkam, and Peitr Arkam, First of his House, was quietly preparing for war.

"His son, Roya, had been fostered in Kaper, under the tutelage of King Norin, and on Roya's infrequent journeys home, Peitr had noted a drastic change, a loss of ambition and a distinct disinterest in becoming King of Alrendria. He was convinced the Magi were involved.

"When Roya disappeared, and Norin announced that his daughter, Yurelle, would wed Makan, Peitr was furious. Makan of House Coryn would be King of Alrendria, a position Peitr knew his own son deserved. Again he suspected the Magi.

"In response to these events, Peitr fostered a hatred of magic in his lands, and though his commands had less effect in Jule, where one of the Mage Academies stood, he gained many supporters, supporters who shunned anything they believed to be of magic.

"Of course," mused Lorthas with a chuckle, "I had the Gift, but I didn't know it at the time. All I wanted was to feed my family." His eyes flashed red. "But I was hated. Hated and feared. People ran from my too pale skin, my 'demon eyes,' my strange, snow white hair.

"I was forced to sneak through the shadows, searching through refuse for food and clothes. At times I stole, but only when our need was great, and never without remorse."

Another smile spread across the Darklord's face. "You know how it is, Dahr. You were hated by the other slaves. You were feared–you *are* feared–because you're different. How many times did you steal when you escaped your enslavement? Did hunger not gnaw your bones until you felt you had no choice? If not for Aryn Odara, what kind of man would you have become? The kind and generous person you are, or something darker. Something crueler. You would have been a monster–"

"No!!!" Dahr screamed, sitting bolt upright. He found himself in his tents, surprised by the sudden change in location. In his mind, he thought he heard Lorthas' fading whisper. "We will speak more of this next time."

He did not know which he feared most: Lorthas' seemingly limitless knowledge of his life, the Darklord's ability to enter his dreams, or the Darklord himself.

When morning came, Dahr was still lying awake. He rose early, washing in the cold river water. The other Guardsmen were up by the time he returned to the camp. They rode northwest, following a tributary of the Danelle and leaving the great river behind.

The next few days passed slowly. The forests became broken, and the land more open. Small streams and creeks were abundant, their waters flowing south toward the Danelle. The plains teemed with animals, and the sky was constantly speckled with the shadows of birds. But there was still no sign of the Garun'ah.

One afternoon, eight days after Jasova found the remains of the Garun'ah family, Dahr rode ahead of the party, eager to be alone. He wondered where the Tribesmen could be. Nomads or not, they had traveled the plains of northern Madryn for days, and had seen only scattered signs of his people. He wondered if they had gone too far north, or not far enough.

Dismounting on top of a grassy hill, he waited for the others to catch up. Closing his eyes, he allowed the warmth of the sun to flow over him, suffuse him with its power. He felt at peace here, a peace he had not known during his time in Kaper. There was a freedom to the Tribal Lands that Dahr relished. He was not yet ready to return to his old life.

He heard the footsteps behind him, but did not turn his head. "What do you want, Elorn?" he asked quietly.

The Guardsman froze, as surprised that Dahr had heard him coming as he was that Dahr had known his identity. "How long will you keep us out here?" he asked in a hoarse whisper. "How long must we follow you through this barren waste in search of the Wildmen?"

Dahr took a deep, calming breath as he opened his eyes. Slowly, he turned and looked down at the stocky Guardsman. Elorn stared up at him defiantly. "There is nothing here!" he repeated. "No sign of your people."

"You may go whenever you wish," Dahr said, his voice like iron.

"I will not disobey my orders," Elorn replied stiffly.

"Then I will order you to leave, if that's what you want." Dahr tried to keep his temper under control. "I don't know what we'll encounter out here, Elorn, and I'd welcome your blade if it comes to a fight, but I won't have you stay if your heart is against it."

Elorn frowned as he considered Dahr's words. Finally, he shook his head. "I will not leave her."

"I can't blame you for that," Dahr replied. "For I wouldn't leave her either, were our places reversed." The others appeared in the distance, riding their horses slowly. "I don't want you as an enemy, Guardsman, but your behavior must change if we are to be friends."

Elorn nodded his head, a single curt bob. He started to turn, but Dahr put a restraining hand on his shoulder. "And Elorn," he said, waiting until the gruff Guardsman had turned back around. "If you ever belittle me or my people again," he growled, "I'll make you regret it."

Elorn's face tightened. "Yes, Commander," he said quietly before walking back to his horse.

"What was that about?" Katya asked after her horse cleared the top of the hill.

Dahr shrugged. "Elorn and I were just discussing which direction will most likely lead us to the Tribesmen."

Katya looked skeptical; her lips pursed together thoughtfully, but she said nothing as Dahr climbed back into his saddle. They rode for a while longer, stopping early, in the shadow of a large forest along the bank of a small stream. "We'll camp here tonight," Dahr announced, dropping down from his saddle.

They set up camp quickly and relaxed in the afternoon sun. Elorn disappeared as soon as his duties were finished, heading off into the forest alone. Vyrina prepared a stew, using venison from the previous day's hunt. As they sat around the fire eating, Katya told the other Guardsmen how she and Dahr had met. Dahr blushed at Katya's recounting of the events in the Dungeon; the redhead's retelling made Dahr sound much more the hero than he actually was.

The Guardsmen laughed at the story, and laughed even louder when they realized that Dahr was embarrassed by it. They sat around the campfire until late in the evening, sharing stories of their adventures. Jasova told them about the battles he fought against the Corsan raiders; Vyrina and Nykeal shared tales of their youth in Kaper, and of all the strange things they had seen in the city.

They retired to their tents early, but Dahr was restless. He tossed and turned in his bedrolls, afraid to sleep lest he encounter the Darklord again. After a while, he gave up on sleep and decided to take a walk. He left the camp, heading toward the thin trees of a nearby forest. The moon above was nearly full; it cast more than enough light to see.

Dahr picked a careful path through the woods, listening to the hooting of owls and the chirping of insects. As he strolled, his shoulders began to unknot, his breathing came more easily, and his eyes began to feel heavy. He was about to turn back toward the camp when a sudden flash of motion caught his attention. Crouching low, he strained to hear any sounds. Soft voices came to him, drifting softly on the cool night breezes.

Bent low, he crept from tree to tree, making as little sound as possible. He saw two shadowy forms ahead of him, and he crouched even lower, not wanting to be seen. He let out a sigh when he realized it was only Elorn and Katya.

"...just don't understand what you see in him," Elorn said, waving his arms expressively.

Katya was sitting on a log, and she threw her head back in exaggerated disgust. "You don't have to understand," she said wearily, as if this were not the first time she had said as much. "You just have to accept it."

Elorn's eyes were piercing and unrelenting. Finally, Katya sighed and said, "Dahr is honest. And just. And noble. He's a thousand other things besides, and each of those things makes me care for him."

When that did not seem answer enough, Katya's voice became almost pleading. "Elorn, you are my friend!" she said, standing and putting a comforting hand on his shoulder. "Don't make me choose between you and Dahr." Her tone left no doubt as to who would lose in such a scenario.

She shook her head suddenly. "But that's not the point!" she demanded, more hotly. "Your behavior is unbecoming in a Guardsman. Dahr is our leader! You will treat him as such."

Elorn let out a shuddering breath. His eyes were hurt, as if he had just been betrayed. "Jasova has already reminded me of my oaths," he said sullenly. "I had hoped not to hear the same lecture from you." He pushed Katya's hands away and stomped into the wood, his body trembling.

Katya was left alone in the clearing. She took a long, slow breath, and sat back on the log. Looking up at the sky, she massaged her temples. Dahr stepped out of the trees behind her, walked silently across the clearing, and put his own hands tenderly on her head. She stiffened minutely at his touch, but relaxed again almost instantly. "How long were you there?"

"Long enough," Dahr whispered. He smiled, though she could not see it. "You don't have to fight all my battles for me," he told her. "I can take care of Elorn myself."

"I know," she replied. "But it's my fault he hates you so."

"Not all your fault," Dahr responded. "There are other reasons, I think, that he has not shared with either of us."

"Perhaps you're–" Katya's words were cut off by a low growl, vicious and intense. Both their heads snapped to the right, and Katya's hand reached for the sword that was not sheathed at her side. Her eyes widened fearfully when the bear walked into the clearing, sniffing the air.

The beast was huge, covered in light brown fur. Despite its great size, it was thin, starved and frothing at the mouth, mad with hunger. Its ravenous brown eyes darted from left to right, scanned the clearing, and finally came to rest on Katya. It growled again, a deep, guttural sound which sent a shiver of fear through Dahr.

"Don't move," he whispered in a tight voice. The bear took one step toward Katya, then another. It crossed the clearing slowly, its eyes locked on her trembling form. Beneath his hands, Dahr felt her body tensing, preparing to run. "If you run, it will chase you," he warned her. "It is starving and will hunt you relentlessly." Her head tilted up marginally, and her eyes strained to meet his. "Wait for me to distract it. Then run."

Dahr took a slow step to his right, then a second, putting some distance between him and Katya. The bear saw, and followed him with its eyes. It sniffed the air again, then decided to ignore Dahr. It stalked toward Katya, saliva falling in streams from its jaws.

Katya tensed, and the bear, as if anticipating her flight, lunged forward faster than Dahr would have believed possible. It swiped its paw and Katya tumbled across the clearing, blood welling from her shoulder. The bear stood on its hind legs, roaring with anger. Upright, the creature was hands taller than Dahr, but he rushed forward, desperate to protect Katya.

The bear stepped forward, and Dahr hurtled across the clearing, letting out a cry of rage. He caught the bear by its massive arm, using his momentum to push the animal off balance. Together, they tumbled to the ground, the earth shaking with the force of their impact.

The beast roared again, flailing left and right, trying to crush its attacker. Dahr struggled to remain atop the animal, knowing that if the bear put its weight on him, he would be finished. With a mighty heave, the bear pushed itself to its feet and knocked Dahr to the ground. He rolled, but the bear was faster, striking a blow to his back with its sharp claws.

Dahr grunted in pain but rolled away and stood. The beast rushed in, roaring in anger. Dahr caught a claw in mid-strike, and struggled to keep the bear at bay. The bear pushed up onto its hind legs, swinging with its other claw. Dahr caught that one as well, and for a moment they were stalemated, arms locked in a desperate wrestling match.

The bear leaned in with all its weight, snapping its jaws fingers from Dahr's own face. Dahr trembled with the effort of holding the animal back. "Sure you don't want to reconsider this?" he grunted to the bear. "We may look filling, but I promise, we don't taste too good."

The bear growled in response, and Dahr dropped to one knee under the weight, struggling to keep the animal away. Behind him, Katya stirred, and Dahr called to her. "Run!" he said between clenched teeth. "I can't hold him much longer. Get away from here!"

"I won't leave you!" she called back, regaining her feet. She searched the ground, stooping to pick up a large, knotted stick. She swung the makeshift club back and forth, testing its weight.

"Go back to the others, Guardsman!" Dahr growled. "That's an order."

Tears filled her eyes, but she nodded and stepped away. The bear roared, leaning forward, and Dahr was pushed off balance. He fell to his back, the animal slavering above him. Katya screamed "No!" as the bear's maw lowered toward Dahr's unprotected throat.

Howls filled the night; dark shapes darted from the trees. The bear roared in pain. It thrashed, confused, facing attacks from all sides, and one claw landed square on Dahr's chest. He grunted in pain, swinging his own fist in retaliation. The bear howled and stepped back warily. The shadowy forms were relentless, dodging in and out of the shadows, striking the bear from every angle.

The bear was driven back slowly, and Dahr stood. He held one hand against his aching side and stared at the bear angrily. "GO!" he shouted, and the animal jumped. The shadowy forms stopped their attacks, but their growls echoed Dahr's own. The bear, outnumbered, let out one more plaintive roar and ran off, crashing loudly through the underbrush.

When the bear was gone, Dahr fell to his knees, gasping weakly. Katya was at his side in an instant, hugging him to her chest. "Are you crazy?" she asked. "What possessed you to do that?"

"Only way…" Dahr gasped between pained breaths, "Stop him… hurting you." She squeezed him tightly, and Dahr clung to her desperately. Bright eyes suddenly surrounded them, watching from the shadows. Katya gasped, afraid again, but Dahr put a comforting hand on her shoulder.

"It's all right," he said. Reaching out his other hand, he beckoned the animals forward. One stepped from the shadows, and Katya recognized the dogs they had encountered in the slavers camp.

"They followed you all this way?" she asked incredulously.

Dahr shrugged. "I guess so."

"Why?" she asked, her voice full of wonder.

Dahr laughed. "I don't know why, and to be honest, I don't care. If not for them...." He let the thought trail off unspoken. Katya shivered, clutching Dahr all the more tightly, and he hugged back, relieved that she had not been seriously injured. *If anything had happened to her...!* "I love you," he whispered under his breath.

She kissed him, forcefully, her fear feeding her passion. When they finally parted, she let out an explosive breath. "I love you, too, Dahr." Her fingers fumbled with the laces of his shirt, and Dahr tried to speak. He wanted to tell her how much she meant to him, how he had never felt as alive as when she was near, how she was one of only a few he trusted completely.

Words failed him, and he surrendered to the fire burning within him. Growling with pleasure, he lowered her to the ground, pulling hungrily at her shirt. The dogs, silent but for their breathing, stepped into the shadows to guard their new master.

Chapter 14

Martyn groaned as he opened his eyes, wincing at the light. He was back in the Emperor's Palace, though he had no memory of how he had gotten there. He struggled to sit up, surprised by how much effort it took to move. He looked around, noticing that he was not in his chambers. He went to stand, but a jarring pain shot through his right leg. He fell upon the bed, lights flashing before his eyes. Sucking in breath after breath, he waited for the pain to go away.

He looked at his leg, but saw nothing wrong. Tenderly, he pressed on his thigh, slowly working his hand down; as he neared his knee, he felt an ache. He went to run his hand through his hair and was once again surprised, this time by the thick bandages wrapped around his head.

Confused, Martyn tried to remember what had happened. Slowly, the pieces began to fall together. The bar. The fight. Getting thrown over the railing. With Martyn's understanding came an equally strong sense of relief. He wondered how he had ever survived the fall.

"So," called a familiar voice, "you decided to wake after all." Charylla stepped toward him, holding a lantern in one hand. Martyn winced at the bright light. Squinting, he watched as the Aelvin Princess set the lantern on a nearby table and began to check his bandages.

"What do you mean?" he asked, looking around in confusion. "How long have I been here?"

The princess did not answer immediately. She continued her ministrations without even acknowledging Martyn's question. Suddenly, her eyes grew distant. A chill passed through Martyn, starting in his head and legs, but quickly spreading through the rest of his body. His breath came in quick gasps, and he shivered despite his attempt not to.

As quickly as it had begun, the sensation disappeared, and Charylla stepped back, appraising the prince. "You will heal, Prince Martyn," she told him. "Though I believe your leg will be tender for a few days more." She reached behind her and grabbed an ornate cane, which she offered to him. "Use this until your knee stops aching. It will speed the recovery."

Martyn accepted the cane, finely-crafted oak, with a steel tip and an ornate handle, carved to look like a cat's head. "Thank you," he said absently, studying the gift intently. With a start, he lifted himself from his stupor and looked into Charylla's eyes. "How long have I been here?"

"You have been in this room for a day," she responded, her lips twisting up in a small smile. "But it has been nearly ten since your fall." Charylla turned around again, walking to the table that held the lantern. When she returned, she carried a tall glass of water, which she offered to the prince. He took it, drinking thirstily.

"Ten days?" he repeated, amazed. He coughed, and each exhalation sent a jolt of pain through his head. Clutching the edge of the bed, trying desperately to maintain his balance, he asked, "How? That is... What happened? How did–"

"How did you survive?" Charylla finished for him. "It is said that Valia protects the foolish." When that answer did not seem to appease the prince, she stated matter-of-factly, "You nearly fell to your death, but knocking yourself senseless on the railing probably saved you."

Martyn shook his head. "I don't understand."

"I will explain," she replied, with a hint of exasperation, "if you give me a moment." After refilling Martyn's glass, Charylla pulled over a chair and sat at his side. "You hit your head on the railing as you fell, which knocked you unconscious. Had you remained alert, you likely would have been tense from fear, and the fall would have killed you." Martyn blanched at the mere thought of falling all that distance to the ground.

"During your fall," the princess added, "you hit a branch several levels down. Hitting that branch deflected you toward the tree, and you landed on one of the lower platforms. Barely." Charylla held her hands about four hands apart, illustrating how close Martyn had been to the edge. "A little more to your right and you would have missed it entirely."

More memories flooded back to him. "What about the fire?"

Charylla seemed surprised by his worry, but her eyes hardened at the statement. "It was brought under control," she said. "Luckily, for both you and the city, an *Ael Maulle* was nearby." She beckoned to the doorway, and an old Elf stepped inside.

"He has checked on you every day since then," Charylla explained, bowing her head to the Elf. "*Ael Maulle* are often protective of those they have healed."

The Elf stepped forward, hobbling across the room. He stopped beside the bed and bowed his head, if only slightly, and looked at Martyn for a long moment. In a quiet, raspy voice, he said. "Good thing it was that I was near. Would have been better for you, though, were my Healing stronger, but my skills lie elsewhere."

"Baerael came running when he saw the flames," Charylla explained, though Martyn could not imagine this withered, old Elf moving any faster than a crawl. "He quenched the fire before it spread to the other levels, then found you four levels below, comatose and on the verge of death. He healed you as best he could and kept you stable until they brought you to me."

"I thank you, Baerael," came Martyn's polite reply.

The old Elf dipped his head again; a smile spread across his wrinkled face. "*Ael Maulle* take their duties seriously, little Human," he replied. "It is Valia's will that we preserve life whenever possible."

"Whether in service of the Goddess," Martyn laughed, though the effort sent a wave of dizziness through him, "or for some other reason, I thank you nonetheless." Baerael bowed again and shuffled out the door.

After the old Elf had gone, Charylla turned her attention back on Martyn. "I do not know who to be more angry with," she said sternly. "You or Treloran. I expect better conduct of you both. You are not common soldiers, no matter what you may wish to be. You are leaders of your people and should conduct yourself accordingly."

"The soldiers, the merchants, even the servants are who give us our power," Martyn replied, reciting a speech his father had made on numerous occasions. "To lead, a ruler must understand his people. To stay in power, a people must respect their ruler. Our powers as kings or emperors do not come from the Gods, no matter what we might like to believe. Our power comes from the people."

Charylla stared at him for a long moment before speaking. "Wise words, for one so young."

"The wisdom belongs to my father," Martyn admitted. "Though I hope in time to see things as clearly as he does."

"Nevertheless," Charylla said, her tone growing more lecturing, "a ruler must behave with more dignity than commoners. He must be a leader to his people. An example." Her eyes flashed angrily. "You, I have no control over, but my son will learn his place in the world." She stilled her rising anger, and a thin smile spread across her face. "I believe Lord Iban wishes to have a few words with you once you are recovered."

Martyn winced at the Guard Commander's name. He did not look forward to the lecture he knew he would receive. For an instant, he wished he and Treloran could switch places, believing that nothing the Aelvin Princess could say would be worse than Iban's wrath. Then, with another look at Charylla's barely-controlled rage, he changed his mind again.

Charylla stood to leave, pushing her chair back to the wall. "Princess!" Martyn called before she left the chamber. She turned around, looking at him expectantly. "Treloran is not at fault for the other night. Your son tried to stop me from fighting. He warned me that jousting was dangerous and foolish. He only joined the game to even the odds and should not be held accountable because the Prince of Alrendria is a stubborn fool."

After a moment's silence, a genuine smile replaced Charylla's cold one. "Thank you, Martyn. I would regret accusing my son of things for which he was not responsible." Then, her lips pursed together thoughtfully. "But there are matters other than the other night I need to discuss with Treloran."

She went to the door, stopping on the threshold. "You need rest, Prince Martyn," she said with a hint of concern. "I am an adequate Healer, but the healing took a great deal of energy from the both of us. You will live, without even a scar to remember your foolishness, but you will be easily exhaustible for the next ten days."

The Elf's eyes glinted mischievously. "Sleep, Prince of Alrendria," she said as she left the room, and Martyn felt his eyes grow heavy. He dropped almost instantly into sleep, wondering if Charylla had used her Gift on him, or if he were simply exhausted.

When next he woke, the light outside the room's only window was dying. Again, Martyn struggled to rise, this time with much less pain than before. He took a step and nearly fell, remembering too late that he needed the aid of a crutch. He looked around, spying the cane Charylla had given him against the table near the bed.

He grabbed it and practiced using it, hobbling around his room in a circle. The pain was not terrible, but every step with his right leg sent a shock through his body, and he kept his eyes closed in anticipation much of the time.

"Are you practicing for a race?" Jeran asked from the doorway, laughing. "I saw some old Elves the other day, walking around with canes just like that one." He looked at Martyn appraisingly. "I think you have a fair chance of winning."

Martyn blushed at Jeran's joke as he hobbled back to the bed. "Glad you finally decided to visit."

"You know how it is," Jeran replied. "Places to go. People to see. Wars to fight." He laughed again, taking a seat beside the prince on Martyn's feather-filled bed. "I've stopped by to see you every day!" he exclaimed, feigning an angered expression. "And twice this afternoon! Until now, you never had enough decency to be awake."

This time, Martyn laughed along with Jeran. "You sound well," Jeran said. "And look pretty good too, considering the fall you took." Jeran shook his head and let out a relieved sigh. "You're very lucky, Martyn."

"You have no idea!" the prince returned, and launched into a retelling of his story. Jeran listened in silence as Martyn recounted the events following Jeran's sudden departure from the archery range.

"Amazing," Jeran said when the prince was finished. "We'll have to try jousting when we return to Kaper. It would be good for the Guardsmen." Smiling, he added, "Though I think we'll keep the beams near the ground."

They laughed together, and Martyn asked what Jeran had been doing since his accident. "The Emperor has me very busy," Jeran said, his voice dropping to a near whisper. "When we aren't discussing the Durange and the Darklord, he's helping me train my Gift. He's also showing me how to control the Readings."

"That doesn't sound like a lot of fun," Martyn said.

"It has its moments," replied Jeran. "There are times when it's difficult, and I wish I could be doing just about anything else. But it's something I need to learn. If I can't control my Gift, I'll eventually hurt somebody with it.

"Besides," Jeran shrugged, "the Emperor is a lax taskmaster. If I want an afternoon or evening free, I have only to ask him, and he arranges it."

Martyn smiled. "Then make sure the Emperor knows you will not be there five days hence," he ordered. "Once my leg heals, I'll want to celebrate!"

Jeran laughed again. "Perhaps we should keep you away from the bars, my Prince," he said seriously. "You have a nasty habit of getting into trouble at those places." Jeran stood and stepped away from the bed. "Come on!" he said, beckoning for Martyn join him. "Your leg will never heal just sitting around. Let's walk."

Martyn shook his head fervently. The idea of hobbling around the hallways where everyone could see his infirmity did not appeal to him, but Jeran waved him forward again. "It would do the Guardsmen good to see you up and about. Many feel that they are to blame for your injury, that at least one of them should have been near."

Sighing in defeat, Martyn hefted himself up, wincing as he put weight on his injured leg. Tightening his grip on the cane, he walked slowly toward Jeran, trying his best to hide his limp. Smiling, Jeran led him from the room and walked beside him through the palace's winding passages.

The prince had been housed near the Alrendrian Guard, on the ground level of the palace. Though not a far walk, Martyn could only manage a slow pace, and it took quite some time to cover the distance. At first, walking was agony, but as his muscles limbered, the pain in the prince's leg faded to a dull ache. Though he would never admit it, Martyn was glad that Jeran had forced him to leave his bedchamber.

Word of their coming preceded them through the halls. Guardsmen by the score turned out to see their prince. They saluted him as he passed, calling out warm greetings. Martyn returned the salutes, not the easiest maneuver with his arm grasping the cane, and he greeted the Guardsmen by name, remembering another of his father's many lectures.

"The Guard are your sword and shield," Mathis had once told him. "Much more important than the weapons at your side. It's their duty to ensure your safety; it's their loyalty that protects you and Alrendria. But like any weapon, they're useless if not cared for. Show the Guardsmen that you care for their well-being, show them you're as loyal to them as they are to you, and you'll have an unstoppable weapon at your disposal. Neglect them, and they'll fall apart."

His father's lectures, so boring when he was forced to listen to them, had been coming back to him more often of late. The words made more sense to him now, and he could see the wisdom that the King had tried so hard to share with him. Martyn was suddenly anxious to return to Kaper, to tell his father that he finally understood, and to thank him for his patience.

Willym, the ranger, stepped into the hall before them. "Glad to see you're well, Prince Martyn," he said, smiling. "Takes more than a little tumble to kill a good ranger." The other Guardsmen laughed at the older man's words, calling out their assent. "We're honored that you visit us, despite your injury."

"It's my injury that brings me here," Martyn said, and a hush fell over the Guardsmen. Fearful of rebuke, or perhaps just expecting it, they wait-ed at attention for Martyn to continue. "I want the Guard to know that they're in no way responsible for my accident." He spoke loud enough that all could hear his words. "Your prince took on a bit more than he could handle and suffered the consequences. The Elves taught me a lesson, and my own foolishness sent me over the edge of that platform."

"That's not the way I heard it!" cried Pylias.

Raeghit nodded. "Word is that you and the Elf Prince were the ones did the teaching."

"Took out three of their best warriors, you did," added Braltur. "With only a couple of bruises between you."

"I heard that the fire blocked off the only exit," said Quellas, a thin-faced Guardsman from the Davinshier Family, part of House Menglor. "When you saw the flames spreading, you jumped down to the next plat-form to find help."

Martyn stared wide-eyed as the Guardsmen related their version of the events. Jeran watched, a wry smile twisting his lips. The prince glared at Jeran, but he laughed along with the Guardsmen, insisting that things did not happen quite the way they described them. Finally, he waved his hands for silence. "Enough!" he called out, laughing. "I thank you for raising my spirits! And my self-esteem! But I'm not an invincible warrior. Besides, if I were, what use would I have for the Guard?"

That silenced the Guardsmen. Martyn smiled, knowing he had them now. "I'd hate to put the lot of you out of work, forcing you to return to the farms and smithies from which you came."

A quiet murmur spread among the warriors. "Lucky it is that you *do* have need of the Guard," Willym said, clapping the prince fondly on the shoulder. "I have no desire to return to my father's mill, and I've been gone a score and a half winters!" The other Guardsmen added their agreement.

Slowly, the warriors returned to their duties, and Martyn turned around, starting back toward his room. "You knew?" he asked Jeran accusatorially.

Jeran laughed. "I heard a few of the stories," he admitted, trying to hide his smile. "I thought hearing about your prowess would speed your recovery. You always did like it when people said good things about you."

Martyn wrinkled his face in mock anger, forcing an evil glare at his friend. They walked in silence through the halls for some time, Martyn's thoughts distant. He thought on the events of the last few days, and the words he had shared with Treloran, and his mood grew pensive. "What do you think she'll be like?"

"Who?" came Jeran's confused response.

"Miriam," replied Martyn. "Princess of Gilead. The girl I'm to marry."

Jeran looked at the prince thoughtfully. "I don't know, Martyn," he admitted. "I've heard her described as beautiful, with long blonde hair and piercing blue eyes. But I have no idea if those words were true, nor do I know what lies beneath her surface." Martyn nodded sadly. "Why are you thinking about this now?"

"Treloran and I spoke of the duties of kings," Martyn told him. "It seems like we have few choices. Most of our decisions are made for us." He looked at Jeran for a long time. "You're lucky, you know. If you marry, you'll marry for love."

"First Seats often marry politically," Jeran pointed out.

"But they don't have to," Martyn returned. "House Odara is strong. A political marriage would not hurt you, but should you decide to marry for love, it won't cost you much, and it will cost Alrendria less." The prince shook his head angrily. "That's what angers me the most," he said at last. "Not that I have to marry Miriam for the sake of Alrendria, but that the choice is not mine."

Jeran stopped Martyn by putting a hand on his shoulder. "My uncle used to say that duty weighs heavily on the soul, and that honor was as much a curse as a blessing." Jeran squeezed the prince's shoulder comfortingly. "He also said that we always have a choice. Some choices are easy, and some choices are not, but the choice is always there."

Martyn looked at him blankly. Finally, Jeran said, "You could refuse to marry Miriam."

"What?" came Martyn's startled reply. "Jeran, you must be crazy. Have you forgotten what we're facing? *Who* we're facing. We need alliance with Gilead more than anything. If the cost of that alliance is my marriage to Miriam, then I have to do it."

Jeran smiled. "Then it seems like you've already made your choice." Martyn frowned, considering Jeran's words. "Uncle Aryn told me that we must sometimes choose paths we don't like. Honor often dictates what choice we make, but it can't force us to like those choices."

They stood in silence for a long time. "Your uncle was very wise."

"No wiser than your father," Jeran replied. "After all, they had the same teachers."

"The Tigers of Alrendria!" called a voice down the hall. "Well met!"

"Astalian!" Martyn said excitedly, looking up. The Aelvin warrior walked toward them, taking long, confident strides. He wore long, brown pants and a dark green shirt, his blonde hair pulled away from his face. A faded, yellow-brown ring, a memento from the joust, circled his left eye. "Martyn, it is good to see you up and about. You look much better then when we last parted company!"

"I feel much better," Martyn admitted. "But it seems that I wasn't the only one to take a fall that night." With a sly smile, he pointed at the Aelvin warrior's eye.

Astalian touched his wound tenderly, flinching in memory of the pain. "A lucky blow! Not enough to drop me from the planks." He clapped an arm around Martyn's shoulder. "We would have won, if not for your fall. I tell you, I nearly went mad when you dropped from sight. I thought the lot of us were going to be put to death for killing the Prince of Alrendria." He laughed suddenly. "That is, if we managed to survive the fire."

Astalian's eyes shifted to Jeran, and the Elf looked him up and down appraisingly. "You must be Lord Odara." As Martyn made the introductions, Astalian's smile broadened. "Well met, Jeran!" he said in an amicable tone, clapping him on the shoulder. "Word of your skill precedes you. I heard how you bested Luran in the wood, and Treloran himself has praised your bowcraft."

The Elf laughed boisterously. "It is rare for Treloran to praise anything!" he added. "So you should take extra stock in the words."

Jeran blushed at the Elf's praise. "I didn't want to fight Luran. He left me no choice."

"Luran rarely does," apologized Astalian. "It was time someone put him in his place. I will lose little sleep over his disgrace." The Aelvin warrior laughed again. "Perhaps next time he will not be so quick to shout 'dishonor.' "

"Perhaps," Jeran agreed. He studied Astalian carefully, inspecting the Elf from head to foot. "And you're the mighty Astalian?"

"None other," came the confident, slightly accented reply.

"I've heard of you," Jeran said. "Many of the Elves speak your name. It is said that you're the greatest of the Aelvin warriors."

Astalian bowed his head formally. "Humility dictates that I refuse such grand praise." The hallway echoed with bold laugher as he added, "But who am I to argue with the words of my own people?" Jeran and Martyn laughed along with the Elf.

Astalian's eyes narrowed, and he returned Jeran's measuring gaze. "Perhaps you would not mind crossing blades with *me* someday." An eager grin spread across his face. "I would welcome the challenge."

"So long as it's a friendly bout," Jeran replied. "I don't want to wager my honor again."

"A friendly duel then," Astalian agreed. "Whenever you wish it." He looked back and forth between the two. "You are well?" he asked, but continued before the prince could answer. "We should celebrate! You have the Goddess' favor, Martyn. Only She could have saved you from death."

Martyn clutched his bandaged head. "I wish she had saved me a bit more gently."

They laughed again, and Astalian inserted himself between the two of them, hooking one arm around each of their shoulders. "I will have a bottle of *brandei* brought to my rooms!" he told them. "We will drink to our people's health and well being!"

Martyn waved the Elf away. "Not tonight, Astalian!" he laughed. "I have but this very day regained my senses, and I'm not eager to lose them again so quickly."

"I, too, must beg your leave, friend," said Jeran. "The Emperor has requested my presence."

Astalian's eyes looked hurt, and he lowered his gaze to the ground. "In five days time," Martyn said hastily, "when my leg is fully restored, Jeran and I will celebrate my recovery. You should join us!"

The Elf's sadness melted away. "Agreed!" he said with fervor. "We will toast to your health and to Valia's wisdom until the Goddess herself comes and asks us to stop!" His eyes danced merrily, and he smirked. "I will even see if I can convince Treloran to join us in our prayers!" Laughing, he clapped them on the shoulders, bid them farewell, and hurried down the hall.

They watched him go, and once the Elf had disappeared, Jeran put his head in his hands and wept. "The Five Gods have forsaken me!" he lamented dramatically. "There are two of them! The Elves have a Prince Martyn too!"

Martyn, confused at first by Jeran's reaction, now stared at his friend with mock anger. Jeran's sobs turned into laughter as he looked at the prince. Shaking his head, Martyn shifted his grip on his cane and started walking again. It was not long before they reached his rooms.

They pushed open the doors laughing, but silence immediately fell over them. Lord Iban sat in the chair next to the bed, staring at the door. His face was expressionless, his eyes stony.

"Lor... Lord Iban," Martyn stammered. "We just went to visit the Guardsmen. Jeran thought it would be wise if they saw me whole and healthy." He looked guiltily at the cane. "Well, almost healthy."

Iban's expression did not change. "Every now and then Lord Odara has a good idea." It was impossible to tell if the Guard Commander thought this was one of them. To Jeran, he said, "Leave us. I wish to speak with the prince." His eyes flashing, he quickly added, "But I will see you on the morrow. It has been a while since our last talk."

Jeran nodded quickly and turned toward Martyn. "I must meet with the Emperor anyway," he said, offering the prince a comforting look. Stifling a yawn, he said, "And I'm quite tired."

"Get your sleep, Jeran," Martyn said as his friend left the room. "You'll need it!" After the door shut, Martyn turned to face Iban. "I suppose you're here to tell me what a fool I am."

"I suppose you will claim that you're not a child, and that you're old enough to make your own decisions. You might also say that accidents happen, and had the entire Alrendrian Guard been on that platform, there would have been nothing they could have done." Iban's face betrayed no emotion; his words were icy, cold, and unfeeling. A shiver ran down Martyn's spine.

"Maybe you will claim the Gods' will cannot be thwarted," Iban continued, exhaling harshly. "And maybe you will say no harm was done. You are alive and well, and we should put this whole thing behind us."

He looked Martyn up and down. "Or do you have a different excuse you wish to use?" he asked, his disappointment evident in the way he shook his head. "How many bar fights is the Prince of Alrendria going to be in before he learns his lesson?" Iban cast his eyes skyward as if expecting the Gods to answer.

"It's not what you think–" Martyn started, but a glare from the Guard Commander silenced him. Steeling himself, he started again. "It was not a brawl," he insisted, meeting Iban's stare defiantly. "It was a joust. A game the Aelvin warriors play. The fire and the fall were accidents, though in hindsight, we should have placed the planks near the center of the platform."

Iban was silent for a long while. "A game," he mused to himself. "Is your life a game as well, Martyn?" Iban stood and paced the floor. "One attempt has already been made on your life. Perhaps two."

"Two?" asked Martyn, confused by the warrior's statement. "My fall was not a clever ploy, no matter what you may believe! If one of the Elves in that bar had wanted me dead, there were better opportunities than during the joust."

Iban folded his hands and pressed them against his mouth. "You're too valuable to Alrendria to risk your life so carelessly," he said in a low growl. "From now on, you will not leave the palace without an escort."

"I am not a child," Martyn snapped.

"No," returned Iban. "You are the Prince of Alrendria. Start acting like it."

Martyn frowned, but did not speak. He took a deep breath to calm himself and said, "You're right, of course, Lord Iban. My apologies. I will allow a Guardsman to accompany me."

"Five."

"Two," the prince replied with a smile. "With Prince Treloran more or less always at my side, that makes four of us. Besides, even if they aren't seen, Treloran must have guards of his own."

"We are not merchants, Martyn, to be haggling over the number of your guards." Iban met the prince's gaze, but Martyn would not back down. Finally, the Guard Commander nodded. "Two," he said gruffly. "But two of my choosing."

"And only when I leave the palace," Martyn insisted. "Within its walls, I'm to be allowed my privacy."

"You drive a hard bargain, my Prince," Iban returned, but a small smile spread across his face.

"How fare the negotiations?" Martyn asked, hastening to change the subject.

"Not much has happened since your injury," Iban informed him, then began to elaborate. As evening faded to night, the old warrior filled Martyn in on the happenings of the last ten days, pausing periodically to ask the prince probing questions, and forcing him to see details he would have missed on his own.

As Iban said, little had been accomplished since the prince's accident. Most of the time had been spent listening to Rafel argue with Luran's replacement, Horeish, who shared the *Hohe Chatorra*'s dislike for Humans. Their discussions had become heated on numerous occasions, forcing Charylla and Iban to intervene, ordering both delegates to silence.

Iban asked for Martyn's assessment of the Elves, then cued the prince in on his own interpretation, surprising Martyn with the complexity of his thought. If he had any doubts about Iban's qualifications as a diplomat, they were dispelled by their conversation.

It was late in the night when Iban left, instructing Martyn to be early to the meeting tomorrow. "It would be a boon to us were you present. Tensions have been strained since your fall."

"I'll be there," Martyn assured him, and Iban saluted, bowed his head with a small smile, and turned away. Martyn did not watch him leave. Instead, he went to the bed and gathered his belongings, intent on returning to his own chambers. The door shut with a bang at Iban's departure.

He tied his clothes in a bundle and walked to the washstand, facing the mirror. Slowly, he undid the bandages around his head, fearful of what he would find. He winced as the last bandage came undone, and the welt became visible. It was a huge knot, swollen and tender, yet it seemed to be healing nicely, the color almost normal. He touched it gingerly, glad to discover that it did not pain him much. He supposed he owed Charylla thanks for his speedy recovery.

"That is a nasty wound, Human," said a familiar voice. "Did that happen during the joust, or when you tried to fly back to the palace?"

Martyn turned, smiling when he saw the Elf from the other night. She no longer wore green leathers, but a dress of white, cut to accentuate her thin, lithe figure. Martyn's pulse raced as he looked at her. His eyes roved over the gentle swell of her breast, the tender curve of her hips. "Truth be told, Lady Elf, I don't remember much of the evening. I'm told my injuries are a result of the fall."

She took a step into the room. "You fight well," she said, "for a Human."

Martyn laughed. "Then we're even, since you fight well for an Elf."

She looked at the pile of clothes on the bed. "You are going somewhere?"

He nodded. "I wish to return to my chambers." He looked around the tiny, spartan compartment. "These rooms are not to my liking." In a friendlier voice, he added, "My name is Martyn."

The Elf blushed suddenly, though Martyn did not understand why. "I am called Kaeille," she said, casting her eyes to the floor. "Would you like some company while you walk to your chambers?"

Martyn laughed, "My Lady Kaeille," he said, offering his best smile, "I can think of nothing more enjoyable than another evening in your company." Her cheeks turned bright crimson, and Martyn had a hard time reconciling the shy girl before him with the tempestuous warrior he had met the other night.

Grabbing his things, he walked toward her, his arm extended. As an afterthought, he added, "But let's stay on the ground this time." She smiled and cautiously took his arm. Together, they walked from the chamber.

Chapter 15

Jeran walked down a smooth, stone-covered path, looking in marvel at the beautiful flowers that dotted the trail. To either side, the Great Trees towered over him, casting shadows over most of what he could see. The scents of roses and honey, and the clean odor of spring, drifted to him on the gentle breeze.

He breathed slowly, relishing the quiet and peace. His days had been long and tiring. The Emperor was a zealous teacher who pushed Jeran to the limit of his abilities, and recently, his nights had been long and sleepless, which only added to his tension. News of Martyn's injury had shaken him badly, and Jeran had spent most of every night at his friend's side. When Elierian cornered him the day before to inform him that the prince had regained consciousness, he had felt as if a great weight had been lifted off his chest.

Martyn, despite his wounds, seemed in good spirits, and Jeran was certain the prince would fully recover. He could finally relax and let life return to normal. Since the prince's fall, Jeran had found concentrating all but impossible. As a consequence, he had been shirking his responsibilities, exploring Lynnaei or lounging in the soft grass of the Vale with the Emperor.

Jeran picked up his pace and began to whistle, a merry tune to accompany his mood. Ahead, the trail branched; one fork headed north, the other east. He stopped, bending to sniff the purple, star-shaped flowers growing in the triangle between the two trails. Standing, he looked at the bright blue sky, watching the giant, puffy clouds drift past. Scratching his chin, he pondered which path to take. After a moment of deliberation, he turned north, but made it little more than a step.

"No!" called a quiet voice. "That's the wrong way. Go this way!" Jeran turned, surprised that he was not alone. An Elf sat a little ways down the eastern path. Her fingers danced across the strings of a lyre, deftly tuning the instrument. She smiled at Jeran when he looked at her.

"What's down that path?" he asked, lifting himself onto the balls of his feet to peer down the trail.

The Elf shrugged. "I do not know," she admitted with a shake of her head. "But that is the way you should go." Finished adjusting her instrument, she lifted it to her chest to test the cords. Sweet notes sprang from the lyre. Satisfied, the Elf began to play, a hauntingly beautiful melody that tugged at Jeran's heart.

He listened to her for a time, then turned down the path she had indicated. He walked silently, listening to the song fade behind him. When the last note died, he quickened his pace, eager to see where the trail led.

He went over hills, past sites of incredible beauty, until another fork appeared before him. He paused again, looking from one trail to the other, deciding at last to take the left fork. He only managed a handful of steps before another voice called out to him.

"Where are you going, Jeran?" asked Jes' musical voice. He turned to face her, surprised that she had found him. Jes wore a gown of gossamer white that shimmered in the afternoon light. A train of lace ran behind it, and the sleeves were likewise adorned with silky, diaphanous material. The wind caught the lace, billowing it in gentle, graceful waves.

Jes' curly, black hair hung loose, falling to the middle of her back. Her milk white skin was smooth and unblemished; her blue eyes, usually so forbidding, appeared warm and friendly. Jeran's pulse quickened at the sight of her, and he forced himself to calm. "I'm just out for a walk," he said, pointing a finger down the left path. "I was going to go that way. Would you care to join me?"

She smiled, and Jeran felt his heart melt. "I'd love to walk with you, Jeran," she replied, striding toward him. "But you're going the wrong way. Let's take this path." She gestured to the right and walked toward the other trail, not waiting for Jeran to follow.

He hurried to catch her, offering his arm, and she took it with a grateful smile. Arm in arm, they walked down the path, sharing the beauties of the Aelvin wood. Birds flew by, only hands from their heads, and one landed on the ground at Jeran's feet. It stared up at him, almost expectantly, bobbing its head slightly and hopping from one foot to the other. Jeran pointed it out to Jes, and she laughed at its antics. They walked on, careful to step around the playful creature.

They did not speak. Jeran did not think he could have, even if he wanted to. He spent as much time looking at Jes as he did the scenery. The warmth flowing from her was even more enticing than the wonders of Illendrylla. She caught him staring at her once, and his face flushed red in embarrassment. Jes gripped his hand comfortingly, but said nothing, smiling fondly.

They neared another split in the trail; this time, paths radiated in all directions. In the center of the crossroads stood a statue, a spire of black and white marble with a sundial atop. They approached the tower from the south, on the largest of the paths. To the north, east, and west ran other broad avenues, though none quite so wide as the one they currently walked. Interspersed between the larger paths were scores of smaller trails, snaking off in every direction imaginable.

"Which way do I go now?" Jeran asked, looking around in confusion.

Jes shook her head and laughed, as if Jeran had made a joke. "Why, we go this way, of course," she replied, turning to the right and heading toward the eastern trail. Jeran did not immediately follow. He looked down each path in turn, and studied the statue rising in front of him.

When he did not join her, Jes turned to face him. Putting her hands on her hips, she asked, "Are you coming or not?" Jeran thought he detected the tiniest hint of irritation in her tone.

Sighing, he started toward her. "That's the wrong way, Jeran," called another voice.

Jeran craned his neck around, his eyes widening when the Emperor stepped from the trees. "What are you doing out here, Grandfather?" he asked, no longer uneasy calling the Aelvin Emperor by such a familiar name.

"I'm here to show you the way," said the thin, raspy voice. The Emperor walked north, beckoning Jeran to follow. Jeran took a step toward the old Elf, then turned to look at Jes, who now stared at him with unhidden annoyance.

Biting his lip, he took another step toward the Emperor. "This is the way you should go," Jes said, her voice sweet, almost lyrical.

"No, no, my boy," the Emperor argued. "This is the correct path."

Jeran stood between the two, not sure which way he should go. He walked toward Jes, hesitated, then turned and started back toward the Emperor. A third voice stopped him in his tracks. "Odara!" it called sharply, and Jeran whirled to face Lord Iban. The Guard Commander wore full battle armor and had his sword sheathed at his side. "Where do you think you're going? This isn't a game! Come with me this instant."

Iban stomped down a path that twisted to the southeast. He went nearly fifteen paces before turning around. When he saw that Jeran was not following, his eyes flashed dangerously. More confused than ever, Jeran licked his lips, then headed in the direction Iban was pointing.

"That would be a mistake, Lord Odara," Charylla said from the northeast. "This is the way you should go." The Aelvin Princess was dressed in thick, green robes and had a crown of gold woven through her elaborately-coiffed hair. She beckoned to him.

"My granddaughter forgets her place," the Emperor said to Jeran. "They all forget who is Emperor of the Forest. Follow me." he said again, leaning heavily on an oaken staff.

"Why would you want to follow an old man like him?" asked Alynna, her lips pursed together in the semblance of a pout. She wore a sheer, red dress, not dissimilar to the one she had worn to his chambers. It was half unlaced, and a generous amount of white cleavage was visible between the folds of cloth. "Come with me, Jeran," she beckoned seductively. "I guarantee that your time will be much better spent in my company."

"You would follow a slip of a girl like her?" asked Jes, her voice hurt. "What of me, Jeran? Have you no desire to learn what I can teach you?" Tears filled her eyes, and she tried to blink it away.

"You will come with me," said King Mathis, dressed in his most regal attire: a shirt emblazoned with the Rising Sun of Alrendria, a white cape similarly marked, and a crown of gold around his head. The King looked at Jeran expectantly. "Duty demands it," he added, starting down a path to the northwest.

"The Child of the Great Eagle should come with me," said a Garun'ah warrior, dressed in tanned hides, his neck encircled with beads. "The Tsha'ma have the answers he seeks." The Tribesman's smile was knowing, confident. "The cub will follow us."

Jeran spun in slow circle, not knowing which way to go. Around him, voices called, each demanding that he follow the path they chose. He put his hands to his head, not wanting to refuse any of them. Wanting to refuse them all.

Alynna, her lips pressed together, stretched out an arm toward him, her eyes inviting. Jes fought both tears and anger as she watched him, hands on hips. The Emperor stared at him confidently, knowing his would be the path that Jeran chose. Iban drew his sword, threatening with steel when words were ineffective. King Mathis looked betrayed; his haunted eyes lowered to the ground.

"I don't want your paths!" Jeran called out suddenly. "I want to choose my own way!"

"Then choose, Jeran," whispered a voice. "Choose, Lord Odara," whispered another. Around him, voices whispered. "Choose… Choose…."

The Emperor suddenly laughed. "Which of our paths do you choose?"

"I don't want your paths!" Jeran repeated, "I want my own!"

Laughter came back to him from every direction. "Your own path!" sneered Luran. "Are you even smart enough to find your own path, Human?" The Aelvin warrior spat on the ground. "You know I do not like you, so you know I would not coddle you. Follow me, boy, and I will show you the right way."

The voices continued, inexhaustible, inexorable. "This way, Jeran…."

"Follow me, Jeran."

"Do you not find what I offer desirable?"

"Trust in my wisdom, Jeran. I have seen a great many winters."

Jeran pressed his hands over his eyes, squeezing them tightly closed. Staggering under the onslaught of voices, he dropped to his knees. "Must I follow one of you?" he whispered.

"Do not waver, Jeran," called a new voice. "You are right to want to choose your own path." Jeran opened his eyes to look at the new speaker. The man, dressed in long, brown robes tied at the waist with a belt of golden rope, seemed familiar to him. Black, shoulder-length hair hung loose, and the man stared at Jeran with sky blue eyes.

Recognition came to him. "You!" Jeran exclaimed. "You're the man from my dream." The man bowed his head in acknowledgment, and Jeran climbed to his feet, looking around with sudden understanding. "This is a dream too," he said, half in question. When the man nodded wordlessly, Jeran asked, "You claimed before to be a guide. What should I do?"

Musical laughter filled the air, seeming to come from every direction. "He's certainly a comical one," chuckled another voice. A woman stepped from the trees, and cocking her head to one side, studied Jeran intently. She wore long robes of vibrant green, cut to accentuate her figure. Her eyes were the color of emeralds and slightly slanted, her lips thin, her cheekbones high and angular. Her hair was golden brown, tied in a tight braid and wrapped over her shoulders.

Her lips twisted up in a tight smile. "Not a moment ago he insisted that he be allowed to choose his own path. Now he wants you to tell him which way to go." She laughed again, and the sound, though at Jeran's expense, boosted his spirits.

The man returned the smile. "The boy is confused," he replied. "I understand his dilemma. He does not know what to do, yet feels like he is being pulled in every direction but the one he wishes to go." The woman nodded in understanding, and the man turned to face Jeran. "They can offer you little advice in this matter. In the end, you must choose which path to take, and accept the consequences of your decision."

The other voices, silent since the pair's arrival, all started to whisper again. "This way!"

"Follow me, Jeran."

"You know I want only what's best for you."

Jeran ignored the voices, but they grew louder, more insistent. "What advice can you offer?" he asked, hoping for some insight.

The man smiled. "When you make your choice, do not choose something you know you will regret. After your choice has been made, do not regret the consequences you could not foresee."

Jeran waited expectantly, hoping for more. When the man was not forthcoming, he frowned, considering his options. "I will go back the way I came," he said with conviction.

"You can never go back!" came a chorus of voices, spoken by all those around him. The sound echoed through the wood, until all that could be heard was the musical laughter of the unknown woman.

The man's smile broadened. "We can never go back," he said, echoing the other voices. "Once our choices are made, they are ours for eternity." The woman turned and walked into the trees. "Choose wisely," the man added, turning to follow.

"Wait!" cried Jeran, and the man turned, one step away from the dark trees. "Who are you?"

The man smiled, warm and reassuring. "A friend," he answered. "I am your friend, Jeran." Without another word he, too, stepped into the trees, fading from sight.

Around him, the voices demanded that he follow them. Jeran did not know which way to go. He spun slowly, and was met with angry eyes... accusing eyes... sad eyes. The statue stood in front of him, rising like an ebony pillar, seemingly taller than before. Jeran stopped spinning and let his eyes focus on the monument, surprised to see a door along the side of the tower. "This way," whispered a voice, and the door slowly opened.

Jeran, assaulted by voices on every side, ran through the door and found himself in a familiar chamber. A fire blazed along the far wall, the flames crackling merrily. A chair sat on either side of the fire, and the silhouetted form of the Darklord bent over a table, pouring wine. Frowning, Jeran walked forward.

Lorthas turned at Jeran's approach, seemingly unsurprised by the visit. He held out one glass, keeping the other close to his chest. Warily, Jeran took it, touching the dark red liquid to his lips, unwilling to show the Darklord how terrified he truly was.

Lorthas smiled at him–a thin, knowing smile–then gestured to one of the chairs, indicating that Jeran should sit. Reluctantly, Jeran took the proffered seat. He waited for Lorthas to sit across from him before he asked, "What are you doing in my dreams, Darklord?"

Lorthas shook his head sadly. "Such anger," he said, his tone calm and soothing. "Such vehemence. You should thank me for offering you an escape from that nightmare." The Darklord sighed, lowering his head sadly. "But instead you offer only accusations and hatred."

"Thank *you*?" Jeran repeated, disbelieving.

Lorthas nodded. "Terrible nightmare, that. I've had many like it over the winters. I know how you feel. Prodded down this path by one person, poked down that one by another. Never free to be your own man. Never free to make your own choices." The Darklord shook his head slowly, as if remembering his own pain. "I would spare you such anguish, Jeran."

"I will not thank you for watching my dreams," Jeran replied flatly. "Nor will I thank you for taking me from them."

"Taking you from them?" the Darklord repeated, surprised. "I only offered a way out. You *chose* to take that escape. I didn't force it on you." The Darklord sipped his wine; the liquid left blood red stains on his lips. "Mark me, Jeran," Lorthas said, "I will never force you to choose. I will never tell you which way you must go. So long as you are in my company, you are free to make your own decisions. Free to make your own judgments."

The Darklord's eyes met his. "Have you considered my request?"

Jeran shrugged noncommittally. "Truth be told, I haven't given it much th–" The word cut off unexpectantly. Try though he might, Jeran could not finish his statement.

Lorthas chuckled, low and grating. Jeran shivered at the sound. "I told you before. When you say something is true in the Twilight World, it must be true." He laughed louder, hiding his mocking smile behind his glass. "I will take your inability to speak as indication that you have considered my offer."

Grudgingly, Jeran was forced to admit that he had thought on the Darklord's words. "And have you decided to listen to my tale?" Lorthas asked. "I will only tell how I remember history. I will leave it to you to decide whether my actions were just or not. Can you get a similar offer from them?" he asked, waving his hand. Beside Jeran's chair, the ghostly forms of Jes, Tanar, and the Emperor materialized.

"After hearing my story, will they allow you to claim my actions were right, should you believe my words hold merit? Would any in Alrendria accept your decision? They say that I am a tyrant," he added, waving his arms dramatically, "but *they* are the oppressors. "*They* are the ones who seek to poison the minds of men."

As the tirade continued, the Darklord's eyes grew stormy. "Should you find me guilty of the crimes of which I am accused, I will accept your judgment, even if I don't agree with it. Would the same be true of them?" The volume of his voice had risen steadily since the start of his speech.

Lorthas stopped, forcing himself to calm. He continued in a quieter, more subdued voice. "Truth," said the Darklord, to emphasize his next statement, "I made mistakes, Jeran. I'll be the first to admit it. I did things during the MageWar of which I am not proud. Things I wish I could take back. But so did my enemies! Would they be so quick to admit their atrocities? I think not."

The Darklord met Jeran's eyes. "What say you?" he asked cordially. "Will you listen to my tale? I assure you that every word will be the truth. Should you doubt it, you have but to ask, and I will offer assurance. You have yourself witnessed how the Twilight World prevents lies."

The Darklord drank deeply, urging Jeran to do the same. "I will not discourage your questions," he added. "I will welcome them. As many and as often as you think necessary." Lorthas' eyes flashed again, this time in anticipation.

Jeran let the silence stretch out, trying to decide what was the best thing to do. "I will listen to your story," he said at last, and Lorthas' smile broadened. "On one condition!" Jeran added, and Lorthas pricked up his head, eager to hear the terms. "You will teach me how to find your dreams," he said after a long pause, "so *I* can find *you* in the Twilight World." This time, Jeran's eyes flashed. "You will not enter my dreams again."

Lorthas laughed. "You are cautious," he said between chuckles. "An admirable quality." The Darklord folded his hands together and tapped his index finger against his lips. "It will be as you say," he said after due consideration.

"You will swear to it?" Jeran prompted.

The Darklord's smile broadened. "Truth," he said to show his sincerity. "I will teach you how to find me in the Twilight World, and I will never again enter your dreams."

Still wary of Lorthas' motives, Jeran asked, "Then what do I do?"

"Relax, first of all, and enjoy your wine," the Darklord told him, sipping his own drink. "It may not be real, but the vintage is exquisite!" Jeran settled back in his chair and folded his hands together, but he did not touch the wine sitting on the small table beside his chair. The Darklord chuckled again. "Always so serious," he said with an amused shake of his head.

"Very well," he said after a brief pause. "Clear your mind and prepare to seize magic. You *do* know how to touch your Gift, don't you?" Jeran frowned, not wanting to answer the question. "I will assume that you have progressed that far in your training," the Darklord said at last, "since you're not very forthcoming.

"You will find that you cannot seize magic in the Twilight World," Lorthas warned. "This place is, after all, only a dream. But when you focus your Will, the dream will subtly change."

Jeran took slow, deep breaths, trying to find the calm he needed to work with magic. It was difficult to come by, the Darklord's mere presence made it hard to relax, harder still to clear his mind of thought. After a long, drawn out silence, he was ready. He took a deep breath, released it slowly, and the world around him blurred sharply.

When it came back into focus, he was surrounded by swirling dots, luminescent spheres that floated through the room. They looked like fireflies, dancing in intricate patterns throughout the chamber. Jeran reached a hand out to one and it flew away, keeping its distance. Some of the spheres faded, growing slowly dimmer until they disappeared completely. Others popped into being before his very eyes. Most were about a finger's width in diameter. Some were smaller, little more than a floating speck of light. A few were broader than the others, their light brighter, so bright in some cases that they cast shadows.

"They're beautiful," Jeran said, reaching his finger toward another sphere. This one did not run away. Instead, it danced around his finger curiously, inquisitively, but never allowed him to touch it.

"Each of those spheres is a dreamer," Lorthas explained. "When they sleep, their spirits float through the Twilight World. It is easy to see them, if you want to, but it is much more difficult to enter them, and even harder still to change the dreams."

"That one there," he continued, pointing to a bright sphere hovering a few hands away, "is the son of a farmer in *Ael Shataq*. The Gift is strong in him, and my Magi are even now going to find him, to bring him to me for training." He pointed to another sphere, this one tiny and dull, barely visible at all. "That is one of my greatest generals. A marvel on the battlefield, but virtually worthless in terms of the Gift."

"How can you identify them?" Jeran asked, awestruck.

The Darklord smiled at the question. "Each sphere is slightly different. In time, you learn which spirit belongs to which person. It is easier if you know the person in the waking world, but given time and patience, one can find just about anyone here." Lorthas sipped his wine. "The hard part is entering their dreams once you find them."

"Is that how you found me?" Jeran asked, fearful that the Darklord could find him at will.

Lorthas nodded, but at Jeran's frightened look, he chuckled and waved his hand dismissively. "I know what you're thinking, Jeran, and you may put your fears to rest. As I said before, finding a person in the Twilight World is easy, but that does not mean spying on them is. Truth, it took all of my considerable skill to enter your dreams the first time, and even untrained, it would have taken but a thought from you to cast me out again. I cannot read your thoughts, nor can I learn anything about your life in the waking world unless you tell it to me."

"And how will I find you?" Jeran asked, wanting the lesson to end.

"That's the true question," replied Lorthas. "If you would wait but a moment." The Darklord's face contorted in concentration. Suddenly, his form shimmered, compacting in on itself and growing brighter. With a whooshing sound, Lorthas' body became one of the glowing spheres.

It was about two hands across, larger than any other in the chamber. The Darklord's voice came to him, sounding as if it were far away. "This is my true form in the Twilight World. Study this sphere until you will know it on sight. Whenever you prepare for sleep and wish to seek me, hold yourself on the edge of seizing your Gift. That will draw you into the Twilight World. Once there, focus your Will as I have shown you and approach this sphere. I will sense your presence, and we will meet here."

Jeran looked at the Darklord's sphere, though in truth it would be impossible for him not to recognize. The sphere burned with a bright, white light and left dark shadows behind every object it touched. Streaks of red, gold, and black, each pulsing to a different beat, interlaced the orb. Jeran stood, walking around the sphere and examining it on both sides. "I will not forget it," he said, the world suddenly blurring around him.

"You are waking," called the Darklord's voice. The sphere shimmered again, and Jeran saw Lorthas' face staring at him. "I have enjoyed our talk," the Darklord said in a friendly tone, his words fading. "I look forward to our next meeting." The world blurred again.

Jeran opened his eyes and found himself in his chambers. He felt nearly as tired as when he had gone to bed. Light poured through the open blinds, and he could see that it was already late morning, far later than he usually arose. Groaning, he climbed from the bed and dressed hurriedly, knowing he was late for his meeting with the Emperor.

Liseyl was cleaning the sitting room when he emerged from the bedchamber. She smiled at him, pointing toward a small table on which sat an array of small pastries, Aelvin delicacies, and a large glass of chilled cider. "Late night?" Liseyl asked, her eyes smiling, "I left some food out for you."

"Restless night," Jeran replied, gratefully digging into the assorted dishes. "How are you finding Lynnaei?"

"It's a city full of wonders," Liseyl replied, her eyes distant. "The children love it! Mika and Ryanda can't get enough. Mika, in particular, wants to climb to the higher levels, but personally, I can't go much above the first or second without growing dizzy."

Jeran laughed. "Perhaps I'll take him with me one afternoon. If you don't mind, that is. The upper levels of the city are something he should see, if he's so inclined. Not many Humans can boast such a privilege."

"It seems we have been nothing but blessed this past season," Liseyl affirmed. "Sometimes it seems like being taken as slaves was the best thing that ever happened to my family." She stopped suddenly, as if her words had just sunk in, and her eyes grew sad.

Jeran crossed the room and put a comforting hand on Liseyl's shoulder. "It's not wrong to enjoy that which is good in your life. Mourn your husband's death, but don't regret the blessings that come from it." Liseyl looked up at him, thankful for his tender words.

"I was given some advice not too long ago," Jeran said, "which I will share now with you." He quoted the dark-haired stranger from his dream. "Make no decision you will regret from the start, and do not regret consequences you could not anticipate." He squeezed her shoulder fondly. "I'm sure the same applies to consequences over which you had no control."

"Thank you, Jeran," Liseyl murmured, pulling away. "Feel free to take Mika with you when next you go to the city." She giggled. "I think he enjoys your company more than mine anyway!"

Jeran smiled, and a thought suddenly occurred to him. "How fare the others?" he asked, embarrassed that he had not concerned himself with their welfare. "Are the children well? The women? Have they adapted to life in Lynnaei?"

Liseyl nodded. "All is well, Jeran," she replied. "You have no need to worry yourself over them. They are all well cared for, treated better treated now than they have been in a long time. They feel as if they're all nobles, their every whim satisfied."

"That's good to know," Jeran said, still embarrassed by his inattention, believing even more strongly that he did not deserve their loyalty. He drained the rest of his cider and headed for the door. "I'll be meeting with the Emperor until late this afternoon. Tell Mika I plan to go into the city two days from now, and that I look forward to his company."

"I will, Jeran," Liseyl responded as he closed the door behind him. He walked down the hall purposefully, taking long, quick strides, until he heard a strange sound. Confused, he stopped in his tracks and looked around. Finally, he discovered the source: a huddled form crouched in the far corner of the hall, sobbing quietly.

He approached slowly. "What's the matter?" he asked, and the figure lifted its head. It was Eilean, Liseyl's eldest. Tears streaked her sky blue eyes, leaving watery trails on her cheeks. Her pale blonde hair was in a state of disarray, her blue dress wrinkled.

Jeran dropped to his knees. "Eilean," he asked again, lifting her head with his hand, "what's wrong? Are you injured?"

She shook her head, trying to pull away. Wiping her eyes with an arm, she composed her features as best she could. "It's nothing, Lord Odara."

"Nonsense," he replied, not bothering to scold her for calling him Lord Odara. "You're crying! Were you hurt? Did something happen?"

"No... No," she stammered, trying to find the words. "It's just... I just...." Her eyes swelled with new tears, and she almost wailed. "I miss my father, Jeran," she said, crying sadly.

He clutched her to his chest, his own eyes watering in response to her unbridled emotions. He rocked her back and forth slowly, doing his best to comfort. "Why are you out here?" he whispered softly.

"I didn't...." she started, breaking off as another wave of sobs wracked her body. "I didn't want Mika and Ryanda to see." She wiped her eyes, sniffing back her tears. "I'm sorry. I shouldn't bother you with such trifles."

Jeran's genuine smile touched her heart. "I shouldn't?" he said, feigning indignity. "Am I not your friend?" Eilean smiled back, but it was a weak one. Releasing her, Jeran sat on the floor with his back against the wall. "I understand what you're feeling," he said after a pause. "My uncle was taken from me, much the same as your father was taken from you."

He looked at her for a long moment, then nodded. "I was even about your age when he was taken," he said, wiping his own eye. "I loved my Uncle Aryn very much. I didn't think I'd ever be happy again."

"But you are?" she asked, hopeful.

He nodded. "I'm very happy, for the most part. I have good days and bad, but they are no worse than anyone's."

"It gets easier then?" came the next hopeful question. "You stop missing him."

"Never," Jeran answered, shaking his head sadly. "Not a day goes by when I don't miss him. Not a night that I forget to pray to the Five Gods to bring him back to me." He looked at Eilean, brushing the last of her tears away with a tender touch. "In some ways I am lucky," he admitted. "I can hold on to the hope that, one day, Uncle Aryn will return. But in other ways, you're the lucky one, since you know for sure what happened."

She sniffed again, and Jeran climbed to his feet. "You will never stop missing your father," he prophesied. "And your memories of him will always be as they are now. But in time, you will accept what has happened, and it will not seem as bad."

Eilean stood as well and smoothed her dress, trying to iron out the wrinkles with her hands. One hand went to her hair, nervously fussing with the stray curls, and her cheeks reddened as she imagined her appearance. Jeran tried to hide his smile. "Peace, Eilean," he said before striding down the staircase.

Jeran nearly ran through the halls, following the now well-known path to the Vale. Elves bowed as he passed, their heads nearly touching the ground. Several Guardsmen walked the halls, and they saluted as he hurried by, but he barely acknowledged them. He descended ever lower into the palace, winding through the red-stoned, labyrinthine halls.

The imposing figure of Charylla stood before the entrance to the Vale. The Aelvin Princess wore white, and a narrow circlet of gold wove through her hair. Dark green eyes, nearly black in the shadowy corridor, bored into him. Crossing her arms over her breasts, she stared at him defiantly.

He bowed to her most formally, not knowing what to expect. "Princess Charylla," he said carefully. "An unexpected surprise. It has been some time since last I saw you. I hope the negotiations fare well."

"What is your purpose here, Mage," she said sternly, her eyes sparking.

Jeran stepped back, repulsed by the barely-controlled emotion in the Aelvin woman's tone. "Princess, I assure you, I am not a Mage." He offered her a small smile and tried to pass.

"Do you deny having the Gift?" she demanded, almost daring him to lie. She moved to intercept him, blocking his access to the Vale. "Do you deny using it since entering our forests?"

Jeran shook his head. "I do have the Gift," he admitted, seeing no other option but the truth. "And I *have* used it, but only in an attempt to train. My Gift is strong, and it manifests without my desire. I was informed that, without training, I could pose a threat to those around me."

"If you have the Gift, then you are a Mage," came the matter-of-fact reply.

"No!" Jeran insisted, trying to explain. "Humans don't require those with the Gift to train their abilities. I have met only a handful of Magi in my life, and on all occasions, I made it well known that I did not want training. Even now I seek only enough control to ensure that my magic can't harm those I hold dear."

Charylla eyed him suspiciously, but let the matter drop for the moment. "What are your plans for the Emperor?"

Jeran shook his head, feigning ignorance. "I don't know what you mean," he said. "The Emperor requested my presence, not the other way around."

"Do not play the fool with me, boy," Charylla said, her voice stony and cold. "I do not doubt that Grandfather has his hand in this as well, but there is more to your visitations than simple curiosity. Grandfather has not entertained anyone in the Vale for over a century, nor expressed an interest in state affairs for winters. Until last spring, that is, when he approached *Ael Alluya* and demanded that the Path of Riches be reopened.

"Why does Grandfather desire so much of your time?" she asked, eyeing him suspiciously. Jeran looked for an escape, but Charylla's eyes were hard, and her tone would brook no deception on his part.

Not wishing to betray the true reason for his visits, not sure even after all he had seen that he could trust the Aelvin Princess, Jeran said the first thing that popped into his head. "The Emperor teaches me control of my Gift." He smiled, happy to have found a way to distract the princess from the truth.

His statement did not have the desired effect. Charylla's eyes narrowed dangerously. "He is doing what?" she nearly yelled, throwing away what little remained of her Aelvin decorum. "Grandfather is too old to act as teacher, especially to one with your strength. How could you have asked such a thing."

Jeran stood, mouth agape, as the Aelvin Princess stormed toward him, continuing her tirade. Fear spread through him in a wave, and he cringed away from the verbal assault. Charylla did not relent, and Jeran slowly retreated, until his back contacted the smooth red stone and he had nowhere else to go.

"...stupid Humans. I cannot believe you would ask such a thing of the Emperor." Charylla leaned in close, stopping only a hand's length away from Jeran. Her eyes were dark green pools, glowing with an inner flame.

Charylla opened her mouth again, but the Emperor's voice cut her off. "That is enough, Granddaughter," he said sternly, hobbling through the now-open doorway, using a cane to support his weight. "It was my decision to tutor Jeran," he explained, "and I have gladly accepted the task. If you disagree, then it is I you should yell at, not him."

Charylla backed away from Jeran and turned to face the wizened, old Elf. "Grandfather," she began, struggling for the words that had so easily come to her a moment before. "It is unwise for you to take on such a task. You are no longer young, and it would pain me were something ill to happen to you."

"Your concern for my well-being is quite comforting," the Emperor said wryly. "But the 'life' you would have me live, just to ensure my continued good health, is so pointless I would almost be happier dead."

The Emperor's words cut deeply. Charylla's face paled, and her eyes lowered shamefully. Sensing her pain, the Emperor softened his tone. "Granddaughter, I appreciate your concern. Truly, it warms my heart. But you cannot lock me in the Vale like a trophy and not expect me to grow restless. There is a world out there, and if I am not to be a part of it, then what is the purpose of having a life?"

Charylla bowed her head submissively, and the Emperor smiled. "But that is neither here nor there," he said, putting his free arm around her shoulder. "Come with us, Granddaughter." He started toward the Vale, turning to face his young apprentice. "Jeran, I think it is time we tell my granddaughter what is going on in other parts of Madryn."

Jeran bobbed his head. "If you think it wise, Grandfather."

"You don't think we can fight a war alone, do you?" the Emperor quipped. With a smile, he led them into the Vale.

Chapter 16

"His story is hard to believe, Grandfather," Charylla said, breaking the long silence that followed the Emperor and Jeran's dark tale. The Aelvin Princess had listened in polite silence, but the whole time, her eyes had betrayed the thought she had just spoken. "The Boundary is impervious," she added, shaking her head. "Lorthas will never be able to break it."

"Lorthas does not have to, Princess." Jeran shifted his weight, trying to make himself more comfortable under her intense, green eyes. The three stood in the center of the Vale, sitting in a tight circle. Bright blue skies shone down on them from above, and a flock of birds swooped overhead, singing a chirping melody. "The Boundary goes against nature. Given enough time, nature itself will find a way to bring it down."

The Emperor chuckled. "It sounds like you've been talking to the twins. Nahrona and Nahrima have often expressed similar thoughts." He turned to Charylla. "They have also said, on many occasions, that anything created by man can be destroyed by man."

"But magic cannot touch the Boundary," Charylla stated adamantly. "There should be no way to destroy it with magic."

"Perhaps. Perhaps not." The Emperor smiled warmly at his grand-daughter. "True, there is no known way to affect the Boundary with magic," he lectured, stressing the word 'known,' "and the Boundary's unpredictable effects make studying magic a challenge even under the best of circumstances. But that does not mean there is no way to weaken it."

An owl dropped down on ghostly wings, alighting on the Emperor's shoulder. He grunted under the bird's weight and craned his neck around. "I am not as young as I used to be," he said irritably. "You have to stop surprising me like that." The owl stared back at him with wide, round eyes.

With a look of exasperation, the Emperor returned his attention to Charylla. "To my knowledge, there have been only a few cursory studies of the Boundary since the Raising. On our side at least. *Ael Maulle* and Magi alike are scared of the Boundary. They will not approach it, not even for academic reasons.

"But just because they are afraid to try does not mean the task is impossible." He chuckled, and the owl hooted in agreement. "In any case, even without aid from us, the twins are right. Given enough time, the Boundary will collapse on its own. It is not a thing of this world."

"Then why...?" Charylla trailed off, unable to find the right words.

"Why were you taught that the Boundary was impervious and impenetrable?" supplied the aged Elf. He laughed again, but this time there was a sour note to it. "Not by my choice, beloved," he assured her. "Not by my choice."

The Emperor's eyes grew distant. "After the Raising, *Ael Maulle* did not want to deal with the Boundary, nor did the Magi, and the armies of the Four Races just wanted an end to the bloodshed. They were elated that the war was over, that the Darklord was imprisoned."

His mind whisked back to those dark, troubled times, the Emperor took a slow, steadying breath. "The Mage Assembly and *Ael Maulle* decided to keep the truth hidden. To bolster morale, they told the allied races that the Boundary would hold forever. They knew it would hold for centuries, and hoped it would hold for millennia. They thought they had enough time."

Sighing deeply, the Emperor shook his head. "They intended to keep the secret only until things had settled, until life had returned to normal. After a generation or two, the Magi planned to prepare the people for the Boundary's collapse. One or two small steps with every passing generation, so that by the time the Boundary fell and Lorthas' hordes poured through the Portal, we would be ready."

The Emperor was silent for a long time; the only sound heard was the whispering of the wind through the trees. "Not all approved of the decision. Aemon was against it, as was I. The *Tsha'ma* as a whole condemned the plan, claiming that the only way to maintain alliance between the Races was to hold the threat of Lorthas over their heads."

Quiet permeated the Vale, and the Emperor lowered his gaze to the ground. "No one would listen. If only they had. If only Aemon and I had fought harder to make them understand."

Again, the Emperor's words trailed off, but this time, a quiet sniffling broke the silence. Surprised at her grandfather's reaction, Charylla reached out a comforting hand, her face betraying concern. Jeran, too, was touched by the Emperor's tears, but knew not how to ease the old man's pain.

The Emperor welcomed Charylla's light touch. Blinking back his tears, he raised his eyes to meet hers. "I am fine, beloved," he assured her. "Momentarily overcome with 'what ifs.' I could spend an entire lifetime considering what might have happened had I done things differently." He laughed again, harshly. "Does me no good, though," he told them. "Do not waste your time on such things."

He shook himself, dispelling his melancholy, and continued his story. "In time, those with the Gift came to believe their own lie. Self-deception is one of the worst things in this world. As the seasons passed, even I allowed the threat of the Darklord to fade from my thoughts, until Lorthas was little more than a distant, irritating memory.

"With the Boundary secure, events unfolded as the *Tsha'ma* predicted. The Four Races went back to squabbling amongst themselves, old hatreds resurfaced, and new hatreds began to form. In less than a decade, everything accomplished during the MageWar had crumbled. The alliance was broken, and the trust between the Races was disappearing.

"We were not guiltless!" the Emperor explained, waving an accusatory finger at Charylla. "As the winters slipped by, our people grew more fearful of other races. We blamed the Humans and Garun'ah for what had happened, glossing over our role in the events leading to the MageWar. We Elves grew less trusting, more haughty as the centuries passed. In time, *Ael Alluya* demanded the closing of the Path of Riches, our last link to Madryn and the other races."

"Grandfather," Charylla exclaimed, "you were against such things all your life! I was barely a child when the Path of Riches closed, but I remember your vehemence, your resolve that it remain an active trade route. Even if our people hold some blame, it is not yours!"

"Was I not to blame?" he asked her. "I am the Emperor of Illendrylla. My word is the word of Valia. The words of the Goddess. You and the others would have me believe my words are law as soon as they leave my mouth." The Emperor's lips twisted wryly. "Yet that does not seem to stop *Ael Alluya*, or anyone else, from twisting the meaning of my words at will, or ignoring them altogether.

"Perhaps I am not the only one at fault," he amended. "But had I used my 'Imperial Majesty,' the Path of Riches would never have closed. For reasons both political and personal, I allowed *Ael Alluya* to do as they wished."

The Emperor touched Charylla's cheek lightly. Fondly. "You always did see me in a better light than I deserve, my dear." To Jeran, he added confidentially, "She has always been my favorite. The brightest jewel in my entire collection."

The princess' cheeks reddened visibly, and she lowered her eyes. Jeran was shocked to see the aloof Aelvin noblewoman so easily embarrassed. "Then these negotiations are just a ruse?" she asked, smoothing her features. "A deception to provide Jeran the opportunity he needed to share Alrendria's knowledge with you?"

"Not entirely, my dear," the Emperor responded. "Though learning what King Mathis knows is an important step, reopening trade with the Alrendrians is more important."

"Why?" Charylla and Jeran asked simultaneously. They shared a look, then turned their eyes back to the Emperor.

"During the MageWar, we barely defeated the Darklord," came the Emperor's steady answer. "At the best of times, it was all we could do to maintain the stalemate. The only thing that held Lorthas at bay was the alliance between the Four Races. If not for our solidarity, the Darklord would now control Madryn."

Charylla nodded in understanding, and Jeran, too, saw the direction of the Emperor's thoughts. "Should the Darklord break free," he said, "he'll find a world already at war with itself. Unless we are united, we will fall."

"Is there time for this?" Charylla asked. "If the Boundary is already weakening, it may be too late for such steps."

"I doubt the Boundary will collapse on the morrow," replied the Emperor. "There are seasons yet, if not decades or centuries, before the Boundary is weak enough to cross. When he enters Madryn, I would like him to find a land at peace, a land with Humans, Elves, and Garun'ah allied against him.

"But the Darklord is not our only threat," the Emperor continued, wagging his finger in warning. "The threat posed by his agents on *this* side of the Boundary is quite real. If the Durange and whatever other allies Lorthas has won are successful in fomenting strife, it will make the war all the easier for the Darklord to win."

Suddenly, the Emperor laughed, and the sound echoed throughout the Vale. "The Three Races are doing a fine job of aiding the Darklord's plans, even without the help of Lorthas' minions. We fight with the Garun'ah. The Humans fight each other."

The owl, disturbed by the Emperor's violent laughter, jumped from the Elf's shoulder. Flapping its wings, it flew to one of the many branches stretching overhead. "When the Boundary falls," the Emperor concluded, "Lorthas may find a world ripe for the taking."

"If our cause is so hopeless," Charylla demanded, her shoulders slumping, "then why the negotiations? Why even try?"

"Because not fighting the Darklord is even worse than losing to him," Jeran answered in the Emperor's stead. Charylla's dark eyes turned toward him, but she said nothing. Jeran felt uncomfortable under the princess' sharp, scrutinizing gaze.

The Emperor nodded. "Jeran is right." He cast his eyes about the forest floor, looking for his staff. "That is why I desired these negotiations, beloved. Not for the trade, though more trade would not hurt. We must use what few winters remain wisely. If we open trade with Alrendria, it is one of many steps toward alliance. In time, both our races may be able to put aside their prejudices and embrace each other as friends."

"What of the Garun'ah?" Charylla asked. "How can we make peace with them? Especially now, when fighting has once more broken out between our races?"

The Emperor struggled to his feet, using the staff to help hold his weight. "I do not know, Granddaughter," he answered sadly. "I had hoped to open talks with the Tribesmen as well, but now that there is fighting, such a thing will be difficult." Jeran and Charylla stood too, one to either side of the Emperor.

"Something about these skirmishes troubles me, Granddaughter," the Emperor admitted, waiting until he had her full attention before continuing. The Tribesmen have never raided over the river. They have always claimed that their lands reach to the Danelle, never beyond."

"Perhaps their opinion has changed, Grandfather."

"Why does it matter?" Jeran asked. "They allow Humans to live on their lands. I've been told that the Garun'ah consider their lands the property of all, and they are merely its custodians."

"The Garun'ah find my people's rigid patterning of nature abhorrent," the Emperor answered, chuckling weakly. "A sentiment you share, Jeran, if memory serves." The old Elf hobbled toward the palace, flanked by his two companions. They followed obediently, unconcerned with their destination, winding through the cobbled paths of the Vale.

"They would allow us to live on their lands," the Emperor added, "provided that we did not try to force the landscape into our narrow view of beauty." Sarcastic laughter once again drifted through the trees. "My people have never been good at compromise," he confided to Jeran.

To Charylla, he said, "It is possible they have changed, my dear, but I find it unlikely. I know the Garun'ah. Truth be told, I am still friends with some of them, as odd as that would seem to some of our people." The Emperor stopped in mid-stride, tapping a finger to his lower lip. "I would almost suspect Luran of fomenting dissent between our races. His hatred of the Garun'ah runs very deep."

The Emperor started walking again, and Charylla hurried after him. "You are not suggesting that Luran is behind the Tribesmen's recent attacks!"

"There is little I do not consider your brother capable of," came the Emperor's stony reply.

"He is your blood, Grandfather, just as I am!" Charylla's voice was hurt, almost pleading.

"Do not remind me, beloved," he replied dryly, then calmed his growing anger. The Emperor patted his granddaughter's shoulder gently. "I do not believe Luran evil, my dear. Just misguided. He will do what he deems best, even if it means plunging us into war with the Garun'ah.

"If only the Orog had not been lost!" the Emperor lamented. "They were so peaceful, so careful and logical. Even the most inflexible were forced to listen to their words, so eloquently were they spoken, so infallible and simple." The Emperor lifted his eyes toward the heavens. "Of all the Races," he inquired of the Gods, "why was it the Orog you destroyed?"

"The Orog?" Jeran and Charylla repeated in unison.

The Emperor looked at them blankly. "Do my words surprise you?"

Both nodded, but it was Jeran who spoke. "The Orog were traitors! Monsters who betrayed us to the Darklord. That's why Aemon imprisoned them behind the Boundary with Lorthas and the rest of his allies."

Jeran's words shocked the Emperor. He opened his mouth, but no sound issued forth. His eyes, disbelieving, shifted from Jeran to Charylla. "Do you believe this as well, Granddaughter?" he managed to whisper, his voice weak.

She nodded slowly, and the Emperor made a sound, almost like a wail. "How could I be so deaf?" he asked. "Have I been so long separated from this world?" He cast his eyes toward the heavens again. "How could you do this to them?" he demanded. "You Shael, most of all! How could you dishonor them in this way!"

"Neither of you know the Orog," the Emperor said harshly, returning his gaze to his companions. "They were neither monstrous nor traitorous; they were the most peace-loving of all the races! The most patient. The kindest. Impossible to anger, but an implacable foe once set to a cause."

As the Emperor's thoughts drifted to memories of the Lost Race, his smile grew wistful. "You are familiar with the stories of knights?" he asked Jeran. "Those tales of chivalry and honor Humans adore so much?"

Jeran nodded his head dumbly. "Human knights are but poor imitations of the Orog." The Emperor's green eyes grew distant, his mind wandering into the past. "I remember the days at the end of the MageWar, when we were preparing to raise the Boundary. Aemon had sent word to the Orog that they must flee their homelands or be trapped inside *Ael Shataq* with the Darklord. The Magi waited, knowing every day's delay gave Lorthas a chance to escape his prison before it was made.

"One morning, following a long and bloody battle, a small, ragged party of Orog approached the Alrendrian encampment. 'Noble Aemon,' called their leader, a barrel-chested man named Chorcak. 'Noble Aemon, I have been sent by the Elders. Our people battle the minions of Lorthas and have been much delayed. The Elders beg you wait no longer. Raise your Boundary, Noble Aemon.'

"The Orog's words paralyzed Aemon. 'I cannot, honorable Chorcak,' he replied. 'The Orog will be trapped within the Boundary, forced to fight Lorthas alone.' The armies of the Four Races heard of Chorcak's arrival, and they assembled in the tens of thousands to hear the warrior's words. The Magi used their Gift to give his words strength, and they carried over the entire assembly.

"Aemon made many protestations, but Chorcak was adamant. 'The Elders say it is better for one race to die that the others may live free, than for all races to live as slaves.' His eyes were strong and confident as they stared at the High Wizard. 'Raise your Boundary, Protector of my People,' he said, and with tears in his eyes, Aemon gave the order to raise the Boundary.

" 'I ask one favor, Honorable One,' Chorcak begged. When Aemon raised his tear-stained eyes from the ground, the Orog said, 'I ask that you give me leave to cross your Boundary before it is raised, taking with me those of my people who wish to follow. My place is within *Ael Shataq*, fighting against the Dark One.'

"In a broken voice, Aemon gave his permission, and Chorcak rallied his people. In the end, nearly all of the Orog accompanied him. Only the wounded and ill remained behind. As the Orog marched north, the other races cheered them."

The Emperor's head raised, as if he were there, looking across the plains at the retreating Orog host. "It was a thunderous sound," he said in awe, a tear in the corner of his eye. "Deafening. Proud. Together, we sang the Orog to their deaths."

Charylla sniffed, and Jeran was forced to scrub tears from his own eyes. "Only a handful of Orog were outside the Boundary when it was raised. A small remnant of a once mighty people. Alone, cut off from friends and family, they soon died out. Less than a century after the Raising, the last Orog was laid to rest.

"And now I discover that even their memory is tarnished." The Emperor wiped his eyes. "Is there no justice in this world?"

"Surely, some have survived," Jeran said, hopeful.

"Lorthas' hatred of the Orog was strong," the Emperor stated. "And his fear stronger. The Orog were immune to his magic, and Lorthas despised what he could not control. For the Lost Race to have survived, it would have taken a miracle."

"Is it too late for us then?" asked Charylla sadly. "Without the Orog, divided by hatred and ignorance, can we hope to stand against the Darklord?"

"Throughout my lifetime," the Emperor said slowly, "there have been three events that brought all four races together, fighting toward a common goal. Only three in over six thousand winters. The first was Aemon's Revolt, when the races united to overthrow the Darklords. The second was for the construction of the Path of Riches. The third was the MageWar, when once again we were threatened with enslavement to a Darklord."

The Emperor looked back and forth between his two charges. "Three times only, and two of those times in war." He shook his head back and forth. "And we are the enlightened beings!" he snapped. "The ones created by the Gods to rule and care for Madryn! Bah!" His anger barely in check, the Emperor's free hand clenched into a fist.

"To be honest, beloved," he said to Charylla, his tone icy, "I do not know if we can succeed. Our 'victory' in the MageWar was sour at best, buying Lorthas time to strengthen his armies and costing us our alliance. If not for the Boundary, we would all be the Darklord's servants. But if our struggle was worth only a few winters of reprieve, then I would have preferred to fight to the last, giving my life in the battle against Lorthas.

"Can we win?" he asked again. "I do not know. But I can answer you this. I will stand against Lorthas even if I am alone in the struggle. If I do not, then everyone who died, everyone who sacrificed themselves in the MageWar, died for nothing. I will not dishonor their spirits by cowering before Lorthas now."

The Emperor stopped at a small, oaken door leading out of the Vale. Jeran's curiosity finally got the better of him. "Where are we going, Grandfather?" he asked, earning him a glare from Charylla.

The Emperor's brow furrowed. "Going?" he asked. "I am going to take a nap. All this talk and reminiscing has fatigued me. As to where you are going...." He let the word hang in the air. "I do not know, Jeran. That is a question only you, and perhaps the Five Gods, can answer." Laughing, he drew open the door and hobbled through, pulling it shut behind him.

"Grandfather?" Charylla said to Jeran once the Emperor was safely away, her lips twisting up in a smile.

Jeran swallowed. "It was his request, Princess Charylla. He claims to grow tired of hearing 'Emperor' all the time."

She turned, her dress billowing with the motion, and started back the other way, gesturing for Jeran to follow. "Do you know what you have started?" she inquired, walking through the thick grasses of the Vale.

"I am just the messenger, Princess," Jeran assured her. "I have started nothing." He stepped onto a stone-lined path, stooping at its edge to pluck a flower, its petals as white as snow. He held the flower out, offering it to Charylla. "A peace offering," he said, smiling weakly. "I have few enough allies here to warrant losing the little trust you have shown me."

She took the flower, weaving the stem deftly through her hair, and bowed her head, her slanted eyes narrow and probing, her lips pressed together in a tight smile. "Grandfather trusts you," she said. "And though our opinions have differed many times, in all but a few cases, he was right." Her smile broadened. "It seems we are to be allies, Jeran Odara, though I must tell you, I fear what your news means for my people."

"Lady Charylla," Jeran replied, offering her his arm, "I can honestly say that I fear what my news means for all the races."

She took his arm in hers, and they started down the path together. "You are very odd," she told him. "Even for a Human."

"I will try to take that as a compliment," he assured her, laughing. The Vale was quiet; even the birds seemed to understand their mood. The few songs they heard were sad, reflecting their thoughts. The Tower of the Five Gods rose before them, its spire disappearing far above.

Charylla led them to another door, this one leading to the twisting corridors of the palace. "Where are you going now, Jeran?" Charylla asked softly, her eyes far distant.

"I will speak with Jes," Jeran said, though he did not look forward to spending time with the raven-haired Mage. "I have not seen her in some time, and she is one of the few aware of my mission here in Illendrylla."

"Ahhh," Charylla responded, nodding her head, as if she had just discovered the answer to a riddle that had long plagued her. "That is probably for the best. Most Magi do not like giving up their students, even when they do not like to teach. I am sure she is eager to hear about your progress with Grandfather."

"What do you–" Jeran started, but was unable to find the right words. "How did you know?" he managed to ask weakly, not sure how Charylla had figured out Jes' secret.

The Aelvin Princess laughed. "She is not as great an actress as she appears, at least, not if one knows which signs to look for. I am embarrassed I did not see what she was before now." Charylla turned and walked away, stopping at the intersection of two hallways. "I will leave you to your Mage, Jeran," she said. "And I ask of you a favor. Be wary of Grandfather's health. He is old, whether he cares to admit it or not, and it would be a tragic thing were he to fall ill."

"Princess Charylla," Jeran replied somberly, "I promise you, I will allow the Emperor to do nothing that will cause him harm."

"Good luck stopping him if he gets it into his head to do such a thing," she murmured, but her eyes were appreciative. "Thank you," she said in a louder voice. "I will bid you farewell, Lord Odara. There is much I need to attend to."

Jeran bowed deeply at the waist, and Charylla turned and walked away on silent feet. When she had gone, Jeran took several deep, steadying breaths, then started toward the Alrendrian apartments.

He walked quickly through the halls, his eyes on the ground and his thoughts on the Emperor's words. And Charylla's. "Lord Odara!" echoed a cry down the hall, followed by the sound of running footsteps.

Jeran stopped, turning his head around. "Bystral!" he said, his thoughtful frown turning up into a smile. "Well met, Guardsman. I have not seen much of you these last few days." Bystral wore green and brown, similar in color to that of the Aelvin warriors. His blonde hair was disheveled, pulled back in a loose ponytail.

The Guardsman stopped in front of him, saluting fist-on-heart. "I have not been here, Jeran," he replied. As he spoke Jeran's common name, his cheeks turned a bright shade of red. "I was in the Great Forest."

"Outside the city?" Jeran asked, surprised. "I thought the Elves didn't want any of us leaving Lynnaei." The Elves had been very protective of their forests since the Alrendrian delegation arrived in Illendrylla, watching from the shadows whenever the Humans left the Path of Riches.

"It was Willym's idea," Bystral explained. "After Prince Luran left to fight the Tribesman, Willym got to thinking. He thought maybe only Luran cared whether we saw the forests. He went and asked that blonde Elf, the warrior...." Bystral trailed off, his face contorting as he tried to remember the name.

"Astalian?" Jeran offered, his lips twitching up in a smirk at the mere mention of the Elf's name.

"That's the one," Bystral nodded. "Anyway, Willym asked Astalian if some of the Guardsmen could see the forests, perhaps take part in an Aelvin patrol. The Elf loved the idea, and told Willym to select half a score of Guardsman to accompany him."

Jeran waved for Bystral to join him. The Guardsman recounted their story as they walked down the hall. "They are like cats!" he said, waving his arms animatedly. "Jumping from tree to tree, running along branches barely a hand across. We tried to keep up with them on the ground," he added, showing Jeran a series of long scratches running the length of his arm, "but the undergrowth has thorns sharp as a blade.

"A few of the more adventurous Guardsmen," he said, his smile indicating that he was one of them, "climbed the trees with the Elves." Bystral genuine laughter echoed through the halls. "After a few days we managed to stop falling, but our best could not keep up with the worst of the Elves."

The Guardsman chuckled, a glint in his eyes. "Poor Raeghit," he said, shaking his head. "He nearly broke his neck trying to jump between two trees."

"A fine tale," Jeran said when Bystral had finished. "I'm glad to see the Guardsman are becoming friendly with the Elves. But from your haste to find me, I doubt you just wanted to tell me you were enjoying your time in Illendrylla."

The Guardsman's face darkened visibly. "No, sir," he replied, his expression growing serious. "There's something going on around the city."

"What do you mean?" Jeran asked, instantly alert.

"I'm not sure," Bystral admitted. "Nor does Astalian seem to know for certain. Our party saw no one, but there were signs of life. People moving across the ground."

"Could it be farmers?" Jeran asked. "Residents of the wood?"

"The Elf didn't seem to think so. He didn't know what the tracks meant, but he seemed concerned, though he didn't share his reasons with us." Bystral blushed again. "It's probably nothing," he admitted. "But I thought you should know that something might be wrong. The Elf was quite silent during our return to Lynnaei."

"If Astalian was silent," Jeran laughed, "then something *must* be amiss!" He shared a smile with Bystral, then clapped the Guardsman on the shoulder. "I'll talk to Astalian when next I see him," he promised. "You should share your concerns with Lord Iban, though. Prince Martyn too."

Jeran sniffed the air tentatively. "But were I you, Guardsman," he added with a smile, "I would bathe first."

They arrived at Jes' door and Jeran stopped. "Going to see the lady?" Bystral asked, his eyes sparkling with mirth. "I hear you've been ignoring her since our arrival in Lynnaei. In my experience, a lady does not like to be ignored." Bystral clasped Jeran's arm in parting. "If the Lord Odara doesn't mind taking advice from a simple Guardsman, don't let your guard down. An angry woman is a deadlier enemy than the most skilled swordsman."

At Bystral's cruel laugh, it was Jeran's turn to blush. "I will take your advice to heart," he managed to say, hiding his chagrin. The Guardsman saluted and continued down the hall, heading toward his own quarters.

Jeran knocked lightly on the door. "Enter," called a cool voice. Jeran opened the door, trying to calm his breathing.

Jes was sitting on the far side of the room, reading a thin book. She wore a white, cotton dress that clung to her body, accentuating its curves. Her black hair hung in loose curls, framing her face. The sight of her reminded Jeran of his dream, and he blushed slightly. "So," Jes said, her eyes never rising, "you have not forgotten that I'm here. That's a comfort."

"I didn't mean to ignore you," Jeran said, closing the door behind him. His heart pounding, he stared across the room at the Mage. "I've been very busy with the Emperor. He's been teaching me how not to seize magic. And how to control my Readings."

"I see," Jes said, refusing to meet his eyes. "I hope you haven't forgotten why you were sent to Illendrylla."

Jeran stiffened at her harsh words. "Certainly not," he replied. "The Emperor and I have discussed why we are here at great length. He's doing what he can to aid us, and just today, the Emperor brought Princess Charylla into his confidence. But for now, there is little to do but wait."

"He did," Jes said, and it was impossible to tell whether she meant it as a question or a statement of fact. "If you have not been discussing our mutual 'friend,' with the Emperor, then I wonder why you couldn't find a moment or two in which to speak with me. To apprize me on the Emperor's intentions." Her words were cold, and Jeran saw that she was angry, but he did not fully understand why.

"I've been busy," he said, his cheeks reddening, his heart pounding even harder than before.

"Personal pursuits?" Jes asked, turning the page. "You seem to find enough time to parade around the city with Prince Martyn and that Elf, Astalian." A moment more of calm silence, then Jes lost her inner war. "We have been in Lynnaei over twoscore days!" Her composure gone, twin blue orbs, almost burning with their own fire, snapped up to glare at Jeran. She slammed the book close and threw it roughly on the table. "I would have thought you'd seek me out at least once since then."

"If you were so concerned, you could have found me," Jeran replied, his own anger rising.

Jes laughed harshly. "You would like that," she responded coldly. "How many women do you need sneaking into your quarters? I prefer to keep the gossip about me to a minimum."

Jeran blushed deep red. Since the first incident, Alynna had found her way into his chambers three more times. Each time she was more insistent, and each time it became more difficult for Jeran to extricate himself. Eventually, he would run out of excuses, or Liseyl would not be around to help, and he would either have to forcefully remove Alynna from his chambers or succumb to her temptations.

Neither prospect was particularly enticing. Jeran had considered having a guard posted at his door, as ridiculous as the idea sounded, to discourage Alynna from entering. "Is that what this is about?" he demanded hotly, hiding his embarrassment with anger. "I don't ask Alynna to my chambers. I don't entice her to my bed or encourage her to slip into my apartments when no one's watching. Alynna means nothing—"

Jes' laughter cut him off. "You seem to forget, Jeran, that we are *not* courting." Her chiding voice hurt him as much as her casual, dismissive wave. "No matter what pretext we needed so that I could train your Gift. You owe me nothing. Certainly, you don't need to offer excuses as to your relationship with Alynna Morrena. If you want to take a flaxen-haired trollop to your bed, it's no concern of mine. I simply think you should have tried to keep me informed of your dialogue with the Emperor."

"Nonsense!" Jeran snapped, more loudly than he intended. "The Emperor himself meets with you regularly. He tells me so himself. What could you learn from me, that he does not share with you?" Jeran eyed her suspiciously. "No," he said, shaking his head. "There is more to this."

"How dare you!" Jes yelled, rising to her feet. She was only a few fingers shorter than Jeran, but standing there, she seemed to tower over him. Fists planted firmly on her hips, she glared at him. "How dare you insinuate...." She broke off, her words fading away. She stared at him furiously, her lips pressed into a thin line. They faced each other, neither willing, nor able, to speak.

Finally, Jes broke the silence. "I apologize," she said, though she did not sound regretful. "You are right, I do meet with the Emperor, and he has kept me up to date on your progress, in regards to both your training and concerning our 'friend.' "

Letting out a deep breath, she unclenched her fists. "I suppose I was angry because you did not deem it necessary to keep me informed yourself. Like it or not, you are my apprentice, even though I have handed your training over to the Emperor for the time being. We Magi are very protective of our students.

"Besides," she added, small spots of color blooming on her cheeks, "I am envious of you." At Jeran's quizzical look, her cheeks grew even redder. "You have no idea how tedious negotiations are," she told him, sighing heavily. "I would much rather spend my days with the Emperor than listen to Rafel argue endlessly with the Elves."

She smiled weakly, and Jeran returned the gesture in kind. "I'm sorry, too," he said. "I should have made more of an effort to see you, to show you how I am progressing. I—" He broke off, unable to tell her that he was afraid of her, afraid she would be disappointed with the little progress he had made in controlling his Gift.

"Speaking of our 'friend,' " he said, trying to change the subject. "I met him again the other day."

"In the Twilight World?"

Jeran nodded. He licked his lips, ready for another argument. "I have agreed to listen to his version of history."

Jes' eyes were instantly disapproving. "That is unwise."

"It's not as bad as it sounds," Jeran assured her. "I made him show me how to find him in the Twilight World, and forced him to promise not to enter my dreams again. He swore he would not, and if something is told as truth in the Twilight World, it must be true. You told me that yourself."

He had thought his words would comfort Jes, but instead, her eyes grew icier. "Not only does he agree to give Lorthas a chance to warp his mind," she said, pressing her fingers against her eyes and shaking her head back and forth sadly. "He now allows the Darklord to give him lessons in magic." Casting her eyes upward, she asked, "What did I do wrong?"

Her eyes returned to Jeran. "You cannot meet with him," she said flatly. "He will only tell you lies."

"Lorthas told me you would say as much," Jeran whispered. "He has offered me a chance to hear his story, his version of what happened, and judge for myself whether or not he was wrong. He claims the Magi have warped history to make themselves appear more noble. He claims you will not want me to hear his tale, because I will know it for the truth."

Jeran met Jes gaze squarely, unflinchingly. "But most importantly, he's willing to let *me* make the decision for myself."

"Of course he is!" Jes blurted out. "What has he to lose? If you believe his story, he gains an ally, a potentially powerful ally, on our side of the Boundary. If you do not believe him, he loses nothing."

"Then it's not the Darklord you don't trust," Jeran said sourly, his mouth turning down in a frown. "It's me."

Jes eyed him warily. "Lorthas' tale may be false," Jeran admitted. "It may be the truth, at least the truth as he sees it. But that's not the point. You don't trust me to make the decision for myself. To determine for myself whether or not his actions were justified. You're not even willing to take the chance that I may understand his motives, as remote a possibility as that may be.

"I'm not as naive as you think, Jes," Jeran said coldly. "I don't believe the Darklord was misunderstood–that his intentions were solely to protect the weak from the powerful. But he deserves the chance to tell his story. And each person–Human, Elf, or Tribesman–has the right to listen, to decide for themselves whether Lorthas is good or evil."

Jes opened her mouth to reply, but Jeran kept speaking, not giving her the chance to voice her own opinion. "If that right is denied, if any one person is forced to choose opposite their own heart, then Alrendria's entire history has been in vain. Without the freedom to choose the path our lives will take, we are slaves. If we will not allow people to choose their own path, then why did we even fight the MageWar?

"Whether we are forced to believe the same things as King Mathis, or the Magi, or the Emperor... How is that any different than being forced to believe what Lorthas wants us to believe?"

Jes stood, mouth agape, as Jeran concluded his speech. "Freedom of choice is the only true freedom," he concluded. "The problem with giving people the freedom to choose their own path is that, sometimes, they choose poorly."

Jeran fell silent, averting his eyes from Jes' intense scrutiny. "Have you been talking to your grandfather?" she asked in a stunned voice.

Jeran shook his head. "I was reading Yassik's *Conversations with Aemon.* The one Aemon kept in his chambers, with his own notes scribbled in the margins." Jeran shrugged. "I guess it's almost like talking to him. He seems to be very wise."

"The wisest person I've ever met," Jes replied absently. She stared at him, seemed to stare through him, while she considered his words. "I still don't like the idea of you conversing with the Darklord. Nor would Aemon, but he would be hard pressed to dispute your argument." She smiled at Jeran. "He hates it when people use his own words against him."

"I'll try to remember that."

They talked for a while longer, Jes telling Jeran how the negotiations were going, Jeran recounting his experiences with the Emperor. Jes seemed pleased with his progress, and Jeran sighed in relief when she said, "It seems like the Emperor is doing much better than I could have. I would like to sit in on one of your lessons, if you don't mind."

Jeran shook his head, and Jes smiled warmly. "Now you'll have to excuse me," she said, starting for the door. "I am to meet with Rafel and the other delegates tonight, and I wish to draw myself a bath before I'm forced to listen to his incessant droning."

Jeran bowed at the waist and let himself out. Bystral met him in the hall. Approaching cautiously, the Guardsman examined him from head to foot. "I see no bruises," he said at last. "Though I thought I heard some yelling a while back. You either managed to calm Lady Jessandra's wrath, or she is quite skilled at torture, knowing where to strike so the bruises will not be seen."

Jeran rolled his eyes. "Bystral, have you nothing better to do than skulk about the chambers of the Alrendrian nobility?"

"Skulk?" replied the brawny Guardsman in a hurt tone. "I was here for my Lord's protection! All know of the Lady Alynna's...interest...in you. I worried that your visit with the Lady Jessandra would end in bloodshed. I was here to rescue you should the need arise."

Jeran groaned. He put an arm around the Guardsman's shoulders and led him away from Jes' apartments. "I want to discuss the possibility of posting a guard outside my chambers," he said as he and Bystral started down the hall. "For some reason, the Lady Alynna keeps confusing my room with her own."

"I doubt there will be many volunteers for that duty," Bystral replied seriously. "It is not wise to anger a woman." At Jeran's confused look, the Guardsman explained. "An angry woman is slightly more deadly than a viper. And Lady Alynna's fangs are by far the sharpest." Jeran groaned again, and Bystral's laughter echoed down the hall.

Chapter 17

"It's amazing!" Mika said, staring down at the treetops. He and Jeran stood on a platform far above the ground, overlooking the city. Thousands of rope bridges were visible below; the tiny silhouettes of Elves crossed back and forth upon them. Thin tendrils of smoke rose from pipe chimneys, a forest of plumes extending into the blue, sunny sky.

"Indeed," Jeran replied, smiling down at the boy, "it's a beautiful sight." As promised, he had asked the Emperor to excuse him for the day so he could bring Mika into the city. Until today, the boy had seen little more than the bottom levels of Lynnaei; his mother's fear of heights had prevented him from climbing higher.

"Can we go higher?" Mika asked, beaming at Jeran and pointing a small finger toward the thin rope ladder that climbed to the very top of the Great Tree. A narrow, round platform sat at the summit, swaying back and forth in the gentle summer breeze. Ropes stretched down from the observation tower, anchoring it to the platform and adding stability.

Jeran hesitated, but finally nodded. "Come on," he said, starting toward the ladder, waving for Mika to follow. "Try not to fall," he added in a stern voice. "If you hurt yourself, your mother will have my hide!"

Mika laughed, running ahead of Jeran. "Mother wouldn't hurt you even if you killed me yourself!" he returned, scrambling deftly up the rungs. "She thinks you're the Five Gods greatest gift to Madryn!"

Jeran groaned as he grabbed the bottom rung. Liseyl and the others were only getting worse. Try though he might, he could not get them to treat him as a normal person. All he wanted to be was Jeran Odara, but between the Guardsman and his 'servants,' the women and children he had freed from the slavers, Jeran Odara was disappearing, and he was becoming Lord Odara, First Seat of House Odara, Warden of Portal and Protector of the Boundary.

The Elves were not helping either. They bowed and scraped more than the Humans, and Jeran was not sure why. *Perhaps because I bested Luran in the duel.* For whatever reason, try though he might, few talked to him as they would a friend, and even fewer as an equal. As he climbed the ladder, he found himself wishing for his old life in Keryn's Rest.

Mika reached the top of the ladder and pulled himself onto the platform. Running to the edge, he grasped the thin rail and leaned out as far as he could, staring down. Jeran winced at the boy's recklessness, but he held his tongue, not wishing to startle Mika and risk his falling. Gritting his teeth, he quickened his pace, careful not to sway the top of the tree overly much.

Grabbing the top rung, Jeran pulled himself onto the platform. As he stood, the platform shifted, swaying hard to the left. Desperately, Jeran reached out to Mika, who seemed oblivious to the motion. When Jeran's hand grasped the boy's shoulder, Mika turned confused eyes in his direction, but they almost immediately returned to the city. Jeran let go, sighing to himself, and took a hold on the rail. He looked out at Lynnaei.

They were two hundred hands above the lower platform, higher than any other tree in this region of the forest. As far as the eye could see, the tops of the Great Trees were visible, green leaves blowing in the breeze. Jeran watched the forest sway, dancing in the wind, and it reminded him of the sea. He, Dahr, and Martyn had once accompanied King Mathis to the coast of Alrendria. Jeran remembered the feel of the coarse, sandy shore, the salt smell and gentle rolling of the blue waters, and the feeling of calm that had overcome him. This feeling was similar, yet subtly different.

To the north was the Emperor's Palace, the top of the plateau even higher than they were. The palace's thousand towers stared down at them from the heavens, but none reached as high as the Tower of the Five Gods. The alabaster spire stood isolated in the center of the plateau, rising so high that its top was lost in the clear, blue sky.

Jeran walked a slow circuit around the platform, careful not to let go his grip on the rail. In every direction, the stark beauty and majesty of Illendrylla struck him dumb. He struggled for breath, his knees wobbled, and he tightened his hands on the rail, afraid that he would lose his balance.

Mika stood similarly transfixed, his eyes wide. Slowly, one careful step after another, Jeran moved to the boy's side. "Do you feel it?" he asked in a whisper, afraid his words would destroy the feeling.

Mika swallowed, nodding his head dumbly. "This is the magic of nature," Jeran told him. "I have felt the same before, on several occasions." Jeran closed his eyes and lifted his face to the sky, allowing the light and warmth to penetrate him. "There are few places left which carry such feelings, Mika. Remember this always."

The boy was silent for a long moment. "I will, Lord Jeran," he said at last, his voice all seriousness.

His eyes still closed, Jeran took several slow, deep breaths and allowed the feeling to penetrate him. He felt the emptiness, the calm, which always preceded the focusing of his will. Sucking in a quick breath, Jeran went through the exercises the Emperor had taught him. Careful not to draw any of the flows, he willed the magic away.

Jeran's time with the Emperor had been well spent. He had progressed far enough in his training that he could hold magic at bay. No longer would he be a threat to his friends by unintentionally seizing magic. But his training had caused a new problem. Now, whenever he seized magic, any more than the tiniest amount, he lost control of his Gift and the magic ran wild.

Usually when that happened, the Emperor was quick enough to take the magic and direct it away from Jeran. But several times now, Jeran had drawn more magic than the old Elf could contain. Two of the Vale's beautiful trees were now charred cinders.

Without the aid of the Emperor, Jeran knew his Gift could run rampant. Here, suspended high above the Aelvin city, he could not begin to guess what damage magic could cause. Taking slow, calming breaths, he held the magic at bay, continuing the exercises long after the feeling had passed, until he was certain his Gift would not manifest itself.

When the magic receded, a slight tingling sensation remained. This feeling was also familiar; it warned him that a Reading was present. In this area, the Emperor had been even more successful. Jeran had almost complete control over his Readings now. They no longer came upon him in surprise, no longer frightened him with their intensity, no longer caused unbearable headaches. He could access them at will or push them away.

Just the other day, the Emperor had given him some great news. "I am no longer going to suppress your Readings," the old Elf had said. "You have progressed far enough. It's time you started taking responsibility for yourself." Jeran had gladly accepted the duty, honored that the Emperor felt him ready for such a responsibility. His training was far from over, though. Now the Emperor was teaching him how to force a Reading from an object, to see its history with a single touch.

Smiling to himself, Jeran opened himself to this Reading. A smell drifted to his nose on the suddenly-brisk winds, and he opened his eyes.

Above, stars shone in a clear night sky, but a thick ring of smoke rising from the forest was beginning to obscure them. Flames blanketed the forest, casting light brighter than the brightest day. Screams and shrieks echoed to him from the distance, and they were but part of the cacophony. The clang of metal on metal. The hiss of water as it attempted to quench the flames.

A ball of fire drifted over Jeran's head, hitting the tree behind him. The top of the Great Tree exploded in flames, and a wave of heat pounded Jeran's back. Streaks of lightning crackled through the forest, the jagged bolts falling from a clear sky.

Jeran forced the vision away, dropping to his knees. The MageWar. It must have been. To his knowledge, the only time that fire coursed through Lynnaei was during Lorthas' attack on the city, nearly nine hundred winters past. He drew a slow, shuddering breath, banished the remnants of the vision, and tried to calm himself by embracing the peaceful feeling he had experienced moments before.

Peace would not return to him. Though the sun once again shone across the sea of green, Jeran saw nothing but destruction, fires scouring away thousands of winters of history. Tears came unbidden to his eyes, and he struggled to force them away. Mika stared at him concernedly, a worried expression on his face. "Lord Jeran?" he called tentatively.

Jeran forced a smile. "I'm well, Mika," he said slowly, regaining his feet. "Just a little dizzy. Let's return to the lower levels. There's much more of the city we have yet to see." Mika's smile returned as he scampered down the ladder, Jeran several rungs behind.

They climbed down several more levels, until they reached one where the branches were broad enough to serve as bridges. This was a merchant level, a level where *Ael Pieroci* had their shops. Crossing from one tree to another, they examined the wares of the Aelvin craftsmen. Mika fell silent, his mood growing steadily darker. Finally, he turned to Jeran. "Lord Jeran?"

Jeran stopped, setting down the tapestry he had been inspecting. "Yes, Mika?"

"What will happen to us when we return to Alrendria? To my mother and me...and my sisters?" He added the last after a pause.

"I will find you a place in Kaper," Jeran replied, ready with an answer. He had already discussed this matter with Liseyl. "I know the King well, and I'm sure he'll find a place for you in the castle." Jeran smiled warmly. "Your mother's a very talented woman," he told Mika. "It would be a shame were her skills not put to use."

Mika nodded, but his eyes still seemed distracted. "You won't stay in Kaper though," he said at last. "At least, not for long. You're the First Seat of House Odara." He stated it as fact, and Jeran decided not to remind the boy that he did not hold the title. Yet. "You'll be going north, to Portal."

Jeran nodded, though he did not like to remind himself. "It's true. I'll have to return to my lands. Lord Talbot already tires of doing my duty for me, and I can do more good in Portal than elsewhere."

Mika nodded his head again, as if he had expected Jeran's words. "I want to go with you," he said confidently. "I want to go to Portal. To be your Guardsman."

Jeran cocked his head to the side, regarding the boy in a new light. "I'm honored, Mika," he said seriously. "But wouldn't you prefer to remain with your mother and sisters? Besides," he added the last with a smile. "You can't be *my* Guardsman. The Alrendrian Guard serves the King and Alrendria, not the Firsts."

"I don't want to serve the King," Mika replied defiantly, "or Alrendria. Only you, Lord Jeran." The conviction in Mika's voice took Jeran's breath away. The boy had spoken from the heart, and no sword, no army, no magic could match the power in those simple words.

"Mother will go with you as well," Mika announced. "Eilean and Ryanda will go where she says. Please, Lord Jeran. Take me with you when you go." His eyes were pleading.

Jeran could not refuse his request. "When I go, Mika, you may come with me. If that's truly what you want."

Mika smiled, a smile so broad and bright that it lifted Jeran's own spirits. A fraction of his earlier peace, the peace ruined by the Reading he had viewed, returned. Jeran put an arm around the boy's shoulders, and together, they walked across the nearest bridge to the next tree.

"Look at that!" cried Mika, pointing to a building crafted into the side of the Great Tree. The shop, supported on beams that ran into the thick trunk, hung suspended in the air, hundreds of hands above the ground. Arrayed on the outside of the shop, and glittering from within its windows, were crystalline figurines.

Mika pulled away from Jeran, running ahead. Jeran followed more slowly, allowing the boy time to explore on his own. As he entered the store, the quiet murmur of voices died away, and all eyes focused on him. "Good day to you," Jeran called out amicably, blushing under all the curious eyes.

In unison, the Elves bowed, bending low at the waist, their eyes locked with his. None spoke. No one moved. Finally, Jeran reached out to the nearest table and picked up a crystal figure cut into the shape of a hawk. He lifted it to eye level and inspected the piece closely, ignoring the eyes boring into his back.

He turned the figurine over in his hands, amazed by the flashes of rainbow color that jumped at him as the crystal caught the light. With Jeran's attention firmly on the crystal, the Elves regained their ability to move. One by one, the patrons disappeared, until only Jeran, Mika, and the Elves who owned the shop remained.

Mika stood face to face with an Aelvin boy. They were of a height, and near the same age, but the Elf was thinner. He stared at Mika curiously, his slanted green eyes sliding up and down. Mika returned the look in kind, his curiosity equal to the Elf's. "You are Human?" the Elf boy said, his words spoken slowly and carefully, as if he were not sure they were the correct ones.

Mika nodded. "Yes, I'm Human," he answered, offering the boy a small smile. "My name's Mika." He extended at hand. "What's yours?"

The Aelvin boy stared at Mika's hand in confusion. The owner of the shop, a tall Aelvin merchant dressed in the yellow and red of *Ael Pieroci*, knelt at the boy's side, whispering something in the fluid language of the Elves. The boy nodded his head at the words and took Mika's hand, shaking it tentatively. "I am Justyn."

"Justyn," Mika repeated the name, smiling at the sound. "Justyn, meet Lord Jeran Odara, First Seat of House Odara." Mika pointed at Jeran as he made the introduction.

The Elf's eyes widened into saucer-like orbs as he stared at Jeran. He quickly ducked his head in a bow and squeezed his eyes shut. When Jeran saw the Aelvin boy trembling, he took two quick steps forward and dropped to a crouch at his side. "Peace, Justyn," he said, trying to comfort the young Elf. "Peace. I mean you no harm."

The boy opened his eyes slowly, his head still bowed. Jeran smiled warmly, extending his own hand. "It's an honor to meet you," he added, ducking his own head down so their eyes were on a level.

Slowly, the Elf's thin hand reached out. When they touched, Jeran closed his larger hand over the boy's and gripped gently. "You have nothing to fear," he assured the Elf. "You may speak to me." He had discovered that many Elves were willing to talk to him, if he gave them permission.

"I am not...not worthy," Justyn replied. "You are...." the boy paused, searching for the right words. "You are *Teshou e Honoure.*"

Jeran stared at the boy in confusion. The merchant translated. "It means 'touched by the Gods.' " Justyn bobbed his head enthusiastically.

Jeran looked at the man, who dipped his head politely. "Touched by the Gods?" Jeran repeated, still confused. "What do you mean?"

"It is a great honor among our people," the Elf explained, "to be blessed by Valia. Or by any of the Gods." Jeran stood to face the Elf, who was shorter than he was and much thinner. "Surely, you are blessed by Balan," continued the storekeeper, "else you would not have been able to stop the *Noedra Synissti*, or defeat the honorable Luran in combat.

"It is said that you spend much of your time with the Emperor," he continued. "And the Emperor, may He live forever, is the Hand of Valia. Her presence in this world. For him to grant you so much of his time is surely proof that the Goddess favors you as well."

"I'm just a man," Jeran said. "No different from any other. No different than you."

The Elf smiled. "The Gods would not favor the arrogant, Great One."

Jeran put a hand to his head, squeezing his temples tightly. "Please," he said, almost begging, "Call me Jeran."

"As you wish...Jeran." The Elf bowed his head again.

"You too, Justyn," Jeran said, looking down at the boy. "You may call me Jeran, too." The boy nodded his head, but did not answer. Jeran smiled weakly, then returned his gaze to the shopkeeper. "And you are?"

"Mastyne," came the reply. Jeran offered his hand, and the Elf took it carefully, bowing reverently.

Jeran ignored the gesture. "Tell me, Mastyne, why do so many of your people speak my language?" Jeran pointed at Justyn. "Even your children know the Human tongue."

"Every Elf is required to learn a second language," Mastyne explained. "It is our way." His cheeks flushed slightly, and he expounded on the hastily-spoken statement. "There is little point in learning the language of the Orog. It is as dead as the Lost Race, something only the scholars wish to learn. Nor do many choose the language of the Wildmen. Many, such as Lord Luran, feel the Garun'ah are savages, and look down on any who show an interest in their ways."

Mastyne shrugged. "That leaves only the language of the Humans," he admitted, almost apologetically.

He glanced at his son. "Justyn, show…Mika…around the shop. You will have few such opportunities to practice speaking with Humans." The boy nodded in acquiescence and waved for Mika to follow him.

Jeran considered the Elf's words while they watched the boys stroll away. "You say *many* believe the Garun'ah are savages." He waited for Mastyne's confirming nod. "You do not share those feelings?"

"I am a simple merchant," Mastyne replied carefully. "I have never faced the charge of the Wildmen, as have *Ael Chatorra*. But to my thinking, the Garun'ah are no more evil than we. Were I to talk to one of them, I would likely learn they think us the monsters." He shrugged again, as if nervous. "I am just a simple merchant," he repeated.

"And a wise one," Jeran countered, earning himself another embarrassed bow. They talked a while longer, exchanging pleasantries and making small talk. Eventually, Mika returned at a run, holding a crystal in his hand.

"Lord Jeran! Lord Jeran!" he cried. "Look at this." He held the crystal out to Jeran, who took it gingerly. Carved to look like a swan, it had a long, slender neck of delicate crystal and eyes of blue sapphire. The entire figurine shimmered, reflecting tiny spots of color against Jeran's face. He turned the figurine over in his hand slowly, admiring the craftsmanship.

"Is this your creation?" he asked Mastyne.

The Elf shook his head. "I am only a merchant," he said with a smile. "It is my wife who is the artisan."

"Isn't it beautiful?" Mika exclaimed. "Mother would love it!"

"It is indeed a work of art," Jeran answered, lifting his gaze to Mastyne. "How much do you want for it?" he asked, searching his pockets for coin.

"It is yours, Great One," Mastyne replied, bowing his head again. "I cannot accept payment."

Jeran insisted. "I can't just take such an exquisite piece."

"When I say that my wife's work was admired by *Teshou e Honoure*, when I tell them you accepted a piece as a gift, my business will triple." Jeran shook his head, but now it was the Elf's turn to insist. "Take it!" he repeated. "My wife will…how do you say it…have my head if I make you pay for her work."

"I have no way to carry it," Jeran said, knowing this was his last excuse. "It would be a tragedy were it to break before I gave it to Liseyl."

Mastyne clapped his hands, and Justyn ran over. The Elf took the crystalline swan from Jeran and handed it to his son. "Wrap this up and take it to the palace. Deliver it to the Lady Liseyl, with our compliments. Tell her it is a gift from her son." Justyn bobbed his head, whispered goodbyes to Jeran and Mika, and disappeared into the back of the shop.

"I thank you," Jeran said to the Elf, whose cheeks flushed red. "If there's anything I can do to repay you…." Jeran let the words trail off, hoping Mastyne would make a suggestion.

"If it would not be too much trouble..." Mastyne started, but paused in the midsentence. Jeran had to encourage him to continue, "I believe these negotiations will be a success, and the Path of Riches will flow again. Many will resist dealing with Humans, but I will gladly welcome the new market.

"If it is not too much trouble." He paused again to clear his throat. "Allow your little friend to return. I would have my son make friends with a Human, so he better understands your people. He is *Ael Pieroci* too, and I would that he were successful in his trade."

Jeran looked back and forth between Mika, at his side, and Justyn, who was even now hurrying from the shop, the packaged crystal tucked under his arm. "Mika is free to return whenever he desires," Jeran said. "I will make sure a Guardsman is available to bring him here at all times."

Mastyne ducked his head again, this time in thanks. "I assure you," Jeran said as he walked Mika to the door, "when the beauty of your wife's craftsmanship reaches Alrendria, you will become one of the richest merchants in Madryn."

"You honor me, Great One."

"Jeran," said Jeran wearily. "Or Lord Odara. Anything but Great One."

"Of course," Mastyne apologized, smiling secretively.

They wandered aimlessly through the tree city, meandering from store to store, across broad bridges, and up and down levels in a seemingly random pattern. Mika led the way, beaming at every new discovery, and Jeran, too, marveled at the intricate layout of Lynnaei.

The lower levels served as storerooms for the businesses and homes above. Goods were raised and lowered in baskets, some only several hands across, others large enough to hold a horse comfortably. Thick ropes connected the baskets to an elaborate pulley system operated with cranks. Smaller baskets, some weighted with stone, but most carrying the refuse accumulated in the upper levels, lowered as the goods went up, helping to maintain stability.

Long, narrow wagons traversed the broad limb-avenues below, carting goods from one district to the next. On the higher levels, brown-robed *Ael Namisa* transported wares in baskets strapped to their backs. They moved busily, rarely stopping, though everyone paused to bow deeply at the waist when Jeran passed.

Flowers grew on every door, their colors showing which class of Elf lived, or worked, in the dwelling. Vines, with flowers of the same shades, snaked up the walls of each structure. Green and blue for *Ael Chatorra*, to show the location of a guardpost. Yellow and red, the colors of *Ael Pieroci*, for a shop or merchant's home. Gold and purple for *Ael Maulle*. Brown and tan for *Ael Namisa*.

The middle levels, where Jeran and Mika spent most of their time, were mainly shops and sentry posts. The homes of the Elves, and inns for guests, were several levels higher, and above them, taverns and thin rope bridges overlooked Lynnaei. There were occasional breaks in trees from where fields of green grass, or crops, could be seen growing far below. Brown-robed Elves tended the fields, appearing like insects from the upper levels of the city.

Vast houses, the homes and manors of the wealthy and powerful, sat on the fringes of the clearings. The homes extended far from the trunks of the Great Trees, so far it seemed like they would fall at the slightest breeze. Balconies lined with narrow rails overlooked the city.

Jeran cupped a hand to his eyes to shade them from the sun. Elves were sitting on the balconies, enjoying the cool afternoon breeze. Some were mending clothes, rocking back and forth in finely-carved wooden chairs. Others read, and still others occupied themselves with chores.

The streets were alive with action. *Ael Pieroci* hawked their wares from storefronts or carts. Artisans and crafters painted or sculpted in the plazas. *Ael Namisa* cleaned and repaired and carried. "It's just like a Human city," Jeran said to Mika.

The boy looked at him oddly. "It's in the trees," he replied seriously.

"Yes," Jeran laughed, "there is that. But otherwise, it's not so different from Kaper."

"Jeran!" called a voice far behind them. Jeran turned, peering through the throng of Elves. Martyn ran up the stairway to the platform, taking the steps two at a time. Breathing heavily, he jogged across the platform. Lisandaer and Raeghit appeared an instant later, hurrying to keep up with the prince.

Martyn stopped next to Jeran and Mika, putting a hand over his gut. "Thought I saw you," he wheezed, gasping for air, pointing down, "From down there. Takes forever to get from one place to another in this city!"

The prince smiled at Jeran's companion. "Hello, Mika," he said, his breathing finally starting to slow.

Mika bowed formally. "Greetings, Prince Martyn," he said reverently.

"You can call me Martyn," he told the boy, glancing from side to side conspiratorially. "When we're alone, at least." Mika smiled, and the prince raised his eyes to Jeran's. "What are you doing out here?" he asked. "I thought the Emperor kept you busy night and day."

"Mika wanted to see the city," Jeran informed the prince. "And Liseyl doesn't care for heights." Jeran clapped Martyn fondly on the shoulder. "What of you? Shouldn't you be embroiled in bitter negotiations?"

Martyn groaned. "Do not speak of such evil things!" he ordered. "I never thought it would be this bad. All the arguing. And over the most inconsequential things. Rafel is the worst of the lot, but even Alynna is starting to get into the game." Martyn's eyes twinkled. "Perhaps if she had something else to distract her, she–"

"Do not speak of such evil things!" Jeran interrupted, imitating the prince.

"It's good to see you, Jeran," Martyn laughed, grasping Jeran's shoulder and squeezing it tightly. His stomach grumbled, and the prince put his hand over it. "Let's find somewhere to eat," he suggested, earning an eager nod from Mika.

They began the long climb to the tavern levels, and Martyn filled Jeran in on the progress of the negotiations. "For all his complaining, it seems Rafel has finally won us an embassy in Lynnaei. Horeish, he's Luran's replacement, was adamantly against such a thing, but Charylla forced him to allow it. We will be allowed to build an embassy and will be given our own district, where shops can be built.

"We'll have access to the forest, but not to any Aelvin settlement other than Lynnaei. The Elves will establish a presence in both Western Grenz and Kaper, and their property in Grenz will have easy access to the eastern half of the city.

"As far as I can tell," Martyn said with a shrug, "that's the only thing of importance. The rest is just a bunch of trivialities. How much of each good must be supplied each season. Exchange rates between Aelvin currency and Alrendrian currency. How many Guardsmen, or Aelvin warriors, will be allowed to accompany the ambassadors. Whether the embassies will be subject to the laws of their own people or the land where they reside." Martyn rolled his eyes. "It's very boring," he said to Mika, who nodded his head seriously.

They reached the topmost level, and Martyn's eyes searched for an empty table. He found one against the far railing, and led the others to it, making sure to take the seat furthest from the edge. Jeran took the seat nearest the edge, his eyes dancing merrily as he leaned back against the rail. "What?" the prince demanded, blushing furiously.

"Nothing," Jeran said, shaking his head. "Are you sure you wouldn't prefer this seat, my Prince?" Martyn sneered at him, then they both broke out in merry laughter. The Guardsmen laughed at the prince's expense, too, but Raeghit also kept himself far from the edge, Jeran noticed.

An Elf appeared immediately, bowing deeply. Martyn ordered for them all, and the servant scurried away, eager to serve. She returned an instant later with five tall glasses: *brandei* for Jeran, Martyn, and the Guardsmen, and a weak cider for Mika. "The negotiations are not the worst part," Martyn confided, drinking deeply. "Lord Iban is."

Jeran sipped his own drink, and his eyes locked with Martyn's, waiting for the prince to expound. "He has me locked up with him all morning!" the prince lamented. "From sunrise until the start of the day's negotiations. And he usually reviews the sessions with me afterward, keeping me till late in the evening."

"What's wrong with that?" asked Jeran.

"Oh that's not the true problem," Martyn said. "Though I wish he would let me sleep a bit later. No, I've learned a great deal from him already. The old fox knows more than I ever would have guessed."

"Then what's the problem?" asked Jeran, his expression blank.

"It's the way he asks me questions," Martyn said. "He asks me what I think, nods his head sagely the entire time I'm talking, then tells me everything I forgot to think about!" Jeran's stern face finally broke into a small smile, and he nodded his head. "You know what I'm talking about?" Martyn asked, relieved.

"Most certainly!" Jeran replied. "Do you think all I was doing during the journey here was setting up Iban's tent and caring for his horse?" Jeran laughed loudly. "Not at all! I've been through the same treatment!"

"And you didn't want to strangle him?" Martyn asked. Mika's eyes grew as wide as saucers.

"Sometimes," Jeran admitted, tousling Mika's hair. "But then something occurred to me. Iban rarely told me I was wrong; he only pointed out things I had forgotten, or neglected, to consider. As time passed, those things became fewer and fewer." Jeran met Martyn's gaze. "He's just trying to teach us how to attack a problem from all sides, so we don't miss anything important."

"I suppose...." Martyn said, his words trailing off. He scratched his chin thoughtfully. "Now that you mention it, it does seem like he doesn't complain as much as he used to."

"See what I mean?" Jeran said, nodding to the Aelvin servant who reappeared, carrying five platters of steaming food. She set them on the table one by one, bowing deeply each time. She turned to go, and Martyn stopped her, offering her a gold coin.

The servant shook her head vigorously, folding her hands in front of her and casting her eyes to the floor. "Take it!" insisted Martyn, but the Elf still refused.

"It's a gift," Jeran explained in a soft voice. "A custom in Alrendria. A reward for service well done." The Elf opened her eyes, her lips pursing tightly together. She seemed to have something to say, but was hesitant to say it. "You may speak," Jeran assured her.

Her voice was high and lilting, but she spoke in hushed tones. "If one's duty is to serve," she asked, confused, "then why would one not serve well?" Her accent was light, her voice musical.

"If you won't take it for serving us," Martyn responded, holding out the coin, "then I offer it as a gift from person to person. Friend to friend." The Elf's cheeks turned bright red, but she took the coin, bowing deeply before she left.

They ate in silence, relishing the finely cooked meal. As time passed, the patrons at the other tables turned their gazes on the five Humans, staring openly. Jeran felt uncomfortable under all those eyes, but Martyn and Mika seemed not to notice, and the Guardsmen were embroiled in their own discussion. To distract himself, Jeran asked, "How much longer do you think the negotiations will continue?"

"Before we return to Alrendria?" Martyn asked, shoveling food into his mouth. He shrugged. "With the way these nobles argue, we could be here for winters." He grabbed his *brandei*, draining the remainder of the liquid in three quick gulps.

"Seriously," he said, setting the goblet back on the table, "We'll likely be here for the rest of the season. I wouldn't expect Lord Iban to return to Alrendria before the start of harvest."

"It's only the beginning of summer," Jeran pointed out. "I thought you said the hardest part of the negotiations were done."

"They are," Martyn replied. Finishing the last of his meal, he pushed the plate aside. "They are. But Iban feels we should take this opportunity to learn about the Elves. 'To facilitate peace between our Races.' " He said the last in a fair approximation of the Guard Commander's voice.

Mika giggled at the prince's impression, and even Jeran smiled. He opened his mouth to comment, but a familiar voice hailed him. "Well met, Tigers of Alrendria!" Astalian crossed the platform to their table, ducking low in a dramatic bow.

"Astalian!" cried Martyn, his eyes smiling. "Where have you been keeping yourself these last days."

"Ah, my dear Prince of Alrendria," came the Elf's reply. "Duty called, and I, ever the obedient servant of my people, answered." He looked back and forth between Jeran and Martyn, grinning slyly. "But where I was is of no matter," he laughed. "It is where I am that is important."

"Astalian," Jeran said, pointing to Mika, "I'd like you to meet someone. This is Mika, a dear friend of mine. Mika, this is Astalian, the greatest of the Aelvin warriors."

The Elf bowed again, sweeping his arm to the side in a dramatic flourish. "Now, my friend, there is no reason to exaggerate. I am only the greatest of the *living* Aelvin warriors." He winked at Mika. "I am sure there was at least one better in all the winters since the Goddess created us."

Mika laughed at the Elf's joke, and Astalian reached over and grasped Mika's hand at the elbow. "Well met, Mika." Mika grasped the Elf's arm, and Astalian feigned a pained expression, dropping to his knee. "Enough, fearsome warrior!" he cried. "I yield!" Mika released the Elf's hand, laughing uncontrollably. Astalian winked again as he stood and turned to Jeran. "He will make a terrifying warrior some day."

"It's an honor to meet you, Sir," said Mika, smiling up at the Elf.

"And you as well," replied Astalian. To Jeran and Martyn, he said, "Have you two plans for the afternoon? Dinner with the Emperor, perhaps? A secret rendezvous in some dusty corner of the palace?"

They shook their heads, and Astalian's eyes brightened. "The Goddess be praised! Then you can come with me! Tonight is *ael Chatel e Valia*." At the blank stares he received, he translated. "The Feast of Valia! The summer celebration in honor of the Goddess!"

He stepped to the side of the table, putting one arm on Jeran's shoulder, the other on Martyn's. "There will be drinking, dancing, and all manner of merriment. We will stand around the fire and watch the night lights, singing songs in honor of the Goddess." With a mischievous look at Martyn, he added, "We can even offer the Goddess a sacrifice, should that be to your liking!"

Martyn looked interested, but Jeran waved his hands. "I'd love to accompany you," he said, shaking his head, "but I'm afraid my young friend's mother may not approve." He looked at Mika, whose smile slowly faded.

"Say no more, Jeran," Astalian said in defeat, his head hanging low. From the corner of his eye he looked at Mika, winked, then whistled a series of notes. From around the platform, *Ael Chatorra* stopped what they were doing and approached the Aelvin warrior. They stopped behind him, forming rank.

"Elsynder," Astalian said without turning around. "We have been neglecting some of our Human guests." He pointed to Mika. "Would you be so kind as to show my young friend the armory. Teach him how we use our weapons. Maybe even take him on patrol with you?" Astalian's eyes glittered as he looked at Mika. "If that sounds like something you would be interested, my little friend."

Mika's smile covered his entire face. "It sounds wonderful!"

Astalian's smile mirrored the boy's. He turned to face the Aelvin warriors. "He is to be shown every honor," Astalian commanded, "and returned to the Emperor's Palace before full dark, delivered to the hands of the Lady...."

"Liseyl," supplied Martyn.

"Liseyl," repeated Astalian, bowing his head in thanks. "Should any harm befall him...." Astalian did not finish the statement, but the sentiment was clear.

Elsynder saluted, smiling at Mika. "It is an honor, mighty Astalian," he said, waving his arm toward the stairs, waiting for Mika to follow.

Astalian's eyes were full of mirth as he looked at Jeran. "Is a patrol of twenty enough to secure your freedom, great warrior of Alrendria?" he asked. "I know your prowess is legendary. Should these meager troops prove insufficient, I can muster a full squad of fifty."

Jeran laughed, shaking his head in defeat. "Twenty will be enough! Besides, if I said no now, I'd have a much greater threat to my safety." He looked pointedly at Mika, who was so eager to join the Elves that he trembled in his seat.

"I can go?" he asked, full of excitement. Jeran nodded, and Mika was out of his seat in a flash.

As Elsynder introduced the boy to the other warriors, Astalian leaned in close and whispered conspiratorially, "Now the fun will truly begin!"

Chapter 18

As Elsynder and the Aelvin warriors whisked Mika away, Astalian took the boy's seat and waved for the serving girl. The brown-robed Elf hurried over, bowing to the new arrival. *"Brandei!"* Astalian said enthusiastically, "A bottle. The best you have. Hot." Directing a meaningful look at Jeran and Martyn, he smiled wickedly. "It goes to your head faster when it is warmed."

Jeran groaned dramatically, covering his eyes with his hand, and Martyn reached over the table to cuff him on the shoulder. "Be nice, Jeran," he said. "We must be polite to our Aelvin hosts." With a sly look at Astalian, he added, "It would be rude of us to refuse an invitation. Especially to a celebration in honor of the Goddess."

Astalian was quick to jump on the prince's cue. "My people take such festivities very serious," he said in an overly serious tone, schooling his features to a strict calm. "The same way they take everything else. If you refuse the invitation...." He let the statement trail off. "I do not know how such a dishonor will be received. You may find yourself challenged to a score of duels."

Jeran removed the hand from his eyes and looked at his two companions incredulously. "You don't think I believe any of this, do you?" Astalian's eyes glittered, and Martyn shrugged shyly. "Very well," Jeran conceded, trying hard not to laugh. "If it's that important to your people."

"You will come with us?" Astalian asked, a bright smile on his face.

"I could use a night away from the palace," Jeran admitted.

The Aelvin warrior shook his head. "I never thought I could convince you! You run from parties like a rabbit from a fox."

Martyn howled with laughter, slapping his knee. "He's right, Jeran!" the prince commented. "Getting you out to have a good time is harder than convincing my father of my innocence."

"Innocence at what?" asked the Elf, confused.

"At whatever it is he thinks I did!"

Jeran tried to ignore them, but both were relentless; their jokes continued uninterrupted until the *brandei* arrived. The bottle of red liquid sat in a steaming bucket of water, the cork already loosened. The servant placed the bucket in the middle of the table, along with six glasses. Martyn smiled at the girl. "Six?" he queried. "Are we to have the honor of your company, m'Lady?"

The Elf smiled, her cheeks once more turning red. "The sixth glass is for me," said Treloran, stepping up from behind the Aelvin woman.

"Acceptable company," Astalian remarked gravely. "If not as desirable." The servant giggled, then hastily clapped a hand over her mouth. Her face turned the same shade as the *brandei*. Treloran cast an evil look at his friend and sat in the table's sixth chair.

"How did you find us?" Martyn asked the prince, his eyes shifting to Astalian. "And you as well? It was pure chance I came across Jeran, yet it seems you two knew exactly where to find us."

A stunned silence followed Martyn's question. "You are joking?" Astalian asked cautiously, his face contorted. To Treloran, he said, "I have difficulty telling when these Humans jest." The Aelvin Prince nodded in agreement.

When Martyn did not laugh, Astalian could barely contain his surprise. "You truly meant it!" he said, almost in question, still half disbelieving. "I told Treloran to find me with you and Jeran," Astalian explained. "But for as to *how* we found you...." He waved his hands in an expansive gesture that encompassed the entire platform. "What do you see, Prince of Alrendria."

Martyn looked around, scanning the platform. Most of the tables were filled, and most of the eyes were trained on them. Martyn suddenly felt uncomfortable.

"Let us forget for a moment that you and Jeran are Humans in a land of Elves. You are Martyn Batai!" Astalian spoke seriously, as if his words were something of which Martyn were not aware. The prince felt his cheeks burning. "Prince of Alrendria, who fought in a joust nearly twoscore days ago and fell from the Great Trees, yet managed to survive."

The Elf's eyes shifted to the left. "Your friend is Jeran Odara," he continued, as if introducing them, "First Seat of a Great House, *Teshou e Honoure*. Touched by the Gods. He is the only person, of any race, to stop a *Noedra Synissti* from killing its target, and he is the Human who defeated Luran, our greatest warrior, excepting me of course, in single combat.

"It is as if you carry the sun on your shoulders," Astalian finished with a laugh. "I could close my eyes and find you anywhere in the city."

"You have more titles than me," Martyn pouted, casting a sidelong glance at Jeran.

"Not by choice," came Jeran's quick response.

"Do not worry, my friend," Astalian replied consolingly, placing an arm around the prince's shoulders. "We will endeavor to add more laurels to your name before night's end." He pulled the bottle from the bucket, sniffing deeply. "Ahhh," he said, filling their glasses, "Just right." Finished pouring, he returned the *brandei* to the hot water and lifted his glass. "To friendship," he toasted.

Jeran and Martyn raised their glasses in unison. "To friendship," they repeated. Lisandaer and Raeghit repeated the toast.

Treloran looked each of his companions in the eye, then lifted his own glass. "To friendship," he stated in a quiet voice, earning himself a clap on the back from Astalian. The six companions drank deeply.

"Did I not tell you!" Astalian said matter-of-factly to the Aelvin Prince. "You have grown to like these Humans. Just as the Emperor thought you would."

"Grandfather is very wise," Treloran said glumly, sipping his *brandei*. "He was right, these Humans are almost bearable."

"Your compliment is greatly appreciated," Martyn replied wryly.

Astalian laughed loudly. "What my gloomy brother-in-arms means to say is that he was wrong, and you Humans are not the evil creatures he thought you were." The Aelvin warrior glared at Treloran, who blushed fiercely under the burning gaze. "But you must forgive his lack of manners. His uncle will not take his change of heart well. Treloran does not look forward to their next meeting."

"What of Luran?" Jeran asked, worried about Dahr. "Has there been any word?" He had no idea where his friend and the Guardsmen were, but if hostilities between the Elves and Garun'ah were renewed, Dahr and the others might be caught in the maelstrom.

Treloran shook his head. "Some brief reports," he answered. "My uncle still searches for the Wildmen."

Jeran nodded, shifting his gaze to Astalian. "I spoke with one of my Guardsmen a couple days ago," he told the Elf, "and something he said concerns me."

"One of the Guardsmen I took on Forest Patrol?" he asked seriously, his demeanor changing in an instant. Gone were the laughing eyes and murmured jests, the carefree attitude and bantering tone. Astalian's back straightened, his head lifted high, and his was voice proud and commanding. This was Astalian the warrior, the legendary Aelvin fighter.

"Bystral told me there were tracks outside the city," Jeran stated. "He also said you were concerned by them."

Green eyes bored into Jeran intently. "It is true," he said at last, the confession difficult. "In several locations there were indications of a large party moving toward the city. They were careful not to leave a trail, but I know what to look for." Astalian drummed his fingers on the table, his *brandei* temporarily forgotten.

"There is no record of a large group entering the city," he admitted. "Which could mean they turned back." His eyes shifted to Treloran. "Or it could mean they know the location of a passage."

"A passage?" Martyn asked.

"During the MageWar," answered Treloran, "several passageways were cut through the city walls, so the Emperor could be evacuated if Lynnaei fell. The locations of the passages were known to very few, and *Ael Maulle* used their magic to hide the openings."

"What does it mean?" Jeran asked. "Do you suspect the *Noedra Shamallyn*? Is Prince Martyn in danger?"

"The *Noedra Shamallyn*...." Astalian repeated, shaking his head. "No. But it may be the *Kohrnodra*."

"*Kohrnodra*?"

"The Brotherhood of Kohr," explained Treloran. "They are a sect of Elves who have forsaken Valia and instead worship her father, Kohr. They believe the Emperor, the Hand of Valia, needs to be removed from power, and a new emperor raised in his place."

"They are a vile bunch," added Astalian. "Purists. They believe anything not Aelvin is corrupt. They wish to restore the Elves to their one-time power, and remove all vestiges of the other Races from our culture."

Astalian turned his head to the side, spitting on the ground. "There have been similar groups in Humans lands," he reminded them. "The Arkamians, who allied with the Darklord, despised all that was not Human. More recently there was another...." The Elf's words trailed off as he searched his memory for the name.

"The Purge of Ra Tachan," Jeran supplied. "The Tachans tried to destroy everything of magic."

Astalian nodded. "The Purge," he repeated, disgusted. He drained the remainder of his glass, smacking his lips together as if to clean the vile word away. "Tonight is the feast of Valia," he reminded them. "Were I *Kohrnodra*, I would want to do something to ruin the celebration."

They drank the remainder of the *brandei* in silence, their thoughts growing ever darker. Finally Astalian stood, pushing his chair back forcefully. "This is nonsense!" he exclaimed, recovering some of his usual exuberance. "It is *ael Chatel e Valia*! I refuse to let the likes of *Kohrnodra* ruin my celebration." In a lower voice, he added, "And I would welcome the presence of five skilled blades, should those fools dare show themselves tonight."

Martyn's eyes danced with anticipation, and even Treloran looked eager for a fight. "Am I the only one who would rather not get a blade shoved through my ribs?" Jeran asked, standing.

"I for one would prefer to keep my skin intact, Lord Odara," Raeghit said with a smile.

Astalian clapped Jeran on the shoulders, and the others stood. Following Astalian, the party traveled down the winding staircase and through the city of Lynnaei. Evening was rapidly approaching, and what little sunlight penetrated the Great Trees was quickly fading. Around them, small orbs began to flicker into being, casting a warm, golden light on the avenues. As always, the many exotic sights of Lynnaei capitvated Jeran. Elves crowded the platforms; their raucous laughter and spirited conversations filled the air. A myriad of entertainers appeared. Jugglers tossed flaming brands over the heads of onlookers and acrobats tumbled along the railings, unconcerned with their height.

Ael Maulle walked the streets, using their magic to strengthen weakening orbs, or creating new ones where extra light was needed. "Some lights burn for decades without dimming," Astalian said when he noticed Jeran's interest. "Others dim after a season or two. It is the duty of *Ael Maulle* to ensure the lights remain constant."

Astalian led them ever deeper into the city, away from the familiarity of the Emperor's Palace. They passed countless Elves, some still hard at work, but most already joining in the celebration. Wherever they went, glasses were raised high in praise of Valia, Goddess of the Elves.

One group of Elves laughed uproariously, their customary reserve temporarily gone. Another was busy hauling a cart laden with casks of *brandei*, wine, and ale toward the site of the celebration. Still another group, purple and white robed *Ael Alluya*, had gathered around a brown-robed Elf. The girl stood on a bench, reciting a poem about Valia's beauty. At the sight, Martyn grew confused, and he tugged on Treloran's sleeve. "I thought *Ael Namisa* were not allowed to speak to the Ruling Class."

"Only if they are spoken to first," corrected Treloran, grabbing a glass of wine offered by a passerby. "But the Feast of Valia is one of our most important celebrations, and everyone is given the right to speak."

"We shed the shackles of our castes," Astalian added dramatically, spinning slowly, his arms held out wide. "And acknowledge all our brethren as Valia's children."

A tall, shapely, Aelvin woman, wearing the colors of the artisan class, mistook Astalian's gesture. She embraced him tightly, pressing her lips to his. "May the blessing of the Goddess be on you, Noble One," she said with a smile, continuing on her way.

"And on you as well," murmured the Elf, brushing a finger along his lips. He laughed merrily and urged them to continue onward. "We are not even near the fires yet!" he exclaimed. Jeran and Martyn shared a look. If this was nowhere near the celebration, they wondered what the true festivities would be like.

A full moon was rising overhead, and the glowing orbs dimmed considerably where the pale moonlight touched. Elves by the hundreds walked with them, more than a few locked together in tight embraces, shamelessly kissing their neighbors. The way soon became crowded. Above and below, the other levels of Lynnaei were similarly packed, with more Elves filtering into the area with every passing moment. After a while, the six companions had to fight just to move forward.

Finally, Astalian had enough. "Make way!" he yelled, startling the couple before him. "Make way for Prince Treloran, Grandson of Emperor Alwellyn." The nearest Elves jumped, pushing against those around them, trying to give their prince some room.

"Make way for Martyn, Prince of Alrendria!" Astalian shouted, and more Elves turned startled eyes in their direction. "Make way for Jeran the Mighty, the Odaran Wolf!" Jeran groaned at the Elf's playful words, but the crowd reacted much more violently. The throng of people surged away from them; hundreds of eyes turned in their direction.

"Make way for the honorable Astalian!" shouted Martyn, already enjoying himself. "The legendary Aelvin warrior!" He smiled at Astalian, who returned the gesture in kind.

Around the six, an empty space formed, nearly ten hands in diameter. The Elves surrounding them stared in awe at their august company, and none dared step inside the circle. "Much better," Astalian laughed, waving his companions forward. The crowd parted around them, almost as fast as they could walk. Astalian led them down another flight of stairs, and they found themselves on the ground. Thick, green grass and brilliant wildflowers blanketed the forest floor.

Astalian walked ahead, stopping underneath a giant, trellised archway spanning the distance between two of the Great Trees. *Ael Chatorra* stood to either side of the arch, guarding the entrance. They bowed formally at Astalian's approach, and again when Treloran and the Humans joined him. "We have been awaiting your arrival," the Elf on the left said.

Astalian nodded seriously. "Has there been any trouble?"

The guard shook his head. "A scuffle near one of the other entrances, but nothing out of the ordinary."

"Keep your eyes open," Astalian warned. "It would be terrible were something to ruin the Goddess' feast." The soldier bowed again, stepping aside so they could pass. Astalian strode boldly into the clearing, followed immediately by Treloran and Martyn. After a brief hesitation and a shared smile, the Guardsmen crossed beneath the archway. Jeran entered last.

The clearing was vast, a broad circle several thousands hands across, ringed by the Great Trees, which stretched equally high around the perimeter. Far fewer people stood within the clearing than without, but it still was difficult to move without bumping into those nearby.

Martyn turned to the Guardsmen. "Feel free to explore. I will be safe enough in the company of Astalian." Raeghit and Lisandaer bowed, but made no move to depart. Martyn, laughing, pointed to a nearby party of Guardsmen. "There are others close enough to offer protection, should I need it. You have served well. Enjoy yourselves!" Saluting fist-on-heart, the two Guardsmen disappeared into the crowd.

Ael Namisa wove deftly through the throng, carrying trays laden with food or drinks. Astalian waved to one servant, who hurried to them, weaving with incredible dexterity through the ocean of people. "The Goddess' blessing on you," she said, extending the tray in their direction.

Astalian took four glasses and handed them out to his companions. Then he turned and kissed the servant on the lips, not as strongly as the artisan had kissed him. "Goddess' blessing," he intoned.

To both Jeran and Martyn's surprise, Treloran also leaned over and kissed the servant, though his was but a light touch on the cheek. "The Goddess' blessing," he murmured.

"And on you, my Prince," she replied, turning to face Jeran and Martyn. She stood there, waiting expectantly.

"It is believed that the Goddess gives of herself to create us all," Astalian explained. "That she crafts each of us with her own hands, like a sculptor shapes a statue. During the feast of Valia, we congratulate the Goddess on her craftsmanship. When you see someone you admire, one who stirs the fires of your passion, you bestow upon that individual a kiss. Valia feels each kiss herself, accepting it in recognition of her handiwork."

"One does not have to embarrass oneself," Treloran assured them. "Any kiss will suffice."

"But," countered Astalian, "the more passionate the kiss, the more you claim to admire Valia's work." He looked at the servant, who waited patiently while the Elves explained the custom to their Human guests. "Not to offer a kiss is to claim the Goddess' creation is not a thing of beauty."

"Astalian finds much beauty," Treloran said dryly. "He offers a great deal of praise to the Goddess."

"I am a simple warrior," Astalian laughed, draining his glass and taking another from the servant's tray, "not an aesthetic. To a warrior, all life is beautiful." He chuckled at his own comment. "Besides, who am I to judge the Goddess on the worthiness of her creations?"

Smiling, Martyn leaned in, pressing his lips to the servant's mouth. She kissed him back, more forcefully than he had intended to kiss her. He jerked back in surprise. "I am beginning to like the customs of your people, Prince Treloran," he told them, gulping his wine.

"Good thing we'll be returning to Alrendria before the start of harvest," Jeran said sarcastically as he leaned in to kiss the Aelvin girl's cheek. "Else we would never be able to convince Martyn to come home." His statement earned a reproachful look from the prince, but sent Astalian into gales of laughter.

The servant disappeared into the crowd, but not before Astalian grabbed two more glasses from her tray, one for Jeran and one for himself. Jeran looked at the still half-full glass in his hand. "I'm not yet finished with this drink."

"You will be," Astalian assured him, "soon enough."

Jeran smiled as he took the second glass, and he followed the Aelvin warrior toward the center of the clearing. The festival amazed him, stunned him speechless. It was as if the Elves had completely discarded their stern facades and social rigidity. Brown-robed *Ael Namisa* drank alongside *Ael Maulle*, and both laughed at crude jokes made by *Ael Alluya*, who wore the purple and white of their class.

Musicians were everywhere. Pipes and flutes, sometimes alone, other times in accompaniment, played music, raucous and merry. Other Elves plucked at the strings of lyranthes, and one garishly-dressed Aelvin musician sat at a huge harp, fingers flying over the strings.

Many Elves danced to the music, though often to a different beat than their partners. Some Elves displayed the colors of their class proudly, but most hid behind brightly-colored costumes and feathered masks. Half-dressed men, their upper bodies oiled and glowing in the moon and fire-light, stared passionately from behind their masks at passing women, many only slightly more dressed than the men.

Everywhere, people were kissing, and sometimes more than just kisses were exchanged. *Brandei* flowed in rivers from the taps on giant casks; wine fell like rain into the waiting mouths of the Elves. Even ale, never a favorite drink among the Elves, was doled out in generous portions. Jeran stared, mouth agape, at the sudden transformation of the citizens of Lynnaei.

"Look at that!" said Martyn, pointing. Jeran followed the finger until he saw Bystral and Raeghit walking toward them, a tankard of ale in each hand and an Aelvin woman under each arm. The women wore sheer skirts, slit high up the side and showing every curve on their bodies. A thin strip of cloth covered their tops, barely concealing small, firm breasts. Masks with matching plumes of red and gold on the sides hid their faces.

"Guardsmen," Jeran nodded in greeting, trying to hide a smile. To Astalian, he said, "It seems some of our people are already setting aside racial prejudices." Bystral blushed at the words, but he made no move to remove his arms from the women.

"If only everyone were as eager to bring our peoples together," replied the Elf. The women giggled at his words, disentangling themselves from the Guardsmen long enough to plant tender kisses on the cheeks of all the men and whisper 'Goddess' blessing.' When finished, they returned to their Human chaperones.

"They are almost different people!" Bystral told Jeran. "I'd never have expected–" He cut off abruptly, blushing furiously, when one of the women ran a hand up his shirt. Pulling her hand out forcefully, he looked around in embarrassment. "Yesterday they were more reserved than the most proper noblewoman. Today–" He was interrupted again when his other companion started nibbling on his ear.

"–they are more forward than a serving wench in the wharves of Kaper," finished Raeghit, eyeing his two companions appreciatively.

"There are only a handful of holidays like this each four-season," Astalian explained. "Most of my people spend the better part of their lives controlling their…passions. When they are given the chance to indulge themselves, they do not waste it.

"*Ael Chatorra* are better than most of the classes," he admitted. "We appreciate life more than the others, probably because we are asked to risk ours in defense of the Empire. Most of us," he added, with a significant glance at Treloran, "do not hold ourselves back. Even when there is no reason to celebrate!"

"Just because you like to share your bed with anything showing half an interest," Treloran retorted, a quaver of anger in his voice, "does not mean I have to."

"You show no interest in anything, Treloran," Astalian replied curtly. He turned to Martyn, but spoke loud enough for the Aelvin Prince to overhear. "I worry for him. If I did not know better, I would guess my young friend has given his heart away. That is not a wise thing for a prince to do, Martyn, as I am sure you are aware. His heart is not his to give."

"Yet you think my loins should be a gift to the masses?" Treloran snarled, glaring at the Aelvin warrior. "I do not need your coddling, Astalian. Nor do I need your protection."

Jeran interceded, stepping between the two before their heated exchange erupted into a full-blown argument. "Enough, my friends!" he said, drawing both Astalian's and Treloran's eyes. "Stop this! You're not enemies."

"Astalian," he said, looking at the blonde warrior. "Your concern for Treloran is admirable. But he is his own man, and must make his own choices." Jeran smiled briefly. "A lesson I learned all too painfully from my own prince."

Astalian seemed shamed. "My apologies, Highness," he said, bowing his head formally. "My suggestions are only out of concern."

Treloran schooled his features, hiding his pain. "I know, old friend," he said, grabbing the Elf's shoulder warmly. "But you are wrong. My heart is mine to give. It is the rest of me which belongs to the Empire."

"Here, here!" said Martyn, extending a full glass of *brandei* to the Aelvin Prince. "To us!" he said to Treloran. "To those whose lives have been taken from them. To those with no choice in who they love. Or what they want to do." He raised his glass high. "To the slaves of the Empire!"

Treloran smiled weakly. "To the slaves of the Empire," he echoed, and they downed the thick red liquid. Treloran's smile broadened, and he shook off his melancholy. "It seems we understand each other, Prince Martyn."

"We are not so different," Martyn agreed.

"I will try to take your words as a compliment," the Elf replied wryly. To hide his laugh, he turned in the direction of the bonfire, which now rose high above the assembly, casting warmth and light to the far ends of the field.

"He is not himself," Astalian confided to the prince. "I worry for him."

"He will be well," Martyn assured the Elf. "Duty is a painful burden at times."

"Truly," replied Astalian sadly, starting after the Aelvin Prince. Jeran and Martyn did their best to keep pace with the dexterous Elf, but were waylaid every few steps by passing Aelvin women demanding the Goddess' blessing.

The bonfire stood before them, a tower of flame rising more than sixty hands into the clear summer sky, its light so bright that one could not gaze directly upon it. Stars shone above, more stars than Jeran had ever seen in his life. A statue stood before the fire, a statue of the Goddess Valia, constructed of living plants.

Jeran stared at the construction, stunned speechless by its detail and beauty. The body was of flowered vines, entwined around an elaborate trellis. White lilies formed the skin, red roses the lips, lilacs the eyes. Valia wore a dress of vibrant, multi-colored petals. From a distance, in the flickering shadows cast by the fire, the statue seemed real. Alive.

Treloran stood to one side of the statue, talking to a woman dressed in green and brown leather armor, with a sash of blue draped over her shoulder. The Aelvin Prince's sullen mood was gone; he spoke animatedly to the soldier, beaming when his comments brought a smile to her face. Jeran frowned, beginning to understand Astalian's concern.

"My favorite Human," called a musical voice, and Jeran turned, stunned at the sight of the Aelvin beauty. But her words were not meant for him; she eyed Martyn confidently, her green eyes playing with his.

"Kaeille!" Martyn said, smiling broadly, his eyes roving her body. Kaeille wore a skirt of sheer blue silk, tight across her hips and hanging low to the ground, though slit high up one leg. A shirt, if it could be called that, consisting of two narrow strips of red, crossed her chest, hiding modest breasts. Skin of smooth, porcelain white gleamed in the firelight. A long dagger was sheathed at her side, and the hilt of a shortsword protruded over one shoulder, but the weapons did not detract from her appearance. If anything, they only served to accentuate it.

Martyn's eyes roved unashamedly over her body, and he stepped forward quickly, placing one hand on either side of the woman's face, and kissed her, hard. Her arms tightened around him reflexively. Jeran watched in astonishment, surprised by the prince's action. He put a hand to his forehead, squeezed his temples, and leaned over to whisper to Astalian. "It seems Treloran is not the only one we should worry about."

The Elf smiled sadly at Jeran's comment. "My heart aches for them," he said honestly, a smile suddenly blossoming on his face, "but *we* are the ones who will have to listen to them complain about their duty." He raised his glass in toast. "To those forced to listen to the woes of princes," he said, trying to find some humor in the situation.

Jeran clinked his glass into the Elf's. "May the Gods have mercy on us," he added, and they both drank deeply.

Martyn finally broke his embrace with the Aelvin warrior. "The Goddess' blessing on you," he said, pleasantly surprised by the blooms of red that formed on her cheeks.

She touched a hand lightly to her lips. "I was not aware you thought so highly of me," she admitted, embarrassed. Suddenly her eyes glinted. "And to think I was only going to kiss your cheek."

Martyn feigned a sad expression while he introduced Kaeille to his companions. Astalian she knew, but when Martyn introduced Jeran, her skin whitened visibly, and her eyes widened into green and white orbs. "I am honored," she whispered reverently.

Trying to hide his own embarrassment, Jeran leaned in to kiss her cheek. "Goddess' blessing," he said, watching as her hand went up to caress her face. "I am just a man," he assured her. "A man fortunate enough to spend time with the Emperor. I am not touched by the Gods." She stared at him blankly, as if he had spoken gibberish.

Martyn's eyes went back and forth between Jeran and Kaeille, his brow furrowed in confusion. "*Ael Chatorra!*" Astalian snapped, and Kaeille jumped to attention. "It is not polite to stare, even at one favored by the Goddess." That earned him an evil glare from Jeran. "Besides," the Aelvin warrior added, "the Prince of Alrendria requires an escort. Someone to keep him from trouble."

"It would be an honor, Mighty Astalian," she said, ducking her head in salute. Taking Martyn by the arm, she led him into the crowd, calling for *brandei*.

"Is that wise?" Jeran asked.

"You and Treloran!" came the irritated response. "You two are cut of the same cloth." Astalian stared at Martyn and Kaeille, huddled close together, whispering to each other. "I will tell you the same thing I tell my chaste, innocent prince. Martyn is young, and before long, duty will force him to set aside his own desire for the sake of Alrendria. Let him enjoy what is offered, so he at least has the bittersweet memories of what was to keep him company during the long nights ahead."

"On some things, Astalian" Jeran said, turning his back on Martyn, "we will never see eye to eye." Suddenly, the stern face of Charylla emerged from the crowd, and Jeran flinched. The princess wore a gown of green silk, her hair piled high atop her head.

"If you can live with our differences, so can–" Astalian cut off when he noticed the princess. He bowed deeply. "Highness," he said in greeting.

She leaned forward, brushing her lips against his cheek. "Goddess' blessing," she said, repeating the ritual on Jeran. They returned the gesture in kind. "Astalian," she said, her face resuming a stern countenance. "I desire your presence on the morrow. I have concerns with *Ael Chatorra* I need to discuss."

"Of course, Highness," came the immediate reply. "But if there is a problem with the troops, it is Luran to whom you should speak."

"My brother is not here," the princess pointed out. After a pause, she added, "And my brother is one of the subjects I wish to discuss."

"I understand, Highness." Charylla whirled around and disappeared into the crowd.

A servant passed, and Astalian halted him long enough to place his half-drunk glass on the tray. "It seems duty places its burdens on me at times as well." He laughed at Jeran's questioning look. "Dealing with the Imperial Family is difficult enough without a hangover."

Jeran laughed. "On that, at least, we agree," he returned, setting his own glass on the tray and clapping an arm around Astalian's shoulders. They walked to the base of the statue and, to protect them from the waves of heat rolling off the bonfire, they stood in the Goddess' shadow. The music grew louder, and more than a few voices lifted in song. Couples danced all around them, twirling in tight circles. Those not dancing were usually giving the Goddess' blessing to every member of the opposite gender who happened past.

Ael Chatorra stood guard at every entrance to the field, and more leather-clad warriors patrolled the confines of the clearing. Still others, like Kaeille, had joined in the festivities, though their weapons were close at hand. "Do you expect much trouble from the *Kohrnodra*?" Jeran asked, pointing to a group of Aelvin warriors.

Astalian dismissed them with a gesture. "A few fights perhaps. Maybe they'll attack a few of the more inebriated on their way home. The Brotherhood of Kohr is a scattered collection of zealots, a hundred small bands of misfits. They are not organized enough to cause serious trouble."

"Then why all the guards?"

"With the exception of the Emperor, and Luran, the entire Imperial Family is here. If something were to happen...." Astalian let the sentence drag out. "Suffice it to say, were something to happen to any of the Emperor's kin, Luran would hold me responsible."

"Ah, Jeran," said Jes, stepping around the side of the statue. "I was not sure if I would see you here tonight." She was dressed in a gown of white that accentuated her shapely curves perfectly. Her hair, freshly cut and curled, hung loose about her shoulders. Twin pools of blue, the color of the sky, stared at Jeran intently, and a slight smile parted her red lips.

Jeran felt uncomfortable under her intense gaze. He stepped toward her, placing a light kiss on her cheek. "The Goddess' blessing," he said, the same way he had said it a thousand times before.

When he pulled back, Jes' smile had turned into a frown. "That's it?" she said, her tone hurt. "I was told the passion behind the kiss was related to the beauty of the one who received the token." She cast her eyes to the ground, fluttering her eyelashes. "I believed you thought more highly of my beauty." She pouted her lips, but her eyes danced mirthfully.

Jeran's cheeks turned bright red, but Astalian came to his rescue. "He is new to our ways, Lady Jessandra, as are you all. I am sure poor Jeran meant no offense." He stepped between Jes and Jeran, embracing her warmly and planting a passionate kiss on her lips. Her eyes widened in surprise at the sudden onslaught of affection, and now it was Jeran's turn to hide his amusement.

Astalian finally pushed Jes away. "The Goddess' blessing," he told her. Jes looked flustered; one hand smoothed her hair while the other straightened her dress. Jeran opened his mouth, a choice comment on the tip of his tongue, but someone grabbed his arm, whirling him around. He felt hot lips press against his. Vise-like arms squeezed mercilessly against his back.

When Alynna finally released him, he sucked in a hasty breath, desperate for air. "The Goddess' blessing," she said, her red lips spreading in a broad smile. Leaning in, she whispered, "Your servant stayed at the palace. I'm not going to let you escape me this time, Jeran."

Jeran extricated himself from Alynna's arms, his face the same shade of red as her painted lips. Stepping back, he saw Jes glaring at him, her lips pressed together tightly. Her eyes shifted to the right, and Jeran swallowed. He hurried to Astalian's side, where he felt more comfortable.

Jes and Alynna stared each other down, their eyes burning with repressed anger. Jes looked even more angrily at Alynna than she had at Jeran. Jeran knew it was just an act, an attempt to maintain the illusion of their courtship, but he found himself stepping away, the flames of the bonfire more welcome than the fire in the women's eyes.

"My suggestion," cautioned Astalian, "as a battle-hardened warrior, is a stealthy retreat. In all of Madryn, the only thing more dangerous than an angry woman is two angry women." Jeran nodded his agreement, and the two of them slipped slowly around the fire, putting as much distance between the women and themselves as possible.

The moon rose to its zenith, but the celebration continued unabated. It began its long journey toward the western horizon, and still the revelry continued. The pipers played, the dancers danced, and Valia received praise for her creations in quantities never before equaled.

Jeran and Astalian mingled with the throng. The Elf introduced him to many of the guests, and Jeran introduced the Aelvin warrior to those Alrendrians they happened upon. When not otherwise engaged, they shared stories of their youths. Jeran discovered that beneath Astalian's exuberant surface beat the heart of a poet, staunchly devoted to the Emperor and his family. Astalian learned some of Jeran's past as well, and his estimation of the young Human improved significantly. "We are not so different," Astalian said as they sat on the roots of a Great Tree, watching the celebration from a distance.

"You and I?" asked Jeran, stifling a yawn.

"Humans and Elves," Astalian corrected. "We live, die, love, fight. In both Races there are good men and bad. Beautiful women. Honorable warriors...." He trailed off, his eyes wandering toward the bonfire, where the distant forms of Treloran and Martyn could be seen, their women still at their sides. "But you and I are much alike as well," he admitted.

There was a blur of motion, and they both jerked upright, instantly alert. A long-shafted arrow quivered between them, its wickedly barbed head lodged in the trunk of the Great Tree. A piece of parchment was tied tightly around the arrow's shaft. "How secure did you say this field was?" Jeran asked, his eyes scanning the clearing for the attacker.

Astalian untied the note from the arrow, quickly scanning its contents. "We must get to the princes!" he said, lunging from his seat and running toward the fire, calling loudly for his warriors. The parchment, forgotten, drifted slowly to the ground. Jeran picked it up, tucked it into his shirt, and followed after the Elf, shouting for the Guardsmen to rally.

Suddenly, a flare of light erupted across the field. The statue of Valia burst into flames, a pillar of fire rising higher than even the bonfire. A wave of heat washed over Jeran, and he coughed, trying to rid his lungs of the acrid smoke. Screams, several of pain, but most of sheer terror, cut through the stillness of the now-bright clearing.

Jeran, undeterred by the heat, ran forward, relieved to discover that few had been caught in the conflagration. Those whose clothing had caught fire were thrown unceremoniously to the ground, the flames quickly extinguished. Aelvin warriors rushed toward the bonfire from all directions, but the Elves of other classes hastened away from the burning figure of Valia.

The crowd pressed against Jeran, but he pushed through undaunted. Shoving an Elf to one side, he stood up on his toes and scanned the field. Most of those remaining near the bonfire were fighting the flames, but three combatants were rolling back and forth across the ground. Jeran recognized Martyn as one of the three. Letting out a groan, he struggled even harder against the oncoming Aelvin throng.

At long last, he shoved his way through the wall of Elves. He ran at full speed to Martyn's aid, but Astalian was a handful of paces ahead. As Jeran watched, Martyn's assailant landed a solid blow on the prince's jaw, stunning him. A well-placed kick took out the second attacker, who Jeran now identified as Treloran. An Elf, dressed in dark green and black, jumped to his feet and took off at a run, heading toward the far side of the clearing and the safety of the Great Trees.

Jeran fell to the ground at Martyn's side; Astalian was already helping Treloran regain his feet. Behind them, the flames were finally contained, and a small force of Aelvin warriors and Alrendrian Guardsmen were forming. "What happened here?"

Martyn flinched at Jeran's touch, then seemed to recognize his friend. With an angry groan, he pulled himself to his feet, ignoring Jeran's question. He scanned the clearing, then pointed to the retreating form of the Elf. "There he is!" he shouted to Treloran. "We can still catch him!"

Treloran followed Martyn's finger, and his jaw set with determination when he saw the Elf's silhouette. He barked some commands and started off at a run. Martyn waved the Guardsmen forward as well, running at the Aelvin Prince's side. Jeran's cry of, "Martyn, wait!" was echoed by Astalian's, "Hold, my Prince!"

Neither prince heard, or they chose to ignore the commands. Groaning, Astalian started after the others, but Jeran could not tell if the Elf intended to stop the princes or join in the attack. Steeling himself, he followed, yelling, "What was in the note?"

"The *Kohrnodra*!" came Astalian's muted response. "The letter warned that the Brotherhood of Kohr planned to defile the statue of Valia. But I fear worse! We must stop this foolishness now!"

They were gaining on the others, passing the slowest of the Humans and Elves. Martyn and Treloran were ahead of the pack, running after the fleeing Elf with reckless abandon. Jeran urged every ounce of strength from his already weary muscles, and sighed in relief when he realized he would catch Martyn before the prince entered the shadows of the Great Trees.

Astalian maintained his lead on Jeran, if only by a handful of paces. As they passed the last of the Guardsmen, with only ten hands between them and the princes, a movement in the corner of Jeran's eye drew his gaze up. At the edge of the clearing, he saw a line of warriors staring down at them from the lowest level of the city. The archers stood along the railing of a broad avenue, watching.

Jeran heaved a deep sigh. When the princes reached the edge of the city, they would be under the protection of the archers above. His relief evaporated when he saw the Elves draw their bows, and he watched in horror as nearly two score arrows were aimed in their direction.

Martyn and Treloran ran on, eyes fastened on the retreating Elf, oblivious to the danger above.

"Astalian!" Jeran yelled. "Ambush above!" He urged himself to run even faster, closing the distance between himself and Martyn. Astalian's eyes flicked upward, and the Elf's surge of speed was even greater than Jeran's.

Jeran reached Martyn just as the *Kohrnodra* loosed their arrows. He grabbed the prince by the collar and threw him to the ground, using his own body as a shield. They grunted as they hit the hard-packed dirt, but the sound was quickly drowned as the night erupted in screams.

Chapter 19

Dahr woke with a start, sweat beading his forehead, and he sat bolt upright, his eyes darting around the tent frantically. *The Darklord!* Once more Lorthas had invaded his dreams, and as always, a nightmare had preceded the white-haired Mage's visit. In this one, Elorn had chased Dahr; jealously and hatred had overcome the Guardsman's loyalty to Alrendria.

When Lorthas appeared, it had almost been a relief to follow his beckoning finger through the gateway and into the stark room with the brightly burning fire and comfortable chairs. Lorthas had asked him to sit, a courtesy he always extended in these nightly visitations, and offered Dahr a glass of blood red wine.

As always, Dahr refused the drink, but settled into the chair, sighing. He knew from experience that he could not escape; his only recourse was to sit in the Darklord's company until he finally woke.

His breathing quickened, came in short, ragged bursts, as their conversation replayed in his mind. "You look tired, little brother." Lorthas' words were tender, concerned. "Your rest has once again been plagued with nightmares? A pity."

The Darklord's sympathy offered Dahr little comfort. "My nightmares are often followed by your visitations," he answered coldly.

"But not always!" laughed Lorthas, his fire red eyes blazing merrily. "I am not the cause of your bad dreams, Dahr. At least, not directly. But your troubled soul is easier to spot in the Twilight World, which is why my visits often follow such events."

Dahr looked at him skeptically, only half-believing the Mage's words. "What do you want of me, Darklord?"

"What do I always want, little brother?" Lorthas asked whimsically. "To talk. To tell my story. To give you a chance to judge for yourself how evil I am."

"And if I no longer wish to hear your tale?"

"Then we sit here quietly until you wake." Lorthas said with a shrug. "Though it would sadden me greatly if you blinded yourself to the truth. There is much potential in you, Dahr. It would be such a waste should you choose to close your mind to other possibilities."

Dahr was silent for a long time. "It seems I have nowhere else to go," he said at last, waving at the featureless, doorless walls.

"Then I may proceed?" Lorthas inquired politely.

Only after Dahr nodded did the Mage speak. "Excellent. Now where was I?" Lorthas' face contorted, and he tapped a finger to his brow. "We have spoken at great length of my childhood, of the taunts, the beatings, the fear. I can see in your eyes you know of what I speak."

Dahr was indeed haunted with memories of his own childhood, though he was loathe to admit as much to the Darklord. "When Aemon appeared from nowhere," Lorthas began, "rescuing me from what would have been certain death, he seemed more a God to me than a man. His grey robes billowed in the breeze; his face was kind, so kind and yet so angry at the abuse I had suffered at the hands of those bullies. His eyes were…so blue, so intense, so full of knowledge." Lorthas' own eyes were distant, as if he were reliving these memories.

"I would have followed him anywhere," Lorthas confided to Dahr. "And I did, for many, many winters. I watched with a profound sadness as he ordered the Magi to abandon the city of Jule. I stared in horror and fascination as Peitr's army poured through the city, destroying everything touched by the Magi.

"I grew up in the shadow of that terrible war, watching Alrendria torn apart with senseless destruction. I saw friends perish in unspeakable ways; innocent beings, both Magi and common, subjected to hideous tortures. For decades I stole into the Arkam Imperium by night, hiding my face, using my gifts to free those condemned to death and slavery."

For what seemed an eternity, Lorthas talked of his forays into the Arkam Imperium, describing scenes of terrible carnage, of mindless cruelty, of painful, slow death. Every innocent freed sent a wave of relief through Dahr, every unjustified death a pang of anguish. He found himself hating the Arkamians as much as he hated the slavers, and he found himself hoping to hear Lorthas tell of another murderer punished, another crime avenged.

That was what shocked him from the Twilight World, waking him so fast that Lorthas did not even have time to whisper his usual goodbyes. Dahr felt numb, nauseated that the Darklord's words had moved him so, disgusted that he shared his hatred with such a man. The understanding that, had he been in Lorthas' place, he would have done the same things sickened him, haunted him, tortured him to the depths of his soul.

Near panic, he gagged, choking down the bile that rose unbidden in his mouth. "I'm not like him!" Dahr whispered fiercely.

A soft hand reached up to touch his arm. "Not like who?" murmured Katya, her eyes opening slightly. When she saw the look of fear and revulsion on Dahr's face, she jerked awake, her arms around him instantly. Dahr fell into her embrace, relishing the feel of her hands on his back, comforted by the press of her bare breast against his chest. "Peace, my love," she whispered, rocking him back and forth.

They sat in silence for an eternity, until the first rays of light peeked over the eastern horizon. "Come, Hunter," Katya said, standing. "We will sleep no more this night. Best get up and prepare for the day's ride."

Dahr stayed seated, watching as Katya dressed. His eyes danced merrily over her naked form, her taut muscles rippling with each movement. She dressed slowly, casting enticing, knowing glances in his directions. Once finished, she sat herself on one side of the tent and said, "Your turn."

Dahr complied, and much to Katya's delight, his cheeks burned red while she stared at him. Together, they packed their gear and folded the tent, then went to the cookfire for breakfast. Jasova, having taken the last watch, sat beside the flames, stirring a large pot of porridge that boiled over the coals. From time to time, he reached into a pack at his side and tossed a scrap of dried meat to the dogs, who sat in a circle around him.

Dahr flushed again as he remembered his first night with Katya. They had returned to the camp the next morning, clothes smeared with damp dirt and bits of leaves still in their hair. The dogs had followed close behind, sniffing the air tentatively as they approached the Humans.

The camp was packed when they arrived, and the five Guardsmen were preparing to mount. Spotting them, all but Elorn had hurried over; the dour Guardsman chose to remain with the horses. "When we woke and discovered that you never returned to camp," Jasova had said, "we began to worry. We thought it wise to come look for you."

Dahr and Katya had shared a look, and Dahr's cheeks turned a bright shade of red. Vyrina's bold laughter had cut across the camp. "It seems something happened after all," she chuckled, her smile wicked. "Good thing we weren't concerned for your welfare last night!" At the Guardsman's jest, Dahr's face had grown even hotter.

Smiling, but keeping his thoughts to himself, Jasova dropped to one knee and extended a hand to the dogs. The pack leader stepped forward warily, sniffing the Guardsman's hand. "It's all right," Dahr said, though he still was not sure if he had spoken to Jasova or the hound. "He can be trusted."

The dogged sniffed, then stepped forward, allowing the Guardsman to scratch his head. Jasova had looked at Dahr quizzically. "Friends of yours?"

Dahr had nodded. "From the slavers' camp. It seems they've been following us." He absently reached down to pet one of the animals. The others crowded in, eager to receive some attention.

Jasova had liked the dogs instantly. He was always giving them treats, scratching their ears, and playing with them. "Still trying to take my friends away?" Dahr asked as he and Katya joined the Guardsman. A broad smile split his face.

Jasova laughed, extending a hand. Three dogs ran forward, each trying to be the first to reach him. "They have enough love for the two of us," he stated. "Though if it came to a fight, I have no doubt whose side they would take."

Dahr and Katya sat, and Jasova dished them bowls of porridge. They ate in silence, listening to the quiet sounds of nature. A rustling from the tents behind them indicated that the other Guardsmen were waking. "Which way do we go today?" Jasova asked, scraping the last of his breakfast from the bowl.

Dahr considered the question. They were still traveling north, though Dahr bent their path more west with each day. During their travels, they had passed the remains of several more camps, and the sites of a couple grisly battles, but had not yet encountered a single Tribesman. The Garun'ah either did not exist in great numbers, were exceptional at hiding, or were not to be found in this part of the Tribal Lands.

"What do you think we should do?" he asked. "Should we continue on or turn back toward Kaper? We are more than three-quarters of the way to the northern sea and have yet to see a single one of my people.

"I was," he continued, setting his jaw determinedly, "and still am, eager to find the Garun'ah. There are things they need to be told, and things I wish to learn about them, but it seems unlikely we will ever find them. Perhaps there are not as many of them as we believed, or maybe we will not find them unless they want to be found." He looked at his companions expectantly.

Jasova did not answer immediately. "We should do as you think best," he said at last. "This is your mission, and therefore your decision. To give up now, after all we've been through?" He shook his head. "Personally, I wouldn't give up our search, though part of me is ready to return to the comforts of Alrendria. But in Kaper, there waits only work for us and loneliness for you."

Katya nodded her agreement. "Is this not the chance you wanted? Time away from the city and the prejudices of man? Take advantage of it, Hunter. Don't let Elorn's constant whining affect your decision."

Dahr lowered his eyes and scratched his chin thoughtfully. "*This* is what I've been longing for," he agreed. "But I feel like we're searching fruitlessly. Perhaps…." The appearance of the other Guardsmen interrupted him. Wardel and Vyrina walked up behind him, stooping to pet the dogs. Elorn stood across the fire, wordlessly dishing a bowl of porridge. Sitting on a fallen tree trunk, he began to eat.

"Which way do we go today, Dahr?" Wardel asked, stretching an arm over his head and yawning.

Vyrina accepted a bowl from Jasova with thanks, then stifled her own yawn. "I suppose there's little chance of finding a hot bath at the end of the day's journey?" Her voice was steady, but her eyes danced merrily.

Dahr smiled back at them. "We go north again today," he said. "Tomorrow, we turn west. Once we reach the Anvil, we will start south, heading first to the east and then the west. If we have met no Garun'ah by the time we reach the Path of Riches, we will return to Kaper."

Jasova nodded. "A reasonable plan." he said solemnly, and two of the dogs barked their agreement. The other Guardsmen did not argue; not even Elorn voiced a complaint.

They finished their breakfast quickly, packed the remainder of the gear, and hit the trail before the sun had cleared the horizon. As they traveled north, the landscape had become more stark. The thick forest had disappeared; only thin copses of trees, dotting the landscape here and there, remained. The plains were rolling, the hills so steep they sometimes seemed like mountains. As the days progressed, the party was treated to majestic views of rolling valleys, lazily meandering streams, and placid lakes teeming with fish.

It was beautiful, this land, far different from Alrendria, even different than the other regions of the Tribal Lands they had traveled. It seemed wild, untouched, almost pristine. Dahr felt his blood stir. He sniffed the air cautiously, almost swooning with the scent of the moist, earthy smell. He felt the urge to push Jardelle to a gallop and run at full speed through the knee-high grass, relishing the feel of the wind in his face, the peaceful aura of nature around him.

Instead, he urged his powerful mount a few steps ahead of the others, just far enough that their conversations faded to a distant hum. The dogs started to follow, but he ordered them back. Reluctantly, they slowed, waiting for Katya and the others. Alone, Dahr took slow, deep breaths, closing his eyes from time to time, feeling the warm sunlight and the soft touch of the wind's fingers on his face. He spent most of the day in quiet reflection.

When the sun started to sink in the west, Dahr pulled Jardelle to a stop at the top of a tall hill. He signaled for the others to halt, then called to Katya, asking her to join him. She came obediently, smiling at him as she drew her horse next to his. Her green eyes were so deep. So beautiful.

"Do you truly believe I'm making the right decision?" he asked. "We haven't seen a Tribesman yet. What reason do we have to believe we will find them to the south. They could still be north of us, or they could be to the east, along the fringes of Illendrylla. Maybe we should–"

Katya's sudden laughter cut Dahr off. He looked at her in confusion. "Before you make your final decision," she said, "I have a suggestion."

"What is it?" he asked hopefully. "I'd be happy for any advice."

"Maybe you should ask him for directions," she laughed, pointing down the hill. "I bet he knows where to find the Garun'ah." Dahr turned his head in the indicated direction, peering down the hill. In the distance, sitting cross-legged on a large boulder, was a man. He sat stone still, watching them silently. Few details could be seen from their distance, but Dahr knew without doubt that they looked at a Tribesman.

He found himself laughing along with Katya. "Have the others wait for me here," he ordered, spurring his horse to a gallop. He flew down the hillside, reining in at the last moment, stopping in a cloud of dust and a shower of loose pebbles.

Dismounting, he approached quietly, bowing deeply at the waist. "*Jokalla* Tribesman," he said without looking up, the Garun'ah word awkward on his tongue. "I come in peace and wish to speak with you." Slowly, Dahr raised his head, surprised to see Kal sitting before him.

"*Jokalla tsalla'dar*," Kal replied. "I have been waiting for you." He glanced around curiously. "You come alone?" he asked, springing lightly from his perch and landing on the ground next to Dahr.

Dahr shook his head, pointing a finger up the hill. "I have six others with me, but I asked them to wait up there so I could speak to the Tribesman alone. Had I known it was you...."

Kal bobbed his head in understanding. "Is the Odara with you?" he asked suddenly, and when Dahr shook his head, the Tribesman looked sad. "A pity. I have blood debt. I had hoped he would be with you."

The Tribesman was quiet for a moment, then raised his eyes to meet Dahr's. "Shall we join your friends?" he asked, standing. Dahr nodded and grabbed the reins to his horse. With Kal at his side, he walked back up the hill. "I was beginning to worry I would never find a Tribesman. We have seen few signs of your people."

"You would not have," Kal informed him, laughing. "You were nearer our lands when you started your journey than you are now. You passed through the lands of the Tacha early in your travels." He gestured down the hill. "If Rannarik had not sent me after you, had you continued north, you would have found only death. A few days more would bring you to the lands of the Drekka."

"The Drekka?" Dahr repeated. "I thought they were destroyed in the MageWar."

Kal's head lowered, almost as if he were ashamed. "Most were killed," he assured Dahr, "but some escaped. The Drekka are hard to kill. Like disease, they spring up from time to time." His brow furrowed angrily. "They grow restless again, the Lost Tribe. They raid the other tribes, as far as the Afelda lands."

Kal gestured to the open plains. "Now we travel the lands of the Channa, but it not surprising that you see no Garun'ah. In summer, Channa travel east, where water is more plentiful."

Dahr took the sudden silence to change the subject. "If Rannarik knew we were coming, why didn't he send you for us days ago? Why did he make us travel all this way?"

"He is *Tsha'ma*," shrugged Kal, as if the word answered the question. "Two moons ago he had a vision. He told me to travel to the edge of the Channa lands. He described this very spot, and told me to wait for you here. Under no circumstance was I to look for you, but wait until Garun brought you to me."

Kal shrugged again. "He did not offer reasons, and I am wise enough not to argue with *Tsha'ma*. Rannarik told me you would arrive alone, or in the company of a few others." Kal slapped Dahr's shoulder amicably. "The Gods had their reasons for delaying our meeting, Dahr. They always do."

They cleared the top of the hill, and the Guardsmen were waiting for them. Jasova, recognizing Kal, bowed low, calling out a friendly greeting. Hearing the Tribesman's name, recognition flashed on Nykeal and Katya's faces. They both hurried over to welcome Kal to the camp.

Dahr introduced him to Vyrina and Wardel, and the dogs all eagerly padded over to the Tribesman, who took the time to stroke each individually. "You will have to tell me how you came to acquire these animals," he said. "They seem...familiar."

Kal's statement trailed off, and he looked at the sky. The sun was sinking in the west, and dark clouds were rolling in from the north. "The day grows late," he said suddenly, "and a storm approaches. We should rest here tonight and start back to the lands of the Tacha tomorrow."

Dahr nodded, ordering the Guardsmen to set up camp. They went about their assigned tasks diligently; not even Elorn complained. Dahr and Kal stood together while the others raised the tents and started a fire. After a while, Elorn returned from a nearby copse of trees, arms heavily laden with logs, and they built a large, hot fire.

"Your friend does not seem happy to see me," Kal said when he noticed the Guardsman's dark glare.

"Elorn is no friend of mine," Dahr laughed. "He was looking forward to returning to Alrendria. Meeting you will delay our return."

Kal laughed in response to Dahr's warm smile. "Why do you seek us?"

Dahr shrugged. "Partly to learn more about the Garun'ah. Other than you and Rannarik, I have never seen another Tribesman. Partly because of the danger which faces Madryn. I hope to convince your people," at Kal's stern glance, Dahr amended himself, "our people, to lend their aid."

When Kal's penetrating glare did not relinquish, Dahr felt himself blushing. "Mostly," he admitted, "it's because the Elves would not let me enter their lands."

Kal laughed loudly, and after a moment of embarrassment, Dahr joined him. "I should have told you the *Onahrre* would never let Garun's Blood into their precious forest." His whole frame shook with laughter. "I could have taken you with me then and spared you the journey!"

They talked quietly until Elorn finished cooking and called them to dinner. Kal ate heartily, putting away nearly as much as Dahr. "You make good food," he said to Elorn, "for a Human." Elorn glared in response, but a stern gaze from Dahr made him accept the compliment graciously.

The Guardsmen were all curious about the Garun'ah, and none hesitated to ask questions. Kal was kept talking until late in the evening, and Dahr made no effort to slow the tide of questions; most were things he, too, wanted to know. The Guardsmen's eagerness spared him from betraying his complete ignorance of the ways of his own people.

As promised, a storm rolled in as night spread its curtain over the sky. "Perhaps it's for the best if we retire," Dahr said as the thunder came closer. "We can wait out the storm in the safety of our tents and start south early tomorrow."

As an afterthought, he turned to Kal. "Have you a tent?"

The Garun'ah shook his head. "Speed was of the essence," he replied, pointing to the sky. "So I traveled with only Garun's blanket for protection." A peal of thunder interrupted the Tribesman. When it faded, he added, "Do not worry. I have been wet before. I will survive."

Dahr opened his mouth, but it was Katya who spoke. "That's ridiculous," she said. "You can have my tent." With a wink, she said, "I rarely use it anyway." Dahr turned bright red at her words; his breathing became labored. Wardel and Vyrina exchanged knowing looks, and Elorn scowled, kicking dirt over the coals of the fire before stomping to his own tent.

Katya laughed at Dahr's embarrassment. "Don't act like such a child," she said, smiling over at him. "It's not exactly a camp secret. Nykeal and Vyrina knew even before we came back to camp that first night; and if Jasova, Wardel, and Elorn didn't know at first, they certainly must have some indication by now!"

Her eyes danced at his discomfiture, and a wicked smile spread across her features. "I promise to be more discrete when we return to Alrendria. If you want me to be." She finished the statement with a wink.

Kal burst out in loud laughter, which only served to turn Dahr a brighter shade of red. "I thank you for your offer, little sister," he said as the first drops of rain fell from the sky. Extending his palm, he added, "And I gladly accept it." He scanned the row of structures. "Which is mine?"

Katya pointed to the nearest tent. With a bob of his head, the large Tribesman ran to the tent and ducked inside just as the wind began to howl. The Guardsmen scurried for their tents, leaving Dahr and Katya alone in the approaching storm. Katya stood slowly, her red hair shining in the dying firelight. She started toward Dahr's tent, looking back over her shoulder. "Are you coming, Dahr," she asked seriously, "or would you prefer to sit out here and get wet?"

With a flirtatious wink and a sway to her hips, she sauntered across the camp and disappeared into the tent. With a laugh, Dahr climbed to his feet and ran to join her.

* * * * * * * * * * * * * * * * * * * *

Kal sniffed the air tentatively, worming his way forward slowly over the wet leaves. "Can you smell them, Dahr?" he asked in a whisper as he neared the edge of the hill. He smiled, exposing white, slightly-pointed teeth and stared at Dahr with a hungry, feral look.

Dahr edged forward, too, peering down into the shallow valley. The forest, thicker than any Dahr had seen since leaving the Great Forest, was dark, the trees heavy with leaves. A cool breeze rustled the branches, and the shadows of songbirds drifted over the ground, flickering in the thin patches of light that penetrated the canopy.

A small stream flowed from the mountains in the west, cutting through the valley, snaking gently between the trees. Dahr strained his ears, hoping to hear the approach of their prey, but the only sounds audible were the babble of water over rocks, the quiet chirping of birds in the trees, and the sound of the wind whispering through the branches. He sniffed the air several times, eager to detect whatever scent Kal spoke of. "I smell nothing," he said at last, disheartened. "Nothing but the trees."

Kal eyed him for a long moment, his expression one of disbelief. "Perhaps you simply do not realize what you smell." He reached over and grasped Dahr's shoulder warmly. "Do not worry, little brother. In time, you will forget about being Human and learn how to be a Hunter."

Dahr cringed at the words 'little brother.' They were the same words Lorthas used to address him in his dreams. "I don't want to forget how to be Human," he replied, almost defiantly.

The dreams–the nightmares–came more often now. Lorthas seemed to be in his dreams constantly, sharing with Dahr the story of his life. Even more frightening to Dahr was the sympathy he felt for the Darklord. He did not trust Lorthas, would never trust him, but the sincerity of his words was too obvious, too heartfelt to be pure fabrication. There were times when he understood the Darklord's anger, his hatred at being ridiculed, his desire to protect those like him. That understanding frightened him more than the Darklord did.

"You do not have to forget," Kal admitted, and when Dahr did not respond, he added, "but you must pay attention. You will learn nothing from me if you constantly enter the sun-dream."

Dahr shook thoughts of the Darklord away. He smiled at Kal, accepting the Tribesman's rebuke. In the days since they joined company, teaching Dahr the ways of the Garun'ah had become Kal's quest. From daybreak until nightfall, Kal was at his side. He eagerly answered, even encouraged, Dahr and the Guardsmen to ask questions, and posed many questions of his own, curious about the Humans' strange habits. When asked about his interest in their ways, Kal had answered, "The Tsha'ma say understanding and tolerance are Garun's highest virtues, next to honor."

Dahr did not mind Kal's lessons, though the price seemed to be the constant reminder that he was not Human. Teasing Dahr about his Human qualities earned nearly as much of Kal's time as teaching Dahr the ways of the Tribesmen. He opened his mouth to retort, but before he could speak, Kal raised a hand, signaling for silence. With his chin, he gestured toward the far side of the valley.

A small herd of deer emerged from the underbrush. Dahr's eyes widened in shock, again surprised by Kal's ability to hunt and track. It was a small herd, only nine deer in all, but all were fat and healthy. A massive buck, a heavy rack of antlers crowning his head, led them. As one, they walked to the stream and lowered their heads to drink.

"Did I not tell you?" Kal asked, smiling smugly. "Deer! We will dine well this night, *tsalla'dar*." The Tribesman's hushed words echoed across the clearing. The buck raised his head, water glistening on his antlers. His eyes darted back and forth, searching for the source of the sound. He sniffed the air, scanning the trees for predators.

Dahr sucked in a breath, pushing himself even flatter to the ground. After a tense moment, the buck lowered his head again. In the quietest of whispers, Dahr asked, "But how did you know where they were?"

"I told you," Kal said, leaning over to whisper in Dahr's ear. "I could smell them." At Dahr's incredulous look, Kal stifled a laugh. "And you could too! I am sure of it!"

Kal's smile turned to a frown, and he peered intently into Dahr's eyes. "You need to spend more time among the creatures of the wood," he guessed, giving Dahr long, hard appraising look. "Your seasons in the man-city have poisoned your nose to nature. Have no fear, little brother. In time, you will learn. You are a Child of Garun." Kal's statement had a finality to it that left no room for argument.

Dahr started to speak again, and again Kal signaled for silence. "Now is not the time for talk," he hissed, turning his attention back to the deer. "Are you ready to hunt, little brother?"

Dahr nodded. Reaching a hand behind him, he grasped for his bow. Kal grabbed his arm. "Today," he whispered, shaking his head, "we will not kill from a distance like the Humans and *Aelva*. Today, we hunt like Garun'ah."

A feral grin spread across Kal's face. "Have you your long-knife?" he asked, and Dahr dropped a hand to his waist, feeling for the hilt of the *dolchek* that Kal had gifted him. He nodded his head and closed his hand around the carved-bone hilt, drawing the blade from its sheath.

Kal's smile broadened. "Good. Now focus on the deer. Find one that interests you. Ignore the others. Reach out to the creature. Feel its breath flowing through your lungs, hear its heart beat inside your chest. You are the Hunter, and it, the prey." He had a hungry look in his eyes. "You will know when the time is right."

Kal turned away, focusing his own eyes on the deer. His breathing slowed, and his eyes grew distant and unfocused. Dahr took a steadying breath as he watched Kal prepare himself. The Tribesman raised himself up on all fours. He rocked back and forth slowly, his *dolchek* clutched tightly in his hand. Sunlight glinted off the cold steel blade.

A breeze gusted past them, and Dahr shivered. Summer was upon them, with midsummer still some time off, but when the winds blew down from the Anvil, the temperature plummeted. Several times their path had taken them into the mountains, and those nights had been bitter cold.

On the coldest, when the winds whipped down from the heights of the Anvil and the Guardsmen huddled around the fire, Kal had sat comfortably in light leathers. Arms exposed, he sat some distance from the fire, chiding the Alrendrians about their thin blood. Dahr, too, did not suffer as much as the Guardsmen, but he was not as comfortable as Kal. When he donned a warm coat one night, Kal's laughter had seemed mocking. "In time, little brother," he had said, "you will learn to love the feel of Kohr's icy fingers."

Their path had led steadily south since joining Kal, though the Tribesman frequently turned from east to west. Kal had no horse, and refused to share a saddle with the Guardsmen. He ran at their side all day, able to keep pace with the horses unless they were at full gallop.

Nearly a score of days after their meeting, Kal drew to a stop, looking around in confusion. "We are well within the lands of my people," he had stated, "but there is no sign of the Tacha." He scratched his hairless chin thoughtfully. "My father would not take the tribe to the winter lands so early. So the Tacha must go to *Cha'khun*."

"*Cha'khun*?" All save Elorn repeated the strange word.

"A meeting of tribes." Kal explained, shrugging. "It is of no matter. It is not much farther to Kohr's Heart. We will find my people there." Without another word, he turned around and jogged to the northeast.

Another ten days had passed since then, and yesterday, Kal had told them that they would reach Kohr's Heart before the next full moon. Their pace, always unhurried, was now even slower. Kal did not rush them from their bedrolls, and he often stopped when the sun was still high in the sky. When Dahr had asked about their speed, the Tribesman had laughed loudly. "You have spent too much time among the Humans, little brother," he said, sounding almost sad. "There is no need to run from place to place as they do. The Tacha are not going anywhere."

Dahr had accepted the answer and let his horse fall back, scanning the thin forests and open plains for Garun'ah. In all their travels, they had yet to meet any Tribesmen other than Kal. Several times, Dahr saw figures on the edge of his vision, shadowy forms that he believed were Garun'ah. When he mentioned the phantom watchers to Kal, the Tribesman had replied, "They are likely Hunters from another tribe. Since they hunt in Tachan lands, they will keep their distance unless we approach. If they wish to speak, they will signal."

"If these are Tachan lands," Dahr had asked, confused, "Why do you allow the other tribes to hunt here?"

"I forget how little you know of our ways," Kal had answered with a frown. "The tribes do not own the land like Humans. To say this is Tachan land means only that we are responsible for its care. If another wishes to use it for food or shelter, that is their right."

"That is why you allow the Humans to live on your lands?" Jasova had asked, his curiosity prompting the interruption.

Kal nodded. "So long as they leave us in peace."

"Anyone can hunt your lands?" This question had come from Vyrina. She and the other Guardsmen had crowded around. "At any time?"

"Only if the Tacha were starving would closing our lands be discussed. But Arik, my father, *Kranor* of the Tacha, would never refuse food to the hungry, no matter how desperate were our people.

"However," he had continued, "those who accept a gift from the Tacha must remember our kindnesses. If such a time came when the Tacha needed help, they would be obligated to give it. That is how it has been since we freed ourselves from the *Aelva*."

"Is that the way of all the tribes?" Nykeal had asked. "Or just the Tacha?"

"The same holds true of all the tribes but Drekka. Only the Lost Tribe goes against the old ways. They refuse to share their land, and they kill any who are not of their tribe." With a smile, Kal had added, "You are lucky I found you when I did. Another day's travel would have put you on the edge of Drekka lands."

Dahr shook himself and brought his thoughts back to the present. Kal was still rocking back and forth, his eyes locked on a large, brown-eyed doe. Dahr edged forward, until his head and shoulders hung suspended over the hilltop.

His eyes were drawn to the buck. The stag drank, his head low over the water. The animal tossed its head when Dahr's eyes settled on it; it looked up the hill, not quite in his direction. Dahr felt his hand tighten reflexively on the hilt of his *dolchek*; the carved bone of the hilt pressed into his palm. His breath came in short, ragged gasps. With an effort, he calmed himself, allowing his muscles to relax and his breathing to slow.

The stag lowered his head, taking slow sips from the stream. The animal's throat contracted with each swallow. Dahr saw the pulse beating in its neck. A growl escaped his throat; saliva filled his mouth.

The deer's head shot up again, and its eyes locked with Dahr's, as if it knew exactly where he lay in wait. Dahr's muscles tensed for action. "Now!" he snarled, leaping down the hillside.

He did not know if Kal followed, nor did he care. The stag bellowed a warning and the other deer scattered, fleeing into the trees. Dahr plunged heedlessly down the hillside, his *dolchek* raised high, a growl of pleasure escaping his lips.

The buck stared at him challengingly, then it, too, turned and ran. Dahr followed recklessly, weaving through the trees, jumping fallen logs, and dodging the thorned vines and sharp rocks that littered the forest floor.

The stag was quick, but Dahr kept the animal in sight at all times. He knew it could not be possible, but it seemed as if he were gaining ground on the swift-footed beast. His breath came in quick, hot bursts; he delved deep into his soul, searching for hidden reserves of strength, driving himself to run all the faster.

The stag turned off the game trail, disappearing into the virgin wood. Dahr followed, plunging through the underbrush, oblivious to the branches that whipped across his face and the thorns that tore at his breeches. The stag was less than ten paces ahead; he could no longer doubt that he would catch the animal.

The stag dodged wildly, frantically changing directions to throw off pursuit, but Dahr was not fooled. It was almost as if he knew ahead of time which way the deer would run.

The deer stumbled, it legs sliding on a bed of wet leaves, and with a cry of pleasure, Dahr launched himself in the air, *dolchek* outstretched. He landed on the deer's flank with a snarl. The animal squirmed beneath him, but Dahr was the stronger. He could smell the animal's rage and fear, but it only served to heighten his desire to kill.

With a bellow of rage, of animal hunger, Dahr raised his blade and brought it down. At the last instant, the deer twisted, and Dahr's killing blow caught the animal in the flank. The stag squealed in fear and pain as the blade dug deep. Warm blood sprayed across Dahr's face, and the buck thrashed back and forth, trying to score a blow with its antlers.

The animal's cries brought Dahr back to his senses. A snarl caught in his throat, and he shuddered. Quickly, to end its pain, he pulled back the stag's head and slashed with the *dolchek*. The struggle quickly ceased.

With no small effort, he rolled himself off the deer and fell to the ground, breathing heavily. He looked at the blood-stained blade in his hands, his similarly stained leathers, covered with briars and leaves. His hair was disheveled, matted to his head with sweat and blood.

Dahr's head snapped back, his *dolchek* fell to the ground, and he let loose a cry of rage, pain, and disgust. The sound echoed through the forest, frightening birds from the safety of their nests. Other animals, those few not scared away by Dahr's hunt, scattered too, leaving behind the sound of rattling leaves.

When the last vestige of his bellow faded into nothingness, Dahr lowered his head to his hands. Deep sobs wracked his body, though no sound escaped his lips. After a time, he heard his own voice whisper harshly, "What kind of monster am I?"

"No more a monster than any creature in Madryn, little brother," came Kal's reply. "Less so than many."

Dahr opened his eyes and raised his head. He had not expected an answer. Kal was staring at him, the doe slung over his shoulders. The Tribesman offered Dahr a reassuring smile before lowering the creature to the ground.

"I *am* a monster," Dahr repeated, gesturing to the deer at his side. "Look what I did!"

Kal squatted next to Dahr and lifted the stag's head, peering deeply into its sightless eyes. Slowly, almost reverently, he lowered it gently to the ground again. "You have killed," he stated, and there was a nonchalance to his voice that constricted Dahr's chest. "It is no different than killing with a bow or with a sword. I have seen you do both. Why should this time make you feel differently?"

Dahr opened his mouth to speak, but no words came to his defense. "Death is a part of life, little brother," Kal said softly. "This deer knew that as well as we. There is no shame in taking this animal's life, so long as you honor the animal's death. Be at ease, *tsalla'dar*. All is well. There is much honor in this hunt."

"No!" Dahr insisted. "I didn't kill with honor. I killed as if I were a beast myself."

"We are all animals," Kal laughed, "though we often try to hide our true nature. Once in a while, we must release the animal inside. If you keep the beast caged too long, it has a way of escaping when you least expect."

Kal stood, offering Dahr a hand. Taking a deep, steadying breath, Dahr grasped the Tribesman's arm and pulled himself to his feet. "Come, little brother," Kal said. "Let us take these deer to camp."

He frowned, staring at Dahr. "Perhaps we should clean you up before returning," he said, changing his mind. "The way you look, the others might think the stag won the fight." With a laugh, he hefted the doe onto his shoulders and headed toward the stream. Dahr offered a tight smile in return. Grabbing the heavy buck, he followed the Tribesman to the cold, cleansing water.

Chapter 20

The survivors were taken to the palace. Rows of stretchers, their occupants moaning in pain, lined the plaza outside the main gates. An army of brown-robed Elves drifted through the throng, bringing water and much needed medicines. Every *Ael Maulle* with a talent for healing had been summoned. Those not at the bonfire were at the palace, their proud golden robes now stained with blood.

Rooms were made available to the survivors of the *Kohrnodran* attack. *Ael Namisa* and *Ael Chatorra* alike carried stretchers, their occupants crying out in pain and fear, inside the palace. Other Elves, those with no further need of accommodation, were solemnly taken to one side of the courtyard, where they lay peacefully, their bodies shrouded in white cloth, awaiting the final rites.

Elves wandered the courtyard, some frantically, some in a daze, searching the injured for friends and family. A few looked among the bodies, their features tormented and anguished. Elierian stood in the center of it all, doing his best to aid the victims, and keeping the onlookers safely away from *Ael Maulle* and their arcane works. The *Volche Namisa* was a calm port in a stormy sea. He had mobilized the entire palace, an army of servants roamed the plaza, helping to reunite families and tend the wounded.

Shouts of joy and tears of relief were numerous, almost enough to drown out the cries of despair. Jeran did his best to block out all sound as he scanned the ground, walking among the seemingly endless rows of injured, searching for fallen friends. When last he had heard, not all the Guardsmen had been accounted for. Nor had all the delegates yet returned.

His eyes darted back and forth until attracted by a not-quite-Aelvin physique. Sucking in a breath, he hurried to the figure. A young *Ael Maulle* approached at the same time, his brown hair streaked with ash and dirt, his gray eyes distant and tired. They knelt together, and Jeran peered down into Raeghit's tormented eyes.

The Guardsman's gaze shifted slightly, almost imperceptibly, in Jeran's direction. Slowly, Jeran drew back the shroud, wincing when he saw the broken shaft that protruded from Raeghit's abdomen. The *Ael Maulle* lowered his hands to the wound, and his eyes grew distant. A look of intense concentration swept across his face, compressing his lips in a thin line.

Jeran put one hand on Raeghit's shoulder, the other on his forehead. After a moment, the Elf looked up, his eyes sad. "I have eased his pain," he said with a shake of his head. "But I will not waste my strength. Others need it more."

"Thank you," Jeran whispered, and the Elf stood, bowing slightly before hurrying on to his next patient. Jeran tried to breathe, but his chest was tight. He pressed his eyes tightly closed, and when he opened them, he saw the Guardsman looking up at him, his eyes alert. "Glad to have you back," Jeran said, surprised by the strength in his voice.

Raeghit tried to pull himself up to a seated position, but he was too weak. With a grunt, he fell back to the ground. Craning his neck forward, he tried look at his injury. "The prince?" he asked weakly.

"Martyn is well," Jeran assured him. "A few bumps and bruises." A brown-robed *Ael Namisa* stopped at their side and offered Jeran a wooden cup filled to the brim with cold water. He accepted it with thanks, holding it to the Guardsman's mouth.

"The Five Gods be praised," Raeghit said, drinking thirstily. He coughed suddenly, spitting up water and flecks of blood. "I wish the same could be said of me."

Jeran tried not to lose the smile he had glued to his face. "I've seen worse injuries," he told the dying Guardsman.

"Not on the living," Raeghit laughed, grimacing in pain. He coughed again, and more blood sprayed across the white linen. Using the corner of the sheet, Jeran wiped the red-flecked spittle from the Guardsman's mouth. "What happens now, Lord Odara?" Raeghit asked, fear tingeing his voice.

Jeran felt tears in his eyes and forced them away. He opened his mouth to speak, but could find no words. Astalian answered for him. "My people believe the honorable go to the Heavens when they die," he explained, stepping out of the shadows, his eyes full of sympathy. "To live with the Gods."

Stooping, the Aelvin warrior put a hand on the Guardsman's arm and squeezed tightly. "I envy you, my friend. By sunrise, you will walk with Valia through the Gardens of Forever. You will hunt with Balan and Garun in the Twilight World."

Raeghit's fear melted away. He looked at Jeran, a renewed hope in his eyes. "Do you think it's true, Lord Odara?" he asked, his strength fading.

"I do," Jeran answered, forcing his smile even broader. "And this I know for fact as well. There are none more honorable than the Alrendrian Guard. When it's my time to die, I'll find you arm in arm with the Gods."

"I am of Alrendria," murmured Raeghit, repeating the Guardsman's oath. "I am the sword that defends her, the shield that protects her. Alrendria before King. Alrendria before House. Alrendria before self."

A wracking cough interrupted the Guardsman's oration. Jeran's tears, which he had held in check since seeing the wounded Guardsman, now fell. Astalian's hand moved to Jeran's shoulder, offering support. "Alrendria offers me freedom," Raeghit continued in a barely audible whisper. "In return I offer her my heart, my soul, my life...."

The Guardsman let loose one final breath, then lay still. "A brave man," Astalian said solemnly, looking at Jeran. "The only thing harder than living with honor is dying with honor." The look on his face said that he believed Raeghit had passed his final test admirably.

With a feeling of intense sadness, Jeran drew the shroud over Raeghit's head. Together, he and Astalian carried the stretcher away, setting it alongside the other dead. "We must find Charylla," Astalian told Jeran. "The princess needs to know what has been discovered."

Jeran nodded in agreement, and they started toward the palace. "Any sign of Jes?" he asked, unable to keep the worry from his voice.

"No," Astalian replied. "But that she has not yet been found means she is likely alive. Most of the dead have been recovered." Jeran nodded again and they walked the rest of the way to the palace in silence, each lost in his own thoughts.

The attack had been well planned; the *Kohrnodran* troops had been placed with exacting precision. Archers had hidden on all four sides of the field, arrayed thickly around the four main entrances. When Valia's living statue burst into flame, the crowd had panicked, and though some had gone in every direction, most had run toward the arches, the quickest way to safety.

The press of bodies was so great that movement had been brought to a standstill. The close-packed, frightened Elves had made easy targets. Once the attack began, the Elves scattered in every direction, heedless of those in their way. Nearly as many had been trampled by their own people as had fallen to the arrows of the *Kohrnodra*.

With danger in every direction, it had taken *Ael Chatorra* quite a while to organize a response. At first, most were concerned with locating Treloran and Charylla; only after the safety of the Imperial Family was ensured did the Elves consider retaliation. By the time sufficient force was brought to bear against the enemy, the *Kohrnodra* had disappeared.

Never before had the *Kohrnodra* dared such a bold and blatant attack. How their numbers, nearly ten score, could have slipped into the city undetected, remained a mystery. How they managed to elude the patrols of *Ael Chatorra* circling the clearing was equally unknown.

They found Charylla in the entry hall. Like the courtyard outside, the hall was filled to bursting, occupied with both the injured and those required for their care. The princess stood in the center of the enormous hall, directing the stretcher-bearers and telling the brown-robed servants where to take the wounded.

Martyn and Treloran flanked the princess, each looking sullen. Neither had been happy about being dragged to the ground, though it had likely saved their lives. Nor were they happy when they were spirited off to the palace, away from the confusion of the fray. Martyn had fought like a lion, demanding that he be allowed to lead the Guardsmen in the attack. Treloran, less animated, but equally as insistent, claimed it was his right as *Ael Chatorra* to seek vengeance against the *Kohrnodra*.

Jeran and Astalian had overruled them. "What enemy, Martyn?" Jeran asked wryly once the prince was safely away. "You wouldn't even know who you were looking for!"

"Your mother will need your strength at the palace," Astalian had told Treloran. "You are *Ael Chatorra*, but you are also *Ael Alluya*. Your duty to the people is to return to the palace." The response had placated neither prince, but both were wise enough not to argue.

"There is no need for both of us here," Astalian had said, turning to Jeran. "Besides, we do not know what other treacheries may be waiting at the palace. Join the princes. I will stay." At his whistle, a squad of Aelvin warriors had appeared. Nearly an equal number of Guardsmen hurried over to join them, seeking action.

"Have the injured brought to the palace," Jeran had suggested. "They'll be safer if the *Kohrnodra* come back." Astalian nodded in agreement before calling out to another squad of *Ael Chatorra*. Hastening to them, already shouting orders, he had quickly disappeared from view.

Jeran had led the princes to the palace, where Charylla was waiting, her eyes shadowy and her white skin smeared with dirt. She had hurried to Treloran, embracing him tightly. "Thank Valia," she whispered. "I feared the worst."

"Those monsters will not get away with this!" she had vowed when Jeran filled her in on what he knew, and she had agreed with his decision to bring the wounded to the palace. "It is the least we can do," she had said, turning toward a brown-robed *Ael Namisa*. "Find Elierian. Have him assemble the servants. We will need stretchers, bandages...."

Jeran had left Charylla and the princes and hurried outside, where the first of a long line of bodies were being laid out. He had directed the Elves until Elierian arrived, then relinquished his duties to the more experienced Elf. As the number of wounded grew, Jeran hurried from one side of the plaza to the other, offering aid wherever it was most needed, always wary of attack.

He had searched the throng of bodies for familiar faces, stopped every party arriving from the site of the attack, asked everyone for news of the Alrendrians. The remainder of the night passed slowly, and more and more of his people were found. More often than not, the news had been joyous.

This time, Charylla saw their approach. "What news, Astalian?" she demanded, her eyes cold, as if all emotion had been burned away.

"Little good, Princess," came Astalian's grim-faced reply. "At least two hundred dead. Perhaps five times that number wounded. We believe we have accounted for all the dead, but the wounded continue to trickle in. Many managed to escape the initial attack and are only now finding their way to the guard posts."

"And the *Kohrnodra*?"

"I am ashamed to admit that they escaped, Highness." Astalian looked more angry than ashamed. "I am unsure how they did. It is as if they knew our every move. Both before and after the attack. Where to hide. When to strike. How to escape undetected."

Charylla's eyes were stormy. "Is it true you knew of their presence?"

Astalian's eyes widened in shock. "I was aware of movements outside the city, Princess," he exclaimed. "I was not even sure it was the *Kohrnodra*, let alone a party this large!"

"It is your duty to know these things," the Aelvin Princess snapped. "I begin to doubt the prowess with which you are so often attributed. The great Astalian should certainly have known of such an attack. Surely, there was something the *mighty* Astalian could have done to stop it!" Her calm demeanor was smashed; her anger had gotten the better of her.

Astalian's shoulders slumped, more so than Jeran believed appropriate. He offered no words in his defense, but throughout the princess' tirade murmured, "I did not mean to disappoint."

Martyn's eyes grew wide at Charylla's relentless onslaught, and even Treloran seemed taken aback by his mother's vehemence. "It is not Astalian's fault," the Aelvin Prince began, but Charylla rounded on him, her anger finding a new target.

"Not his fault?" she repeated. "Whose fault is it then? Astalian is *Hohe Chatorra* in your uncle's absence." Treloran stepped back, his eyes wide. "Do not think you are going to escape so easily!" she snapped, her anger temporarily redirected. "You are the Emperor's heir, Treloran! What right have you to risk yourself in such a manner? What if something had happened? What if your death was what they wanted all along!"

"Please, Princess!" Astalian begged. "Do not take your anger out on Treloran! He is not at fault, nor does he deserve your temper. Surely, you can see he was only doing his duty, even when chasing the—"

Charylla's hand drew back, and she slapped Astalian, hard. "How dare you speak to me in such a manner?" she demanded, her eyes flashing. Astalian raised a trembling hand to his mouth; when he lowered it, it was covered with bright red blood. "If anything had happened to my son," Charylla sneered, "you would have had more to worry about than a swollen lip."

Astalian's eyes flashed, but he steadied himself. Squaring his chin, he met Charylla's gaze levelly. "I did not mean to disappoint," he repeated.

Outraged by his tone, Charylla's arm snapped backwards again, ready to strike. It was caught at the last instant, held fast by a withered, gnarled hand. The Emperor stared at his granddaughter with a mixture of surprise, sadness, and disappointment. "What goes on here, beloved?"

"Grandfather," whispered Charylla, stunned, her cheeks reddening in embarrassment. "What are you doing here?"

"I am old, child, not deaf." He said sarcastically. The cries of the wounded echo throughout the palace. They can be heard even in the heart of the Vale." He release Charylla's hand and reached out toward Astalian. Touching the Aelvin warrior's face, he closed his eyes and seized his Gift. Allowing a trickle of magic to flow through his fingers, the Emperor healed the Elf's wound.

"Thank you, Eminence," Astalian whispered, his voice full of love.

"The pleasure was mine," replied the Emperor. "Tell me what happened."

He listened in silence as Jeran and Astalian filled him in on the night's events, with the princes adding what comments they could. The Emperor's face tightened visibly at the mention of the *Kohrnodra*, and a tear formed in his eye when Treloran described the statue of Valia in flames. "How many dead?" he asked hoarsely.

"Near two hundred Elves," Astalian answered. "Five times that in wounded."

"And the Humans?"

"Six dead. All Guardsmen. Another ten or so with injuries. All but one are expected to survive."

"Jes is missing," Jeran added. "I've been searching for her since the attack, but she is not to be found."

The Emperor met his eyes. "You are worried for her?"

"It isn't like her to vanish in this manner," Jeran answered. "Were she well, she would be here, among the wounded." Martyn nodded his agreement.

The Emperor closed his eyes. He remained silent for a long time, then blinked and said, "She is well, and on her way to the palace as we speak." He reached out, patting Jeran's arm comfortingly. "So you need not waste your concern on her."

His eyes shifted back to Charylla. "You still have not told me why you struck Astalian."

Charylla's cheeks turned an even brighter shade of red. "He was negligent in his duties," she said flatly, though her voice lacked its earlier conviction. "I was chastising him for his poor judgment."

"It is you whose judgment is lacking, my dear," came the Emperor's stony reply. "Astalian has served this family honorably for decades. In my lifetime, I have not had a more skilled and valued warrior at my side. He is no more capable of neglecting his duty than he is capable of betrayal."

Charylla's eyes lowered shamefully. "Of all my family," chided the Emperor, "you are the last I would have suspected of such foolishness. For many reasons. If you have yet to learn control of your emotions, perhaps you need spend more time among *Ael Maulle*."

"My apologies, Grandfather."

"I am not the one to whom you owe an apology," returned the old Elf.

Swallowing her shame, Charylla lifted her eyes to meet Astalian's. "I beg your forgiveness," she said weakly. "My words were spoken hastily. Your honor was never in question."

"I did not mean to disappoint," he said, bowing his head, a tenderness to the words that had not been there before.

"If you will excuse me," the Emperor said, "I should be with my people." He walked away, leaving the five of them standing in silence, and circled the room, stopping to talk with the wounded, offering them words of comfort or resting a wrinkled hand upon their brows. Wherever he went, whispered words of greeting preceded him, and a hushed, awed silence followed him.

Martyn watched the Emperor work his way around the room. "They adore him," he said. "I hope my presence offers such comfort when I take the throne."

"Then watch, Prince of Alrendria," Charylla said. "Watch and learn. For you will find no better teacher in the whole of Madryn." The Emperor, as if hearing her words, turned to gaze adoringly at his granddaughter. She smiled back, her anger dissipating.

Turning to Astalian, she apologized again, the smile still on her lips. "Your honor was never in question, noble Astalian," she repeated, and his eyes brightened visibly. "There is still much to be done," she added, suddenly looking exhausted. "And dawn is not far off. The princes will stay at my side, so all who enter can see that they are safe. Their welfare is nearly as important as the Emperor's."

When she mentioned the Emperor, she looked up, her eyes once more seeking his comforting form. He stood at the entrance, talking with several *Ael Chatorra*. With a bow of their heads, they stepped aside, allowing him to pass. Charylla groaned. "He cares not at all for his own safety," she grumbled. "One of these days, he will walk into an assassin's arrow."

Astalian smiled. "I will speak with *Ael Chatorra*. The Emperor will have a constant guard. Do not fear for his safety, Princess." He hurried off, whistling for his soldiers.

"Mother," Treloran said, "perhaps Martyn and I should follow the Emperor's example. If we are seen–"

"You will stay at my side," she snapped, regretting her tone instantly. "Just this once, Treloran, heed my words. The first thing the eyes of the wounded seek are you and Martyn. Whether true or not, many believe this attack was meant to take one, or both, of your lives." She looked into Treloran's eyes, then into Martyn's; both were eager to do more than stand idly while others worked around them. "Very well," she sighed. "But keep yourselves visible at all times."

They promised to do so as they hurried to the nearest litter. "It seems Grandfather made a wise decision," Charylla said to Jeran, laughing quietly. "I do not even think they realize that they are still at each other's side."

"They have much to learn from each other," Jeran replied. "And much more in common than either cares to admit."

Charylla's eyes met his. "Are you sure you are Human? You talk like an Ancient, the oldest of Elves."

Jeran laughed. "Perhaps I've spent too much time with the Emperor."

"It is not possible to spend too much time with Grandfather," Charylla replied lightly, joining in his laughter. Suddenly, her eyes grew serious. "I am sorry for your loss," she said, referring to the Guardsmen. "More precautions should have been taken."

"I regret the loss of life," Jeran told her, "but the blame belongs to no one. You could no more have stopped this attack than I." A Guardsman, her upper body wrapped in bandages, walked past, clinging to the arms of a brown-robed Elf. "I only hope this tragedy does not ruin the trust we are trying to build."

"You have the support of the Emperor," Charylla told him. "And if there were yet any doubts, you have my support as well." They looked at each other, sharing a mutual respect. "I have learned much about Humans since your arrival. Luran is wrong. You are not inferior."

Jeran laughed aloud. "I will take that as a compliment, my Lady."

"That is not what I meant," she returned, slightly embarrassed. "I would be honored to have your people as an ally, even in a time of peace. And with the Darklord's prison weakening... I cannot imagine fighting the battle without you at our side.

"You came seeking unity," she added. "If it is within my power, you shall have it. And this time, perhaps we can make a peace to survive the ages."

"Then my mission was a success, Princess," Jeran told her. "King Mathis will be overjoyed." Elierian appeared as if from nowhere. Bowing to Charylla, he began to list a series of items that were in short supply. Jeran took the opportunity to slip away. He wanted to find Jes, to make sure she was really all right.

He stifled a yawn. With the battle ended and the *Kohrnodra* gone, perhaps they could find their bedrolls for a time, once the wounded were dealt with. Stepping outside, he was surprised to find the courtyard nearly empty. The bodies had been taken away, and all but a few of the injured had been moved. Rosy tendrils of light were rising in the east; dawn was but a few moments away.

The quiet songs of morning birds drifted to him from the distance. He looked down at the forest city, surprised by the feeling of tranquility that washed over him. Closing his eyes, he could almost forget about the tragedy, the death of friends. Almost.

"Ah, there you are," said a voice behind him.

"We have been looking for you," added a second, almost identical to the first.

A small smile spread across Jeran's face, and he turned to face the twins. Nahrona and Nahrima stood side by side, their golden robes smeared with dirt and stained with blood. Their eyes were bright and focused, but their shoulders slumped, as if they were on the verge of exhaustion. Were his life at stake, Jeran could not have told them apart.

"Much death tonight," one said.

"A terrible tragedy," affirmed the other.

"There is more to come."

"Much more."

"What do you mean?" Jeran asked. "More tragedy tonight? Do you know of another attack? Why haven't you–"

"No child," said the first. "Tonight's tragedy is over."

"So far as we know," added the second.

"But yours is just beginning."

"There is much pain in your future."

"Much suffering."

"Me?" Jeran repeated, shocked. "What suffering? How do I prevent it? What do I have to do?"

"Prevent it?" answered the Elf to his right. "You cannot prevent it."

"Hush, Nahrona," the first counseled when he noticed Jeran's eyes widen in fear. "You are frightening him." To Jeran, the old Elf said, "We do not know the nature of your suffering, only that its time grows near."

"It hangs around you like a shroud," Nahrona added, "dancing at the edges of your aura."

"Nor do we *wish* for you to suffer," Nahrima stated, casting a slightly irritated glance at his brother. "But you cannot expect to forge a sword without passing it through the fire."

"But that is not why we came," Nahrima said after a long pause. "We wished to say goodbye. Your time with us will soon end."

"I don't understand," Jeran said, his face contorting in confusion. "Lord Iban told me that we'd be staying in Lynnaei until the end of summer. We still have more than half a season before we return to Alrendria."

"Nevertheless," Nahrona told him, "your time with us grows short. We wished to say goodbye."

"And offer some advice," Nahrima added.

"Advice?" Jeran prompted, thoroughly confused.

"There will be a time of great despair," Nahrima told him.

Nahrona smiled sadly. "A time when you will feel as if all is lost."

"Do not give in to temptation," warned Nahrima. "Do not surrender to your fears. To your suffering."

"It is when life is bleakest that we find our true selves," Nahrona said. "When the weight of the world crushes you, remember what you fight for."

"Remember *who* you fight for."

"Those memories will give you strength."

"They will see you through the dark times."

As one, the Aelvin twins reached out, each placing a hand on Jeran's shoulder. They smiled warmly. "In your absence," Nahrima promised, "we will do all we can to ensure that the peace you started here grows."

"If you survive your tempering–" Nahrona started.

"When, brother," Nahrima interrupted. "When!"

"Once you finish your tempering," Nahrona amended, "we will be there to aid in your training."

"When the battle is finally joined," they said in unison, "you will be ready." The two Elves squeezed his shoulders with more strength than it seemed possible from such frail bodies. Silently, they turned and walked off, leaving Jeran dumfounded.

He stood there a long time, lost in his own dark thoughts. A hand grasped his shoulder roughly, and Jeran whirled around. Lord Iban stood behind him, covered in dirt and leaves, his leather armor scratched and pitted. After the attack, he had insisted on joining the Elves in their search for the *Kohrnodra*. "Where is Prince Martyn?" he asked gruffly.

"In the palace," Jeran told him, looking the grizzled old warrior up and down. "You did not find them?"

"No," spat Iban angrily. "Not as much as a broken branch. This attack was well planned. I could almost believe...." He let the statement trail off, refusing to share his thoughts.

"What is the final tally?" he asked.

"Six dead," Jeran informed him. "All Guardsmen. Nearly twice that in wounded."

"The representatives of the Great Houses?"

"All are well," Jeran assured him. "Alynna has a couple of scratches. Rafel, a black eye he claims came from the blow of a *Kohrnodran*."

"That fat idiot probably fell," Iban grumbled. "Or insulted one Elf too many."

Jeran hid his smirk. "Jes is missing," he said. "She hasn't been seen since the attack."

"I most certainly have been seen since the attack," she announced, stepping out of the shadows to Jeran's left. "Just not by you." Her white dress was nearly black with dirt and torn in several places. Otherwise, she looked whole and healthy.

"I wish to speak with you, Odara," Lord Iban said, casting a glance in Jes' direction. "Tomorrow," he added. "Tonight, I will deal with the prince." He bowed to Jes and stormed toward the palace.

"Where did you go?" Jeran demanded. "I was worried that something had happened to you. That the *Kohr–*"

"I wasn't aware that I had to keep you informed of my movements," Jes interrupted, her red lips twisting up in a wry smile. "But your concern is appreciated." She turned away and started toward the palace. Jeran hurried to follow, slowing when he reached her side. "If you must know, I went to meet some of my...friends." She did not have to tell Jeran which friends she meant.

"Aren't you trying to hide your Gift?" Jeran asked.

Jes looked at him out of the corner of her eye. "In the aftermath of the attack," she said, "I thought it safe to use a little magic." Her smoldering gaze intimated that she did not feel the need to justify her actions to him. "An attack of this magnitude had to be brought to the attention of the Assembly."

"Why?" Jeran asked. "What concern is it of theirs?"

"All that occurs in Madryn is the concern of the Magi," she informed him coolly. "But in this case, I suspect that the *Kohrnodra* have organized at the order of our enemy. For millennia, the Brotherhood of Kohr has remained a loosely knit web of dissenters and religious fanatics. I cannot believe the timing of this attack to be coincidental."

They entered the palace, and again Jeran was surprised to find the room nearly barren. Only a few wounded remained, awaiting *Ael Namisa* to show them to their rooms. The deafening din was gone, replaced by a tranquil silence. Charylla still stood in the center of the chamber, Astalian at her side. The Emperor was there, too, talking to Lord Iban and the two princes.

At Jes' and Jeran's approach, Charylla looked up, and she smiled. "You have finally been found," she said to Jes. "At last, Jeran can stop worrying."

Jeran flushed at the princess' words. He tried to stammer a retort, but a sudden crash at the door drowned out his words. Everyone whirled to face the entranceway, and those who carried weapons reached for them reflexively.

Luran stood before them, dressed in full battle armor. The giant wooden door quivered from the force he had used to push it open. In one hand, he held his sword; in the other, he clutched a body. Sneering, he threw the Elf toward them. It slid across the floor with a sickening squeal, coming to rest at their feet.

The *Kohrnodran* stared up at them lifelessly. "What is the meaning of this," Luran snarled. "In my absence, can I not even rely on the defense of Lynnaei?" He stared at the Emperor icily. "I told you that allowing Humans to come was a mistake, Grandfather."

The Emperor frowned. "How dare you blame them for this attack."

Luran's bitter laughter echoed through the hall. "I do not blame the Humans, Grandfather," he said harshly. "The blame lies with Astalian. He commanded *Ael Chatorra* in my absence."

Astalian pushed his way to the front of the assembly. The sorrow and shame he had showed Charylla was gone, replaced by anger and disgust. "Which do you question, Luran," he asked, "my honor or my abilities?"

"I question neither," Luran snarled. "I know that both are lacking."

Astalian's hands tightened into fists. "Perhaps if you had stayed in Lynnaei instead of chasing your parent's ghosts–"

"I will not take such insults from the likes of you," Luran screamed, his hand tightening on the hilt of his blade.

"Is your thirst for Garun'ah blood finally sated?" Treloran asked his uncle, stepping forward, interposing himself between Luran and Astalian. "Have you finally managed to avenge the death of your parents? Or did you merely lose the lives of more Aelvin warriors?" He looked at his uncle angrily, goading him to action. "Do you now seek to wet your sword with the blood of your own countrymen?"

Luran trembled in rage. He was so incensed that he could not speak, and he stared blankly at Treloran, hurt by his nephew's betrayal. Then his gaze, sharp as daggers, returned to Astalian. The Aelvin warrior did not seem to notice. "Did you even find the Tribesmen?" Astalian asked, smirking. "I sent scouts of my own to the Danelle, but they found no signs of the Garun'ah on our side of the river."

Luran lifted his blade higher, his knuckles white. Everyone else stood awestruck, listening to the exchange between the two greatest Aelvin warriors. "Nor was there any sign of you and your troops," Astalian added. "Tell me, Luran, where were you exactly?"

"I do not need to explain my actions to the likes of you," Luran snarled, starting across the chamber, his blade raised before him. "Your scouts need more training. I was on the Danelle, and so were the Garun'ah. Should you desire proof, I can show you their carcasses.

"But first, I will make you regret insulting my honor." He charged forward, and only now did Astalian reach for his own blade.

"ENOUGH!" shouted the Emperor, and Luran came to an abrupt halt. The Aelvin Prince struggled against unseen bonds, and he glared at his grandfather. "There has been enough bloodshed tonight. Drop you sword, Luran."

"He has insulted my honor," Luran repeated. "I have the right to–"

"I did not tell you to speak, Grandson," the Emperor said wearily. "I told you to drop your sword." Luran stiffened at the interruption, his eyes growing even more angered. After a tense moment, the sword clattered to the floor. "As for your honor," the Emperor added, "even *I* am beginning to doubt its existence."

"Grandfather?" Luran called, the pain caused by the Emperor's words apparent in his voice.

"My father used to say, 'A man who cries 'honor' at every insult is a man with something to hide.' " The Emperor's eyes shone bright green. "What is it that you hide, Luran?"

"Grandfather!" Luran pleaded. "Everything I do is for Illendrylla. I have only the Empire's wishes in my heart."

"I am sure that is what you believe," the Emperor replied. "I do not question your convictions, Luran. Only your methods." The old Elf remained silent for a long time, considering his options. "I am relieving you of your duties. You are no longer *Hohe Chatorra*."

"NO!" Luran wailed, his anger returning in full force.

"It is not a permanent demotion," the Emperor assured him. "You need time to reflect upon your actions. Time to find peace within yourself. When you have demonstrated to me that you are ready, you can return to your place as the head of *Ael Chatorra*."

The Emperor turned to Astalian. "I would name you *Hohe Chatorra* in Luran's absence, if you are willing to accept the responsibility."

"It would be an honor," Astalian replied solemnly, his eyes locked with Luran's.

"I will release you now, Grandson," the Emperor informed Luran. "I suggest that you go directly to the Vale. Commune with the Goddess. She will show you how to balance your life."

Luran stiffened as the Emperor released his magic. He stared angrily at everyone present, his gaze sweeping slowly from left to right, his eyes burning into those who had witnessed his shame. Hands clenched into fists, then released. Clenched again. He turned on his heels and ran from the chamber, not even bothering to pick up his sword.

Chapter 21

"Well," Martyn said after Luran stormed away. "I don't think he's taking his demotion well at all." All eyes turned on the prince and he shivered, uncharacteristically embarrassed by the attention. His cheeks burning red, he offered the assembled Humans and Elves a shrug of the shoulders. "Well, he isn't!"

"Perhaps I was too harsh on him," the Emperor muttered, scrubbing his eyes wearily. "Perhaps I allowed anger to control my decision."

Charylla reached out to the old Elf, her hand sliding comfortingly around his shoulder. "If anything, Grandfather, you have been too lenient with Luran. He has allowed *his* anger to blind him."

"The Emperor cannot afford to have his *Hohe Chatorra* guided by hatred," Astalian added. "Else he will find his empire constantly at war."

Elierian, bowing low, offered his own consolation. "Prince Luran will certainly use his time wisely. A season or two of meditation will calm his spirit."

"Were I in your place," Iban told the Emperor, "Luran would not have escaped so lightly." After Iban, the voices in the chamber stilled.

"Is this what I am reduced to?" the Emperor asked, though his tone was jovial. "The Emperor of Illendrylla, forced to take counsel from lowly Humans and Aelvin children." His eyes, filled with gratitude, roamed over those assembled, and he smiled. "Your words bring me great solace."

"Come, Grandfather," Charylla requested, taking the aged Elf's arm. "Let me escort you to your chambers. It has been a long night." To Astalian, she added, "I still desire a word with you, *Hohe Chatorra*, though in light of last night's events, if you wish rest before our meeting–"

"If it pleases you, Princess," Astalian interjected with a polite bow, "I will accompany you now. We can discuss your concerns after escorting the Emperor to his apartments." Gone was Astalian's earlier shyness when addressing Charylla; he met her eyes confidently, and it was she who broke their locked gazes.

At the Aelvin warrior's words, the Emperor frowned, and he directed an intense, lingering gaze at his self-appointed escorts. Absently tapping a finger to his thin lip, the Emperor mumbled farewells to those in the hall and allowed himself to be led from the room, Astalian on his right arm and Charylla on his left.

Elierian, eager to be about his duties, disappeared as well. Jeran, stifling a yawn, stretched his arms high above his head. "I think I shall follow the Emperor's example," he said, rubbing his eyes. "The sky is already growing light, and I think I'd prefer to be wrapped in my blankets before it clears the horizon."

He extended a hand to Jes. "M'Lady," he said formally, a small smile on his face. "Would you allow me the honor of escorting you to your chambers?" He had meant it as a jest, but Jes surprised him by accepting his arm. After bidding farewell to those remaining, she let Jeran lead her away.

"I believe they have the right idea," Martyn admitted, starting toward the stairs. "I, too, shall seek my bed."

Iban cleared his throat, and the sound froze Martyn in his tracks. "Are you forgetting our morning meeting, my Prince?"

Martyn turned around slowly, half expecting to see the Guard Commander smiling, but was instead confronted with Iban's most serious, and sincere, expression. "You must be joking!" the prince scoffed. "In light of last night's events–"

"In light of last night's events," interrupted Iban, "I think our morning meeting is even more important than normal." He folded his arms across his chest, as if waiting for Martyn to argue.

The prince glared at him, but wisely held his tongue. "Very well, Lord Iban," Martyn said with a resigned sigh. "If you think it wise." The slightest hint of a smile broke Iban's grim countenance, and without another word, he turned and strode from the chamber. Groaning, Martyn followed.

Iban walked quickly through the narrow, stone-lined halls of the palace. The gait suited Martyn, who was certain he would fall asleep the moment he stopped moving. The *Kohrnodran* attack notwithstanding, the night had been a long one, and the prince's excesses at the feast were not helping matters. During the excitement of the attack and its aftermath, he had not noticed, but now, his head throbbed and his mouth was dry. Several times, he had to fight waves of dizziness and nausea.

They entered the small, sparsely-furnished chamber where they met each morning. Crossing the room silently, Iban took his customary place in a large, well-cushioned chair and gestured for Martyn to sit as well. While he waited, the Guard Commander folded his hands together and absently tapped his knuckles against his lip.

Martyn sat as instructed, casting his eyes about the room. The room had few wall hangings, and no furniture other than the two chairs. He wondered, briefly, if Iban had chosen this chamber because it contained so few distractions. Finished his inspection, he met Iban's gaze squarely, determined to make the Guard Commander speak first. His thoughts drifted to the many other mornings he had spent in this chamber.

Iban insisted on meeting at sunrise, long before the delegates assembled for the daily negotiations. Martyn hated rising so early, but could find no good reason to argue with the Guard Commander. 'Astalian and I did not return from a night of debauchery until just a few moments ago,' was not an excuse that would earn Iban's sympathy.

Besides, Martyn had to admit that he enjoyed his meetings with the old warrior. Iban had a keen eye and a sharp wit. As skilled at politics as he was at warfare, the Guard Commander's vast store of knowledge continually surprised Martyn. "Always keep how much you know a secret," Iban had once counseled. "Keeping your opponent ignorant of your abilities is nearly as important as knowing his."

They spent the first part of every morning discussing the previous day's negotiations. First, Martyn had to describe all the main points, focusing primarily on those items that had elicited the most argumentation. Then he had to offer explanations for the debate, attempting to explain why Horeish was against an Alrendrian Embassy in Lynnaei, or why Rafel wanted the Elves' promise not to establish trade with the other Human nations, except through Alrendria.

Iban generally listened to Martyn's opinions in silence. Occasionally, he offered a suggestion, prodding the prince toward a more logical conclusion than the one he had drawn for himself. After Martyn finished, Iban critiqued his evaluation and furnished his own interpretation.

In the beginning, Martyn was dismayed by how often Iban thought him wrong, and how often the Guard Commander's words rang true in his ears. But as the days passed, Iban's corrections had grown fewer in number. Now there were mornings when the grizzled warrior did little more than nod at Martyn's assessments.

The second part of each session was spent in discussion of the Elves and their society. Each day, Iban demanded five new things–whether they be customs, traditions, laws, or merely the prince's own observations. Despite the requirement, the Guard Commander was never satisfied until Martyn mentioned at least half a score. "Know your enemy," Iban told him on numerous occasions. "The more you know of your adversary, the more likely you are to defeat him. Those words are as true at the negotiation table as they are on the battlefield."

Their discussions were often interesting, and Martyn learned a great deal. "Don't just *observe* these things," Iban once warned. "Understand them. Both the meaning and the motivation." Together, they dissected the Elves and their culture, seeking understanding and advantage.

"It's not enough to know what your opponent wants," Iban said on another occasion. "You must understand *why* he wants it. With that knowledge, you will always find yourself the victor."

The third part of each morning was Martyn's favorite. Lord Iban talked, not of events in Illendrylla, but of the court in Kaper. "You're old enough now," Iban said one day, scratching his salt-and-pepper beard, "to take an active role in your father's governing. To do so, you must know your subjects."

Iban talked at great length about the Great Houses and the Families that comprised them. He described each Family in detail, their main imports and exports, and the defenses erected around each of their holdings. Once, when Iban launched into a lengthy discussion on the defenses of Portal Keep, Martyn had interrupted. "Portal is part of House Odara!" Martyn had stated, trying not to laugh. "You don't expect that I'll ever fight Jeran, do you?"

Iban's face had grown deadly serious. "No, Prince Martyn, I don't think you and Jeran will ever come to blows. But if Lorthas breaks free of his prison, his first target will be Portal. If the Darklord can secure and hold the citadel, it will be virtually impossible to rout him from this side of the Boundary." Martyn's smile had faded, and he listened in attentive silence to the remainder of Iban's lecture.

Mostly, Iban talked about the nobles, outlining their strengths and weaknesses, their motivations, their vices. Martyn learned of scandals and crimes, hidden deeds of heroics, and exaggerated stories of benevolence. "This is all quite interesting," Martyn once said in response to a particularly embarrassing story. "But how am I to use this information?"

"Under the right circumstance," came Iban's instantaneous reply, "such information can be used to motivate a hesitant vassal, or ensure their aid in times of wavering loyalty."

"These are my vassals, not my enemies!" Martyn exclaimed. "They're sworn to protect Alrendria and the King. Surely, you don't think they would renege on their vows."

Iban's frown had been cold and dispassionate. "Each will serve in their own way, according to their interpretation of the oath." The Guard Commander had leaned forward, and his voice dropped to a near whisper. "If it comes to war with the Darklord, or even just the Durange, do you think all the nobles will flock to your cause?" Martyn went wide-eyed.

"Oh some will," Iban admitted, smirking at the prince's stupefied expression. "Perhaps many. But there will be others who offer excuses."

"But the Alrendrian Guard foreswears all bonds to House and Family," Martyn pointed out.

"True," Iban replied, "but it takes more than soldiers to win a war. You need swords and arrows, armor and horses, food and grain. Thousands of other supplies, and the men who work with those materials. Steel does little good without a blacksmith to forge it, and even if you have a forest and a flock of birds, you still need a fletcher to fashion arrows."

"I see what you mean," Martyn replied, embarrassed that he had not considered such matters.

"*Those* people have not foresworn their allegiance in favor of Alrendria."

"I understand!" Martyn had snapped, more harshly than he intended.

"Good," Iban returned, just as brashly. "See that you never forget it. I doubt any of the Families would completely ignore a king's request for aid, but many will offer excuses and send less than you ask. Some will claim they do not have the resources, others will insist the goods are in greater need elsewhere."

The hint of a wolfish smile had twisted the corners of Iban's lips. "There will be as many excuses as nobles," he said, "and the excuses will rarely match the true reasons."

Iban's eyes glinted mischievously. "Listen to the nobles' excuses," he encouraged the prince, "but don't believe them. If one claims a poor crop, offer to dine with him. If the meal is poor, then he likely tells the truth." At that, Iban had barked a quick, heartfelt laugh, one of the few Martyn had ever heard from him. "Even the rich can't eat when food is truly scarce."

"That's why you must keep this knowledge!" Iban had explained. "To use it when you must. To motivate and coerce." He wagged a cautionary finger in Martyn's face. "But methods of this sort should only be used as a last resort, else you'll rule a kingdom where gossip and blackmail are the favored tools of the nobility."

"How do you know all this?" Martyn had asked one afternoon. "In all my life, you've rarely been in the castle. How can you know so much about the nobility?"

"I've been all across Alrendria," Iban told him. "Both before and after joining the Guard. Besides, you don't need to gather information first hand. There are a thousand other sources of reliable information."

"Like servants?" Martyn asked. "Sionel is always telling me how much the servants know."

"Servants are one source," Iban nodded, "but only one, and far from the best. Their information is reliable, but they are often loyal, and will talk to their patron of any encounters they have. You are better off learning what you can from innkeepers... Barmen... Mistresses."

"It isn't easy for a king to speak freely with tavern keepers or mistresses," Martyn chuckled.

"No," Iban agreed. "That's why you need someone to do it for you. There is a man of my House, Zarin Mahl, quite skilled at gathering information, and even more adept at determining which information is reliable, and which is drivel. When we return to Kaper, I will introduce him to you. Perhaps you'll find his services advantageous."

Now, though, Iban offered no words of advice, and Martyn quickly grew bored. He stared across the room at the Guard Commander, his irritation growing. He had come to respect Lord Iban during the journey to Illendrylla, and did not wish to upset his mentor, but he did not want to sit here all morning either. Stifling another yawn, he made to stand.

"I did not come here to stare at you, Lord Iban," he said matter-of-factly. "Yesterday's negotiations offered no new issues. You know what I learned of Aelvin society last night. If you're still unaware of the particulars, you likely wish to remain so. And quite frankly, I'm more interested in sleeping today than in learning about the Alrendrian nobility."

"In light of what happened last night," Iban said quietly, "I think you should confine yourself to the palace."

Martyn was on his feet in an instant. "What!" he exclaimed in a near yell. "You certainly don't think I had anything to do with what happened!"

"Of course not," Iban answered, not even flinching at Martyn's stern glare. "I know you're not responsible. But I never expected that an attack of such magnitude was possible within Lynnaei. I even doubt such a thing will happen again, but I cannot risk your life on a guess." He met Martyn's gaze squarely. "You should confine yourself to the palace."

"No," Martyn said flatly. "It's my duty to learn about the Elves." He mimicked Iban's voice. " 'Knowing your allies is as important as knowing your enemies. Perhaps more important. If we are to form a lasting peace with the Elves, we must understand them.' Your words, Iban," Martyn stated angrily. "Not mine."

"Astalian is going to suggest the same thing to Treloran," Iban assured Martyn. "Neither of us believes you are safe in Lynnaei."

"Is that supposed to make me feel better?" Martyn asked, pacing the chamber. "Am I supposed to be comforted? It's all right to coddle me, to clutch me to your breast like a helpless infant, just because the Elves are going to do the same thing to Treloran?" Martyn shook his head emphatically. "I refuse."

"Have I taught you nothing?" Iban snarled, the first hint of anger entering his tone. "I thought you were now a man, not the arrogant, selfish child I took to Illendrylla." Iban snorted in disgust, tapping his fist against his chin with ever-increasing force. "I hate being wrong."

"What do you mean?" Martyn demanded. "It's my duty to show strength in times of trouble. It's my duty to learn about the Elves. It's–"

"It's your duty to remain alive until we return to Kaper," interrupted Iban. "It's your duty to survive to take your father's throne. To rule Alrendria after his death." Martyn fell silent, listening, really listening, to Iban's words. "Those other things are duties as well," Iban admitted, "but preserving your life takes precedence over them all."

For a long time, Martyn stood motionless. Finally, he retook his seat. "I apologize, Lord Iban," he said sincerely. "I spoke rashly. As usual, you are correct. But I still think it folly to confine me to the palace. If we act as if we're afraid of the *Kohrnodra*, then their attack was nearly as successful as if I had fallen to one of their arrows."

Iban stopped tapping his hand against his chin. He met Martyn's confident gaze. "You have a suggestion?"

"I will continue my daily excursions," Martyn informed him, "but not without an escort of Guardsmen or Aelvin warriors."

Iban considered the proposal. "A score of Guardsmen," he returned. "At all times."

"Ridiculous!" laughed Martyn. "You're almost begging for the *Kohrnodra* to take another shot, if only to prove they can." He scratched his chin. "Five guards at all time, of my choosing."

"Ten," countered Iban, "All Guardsmen. If you want to take Elves in addition to the ten, feel free."

"Ten," Martyn agreed, "But my choice, Elves or Guardsmen."

"The Guardsmen's first concern is your safety."

"The Elves know the land better," Martyn returned with a smile, "and they're not afraid when they have to run along the narrow bridges high in the city. Besides, the Aelvin warriors know I'm friends with both their prince and their commander. It's unlikely that any would let me come to harm."

Iban took a moment to consider the prince's proposal. "Eight Guardsmen, two Elves."

"Four Guardsmen, four Elves," replied Martyn. "The final pair at my discretion."

"Agreed," Iban said with a broad grin. "It's nice to know you occasionally listen to what I have to say."

"Agreed," Martyn echoed, ducking his head to Iban. "Though to be honest, I'd have conceded the last point had you proved obstinate." Once again he made to stand.

"There is one more matter, Prince Martyn." Iban spoke quietly, an uncharacteristic hesitancy in his tone. Martyn took his seat, staring at the Guard Commander warily. After a long, calculated pause, Iban said, "It's been brought to my attention that you're spending a great deal of time with an Aelvin warrior."

Martyn's eyes narrowed reflexively, but he tried not to act suspicious. "I'm just following your advice," he said lightly, trying to keep his smile even. "What better way to understand the Elves than by getting to know the people? There's only so much one can learn from the nobility."

"This particular warrior, the one to whom I refer, is a woman." Iban watched Martyn carefully, the way one would watch a rabid dog.

Martyn refused to rise to the bait. "Unlike some," he said, forcing a laugh, "I do not discount a woman's opinions. Nor do I feel they have no place on a battlefield. On the contrary, I find that women offer interesting perspectives in both military and social matters."

"I agree with you, my Prince," Iban said, his gaze piercing. "However, I have heard that your relationship with this Elf is not purely platonic."

Martyn blushed. Knowing the game was over, his expression hardened. "And if it is not?"

"Then I feel it is my responsibility to remind my prince of his obligation to Princess Miriam of Gilead."

"Astalian said much the same thing to Treloran," Martyn replied blandly, struggling to keep his anger in check. With Iban, calm words and rational thought worked far better than rage. "I will answer in much the same way as the Aelvin Prince. My body may belong to Alrendria, but my heart is mine to give."

"When last I checked," Iban replied coldly, his lips twisting up in a wry smile, "your loins were not attached to your heart."

Martyn's cheeks turned bright red, and he cast his eyes to the floor, no longer able to meet the Guard Commander's stern glare. "It's not like that!"

"Perhaps," Iban allowed. "But it will be like that before too long. I have seen you with this Elf, and I'm not yet so old that I've forgotten what it's like." Cold eyes softened somewhat. "My concern is not for Alrendria, Martyn. It's for you."

Martyn slammed a fist into the side of his chair. "Why must I give up so much for Alrendria?" he asked, anger overcoming him. "No one else is forced to make such a sacrifice. Political marriages are rarely arranged anymore. Except for kings, that is."

"Must you really ask why?" Iban's words were surprisingly soft, even sympathetic.

After a long moment, Martyn shook his head. "No," he admitted. "I know the reasons all too well. We need alliance with Gilead in case it comes to war with the Durange. The only way to cement such an alliance is through marriage."

The prince fell silent, in somber reflection on events he knew must be. "But my heart is mine to give, Iban," he insisted. "No one can take that right from me."

"Your words are true, Prince Martyn, but have you considered the Elf's feelings? What's to happen to her when you wed Miriam? Will you set her aside? Spurn her love? If you truly care for her, how can you force such a future on her?"

"There are other options!" Martyn insisted. "Many kings before me have had consorts. Mistresses. Some were even public!"

"Just because a thing has been done before," Iban scolded, "does not mean it is the right thing to do. Or the honorable thing. Alrendrian Kings have had mistresses," he admitted, "but very few were public, and none to my knowledge were of another race.

"You could sneak to your Elf's chambers," Iban suggested, nodding as if it were a marvelous idea. "Creep through the shadows of Kaper like a thief. But what of Miriam? She is a woman, too, though you have yet to meet her. She will have feelings for you, for good or ill." Iban paused, waiting until Martyn met his icy blue eyes. "There have been a few mistresses in Kaper Castle, but fewer queens who approved of them."

"I can't help my feelings," Martyn snapped. "Nor can I help Miriam's. We will do this thing because we must. I am forced to marry her, not love her."

"And you will love who you want?" Iban asked, shaking his head sadly. "You blind yourself, Martyn. You haven't even met your betrothed, and you refuse her a chance. Perhaps, if you entered your marriage with an open mind, you could love her, and she you."

"And if I love another?"

"That is regrettable," Iban answered. "Even if you take your Elf to Alrendria, she will be little more than your public plaything. An oddity in the court, much like Dahr was after coming to Kaper. Even though you sometimes envied your friend for the attention he received, ask him if he shared your enthusiasm." Iban paused long enough for his words to sink in. "Then imagine what the people would say of your Elf. The King's Pet. The Aelvin whore. Is that what you would have her called?"

Martyn's hands squeezed the arms of his chair; his eyes locked with Iban's. He wished he were somewhere else, anywhere but here with the infallible, ever-practical Guard Commander. "If the Elves have an embassy in Kaper, she will not be such an oddity."

"Perhaps," Iban replied. "But she would still be your mistress, and that alone would occasion gossip." Iban took a slow, deep breath and tried again. "And what of Miriam? What will she think of your mistress? Duty to Alrendria dictates whom you must wed, but you have a duty to your wife as well, whether or not she's the one you would have chosen. Honor demands that you carry out your duties. Honor requires you keep your vows to–"

"Honor and duty. Duty and honor!" Martyn yelled, jumping to his feet. "That's all you talk of! I will carry out my duty to Alrendria, have no fear. But what of the obligations I have to myself? Alrendria is supposed to be a land of freedom, yet its king is a slave!" He stormed toward the door. "I have had enough talk for one day, Lord Iban."

"What is honor?" Iban asked as the prince reached the door. Martyn stopped, his hand frozen on the handle. When Martyn did not answer, Iban asked again. "What is honor to you, my Prince?"

Martyn slowly turned, stopping when his eyes met Iban's. At the prince's blank expression, Iban rephrased the question. "If honor were a thing, what would it be?"

When Martyn still did not answer, Iban smiled. "Then come here and sit, my Prince, and I will tell you a story. It will not offer an answer to your current dilemma, but it may help you better understand your options." Reluctantly, Martyn returned to his chair, sitting once again upon the plush cushion.

"What do you know of the BattleMagi?" Iban asked, and at Martyn's blank expression, he chuckled. "Little, I see. BattleMagi were Magi who trained their Gifts for use in war. There were few who had the ability, and fewer still who entered the training, for becoming a BattleMage carried with it a dire consequence.

"BattleMagi could form bonds with those under their protection. The bond increased the stamina of the ungifted, and it quickened their healing. Most importantly, those bonded always knew the whereabouts of their Mage, and it allowed him to feel his people's presence, too."

"That doesn't sound like too bad a bargain," Martyn mumbled.

"No," Iban admitted, "but I have yet to finish. The BattleMagi could offer all these advantages through their bond, but at a grave price. In exchange, they felt the pain of their people as if it were their own. Every blow in battle was sensed, every hunger pang felt, every death cut through the soul of the BattleMage like a knife in his own heart.

"This bond made the BattleMagi consider honor the greatest virtue. They conducted themselves with honor, and were keenly aware of the consequences their actions would have, especially on their people. A true BattleMage would do nothing to endanger lives unless he felt the cause just, the potential loss and suffering necessary."

Iban continued the story through Martyn's stunned silence. "The final phase in the training of BattleMagi was coming to terms with personal honor. In it, the apprenticed Magi sat in a circle and discussed what honor meant to them. They shared their thoughts, and they shared their fears. If they deemed themselves, or were deemed by their brethren, unwilling to accept the risks, or unworthy to take responsibility for the lives of others, they were put to death."

"Put to death!" exclaimed Martyn. "What do you—"

"Put to death," repeated Iban, silencing the prince with a harsh glare. "Their previous training could not be taken away, and a BattleMage who had no concept of honor, no regard for human life, could not be allowed to wander free.

"The first of these rituals, before it was even a ritual, was conducted by Tyre, the greatest of the BattleMagi. He sat at a fire surrounded by seven apprentices, all at the end of their training. 'What is honor?' he asked them, his eyes hinting at a great understanding.

" 'Honor, Sir?' asked one student, his question echoed by the other apprentices.

"Tyre nodded sagely. 'Honor,' he repeated. 'If it were a thing, what would it be.'

" 'Honor is an eagle,' stated the first apprentice, 'proud and strong, soaring on great wings.'

" 'It is a shield,' said the second. 'It defends us. Keeps us safe.'

" 'No,' said the third. 'It is a rock. A heavy rock, secured to me with a chain of iron. I am a man in water, struggling for each breath, and honor pulls me down.' He looked into the sad, blue eyes of his master. 'Honor is a test,' he concluded. 'A struggle for survival.'

" 'It is the summit of a great mountain, commanding a view of all the land.'

" 'Honor is a mountain cat,' said another, 'ferocious and beautiful. But if you aren't careful, it will bite you.'

" 'Honor is like my mother,' the sixth said, eliciting laughter from his companions. 'It protects me when I am scared, it offers me guidance when I am unsure, and it makes me feel guilty when I do something wrong.'

"There was a long silence before the last apprentice spoke. 'Honor is a thief,' he said softly, after long consideration, 'and it's a tyrant. Honor takes your freedom, and it demands you live by its rules. It dictates every decision, watches your every move, and makes you question your own motives. It is a torturer, delighting in your suffering.'

"He looked at his companions, his own words rending his heart. 'A man without honor is hardly a man, and yet is accepted. A man with honor is revered and yet pitied for his self-sacrifice, simultaneously lauded and shunned, lest his honor force him to pass judgment on another. If even once he falls from honor's path, he is deemed the lowest of men, despised for his betrayal.'

" 'Honor is a sickness,' he continued, trembling from the conviction in his voice. 'It pits man against man. It is an excuse, a thing created by man, justification for war and suffering.' Tears fell from the apprentice's eyes. 'Honor is a God,' he concluded. 'An unattainable ideal that we will never truly realize.'

"An unnatural stillness followed the apprentice's declaration. 'Honor is all of these things,' Tyre told his apprentices, 'and it's a thousand other things besides. To me, honor is a sword. A sword is forged to defend one's life. It is used to defend the lives of others. To protect the weak and innocent.'

" 'A sword's blade can cut both ways,' Tyre continued. 'In the hands of a man who understands it, it will do no evil, but if not used properly, it can harm anyone, including the person who holds it.'

"His students listened in awe. Some even claimed that a heavenly light surrounded the BattleMage while he spoke. 'But a sword is just a thing,' he reminded them. 'On its own it can do no harm. It is the swordsman who controls its strokes, the swordsman who dictates where the blade falls and what its target will be.'

" 'So it is with honor. Honor protects us. It protects others. If a man understands honor, it can be wielded with deadly accuracy, and it will harm only those who deserve punishment. If it is not understood,' Tyre warned, 'if it is not wielded properly, honor can hurt not only the innocent, but also those who would use it as a weapon.'

" 'We BattleMagi are weapons, too. Much like a sword. Much like honor. Our Gift forces an obligation onto us. It is our responsibility, our duty, to learn control of our powers, to understand them. To understand ourselves. Only with that knowledge will we truly be able to protect Madryn, to serve the Four Races in our role as defenders.'

"He gazed at them all with pride, and a smile touched his lips. 'Learning to master any weapon takes time, patience, and dedication, whether you talk of the blade at your side or of yourself. The Sword of Honor is perhaps the toughest to master. It may take a lifetime, even a Mage's lifetime, to learn how to wield it properly.'

" 'Perhaps it can never be mastered,' lamented the seventh apprentice. 'Perhaps honor is something we'll never truly understand.'

" 'Which is more important,' Tyre asked, 'the having of a thing, or the earning of it? You may be right. True honor may be beyond our reach, but so long as we strive to attain it, we better ourselves. We walk closer to the path the Gods have chosen for us.'

"A long silence followed while the apprentices considered their master's words. 'I cannot....' the seventh apprentice said after searching his soul. 'I cannot trust myself. Not with the lives of others. Not even with my own meager Gift.'

"He looked around the fire, meeting the troubled eyes of his fellow students. Finally, his gaze settled on Tyre. 'How can I be trusted with this responsibility?' he asked. 'How can any of us be trusted with your Sword of Honor? What damage might be done if we strayed from the path, or corrupted honor with our own mortal desires?'

"He stood," Iban said, his voice echoing through the chamber, "brushed the dirt from his dark leather armor, drew his belt knife, and drove the blade into his heart. His companions jumped to their feet as he fell, begging Tyre to summon a Healer, to use his own Gift to keep the apprentice from death.

" 'No,' Tyre said. 'This is what he wishes. I will not steal his choice from him.' Tyre stood, walked to his dying student, and knelt at the young man's side. He brushed the apprentice's brow with a kiss, then bowed his head in prayer. After a moment, he stood and walked away.

"He stopped at the edge of the firelight and posed a question to his six remaining students. 'Consider this,' he said. 'Who is more honorable, a man who spends his life trying to understand honor, or a man who knows he will never attain such understanding and takes his own life, lest he be tempted to use his powers in a dishonorable way?' "

Martyn tried to work some moisture back into his mouth. "What's the answer?" he asked, breaking the silence that followed the story's conclusion. "Which is more honorable?"

"I have no idea," the Guard Commander admitted. "Perhaps it's something each man must decide for himself."

"Wha... What does this have to do with me?"

"You will make choices throughout your life," Iban explained. "We all do. No matter what you choose, you will find justification for your choice." Iban sat back and folded his hands in his lap. "Consider the consequences of each choice,' he advised, "not only for yourself, but for others as well. No decision, no matter how trivial, affects only one soul."

Martyn stood and started for the door. "And in this matter, you think the best thing for me to do is to forget Kaeille?"

Iban's voice followed him. "In this matter... In this matter, I only wish to spare you pain, my Prince. I don't know how you should decide. I'm not even sure how I would decide, were I in your place. But no matter how you choose, your decision will affect more than yourself.

"Think of your Elf," Iban counseled him. "Think of Princess Miriam. Think of your father, your friends, Alrendria. And think of yourself as well. Weigh your decision carefully." As Martyn opened the door, Iban rose to his feet. "If you do that, I know you will make the best decision. Like it or not, you are a man of honor, Prince Martyn."

The last thing Martyn saw before he closed the door was Lord Iban saluting him, fist-on-heart.

Chapter 22

Jeran sat in the Vale, a jagged piece of rock in his hands. Nearly ten days had passed since the *Kohrnodran* attack, and Jeran had spent most of that time in quiet seclusion, continuing his training with the Emperor. The twin's dire predictions weighed heavily on his soul, and he wanted to be prepared for whatever was to come.

He looked at the stone, turning it slowly end over end, inspecting it from every angle. It was gray, with flecks of color throughout, pitted and scarred. He traced a finger along one edge. It was cool to the touch, sharp at the edges and smooth along the flatter surfaces. It seemed no different from any other rock.

But he could feel the image trapped within the stone. He slowed his breathing, as the Emperor had taught, and focused his mind on the stone, trying to coax out its story. Cupping the shard in both hands, he closed his eyes and extended his perceptions outward, into the very rock.

He felt the familiar twisting feeling that accompanied his Readings. Unsure of what to expect, he opened his eyes.

He was no longer in the Vale. No longer in the Great Forest. In fact, he was somewhere he had never before seen, or been to. He stood in the center of a vast city, surrounded on all sides by palaces of unimaginable beauty. People passed him, heading in every direction, but they paid him no mind. Jeran even stepped out of the way of a passing carriage before he remembered he was not really there.

His body still sat in Valia's garden, under the watchful eyes of the Emperor, but his mind had been transported into the past, to a place and time with which Jeran was not familiar. To the time of an event so powerful, it had left an imprint on the very rock around where it occurred.

Unlike his earlier Readings, the visions that had nearly incapacitated him on the journey to Illendrylla, this Reading had been induced. This was his final test, the only remaining task he had yet to master. If successful, he would have full control over this aspect of his Gift.

He looked around, trying to get a feel for the place, an idea of the time and location. To his left stood an elaborate structure. Constructed of smooth, white stone, the palace stretched into the heavens, its many towers and balconies overlooking the rest of the city. A staircase of solid marble, more than a hundred hands across, rose to intricately-carved double doors of burnished oak.

The doors stood open, and men and women both walked unmolested through the giant archway. Some wore the insignia of Guardsmen, others were dressed in dark grey robes, but the majority wore only the clothes of commoners and craftsmen.

Humans were not the only race walking the streets; Jeran saw the familiar forms of Garun'ah, too. One Tribesman, a giant, standing taller than even Dahr, walked right past Jeran, a gray wolf loping at his side. Other creatures, not quite as tall as the Humans but broad and heavily muscled, walked the streets as well.

Jeran had never seen an Orog except in his visions. No Humans save the Magi had; the Lost Race had been sealed within Ael Shataq *centuries ago, when the Boundary was raised. But there was no mistaking them. Gray-skinned, high-browed, and powerfully muscled; they walked in pairs, oftentimes carrying huge bundles of tools on their backs. Polite and deferential, they placed each step deliberately, but quickly moved out of the way of other passersby, bowing respectfully as they did so.*

Jeran looked around some more, seeking additional clues. A grassy square, open to the city on all sides, surrounded him. In the center stood a large statue, carved in the shape of a man. The man wore robes, and he stood with one hand reaching up to the heavens, his eyes fastened on some far distant object.

Words were inscribed on the base of the statue, and Jeran started toward it, but a crash of thunder stopped him in his tracks. Confused, he looked up, but saw only blue skies dotted with large, puffy clouds of white. Shaking his head, he started forward again and heard another distant crash.

Others seemed to notice the sound as well. All around him, people looked at the sky, shaking their heads in puzzlement. An excited murmur began to spread, rising in volume as the crashes grew louder and more frequent. Suddenly, one woman pointed up, her eyes wide with fear. Jeran turned in the direction of her shaking finger, and his mouth dropped open.

Dark, ominous clouds boiled toward them from the north, against the wind. The clouds swept forward, moving with incredible speed, filling the sky from horizon to horizon. Large bolts of jagged lightning, followed by terrible crashes of thunder, streaked across the sky. As the clouds obscured the sun, the light in the plaza dimmed. At first, the darkening was hardly noticeable; within moments, the day was no brighter than twilight.

The murmur had grown more excited, and several people were hurrying from the square, seeking the safety of their homes. The clouds continued to spread, blocking all light, leaving the city in complete darkness except when illuminated by lightning. Hail, chunks of ice as large as apples, began to fall, clattering against the paving stones.

With the fall of the first hailstone, the rest of the assembled people scattered, seeking cover. The wind picked up, howling through the square, strong enough to blow over carts and toss people roughly to the ground.

That was when Jeran heard the first screams.

The cries were distant at first, faded and intermittent, but they grew louder. Jeran stood through the tumult, unaffected by the weather, watching in surprise and horror as flames rose in the north, so bright they could be seen over the top of the palace.

Lightning flashed twice, in rapid succession, and then again. One jagged bolt struck the palace to Jeran's right, and stone crumbled, falling to the ground with a loud crash. Lightning showered the square, raining destruction on the buildings. The hail fell faster, its clatter nearly loud enough to drown out the thunder reverberating through the streets.

Jeran looked up and was swallowed in light as a bolt of lightning passed through him, shattering the statue into a thousand pieces....

Jeran dropped the stone, gasping in a deep breath. It fell to the ground, clattering loudly on the loose pebbles at his feet. He wrapped his arms tightly around his chest and rocked back and forth. The Emperor was at his side in an instant, withered hands placed comfortingly on Jeran's shoulder. "What did you see?" he asked in a sympathetic voice.

"Death," came Jeran's reply. He outlined the scene. The square. The palaces. The people. And finally the strange, unnatural storm. "There were Guardsmen," he told the Emperor, "so I was in Alrendria. But there were Orog, so it must have been before the Boundary was raised. In fact, there were very few warriors at all, so the vision was likely from a time before the MageWar."

"The statue seemed central to the vision," Jeran continued. "It was at the center of the square, and the vision came to an end with its destruction." He looked at the stone. "I would guess the stone was once part of the statue."

The Emperor smiled and squeezed Jeran's shoulder. "You have successfully induced a Reading," he told him, "from an object more than a thousand winters old. If you can sense and activate an imprint that old, your mastery of Reading is nearly as good as mine."

"But where was I?" Jeran asked, shaking off the fear and sadness that had flooded him.

"Tyrmalin," answered the Emperor sadly. "It was a Mage Academy. One of the most beautiful cities in all of Madryn. Each building was a work of art, sculpted to accentuate the landscape. Nothing was out of place or unnatural." The Emperor's eyes grew misty. "Aemon tried to build Shandar with the same consideration. Although he came close, he could never recapture Tyrmalin's unique beauty."

"But the storm...." Jeran's voice caught when he saw the pained expression on the old Elf's face.

"Lorthas," spat the Emperor, the word coming out like a curse. "He attacked without warning, razed the city to the ground. Thousands were slaughtered. It was the first battle of the MageWar, if you can even call it a battle."

The Emperor broke off his narration and took several deep, slow breaths. "In truth, the Darklord only intended to destroy the Academy. Aemon was supposed to be present, along with many of the Elder Magi. Lorthas hoped to knock out the leaders of the Mage Assembly with one well-timed attack.

"It probably would have worked," the Emperor admitted, "but he attacked one day too late. Aemon had called for a meeting of the Assembly the day before, asking all Magi to meet him in the Hall. You are familiar with the Hall?"

Jeran nodded. "Carved into the rock of Aemon's Shame?" he asked. "Overlooking Shandar?"

"That's it!" the Emperor agreed, nodding. "Though Shandar had not been built yet, the Assembly Hall was already there. Aemon wanted to discuss Lorthas, who, in the winters prior to the attack on Tyrmalin, had grown increasingly militant, increasingly convinced that the only way to save the Magi from extermination was to take control of Madryn."

The Emperor's eyes grew introspective. "Had Lorthas attacked a day earlier, he would have succeeded. Had the meeting at the Hall been on any topic other than Lorthas, he would have been summoned, and would have known not to attack."

He shrugged, shaking off his sudden melancholy. "When Lorthas learned that the Magi were not in Tyrmalin, he was furious. With the element of surprise gone, he knew he was in for a long and bloody war.

"In his rage, he destroyed Tyrmalin, leveled the city, destroyed the palaces. Any who refused to join Lorthas were taken as slaves if not killed outright." The Emperor rubbed a hand roughly over his eyes. "Tyrmalin was one of my favorite places," he confided to Jeran. "Second only to the Vale. I have never forgiven Lorthas for its destruction."

The Emperor picked up the rock reverently, as if it were an icon. "After the MageWar, I returned to Tyrmalin. Or where Tyrmalin had been. The centuries of warring had not been kind to Madryn, and scavengers had taken most of what survived the initial attack." The Emperor held the rock up to eye level. "I walked the ruins for days, trying to invoke a Reading not filled with war and suffering.

A hard, angry glint entered the aged Elf's eyes. "This rock was the best I could find," he said, tapping a finger against it. "Lorthas' attack had washed away all other memories of Tyrmalin. All the images of beauty, peace, and love were gone. This stone, this tiny fragment of statue, held within it the last blissful moments of the legendary city. The last peaceful moments in Madryn for a long, long time."

The Emperor stood, groaning audibly, and tucked the stone inside his robes. He extended a hand to Jeran. "Come," he said. "We are done here for the day."

"What of my training?" Jeran asked, climbing to his feet.

"You have learned all I can teach. Your ability with Reading almost equals my own. The rest will come with time." The Emperor turned away and began to shuffle down the stone-lined path.

Jeran hurried after him. "Then we should work on my Gift. I don't know how much longer I'll be here, and I need to learn all you can teach me before I go. I can make more progress if I try harder. Please," he almost begged. "I need more training if I am to learn control."

The Emperor laughed so hard he coughed. He doubled over, a hand clasped to his stomach, until the wave passed. "You are a treasure, Jeran!" he said, still smiling. "In all my life...." He let the statement trail off and continued his slow, scuffling walk through the Vale.

"Please, Grandfather," Jeran asked again. "I'm afraid of what I might do with my Gift if I don't learn how to control it."

"Jeran," replied the Emperor in a commanding voice, not bothering to turn or slow down, "you are more dedicated than the most devout *Ael Maulle*. You have learned more this summer than most with the Gift learn in a four-season! Or even two four-seasons!"

His voice became quieter, more sincere. "You are no longer a threat to anyone," he assured him. "You can extend your perceptions without fear of your magic running wild. You know how not to draw the flows. Never again will magic surge through you without you telling it to."

"But there is still more I need to learn."

"There will always be more you need to learn," countered the Elf. "But as your skill grows, so does your strength, and I am not as young as I used to be. A thousand winters ago, I would have trained you day and night, if that was what you desired. But no longer!" He smiled weakly and shook his head. His voice lacked spirit, as it often did when he spoke of his age.

"Your Gift is no longer a threat," he repeated, "except, perhaps, to your enemies. All you have left to learn is how to maintain your hold on magic. And while that is both the hardest–and most interesting–phase of an apprentice's study, sadly, I no longer have the strength to teach you."

"Then how will I learn?"

"Practice," came the reply. "The same as anything else. Practice when no one is around. Practice when other Magi are available. Sometimes the magic will rush through you in a torrent, and you will have to release it. Other times it will fade away, no matter how hard you try to keep your grip."

"I will not lie to you, Jeran," the Emperor said, "It will be winters before you can hold magic for more than a moment or two. If you try to, it will run wild, releasing itself with unpredictable results.

"For some, it takes decades of diligent training before they master holding magic. But the more you seize it and the longer you hold your focus, the greater strength and control you will acquire. Repetition is the key. Repetition and practice.

"But not today!" he asserted when he saw the gleam in Jeran's eyes. "Today, there is something I want to show you." The Emperor disappeared around a bend in the trail, and Jeran hurried to follow. As he cleared the brush, the ivory tower in the center of the Vale appeared, reaching into the heavens, its top so far distant it was invisible.

"The Tower of the Five Gods?" Jeran whispered in awe. "You wish to show me the tower? I thought none but Elves were allowed to enter."

"Few have seen the world from the tower's peak," the Emperor answered, "Elves included. But there's no law which holds the tower off limits to the other Races." The Emperor laughed again. "We just do not have as many visitors as we used to."

The Emperor stepped up to the smooth stone, reaching out a hand. As his fingers contacted the tower, a door appeared, sliding in and over, allowing them access. Breathlessly, Jeran followed the Emperor inside, his eyes instantly going up. A wide staircase wrapped around the interior of the tower, but the view to the top was obscured. "There are five levels to the tower," the Emperor explained. "One for each of the Gods. Though in truth," he admitted, "they are to give us a chance to rest. The climb to the top is quite arduous!"

The old Elf grimaced as he looked at the long, winding staircase. With an audible sigh, he stepped forward, mounting the first step. One foot after the other, he climbed the stairs with surprising speed. "What do you know of the Gods?" he asked. "Have you heard their story before?"

"No," Jeran admitted, shaking his head. "I know little more than their names. And most of what I've learned has been since arriving in Lynnaei." His cheeks turned a light shade of red. "The Gods do not receive as much attention in Alrendria as they do here."

"It has always been so," the Emperor replied, shaking his head, "and for reasons you will understand once I've finished their tale." He turned his head enough to look deep into Jeran's eyes. "But no matter the reason, it is still regrettable. You Humans sacrificed much when you turned your eyes from the Heavens."

As he climbed, he began the story of the Gods. "In the beginning there was only Kohr, the All." The Emperor's voice sounded distant and measured, as if reciting a tale long since memorized. "For eons He traveled the empty universe, delighting in the vacuum.

"But even a God grows weary of eternal nothingness. In the timelessness of space, He grew lonely, and yearned for a companion with whom to share His solitude. Finally, a solution occurred to Him. 'I shall create myself a wife. One to share this universe with me. My equal.'

"And so He created Shael, the Mother. And in every way was She Kohr's equal, but also His opposite. Where Kohr would use force, Shael used compassion. When Kohr's anger rose, Shael retaliated with laughter.

" 'You are indeed worthy of my attention,' Kohr remarked upon the conclusion of their first argument. 'Together, there is nothing we cannot accomplish.'

"Another eternity passed as Kohr and Shael traveled the Heavens, creating the After World. Their arguments were numerous and varied; Their reconciliations shook the Heavens." The Emperor described for Jeran, in great detail, those places the Gods had created. "When all was finished, They looked at all They had wrought, and knew it was good.

" 'We should create a world,' Kohr said one day, 'and populate it with all manner of life. What fun we would have, watching our creation grow and develop.'

"Shael gave His words careful consideration. 'I will create this world with you,' She told Him. 'For I would gain much joy by watching such a place. But....' A mischievous gleam entered the Goddess' eyes. 'I will not agree to such an undertaking until you accept my conditions.'

" 'Conditions?' repeated Kohr. "I need not bargain with you, my wife. I am the All.'

" 'Then create this world yourself,' said Shael indifferently. 'For I want no part of it.'

"Kohr frowned. 'Name your conditions.' "

Above them, the stone of the first landing was growing near. The Emperor paused, using the break to take several slow, deep breaths. Then he continued the climb. " 'I have three demands,' Shael told Her husband, 'and you will agree to all, or there will be no world. First, what is made cannot be unmade. All which is done cannot be undone.'

" 'Agreed,' laughed Kohr, His voice shaking the Heavens.

" 'Second,' the Goddess continued, ignoring the God's laughter. 'None in the Heavens will intervene directly with Our creations. Should one of them displease you, you shall not change them to suit your whims. Each must be allowed to develop in its own way.'

" 'And what of indirect means?' inquired the All. 'Though I may not change this world to suit my whims, will you not allow me to talk with our creations, to instruct them in their errors?'

" 'Should you confine your influence to scholarly discussions,' replied the Goddess, 'and forego the use of divine power, I will not refuse you the right to commune with our creations.'

" 'Agreed!' said Kohr, His laughter even louder. 'I thought your conditions would be more demanding! Which of our creations, when confronted with my Godly wisdom, would refuse the Will of his Creator?' Shael returned the God's smile silently. 'Name your third condition!'

" 'If I create this world with you,' Shael said, 'you will create a child with me, another God with whom to share our creation.'

" 'I will not confine you to one child," Shael added with a twinkle in Her eye. 'Should you desire a multitude of children, I will consent.'

"Kohr pondered this last request for a long time. 'It is agreed, my wife. Let us create a world, and then, together, we shall create a child to help us rule it!' He offered His hand, and the two Gods strode off together, ready to create our world."

They cleared the first landing, and Jeran stared in awe. Large, ornate windows lined the wall, evenly spaced, broken only where the staircase continued its ascent into the heavens. Painted murals hung between the windows, depicting many of the scenes in the Emperor's tale. In the center of the room stood a statue of marble: a motherly woman of stunning beauty with deep, sad eyes and a slight, knowing smile on her lips.

"This is Shael's Tier," said the Emperor. "Where we pay homage to the Mother." He knelt at the statue's feet, bowing deeply. Jeran mimicked the elderly Elf, not quite sure what he was supposed to do. After a moment, the Emperor stood. "Go and look through the windows, Jeran," he ordered. "See how the world looked in its first days."

Jeran did as he was bid. The windows sloped slightly upwards, so the Vale below was invisible. On all sides was a world of stark red stone, devoid of vegetation and life. Above was a sky of blue, dotted with wisps of clouds. None of the palace's towers were visible, nor could any guards be seen walking the ridge above. Jeran could almost imagine he was in the early world, before the Gods created life.

"Come," beckoned the Emperor. "There is yet much to see." The old Elf started up the stairs, and Jeran hurried to follow. With Jeran at his side, the Emperor continued the story.

"First, the Gods created the world," the Emperor said, his voice once again falling into a measured pace. "Kohr created the land, Shael the water. Kohr stoked the fires of the sun, and Shael gave breath to the cooling winds." The Emperor talked of the world's birth for quite a while, telling how Kohr had raised the mountains, and how Shael had created the rains. How Kohr used wind and water to create storms, and how Shael hollowed out caves in the earth to provide shelter.

The Emperor's descriptions of Madryn's creation were vivid, almost as if he had been there to witness this miracle personally. But even more intricate were his descriptions of the creation of life. "When at last the world was done," the Emperor intoned, "the two Gods looked at Their creation and knew it was good. Shael turned to face Her husband. 'This world is beautiful, and yet it is dead. Let us bring life unto it.'

"Kohr nodded his agreement. 'But all which lives will die, my wife,' He warned. 'For no thing has lived until life is gone. No thing is truly missed until it is past.' He knew His wife would never want Her creations to suffer, and he braced himself for the argument He knew was to come.

"To His surprise, Shael agreed. 'All things must die, my husband,' She told Him. 'But upon their death, they will rise to the Heavens, to share eternity with us.'

" 'Only those who please us will ascend to the Heavens,' countered Kohr. "I have no wish to spend eternity surrounded by creatures who squandered their lives.'

" 'So long as the creature pleased one of the Gods,' Shael concurred, 'it can join us. All others will be sent to the Nothing.' Then the two Gods breathed life into the world. First came the plants. Moss and lichen, shrub and flower, tree and vine; the Gods created them one by one, and each, they saw, was good.

"Then came the animals. From fishes to birds, from frogs to lizards, from mice to tigers were the animals created, though here the Gods' ideas differed. Shael's creations were kindly and cautious, Kohr's aggressive and ferocious. 'Ha!' He laughed. 'My beasts are hunters; yours are but the prey.'

" 'Mine are the givers, and yours the takers,' countered Shael, Her eyes mocking. 'Should your creations die, mine will live on; but should mine die out, yours will quickly follow.'

"Kohr stared angrily at His wife, unhappy at being bested. When His anger passed, He looked upon the world They had created. 'We are finished, wife.'

" 'Not quite,' came Shael's reply. 'This world needs a caretaker, someone to tend it in our absence, to help maintain its beauty.' The Goddess knelt and drew to herself a handful of clay. With tender care, she sculpted two figures and breathed life into them. And so were the Orog created. 'My people,' Shael said to them, and the Orog basked in Her glory. 'Go throughout this world and prosper. I charge you with only one task. Maintain the balance. There is a harmony to all things, a balance to all Creation. It is your duty to maintain that balance, both in the world around you and within your own souls.'

"And so did the Orog go unto the world," said the Emperor. "And they kept their word to the Goddess Shael, striving diligently to maintain the balance in all things.

"Kohr watched the Orog depart, then prepared to retreat into the Heavens. 'Now we are done!' He said with a note of finality.

" 'And what of Our child?' Shael reminded Him. 'What of your promise to create another God?' Kohr hesitated, but in the end found no way to escape His oath. From Their union rose the Goddess Valia, the Gardener. Tall and lithe, fair of hair and green of eye, She had both Her mother's compassion and Her father's temper.

"She looked down from the Heavens in awe, reveling in Her parents' creation. 'What a world of stunning beauty,' She told Them. 'Might I see more of it?'

" 'Of course, my Daughter,' answered Kohr, and He showed Valia how to move through the Heavens. The Gods toured creation, the two elder Gods teaching the young Goddess of the world. This was a time of serenity, a time the world has scarcely known.

"Shael and Valia were as close as any mother and daughter, but Kohr found a special place in his heart for his firstborn. Often, when Shael left to visit the Orog, Kohr and Valia traveled the Heavens, reveling in creation.

"But Valia loved the world more than the Heavens, and plants more than any other of her parents' creations. 'Animals are disgusting things,' She once told Her mother, 'Forever soiling themselves and making such irritating noises. The truest beauty in nature is that of the silent flower.'

"Valia spent much time in the world, meticulously growing and molding the vegetation into Her ideal of beauty. Whole forests were reshaped by Her touch; thousands of new blossoms were created with each breath. The Orog, who worshiped Her second only to Shael, called her the Gardener.

" 'You spend too much time on the beasts and in the rocks,' she chastised the Orog one day. 'And though your work is splendid, I feel greater devotion must be given to nature's true beauty.' She called two of the Orog forward, one male and one female. After studying them for a long time, she snapped her fingers and the Elves were born.

"The Elves were taller and thinner than the Orog, with far greater dexterity and agility. The Orog stared in surprise at their cousins' sudden appearance, and the Elves stared back, equally shocked by their existence. 'My people,' Valia said to Her Race, and they fell to their knees in worship. 'There is a whole world of beauty, and I, even though a Goddess, am unable to enjoy it all. When I am called to the Heavens, who is left to tend the gardens of this world? If I train you in its care, will you not share in the burden of its maintenance?'

"The Elves agreed, and Valia taught them Her ways." The Emperor stopped his oration, and Jeran was surprised to find himself standing on the second landing. He had been so absorbed in the tale that he had not noticed their arrival. "This is Valia's Tier,' the Emperor told him. "Here we honor the Gardener."

This level was much like the first. Murals lined the walls between the evenly spaced windows. In the center of the chamber stood a living statue of Valia, not unlike the one at *ael Chatel e Valia*, but this one was even more lifelike than the other. Jeran blinked in surprise, certain he had seen the Goddess' chest rise and fall as she drew breath.

Once again, the Emperor knelt at the statue's feet, and Jeran did the same, offering a silent prayer for Valia's blessing. Standing, he crossed to the windows and looked out. They were nearly level with the top of the palace, but it was hard to see much beyond the top of the plateau. These windows, unlike the one on Shael's Tier, sloped down, offering a stunning view of the Vale. Valia's Garden lay beneath them in all its splendor, its perfectly arranged vegetation so beautiful it brought tears to Jeran's eyes.

"We still have quite a ways to go," the Emperor told him, starting toward the stairs, and Jeran had to pull himself away from the window. He cast one last look at the statue before taking the steps two at a time, hurrying until he walked once more at the Emperor's side.

"Kohr grew sad at His daughter's absence," the Emperor said, continuing his tale. "He had grown fond of Their time together, and missed it greatly. A thought occurred to Him. 'Since I found such joy in my daughter,' He said to Himself. 'Then surely would I find even more joy in a son.'

"He approached Shael and said, bluntly, "I desire another child. A son.'

"Shael eyed Him curiously. "If that is what you desire, my husband,' She said, 'I will certainly not argue with you.' She looked Him up and down appraisingly. 'But be sure this is truly what you wish. Once done, it cannot be undone.'

" 'I know my own heart, Wife,' Kohr told Her blandly, striding boldly across the Heavens. She yielded to Him, and Their melding rocked the Heavens. From this union were born not one, but two, sons. Balan and Garun. The Twins.

"Balan was the elder. Taller than Kohr, He nevertheless had His mother's narrow frame. His eyes were bluer than the sky, His hair as dark as night. He was soft-spoken but implacable, born with Shael's wisdom and Kohr's stubbornness.

"Garun was the giant of the Gods. Broad of shoulder and thickly muscled, with hair and eyes the same shade of chestnut brown, He towered over his family. His great size was matched only by His love of life, and He viewed the Heavens with a sense of awe.

"Upon their birth, the Twin Gods looked about in wonder. Satisfied with their existence, the twins shared a knowing, understanding glance. Garun began to study His newly-acquired form; Balan studied the Heavens assiduously. Finally, he spotted Shael, and a smile touched His lips, though His face wrinkled in confusion. 'Who are you?'

" 'I am Shael,' She replied. 'Your Mother.'

" 'And I am Kohr,' thundered the God, His voice shaking the Heavens. "The All. First of the Gods. Father of the Universe.'

"Balan looked His father up and down. 'Hmm,' He grunted, His eyes shifting back to Shael. 'A pleasure to meet you, Mother.' He bowed His head politely. 'I am Balan. My brother, the one assiduously studying the construction of his arm, is Garun.'

" 'How dare you ignore me!' Kohr shouted, His temper flaring. 'I am the All! You will show me respect.'

"Balan turned to face His father. 'What have you done to earn my respect?' His question was meant earnestly.

" 'I am your father!' Kohr sputtered, His rage increasing. 'Without me you would not exist.'

" 'For which I thank you,' Balan said, bowing His head. "But other than your part in my birth, you have done little.'

" 'I created the universe,' replied Kohr, 'the Heavens and the world below.'

" 'Mother is responsible for as much of the universe as you.'

" 'I am the All!' yelled Kohr, 'and you are but my son.'

" 'You have no powers which I do not possess,' Balan stated, His voice icy calm. 'Nor does a longer existence guarantee you admiration.'

" 'What have you done in comparison to my achievements?' Kohr demanded, His eyes as sharp as daggers.

"You have created more than I, Father,' Balan admitted, 'but you have existed since the dawn of time, and I am but newly born. Besides,' He added with a smirk, 'you have all but ignored your creations since the day you spawned them from the Nothing. Respect is not a measure of how much you create. It is a reflection of the love and esteem that you bestow upon your creations.' "

The Emperor craned his neck around to meet Jeran's eyes. "Suffice it to say, Kohr was not fond of His oldest son. He and Garun might have gotten along well enough, but the twins were virtually inseparable, and Kohr could hardly stand to be in the same place as Balan.

"In any case, like their sister, the two new Gods were more enthralled with the world below than with the Heavens. At their request, Shael showed Them how to pass between the worlds, and They left their father's ravings behind.

"They appeared in a field of clover, startling a herd of deer. As one, the herd bounded toward the nearby forest, into an ambush by a pride of lions. 'What beautiful creatures!' Garun exclaimed, watching attentively.

" 'Which ones?' asked Balan, not sure if his brother spoke of the deer or the lions.

" 'Both,' came Garun's reverent answer. 'And what a beautiful game they play.'

" 'Who are you?' demanded Valia, stepping from the trees, a small contingent of Elves at Her heels.

" 'I am Balan, and this is Garun. We are your brothers.'

"Valia looked at them for a long time. 'Greetings,' She said, inclining her head slightly, then turning and starting back toward the wood. 'Try to watch your step. I would not want you walking on my flowers!' She disappeared into the trees. 'Once you have acquainted yourselves with existence, my brothers, seek me out. I will gladly guide you.'

"The Twin Gods explored the world, often accompanied by Shael or Valia. Their mother taught them of the world, and from the Orog, they learned of the Balance. But when Valia showed them her gardens, Garun scoffed. 'You waste your time on these plants, Sister! The true beauty of nature is the animals. The cycle of life and death.'

" 'Animals are unruly,' Valia chided, Her tone patronizing. 'They are dirty and disrespectful. Not deserving of our love.'

" 'Your Elves are animals,' Garun pointed out. 'Do you not love them?'

" 'My Elves understand beauty,' countered the Goddess. 'They appreciate the nuances of perfection. Perhaps you do not see the splendor of my gardens,' She laughed, 'but you are young, little Garun. Have patience.'

"Garun glowered at His sister's mocking tone. 'Your plants are lovely,' He told Her, 'but their beauty is forced. It pales in comparison to the beauty of true nature, where flora and fauna live in harmony.'

"He stormed from the gardens, and Balan hurriedly followed. 'Do not allow her to unsettle you, brother,' Balan said, laying a comforting hand on Garun's shoulder. 'Her opinion is different than yours, that is all. Do not allow mere words to drive a wedge between you.'

" 'Like you and father?' Garun asked with a smile.

" 'I have never faulted father for his beliefs,' Balan replied, 'only for his actions.'

" 'If Valia can have a Race,' Garun inquired, 'then why can I not? I will make a Race of my own, and teach them the true ways of nature. Like the Orog, they will strive to maintain the Balance, and unlike the Elves, they will seek true beauty.'

"Garun closed His eyes, and before Him sprang into being the first Garun'ah. Taller than the Elves, nearly as broad as the Orog, they stood before their God, marveling at the land around them.'

" 'What of you, brother?' asked Garun. 'Do you not want a Race?'

"Balan considered His brother's question. Suddenly, another Race, the Humans, popped into being. Neither as tall as the Garun'ah, as broad as the Orog, nor as lithe as the Elves, Balan had taken the characteristics he most admired from each of the other Races and put them together.

"The Humans and Garun'ah looked at each other curiously, and the Gods introduced them. 'What will you teach your people, Balan?'

" 'I will teach them to seek truth,' the elder God said. 'For truth is the only true beauty. Knowledge will be their religion, honor their sword, truth their shield.' He looked at His creation with great pride. 'I see in you great potential, my children. Seek truth and follow your heart, for they will not lead you astray.' "

Jeran and the Emperor arrived at the third level. Like those before, scenes of the Gods' story were painted on the walls, but unlike the other levels, this tier had more than one statue. In the center of the room stood a giant bronze figure, twice as large as the statues of the Goddesses. Garun, in all his splendor, looked down at them, a expression of amusement and eagerness on his face. Cluttered around him were statues of many different animals; each looked at the God adoringly.

"This is Garun's Tier,' said the Emperor. "Here we pay homage to the Hunter." They knelt at the base of the statue and offered a prayer to Garun, then Jeran went to the windows. The towers of the palace circled them, a thousand different shades of color. The Great Forest was visible over the top of the plateau, its trees reaching out in every direction. Birds wheeled in lazy circles, floating on the currents of air that blew around the tower.

The Emperor was once again on the staircase. "Kohr summoned the Gods to the Heavens," he told Jeran, "to discuss what had just been done. 'Is it wise to allow these new Races free reign over the world?' He asked.

" 'What is done cannot be undone,' replied Balan.

" 'You had no right to create these Races without permission!'

" 'Whose permission did you ask before creating the universe, Father? Did Valia seek your advice before bringing her Elves into being?'

"Kohr's eyes flashed with anger. 'You have instructed your people to seek truth and knowledge,' Kohr said. "Better to set them a more specific task, as have your brother and sister.'

" 'Your counsel is most appreciated, Father,' Balan said dryly. 'But as usual, I disagree with it. Truth and knowledge will lead my people to enlightenment.'

" 'It will lead them only to pain and suffering.'

" 'What do you fear, Father?' Balan asked, earning Himself a hateful glare. 'Do you fear what they will learn? Do you fear that my Race, or all Races, might discover that true power does not come from the Gods, but from within themselves?'

" 'I fear nothing!' shouted Kohr, and with a supreme effort, the All calmed his voice. "Except the foolishness of my children. Who will watch this world if we are not here? Who will protect your creations from themselves?' He looked at each of his children in turn. 'No answers? Then I will solve this problem for you.'

" 'I am not sure that these Races are better off with you as their protector,' Shael laughed, goading Her husband. 'Maybe you had better leave them to their own devices.'

"Kohr waved His hand, a smug expression on his face. 'To each of your Races,' He said to His children, 'I have bestowed some of our own power. A gift. The ability to create and destroy as do the Gods. To those so Gifted, I exact a duty. They are charged with the protection of this world and those who inhabit it.'

"He turned to Shael. 'Since you think these creatures are better off without my aid, I have refused this Gift to your Race. Time will tell whether or not they would have benefited from my intervention.' With that, the Father of All disappeared into the Heavens.

"The other Gods returned to the world below, each spending time with the Race they had created. They searched out those gifted by Kohr's touch, and taught them how to harness their Gift. They explained the nature of magic and informed the Gifted of the responsibilities that accompanied their newfound skills.

"Many winters passed, and the Races spread across the world. Of all the Gods, Shael visited the world least, save for Kohr. The Orog, the first Race, had existed far longer than the Races of her children, and they had learned from Her as much as She wished to teach. Yet She visited from time to time, because She took comfort in their gentle ways.

"Valia tended her gardens and instructed Her Elves in their care. She ingrained in them a rigid perfection, a desire to see each thing in its place. She sought out Garun and Balan only on rare occasions, and all but ignored Her brothers' Races.

"Garun, too, traveled with his people, teaching them the way of the world, instilling in them a respect for the delicate balance of nature even stronger than the Orog's, though of narrower focus. He could often be found hunting with the Tribes, or sitting around the campfires of the Garun'ah, drinking and laughingly telling stories of the Heavens.

"He and Balan remained close, as did their Races, living side by side throughout the ages. The bond formed between the Humans and Garun'ah has been strong since those first days, when the Gods walked among us.

"Had Garun his way, He would have kept his elder brother by His side at all times, but Balan was a solitary figure. Whenever possible, He slipped away from His brother's camps and wandered the vast wilderness. Sometimes, those of His Race seeking wisdom accompanied Him. Other times, He traveled alone.

"On one journey He was accompanied by a scholarly disciple, one of the Gifted. Seeing His companion's discomfort, Balan bade him sit upon a rock overlooking a stream. 'What troubles you, little brother?' asked the God, His eyes sympathetic.

" 'My quest for truth,' came the sullen reply.

" 'Is the truth so painful then?' Balan asked, a sad smile twisting the corners of his mouth.

" 'It has occurred to me,' said the man, 'that all which you teach us to strive for–truth, honor, compassion–all have their opposites in this world.

"The God's words were gentle. 'No thing exists which does not have an opposite.'

" 'Of course, Master,' replied the student. 'But in your presence, in the presence of any of the Gods, one finds it impossible to be deceitful. To steal. To cause unnecessary harm.'

" 'This troubles you?'

" 'Not of itself,' came the confident reply. 'I have no wish to become an evil man. But you have always said that the earning of a thing, the striving to attain it, is more important than the having.'

" 'I have always found it so.'

" 'And yet in your presence, there is no need to struggle. All desires, all temptations, flee.' The student lowered his face; tears welled in his eyes. 'I do not wish to lose the comfort of Your gaze. Nor do I wish to undertake the struggle and find myself lacking.' The Mage lifted his head and met Balan's intense stare with one of his own. 'But I do wish to *earn* my place in the Heavens,' he stated boldly, 'not have it handed to me because I lived in your shadow.'

"For a long time, Balan sat in silence," the Emperor said, stepping onto the smooth cold floor of the fourth tier. " 'I will consider your words,' Balan said at last. In a flash, He disappeared, returning to the Heavens."

This level was significantly smaller than those below, a tribute to their great height. Between the windows, the paintings depicted scenes from the story of the Gods, from the creation of the Magi to Balan's sudden departure. Otherwise, the room was empty, save for the single statue in its center. "This is Balan's Tier," recited the Emperor. "Here we pay homage to the Scholar."

Forged of solid silver, the statue was of a man seated in a throne of marble. Balan's elbow rested on his knee and his chin was supported on his fist. His expression was thoughtful, his eyes distant. The statue radiated patience and understanding.

Jeran was the first to kneel at the statue's base, followed quickly by the Emperor. He offered a prayer to the God, then went to the windows. He could see all of Lynnaei below, and beyond, the trees of the Great Forest filled his view. It was almost impossible to tell where the city ended and the forest began. Only with the Emperor's aid could Jeran see Lynnaei's living wall.

"Come Jeran," said the Elf, waving his hand. "We are almost done." He started up the winding staircase, a groan escaping his lips with every few steps. His breathing was short and quick, but that did not stop him from resuming the story.

"Balan returned to the Heavens and called for His family to attend Him. He related to Them His disciple's concerns. 'I think it best if we left the world,' He told Them. 'Our tasks there are done. It is time to let it develop on its own.'

" 'I will not abandon my gardens!' Valia said defiantly.

" 'I understand your concerns,' answered Garun, uncustomarily going against Balan's wishes, 'but I have no desire to leave my people. There is much joy for me in the world.'

" 'I have not visited your world in eons,' said Kohr. 'I have taken no active part in its development since the time of creation.' He looked at His son with a wry smile. 'I have no interest in it, but I will not force your siblings to abandon their world.'

"It was a long time before Shael spoke. 'Your brother is right,' She told Valia and Garun. 'Our time in the world is past, though it pains me to admit it. We must give it to our Races, and trust that they will care for it as we have.'

"Though They did not agree with Shael's decision, neither Valia nor Garun was willing to argue with the Mother. Sadly, They made Their last trip into this world, to bid farewell to Their Races.

" 'You will be missed, Honored One,' said the Orog when Shael informed them of her departure. They bowed to the Goddess, then quietly went back to their work.

" 'What will we do without you?' lamented the Elves. 'How will we know perfection if not in the reflection of Your eyes? How can we continue to tend Your gardens without Your aid?'

"Valia looked at Her people fondly. She waved Her hand, and a magnificent garden materialized—every plant, every flower, every vine laid with exacting precision. 'This is my garden,' She told Them. 'So long as you strive to match its splendor, you will never fail me.'

" 'Care for my brothers' Races,' She whispered in a quieter voice. 'They are younger than you, and need much guidance. Help them to mature as you have. Be to them a guide, a teacher, and above all, a friend.' With one last smile of adoration, She returned to the Heavens.

"Garun's people were similarly worried. 'We will never be able to maintain the balance without Your aid! You understand the hearts and minds of our lesser cousins. Without their insight, we will be as moles, stumbling in the darkness.'

" 'A mole's other senses compensate for his poor sight,' Garun laughed heartily. 'Fear not, my children, for I have anticipated your request. In some of you, I have instilled a special power. Those so chosen will commune with the beasts of the forest and the birds of the sky. They, and the *Tsha'ma*, will be your guides. Heed their words, for they speak with me directly.'

"He looked over the vast throng of His people. 'Live with this world,' He told them, 'not in it. Take no more than you return. I will wait for you in the Twilight World.' There was a bright flash, and Garun was gone.

" 'What words do you have for us?' the Humans asked Balan. 'What instructions?'

"Balan smiled. 'Seek the truth at all times,' He told them, 'yet be wary of it. There are few absolute truths; the rest are as variable as the winds. Follow your heart. Your soul knows what is right even when your mind does not. Learn to listen to your inner voice.'

"As Balan prepared to leave, His disciple approached. 'Master,' said the young man, tears in his eyes. "I am sorry. I never meant for my words to send you away.'

" 'You are injured,' Balan remarked, and indeed the man was hurt, His body covered with cuts and bruises. The God reached out and healed the man's injuries. 'How did this come to pass?'

" 'When it was learned that my words are what sends you from us, there were some whose anger grew uncontrollable. They believed that I had displeased you, and that if I were punished, you would not go.'

"Balan, ever patient, ever calm, grew enraged. 'Whoever would harm this man in my name knows nothing of his God!' He said in a voice of cold iron. 'Cast not your eyes toward the Heavens! Do not search for me among the stars. Those who do so will find only emptiness, and upon their deaths, their souls will return to the Nothing.

" 'Those who seek me must look within themselves. The path to right-eousness does not lie within our actions, but within our intentions.' He knelt next to His disciple. 'You understand my teachings better than any other. You are ready to join me in the Heavens.'

" 'If it pleases you, Master,' the man replied. 'I would stay until my life's natural conclusion. Perhaps in time, I can help others to learn your ways.'

"Balan smiled, and a warm glow suffused His people. 'When you are frightened, or worried, or confused,' he said, touching a hand to his chest, 'seek me here. I am never far from you.' In a flash of light, he was gone."

A door brought Jeran and the Emperor to a stop. The top of the tower was almost pitch black, only the tiniest hint of light remained. The Emperor stretched a hand out to the door's handle. "Come, Jeran,' he beckoned, throwing open the door. "See how the Gods view our world."

Chapter 23

Jeran winced, the transition from near total darkness to blinding light sending lances of pain through his eyes, but he followed the Emperor through the doorway. Squinting, his hand shading his face, Jeran kept his eyes locked on the floor until they had adjusted. When he finally straightened, the scene before him took his breath away.

The Tower of the Five Gods stood thousands of hands higher than anything in the vicinity. Its turret, almost always shrouded in mist, was clear today, and it offered a stunning view of the land below. The Great Forest spread out in every direction, the distant treetops looking like blades of grass. The forest filled their view in every direction, and still it seemed insignificant. Small.

Jeran circumnavigated the tower, awestruck. He had climbed high in the mountains of the Boundary, he had stood atop the highest rampart in Kaper, but neither of those things had prepared him for what he now saw. Birds, tiny black flecks, circled far below, weaving around the tower on currents of warm air. Above, the sun seemed larger, brighter, closer. The horizon curved gracefully in the distance, forming a delicate arc.

A flash of light, far away, caught his attention, and Jeran stopped on the eastern side of the tower. He saw another flash. Then a third. The flashes were random and intermittent, but occurred frequently enough that Jeran knew they were not his imagination. "What is that?" he asked, not expecting an answer.

"It is the Eastern Ocean," came the Emperor's reply. "The sunlight reflects off the waves."

"The Eastern Ocean!" Jeran exclaimed. "The sea is more than twenty day's travel from Lynnaei! How high are we?"

"Higher than any living thing on the face of Madryn," responded the Emperor in his quiet, calm voice. He turned and started toward the center of the tower. Jeran turned as well, noticing the statue for the first time.

The door opened through the statue's base, and atop the platform stood a giant figure, dressed in robes of silver. The craftsmanship was superb; the statue was lifelike, almost real. Timeless, all-knowing eyes followed Jeran, boring into his soul. The figure's skin was gold, his hair streaked with bands of silver. In one hand he held a staff, jagged like a bolt of lightning, and in the other, a sphere with the outline of Madryn on one half and another, unknown shape opposite it.

"This is Kohr's Tier," the Emperor said reverently. "Here we honor the Father of All." He knelt at the base of the statue, prostrating himself before Kohr. Jeran knelt as well, but could not take his eyes from the God's image. He offered a silent prayer, then stood, swallowing the knot in his throat.

When he finally had full control of his muscles, Jeran walked to the edge of the tower and carefully leaned over the wall, trying to look straight down. The top of the palace was far below; the turrets of other towers appeared as little more than colored dots on a plain of flat, red stone.

Wanting to see the Vale, Jeran leaned out even further, and his head hit something hard. Pulling back in alarm, one hand rubbing his head. "What's that!" he exclaimed, reaching out a hand to feel the invisible barrier.

The Emperor chuckled. "It's a wall built long before my birth by *Ael Maulle*, or perhaps by Valia herself. No one knows for sure."

"But why?" asked Jeran. "Is it to keep people from falling?"

"That's what everyone thinks," admitted the Emperor. "And I'm sure that was one reason for its construction, but it serves an even greater purpose. The wall begins at Valia's Tier and stops about thirty hands above the top of Kohr's statue.

"So it *is* to keep people from falling," Jeran said. "Or jumping."

"As I said, that is one reason. However, the wall serves an even greater purpose. Once, a long time ago, a very young and foolish Elf used his magic to transport himself to the top of the barrier. He stood above the statue of Kohr, stood higher than anyone before him.

"All was well until the Elf tried to breathe." The Emperor gestured around him. "At this height, there is no air. The magic of the barrier allows us to breathe and prevents others from suffering the fate of that poor Elf."

"What happened to him?" Jeran asked, his interest piqued.

"He fell to the top of the barrier," replied the Emperor, his face blank, "writhing in agony, trying to draw breath. His struggles took him near the edge, and if not for the fortuitous appearance of his father and an *Ael Maulle*, he would surely have fallen to his death."

Jeran smiled when the Emperor's cheeks turned red. He reached out and touched the barrier again. "It's an amazing feat."

"Truly," agreed the Emperor, reaching out to touch it, too. "In fact, this barrier was the inspiration for the Boundary. During the MageWar, Aemon came here to clear his head, to rest and regroup his thoughts. One afternoon, we sat atop the tower, looking out at the world, and Aemon walked to the barrier and laid a hand upon it, much as you are now.

" 'If the Magi of old could create a barrier like this,' he asked, 'then why can't we? But instead of a barrier against man, we shall create a barrier against magic. A boundary. Something we can trap Lorthas behind. It may not be permanent, but this barrier has lasted for millennia! It will give us the respite we need.'

"His words rang true to me," the Emperor told Jeran, "and together, we began working on its construction. It took seasons to figure out how it could be done, and winters to convince others of its necessity." The Emperor rubbed a wrinkled, spotted hand over his face, his eyes sad. "But I did not bring you up here to discuss history," he admitted guiltily.

"There's something else?" Jeran asked, still looking around in awe. "You've already shown me so much, Grandfather."

"I'm afraid this cannot wait." The Emperor withdrew a folded parchment from his robes and handed it to Jeran. "This arrived today. It came to me, but it is addressed to you, and though I have not read it, I fear it can only mean one thing."

Jeran turned the parchment over in his hand. It was fine paper, smooth and sturdy. A seal of golden wax, in the shape of a flying eagle, held the letter closed. Jeran's name and titles were written across the parchment in a flowing, curved script. Nervous, Jeran licked dry lips and broke the seal, steeling himself to the letter's contents.

Jeran Odara

I fear I bear dire news. One of my gifts is a Talent called Divining, which allows me, upon occasion, to see bits of the future. It gives me insight into the consequences of certain actions, or inactions.

I have had such an insight concerning not only you and your friends, but all of Alrendria. I thought it wise to share this vision with you.

In less than a season, an event will occur, resulting in the death of those sent in search of the Garun'ah. This event focuses upon your not being there. That is, they **will** *die if you are not there. Furthermore, should they die, war between Alrendria and the tribes will begin, and the peace you are so fervently fighting for will never come to pass.*

In all fairness, I must offer warning. My vision only told me what will happen if you are not there. It says nothing of what will happen if you are. Some, or all, of those sent to the Tribesmen may die regardless of what you do. If you choose to go, you may die. There is even a chance your presence will have no effect.

Such an event, if allowed to occur, could prove disastrous to our common cause. I thought it best to share my vision with you, but the ultimate decision is yours to make. I have sent a guide who will take you to the Garun'ah. Should you choose to go, you are to meet him outside the gates of Lynnaei. If you are not there by midnight, he will assume you have decided to stay.

I request that you tell no one of this letter. Should you choose to go, I advise you to limit the people aware of both your departure and your destination. Many of those with you, out of concern for your safety, will delay you, and time cannot be spared.

May the Gods be with you, my grandson.

– Aemon

Jeran read the letter twice, his mouth dry, then looked at the Emperor. "Do you know what this says?" he asked, a quaver in his voice.

The Emperor shook his head. "I do not know its contents, but its arrival can only mean your time with me is at an end." He shuffled over and placed a hand on each of Jeran's shoulders. Green eyes met blue, and a prolonged silence ensued.

Jeran was the first to speak. "Grandfather," he said, his voice heavy, "You... I just... I can never thank you for all you've done. Not only for me, but for Alrendria. I've learned so much since coming here, and I have you to thank for it."

"Jeran, Jeran," sniffed the Emperor, "I'm the one who should be thanking you. I've enjoyed the days since your arrival more than any in the last millennium. You've brought excitement back to Lynnaei, and more importantly, you've made me feel useful again. You're a dear friend, as important to me as your true grandfather."

At the Emperor's praise, Jeran's eyes watered. The Emperor sniffed as well, then laughed. "Look at us!" he chuckled. "One of the oldest things in this world and one of the youngest, both standing here trying not to cry!" The Elf's laughter was infectious; Jeran could not help but feel better.

They embraced, and the Emperor pressed dry lips against Jeran's forehead. "Go!" he commanded, his voice heavy with emotion. "I'm sure you have much to do before leaving Lynnaei. I will stall for you as best I can, but I doubt your departure will remain secret for long."

Jeran bobbed his head and started for the stairs. "Wait!" called the Emperor, and Jeran stopped. The aged Elf walked over and grasped Jeran's arm. A tingling sensation ran through his body and a black hole appeared in the floor. Jeran and the Emperor slowly descended through it.

The next thing he knew, they were standing at the base of the tower, looking out at the Vale. "How...." Jeran started, then changed his question. "Why didn't you use your magic to take us to the top?"

The Emperor wiped sweat from his brow. "Two reasons," he answered. "One, it's relatively easy to Gate oneself, but it grows significantly more difficult as you try to transport others. And two, part of appreciating the tower is the walk up the stairs, listening to the story of the Gods, examining the world from each of the five tiers. Had I transported us directly to the top, you would not have seen it in the same way."

Jeran nodded in understanding. "We will meet again," promised the Emperor. "Though I have far fewer winters ahead of me than behind, the Goddess has promised me a reunion before she calls me to join her." Jeran hugged the Emperor again, then started down the nearest path at a run.

The Emperor watched him go. "What have I done?" he whispered when Jeran had disappeared, putting his head in his hands. "I am so sorry, Jeran. So terribly sorry."

* * * * * * * * * * * * * * * * * * * *

"Martyn!" Jeran shouted, throwing open the door to the prince's chambers. "Martyn, where are you?" The room was in a state of disarray. Clothes littered the floor, books and other items lay scattered about, and a stain of dark red puddled beside a shattered glass.

Bright moonlight filtered in from the open balcony. Jeran, suddenly wary, tensed. "Martyn?" he called again, taking a cautious step forward.

The prince appeared in the bedroom door, pulling a shirt on over his head. "Jeran?" he asked. "What are you doing here? It's the middle of the night!" He crossed the room at a jog, scrubbing a hand through his hair to comb it, and waved to a overturned chair.

Jeran refused the proffered seat. "No time," he told the prince. "I'm leaving."

Martyn cocked an eyebrow. "You just came here to check on me?" he asked incredulously, his voice indignant, his gaze hard. "While I'm touched by your concern, my friend, I'm not a child anymore. And you're not my mother!"

"No, Martyn!" Jeran laughed. "I'm leaving Lynnaei. Tonight."

Martyn was instantly serious. "Why?" he asked. "Are you in trouble? Has something happened?"

Jeran told Martyn of the letter from Aemon, outlining the danger Dahr and the Guardsmen were in, and the consequences their death would have on the peace Alrendria sought with the other Races. "So you're going?" Martyn asked, though it sounded more a statement than a question.

Jeran nodded. "As secretly as possible. Both Iban and Jes would try to stop me, or try to send a large complement of Guardsmen as escort. Aemon said I'm better off alone, and if tensions between the Garun'ah and our soldiers *are* strained, I'm inclined to agree with his assessment."

"You shouldn't go alone," Martyn said, his eyes brightening noticeably. "*I'll* accompany you!"

Jeran laughed again. "Do you want Iban to execute me?" he asked, shaking his head. "I appreciate the offer, but your place is here. Besides, Aemon sent a Mage to escort me."

Martyn opened his mouth to protest, but checked himself. He reached out and clasped Jeran's arm just beneath the shoulder, an Aelvin gesture. "Good luck," he said, offering his friend a warm smile.

Jeran returned the gesture, squeezing the prince's arm tightly. "And to you, my Prince," he replied. A shadow at the edge of his vision caught his attention, and Jeran's eyes swiveled right. Kaeille stepped from the bedchamber, pulling on a robe. The front was yet undone, exposing a flat stomach and two small, firm breasts.

Jeran turned away from the Elf's porcelain white skin, locking his gaze on Martyn. The prince's cheeks were crimson. "Oh, Martyn…." Jeran whispered, shaking his head and stepping away.

Kaeille's eyes were downcast as she fumbled with the laces to her robe. "Is all well, Martyn? When you did not return to be–" Spotting Jeran, her speech broke off, and her cheeks blossomed with color. "*Teshou e Honoure,*" she murmured. Her eyes went wide, and her body started trembling. She drew the robe more tightly across her body.

"Jeran," Martyn said, his body stiffening, "it's not what you think. I... I think I love her." He swallowed, his breathing shallow. "Don't be angry."

"I'm not angry," Jeran told the prince, his eyes shifting between Martyn and Kaeille. The Elf was still trembling, unable to meet Jeran's eyes, but she looked at Martyn warmly. When Martyn broke his gaze with Jeran to look at her, his smile lit up the room. "I'm not angry with you," Jeran repeated. "I feel sorry for you."

Martyn looked at Jeran in shock, then nodded in understanding. He opened his mouth to speak, but was interrupted when the door flew open and Astalian walked in. "There you are!" exclaimed the Aelvin warrior. His eyes flicked instantly to Kaeille, and his lips pressed together tightly, but he held his tongue.

To Jeran, he said, "I thought I might find you here. All is ready, just as you asked. *Ael Chatorra* will let you pass through the western gate, and the first Elf who claims to have seen you will answer to me."

Jeran clasped Astalian's arms in parting. "I can't thank you enough, my friend."

"I still think this is madness!" Astalian exclaimed. "It will be tough enough to get through Illendrylla undetected, but if there is trouble with the Garun'ah, you'll be able to do little to stop them alone. Let me send some warriors with you. Or better yet, I will accompany you myself."

"I think I'd do better in the Tribal Lands without an army of Elves at my side," Jeran laughed, smiling at the Elf. "In truth, I'd welcome your company as much as Martyn's, but you are *Hohe Chatorra*. Your duty is to Illendrylla."

Astalian nodded in resigned agreement. They stood in silence for a moment, until Astalian finally said, "You are a good man, Jeran Odara. May the Goddess grant you success."

"Peace and long life, Astalian," came Jeran's friendly reply.

The Elf's eyes glinted dangerously, and his gaze took in both Jeran and Martyn. "When things have calmed, I will bring Treloran to Kaper, and you can show us your city as we have shown you ours." His smile was predatory. "We will shake the walls of Kaper!" he told them prophetically.

Jeran returned the smile, looked at his friends one last time, then hurried from the room. He stole through the palace corridors, careful to keep out of sight. Twice, he had to duck into the shadows to avoid running into parties of Guardsmen, and once he turned a corner to find himself facing five *Ael Namisa*, busily scrubbing the corridor floor. The Elves stood at his arrival, bowing deeply at the waist, but they let him pass without making a sound.

As he was leaving the section of the palace where the Alrendrians dwelt, he nearly ran into Lord Iban. The Guard Commander came barreling around the corner in front of Jeran, grumbling under his breath. Jeran flattened himself against the wall, hiding behind a marble bust of a great Aelvin Mage. Iban stormed down the hallway, completely unaware of Jeran's presence, yet Jeran did not dare take a breath until the Guard Commander's footsteps had faded in the distance.

Jeran made it out of the palace without further incident. He hurried through the starlit night to the stables, where two *Ael Chatorra* waited for him. His horse, already saddled, stood between them. At his approach, they handed him the reins. "Your packs have been filled with provisions and supplies," said one. "The items you gave to Astalian are with them."

Jeran nodded as he climbed into the saddle. His Aelvin sword hung to one side, a warbow dangled from the other. The second Elf handed him a large canteen. "*Brandei*," he explained. "A gift from the *Hohe Chatorra*. He says you may have need of drink stronger than water."

Jeran took the flask. "My thanks," he said to the Elves, heeling his horse to a fast walk. As quietly as possible, he worked his way through the city, heading west across the twisting, unpopulated ground. The quiet sounds of a sleeping Lynnaei drifted down from above, and the lights of the city offered just enough illumination for him to see.

It took a while to reach the western gates. The moon was high above, but only a fraction of its light filtered through the Great Trees, making navigation difficult; but eventually, the giant wall appeared before him, a line of black stretching from north to south. *Ael Chatorra* walked the higher levels, ever alert. As he approached, he marveled again at the construction, the precise weaving of trees, vines, and thorns that provided the Elves with a living barricade.

A guard in forest green leather armor stopped him at the gate. "Halt!" Jeran reined in at the commanding voice. The Elf approached, inspecting Jeran and his mount carefully. "Lord Odara," he said finally, dipping his head in respect, "the *Hohe Chatorra* said you would pass this way tonight."

"Yes," answered Jeran. "I must leave Lynnaei at once."

"Is there trouble?"

"Nothing which concerns the Elves," Jeran answered. "A friend of mine needs help."

"Perhaps you would prefer an escort," suggested the guard. "The Great Forest, though well patrolled, is vast. You have already battled both the *Kohrnodra* and the *Noedra Shamallyn*. You know of what they are capable."

Jeran waved off the guard's kindness. "It's not necessary, though I thank you for the offer. It would, however, be appreciated if you kept my passage a secret."

"The *Hohe Chatorra* made it clear what would happen if we admitted to seeing you." The Elf waved him through, calling for his companions to open the gates. "Stay on *Ael Shende Ruhl*," he warned. "The forest is impassable to those unfamiliar with it."

"Plus," Jeran added with a smile, "you Elves are quite protective of the wood. I'd hate to be mistaken for a trespasser. Luran's orders were to kill all trespassers in Illendrylla, were they not? And though he is no longer *Hohe Chatorra*, I suspect there are many who will still obey his wishes."

"You did not waste your time in Lynnaei, Lord Odara," the Elf said. After Jeran passed, he gave the order for the gates to be closed. "The Goddess' blessing on you."

Jeran spurred his horse to a fast trot, his eyes scanning the darkness for his guide. Once the wall had faded behind him, he slowed–first to a walk, then to a halt. Spinning his mount in a slow circle, he peered deep into the shadowy trees for any sign of life, but his search was in vain. There seemed to be nothing alive in the vicinity.

Fearing that the Mage had already departed, Jeran took a deep breath and extended his perceptions. With the focusing of his Gift, the night seemed suddenly brighter, friendlier. Jeran reveled in the feeling. He took several slow, deep breaths, relishing the many overlapping fragrances of the forest, all but hidden until he focused his magic.

He sent his perceptions forward, down the Path of Riches. He sent them back, toward Lynnaei. To his left and right, deep into the Great Forest. Despite his effort, he saw no one but himself. Straining, he pushed his perceptions to the limit of their range, hoping for some hint of his unknown companion's location.

"What are you looking for?" asked a familiar voice, startling Jeran back to his body. Opening his eyes, he nearly fell from the saddle. Standing before him was Tanar, the reins of a large, white horse in his hands. Tanar wore dark brown, rumpled robes and looked at Jeran with clear, blue eyes, a knowing smile on his face. "You need more practice," Tanar told him, scratching his close-cropped, white beard. "Extending your perceptions is fine, but you should always be aware of what goes on around you."

"Tanar!" Jeran exclaimed, jumping from the saddle. He crossed the distance to his old friend in a heartbeat, embracing the Mage tightly. "I didn't know you were going to be my guide!"

"Nor did I until recently," the old man replied. He stepped back from Jeran, and a small ball of light appeared above his head. "Let me take a look at you," he said, his eyes darting up and down. "You're almost a different person!" he exclaimed. "No longer the boy I left in Kaper."

"*You* haven't changed a bit," Jeran countered. "I'd almost swear those are the same robes you wore on our flight down the Anvil!"

"There are some advantages to being a Mage," Tanar said, smoothing his robes. "I've looked pretty much the same for the last thousand winters, though my hair keeps getting whiter!" They laughed together, and for a while stood dumbly, glad to be in each other's company again.

Tanar cleared his throat. "We had best be going," he said to Jeran, climbing into his saddle. "It's a long way to the Garun'ah, and once Jes finds out you're gone, we won't be able to get away without a fight!" Jeran nodded his agreement and hopped into his own saddle.

They started down the Path of Riches at a fast walk. "What have you been doing these past seven winters?" Jeran asked. "I would have thought you'd stop in to visit Dahr and me at least once!"

"Don't think I didn't want to!" Tanar responded, somewhat guiltily. "I would have gladly spent time with you had I been able to spare a moment." His expression grew dark as he outlined his activities since their parting. "I've spent the better part of the last seven winters trying to convince the Assembly of the threat posed by Tylor and Salos Durange.

The look on his face said that he had been less than successful. "I've also spent a lot of time at the Boundary," he added, "trying to assess how fast it's failing."

Jeran swallowed fearfully. "How long do we have?"

Tanar shrugged. "Who knows. The Boundary is one of a kind. I have no reference on which to base its deterioration. If left to nature, I would guess we still had centuries, but despite all I know, I'd only be half-surprised if it collapsed tomorrow!

"Enough about the Boundary!" Tanar said with a decisive wave of his hand. "We'll have plenty of time to talk of such things. Tell me of your life! What have you been doing? What have you learned? How is it you come to carry an ancient Aelvin sword, instead of a well-forged Alrendrian blade? Tell me everything, Jeran!"

"I don't know where to begin!" Jeran said, smiling at the old man. "Of course, you know King Mathis offered to adopt Dahr and me, else you would not have left us in Kaper. He treated us like his own sons, and we learn–"

A cry from behind interrupted their reunion. "Lord Jeran! Lord Jeran!"

"Mika?" Jeran said, confused. He wheeled his horse about.

Another rider appeared in the distance, galloping recklessly down the Path of Riches. Mika leaned far forward in the saddle, calling out Jeran's name and urging his mount for even greater speed. When he saw them, he reined in quickly, stopping in a shower of loose pebbles. "Lord Jeran!" he said again, sounding relieved.

"Mika, what are you doing here?" Jeran asked. "Is everything all right?"

"You told me I could go with you when you left!" the boy replied breathlessly. "I saw you in your chambers today, packing up your things. I knew you were planning to leave, but you were in such a hurry you forgot to tell me!"

"Mika," Jeran said solemnly, "there is great danger where I'm going. I said you could come with me to Portal, not into the Tribal Lands. I wish I could take you with me, but I cannot!"

Mika's face fell. "You said when you left, I could go with you!"

"Your mother will be worried!" Jeran told him.

"I left a note for her," the boy replied. "So long as she knows I'm with you, she won't worry."

Jeran pressed a hand over his eyes, squeezing his temples tightly. Mika's note would surely betray his departure. It was only a matter of time before his disappearance was discovered. He turned to Tanar. "We have to turn back," he told the old man. "I have to return Mika to Lynnaei."

Tanar's expression grew blank, his eyes distant, and he entered one of the trance-like states Jeran had grown accustomed to seeing during their flight from Tylor. They stood in silence until Tanar pulled his perceptions back to his body.

"It's too late!" he told Jeran. "They already know you're gone. The woman found the note and sought Iban. Even now, he's mobilizing the Guardsmen, preparing a search party. The Elves and Prince Martyn are remaining tight-lipped about your destination, but only a fool would think you had taken to the wood. The Great Forest is all but impenetrable to those unfamiliar with it."

"Couldn't you use your Gift to send Mika back?" Jeran asked hopefully.

Tanar shook his head. "Jes is already searching for us. As is Princess Charylla. I will need to use my magic to keep them from finding us. Creating a Gate is just the thing they need to pinpoint our location."

Jeran's eyes sought Mika. "It looks like we have no choice," he said with a sigh. "You're coming with us." Mika's eyes brightened, though, sensing Jeran's mood, he fought to keep the smile from his face. "But you had better hope they don't catch us," Jeran warned. "And when we return to Kaper, pray that Lord Iban and your mother don't take their anger out on me. Whatever I suffer, I'll make certain you suffer ten-fold!"

Jeran flicked his reins, and his horse started down the Path of Riches, leaving Tanar and Mika behind. The old man looked the boy up and down. "If I were you, my boy," he advised, "I'd pray to all five Gods." He heeled his horse, starting after Jeran. "And I'd start praying now."

Interim

King Mathis sat at his desk, drumming his fingers on the polished wood. Across from him sat his grandmother, Sionel, wearing a gown of grey-blue, the same shade as her eyes. Her lips pressed together tightly; she looked upon her grandson with a grim intensity.

Next to Sionel sat Mathis' cousin, Joam Batai, Commander of the City Guard, wearing leather armor with the Rising Sun of Alrendria stamped on its breast. He leaned over the table, hands folded together, and tapped his knuckles against his lips.

"Where do you think they are?" Mathis asked, his eyes never leaving the desk. "It's been so long since we've had word. Are they still in Illendrylla? On their way back? How do they fare? Are the negotiations going well?" He slammed his hand against the desk with a loud thud. "I can't stand this waiting!"

"Why do you insist on torturing yourself, Mathis?" Sionel asked, her voice chiding. "You have faith in Geffram, and you have faith in the Alrendrian Guard." She reached across the desk and patted his shoulder fondly. "I know you're worried about Martyn, as am I. But there's nothing we can do about it. They're in the hands of the Gods now."

"And the Elves," muttered Joam.

"And the Elves," concurred Sionel, casting an irritated glance in Joam's direction. "Either way, nothing we can do will change their fate." To Mathis, she added, "Martyn is no longer a child. He's capable of caring for himself. And his friends are with him. Alic and Aryn—"

She paused; confusion marred her pristine features. "No, no," she corrected herself. "Alic and Aryn were *your* friends, weren't they. Martyn's friends are... Jeran and Dahr! They are with him, Mathis. They will let no harm come to him."

"Dahr was refused entrance into Illendrylla," Joam reminded her. "He and six of the best Guardsmen are wandering the Tribal Lands."

Sionel's head snapped to the side. "Joam Batai!" she said sharply, glaring at the battle-hardened veteran. "Having children of your own will not spare you, should you insist on angering me. You have suffered more than one spanking at my hands, and my patience grows ever shorter as the seasons advance. If you insist on ruining my every effort to cheer Mathis, you may leave. Now."

Sionel's harsh words startled Joam. He opened his mouth to reply, but could find no words to defend himself. "My apologies," he said meekly, lowering his eyes in shame.

Mathis laughed out loud. "Grandmother," he said, "I've seen Joam stand alone against a charge of cavalry. I've seen him bark orders to Guardsmen and nobles alike. He even defies *me* whenever he thinks it appropriate! Yet a few words from you has him cowering like a frightened rabbit. How do you do it?"

"You have to start when they're young," Sionel told him. "If you command them as children, it tends to last throughout adulthood." She looked at Joam with a fond smile. "If you wait till they're older, it becomes much harder. My bullying is not nearly as effective on Brell Morrena."

"Brell," Mathis growled, thoughts of the nobleman darkening his expression. "I know, in his own way, he wants what is best for Alrendria, but if I could strangle him without bringing down the wrath of House Morrena...."

"You would have to fight me to be the first in line," Joam assured him, the words delivered solemnly.

"I don't know what to do with him," Mathis admitted. "I think it was a mistake to warn him of Tylor's escape. He insists, almost daily, that we recruit more soldiers for the Guard. He demands that we strengthen strategic locations, most of which, in his opinion, are located within the bounds of House Morrena. If he had his way, he'd trumpet news of the Boundary's fall across Madryn."

"Brell is a powerful member of House Morrena," Joam said, trying to reassure his cousin. "Second only to Jysin. We'll need all the Houses behind us when the fighting starts. As much as I hate to admit it, telling Brell was a necessity."

"What of Miriam?" asked Sionel, steering the subject away from the Durange. "When will she come to Kaper? You must wish to cement our alliance with Gilead before news of the Boundary is common knowledge."

"Iban will leave Illendrylla at the beginning of Harvest," Mathis informed them, "if not before. The betrothal will be made formal as soon as Martyn returns to Kaper, and Tarien will leave Aurach once the snows have cleared. With a little luck, Martyn and Miriam will be wed by the spring equinox."

A sly smile spread across the King's face. "You never told me what you thought of her, Grandmother."

"A delightful girl," Sionel answered slowly, tapping a finger against her lip. "Very beautiful. Knows all the proper etiquette. Always has something nice to say. And quite infatuated with Martyn, or at least with the stories she's heard of him.

"She's very eager for this marriage to take place," she added. "All her life, she thought she would be betrothed to Ryan Durange, to strengthen the ties between Gilead and Ra Tachan. There's a lot of bad blood between those lands, you know."

A small frown pulled at the corners of Sionel's mouth. "Not too ambitious, though," she admitted, her finger stopping its busy tapping. "Oh, Miriam's far from dim-witted. Has a good head for politics, that one, and for strategy as well, but she thinks such business is man's work. Daydreams a lot. She won't be like Cerril, taking half–or more!–of your burdens away. Running the castle when you're off at war.

"Not the best match for Martyn," Sionel concluded, shaking her head. "Not the best match by a long shot. But far from the worst. Martyn's a little flighty himself. He might have done better with a wife who was more grounded." She shrugged her shoulders. "They're both young, and have a lot of growing to do. They may yet surprise us."

A knock on the door interrupted Mathis' next question. "Enter!" he called, surprised when Konasi stepped into the chamber. The Mage kept mostly to himself, and rarely visited the King unless he was alone.

"King Mathis," acknowledged Konasi, bowing his head respectfully. "Lady Sionel. Master Batai." He held a rolled parchment out to the King, sealed with the sigil of House Velan. "I have received word from the Lady Jessandra. She instructed me to bring this to you immediately. I am to await your response."

Mathis accepted the parchment and broke the seal. Fighting a growing wave of anxiety, he unrolled the letter and read it. His frown deepened, and he handed the parchment to Joam, a look of anger on his face. To Sionel, he said, "There has been another attempt on Martyn's life."

"It seems," interjected Joam, drawing an angry glare from the King, "that the attack was not aimed at Martyn specifically. He was merely one of the unfortunate targets."

"Nevertheless," retorted the King, "Martyn's safety is of great importance. Perhaps it would be best to order Iban home."

"Lady Jessandra claims the negotiations are nearing an end," Joam pointed out. "She also says they go in our favor. The attack has increased support for trade among the Elves. I think it foolish to withdraw our delegation now, when they're so close to gaining what we desire."

"I'm afraid," Mathis admitted. "What if something happens to Martyn?"

"Is he any safer here?" Sionel asked. "Do you think Kaper unassailable? Is Martyn invincible while walking Alrendrian soil? He could take an arrow, or succumb to disease, or fall from his horse at any time. You can't protect him forever, Mathis, and he will resent it if you call him home before the mission is complete."

"He has a duty to Alrendria," Joam added. "He is a symbol; if he shows fear now, what does it say of Alrendria?"

"He must stay alive," Mathis argued, "at least until he has an heir of his own."

"He is a long time out of swaddling clothes," Joam replied, a mischievous glint entering his eye. "Besides, if the worst were to happen, you're still capable of siring children. It's not too late to find you another wife."

Mathis shuddered at the thought, not eager to be wed or a new father. Sionel interrupted his vexed retort. "What else is there, Mathis? Something else troubles you. Let me see that!" She snatched the parchment from Joam's hands and quickly scanned the contents. "Oh my," she whispered.

"Jeran has deserted," Mathis said, repeating what he knew his grandmother had just read. "He packed up in the middle of the night and stole out of Illendrylla. The Emperor, and at least some of the Elves, aided him. No one, Martyn included, is willing to share knowledge of his destination. One of the freed slaves, a boy, went with him. Jes searched, but was unable to locate them. Iban is even now preparing to give chase." Mathis' cheeks were flushed with anger.

Sionel set the paper down on the desk. "Do you trust Jeran?" she asked calmly.

"Wha... What?" sputtered Mathis. "Of course I trust Jeran! It's like he's my own son."

"Do you think he'd have left without good reason? Even if he chose not to share those reasons?"

Mathis frowned. "No."

"Then perhaps it is wisest to let him go."

A sullen frown marred Mathis' features. "I don't like this."

"That's all right," Sionel answered, winning a smile from Joam. "You don't have to."

Reluctantly, Mathis penned a letter to Iban. Sealing it with his sigil, he handed it to Konasi. "This is for Lord Iban," he said, "but you may deliver the same message to Lady Jessandra. Jeran is not to be followed. The mission in Illendrylla is of more importance. The negotiations are to be concluded, and Iban is to return to Kaper at the appointed time."

"You would let him run free?" Konasi asked; more than a touch of anger infused his tone.

"If you wish to track him, you have my permission. Otherwise, those are my orders." Konasi bowed stiffly and departed. After he was gone, Mathis paced the chamber, moving at a quick, frustrated pace. "Joam!" he called out suddenly. "A letter arrived from Tobin the other day. I'd like your opinion on something he said."

Joam followed Mathis to a small table on the far side of the room, leaving Sionel alone. The old woman's eyes were distant and blurry, only half-focused on the door. The smile on her face was triumphant, but the sadness on her eyes overpowered it.

* * * * * * * * * * * * * * * * * * * *

"King Tylor!" called a soldier, riding into camp at a full gallop. Tylor turned to face the man, who jumped from his horse and landed at the Bull's feet. Dropping to his knees, the soldier bowed his head low.

"Speak," Tylor commanded. Wiping sweat from his brow, he cast a quick glance at the sun. Though it was just clearing the top of the Anvil, it beat down upon him and his men. The heat had been unmerciless these last few days, hotter than even he enjoyed, and Tylor was far more partial to the warmth than the cold. With midsummer only a few days away, it would be a long time before temperatures fell.

"There's a messenger for you, my Lord," the soldier said breathlessly. "He waits in the trees."

"Have him brought to me," Tylor demanded.

"He will not come," replied the soldier. "He says you must go to him."

"Is that so?" mused Tylor, his lips twisting in a wry grin. "Then let him wait. We will pass by him once the camp has been struck." Tylor turned to walk away.

The soldier stopped him. "My Lord!" he insisted. "The man mentioned the High Inquisitor by name. He says he has vital news."

Tylor stopped. Scratching his clean-shaven chin, he squinted his good eye as if trying to see the messenger from where he stood. "He called my brother by name?" he asked, and the young warrior nodded excitedly. "Fetch my horse," Tylor commanded, his good mood suddenly soured.

The man ran off, returning moments later with the Bull's black stallion in tow. Tylor leapt into the saddle and urged the horse to a run. Soon the camp was far behind him, and he was climbing a steep trail into the foothills of the Anvil. As he neared the crest, he entered a dark copse of trees, and he slowed his mount to a walk. "Show yourself!" he demanded, dropping to the ground.

There was no sound, no movement, no indication of a messenger. Tylor spun in a slow circle, peering deep into the dark underbrush. He stopped, his eyes locked on a particularly dense section of the wood. "I said show yourself." His voice was nearly a growl.

A figure emerged, dressed in robes of black, a cowl covering his head. Bright green eyes stared from within the shadows of the robe. "Your Gift, though untrained, is quite impressive. Magic runs strongly in your family."

"I have no magic," Tylor spat vehemently.

"Only one with the Gift could have sensed where I hid," replied the messenger, his voice a sibilant whisper.

"Perhaps you are not as skilled as you believe," the Bull snapped. "I have no magic."

"Suit yourself, Prince of Ra Tachan."

"King of Ra Tachan," Tylor corrected, glowering.

Green eyes stared at him mockingly. "When last I heard, it was your brother who sat the throne in Tacha."

"A triviality," Tylor responded. "He merely occupies the chair until my arrival."

"Hmm...." the messenger said consideringly. "Do most Human kings skulk through the wilderness, hiding in the shadows of the Anvil, afraid to show their face?"

"I did not come here to banter with you, Elf," Tylor growled. "Nor do I wish to debate the nuances of Lorthas' plans. What is it you wish to say?"

"Are you so familiar with the Master?" sneered the Elf. He waved his hand irritably. "No matter. You wish me to get to the point? Very well. Two attempts have been made on the life of Prince Martyn of Alrendria. Both have failed."

Tylor laughed. "I should have known you Elves would be no match for the Alrendrian Guardsmen."

"Remain silent until I have finished!" the Elf commanded, waving his hand mystically.

Tylor tried to retort, but found his mouth sealed shut against his will. A shadowy smile spread across the Elf's face. "A *Noedra Synissti* has never before failed to kill his target. Since the assassin died in the attempt, we were unable to punish him for his failure. His family was forced to suffer the consequences."

The Elf waved a finger, and a bag floated forward. It dropped to the ground at Tylor's feet and opened. A bloody, slightly-pointed ear rolled across the ground, coming to a stop at Tylor's feet. The Bull looked at the severed ear, then glared at the Elf in disgust. "The *Kohrnodran* attack worked as planned," the Elf said, "and but for the intervention of Jeran Odara and Astalian el'e Myndalion, both princes would be dead.

"Salos sought me out in the stronghold of the *Noedra Shamallyn*," the Elf continued, ignoring Tylor's ongoing attempts to speak, "a location unknown to all but a few. He came bearing tidings from the Master. We are ordered to make no further attempts on the lives of the princes."

"What!" yelled Tylor, his mouth once again under his own control. "The Prince of Alrendria must be killed!"

"My people have been given a new target," the Elf explained. "As much as I would like to aid you in your mission, the Master's desires supercede yours." A dark smile spread across the Elf's face. "However, the Master did not say the Prince of Alrendria could not be killed, only that we must not be the ones to kill him. Our efforts are to be focused elsewhere. Should an opportunity arise, I promise that the Prince of Alrendria will taste the steel of the *Noedra Synissti*."

"How very kind of you," Tylor said wryly, his gaze hard.

"Moreover, I wish to strike a deal with you."

Tylor frowned consideringly. "Go on."

"The Alrendrians will return to Kaper before the season changes. Should you wish it, I will apprize you of their departure from Lynnaei. You can lay in wait for them on the Path of Riches, and ambush them at your leisure."

"And what do you get out of this bargain?" Tylor mused aloud.

"Salos claims there is a good chance that the Aelvin Prince, Treloran, will accompany the Alrendrians to Kaper. Should this prove true, we would be most...grateful...if something dire were to happen to him."

"If your assassins are so good," asked Tylor, "then why not kill this prince yourselves?"

"Attacking the Emperor's kin, especially within the walls of the Lynnaei, is a difficult and dangerous task, even for those as skilled as the *Noedra Synissti*. Outside of Illendrylla, away from the protection of the Emperor and the Princess Charylla, the prince will prove an easier target."

The Elf smiled cruelly. "It would only benefit the Master's plan if the Elves could blame the Humans for the death of their prince. Peace between the Races would be much harder to establish."

Above, a hawk cried out angrily. Tylor glanced up at the sound, but the Elf ignored it. "To make the attack easier for you," the *Noedra Shamallyn* whispered, a feigned look of sympathy in his eyes, "I will station warriors at the edge of Illendrylla. Once the Alrendrians pass, they will signal you. You will know their exact location. The Humans will have no chance to escape."

Tylor scratched his chin while he considered the Elf's request. "You are still indecisive," said the Elf. "Allow me to sweeten the deal. I know the location of Jeran Odara. He is now separated from the other Alrendrians, alone and unprotected."

Tylor's eyes brightened at the mention of his adversary. "I see you are interested!" the Elf said triumphantly. "If you kill the princes, I will take you to him. Moreover, I offer you the woman he loves, the Lady Jessandra Vela, First Seat of House Velan. Would it not make your revenge all the sweeter if you could force him to watch while his beloved suffered?"

Tylor's grin spread from ear to ear. "My brother is far too liberal in discussing my weaknesses."

"Then we are in agreement?"

"We are agreed."

"Excellent." Darkness swelled around the Elf, and he disappeared. Tylor's spine tingled, a shiver he felt every time magic was used around him. Smiling, his good humor returning, he mounted his horse and rode back to the camp.

"Halwer!" he yelled to his Aide, who came running at full speed. "Order the men to strike camp. We must increase speed!"

"We are no longer going to Tacha, I presume," Halwer said, half in question.

"No. We have a more important target now. Tacha can wait. Little Ryan can tend my throne a while longer." Tylor's eye gleamed with excitement. "I have him, Halwer!"

"Sir?"

"After eight winters, I will bring Batra's killer to justice! And at the same time I'll deal Mathis a blow he will never forget!"

* * * * * * * * * * * * * * * * * * * *

There was a shimmer of light–silver speckles rotating in a clockwise circle–and Aemon stepped into the room. Emperor Alwellyn smiled at his arrival. "It is rare for me to beat you to one of these meetings, old friend."

"*Old* friend?" laughed Aemon, embracing the Emperor fondly. "Look who's talking!" As he walked the aged Elf to his seat, he explained. "I would have been here sooner, but it's not easy to slip away without him noticing. You trained him too well!"

The Emperor smiled. "You told me to teach him what I could. Whatever I thought would aid him. I thought being able to detect the use of magic would be a boon." The Emperor took his seat, groaning as he lowered himself into the chair. "But he deserves the credit. In all my life I have not seen a more gifted student."

"Except me," corrected Aemon.

"Including you!" retorted the Emperor, and they shared a laugh. Further conversation was interrupted by the screech of an eagle. It flew through the open window, alighting on the sill, and stared proudly at the two old men.

"And how fares your charge, Rannarik?" Aemon asked. "Has he reached the Tacha?"

The eagle jumped from the windowsill, shimmering as it fell. "Dahr has yet to join the Blood," Rannarik said, striding quickly across the floor. "But they are not far from the Tacha. Kal leads them to *Cha'khun*, where the tribes gather even now."

The *Tsha'ma* embraced them both, first Aemon, then the Emperor. "It is good to see you, my friends."

"And you, Rannarik," agreed the Emperor. "How was your flight?"

"The skies were good today," the Tribesman replied.

The door to the room opened, and two women entered, one short and the other tall. The short one leaned on a walking stick. "So," she said gruffly, hobbling across the room and taking her seat, "you decided to show up after all!"

"Now, now," chided the other woman in a graceful, stately voice, "I'm sure they all have good reasons as to why they're late. Getting angry will do us no good. Besides, my dear, I was quite enjoying our chat."

The little woman looked up at her tall companion, and her stern expression instantly softened. Smiling, she winked, then her frown returned. "They always have excuses," she returned, "but the excuses never hold up under inspection. Probably forgot how to get here. They're not as young as they used to be, you know. And they're men, so the Five Gods know they wouldn't ask for help!"

Aemon ignored her comments. "How are things in your part of the world?"

"Quiet," was her instantaneous reply, and this time her anger was not feigned. "Too quiet. No one can figure out where they're hiding."

Aemon frowned, and his eyes shifted to the taller woman. "And you?"

"As well as can be expected," she answered. "There's a lot going on right now, and I'd be a fool to think I knew all the plots and subplots, but so far I've managed to nudge everyone in the direction we need them to go."

"At least there's *some* good news!" Aemon said, stopping when a door materialized on the far wall. It opened, and another man walked in. Large and corpulent, the man wore thick, billowing brown robes. Sweat instantly covered him, and he shuddered. Withdrawing a rag from his robes, he daubed his forehead.

"Did I miss anything?" he asked, calling out greetings.

A vertical slash of blue appeared in the center of the room. Recognizing it, Aemon took a deep breath and sighed sadly. "No, my friend," he said. "Unfortunately, I think the excitement is just about to begin."

The slash opened, and Jes stepped through, dressed in a gown of white. Her eyes scanned the room angrily, locking on Aemon. "Where is he, old man? Don't sit there with that blank expression on your face! I know you have something to do with this!" Her eyes swiveled to the Emperor. "Both of you are in on it!"

"Jes... Jes... Jes," Aemon said in a soothing voice, shaking his head slowly. "I'm sure I don't know what you're talking–"

"Don't play games with me!" she snapped. "I want to know where you sent him and why!"

"Jes," Aemon said again, this time more sternly. "I won't tell you. I can't allow you to track him down. What must be, must be!"

"You and your 'must be's,' " she snarled, pacing the floor angrily. "Your divinations grow tiresome, old man. When have they ever caused anything but strife." Her eyes grew suspicious. "You know he'll be safe? Whatever fool mission you're sending him on, you at least know he'll be safe!"

A tense silence followed, broken when Aemon lowered his eyes to the floor. Jes could barely contain her rage. "You have no idea what will happen to him, do you?"

"I know what will happen if he doesn't go!" Aemon replied defensively.

Jes' voice became pleading. "He's just a boy, Aemon! Little more than a child! Whatever you're planning, he's not ready!"

"If you're being attacked," Aemon said in a lecturing tone, "you might want a sword, but if a stick is all you have at hand, a stick is what you use."

"Is that all he is to you?" she fumed, a hard edge to her voice. "A tool? A weapon?"

"Of course not," Aemon replied sharply. "You know how much he means to me. And I know how much he means to you. But we have no choice. If Jeran doesn't go where he needs to, if what I've foreseen comes to pass, the Races will be shattered, Alrendria will fall, and all will be lost."

"And if Jeran does go?"

Aemon's eyes were cold. "Then we still have a chance."

"A chance?" Jes repeated incredulously. "You risk him for a chance?"

"A chance," Aemon confirmed. "A chance is better than certain defeat. A chance is better than letting Lorthas win."

"And what chance does Jeran have?" Jes inquired, her eyes twin daggers staring into Aemon's soul.

"Jeran...." Aemon's voice cracked. It was a moment before he could speak. "Jeran's fate will be with the Gods." He stood and grabbed the still-pacing Jes, forcing her to look him in the eyes. "Don't make this more difficult than it already is," he begged. "We've prepared him as best we can. We're preparing him still. If there were any other choice, don't you think I'd take it?"

Spots of color blossomed on Jes' face. Embarrassed, her eyes sought the floor. "Tell me what you've seen," she said meekly.

"Later," Aemon replied. "We have other matters to discuss."

Chapter 24

Seven days after the hunt, they found the Tacha. Late one afternoon, as evening was lowering her veil across the world, Kal stopped in mid-stride. His eyes dancing with excitement, he raised his chin high, tentatively sniffing the air, and a broad smile spread across his face. "We are there!"

He took off at a run, scrambling up the hillside, jumping rocks, and dodging trees. "Hurry, little brother!" he cried, craning his neck around, his tightly-woven braid bouncing behind him. "We are home! Hurry!"

Dahr spurred his horse to a gallop, signaling the Guardsmen to follow. Pushing the mighty stallion for every bit of speed, Dahr slowly closed the distance between himself and the Tribesman. The dogs kept pace with him, but Katya and the others fell behind, their horses unable to maintain speed on the steep slope.

Reaching the hill's peak, Kal came to a sudden stop, forcing Dahr to pull back hard on the reins and lean to the side, turning Jardelle away from the Tribesman. He skidded to a stop, sending a spray of loose stones into the air. "Look, little brother," Kal said, beckoning him forward. "Come and see your people!"

Dahr dismounted and stepped forward, looking out over the valley. Before him, the land sloped down in all directions, forming a deep bowl. For as far as the eye could see lay grasslands dotted with thick strands of green forest. To the east, the trees were marginally thicker, following the snaking path of a river, the westernmost tributary of the Danelle. To the west, the plains of northern Madryn stretched on endlessly.

A lush and open plain, a sea of grass blowing in the summer breezes, descended into the valley. Two thirds of the way to the bottom, the grasslands gave way to dense, multicolored forest, thick with foliage. Though harvest season was yet some time off, the leaves here were beginning to turn. A mélange of colors assaulted Dahr, filling him with a sense of peace and tranquility. Colors ranging from vibrant yellow to light green to deep red covered the valley, mixing together in subtle harmony.

A thousand hands from the edge of the lake, the forest abruptly stopped, forming a perfect circle around the vast lake that lay centered in the bowl. As Dahr watched, the center of the lake began to bubble and churn, and a geyser erupted, spraying water high into the air. "Kohr's Heart," Kal said reverently. "Madryn will exist so long as it beats."

Fires dotted the landscape intermittently, and the smell of roasting meat drifted to Dahr's nose, making his stomach growl. Small figures, thousands of them, wandered the field below. Children played in small packs, older men and women tended the fires. Small bands of hunters passed each other, some leaving in search of game, others returning triumphantly with their catch tied securely to roasting poles.

Dahr was more stunned by the Garun'ah than the roiling waters of the lake. "Is that the Tacha Tribe?" he asked breathlessly. There were enough Tribesmen to fill a city, even one the size of Grenz or Kaper. "There must be thousands of them! Where do they all live?"

"They live in the tents," Kal replied in a strange voice, as if he did not understand the question. He stared into the valley for a long moment. "That is not all of them," he told Dahr after his inspection. "There are also the Hunters, and those who have yet to arrive, or were not summoned to Cha'khun." Kal squinted, peering down into the valley, and his brow furrowed in concentration as if he counted those present. "But the greater part of the Tacha are below us."

"There are so many of them," Dahr whispered in awe.

Kal practically beamed with pride. "The Tacha are strong," he affirmed. He looked at Dahr wryly, and barely containing his laughter, asked, "Why are you so amazed? Raised in a Human city, you are used to seeing so many creatures in one place. Even if all Tacha—if all of the Blood in every tribe, the heartless Drekka included, were here—we would number less than the least populous Human land."

Dahr shrugged. "Maybe it's because we have seen few Garun'ah since entering the Tribal Lands," he said after a moment's consideration. "Or maybe it's because it's so open here. There's not so much space in a city. Even though there are many people, most are hidden behind buildings. This is the first time I've seen so many people in one place. And more will be coming?"

Behind them, the Guardsmen were approaching, the steps of the horses rustling the dry grass. "The Channa. Or the Afelda," Kal said with a nod. He shrugged his shoulders and added, "Perhaps both. They are strong tribes, but only the Channa can match the Tacha in number."

"What of the other tribes?" Dahr asked. "Were they not summoned to the Cha'khun?"

"My father would not call the Drekka," Kal said blandly. "Nor would the other tribes come if the Drekka summoned them. As for the Sahna, they are fewer in number, and keep far from the rest of the Blood. It's is rare to summon them, or the smaller tribes, to Cha'khun. Yet...."

Kal broke off, lost in thought. "Yet my father listens to Rannarik's advice, and the Tsha'ma said that all the tribes should gather." He smiled apologetically. "I have been long from the tribe," he admitted. "We must meet with my father. He will know the answers we seek."

The Guardsmen crested the hill and saw Kohr's Heart. Katya, wide-eyed and open-mouthed, edged her horse closer to Dahr's, and reached out to take his hand. Kohr's Heart erupted again, and Vyrina sucked in a surprised breath. Wardel laughed at her reaction, earning himself a punch in the shoulder and an angry glare.

Jasova moved to join Dahr. "Now I know why we couldn't find the Garun'ah," he laughed. "They're all here!"

Dahr returned his smile. "This is but a fraction of the Tacha Tribe," he told the Guardsmen. "The rest are on their way, and at least one more tribe comes to join them, if not more."

"We had better hope they're friendly," Elorn grumbled, "else we may find it difficult to escape." Kal glared at the dour Guardsman, and Elorn fell quiet.

"Good old Elorn," joked Nykeal. "Able to find the advantages to any situation."

Vyrina pursed her lips thoughtfully. "What if he's right?" she asked. "As much as I hate agreeing with him, if the Garun'ah attack...." She let the thought trail off.

"I doubt it makes little difference now," replied Jasova. "If they wanted us captured or killed, it wouldn't be hard for them to catch us." He pointed back the way they had come. Several Garun'ah hunting parties were visible behind them.

Kal looked at them in shock. "Do Humans have no faith in their hosts?" he asked, his expression serious. "If I traveled Alrendria, would I have to fear attack around every corner? You are my guests! The guests of the *Kranach* of the Tacha. You have nothing to fear."

"We meant no disrespect, Hunter," Katya assured him. The other Guardsmen, even Elorn, nodded their agreement.

"Let us continue," Kal suggested, dropping the matter. "I can smell the food from here, and I get no less hungry standing on this hillside." He turned to face them, spreading his arms wide. "Welcome, Alrendrians. Enjoy the hospitality of the Tacha. Our fires are yours to share."

Turning to Dahr, he offered a special welcome. "Welcome home, *tsalla'-dar*. The fires of the Tacha are yours to share." He bowed his head politely, then started down the hill at a fast walk.

Dahr climbed into his saddle and followed, signaling the others to keep close. As they began their descent, all activity in the camp stopped. Every eye turned toward the newcomers. Uncomfortable under the intense scrutiny, the Guardsmen shifted uneasily in their saddles, stopping only at Jasova's command. "Stand firm, Guardsmen!" he snapped. "We're the Alrendrian Guard!"

Dahr thanked the subcommander for his words, but found they did not ease his own growing discomfort. And as they continued down the hillside, their resolve weakened even more. Elorn hunched in the saddle, his hand on his sword, his eyes shifting back and forth as if expecting an ambush at any moment. Jasova and Nykeal rode close to each other, taking comfort in their proximity. Wardel's face was blank, but sweat beaded his brow, and Vyrina held her bow loosely, ready to notch an arrow at the first sign of trouble. Even Katya's hand drifted toward her sword on several occasions.

The hounds were nervous, too. Their eyes sought Dahr's for guidance; their occasional whines and yaps echoed in Dahr's ears.

Determined to set a good example, Dahr straightened his back and raised his head high. Holding Jardelle's reins loosely, he stared at the Tribesmen steadily, keeping his hands far from his weapons. He hoped he looked more confident than he felt. As if reading his thoughts, Kal turned and offered him a reassuring smile.

As they neared the bottom of the valley, it became apparent that the 'trees' were actually tents, and the forest nothing more than the Garun'ah encampment. The tents, fashioned from thick canvas, their colors ranging from forest green to bright yellow, were arranged haphazardly, with no obvious pattern. Small clusters stood together in some areas, in others, a single tent stood alone, isolated from its neighbors.

From the valley, the tents stood out, their odd designs and wild colors drawing attention to them. But from the top of the hill, they had appeared as a forest, blending seamlessly into the surrounding countryside. Dahr wondered how many of the distant groves they had passed in their travels had been real, and how many had been well-camouflaged encampments.

As they entered the tents, a wall of Tribesmen formed around them. All movement stopped as they passed; all eyes fastened on them. Hundreds of heads followed their passage, watching the Alrendrians march deeper into the tent-city. Occasionally, a Tribesman called out to Kal, and he returned their greetings, but the march through the camp was otherwise silent.

Dahr took the opportunity to study the Garun'ah. All were tall and well muscled, with angular features. Their eyes were the characteristic almond shape of the race, their cheekbones prominent. Their hair was uniformly straight, ranging in color from white-blonde to midnight black, with some white and silver mixed in, though black was by far the most common shade. Their skin, dark and tan, did not have the range, from ivory white to ebony black, that Dahr had grown accustomed to seeing among Humans.

The men were beardless, which came as no surprise. Though Jeran and Martyn had been shaving for winters, Dahr had yet to bring a razor to his own face and had not the slightest stubble to show for it. Most Tribesmen wore their hair in tight braids that hung halfway down their backs. Only a few wore their hair loose.

The Garun'ah dressed in light furs, their arms bare, exposing broad arms and powerful muscles. Many wore beaded necklaces around their throats, often with delicately-crafted pendants dangling against their chests. All had weapons belted or strapped to their sides: axes, *dolcheks*, spears, and even a few swords.

The women were even more astonishing than the men. Each was tall, not as broad as the men but still powerfully muscled, the shortest nearly a match for Katya in height. Their cheeks were higher and more pronounced than the men, their skin dark and exotic, their eyes mysterious. They were well curved and amply endowed.

They, too, wore brown furs, though more of their skin was covered than the men. The women wore their hair, which was almost universally dark, loose around their shoulders. They did not wear the necklaces that were so common on the men, but many wore gold and silver bracelets on their arms.

Despite their allure, the Tribeswomen appeared no less daunting than the larger males. Perhaps more so. Many had long-knives, *dolcheks*, sheathed at their waists, or held spears in their hands. Their eyes were stony, dark and depthless. Dahr was certain they would fight just as ferociously as the men, were they forced to.

Many eyed the Alrendrians appraisingly, and more than a few eyes fastened on Dahr. Small smiles turned up the corners of their mouths, and their eyes sparkled. The stares Dahr received were not confined to the younger women; many older Tribeswomen sized him up, too. One wrinkled, stooped, white-haired Garun'ah frowned at him thoughtfully. Her eyes shifted between Dahr and the buxom, dark-haired girl at her side.

To Dahr's surprise, he found himself staring back unabashed. He met their gazes one by one, his smile a reflection of their own. A few lowered their eyes, their cheeks turning red, but most stared back with redoubled intensity. He was enjoying himself until he noticed Katya's eyes on him, her expression stony. After that, he tried to keep his gaze fastened on Kal's back.

The Alrendrian men were not the only one attracting stares. The Tribesmen stared boldly at the Guardswomen. Vyrina's face was flushed, and she stared nervously at the ground. Nykeal returned the stares, but her hand sought Jasova's.

Katya sat her saddle casually, staring defiantly at the crowd. Several of the Tribesmen watched at her openly, one quite intently. A growl rose from deep within Dahr's throat, surprising him with its intensity. The Garun'ah must have heard it. The warrior's head snapped around, and his almond eyes met Dahr's. They stared each other for a long moment, then the Tribesman bowed his head and stepped away, disappearing into the crowd. Dahr turned his gaze on Katya, who shrugged her shoulders and smiled at him suggestively.

Children pressed their way to the front of the crowd, eager to see the strangers. Small boys, bare-chested and sun-darkened, pushed to the front of the throng to stare at Dahr with hauntingly adult eyes. The younger children all had short hair; the older ones wore theirs in loose ponytails. All but the youngest carried small knives at their waist and looked as if they knew how to use them.

The girls were more cautious than the boys. They preferred to hide behind the adults, their heads peeking out from time to time. Many wore deer-hide dresses adorned with strands of beads. The younger ones carried dolls. Dahr smiled at one girl, an adorable child of only several winters who reminded him of Ryanda. The girl smiled back, but ducked behind the protection of her mother's legs.

Kal led them through the camp slowly, walking with his head held high, his braid whipping behind him in the strong summer breeze. More Garun'ah poured into the area, forming a path through the maze of tents. As they passed, the Tribesmen filled in behind them, cutting off all escape.

Elorn drew his horse closer to Dahr's. He still gripped the hilt of his sword tightly, and his eyes darted frantically from left to right. He was tense, ready for an attack at any moment. "I don't like this," he said in a harsh whisper.

"We have little choice, Elorn," Dahr replied. "You must have faith."

"Faith will not protect us if these savages decide to attack."

Dahr's head snapped around. "Do I have to remind you that these 'savages' are my people? And our hosts? You will watch your tongue, Guardsman, or I'll make sure you can't use it." Elorn's jaw tightened, but he had the decency to look embarrassed. He let his horse fall back.

Dahr looked at the other Guardsmen, and was relieved to find them handling the situation better than Elorn. Jasova and Nykeal rode close to each other, but no longer held their weapons. Wardel was eyeing the crowd, smiling at every pretty girl who caught his attention. Vyrina was staring at Dahr. She seemed uncomfortable in the alien surroundings, but smiled at him, trying to hide her fears.

The walk through the Garun'ah camp seemed eternal. They snaked through the tents, following no obvious pattern, but always headed in the general direction of the lake. In time, they stopped before a large, green tent, the same shade as the grass. It blended into the landscape, hard to see even from a short distance.

Two Garun'ah warriors guarded the tent, one to either side of the flap. Lines of dark paint highlighted their faces. Each held a spear in one hand, the points gleaming in the sunlight. They stood unmoving, like statues, ignoring the approach of the Alrendrians.

Kal stopped near the lake, just outside a tent, and raised his hand to halt the procession. Dahr reined in his horse, and the other Guardsmen stopped behind him. At an order from Jasova, they dismounted, forming a semicircle behind Dahr. "This is the tent of my father," Kal told them, pointing to the tent. "Arik *uvan* Hruta, *Kranor* of the Tacha." Kal beamed with pride as he recited his father's title.

Dahr dropped lightly to the ground, patting Jardelle on the neck fondly. "Stay here, boy," he said to the animal, letting go the reins and looking at the lead hound, which stood at his side. "Stay," he said sternly, and the animal dropped to its haunches. The other dogs did the same.

Dahr walked forward to stand next to Kal. The Guardsmen followed, but kept several paces back. Before, the silence had seemed eerie, with thousands of eyes upon them. Now, it was oppressive. Of the thousands of Garun'ah present, not one spoke; the Guardsmen remained silent, too, their eyes cautious and wary. Even the wind had stopped blowing.

The silence pressed in on Dahr from all sides. The feel of a cool breeze on his skin would have been most welcome, and he would gladly have suffered through a storm, so long as it ended the all-encompassing stillness.

Nevertheless, he stood with his back straight, waiting with an outward expression of patience for whatever was going to happen. Behind him, the Guardsmen shuffled back and forth nervously, but were wise enough to hold their tongues.

He found himself remembering a conversation from his dreams, during one of the Darklord's many visitations. "You have no idea how lucky you are, little brother," Lorthas had said. "The Garun'ah are a primitive race. Savage. Primal. They let their emotions rule them and ignore their reason. They're obsessed with their limited interpretation of the Balance, and they give no thought to the deeper meanings of the universe.

"Oh, they have their uses, I suppose. If you need something heavy moved, or if you want to smash something to pieces, there are none better than the Tribesmen. They are honorable, for the most part, and brave to a fault. They have so much potential, and yet they choose to limit themselves."

The Darklord had laughed. "You have no idea how lucky you are!" he repeated. "You have the best of both races. The strength, size, and honor of a Tribesman, coupled to the logical and rational thinking of Humans. You're no Half-man, Dahr, you're twice a man. They don't hate you because you're less than them, but because you're more."

The flap of the tent pulled aside, interrupting Dahr's memory, and Arik, *Kranor* of the Tacha Tribe, emerged. Kal's father was the largest being Dahr had ever seen. He towered over Dahr, and even Kal, who stood a few fingers taller, had to look up to meet the *Kranor*'s eyes. Arik was broad, bulging with muscle, his arms as thick as tree trunks and his hands nearly as large as Nykeal's head.

His hair was mostly gray, with highlights of chestnut brown interspersed throughout. It hung loosely, nearly to his waist. His almond-shaped eyes were brown, youthful and lively. His skin, darkly tanned, was only slightly lined, his face hard and angular. A scar ran down his neck, starting at his right cheek and disappearing beneath his shirt.

He wore hides, the leggings mottled brown, the color of a forest floor. The sleeveless shirt was darker, tied with laces in the front. A cloak of bearskin draped over his shoulders, fastened in front by a pendant of gold molded in the shape of a claw.

The head of the fearsome creature hung limply, but it could be drawn over the *Kranor*'s head like a helmet. Dahr imagined what it would be like facing an attack from Arik–a giant, charging across the battlefield in a wild fervor, looking more like an animal than a man.

A bone-hilted *dolchek* sat comfortably in its sheath, and Arik had a large, double-bladed axe strapped across his back. The *Kranor's* intense brown eyes scanned the crowd, then locked on Dahr, seeming to bore into his very soul. Dahr fought the urge to recoil from the giant's emotionless stare.

Trying to appear as confident as the Tribesman, Dahr stared back, struggling to keep his breath even, to slow his heart enough that its beating could not be heard on the far side of the lake. Eventually the Tribesman's eyes shifted to Katya, then to Wardel. Arik looked at each Guardsman in turn, his expression never wavering. To their credit, not one of the Guardsmen flinched under the Tacha chieftain's scrutiny.

At long last, the giant's eyes settled on his son, and the hint of a smile twisted the corners of his mouth, breaking his stony appearance for the first time. "Why have you brought Humans to *Cha'khun*, my son?" he asked in a deep, bass voice, powerful and commanding. Though spoken only slightly louder than a whisper, the words echoed across the valley like thunder.

Kal did not answer right away, and the silence stretched out interminably. "The *Tsha'ma* Rannarik instructed me to bring the Alrendrians to you. When we arrived in the Summer Lands, the Tacha were gone. You would not yet have taken the Blood to the Winter Lands, so I knew the Tacha traveled to *Cha'khun*. Keeping my word to the *Tsha'ma*, I followed, and brought the Alrendrians here."

"Rannarik said nothing to me of Humans," Arik replied, his mouth tightening. "Only that you had gone on business of the *Tsha'ma*." The *Kranor* fell silent, and his eyes roved over Dahr and the Guardsmen again. "Since the time of Jolam, only the Blood have journeyed to Kohr's Heart. You break custom bringing them here, and risk earning my anger. Why?"

Dahr opened his mouth to explain, but Kal anticipated his intention and silenced him with a gesture. "I bring them because the Alrendrians bear news vital to the Blood. News that all *Kranora* must hear! Here, at *Cha'khun*, the Alrendrians can share their news with all the tribes."

Kal looked at Dahr, his expression grateful. "I bring these Humans to *Cha'khun* because they freed me from the Soul-stealers. I owe them blood debt."

Arik grunted, his eyes scanning the seven Alrendrians. "That one," he said, leveling a finger at Dahr, "is a child of Garun. Why does he travel with Humans? Why does he dress in their clothes and ride their beasts?"

"He was lost to the tribes," Kal explained. "Taken by the Soul-stealers or lost in a raid. He was raised by Humans, first in the southern mountains, then in Kaper, by the King of Alrendria himself. He comes to deliver a message."

Arik folded his hands together and hid his mouth behind the fist. He stood motionless, silent for a long time, considering his son's words. Stepping forward, he glowered at Dahr. "What do you want here?" he asked in a cold voice, a scowl on his face. "What is your true purpose, Half-Man?"

"I wish only to deliver my message," Dahr began, ignoring the *Kranor's* comment. "Deliver my message and learn a little of my people."

"Your people?" Arik scoffed. "You dress in Human garb. Talk the Human tongue. Ride a Human beast." He sniffed the air around Dahr, wrinkling his nose in distaste. "You even stink like a Human." Arik's arm snaked out, and he grabbed Dahr by the chin, forcing his head to the side. Leaning in close, he repeated, "What is your purpose here, Half-Man?"

Dahr's stomach tightened, and blood rushed to his head. He grabbed Arik's arm and broke the *Kranor's* grip, pushing the larger man away. "My name," he growled, "is Dahr Odara. As Kal told you, I come with a warning from King Mathis of Alrendria."

Dahr meant to stop there, but his temper took hold. Before he could stop himself, he opened his mouth again. "I thought the Garun'ah were an honorable race," he snarled, his words loud enough to carry. A murmur arose from among the Tribesmen. "A race of proud and noble warriors. So far, you have yet to live up to your reputation!"

He squared his jaw and met Arik's stony gaze with his own. "As for myself," he concluded, "I'm not sure why I'm here, but I know it's not to be insulted. If another Tribesman, including you, Arik *uvan* Hruta, calls me Half-Man, I will make them regret it."

Dahr regretted the words as soon as they left his mouth, but there was nothing he could do to bring them back. He tensed, expecting the worst. Instead, a broad smile spread on Arik's face, and deep, booming laughter reverberated throughout Kohr's Heart. As if in answer, the geyser erupted behind the *Kranor*, showering the lake with a gentle mist.

"It takes great courage to threaten a *Kranor* in the center of his own camp," the giant Tribesman said. "Even when he insults you first. It is proven. You are of the Blood. I meant no disrespect, Dahr Odara of Alrendria. I only wished to test your mettle."

Arik raised his head to address all the Guardsmen. "Well come to the fires of the Tacha. For as long as you share our tents, you will want for neither food nor drink." He raised his head even higher and addressed the whole of the Tacha Tribe in Garu.

Kal whispered a translation for the Alrendrians. "Tonight we feast in honor of the Ambassadors of Alrendria. Tomorrow we feast the arrival of the Channa. In less than a moon, the Afelda will arrive, and the Sahna not long after. Then, *Cha'khun* will begin."

The crowd cheered his proclamation. Arik reached out a hand and clasped Kal's shoulder. "You have done well, my son," he said in the Human tongue. "It is good to see you again." Kal bowed his head in embarrassed pride. Arik, smiling warmly, turned his eyes toward Dahr. He bowed his head respectfully, then turned and disappeared inside his tent.

Chapter 25

Dahr ran, jumping recklessly over rocks and fallen trees. The plains spread out around him, offering scant cover, providing him with no place to hide from the creature that chased him. He heard its thundering scream behind him, and he pushed himself for ever greater speed, hoping against hope to outrun the beast.

He felt the creature's fetid breath on his shoulders, smelling of death and blood. It roared, and Dahr fell to the ground, knocked from his feet by the fury of the howl. He curled up in a ball, afraid, his whole body trembling.

The monster stopped behind him, sniffing the air like an animal. Dahr heard its snorted breaths, felt the drops of hot saliva that dribbled from its mouth. Trembling, he turned over, forcing his eyes open.

He stared up at his own face, his own body, only twice as large. The giant stood over him, glaring at Dahr with disdain. "You are pathetic!" it growled, spitting on the ground. "Always running. Always searching for another way. I am a Hunter!" The beast roared, and Dahr cringed back. "A warrior! Yet you cage me! Enslave me! You are no better than the Soul-Stealers!"

"I will not be a monster!" Dahr screamed back, summoning his courage. "No better than an animal!"

The giant picked Dahr up by the shirt and held him at eye level. "You pretend bravery?" it snorted, laughing cruelly. "You will not win. You cannot control me all the time. Soon I will take over, and we will be what we were meant to be!" It sneered again, and with a wicked smile, threw Dahr.

"NO!" Dahr screamed, tumbling across the ground. His eyes snapped open and he sat up, almost immediately aware that he was not yet awake. Familiar stone walls surrounded him, and a fire crackled at the far end of the hall.

"No?" asked Lorthas questioningly, rising from his chair near the fire. "You would prefer to go back to your dream? Was this one pleasant? About the curly-haired Guardswoman, perhaps?" He smiled, his lips pulling into a thin line. "It will be difficult, little brother, but I think I can manage it." He raised a hand as if to make a gesture.

"No!" Dahr exclaimed, perhaps too quickly, pulling himself to his feet. "The dream is done," he said to the Darklord, pretending a casualness he did not feel, trying to hide his fear. Walking across the room, he sat in the plush, red-cushioned chair across from Lorthas. "There is little point going back there now."

"As you wish," Lorthas replied, his grin broadening. A glass of blood red wine sat on the table at Dahr's side. He took it and drank deeply, using the liquid to wash the taste of terror from his mouth. Lorthas watched silently, and when Dahr had finished and settled back in his chair, he asked, "Have you joined your people yet?"

Dahr warily eyed the Darklord. "Perhaps," he answered cryptically.

Lorthas laughed, warm and friendly. "Still suspicious of me?" he asked with a chuckle. "Since we met, have I ever threatened you? Even once? I only want what's best for you, little brother. What's best for all Madryn!"

"Is that why you sent the Bull of Ra Tachan after us?" Dahr retorted. "Is that why he amasses an army in secret? For the good of Madryn?"

Lorthas' face drew tight, and his lips pressed together. "That dim-witted clod!" he said angrily. "I haven't spoken to Tylor since demanding he leave *Ael Shataq*. He is a fool, and fools should not be tolerated."

Dahr eyed Lorthas skeptically, but chose not to gainsay the red-eyed Mage. "I should have punished him for his crimes," Lorthas admitted. "I should have made him pay for the things he tried to do in my land. But despite his treacheries, I did not have the heart to kill the poor creature. All I could do was banish him from my world."

Lorthas spread his arms wide in supplication, entreating Dahr to believe him. "I am not the same man I was when imprisoned behind the Boundary. The long winters have changed me, little brother." His smile returned. "And you know my words are truth. The Twilight World will not allow me to lie."

The Twilight Word did prevent you from lying, Dahr had discovered. Everything you said had to be true, else you found your mouth frozen, your tongue tied in knots. "It really isn't fair, you know." Lorthas lamented. "Sending all your criminals and traitors through the Portal. It's difficult enough to build an enlightened society without having to stop every few seasons to put down rebellions stirred up by your newest dissidents!"

Dahr considered the Darklord's words as he drank more wine. He did not want to believe Lorthas, nor did he want to trust the words of the Darklord, but he *knew* it was impossible to lie in the Twilight World. He sat back in his chair, a frown on his face.

"Now what were we discussing last time...?" the Darklord mused, scratching his chin. "Ah yes, I was telling you of my adventures in the Arkam Imperium." For most of the summer, the Darklord had been telling Dahr of King Peitr and the Arkam Imperium. The tales often curdled Dahr's blood and made him grind his teeth in anger.

"The atrocities Peitr committed during the war with Alrendria were numerous," Lorthas told him. "All who supported Alrendria were tortured and enslaved, or simply killed outright. Their sufferings were imaginative. Peitr had a flare for the dramatic."

Lorthas had described tortures in vivid detail, tortures he had sometimes been forced to watch. Fathers forced to choose which children would live and which would die. Mothers given a choice–allow themselves to be used by Peitr's soldiers or have their daughters taken in their place. Children used as shields, forced to walk before the Arkamian armies, preventing the Alrendrians from firing arrows indiscriminately.

"But the Magi suffered worst of all," Lorthas explained, his voice growing angered. "They were given no choices. They were hunted like animals. Tracked day and night by remorseless, relentless soldiers. If found, they were murdered. Their families were murdered. Their neighbors and friends were murdered."

Lorthas took a deep, calming breath and continued. "Back then, I could not forgive Peitr for his actions during the war." Another silence echoed through the chamber, and Lorthas stared thoughtfully into space. "But now I could. I've learned first hand what war can do to a man. What horrors a person will commit in the name of his cause.

"But Peitr never stopped. Even when the war was over, the killing continued. Even when all the Magi had escaped the Imperium, his soldiers hunted them, killing any they suspected of having the Gift." The Darklord's head dropped into his hands, and his voice shook with emotion. "For seasons we stole across the border like thieves, bringing the innocent to freedom. For decades I aided those who wished to escape the Imperium's rule, going even before I had full control of my Gift.

"In the end," Lorthas lamented, "it made little difference. For every one saved, ten were killed. If only I could have done more...."

The ensuing silence was deafening. The room pressed in on them from all sides. "How does any of this justify what *you* did?" Dahr demanded, drawing on his reserves of courage. "The atrocities you committed during the MageWar were as bad as anything the Arkam Imperium did."

"I know...." Lorthas whispered, sounding ashamed. "I know." Blood red eyes stared at Dahr, begging for forgiveness. "There is so much of the story you have yet to hear, little brother. So many seasons of pain. A thousand times a thousand unfortunate events led me to my foolish decision."

The Darklord's eyes suddenly flashed. "You were a slave, were you not?"

Wary, Dahr nodded. "If you could have killed the slavers who murdered your parents, would you have?" After a long hesitation, Dahr nodded again. "When you attacked the slavers' camp, did you feel guilty about the deaths you were causing?" This time, Dahr could not nod. "If you could have made them suffer more for their crimes, would you have? If you could kill every slaver, would you?"

Dahr opened his mouth. He wanted to tell Lorthas he would not kill without feeling remorse. He wanted to say he would never kill for the sake of killing, nor enjoy watching anyone, even a slaver, suffer. He wanted to say these things and a hundred more besides, but no words came out.

"You do not have to answer, little brother," Lorthas assured him. "Your silence is answer enough." The Darklord smiled warmly, triumphantly. "And you *are* justified, little brother. Enslavement is the worst punishment, the worst fate I can imagine. To have your freedom, your right to make the most basic decisions, taken away...." The Darklord shook his head sadly. "I do not envy you your childhood, Dahr.

"But," the Darklord continued, not allowing Dahr a chance to speak, "if you could talk sense into the slavers? If your words could change their hearts, if you could guide them with your experience and wisdom, would you choose that path, or would you still kill?"

"I...." Dahr paused, searching for the truth. "I don't like killing," he said at last. "If there were another way, I'd gladly take it. But most slavers wouldn't listen."

"True," replied Lorthas. "Most people listen to reason only when it suits their purposes. Most would rather blunder about on their own than listen to the voice of experience." He folded his hands in his lap, staring at Dahr thoughtfully. "I did not want to fight the MageWar," he stated. "I wanted only to guide the Races of Madryn. To protect them from the evil within themselves.

"But there were...misunderstandings. I was rash and hot-blooded in my youth. When my proposals did not gain instant approval, I said some things I have long regretted. My words put me at odds with my teacher and oldest friend, the High Wizard Aemon." Lorthas spread his arms wide, shrugging his shoulders. "When I think about all that's happened because of my temper...."

Lorthas fell silent, his eyes heavy with tears. "I tell you truly, there are a thousand things I'd take back if I could, a thousand others I'd change. But despite my powers, I have no control over time. I can only hope to correct my mistakes in the future."

The room began to blur. "Good morning, Dahr," Lorthas said, wiping the sleeve of his white robe across his eyes. "And goodbye. We will talk again soon."

A hand shook him roughly. "You sleep more than the Elders, little brother," Kal said, chuckling. "Come, it is time to meet your people."

Kal left the tent, and Dahr threw off his blankets. He dressed hastily, surprised that Katya had not wakened him when she had risen. Splashing water on his face, he drew aside the flap and stepped out into a brightly lit, hot summer day.

"So, the mighty warrior finally rises from his pallet!" Elorn said smugly. The Guardsmen sat around a small fire, cooking breakfast; the dogs lay in a semi-circle around Dahr's tent. The tents were arranged in a circle, the white material appearing out of place amidst the brightly-colored tents of the Garun'ah. At Dahr's appearance, the nearest hound lifted its head. Dahr reached down and scratched the animal behind the ears, yawning.

"Was that a joke, Elorn?" Katya asked, surprised. She turned toward the other Guardsmen. "I think Elorn made a joke!" To Dahr, she said, "I told you he'd come around."

Dahr returned her warm smile, taking a seat at her side. He was handed a bowl of thick porridge, which he devoured hungrily. Kal stood to one side, watching silently. "Now that we've found the Garun'ah," Vyrina asked, "what do we do?"

"Personally, I plan on enjoying myself!" Wardel said with a laugh. "Did you see the way those women were looking at us yesterday?" he asked Jasova. "I'm eager to talk to them privately." With a half embarrassed, half comical look at the women, he added, "To learn the ways of the Garun'ah, of course."

Jasova put a hand on Nykeal's arm. "Tell me what you learn," he requested, directing a smile at the blonde-haired Guardswoman. "For I dare not leave Nykeal alone! I saw how the Tribesmen stared at her." Nykeal beamed at the comment.

"Be careful, friend," warned Kal. "Take time to learn our ways before you act, else you may return to Alrendria with a Garun'ah bride!" Wardel's eyes widened in surprise and fear, and Kal burst into laughter.

"Were you joking?" Wardel asked, unsure whether the Tribesman laughed at his statement or the Guardsman's reaction. He turned to the others. "Was he joking?"

"I, too, am eager to learn of the Garun'ah," Katya told them. "Though my interests are somewhat different than Wardel's. Perhaps it would be best if we each went our own way, to learn as much as possible. We're Alrendria's first representatives to the tribes in nearly twenty winters!"

"I don't think separating is wise," Elorn said. "We don't know how the Tribesmen will receive us." Casting a nervous glance at Kal, he added, "Though Kal has proved himself nothing if not honorable, we cannot assume all Garun'ah will welcome our presence as he has."

"You have been given guest rites by the *Kranor* of the Tacha," Kal said, lecturing them as if they were children. "No matter their feelings, no Tacha will harm you while you are under my father's protection. So long as you remain at *Cha'khun*, you have nothing to fear."

"And the other tribes?" Nykeal asked. "Will they honor your father's promises?"

Kal scratched his chin. "There has never been violence at *Cha'khun*," he told them. "But there are no proscriptions against it, as there are in Grenz or along *Ael Shende Ruhl*. If they desired, those of the other tribes could attack."

"Wonderful," Elorn muttered sourly.

"But," Kal continued, "if they attacked, my father would lead the Tacha against them. So long as you are here, you are of our Tribe." He stepped closer, putting one hand on Jasova's shoulder, one on Nykeal's. "You have nothing to fear."

"That's good," Elorn replied dryly. "Instead of fighting a couple opponents, we'll be trapped in the middle of a tribal war. I feel *much* safer now."

"Twice in one morning!" Katya applauded. "I think your sense of humor is coming back, Elorn!" He looked at her sternly, but her comical expression forced a small smile to his lips.

"Well, I think I'll be going," Wardel said, standing. "There was one girl in particular who caught my eye. I think I'll see if I can find her." He started to walk away, but stopped to pat Kal on the shoulder amicably. "Thanks for the warning, friend!" He winked, then hurried out into the camp.

Jasova stood as well, offering a hand to Nykeal. "I thought a walk around the lake would be nice," he told her, bowing formally and affecting the manners of the nobility. "Would you care to accompany me, m'Lady?" She giggled, allowed him to pull her to her feet, and they made their good-byes, starting in the direction of the lake.

Around them, the Garun'ah were coming to life. Though most had been awake since dawn, the camp remained eerily quiet until the sun had cleared the horizon. Now, parties of hunters were forming, planning their routes for the day. Those not accompanying the hunts busied themselves with other tasks. Few remained idle. One Tribesman, a short, broad-shouldered warrior, approached the Alrendrians. Stopping at the edge of the Human tents, he folded his arms across his chest and stood silently, his eyes locked on the Humans.

Elorn eyed the newcomer warily. "Come, Elorn," said Katya. "Since you're in a good mood for a change, why don't we set up a practice ring." She rubbed her sword arm dramatically. "All these days in the saddle have left me weak. I could use some sparring."

She kissed Dahr on the cheek. "I will leave you and Kal alone today," she told him. "Give you some time to acquaint yourself with your people." To Kal, she said, "The days I give you, my friend, but at night, he's mine!" Dahr blushed bright red as Katya and Elorn departed, leaving him, Kal, and Vyrina alone.

"A formidable woman," Kal murmured, chuckling to himself at Dahr's discomfiture. "Come, little brother. There is much to see." Dahr turned his eyes on Vyrina, who sat alone of the grass-covered ground.

"I'll be fine," she told him, reading his mind. After throwing water on the fire to quench the flames, she waved for him to go. "Don't worry about me," she insisted. "I don't need a nursemaid, and I'll survive a day on my own. Besides, someone needs to check on the horses!"

The Tribesman took this moment to approach. He was short, barely eleven hands in height, but broader than Dahr. His hair was dark, as were his eyes, and he wore it in a braid which fell nearly to his waist. A double-bladed axe was slung through a loop in his belt, the metal gleaming in the sunlight. He looked to be slightly older than Kal, but approached shyly, like a nervous child.

He looked at Kal and Dahr, bobbing his head in greeting, then turned his dark eyes on Vyrina. "Please," he said in the Human tongue, his voice heavily accented. Vyrina looked up, aware for the first time of the Tribesman's presence. "Please to be...honored...to be show you camp."

"What?" Vyrina asked, confused, her eyes going wide.

The Tribesman stared at her for a moment, licking his lips nervously, then his eyes sought Kal's. He rattled off a long speech in Garu, the words all but incomprehensible to Dahr and the Guardswoman. Kal listened stoically, then turned to Vyrina. "He says he would be honored to show you our camp. He watched us pass yesterday, and says one of the Human *darihna*, one of the woman warriors, stood out like a gem. He says Garun visited him with a vision, telling him to show the *darihna* our ways."

"A gem?" she asked, looking at her stocky, muscled frame and running a hand through her close-cropped hair. "He must mean Nykeal or Katya." She pointed toward the lake. "Tell him they went that way."

Kal relayed Vyrina's message, and the Tribesman chuckled. He rattled off another speech in Garu, which Kal translated. "He says the other *darihna* are too soft for his tastes. They look too delicate to touch. The vision was meant for you, and he would be honored to teach you of the Blood."

The Tribesman hastily added something else. "He apologizes for his poor grasp of your tongue," Kal said. "He has spoken to Humans only a handful of times, and not in many moons. If you are patient, he promises to better his speech."

The Tribesman bowed his head deferentially, his eyes locked on Vyrina. She turned to Dahr, who merely shrugged his shoulders. Standing, she returned the Tribesman's bow, then touched her chest, "I am Vyrina."

The Tribesman smiled. "Frodel," he replied, slapping his chest, "Frodel *uvan* Merck." She joined him, and together, they walked from the clearing, Frodel's bass voice fading in the distance. "Pleasure...to be meet you."

Dahr watched them go. "Do all Garun'ah speak the Human tongue?"

"Not all," replied Kal. "But many speak *Huma*. At least a few words." The *Kranach* laughed. "You, or rather they, give us little choice. There are many Humans in the Tribal lands, some who visit and some who dwell here. Few learn our language. If we wish to speak with them, we must know theirs."

In the distance, a horn sounded. "Come, Dahr," Kal insisted, beckoning. "It is time you met your people."

Dahr stood, and the dogs jumped to attention, starting toward him. "Stay!" he said sternly, and they stopped, though the lead animal seemed unsure. "I'll be fine!" he insisted, and the beast dropped to its haunches, its tongue lolling out of its mouth. The other animals followed their leader's example, laying on the ground.

Kal looked at him curiously. "They're well trained," Dahr said, answering the unspoken question. "Shall we?" He waited for Kal to lead, following the Tribesman into the tent city.

They wove through the colored tents, and as they passed, all eyes turned to regard them. Everywhere he turned, stony, expressionless faces and dark, knowing eyes found him. One woman, an aged, toothless hag, was sewing together hides. She stopped when Dahr passed and pointed a crooked, wrinkled finger at him. She spoke in Garu, the words incomprehensible to Dahr, and started cackling.

"What did she say?" Dahr asked when Kal's mouth drew up in a grin.

The Tribesman shook his head, trying to keep himself from laughing. "She said she must not be working as fast as she used to," he answered with a laugh, "if we now dress our warriors in flimsy man-clothes."

A pained howl drew Dahr's attention, interrupting the glib retort he had planned. He hurried to the sound, wincing as another howl pierced through the still, morning air. He quickened his pace, loping through the tents at a fast jog, Kal trailing behind.

He stopped next to a Garun'ah boy of no more than ten winters. At the boy's side lay a monster of a dog, almost a wolf, whining in pain. The beast was huge, with dark, shaggy hair and crystal blue eyes. It looked at Dahr in agony.

"What's wrong?" Dahr asked the boy, who jumped back, eyes widening. He stared at Dahr in surprise, his mouth hanging open. "What's wrong?" Dahr repeated, but the boy stared at him blankly.

Kal arrived. He spoke to the boy in Garu, and the child replied, hesitantly at first. "He does not know," Kal told Dahr when the child finished his explanation. "The dog was healthy yesterday, when it returned from the hunt. This morning, it was too weak to stand."

The Tribesman looked at the dog sadly. "Of his father's pack, this is the boy's favorite. When the hunters return from today's hunt, he fears his father will send the creature to Garun." Kal's voice dropped to a whisper, though the boy could not understand his words. "Perhaps it is for the best. It is wrong to let an animal live in agony."

Dahr dropped to the ground beside the dog and put a hand on each side of the beast's massive head, staring into its pained, panicked eyes. The dog whimpered, and Dahr stroked its flank carefully, his hand probing even as it comforted. The beast's cries quieted, and Dahr slowly circled the animal, his hands searching for the source of the problem. Both Kal and the boy watched with confused and curious expression on their faces.

The dog lifted its head, following Dahr with its eyes. Suddenly, Dahr froze, his hands on the animal's head. Closing his eyes, he took several slow, deep breaths, then scratched his chin thoughtfully. With a determined nod, he reached to his belt and drew the *dolchek* Kal had gifted him.

"Aiiieee!" screamed the boy, tears welling in his eyes.

"Not in front of the child!" Kal said quickly, but Dahr paid him no heed. With a quick motion, he lifted one of the dog's rear paws and slashed it across the pad. Thick, green pus oozed from the wound.

Dahr massaged the paw, forcing more of the infection from the wound. He made a series of small cuts, and each brought another cry from the helpless animal. "Bring me some fresh water," he said to Kal, "and a strip of cloth." Kal ignored him; he stared at Dahr, a thoughtful expression on his face. "Now!" Dahr insisted; Kal shook himself and jogged off into the tents.

Dahr continued his ministrations, digging deeper into the wound, feeling around with the tip of his blade. The dog howled when the knife hit against something solid. Gritting his teeth, Dahr reached into the cut and drew out a long, curved splinter of wood. The dog yelped when the splinter pulled free, then fell silent.

Dahr massaged the paw until Kal returned, carrying a large bucket of water. After using the water to wash the wound, Dahr wrapped the strip of cloth tightly across the paw. The boy looked at him gratefully. "*Danko*," he whispered, the tears in his eyes now of joy.

"My pleasure," he said, and Kal translated. Standing, Dahr washed his own hands in the bucket. "Tell the boy to clean and wrap the wound twice a day. If he does, the dog should recover quickly." Kal repeated the words to the boy, who nodded his head eagerly.

They continued their walk through the camp. "How did you know?" Kal asked.

"What?"

"How did you know where to find the injury? How to fix it?"

"I spent much time with the animal trainers in Kaper. After a while, you learn the signs. One of the King's hounds accidentally stepped on a caltrop once, and the wound grew infected. It acted in much the same way as this dog."

Kal considered Dahr's explanation, but his gaze remained disbelieving. Any further questions he had were interrupted by the passage of a hunting party. Twelve Tribesmen, all dressed in leather and hides, spears in their hands and *dolcheks* at their sides, had gathered in front of a tent. "*Jokalla, Kal!*" one man cried, rushing to their side and gripping Kal's shoulders tightly. "*Jahrne uva Dar?*"

He was shorter than Dahr, and not as broad. His hair was red-brown, and his eyes, only slightly darker. A short spear hung at his side, but he wore only a loincloth. His well-toned muscles were anointed with oil. They glistened in the sunlight.

Kal shook his head in answer. "Not today," he replied. "Dahr, this is Olin, son of Trayk."

The Tribesman examined Dahr from head to toe. "He is one of the Lost?" he asked, his voice heavily accented.

"He was lost to us long ago," Kal nodded. Turning to Dahr, he said, "As a cub, Olin was taken by the Soul-Stealers. He suffered much while in their care, but managed to escape. Alone, a child of nine winters, he crossed the Tribal Lands in the heart of winter, alone and weaponless. His blood called him back to us."

Olin reached out and grabbed the thick material of Dahr's shirt. Pinching it between his fingers, his eyes scanned Dahr's outfit a second time. "Has living with Humans thinned his blood?" he asked curiously.

Dahr knocked Olin's hand away. "No more than it worsened your manners," he replied, a bit too harshly.

Olin stared at him, his expression cold, but Dahr met the gaze stoically. Suddenly, the warrior laughed. "It may be thin," he said, clasping Dahr's shoulders fondly, "but it is Garun's blood flowing through your veins!" Dahr frowned, confused at the Tribesman's rapidly changing mood, but he gripped Olin's shoulders in greeting. "Will you join our hunt, Dahr?"

"We await the arrival of the Channa," Kal told him. A loud horn blast came from the north, punctuating the *Kranach's* words. A series of notes followed, reverberating through the valley.

"Then you do not have long to wait," Olin replied, bobbing his head in parting. "We will hunt together another time!" he told them, rejoining his men.

Dahr watched as the party of Tribesmen hefted their gear and started running for the hill, eager to be on the hunt. Kal shook him to get his attention. "It is time to greet the Channa," he said, turning north and moving at a fast walk.

Chapter 26

Kal and Dahr walked north through the camp, eventually leaving the tents behind and starting the long climb up the valley's sloping side. Few Tacha joined their pilgrimage; the Tribesmen continued about their various tasks as if oblivious to the horns. The throngs, which had assembled to watch the arrival of the seven Alrendrians, completely ignored the impending appearance of the Channa.

Those who did rush to the edge of the camp were children, mostly young boys, who formed a line around the tents. Standing straight-backed and proud, they watched the horizon, one hand on their belt knives. "What are they doing?" Dahr asked.

"They are defending the camp," Kal explained, tousling the hair of the nearest child. "When our warriors are on the hunt, it is the duty of the *Tor Darnach*, Those Who Will Be Hunters, to protect the tents." The boy beamed up at Kal, and the older warrior returned the smile.

"What of your women? They looked formidable enough."

"You have no idea," Kal murmured, then said in a louder voice, "If the tents were attacked, all who could hold a blade would protect them."

They passed the ring of children and continued up the hillside. Another horn blast echoed in the distance. "But there is little risk," Kal admitted. "Among the Blood, battles are fought among the Hunters. The tents and those too young, too old, or too weak to fight are left alone."

"You don't attack the tents?" Dahr asked, following his first question with a second. "Only the men fight? I thought you said your women were formidable fighters!"

"Only the Hunters fight," Kal corrected. "And though many young men desire to be warriors, no few women take up the spear, too." Behind them, the children parted, and the giant figure of Arik emerged from the tents, his long legs carrying him quickly up the hill.

"Our crafters and artisans remain with the tents," Kal said, continuing his explanation. "If there is battle, those with skills other than the blade are spared. The victorious return to their tents, and the vanquished seek others of their own tribe or join the victors'."

Dahr compared the Garun'ah system of battle to the Human one. On the surface, it seemed to have many advantages. "What if someone *did* attack the tents?" he asked, frowning. "Don't you worry about the safety of your families?"

"Only *Onatsal* would attack children," Kal growled. "Only a coward would kill pregnant women and toothless men instead of warriors." His eyes narrowed, and he took several deep breaths to calm himself. "But it is not as much of a problem as you think. There has been little fighting among the Blood since before the MageWar. For eons we have been bonded in our hatred of the Drekka."

Dahr was confused. "Aren't the Drekka a tribe?"

"They are no Tribe of Garun," Kal snarled, his voice once again crackling with emotion. "They turned away from Garun's teachings long before the MageWar."

"But in Alrendria, it is said that the Garun'ah are a fierce people," Dahr admitted. "Always at war with something." He blushed. "I myself am easy to anger and have lost myself in battle on several occasions."

"There *is* fire in the blood of Garun!" Kal laughed, putting an arm around Dahr's shoulder. "And sometimes the flames burn too hot. On many occasions, even within the Tacha, offense is taken and blows are exchanged. But rarely are blades drawn."

Kal looked Dahr in the eyes. "The children of Garun have quick tempers and a strong sense of honor, but those facts do not make them bloodthirsty monsters."

His dark eyes penetrated deep into Dahr's soul. "The Blood Rage frightens you?" he said slowly, half in question, and Dahr turned away.

Kal clapped a hand against Dahr's shoulder. "If you soak a rag in oil and wrap it around a stick," he said, seeming to change the subject, "you make a torch. When you touch fire to the torch, it brings light and heat. But the same oil, if poured over your head, will burn you to ashes.

"The fire in your blood is a different kind of fuel. It can aid you. Give you strength when you need it. Or it can destroy you." Kal squeezed Dahr's arm fondly, then stepped away. Arik joined them, and Kal nodded to his father in greeting. "You must harness it," he said in conclusion, "or it will consume you."

"You speak of the Blood Rage?" Arik asked, his voice a booming bass.

When the *Kranor* spoke, Dahr looked up. Arik, dressed in much the same manner as the day before, towered over him, his expression severe. His eyes, however, were sympathetic. "Yes, Father."

"It must have been difficult," Arik said to Dahr, "growing in the lands of man. Living in stone tents. They would not understand. Few among the Humans have experienced the Blood Rage. Fewer hear the call of nature. The Voice of Madryn. How did you survive?"

"By fighting, mostly," Dahr replied guiltily, his cheeks turning a bright shade of red. "After Jeran and I went to Kaper, I was always getting into fights. Children... Adults... Servants... Nobles... Once my temper was sparked, it wasn't long before I lost control, no matter how hard I tried to ignore the taunts." Suddenly, he laughed. "I'm afraid I did little to improve the Humans' opinion of the bloodthirsty Garun'ah."

Arik laughed deeply at Dahr's words, a sound like distant thunder. "And does your temper still run out of control?"

Dahr shook his head. "One day, King Mathis came upon me just before I lost my temper." Ashamed by the memory, Dahr's eyes sought the ground. "The other boy was much smaller than me. If I had hit him...." He paused, took a deep, shuddering breath, and looked at the Tribesmen, his eyes begging for forgiveness. "I didn't want to fight, but he was calling me names. I couldn't think clearly."

"Words cut deeper than any blade," Arik stated. "Especially when one is a child."

"Many would claim the other boy struck the first blow," Kal agreed. "Though his could not be seen."

Dahr smiled thankfully. "The King pulled me aside. 'If you have so much energy,' he said, 'then I had best put it to good use. There's a horse causing my trainers a great deal of trouble. Go to the stables, and tell Tillik I sent you to work with the Nightmare.'

"That horse almost killed me!" Dahr laughed. "But I managed to break her. By the time I finished, my rage was gone. From then on, whenever I grew angry, or whenever the walls of Kaper seemed too oppressive, I sought the comfort of the animals. When I was with them, nothing else mattered."

Another series of horn blasts accompanied the end of Dahr's story, much closer than the last. "You see, my son," Arik said to Kal. "Even in the stone prisons the Humans call home, he was drawn to nature. No matter what Humans build, they cannot deafen the Voice of Madryn."

"I don't understand," Dahr said. "What's the Voice of–" They crested the hill and Dahr fell silent, struck dumb by the sight before him. His question forgotten, he stared in awe.

Below them, moving slowly toward Kohr's Heart, was a sea of people, a relentless tide of men. The Channa stretched from horizon to horizon, their front ranks near the bottom of the hill, the rear of the tribe still invisible in the distance. Small groups approached the edge of the host, adding their meager numbers to the throng.

They walked slowly, in no hurry to reach the meeting ground. Wagons, heavily burdened with food and supplies, rumbled alongside the Tribesmen. Dogs ran in packs, and a few hunting birds soared lazily in the warm, summer sky. "I know now why the Channa were so slow to come to *Cha'khun*," Arik announced. "Yarchik must have summoned every last of his people to join him."

The first rows of Tribesmen stopped at the bottom of the hill, forcing those behind them to halt as well, and a tense silence descended upon them all. Dahr heard nothing–not the chirping of insects, nor the barking of dogs–nothing but the pounding of his own heart. "What are they waiting for?" he whispered to Kal.

"They will not join us until Yarchik has given them permission," Kal replied. "They await his arrival."

Dahr looked around, suddenly quite aware of their isolation. He, Kal, and Arik stood alone at the top of the hill, with the Tacha, seemingly oblivious to the approaching horde, far behind. Other than the wall of children, Arik's people showed no interest in the Channa's arrival. The Guardsmen were unaware, or too far away to offer aid if trouble started.

Dahr frowned, his hand dropping to the *dolchek* at his side, and he wished that he had not left his greatsword in his tent. He had no reason to distrust the Channa, yet he could not shake his feelings of uneasiness.

The Channa parted, and a small group of Tribesmen appeared, carrying a litter between them. A series of notes rang out from the center of the Channa, and Dahr jumped at the sound, the shrill notes ripping through the still morning air. The litter started forward, followed by a handful of Garun'ah and a train of wagons.

Kal looked at Dahr, his brow furrowed in confusion. "These are not our enemies, little brother," he said quietly. "Try not to look as if you wish to drive your *dolchek* through their hearts." Dahr blushed and smoothed his features, trying to hide his fear.

Though the four litter-bearers were each young, well-muscled warriors, tall and tanned, with brown hair tied back in braids, it took them some time to carry the litter up the hill. Dahr watched their approach warily. Weaponless save for the *dolcheks* at their sides, the bearers still looked dangerous, but it was the man on the litter who had Dahr on edge.

In the center of the palanquin sat a withered old man. Thin white hair hung loose about stooped shoulders and leathery skin, spotted with age and heavily wrinkled, covered his body. His legs lay still, shrunken and useless; his arms, though still broad, were limp, the flesh loose. But the Tribesman's eyes were lively; nothing seemed to escape their notice.

He leaned forward in his seat, squinting as he looked at those come to meet him. "*Jokalla, Arik uvan Hruta,*" he said, his voice raspy but strong. The aged eyes turned to Kal. "*Jokalla, Kal uvan Arik.*" Those eyes turned toward Dahr, but the man said nothing. He leaned in even closer, staring.

"Greetings, Yarchik *uvan* Greltar," Arik thundered. "I welcome you to Cha'khun."

"Have I gone to the wrong place?" the old man asked, his voice wheezing. "Have I led my people to the stones of Grenz or the legendary walls of Kaper?" Deep brown eyes peered at Dahr, but the words were for Arik. "Have you forgotten which of the Gods' blood flows in our veins? Why do we speak *Huma*? Why do you dress your Hunters in the clothes of Man?"

Arik chucked, a deep rumble. "Always has your humor brought light into our lives, Honorable Yarchik." He pointed to Dahr. "We speak the Man-tongue in honor of our guest, Dahr Odara. He is one of the Lost, raised by the king of our long time ally, the land of Alrendria. He bears grave news and wishes to share it with the Blood."

Yarchik frowned, his eyes all but disappearing in the folds of skin. "You allow outsiders to *Cha'khun*?"

"Dahr is of the Blood," Kal quickly replied.

The old man's eyes swiveled to the younger warrior. "So," he said, his voice a rasping chuckle, "the *Kranach* of the Tacha has gained a tongue since last I saw him. Your friend has come alone? He was sent from Alrendria with news for all the tribes to hear, without the aid of a single companion?" Kal lowered his eyes in shame. "I am old, little Kal, but not witless."

"It was not a light decision," Arik answered, hiding a smile, "but the *Tsha'ma* were insistent. They communed with Garun and told me to ignore tradition, or this would be the last *Cha'khun*."

"So they were," came Yarchik's answer. "Jakal insisted I answer your summons though I was not inclined to leave our Summer Lands." He briefly cast his eyes toward the heavens. "The stars are in agreement," he added. "They told me a stranger would come, a man without a past, in search of himself, bearing tidings of a storm the likes of which has never been seen."

Yarchik turned to fasten his stony gaze on Dahr again. Dahr quickly grew uncomfortable under the old man's piercing, unreadable expression. "The stars told me to ask this stranger a question," Yarchik announced. "And to judge him on his answer."

He leaned in, his head only a few hands from Dahr's. "The words of Garun, passed from father to son for generations untold, tell of twenty virtues. Together, these virtues form Honor in its purest form." The old man pressed even closer, until it seemed he would fall from his litter.

"The children of Garun strive to attain this divine form of Honor," Yarchik continued, "and yet all fall short of Garun's ideal. Once, long ago, when the Gods still walked our world, a young warrior approached the Hunter. 'Honorable One,' the child-warrior lamented, 'I have failed You. My life is full of transgression. My every action defies Your word. I desire glory for myself and not the tribe. I wish for that which belongs to others. I have killed without purpose, because I could, and it brought me joy.'

"The warrior fell to his knees. 'I will never walk the Twilight World with You, mighty Garun,' he moaned. 'I beg forgiveness, and pray that You burn away my sins with Your fire.'

"Garun smiled at his child and reached down to stroke the young warrior's head. 'Your regret is punishment enough,' He said, His voice sympathetic. 'None live their lives without error. Always will there be temptations. Always will there be desires. Times will be when you are strong, and can hold at bay your darker urges. Times will be when you are weak, and will lose sight of your honor.'

" 'This world is a test,' Garun told his people. 'A place to separate the honorable from the dishonorable. Those with honor will join us in the Heavens; those without will return to the Nothing.' He dropped to his knees at the warrior's side. 'Fear not, little one, for your life, though far from perfect, has been an honorable one.'

" 'It is not so, Master,' argued the warrior. 'I have no honor. I beg for punishment, that I may once more walk in the light without shame.'

" 'Had you no honor,' the Hunter said, 'you would not regret your actions. Nor would you desire justice. As for your punishment…. Your shame brings you more hurt than my wrath ever could. Rise, little one, and rejoin your brothers.'

"The warrior stood, tears in his eyes, and as he rejoined his people, Garun addressed them. 'Blood of my Blood,' He said. 'Regret your errors, but do not fear them. There are times when you will stray from the path of honor. Times when honor itself demands you sacrifice your virtue.'

" 'I have given you My law, those things for which the righteous must strive. Only one is incorruptible. Of the twenty Virtues, there is but one from which you must never turn.' " Yarchik smiled, a toothless, terrifying smile. "Tell me, *tsalla'dar*, of which virtue did the God speak?"

Dahr stood, horrified, mouth agape. He had never heard of Garun's Virtues, nor had he any clue which was the most important. He stammered, unable to find his tongue. "Speak!" snapped Yarchik. "If your Blood is true, you have no need to fear."

Brown eyes flashed, full of life. "I will know whether your words are from the heart," he warned in a feral growl.

Dahr dredged his mind, desperately searching for the correct answer. "SPEAK!" shouted Yarchik, and even Arik winced at the heat in the old man's voice.

"Loyalty!" Dahr said, the word coming to him unbidden. He continued, unable to stop himself. "All may be sacrificed save loyalty. Once given, it cannot be taken away. Should all else be lost, you must remain true to your bond. Should you stray from the path of righteousness, still must your loyalties remain true. Should those who earn your trust turn from the Light of Honor, still must you remain loyal to their memory, even as you drive your *dolchek* through their hearts."

Dahr fell silent, shocked by his own words; Kal stared at him wide-eyed, and Arik looked upon him with a newfound respect. "Hah!" Yarchik laughed. "The God's words from the mouth of the Lost. The time of the *Prah'phetia* is truly upon us."

He reached out a withered finger and poked Dahr's chest. "You are the true blood of Garun," he said. "The Channa will listen to your words."

Turning to Arik, Yarchik said, "I hear your summons to *Cha'khun*, *Kranor* of the Tacha. As we have since the birth of our race, the Channa have answered your call. I bring food enough to last half a season, and gifts for our Tachan cousins. Blood calls to Blood. We are the children of Garun. Though our tribes are different, our hearts beat as one."

"So it has been," intoned Arik. "So shall it remain." The giant warrior stepped forward and clasped the old man's shoulders. "Your arrival lightens my heart, *Kranor* of the Channa," Arik replied. "Your wisdom is without equal, your blade unmatched. I welcome you to *Cha'khun*."

The old man grabbed Arik's shoulders. His grip was tight, but his hands trembled on the younger man's arms. "My wisdom I grant you," he coughed, "but my blade I can barely lift. A child could best me, should he wish it."

The elderly Tribesman's eyes grew dim and distant. "I rule the Channa on the strength of my past, a shadow of the warrior I once was. My right to rule should have been challenged long ago." He met Arik's eyes squarely. "Soon, I will walk the Heavens with Garun."

Arik's eyes grew sad, but it did not show in his voice. "The God waits in anticipation of that day." The *Kranor* frowned, and a shadow passed over his face. "Who will rule the Channa in your stead?" he asked quietly.

"Norvik is *Kranach*," Yarchik replied, his voice sharp. "But Kraltir will challenge him, I am sure."

Arik's expression darkened. "Who will win the challenge?"

"Only Garun knows, old friend." Yarchik rapped on his seat, and the litter-bearers obediently turned him around. "We are welcomed to *Cha'khun*," he thundered to his people in a voice that belied his aged appearance. "Let us join our Blood!"

The Channa began the slow march up the hillside; the first wagons, those that had stopped some distance behind Yarchik's palanquin, rumbled forward. A black-haired warrior, a wickedly-curved axe in his hand, marched before them. His eyes were pools of darkness, his face tight, his lips compressed in a sneer.

He walked proudly and looked at the two *Kranora* as one would look at equals. The Tribesman's gaze passed through Dahr, as if he did not exist. "*Jokalla, Arik uvan Hruta.*" His head bobbed deferentially, but his eyes never left the giant Tribesman. The edges of the Tribesman's lips twitched up in a small smile.

"We speak *Huma*," Yarchik told the newcomer, "in honor of our guest, Dahr of Alrendria."

Black eyes turned toward him, as if noticing his presence for the first time, and the sneer returned. "Outsiders have no place at *Cha'khun*," the man said in a thickly-accented voice.

"Dahr and his companions have been welcomed by the Tacha," Yarchik replied. "I respect the *Kranor*'s wishes. So should you, Kraltir." The old man's eyes flashed. "Unless you wish to challenge my right to rule?"

"I honor the wishes of the mighty Arik," Kraltir said. "Though why he welcomes the Lost into his tribe is a mystery only Garun can answer." To Dahr, he said, "You should have stayed among the Humans, Half-Man."

Dahr tensed, but ignored the comment. Angered that his words had no effect, Kraltir turned his eyes on Arik and Kal. "We come bearing gifts for our cousins, the Tacha. These we gathered along the edge of the Tribal Lands." He waved, and his companions spurred the horses, drawing the wagons past. Dahr tensed as he recognized the design of the carts, and he struggled to control his rage when he saw what was in them.

Aelvin eyes, tired and defeated, stared back at him from behind the bars of the slavers' wagons. One by one, the wagons rolled past, each filled to capacity. Both Kal and Arik's eyes narrowed, and even Yarchik stirred in uncomfortably; Dahr suspected that the elderly *Kranor* had not known about the Aelvin prisoners. "They attacked without provocation," Kraltir explained, "while we traveled the Danelle, coming over the river in a shower of arrows. More than one Hunter fell in their vile ambush. Who knows how many there were, but these few we took prisoner. I offer them to you, *Kranor* of the Tacha, to do with as you see fit."

Defiant green eyes stared back from one of the wagons. Dahr's gut clenched; the longer he stared at the haggard, tired eyes beyond the bars, the more his anger swelled within him. He started forward, and Kal put a restraining hand on his arm. "Do nothing!" he hissed. "Say nothing! You walk thin ice if you challenge Kraltir. He has given himself to the Blood Rage. Wait at least until my father accepts these prisoners as a gift."

Dahr shrugged off his friend's arm and stared at Kal angrily, but he held his tongue until Arik spoke. "Garun teaches that all life is precious," the giant warrior said. "That no one being should hold dominion over another. You do not own these children of Valia, so they are not yours to give. Your knowledge of our ways is poor. Perhaps you would be wise to spend more time with the *Tsha'ma*, and less on the hunt."

He turned to Yarchik. "I would not burden you, Honorable One. Allow my people to tend to the *Aelva* until we decide their fate." Yarchik nodded, and Arik turned to address his son. "Take the wagons below," he commanded. "Be sure the *Aelva* are fed and watered. If they are injured, tend their wounds." Kal nodded and started down the hill, beckoning for the Channa to follow with the wagons.

Kraltir trembled with rage at Arik's calm dismissal, and he strode forward boldly, his eyes burning with ferocity. Yarchik's wrinkled hand darted out, faster than the eye could follow, and seized Kraltir's vest. "Remember your place," the old man warned in a growl. "You are not *Kranor* of the Channa, nor even *Kranach*."

A fire entered Yarchik's eyes. "Go," he commanded, "before your tongue brings more shame to your tribe." Kraltir's trembling increased, but he turned and wordlessly stomped down the hill.

The Channa started forward en masse, climbing the hill proudly, slowing only long enough to bow formally to Arik as they passed. Most were heavily burdened, carrying large sacks of grain over their shoulders or leading long trains of animals–cows, pigs, and sheep. Many passed without stopping, but some paused to offer Arik a gift. Woven rugs, golden trinkets, weapons and hides soon piled up around the *Kranor*.

Kraltir, now burdened with a sack of grain, glared at them as he passed. He stopped next to Dahr. "Keep your distance from me, Half-Man," the Tribesman snarled. "I do not trust your kind." A loud growling arose from behind Dahr, freezing Kraltir in place.

Dahr looked down, surprised to see his dogs behind him, hackles raised. The lead hound growled again, baring sharp, white teeth. Emboldened, his anger resurfacing, Dahr stepped forward. "Best you keep your distance from *me*, Tribesman. I would hate to cost the Channa a good grain carrier."

Yarchik's dry laughter came to his ears. "Again you forget your manners, Kraltir," the old Tribesman said. "And again the Lost One turns aside his anger. You would be wise to leave him be." The *Kranor*'s eyes hardened. "Warriors have been challenged for much less insult than you offer."

Kraltir snarled, but heeded his *Kranor*'s advice and stomped sullenly down the hill, disappearing into the tent city. Katya, having seen the dogs leave the tents at a run, had decided to follow. She stepped to Dahr's side. "A charming fellow," she said wryly. "We must introduce him to Elorn."

Dahr ignored her jest and turned to Yarchik. "I thank you, Honorable One," he said, using Arik's title for the aged Tribesman.

The old man waved his hand. "It is I who should thank you, Dahr," he replied. "Already has Kraltir given you cause to challenge him, and I fear he will provide more reason before *Cha'khun* ends." He rapped on the side of his palanquin, and the four bearers lifted him, ready to take him into Kohr's Heart, where the first of the Channa were setting up their tents.

"Perhaps it would be best," Arik said, weighing his words carefully, "if someone challenged him."

Yarchik nodded in agreement, but his expression was sad. "Perhaps."

"You must want someone to put him in his place," Dahr said. He felt odd talking so familiarly with the Garun'ah leaders, yet he did not stop his questioning. "Earlier, you said that Kraltir would challenge the *Kranach* after your death. Surely, if it were within your power, you would want to protect your son from such a challenge."

Yarchik's face grew even sadder. "It is not my son I wish to protect," he replied, his head dipping low. "Though it shames me to say it. It is the fate of the Channa that worries me." He rapped on the side of the palanquin again, and his litter-bearers started down the hill.

Arik's eyes followed the old man down the hill. "Norvik, *Kranach* of the Tacha, is Yarchik's great-nephew." At Dahr's startled look, Arik smiled weakly, the scar on his neck pulling tight. "This is not a Human land," he explained. "The Blood choose leaders on ability, not lineage. That Kal is my *Kranach* is a source of great pride, but the decision had little to do with my position as *Kranor*."

"But if the Norvik is not Yarchik's son...." Dahr, confused, let the statement trail off.

"Kraltir is Yarchik's blood," Aril explained. "The last of his seven sons. If he challenges Norvik and is successful...." Worry creased Arik's face, the expression seeming out of place on the face of the giant. "A sad day it will be for the Channa, if Kraltir becomes *Kranach*."

Arik's eyes locked on Dahr's. "Be wary, Dahr Odara of Alrendria." Dahr heard the omen in the giant man's voice. "An ill wind blows from the tent of Kraltir *uvan* Yarchik. And it comes for you."

Chapter 27

Martyn stretched, groaning lazily. Sunlight streamed through the open window, and he knew he was late for his meeting with Iban. Yawning, he cupped a hand over his mouth to stifle the sound. He did not want to rise; it had been a long night, and he had gotten little sleep.

Kaeille rolled over, running cool fingers up Martyn's bare chest. Closing his eyes, relishing her gentle touch, he groaned with remembered pleasure and drew the covers down. Porcelain white skin, lighter than most Elves', covered hard muscle and soft curves. Martyn stroked her short, black hair and she stirred, smiling.

Emerald green eyes half opened, and she smiled down at her naked body unashamedly before drawing the sheet up. "There is a chill in here," she scolded him, but her eyes danced with laughter. She turned to the window, listened to the birds sing. "You are late."

"I know," Martyn replied with a nod. "I couldn't bring myself to leave you." He yawned again, and offered Kaeille a rakish smile. "Besides, someone kept me up again last night. I never seem to sleep anymore!"

Kaeille pouted angrily, but her eyes sparkled. "You will sleep soon enough, Prince of Alrendria. Before long, you will return to your home. Then," A taunting smile ghosted across her face, but more than a hint of sadness entered her voice. "Then you will long for my company in your bed."

Martyn frowned, his good mood gone. "Without you...and Treloran...and Astalian...I'll be...Kaper will be very lonely."

"Is there no one you long to see in your homeland?" Kaeille asked, stroking his arm.

"My father," he answered, "and my greatmother Sionel. But...." The prince fell silent for a moment. "Jeran and Dahr are my only true friends, and they won't be waiting for me when I return. They are off having adventures, and I'm here."

"I remember a time," she replied, "not so long ago, when the mysterious city of Lynnaei seemed a grand adventure."

"It's not that. It's—" He broke off his statement, searching for the right words. "I miss my friends, that's all."

With an exaggerated sniff, Kaeille blinked back tears. "You have been separated from one friend for a season. The other, little more than a score of days. Am I such a poor replacement?" Her lower lip quivered playfully.

Martyn looked at her, suddenly nervous. "No, no!" he insisted. "It's not that! I swear!"

"You are too easy to frighten," she told him, laughing musically.

Martyn, grimacing, stood to dress. Pulling on his shirt with his back to her, to hide his frown, he asked, "What is to become of us? When I return to Kaper, do I forget this ever happened? Will you find someone else once I'm gone?"

Her tone was unreadable but cold. "Is that what you wish, Prince of Alrendria?"

Martyn turned, smoothing the wrinkles from his outfit. "Of course not!" he exclaimed, the pain apparent in his eyes. "You... I... You..." Again he found himself without words. "I cannot imagine losing you."

"But?" She sat up, the blankets falling, exposing pale, white flesh.

Martyn's pulse quickened. "But I'm Human and you're an Elf," he answered. "I'm the Prince of Alrendria, and you, a warrior of Illendrylla. Your home is here and mine is Kaper, so far away." He pressed his lips together, committing himself to the truth. "I am promised to Miriam, Princess of Gilead."

Kaeille smiled, her eyes full of love. "Do I look a fool to you, Martyn?" she asked. "I may be just an Elf, and *Ael Chatorra* at that, but I know how the world works. Do you think Prince Treloran can choose his own bride? He will be given to whomever the Emperor decides. The Emperor's choice will be based on the needs of Illendrylla, not on love."

"You knew?" Martyn asked incredulously.

"You *do* think me a fool!" she said, her tone light. "Those of the ruling class must often sacrifice themselves for duty. But their love is theirs to give to whomever they choose. I will not be able to take your name, our families will not be as one, but your love will be mine."

"I am to *marry* Princess Miriam," Martyn repeated, not sure that Kaeille understood.

"And you will have to give her children," she added, cocking her head to the side, looking at him as if he were the strange one. "And parade her before your people like a trophy, or a precious heirloom."

A wicked gleam entered the Aelvin warrior's eye. "But it will be me you come to for comfort," she added. "Me you seek when you desire companionship. I will not have your name, but I will have you. You have captured my heart, Prince of Alrendria."

He stared at her wide-eyed. "You mean... You... You *want* to be my mistress?"

"Your consort," she corrected. "I do not wish to share you, Martyn," she explained. "I would much prefer to be your wife. To have you to myself. But if that cannot be, I would rather have a part of you than none at all."

"And this is...acceptable...to your people?"

"It is no longer common," Kaeille answered, "but it is not unheard of. Princess Charylla's husband had a consort, and it seems likely that Treloran will as well."

"Leura," Martyn said quietly.

Kaeille nodded. "He would take her as wife," she told him, "if he had a choice, but the Emperor will likely offer his grandson to a daughter of Cyredyne. He is *Ael Alluya,* and his wife a prosperous *Ael Pieroci.* Together, they have much influence in Illendrylla."

"But if he can have her as consort," Martyn asked, confused, "why is he so upset?"

"He does not want her as consort!" Kaeille replied, looking at Martyn as if he were a fool. "Their children will go unrecognized, and she will never have his name." Her eyes grew dangerously hard. "Had you the choice, would you not take me as your wife?"

He flashed his best smile. "Of course I would, my sweet!" he replied, holding up his hands in surrender. He turned his back again, this time to hide his embarrassment, and tied the laces of his boots. Kaeille stood, wrapping a thick robe around her body.

Martyn embraced her. "Humans are not as tolerant of mistresses... of consorts...as Elves," he warned her. "It would make me happy if you were with me, but you must understand what you face."

Hot, red lips pressed against his. "Later," Kaeille said, sliding a finger down his cheek. "You can explain it to me later. Lord Iban will already be angry with you, and I must report to Astalian." Martyn smiled and drew the Elf to him for another kiss.

He started for the door, but it opened before him, and Lord Iban strode in. His eyes instantly locked on the prince. "So," the Guard Commander said icily, "you are awake, my Prince. I was beginning to worry." Iban expression grew grim. "I thought I had made it clear how little I enjoy wasting my time waiting for you to grace me with your presence."

A movement caught the Guard Commander's attention, and his eyes looked past Martyn. Seeing Kaeille, Iban's lips pressed together tightly, but he said nothing. "If you can find the time, Prince Martyn," he said coldly, "I will be waiting in our meeting room." He turned on his heel and left the prince's chambers.

Martyn hurried after him. "My apologies, Lord Iban," he said, nearly jogging to stay at the old warrior's side. "I overslept and was just on my way to join you." Iban ignored him. "About Kaeille," he said, swallowing, trying to keep the nervousness from his voice. "It's not what you think. I–"

"Say nothing," Iban warned, silencing the prince. "You've made your decision, Martyn, and you will have to deal with the consequences. Both of you will." The Guard Commander stopped in mid-stride and turned to face Martyn. His voice softened. "Like as not I would have made the same choice at your age. Now...." Falling silent, he gripped Martyn's shoulder tightly. "Now I just hope you never come to regret your decision."

They continued down the hall silently, Martyn brooding on Iban and Kaeille's words. He could not imagine a life without the lithe, cynical Elf; she complemented him well, her strengths accentuated his own. In a perfect world, he could take her to wife, love her the way he wanted to, and damn the desires of his father, his duty to Alrendria.

But this world was far from perfect. Alrendria needed him. His father needed him. *Can I condemn Kaeille to a life among Humans, belittled not only for her position, but for her Race as well? Will I be able to so easily ignore Miriam, a stranger, but from all reports a beautiful and clever woman? If we must wed, how could I force Kaeille upon her? How would she feel, being set aside for an Elf, without ever having a chance of her own?*

Dark thoughts plagued the prince. *Would either have the life they deserve? No matter what I did, would either be happy? Would I?*

Martyn's frown deepened, and he wondered, not for the first time, if he had made the right choice. *What would Jeran do in my place,* he asked himself, scowling at the answer that popped unbidden into his mind. *His duty, no doubt. Jeran always does the right thing.*

An angry voice shouted through a half-open door to Martyn's left. "...stupid fool! This was my best suit! What am I to wear to today's negotiations?" Martyn's frown, already deep from his dispiriting musings, grew deeper. He stopped and turned toward the door. Slowly, he reached out and gave it a little push, watching as it quietly swung open.

Rafel stood with his back to the door, dressed in nothing but lacy, white underclothes. In his hand he held an outfit of brilliant purple, the shiny material marred by a dark splotch that covered the chest, and his eyes shifted between the ruined outfit and boy at his feet. An endless string of oaths issued from the nobleman's mouth, and his free arm flapped up and down animatedly.

A young man, one of Rafel's servants, knelt on the floor. A boy of fourteen winters, with blonde hair and dark eyes, he was trembling at Rafel's tirade, his eyes begging forgiveness. "Please, Sir," he said, his voice barely a whisper, "I did not mean—"

"How dare you interrupt me!" Rafel screamed, backhanding the boy and knocking him aside. The servant crashed to the floor, sobbing, his hands clasped over his face. Hitting the boy dislodged the outfit from Rafel's grip, and the purple suit fell to the floor, landing amidst a small pool of liquid and shards of shattered pottery.

Rafel hastily retrieved the garment, holding it up for inspection. His face turned purple-red, nearly the same shade as the doublet, when he noticed the two new stains. "You clumsy oaf!" he snarled. "Look what you've made me do now." Furious, he wadded up the silken outfit and threw it into the hearth.

The boy climbed to his knees; a thin trickle of blood ran down his face. "I am most sorry, my Lord," he said, tears welling in his eyes. "It was an accident."

"An accident!" Rafel scoffed. "Do you think me a fool, boy? I hear what you say when you think I'm not listening. You *want* me to look a fool in front of the Elves!"

"No, my Lord," the boy pleaded. "It's not true. I desire only prosperity for you and your House!"

"You call me a liar?" Rafel demanded, preparing to strike again. "I've had enough of your impertinence!" He drew his arm back, balling his hand into a fist.

Martyn rushed into the room, grabbed Rafel's hand, and whirled the larger man around. "What's the meaning of this," Rafel began, cutting off when he saw Martyn's fiery blue eyes staring at him.

Martyn squeezed Rafel's arm tightly, and the fat man ground his teeth at the pressure. "What are you doing, cousin?" Martyn asked, each word spoken slowly.

"Disciplining a disrespectful servant," came Rafel's tart reply. He wrenched his hand away from the prince and looked at his forearm. Small, red circles had formed where Martyn's fingers had dug into flesh. Irritated, Rafel rubbed his arm. "For what he has done, he deserves much worse."

"And what is this boy's transgression?" Martyn asked calmly. Though he stood a few fingers shorter than the corpulent Rafel, he felt as if he stared down at the older man.

"My Prince?"

"What has he done to deserve this?" Martyn looked at the red welt forming on the servant's face, the slowly-drying blood on his lips. The child was too frightened to wipe his face.

"He defies me at every opportunity," Rafel stated, puffing out his chest indignantly. "He is lax in his duties. Irresponsible. Every chance he gets, he maligns me. Just now he willfully spilled a pot of tea–"

Martyn turned his cool gaze on the boy. "Is this true?" he asked, cutting off his cousin.

Rafel's eyes widened. "You doubt my word?" he sputtered in surprise.

"Silence!" Martyn ordered, his eyes remaining on the boy. "Is what Rafel says true?" he repeated. "Speak the truth and no harm will befall you."

The child summoned his courage. "He lies, Your Majesty," the boy said. "I am ever a faithful servant, attentive to my duties. The tea was an accident. I tripped. I did not mean to...." The servant's speech broke off. Sobbing, he dropped his head into his hands.

"Lies!" Rafel said, lunging at the boy. Martyn intercepted him, shoving the nobleman aside. Rafel hit one of the room's sofas with a crash, upending the furniture, and tumbled to the ground. "You would trust this boy's word over mine?" Rafel snapped, his eyes angry. "I am noble born and he is but a commoner."

"I would trust the truth," Martyn replied.

As Rafel regained his feet, his eyes locked with the prince, and his hands trembling with rage. "What does it matter if I strike him?" he asked. "He is nobody. A servant."

"He is a man," Martyn answered, his voice carrying power and authority. "No matter his station, he is still a man." Angry eyes bored into Rafel. "If you think yourself his better, you are a fool."

Martyn looked at the boy. "Gather your things," he ordered, "and report to Mistress Liseyl, the woman who commands Lord Odara's servants. You know of whom I speak?" The child nodded. "Tell her you are there at my command, and ask her to find you room among her people." Standing, the boy backed out of the room. He still trembled, but not so much as before.

"You have no right–" began Rafel, but the prince cut him off.

"*You* have no right," snapped Martyn, maintaining a thin control over his temper, "to treat this child so. You are noble born, my father's choice to represent House Batai in these negotiations! You are expected to act with a measure of dignity and decorum."

"Do you know to whom you are speaking, boy?" Rafel sneered. "I am Rafel Batai, Third Seat of our House."

"And *I* am Martyn Batai, Prince of Alrendria," Martyn replied coolly, his voice even.

Martyn's commanding tone, his authoritative demeanor, shocked Rafel, and the nobleman's voice lost its haughty edge. "He is *my* servant," Rafel stated. "You have no right to take him from me." He winced as he spoke, hearing the obsequious whine in his own voice.

"Count yourself lucky I do not take them all," Martyn returned, wagging an admonishing finger at the corpulent nobleman. "Mark my words, Rafel. If you mistreat another servant, if I even suspect such a thing, I will remove them from your service. When we return to Kaper, I will bring this matter before my father. We will see how long you remain Third Seat of House Batai once you've earned the King's disfavor.

"Dress yourself," Martyn commanded, glancing at the soiled outfit lying on the hearth. "I don't care if you wear those dirty rags or another of your garish outfits, but be sure you're on time for today's meeting." He stormed from the chamber, slamming the door behind him.

Iban was waiting in the hall. "That could have been handled with more tact, my Prince," he said, shaking his head sadly.

"He irritates me," Martyn replied, his temper still on edge. "I can't fathom why father sent him here!" He met Iban's stony, unreadable eyes. "What would you have had me do, Iban? Allow him to manhandle his servants? Ignore his words?"

"No," the Guard Commander admitted. "I would have handled it no differently than you, save I would have attempted to be more… diplomatic. As to why Rafel is in Illendrylla…." His stern expression broke into a broad grin. "Let's just say your father finds him irritating, too."

The words, delivered in such a grave tone, made Martyn chuckle. His anger melted away as he and Iban continued down the hall. "What would you have done?" he asked, seeking the older man's advice.

"Rafel offered you few options," Iban replied. "Your best course of action would have been to disarm his anger. Perhaps with a joke. Then you could have discussed things more rationally."

Martyn eyed him suspiciously. "Do you find such a thing effective?" he asked wryly.

"Often," came Iban's calm reply. The grin was gone, but the Guard Commander's eyes laughed at the prince. "Once he was calm," he said, continuing his explanation, "your commands would not have seemed so threatening, and you might not have found it necessary to threaten him."

"And the boy?" prompted Martyn. "How does any of this aide him?"

"Tomorrow, or the day after, you could have requested that Rafel release the boy from his service. Any excuse would have sufficed. You need a new valet. The Elves are giving you a horse and you need someone to care for it. Rafel would have gladly given you the child, thinking you now in his debt."

Martyn considered the old man's words. "I don't see how it makes much difference," he said, the words ringing hollowly in his ears. "The results were the same."

"Sullenness does not become you, Martyn," Iban told him. "Nor does short-sightedness. You have earned yourself an enemy today. Perhaps for your father as well. Rafel will not take kindly to your harsh treatment, nor will he likely forget it."

"Surely, you don't think my words would put Rafel at odds with father!"

"Who's to say? Rafel knows the King has little love for him. Your threats may not have caused more damage, but they certainly did not help matters." Iban opened the door to their meeting room, and Martyn preceded him into the chamber. The Guard Commander met his eyes. "As prince, and later as king, you must consider the consequences of each action carefully. Your every word will have unforeseen effects."

The Guard Commander took his seat, and signaled for Martyn to do the same. "We will need every ally for the struggle ahead."

"Rafel will not side with the Darklord," Martyn said adamantly. "No Batai would!"

"When the battle with Lorthas begins," Iban replied, "anyone not wholly with us will be an enemy. It won't matter if they sit at Lorthas' hand or plot their own petty vengeance." Settling back in his chair, he shifted the topic.

They talked away the remainder of the morning, their discussion ranging from the attitude of the other nobles to the nearly-concluded negotiations. Lord Iban even wondered aloud about Jeran, the first time he had done so without grimacing since Jeran and Mika had run off.

There was a knock on the door. "Enter," Iban called, and the door swung open on soundless hinges. Treloran strode in, dressed in a fine, green doublet. He bowed to Iban and Martyn, but held his tongue until Martyn bade him to speak.

"I am to invite you to today's parley," he said. "Mother believes our business is concluded, and suggested that we celebrate our mutual success."

Martyn grinned broadly at the Aelvin Prince's statement. Iban grinned as well, though his was more controlled. "Am I to assume your words mean the Elves have conceded to our final demands?" the Guard Commander asked.

Treloran smirked, but kept his voice even. "You are most astute, Honored Human," he said, his once-genuine arrogance now feigned. "Horeish has been made to see the wisdom of your requests."

Iban stood, a victorious smile on his face. "Then it is finished. Come, Martyn," he added, waving for the prince to join him. "Let's conclude these negotiations and celebrate the first step toward the union of our Races."

Martyn followed Iban from the chamber; he and Treloran walked side by side through the palace. "It pains me to say this, Human," Treloran said, looking at the prince, "but I think I will miss you once you return to Alrendria."

"Your words are touching, Elf," Martyn mumbled, faking an angry glare. He laughed suddenly, and the Aelvin Prince smiled in return. "To be honest," Martyn added, "I'll miss you, too. I've gotten used to you following me around like a well-trained puppy!" Now it was Treloran's turn to offer a dark glare.

Entering the hall, they found most of the Aelvin delegation waiting for them. Only Horeish was absent. Charylla, dressed in a gown of light blue, smiled at their arrival. "Honored guests," she said in welcome, gesturing to the table. "Join us in celebration! We twelve have done what no others of our Races have been able to do since I was but a child. For the first time in three centuries, goods will flow down *Ael Shende Ruhl*.

"Sit," she commanded. "Sit! The others have been sent for. Food and drink are being brought." She smiled at Treloran, noting how he and Martyn stood together, not because they had to, but because they wished to.

"Will Horeish be joining us?" Martyn asked.

Charylla's face darkened. "No," she said, shaking off her anger. "My brother is protesting our decisions. He says if Humans are welcome in Lynnaei, he is not. He is gathering his followers, those few deluded souls who still listen to his words, and leading them from the city."

Treloran sighed. "Luran will calm, Mother," he assured the princess. "Uncle has always been quick to anger."

"And even more stubborn than Grandfather!" Charylla added, her eyes brightening.

"I shall try not to take offense at that remark, Granddaughter," the Emperor said, shuffling into the chamber and smirking at her surprised expression. "You did not expect me to miss the celebration, did you, my dear? You forced me to stand aside during the negotiations, but you would not deny an old Elf a glass of wine in honor of your achievement, would you?"

She shook her head. "No, Grandfather." Standing, Charylla hurried to the Emperor and escorted him to his seat. "But how did you know?"

He smiled devilishly. "Did you truly expect me to sit through these talks without eavesdropping?" Charylla started to stammer a reply, but the Emperor waved her to silence. "I know what you are thinking. Your wards were quite difficult to breach undetected, my dear, but I do have a few more winters experience than you."

Charylla flushed. "As always, I am in awe of your abilities, Grandfather."

"And as always," he replied, taking a seat at the head of the table, "I appreciate your awe."

The last of the delegates arrived, followed by an army of *Ael Namisa* carrying trays of food and dust-covered bottles of wine. They all took their seats, and Lord Iban apprized them of the events that had brought the negotiations to a sudden close. Smiling, he raised his glass, filled with dark, Aelvin wine, and offered a toast. "To our gracious hosts. So long as Valia's children rule with dignity and honor, shall we find within them the greatest of allies."

As one, they drank. Charylla started to lift her glass, but it was Treloran who was first to rise. "To our Human friends," the Aelvin Prince said. "For infusing Illendrylla with a fraction of their limitless life. For blessing us with the strength of their friendship and the wealth of their goods. And for showing a stubborn prince there is more to life than resentment and misplaced anger."

The delegates cheered, drinking deeply, and Charylla stared at her son with open shock, her lips spread in a broad smile. The conversation soon shifted to more trivial matters, and the Humans and Elves talked, not as different races, but as friends.

"When will you leave for Alrendria?" Charylla asked, turning to Lord Iban.

"Soon," he replied. "Though I am loathe to leave the beauty of your city behind me." He gestured around him, though Lynnaei was hidden behind the room's stone walls. "These are memories I will cherish until my death. A wonderful achievement for the twilight of my life...."

His words trailed off, and Iban's gaze grew wistful. Shaking his head, he smiled at the Aelvin Princess. "But we have been long from home," he added. "I would have Martyn returned to Alrendria as soon as–"

"You will leave at the next full moon," the Emperor said, cutting off Iban. "Forgive my interruption. I meant no offense. But you must stay. I insist."

Iban stared at the Emperor, a contemplative look on his face. "Of course we will stay, Your Eminence," Iban replied in a calculating manner, smiling. "None will complain of a few more days in Your beautiful city. I, myself, will relish the opportunity to explore Lynnaei. Often were we locked in this chamber until late in the evening, or too exhausted upon the conclusion of our talks to avail ourselves of the wonders around us."

"Then it is settled," the Emperor said. He smiled at the assembly. "The night of the next moon we will hold an audience in the Great Hall. There will I disclose to Our people the results of these negotiations. Until then, We will be blessed with the pleasure of your company.

"Perhaps, Lord Iban," the Emperor added, "you would honor me with your company for the midday meal tomorrow. Things have been so hectic since your arrival, I feel I have neglected you."

Iban bowed his head politely. "As you command, Emperor," he said with a smile. "It would be an honor."

"Yes," the old Elf sighed wearily. "It always is."

Chapter 28

Dahr paced outside his tent, his expression sour. The dogs followed him, ears pricked up, whining nervously. The day, dark and overcast, punctuated by the distant rumbling of thunder, matched his mood.

"There's nothing you can do," Katya told him, stretching out on the lush grass. The other Guardsmen were gone–Jasova and Nykeal on one of their numerous walks and Vyrina on a tour of the tent-city led by Frodel, her Garun'ah guide. Elorn and Wardel had departed, in opposite directions, immediately following breakfast. Neither had been seen since. "I'm not even sure why you'd want to," she added, yawning.

Dahr stopped in mid-stride. "They're caged," he said, his voice a near growl.

"They're prisoners," Katya replied, sitting up, surprised by the vehemence in his tone. "They attacked the Channa without provocation."

"Or so Kraltir would have us believe," Dahr murmured harshly.

"That one bears watching," Katya agreed, "I grant you that. But the other Channa confirm his story. The Elves attacked them." She stood and went to him, but his heated gaze stopped her a hand's length away. "What would you have them do? Let the Elves free, so they can attack again?"

"No," Dahr answered. "But there must be another way."

"They are well cared for by the Tacha," Katya added. "Fed and clothed, given plenty of water. Their wounds are tended. They are allowed, under guard, to leave the cages and exercise. Things could be much worse."

"They are caged," he repeated, snarling.

"They are *alive!*" Katya returned, her own irritation starting to show.

Dahr took a calming breath. "Sometimes," he said, his voiced pained, "life is not enough. The Garun'ah seemed to understand that, and yet...." He trailed off, his thoughts distant. Behind him, one of the dogs whimpered, and absently, Dahr reached down to stroke the beast's head.

"Why?" she demanded, her eyes probing. "First, you risk Iban's wrath to track down and free those captured by slavers; now you risk our tenuous safety among the Tribesmen? Why is it so important to you?"

Dahr's frown deepened. Reluctantly, he pulled off his shirt, exposing the scar on his shoulder. "Do you know what this is?"

"It's a burn," Katya answered brusquely, thinking Dahr meant to change the subject.

"It's a brand," Dahr replied. "The flying condor of Lord Harol Grondellan, a Rachannen nobleman." He traced the brand with his finger, memories coming unbidden to his mind. "The Rachannen brand all their slaves," he told her. "It makes it easier to track them down if they escape."

"Oh, Dahr," Katya cried, her anger melting into sympathy. "Why didn't you tell me?"

"It's not something I'm proud of," he said. "Nor is it something I care to relive. In all of Alrendria, only a handful know the truth."

She grabbed him, pulling him into a tight embrace. Her lips sought his, and they pressed together, finding comfort in each other's arms. Finally, Katya pulled away, drawing Dahr to the ground. "Tell me," she requested, her voice almost pleading. "Tell me everything."

He told her. He told her of his parents, his childhood in the shadow of Mount Kalan. He told her of the slavers, his family's mad dash through the forest, his father's courageous sacrifice, his mother's dying words. He told her of Gral, the slaver, who had killed his mother, tormented him, destroyed their lives. Gral who, winters later, had led the slave caravan Dahr had set out to rescue.

He told her of his seasons with Lord Grondellan. The hunt. The mountain cat's attack and his terrified flight across Madryn, the whole time certain he would be recaptured, punished, and killed.

She listened in rapt silence, and by the end, tears streamed down her face. Dahr caressed her cheek tenderly, wiping away the tears. "I have never seen you cry before," he said, his own voice catching in his throat.

"Does that mean it cannot happen?" she sniffed. "I'm not stone," she added, forcing a smile. "You confuse me with Jeran. He's the one made of ice."

"Jeran isn't ice," Dahr replied, his voice heavy, speaking from painful experience. "Nor stone. He, too, knows how to cry." He pulled her close to hide his own tears, relishing the feel of her body next to his.

"Do you understand now?" he asked, his voice choked. "I know how they feel. I, too, once lived in a cage. No man should live without freedom. That's why I rescued the slaves. That's why I want to free the Elves."

A prolonged silence followed in which they clung to each other, drawing strength. "Am I interrupting something?" Wardel asked, striding back into the camp, a wry smile on his face.

Katya wiped away her tears. "You're always interrupting something, Wardel," she riposted, laughing. "How goes your hunt? Have your charms won the affections of the Tribeswomen yet?"

The Guardsman's grin faded. "They're a strange race, these Garun'ah. One moment, the women are more forward than a barmaid in the wharves of Kaper, the next, more reserved than a highborn lady!"

"Different land," Katya reminded him, "different customs. Kal was right. You should spend some time learning about the Tribesmen–and women!–before you get yourself into trouble."

"Easy for you to say!" Wardel laughed. "You have no idea what I'm going through! You've already found yourself a Tribesman, and he was raised Human!" Dahr tried to glare at the Guardsman, but Wardel's mirth was infectious.

"Did we miss something?" Jasova asked, entering the camp hand in hand with Nykeal. Another peal of thunder echoed through the valley.

"Dahr and I were discussing the Elves," Katya told them. "What are your thoughts?"

"They attacked the Tribesman," Wardel shrugged. He grabbed a basket of fruit, a gift from one of the Tribeswomen, and rummaged through it. Withdrawing a large, red apple, he smiled greedily and took a bite. "We heard reports of fighting between the Elves and Garun'ah before we left for Illendrylla."

"But should they be kept in the cages?" Katya prompted.

"They're prisoners," Wardel answered. "Where better to keep them." Katya smiled at Dahr triumphantly.

"The cages are small," Nykeal said as she unlaced her boots. "And there were a lot of prisoners. It must be very cramped. Couldn't the Tribesmen find somewhere else to keep them? In a tent or something?"

"My Nikki," joked Jasova. "Always so concerned with the enemy's comfort." She hit him playfully, and he raised his hands in surrender, backing away.

"And you, Jasova?" asked Dahr. "What are your thoughts."

The subcommander scratched his beard. "Wardel and Nikki both make good arguments," he stated. "On the one hand, they are prisoners of war. The only options are to release them, kill them, or keep them captive. Killing them seems excessive, and freeing them only gives them opportunity to attack again, killing more Garun'ah.

"Which leaves imprisonment. The cages are convenient," he continued, tapping his chin. "Where else can the Elves be quartered without constant supervision? If set free in the camp, what's to stop them from attempting escape?

"But the cages *are* cramped," he countered, arguing with himself. "Demeaning. It's no way to live. Personally, I'd prefer death. The only alternative, as I see it, is...." His words trailed off, and his eyes lifted over the others. A smile spread across his face. "I think we have a visitor," he said suddenly, pointing.

They all turned to see what Jasova was talking about. A young Garun'ah, who Dahr recognized as the boy whose dog he had helped, stood to the side of their tents. The boy, just a finger or two taller than eight hands, had light brown hair and matching eyes. He wore no shirt, and though young, hard muscle already covered his torso. He held something in his hand.

His eyes scanned the Humans, a mixture of fear, curiosity, and false bravery on his face. Spotting Dahr in the grass, he started forward, his arm extended, offering the object. *"Danko, Darloka. Mahn Hunssa est ghut weder."* At Dahr's blank expression, the boy swallowed nervously. In a heavy accent, he said, "Thank you."

Dahr took the gift, a rock, amber in color and transparent. A small hole had been drilled through the center of the stone, through which a tightly-braided leather cord was woven. As Dahr examined it, the stone caught the light of the sun, reflecting it back in a shimmer of golden light. He looked at the child uncomprehendingly.

"It be... It is... *shenda* stone," explained a new voice. Frodel walked up, Vyrina a few steps behind. "It symbol among Blood. It mean you done service, and he now owe debt. You dress...You wear *shenda* in honor of debt. When you feel he repay, you return."

"But, I did nothing–" Dahr started, but Frodel's deep voice cut him off. "You saved life of...pat...pet. It greatly hurt pride if refuse."

Dahr lifted the stone to the light, inspecting it again. Brushing his hair aside, he tied the leather cord around his neck, bowing his head to the child. "Thank you," he said, and after a short pause, *"Danko."*

The boy beamed in joy, turned, and ran from the tents, calling out to his friends. "He think it great honor," Frodel told the Humans, his smile following the boy. "He first to give *shenda* to *Cho Korahn Garun.*"

The Guardsmen looked perplexed, but no more so than Dahr. *"Cho Korahn Garun?"* he repeated.

"The Heart of the Hunter," Frodel translated. "Chosen of Garun." His face flushed. "It not easy say in *Huma*. It said *Cho Korahn Garun* be sent by Garun to lead Blood in darkest night."

"And you think Dahr is this *Cho Korahn Garun?*" Wardel laughed. A stern glare from Katya silenced him.

Frodel frowned. "It possible," he answered, unwilling to commit himself.

Dahr shook his head. "I wasn't chosen to do anything. Especially lead the tribes."

"We see," came the Tribesman's response.

A long silence followed. "Jasova," Katya said, seeking to ease the tension, "you were going to share your opinions of the Elves' imprisonment."

Frodel's face darkened at the mention of the Elves. "As I was saying," Jasova continued, clearing his throat. "Were I in charge of the Elves, my options would be few and poor. Honor prevents me from killing them, and keeping them trapped in cages chafes at my morality. If I release them, they may turn on me, or attack again. The only alternative is to secure an oath."

"To what effect?" asked Nykeal.

"If they swore an oath not to attack," Jasova explained, "never to raise a blade against me or my people, except in defense of their lives, I would let them go."

"You assume that the Elves would keep their word!" scoffed Wardel.

"They are just as likely to keep their word as a Human," Jasova returned. "Or a Tribesman!"

Frodel rounded on the Guardsman. "The *Aelva* have no honor!" he growled. "They not keep oath!" Rage consumed him, made him tremble, and he fought to maintain control. "Compare them to Blood great offense."

Jasova remained steadfast against the Tribesman's angry gaze, though Nykeal slowly reached for the blade at her side. "How many Elves have you met?" he asked calmly. "Other than those in the cages, how many have you talked to?"

The question seemed to stun the Tribesman. "None," he admitted. "All know *Aelva* be heartless, honorless demons!"

"And the Garun'ah are without fault? You seem happy enough to keep the Elves locked in those cages."

"If one capture wild animal," Frodel returned, "one not put it in bedroll."

"There isn't any proof they attacked the Channa!" interjected Nykeal. "Save the word of Kraltir."

"No Tribesman tell falsehood," Frodel stated coldly, fighting to hold the Blood Rage in check. "*Aelva* deserve cage."

"And were your positions reversed," Dahr whispered, his voice barely audible, "would you deserve the cage, Frodel? Would you wish to spend your life behind bars of iron?"

Dahr's words stunned everyone to silence, and the Tribesman's attack faltered. "No," he admitted. "It be the little death. My body would live, but heart would die."

"Kal has been telling me of the life of Garun, when the Hunter walked the world. He taught that all life is equal, that all creatures are part of the Balance." Dahr's eyes met the Tribesman's. "Look into my eyes, Frodel, and tell me you truly believe the Elves are less than the Garun'ah. Do their hearts not beat as yours? Are they incapable of honor?"

"They...attack Blood."

"The Elves claim that Kraltir attacked them. Do we discard their word simply because they're Elves? Even if they did attack first, would you not accept their pledge, as Jasova suggested? Were it you in the cage, and you were offered your freedom, would you swear to do no violence? Would you honor your word?"

"No true child of Garun oath-breaker!" Frodel snapped, some of his earlier anger returning.

Dahr's voice remained calm. "Then how can you not offer them the same choice?"

Frodel tried to argue, but no words came to his mouth. His eyes widened in shock, then lowered to the ground in shame. "With so few words have you turned my heart."

"This is not the only evidence we have of Aelvin aggression!" Wardel reminded Dahr. "We saw the remains of several attacks on our journey here. Remember the arrows? The Aelvin runes?"

"Did we see what we thought we saw?" Dahr asked. "I have often wondered." He scratched his chin thoughtfully, the set of his jaw hardening. "There is one way to be sure." He stood and walked to his packs, rummaged through them, and stood with the black-shafted arrows in his hand.

"What do you intend to do?" Vyrina asked.

"I will ask the Elves what they know of these. We will learn the truth."

"And if the Elves say they had nothing to do with the attacks?" Katya asked. "If they deny those arrows are theirs? How will you know if they lie?"

"I will know," Dahr insisted, his eyes flashing with animal ferocity. "If they can be trusted, I will set them free."

"And if they are responsible for the attacks?" Jasova queried. "If they can't be trusted?"

Dahr's eyes were fire. "Then I will set them free." The words were the same, but this time, his tone was cold and dark. "I will suffer no creature to live in a cage." So wild was the look Dahr gave them that the Guardsmen stepped back. "One way or another, the Elves will sleep free tonight."

He stormed away, in the direction of the wagons, the arrows gripped tightly in his fist. "Dogs!" he barked, and the pack stood as one, padding silently behind him.

In the wake of his departure, Frodel murmured, "*Cho Korahn Garun!*"

Dahr stomped through the camp, heedless of his path, drawing many eyes as he walked. The giant in Human garb. The outsider. The Lost One, now returned to his Blood. Many were curious as to his destination and wondered at the stark and angry expression on his face, but they respected his privacy. They would know when it was their time to know.

A few, however, did follow. Frodel and Katya, and the other Guardsmen, though they kept a respectful distance. Kal, who saw Dahr in the distance and guessed his destination. Kraltir, who had been watching the Lost One suspiciously. And another, who chose to remain hidden in the shadows.

Dahr arrived at the wagons and paced them from start to end, searching for a pair of defiant green eyes. He found them in the first wagon. "Why did you attack the Garun'ah?" he demanded, his voice cold, harsh.

The Elf turned to face him. He was tall, though it was hard to gauge his height in the cramped confines of the cage. Blonde hair, dirty and stringy, hung to his shoulders, which were wrapped in a thick, white bandage. A second bandage, blood-stained, covered his leg. Lips, thin and red, pressed into a thin line, but it was the Elf's eyes that first caught Dahr's attention, and held it. They were an intense, passionate, and vibrant green.

"So," the Elf said, his lips twisting into a small grin, "one of you, at least, can speak a civilized tongue."

"Do not bandy words with me, Elf," Dahr growled, a sound echoed by his dogs. "Why did you attack the Tribesman?"

"Why would we not?" the Elf glowered. "The Wildmen respect no borders. They have no conscience. They have no honor."

Dahr was taken aback by the conviction of the words. "I would not say such things too loudly," he whispered, his eyes hardening. "The Garun'ah are touchy about their honor." The Elf snorted in reply, but Dahr' ignored the sarcasm. "You claim the Garun'ah attacked you?"

"Yes!"

"You did not attack them on their journey up the Danelle?"

"These Garun'ah, we attacked," admitted the Elf. "Before they could raid our lands."

"The Garun'ah have not raided your lands!" snarled Kal, stepping up to Dahr.

"They have!" spat the Elf, his voice growing colder. "I have seen the handiwork of the Wildmen! I have heard tales worse than what I saw."

"I have heard enough of your lies, *Onahrre*!" Kal said through clenched teeth. "You are lucky that–"

Dahr waved him to silence. "Leave him be, Kal. I want to hear what he has to say."

Kal rounded on Dahr. "Why would you listen to the words of the *Aelva*?" he asked, his nose wrinkling in distaste.

Dahr took a deep, calming breath. "I would ask this thing of you, Kal. Let me talk to the Elf without interruption. Listen to his words. Listen for the truth."

Kal stared at him for a long time. "Because of the blood-debt I owe you, little brother," he replied carefully. "For no other reason do I listen to the *Onatsal*."

"You say the Garun'ah attacked you?" Dahr asked, turning to face the Elf. "Describe the attacks."

The Elf was hesitant. "Why should I describe what the Tribesman already knows?"

"Because your life and freedom hang in the balance."

The Elf pursed his lips and nodded. "Very well. They cross the Danelle at night, like thieves, attacking the weak, the innocent. Whole villages are destroyed. Women and children torn apart as if by wild animals." He looked at Kal in disgust and spat upon the ground. "They *are* animals!"

Kal, enraged, trembled and lunged toward the cage, his teeth bared in a snarl. Dahr intercepted him, cutting him off with a gesture. "You have seen these attacks?" he asked. "You have witnessed them?"

The Elf frowned. "No," he admitted. "But I have seen the aftermath. And Prince Luran, our *Hohe Chatorra*, has fought the Tribesman. He has seen their murderous rampages firsthand." He glared at Kal. "Who else could it be?"

Dahr stepped closer to the bars, less than a hand away from the Elf. "Listen to my words, Elf, and know them for truth. The Garun'ah do not attack women and children, nor do they torch villages of innocents. The Hunters fight only other warriors, and the defeated are free to seek their own." He turned to Kal. "Tell him."

Kal frowned. "He speaks the truth. No true child of Garun would attack the helpless."

"Why should I believe your words?" the Elf asked skeptically.

"I give you my word," replied Dahr, speaking formally, "as Dahr Odara, of House Odara, raised by the King of Alrendria, who even now has a delegation in the city of Lynnaei at the request of your Emperor." He straightened, sucking in a breath, his name a source of great pride.

Another Elf leaned forward to whisper in her leader's ear. "Jilerin escorted the Alrendrians to Lynnaei," the Elf said, frowning contemplatively. "She claims that your words are true, that you should be trusted." He paused, looked at them. "For some reason, I am inclined to agree with her."

"Good," Dahr answered, the fire in his eyes rekindled. He took one of the arrows in his hand and drove it into the wood of the wagon. "Then tell me what you know of this."

The Elf inspected the arrow. "What do you want me to say?"

"We found this arrow in the body of a Tribesman," Dahr explained, lifting his hand to show them the others. "All along the Danelle, well within the Tribal Lands, there was evidence of fighting."

"Interesting," replied the Elf, reaching out to touch the black shaft.

Kal looked at Dahr angrily. "Why did you not tell–"

Again Dahr waved him to silence. "You claim these are not Aelvin?"

"The runes are Aelvin," replied the Elf. "The arrows are not. These characters are gibberish. They make no sense." He ran his hand the length of the shaft. "And the wood is wrong."

"Why would any other than an Elf carve *Aelva* letters on their weapons?" Kal asked suspiciously.

"I do not know, Tribesman," the Elf admitted. "But then again, why would an Elf? Only the *Noedra Synissti* put runes on their arrows, and they but name the target. Never are the characters nonsensical, like those you hold in your hand." His eyes flashed defiantly. "You captured many of our weapons. Look at them! You will find none inscribed with runes."

Kal frowned, but called to one of the Tribesmen guarding the Aelvin prisoners. In Garu, he asked the man to inspect the Elves' weapons. The Hunter hurried away, to where the Elves' gear was stored.

Dahr described to both Kal and the Elf the signs of battle, the bodies and ruined encampments that they had encountered on their journey to find the Garun'ah. "My people would not venture so far into Tribal Lands," the Elf told them. "We only attack the Tribesmen along the river on orders from Prince Luran. To prevent them from raiding Illendrylla."

"The tribes have no interest in your forests, Elf," Kal replied. "The attacks upon your people were not caused by the Blood."

The guard came running back, calling out excitedly in Garu, then returned to his station. "He says the weapons have no characters," Kal explained, his frown deepening.

"If the Tribesmen were to let you go," Dahr asked suddenly, "would you return to Illendrylla in peace? Would you swear an oath never to lift a blade against the Garun'ah, except in defense of your own lives? Would the other Elves?"

The Elf looked at Kal, then Dahr, considering the proposition. "I would swear such an oath," he said seriously. "As would my companions."

Kal grabbed Dahr by the shoulder, spun him around. "Whether or not these *Aelva* are responsible for the slaughters you saw, they attacked Kraltir and the Channa. You would have me release them to kill again?"

"Have you been so long free of the cage that you forget how it chafes the soul?" Dahr snapped, a thin thread holding his anger back. The words shocked Kal, and the *Kranach*'s eyes lowered. "I have found a way to set these Elves free," Dahr explained. "To guarantee they'll do no harm against the tribes."

"They are *Aelva*!" Kal said, but much of the strength had left his voice.

"They would give their word, and still you would refuse them freedom?" Dahr sneered disdainfully. "You are no better than the Soul-Stealers."

Dahr's words cut deep, and his contemptuous tone was more than enough to evoke the Blood Rage, but Kal did not take offense at the comment. Instead, he stared shamefully at the ground. "What do I know of Aelvin honor?" he asked in a subdued voice.

A tense silence followed. "I am a son of Valia," stated the Elf in the cage. "But I am also *Ael Chatorra*. The Protectors follow the teachings of the Hunter. Our honor is our life."

Kal raised his head and looked the Elf in the eyes. There was a long, tense silence. "Speak your oath, Elf."

"On my honor," the Elf said, raising his eyes toward the heavens, "I swear to return to my lands peacefully, to inform them of what we have learned. On my oath, I will raise no weapon against a child of Garun, save in the defense of my own life, or to protect the Empire."

He looked at Kal. "Is that sufficient?"

Kal nodded and the Elf turned to his companions, and one by one, they made the same oath. After the first wagonload had finished, Kal freed them, leaving Dahr to witness the oaths of the others. He went to the Hunters guarding the Elves; one he sent to find his father, another Yarchik. Several more he ordered to gather supplies for the journey to Illendrylla.

The *Kranach* returned with Katya and Frodel at his side. The two joined Dahr, eager to discover what had happened. By that time, only one of the six wagons had yet to swear the oath. Once their pledge had been given, and they were free of the cage, the Elves were forced into a tight cluster, surrounded by Garun'ah warriors. Only their leader was allowed to stand apart; he came forward to join Dahr and his companions.

Dahr stood with his back to the Elves, facing Kal and the Aelvin warrior. Katya came to his side, and he put his arm around her. Frodel and the other Tribesmen kept their distance, wary, their hands near their weapons.

"You will be given an escort to the river," Kal told the Elf. "Your weapons will be returned when you reach the Danelle."

"It is a good thing you have done this day, Tribesman," the Elf said, his eyes losing some of their suspicion. "I… I thank you." He frowned in thought and swallowed nervously. "I owe you my freedom, Tribesman. Have you a name, so I might know to whom I owe a debt?"

"Kal," came the stoic response. "Kal *uvan* Arik."

"I thank you, Kal *uvan* Arik. Should you ever need aid of the Elves, ask for Nebari el'e Salerian. I would repay this debt."

A small smile touched Kal's lips. "Perhaps you do follow Garun's teachings. I will remember your name, Nebari. You remember your oath."

"I will," he replied, glancing to his left, at Dahr. He ducked his head respectfully, and Dahr returned the gesture.

Suddenly, Nebari's eyes hardened. In one swift, fluid motion, he reached grabbed Kal's *dolchek* and threw it at Dahr.

Chapter 29

Dahr shoved Katya to the side, knowing it was too late to dodge the blade himself. Kal shouted a warning, too late, and grappled with the Elf, who offered no resistance. A cry went up among the Garun'ah even as the dagger flew harmlessly past Dahr, missing his chest by less than a hand's length. He turned, following the blade's flight.

The *dolchek*, with a sickening gurgle, embedded itself in the throat of an Elf who had been running forward. In his hand he clutched a tiny blade, missed during his capture. The blade was raised high, aimed for Dahr's unsuspecting back.

Dahr swung an arm, disarming his attacker, and the Elf fell to the ground, his free hand clutching at his throat. He mewled weakly, blood bubbling around the hilt of the *dolchek*.

The attack enraged the Garun'ah. Weapons, with the singing sound of steel on leather, were drawn, and the Elves were herded into a tight knot. They pressed together, eyes wide, trembling in fear, voices raised in a panicked cry. The Tribesmen advanced, oblivious to the fallen Elf.

Kal's hands were around Nebari's throat. "*Onahrre!*" he spat. "This is what we get for trusting the words of the *Aelva!*" He throttled the Elf, unaware, or not caring, about Nebari's true target.

Nebari, resigned to his fate, made no attempt to fight back. Emerald green eyes stared stoically at Kal.

"Hold!" Dahr shouted to both Kal and the other Garun'ah. "Hold I say! He meant no harm! He killed an Elf with his attack! An Elf!" The gathered Garun'ah slowed their advance, uncertain. Some noticed the Elf, his blade only a finger's length from his lifeless hand, and doubt crept across their faces. Hesitating, they lowered their weapons, if only marginally, and stared at each other, at Dahr, at Kal, no longer sure of what to do.

Kal did not hear Dahr, so lost was he in the Blood Rage. Eyes clouded over with fury, he tightened his grip around Nebari's throat. His murmured words were no longer intelligible; they were audible only as growls.

"Katya, protect the Elves!" Dahr shouted, running toward Kal. She obeyed instantaneously, and to Dahr's surprise, Frodel followed. At his side, Fang growled, and the pack changed direction, forming a semicircle around the Aelvin prisoners. Together, they and Katya kept the Tribesmen away.

Dahr, reaching Kal, seized the *Kranach*'s hands and broke his grip on Nebari. Wrenching a hand free, Kal lashed out in anger, stunning Dahr with a blow across the face. "How can you still side with the Honorless?" he snarled, lunging at Nebari again.

Nebari remained calm, refusing to do so much as shield his face from the Tribesman's claw-like hands. Dahr struggled to hold Kal down, but the *Kranach*, his strength enhanced by anger, could not be overcome. Wincing, Dahr whispered, "Forgive me," as he smashed a knee into Kal's head.

Kal reeled back, stunned, and Dahr was on him in an instant. "He killed an Elf," Dahr yelled repeatedly. "An Elf!" At first, Kal fought ferociously, clawing, scrabbling across the ground, desperate to end the Nebari's life. But in time, Dahr's words sank in, and Kal's breathing slowed. He ceased his struggles, looked across the clearing, and saw the body of the Elf.

He also saw Kraltir trying to force his way past Frodel, inciting the other Tribesmen to attack. "You can release me, Dahr. The Blood Rage has passed." Dahr looked doubtful. "We have a more important problem to deal with, little brother," Kal told him, gesturing with his chin. "I do not have time to convince you of my sincerity."

Dahr turned, groaned when he saw Kraltir, and released Kal. Climbing to their feet, they ran across the camp, jumping over the supine forms of Nebari and the crumpled Aelvin assassin. Ahead of them, Kraltir shoved Frodel aside and lunged at the Elves, his *dolchek* flashing in the sunlight.

Katya intercepted him, grabbed the Tribesman's outstretched arm, pivoted and tossed him. Kraltir landed with a loud crash, the wind knocked from his lungs. The Garun'ah gasped, and a murmur of surprise rose among the crowd.

Kraltir was not impressed. "You dare attack me with your feeble Human tricks?" he spat, climbing to his feet. His *dolchek* was no longer aimed at the Elves, but at Katya's chest. "You will suffer for your insult!"

Katya crouched, drew her sword. "Kraltir!" Kal shouted. "Sheath your *dolchek*. The Elves have not broken oath. You have no reason to call them out."

"They are *Aelva*," Kraltir replied without turning his head. "That is reason enough. And for now, they are not my target. This Human dishonored me. I will win my honor back in blood."

"We want no one hurt," Dahr insisted, and his dogs, in unison, growled at the Tribesman. "Katya meant no dishonor. She was following my order to protect the Elves."

"Whether she meant dishonor or not," Kraltir laughed wickedly, "dishonor she gave. I will enjoy making her pay for it." Katya's eyes flashed, and a smile spread across her face. Licking her lips, she adjusted the sword in her hand and prepared for the fight.

Dahr knew that Katya could take the Tribesman in single combat. Few Guardsmen were more skilled with a sword; even Jeran had been hard pressed to beat her. But the thought of her losing–by mistake, accident, or simply because Kraltir was the better–filled Dahr with an unreasonable fear. "She followed my orders," he repeated sternly. "If you are dishonored, it is by my hand."

Katya's gaze shifted to him, her expression a mixture of anger and love. Kraltir turned slowly; his eyes peered into Dahr's soul. "She is your *bavahnda*?" he asked. "Your woman?"

Dahr laughed. "If any can claim Katya, I can," he said, shaking his head. "Though I am not so foolish as to do so."

Kraltir considered his words. "I accept your challenge, Half-Man." His eyes turned back to Katya, but this time, they appraised her lasciviously, roaming her every curve. "When you lie dead beneath my blade, I will gladly take one with so much spirit to my tent." To Katya, he added, "There are many ways to repay a dishonor. Some are not unpleasant."

Dahr felt his blood boil, but turned to Kal questioningly. "If a Hunter loses a challenge," the *Kranach* told him, "all which is his goes to the victor."

"Absolutely not!" Dahr exclaimed, looking for a way out. Behind him, Frodel stood beside Nebari, was even now helping the Elf stand. "Katya is not mine to give, and if she were, I would still not allow it. Nor would she!"

"You see!" shouted Kraltir. "The Lost One betrays the ways of the Blood. He is no child of Garun!"

"I understand your concerns, little brother," Kal said. "But this has been the way of our people since Garun walked with us. Besides," he added with a smile, "it is not as if you will lose to the likes of Kraltir!"

Kraltir's eyes hardened at Kal's jibe. "Kal's right, Dahr!" Katya said, stepping forward and adding her own assent. "You can't lose to an oaf like this." Leaning in close, she whispered, "And if by some accident you *do*, he'll learn how hard it is to get me to his tent." She sounded almost eager.

"I accept your challenge," Dahr said, turning to Kraltir, who smiled cruelly.

The Tribesman raised his *dolchek* and ran a finger down the length of the blade. "You are weaponless," he commented wryly, sneering at Dahr's empty hands. "What kind of warrior leaves his tent without a blade?"

"I did not think a weapon necessary in a place where I was welcomed." Fang stepped to Dahr's side, baring her teeth. "Go!" Dahr commanded, looking down at the dog. "This is my fight." Fang looked up, whined once, then turned and loped back to join the other hounds.

"Shall I wait while you run to your tents?" Kraltir asked condescendingly, as if speaking to a forgetful child.

"Dahr can meet you with my blade," Kal said, and a startled murmur spread throughout the crowd. The *Kranach* went to the fallen Elf, dropped to his knees, and withdrew the bloodied blade. He offered it to Dahr, hilt first.

"Thank you," Dahr said, waving Kal away, "but I don't need it." His eyes burned with an inner fire. "I would not make this challenge too easy."

Shocked silence filled the clearing. It stretched out, until, at long last, Kal laughed. Deep and rich, the sound echoed, reverberating off the slave wagons. Kraltir's smug expression faded. He hefted his *dolchek* and charged.

Dahr sidestepped easily, using the skills he had acquired under the strict training of Joam Batai. "A sword is a fine tool," Joam used to say, "but in the end it's only a tool. The true weapon is the warrior himself."

Kraltir stopped, pivoted, and charged again. Once again Dahr stepped aside, blocking Kraltir's slash with one arm. With his other hand, he landed a solid blow in the Tribesman's midriff.

Kraltir grunted and spun away. Tossing his blade from one hand to the other, he circled slowly, using the time to regain his breath. Dahr watched him warily, eyes on the blade. Gritting his teeth, Kraltir tightened his grip on the *dolchek* and charged a third time.

Again Dahr dodged, but this time, Kraltir was ready. At the last instant, the Tribesman changed the direction of his attack, his arm coming in low and fast.

Dahr jumped back, frantically blocking, but the move pulled him off balance, and Kraltir slammed an elbow into his back. The Tribesman followed the blow with a solidly-planted knee to the stomach.

Dahr folded, but did not release his grip on Kraltir's blade. Using his momentum, he rolled over his own shoulder, wresting the blade from the Tribesman's grip. Standing, blade in hand, Dahr breathed heavily. He studied Kraltir's *dolchek*, using the moment to regain his own breath.

Kraltir retreated several steps. He stood facing Dahr, his eyes burning with hatred. "You would steal my own weapon and use it against me?" he asked scornfully.

"Is that more dishonorable than fighting an unarmed man?" Dahr replied, trying to maximize his rest. Kraltir's blows had knocked the wind from him, left him unsteady. He looked at the blade again. "Don't worry, Tribesman. I only wish to even the odds." He pressed his thumb against the blade, snapping it at the hilt.

Collectively, the Garun'ah gasped. "You would offer such insult?" Kraltir demanded, his eyes wide and wild. "I only planned to shame you, Half-Man. Now, I will send your soul to Garun!"

"Do you plan on talking me to death?" Dahr asked, tossing the pieces of *dolchek* to the ground, his own anger resurfacing. "I have more important things to do than waste my time on you, Kraltir. If you plan to kill me, then be about it. If you're nothing but bluff and bluster, return to your tent and keep from my sight!"

Enraged, Kraltir let out a violent scream. His hands clenched into fists and he charged, his eyes clouded over with rage. Dahr watched the advance, seemingly without concern. He did not move, nor ready himself for the attack, nor prepare an attack of his own. He merely stood there, watching as the furious Tribesman crossed the distance between them at a dead run. Kraltir snarled, lunged, and launched himself into the air, his hands outstretched.

At the last possible instant, Dahr ducked, grabbed Kraltir by the throat and chest, and stood, heaving with all his strength. The Tribesman flew through the air, arms flapping wildly, and smashed into the side of a slave wagon. The wall caved in with a shattering crash, and Kraltir disappeared.

Voices quickly filled the silence; even the Elves seemed impressed. Katya rushed over to Dahr, the dogs at her heel. They crowded around him, but Katya pressed in closest. "I knew you'd win," she told him, her eyes growing stormy. "I can fight my own battles," she snapped, slapping him hard on the arm. "I'll not warn you again!"

Kraltir climbed from the wagon, blood oozing from a gash on his head. Unnoticed, he dropped to the ground and wrenched loose a jagged chuck of wood. Stomping toward Dahr, he raised the cudgel threateningly.

Kal was first to see him approaching. "Ware, Dahr!" he shouted, and Dahr tensed, instantly alert. Kraltir, grimacing at Kal's forewarning, clenched his cudgel tight and increased his speed to a shambling run.

"Hold, Kraltir *uvan* Yarchik!" a voice thundered across the clearing. The dogs howled at the sudden voice, and the Elves stared at the sky in surprise. The Tribesman, excepting Kraltir and Kal, lowered their heads, touching the fingers of their right hand to their brow.

Kraltir did not stop, though his steps wavered. He continued his advance, raising his club to strike. Dahr prepared to defend himself, and the voice thundered, "Have you no honor, Kraltir? You have been bested. Hold!"

Kraltir stopped, as if frozen in place. He stood there for a long moment, arm raised above his head, eyes furiously burrowing into Dahr. Finally, he released his grip and the cudgel dropped to the grass. "That is better," said the voice, and Kraltir slumped, his arm dropping to his side.

A man, short for a Tribesman and thin, more of a match for the Elves in size, stepped out from behind the wagons. His hair was yellow, the color of the midday sun, and his almond-shaped eyes were deep, vibrant blue. His skin was light tan, but his bones had the harsh angles of the Garun'ah. He wore leathers and hides and had beads and feathers woven through his hair. The tiniest hint of stubble was visible on his chin.

He joined Dahr and Katya, bowing his head formally. "*Jokalla, tsalla'-dar*. I am Jakal, son of Lyt. I am *Tsha'ma*." He looked at the Humans' uncertain expressions, their confusion, and laughed aloud. "You wonder at my coloring?" he asked them, running a hand down his jaw line. "My wild and unkempt beard?"

At their nods, he explained. "I am the Blood of Garun, but some of Balan flows in my veins as well. My greatfather's mother was Human-born." He laughed warmly. "Over the generations, most of the Human traits have been bred out, but the coloring remains."

Again, the finger traced its way down his cheek. "More of an annoyance, this. I cannot understand how Humans live with such things."

Smiling warmly, he turned to Nebari. "Tell me, *Ael Chatorra*, why did your warrior break his oath?"

The Elf shook his head. Confused, he looked at his companions, but they returned his questioning gaze blankly. One warrior spoke in the language of the Elves, smiling, and a nervous chuckle spread among the others. Nebari frowned, and the laughter quickly muted.

A wry smile touched Jakal's face. "I may be short for a Wildman," he said, staring at the Elf who had spoken. "But I assure you, I am not a Human in... How did you put it? Wolf's clothing?"

An anxious whisper sprung up among the Elves. "You speak Aelvin?" Nebari asked, impressed.

"I am full of surprises," Jakal replied, his eyes once more dropping to the body of the Elf. "I am *Tsha'ma*."

Nebari picked up the cue. "I do not know for certain," he replied. "No true *Ael Chatorra* would break an oath once given. Certainly not so blatantly." His frown grew, and he scratched his chin. "May I inspect the body?"

Jakal nodded and Nebari approached the corpse, turned it over, and looked into its eyes. The blood was already darkening, the eyes had glazed over. Sneering, he searched the traitor's pockets, then began to undress the body.

Kraltir spat on the ground, and even Kal looked mildly disgusted. "You would so desecrate the body of one of your own?"

Dahr's brow furrowed in confusion, and Nebari all but ignored the statement. It was Jakal who spoke. "When a riddle presents itself, *Kranach*, discovering the answer is of much importance. In these dark times, with a storm on the horizon, we need answers more than those who walk with the Gods need their honor."

Kal nodded at the sagely words, but Kraltir spat on the ground again. Finally, when the Elf was all but disrobed, Nebari stepped back, his expression one of distaste. "There is our answer," he told them, pointing.

A tiny spider was tattooed on the man's inner thigh. "He is *Noedra Shamallyn*," Nebari said, his nose wrinkling at the word. "Those who would ally themselves with the Darklord."

"You know this from the mark?" Kal asked.

Nebari nodded. "It is said that all of the brotherhood wear such a sign, but the location varies from individual to individual. They need a way to identify themselves to friends, but must keep their identity secret."

"Could these Shadow Knights have another among your people?" Jakal asked, a contemplative frown creasing his face.

Nebari hesitated. "I would think it unlikely," he told them. "The *Noedra Shamallyn* are few. Though a few may skulk in the shadows, I would not believe it possible to find two such vermin in one place."

"But it is possible?" Jakal pressed.

"Yes."

"Is there any way we could find out?" Dahr asked.

"Only by searching for the tattoo," Nebari answered. "Even then, I cannot guarantee such a measure would locate all of the foul creatures." He looked at his troops and hesitated. "I will order them to disrobe, if you would like." Turning to his soldiers, he asked, "Who will submit themselves for inspection?"

At first, only a couple of prisoners volunteered, but after a moment or two, more stepped forward. One or two at a time, cheeks red with embarrassment, mortified expressions on their faces, the Elves slowly agreed, until they all stood together again. "It is the only way to be sure," Nebari told them, sounding apologetic.

"I will not look upon the hideous, naked bodies of the *Aelva*!" shrieked Kraltir.

"Nor would I wish to embarrass your people without just cause," added Jakal in a calmer, friendlier voice. "Long has it been since I shared my days with the children of Valia, but well do I remember their modesty. In public, at least."

Several of the Elves lowered their eyes at Jakal's comment, but none chose to respond. "We could use one of the tents," Dahr suggested. "Nebari, you, and I could have the Elves brought to us one by one, so we could inspect them privately. If they're not *Noedra Shamallyn*, they can be released."

"Wise words, *tsalla'dar*," Jakal stated. "See to it."

"Frodel, line the Elves up and send them to the tent," Dahr ordered. "Katya. Kal. As we release the Elves, take them to the other side of the wagons. Permit no talking until the last of the Elves have been inspected." They nodded in understanding.

"You seem awful eager to undress the Elves," Katya said before walking away.

"I don't look forward to this, beloved."

"I wonder," she mused, casting her eyes at the lithe Aelvin women.

Jakal commandeered a tent for their purposes, and the three of them stepped inside. "Do you wish to inspect me as well?" Nebari asked as they entered the tent; he was already unlacing the ties on his shirt.

Dahr watched him for a moment. "That won't be necessary."

Nebari hesitated. "It is the only way to be certain."

"Nebari," Dahr laughed quietly, "I have no wish to see any of your people disrobed. If they are willing to undress and submit themselves to inspection, we can assume they have no revealing tattoos. If they hesitate...."

Understanding dawned on the Elf, and a smile brightened his features. "Wisdom and cunning," Jakal laughed, nodding his head approvingly. "A dangerous combination. Do not worry, friend Elf. My Gifts will aid us in our search. I will see the truth in the words of your people. If one proves false, I will know of it."

They called for the first Elf, who entered willingly. Without protest, without even waiting to be told, she unlaced her shirt. As it fell to the ground, both Dahr and Nebari averted their eyes, their cheeks flame red. The Aelvin woman's hands fumbled with her pants, and Jakal broke his appreciative stare long enough to say, "Enough! She has nothing to hide."

The Aelvin warrior looked at Nebari in confusion. "We seek a traitor here, Venetia. If you wore the spider, you would not be so quick to show us. Dress, and do not betray what you have learned." She nodded, dressed, and stepped outside, where Kal and Katya intercepted her.

They called for another Elf. And another. The Elves came in one by one, and though some were not as eager as Venetia to remove their clothing, their hesitation was bred of modesty, not treason.

On and on the Elves came, without incident. After more than twoscore had been inspected, a man, thin of frame, with dark eyes, entered the tent, sweat beading on his forehead. "This is ridiculous," he said, his hands on the ties to his shirt. "Nebari, you know I am the Emperor's servant. Why do you let them waste our time."

Nebari frowned. "Do not make this more difficult than it is, Phraetys."

The Elf removed his shirt, and after spinning slowly, so all could see he was unblemished, he reached for the ties to his pants. Licking his lips nervously, he hesitated. "Nebari!" he implored, his face turning red.

"Enough!" said the Aelvin commander. "You will undress and submit to inspection. That is an order, *Ael Chatorra*." Phraetys looked at him forlornly for a moment, then made a dash for the rear of the tent.

Six hands from the back flap, he stopped, frozen in place by Jakal's magic. "I think we have caught ourselves a spider," the *Tsha'ma* said, using his Gift to pull the Elf to the center of the tent. After removing the rest of Phraetys' clothing, Nebari and Dahr searched him. They found a black spider tattooed beneath his left buttock.

"Dress him," Jakal said. "I will use my Gift to hold him in place and seal his mouth. We will examine the others, then discuss what is to be done with this...." He frowned, unable to find the right word to describe the creature before him.

"Traitor!" finished Nebari, glaring at Phraetys with unhidden hatred. Escorting him to the tent's flap, as the *Tsha'ma* had suggested, Nebari handed Phraetys over to Kal, who took him to join the others. The remainder of the Elves were called, but all eagerly proved their loyalty to the Emperor.

Once finished with the last Elf, the three left the tent and went to where the prisoners were lined up. Katya and Kal studied their approach, wondering what was to happen next.

They pushed their way through the Elves, searching for the traitor. Suddenly, Jakal began to laugh. "Here he is!" he called, "but the poor Elf has fainted!" He released his Gift, and Phraetys dropped to the ground.

"A traitor?" asked Kal.

"*Noedra Shamallyn*," confirmed Jakal.

"What would you do with this beast?" Kal asked, turning to Nebari.

"Kill him," Nebari said, his voice half command, half request.

"Kill him," echoed the other Elves.

"He's your traitor," Jakal said to Nebari, "and so the final decision falls to you. But I would ask a favor. Leave him with me. The *Tsha'ma* will discover what he knows. Should we learn anything useful, we will bring the information to the Elves. Perhaps together, we can rid this world of those who would serve darkness."

Nebari reached around his neck and unfastened a golden chain. He pulled the necklace from his shirt, exposing a medallion of finely-wrought gold and silver. "This amulet is my insignia of rank," Nebari said, offering it to Jakal. "Should you learn anything of value, have your messenger wear this as a token of your intentions. With it visible, he will be able to near our lands without being attacked.

"I would caution you not to send him across the Danelle. Prince Luran, the *Hohe Chatorra*, has issued a standing order to kill all Wildmen… Tribesmen, who cross into Illendrylla. I would not want your blood on my hands."

Jakal took the amulet, bowing his head in gratitude. Phraetys' body rose from the ground, lifted by magic, and a dark form rushed toward it.

"This *Aelva* monster must be destroyed!" Kraltir shouted, stabbing with the broken blade of his *dolchek*.

His hand froze a finger's length from the Elf's body. Jakal, his eyes flashing with renewed anger, removed the blade from Kraltir's hand. "I tire of using my Gift to remind you of your honor, Kraltir."

"And I tire of people having to remind you of your honor!" snapped Yarchik. His litter appeared above the crowd, carried on the shoulders of his bearers. "You are given more than ample opportunity, and still you bring dishonor to our tribe."

The *Kranor's* eyes were hurt, angry, and disappointed. "Now you have challenged–and lost–to Dahr Odara, a guest among our people. Your honor and your possessions are forfeit. You have no patience, my son. You have lost your way. Your honor."

Yarchik shook his head sadly. "You will leave *Cha'khun*," he said sternly, "to seek Garun's advice. Go, my son, and seek the Hunter's wisdom."

"Father, you have no right–!"

"Go! Do not return until a full moon has passed. Only then will I listen to your words. Only then will I decide whether to let you rejoin the Blood. Until then, you belong to no tribe."

Kraltir snarled, glared at the crowd, and started to storm away. "Remember, my son," Yarchik said quietly, his voice subdued, "you live because Dahr chose to enter your challenge weaponless. If you force challenge again, he will meet you with *my* blade!"

Kraltir stared daggers at his father, then directed his hatred at Dahr. With a howl of rage, he ran from the camp.

Yarchik turned to Dahr. "I have made you an enemy today."

"It is no matter," Dahr told the withered Tribesman. "Kraltir has already decided I'm his enemy."

"Nonetheless, I side with you, so his rage will only grow. I can do little to repay my debt." He frowned, and his eyes, glistening with tears, were distant. "I know not your message to my people, but I promise my aid in whatever manner you may need."

Dahr flushed. Swallowing nervously, he said, "I thank you, Honored Yarchik."

"It is time for our Aelvin guests to depart," Jakal said, as if the Elves were long time friends and not prisoners. "They have a long road before them."

"Are all Elves as honorable as you?" Kal asked, turning to Nebari.

"No," the Elf replied. "Some are more so, some less." He looked at the unconscious form of Phraetys, and then the tiny silhouette of Kraltir as the Tribesman made his way out of Kohr's Heart. "Perhaps it is the same with both our peoples." Bowing his head respectfully, Nebari smiled. "Peace and long life to you, Kal *uvan* Arik."

Kal gripped the Elf's arm at the elbow. "Good Hunting, Nebari el'e Salerian."

An honor guard ten Hunters strong was called to lead the Elves to the Great Forest. "Let no harm come to them," Jakal cautioned. "Until they walk Aelvin soil, they are your responsibility." The Garun'ah warriors nodded in understanding, and the party started to make their way east.

With the Elves gone and the danger averted, the Tribesmen slowly returned to their daily tasks. Jakal stared at Dahr, his eyes searching, probing. Phraetys hovered at his side. "When the Hunters gather at the heart of the Father," he recited, speaking in measured cadence, "and the tempest threatens unseen on the horizon, shall a pair of spiders seek to destroy what is already lost. When the Blood Rage burns, shall He with one hand cool the fires of the Blood and with the other, fan them to flame.

"Child of one God, raised by another, He shall return the souls of the caged and sow the seeds of forgiveness. At his request shall a son of Garun and a son of Valia set aside their hate and embrace as friends. His coming shall herald the return of *Tier'sorahn*. He shall bathe us in the light of salvation even as He drowns us in blood.

"These are the signs of the coming. These are the signs of *Cho Korahn Garun*. Pray for the *Korahn*, for only through Him shall we hear the voice of Garun. Fear the *Korahn*, for the words of the Hunter are truth. With His voice shall the *Korahn* scour away our illusions.

"Weep for the *Korahn*, for He will carry us to Heaven, or scorch us into the Nothing!"

Chapter 30

"...and so, night after night, season after endless season, I crept through the shadows of the Arkam Imperium, freeing those enslaved by Peitr and his descendants."

Jeran sat in the chair, his hands folded together and pressed against his lips. As he listened to the words, he felt anger stir within him. He sighed, the air hissing against his fingers. "Do you truly expect me to believe all this?" he asked skeptically.

"Whatever do you mean?" Lorthas responded, his arms spread in supplication. The Darklord leaned back, his fire red eyes boring into Jeran.

"You really do!" Jeran said, genuinely shocked. "You really think of yourself as a savior."

"My intentions were honorable!" Lorthas insisted, his words spoken in a practiced, measured tone. "I only wanted to save the Magi, the innocent, from certain death." He paused, and his eyes grew distant. "You never knew the Arkamians, Jeran. They're not the same today as they once were. A brutal, fearsome people. Those whose lives I saved blessed me for my intervention!"

"Of that I have no doubt!" Jeran told him, his voice laced with sarcasm. "But a good deed does not cancel an atrocity. A decade of benevolence, a century of kindnesses, cannot atone for your innumerable evils, Darklord."

"My actions have always been for the good of Madryn!" Lorthas replied, the tiniest hint of frustration breaking through his calm facade.

"Yes," Jeran replied wryly, "I'm sure that's what you believe." He lowered his hands and met the Darklord's eyes with his own steady glare. "I'm not so sure I'd get the same answer from those whose lives you cut short."

"Mistakes were made," Lorthas admitted. "I've told you as much since our first meeting." Sipping his rich, red wine, Lorthas composed himself. "No man is so evil," he recited, "that his soul cannot know redemption."

"You now offer me quotes?"

"From the mouth of High Wizard Aemon himself," replied the Darklord with a smile. "Here is another, from King Makan of Alrendria. 'Even in the darkest night, there is a hint of light. Should one search long enough, he will find the dawn.' "

Jeran stared at him blankly. "Is this supposed to soothe me?" he asked. "Should I now bow to you, Darklord, because you offer me words from the past, spoken by men of greatness?"

"Close your heart against me if you must, Jeran Odara," Lorthas said sadly, "but do not close your mind. I have learned from my mistakes. I will not make them again."

For a moment, Jeran let his anger fade. "I doubt your sincerity."

"Good," came Lorthas' reply. "I would count you a fool if you did not. But if you only doubt, it means my words may yet prove themselves. That's all I want. A chance for the truth to be known."

The Darklord bit his lower lip and shook his head. "I've made many decisions I regret, Jeran. Would that I could take them back and live my life again. Things would be much different." Sighing deeply, Lorthas shoulders slumped, and he look genuinely regretful. "Alas," he lamented, "I do not have such powers. Perhaps not even the Gods have such powers."

They sat in silence; fiery red and cool blue eyes stared at each other across the chamber. "I've heard enough of your forays into the Arkam Imperium," Jeran said at last. "I acknowledge your bravery, sacrifice, and good intentions in saving those hunted by the Arkamians. It's time you continued your story."

Lorthas smiled. "Very well. I had planned on moving on anyway."

"Of course you did."

The Darklord's smile broadened. "Such sarcasm! Such petulance! If I am the monster you believe me to be," he asked, his voice ever calm, "then how can you justify speaking in such a manner? I am the Darklord Lorthas, remember? The Terror of Madryn!"

"By your own admission," Jeran countered, "you cannot harm me in the Twilight World."

"Ahhhh!!!" hummed the Darklord, his eyes flashing merrily. "Then your bravery comes from an overdeveloped sense of security. Does my being trapped behind the Boundary add to your courage? Were this the real world, and we sat across from each other, perhaps you'd be more careful in choosing your tone."

Lorthas laughed, and the sound grated in Jeran's ears. "I should have known as much," he admitted, chastising himself. "People are universally brave when they aren't afraid. The true test of a man's mettle comes when the sword is at his throat." The laughter continued. "You'd be surprised what an honorable man will say–or do!–when his life hangs in the balance."

"Get on with your story, Darklord!" Jeran snapped irritably.

"Children are always so impatient!" Lorthas said to himself, loud enough to be heard, then he bowed his head dramatically. "As you wish, my friend."

"We are not friends, Darklord."

"Of course. My apologies, Jeran."

Shifting in his chair, Lorthas adjusted his robes. "After a decade or two, things in the Arkam Imperium settled. Those with the Gift had escaped or had been murdered. The lost Magi were mourned, honored for their aid, and praised for their unyielding concern–not for themselves, but for the good of Alrendria.

"Such idolatry was not to last," Lorthas said sourly. Beside him, the fire crackled ominously. "Peitr's ideology was like a plague. In less than a century, the Arkamians changed from a tender, caring people into a hateful one. At the end of the Secession, they were oppressed slaves, struggling against a loathsome emperor. In a heartbeat, they metamorphosed into mindless automatons, blindly serving their glorious leader."

Jeran rolled his eyes. "I would hardly compare a hundred winters to a heartbeat."

"No," mused Lorthas. "Of course you wouldn't. But you will. You have the Gift, Jeran. Once you Slow, you'll understand." He sipped his wine, encouraging Jeran to drink as well. "A century may be three or four generations to the commons, Jeran, but to us they pass in an instant. Why, there are times when it feels like I was sealed in my prison but yesterday."

He frowned suddenly, consideringly, then continued his story. "The disease of hatred did not stop at the border of the Arkam Imperium. It slowly spread into Alrendria. As the seasons passed, the hearts of the people there hardened against us, too.

"Oh, it started innocently enough. At first, their fear was little more than a nuisance. They'd hide in the shadows when a Mage walked past, refuse to look us in the eye, or perhaps even tremble when they stood before us, as if waiting for us to unleash our terrible magics on them.

"Do you know how painful it was?" Lorthas asked. "Can you even fathom the feeling? People you spent your life protecting, people to whom you offered your love, your life, regarding you with fear and disgust.

"Eventually, their fear grew beyond mere irritation. The laws of Alrendria, long biased against the Magi, were strengthened. Not in a day, nor even in a century, but they were strengthened nonetheless. Doubtless, the commons who made the changes thought them wise, the next logical step in their protection from the wiles and deviltry of the Magi. Likely, they did not even see what they were doing; limiting our movements, preventing us from governing, turning us into slaves!

"The Magi chose to turn a blind eye to the crimes of the commons," Lorthas added, becoming more animated. His eyes flashed with renewed anger. "Aemon... Always the peacemaker. Always the diplomat. Always the fool! Aemon ignored the signs, refused to see what was going to happen. But I saw. I saw!"

"And you decided to take matters into your own hands," Jeran stated, knowing, almost hoping, he would anger the Darklord.

"I decided to protect my people," Lorthas snapped. "And Aemon, as usual, refused to listen to reason. 'Their fear will pass in time,' he said to me. 'Give them time, Lorthas, and they will see the folly in their ways. They are young, and do not have the benefit of our experiences.'

" 'Does that excuse what they're doing to us?' I demanded. 'What they will do to us if they're not stopped?'

" 'If you fight them, it will only fuel their hatred. We are all Human, Lorthas, equal in the eyes of the Gods. Give them time, I beg you. They will learn we are not monsters. Through our actions, we will teach them!' "

Lorthas' eyes were dead, cold. "I gave them time," he said, his voice a harsh whisper. "As usual, I heeded Aemon's advice, and as usual, the old man was wrong!"

"You don't think highly of High Wizard Aemon?" Jeran asked.

"He is not a god," Lorthas replied. "No matter what the fools outside *Ael Shataq* would make of him. Aemon, your grandfather, is a man, wrong as often as he is right, and uncounted thousands have paid for his mistakes with their lives."

"And *your* hands are clean? You consider yourself Aemon's better?" Jeran asked, trying to hide the tremor in his voice. He wanted to see beyond Lorthas' controlled exterior, but he was afraid of the Darklord, despite the assurances he had received concerning his safety.

At Jeran's words, Lorthas' eyes bulged and his mouth opened, baring small, pointed teeth, but he snapped it closed without speaking. He hid behind his glass and looked at Jeran over the rim, delving deep into his soul. "Aemon was my teacher," he said, his voice calm. "A man of great power and great ideals. But he was a *man*. His faults were numerous, and even he has his biases.

"Were I to choose his greatest weakness, it would be his faith in the spirit of man. He often sees more to a person than what is there. He saw love and innocence in the commons of Alrendria, pacifists and friends among the horde poised to destroy us."

Lorthas paused, smiled slightly, and attempted to sound repentant. "Perhaps," he said modestly, "he even saw more to me than what exists."

"But you did not agree with him?"

Lorthas shook his head. "Aemon and I often disagreed, and on more subjects than just the moral code of humanity."

"So, you do not think all men are equal?" Jeran said, setting his snare .

"I never said– "

Jeran interrupted. "Aemon did not want to force his values onto others. Nor did he wish you to do so. Freedom is the founding ideal of Alrendria."

"They are but children to one who lives as long as a Mage!" Lorthas said, his composure slipping. "They need to be led by the hand, shown the correct path. Who better to show them the path than us?"

"You do not teach, Darklord. You command! You lead through fear. You are–"

"They are sheep!" Lorthas yelled, slamming his glass on the table. It shattered, sending shards flying in every direction; wine dripped from the table like blood. "And like ignorant beasts they follow the loudest voice!"

He stood, pacing between the two chairs. "They are sheep," he whispered again, a measure of his control returning. "And we are lions."

He turned his back to Jeran, facing the fire. "I heeded Aemon's misguided advice, but I also prepared for what I knew would come. Slowly, quietly, I enlisted the aid of those few who would listen, preparing them for the coming storm, when the tides of humanity would wash over the unsuspecting Magi and crush them in their tiny fists."

"And when they did not attack fast enough," sneered Jeran, his voice ice, "you attacked in their stead."

Lorthas feigned surprise, and he almost looked genuinely confused. "Whatever do you mean?" he asked innocently.

"When Alrendria did not turn upon the Magi, when the 'tides of humanity' did not rise up against you, when Aemon's words were shown to be true, it was you who brought death and destruction!"

Lorthas started to speak, but Jeran cut him off. "I have held a piece of Tyrmalin in my hand, Darklord! I have seen your attack with my own eyes." The gaze Jeran leveled on the Darklord was stony. "Tell me, Darklord, and tell me truly, how was the murder of innocents, the destruction of a Mage Academy, for the good of all Madryn?"

Jeran's eyes bored into Lorthas'. "Tell me truly," he asked cynically, "who is the monster?"

"RAHHH!!!" Screaming, the Darklord easily lifted Jeran from his seat and held him at eye level. "Damn that accursed Elf. He, too, poisons you against me!" Jeran tried to cry out, but his voice was frozen. He stared helplessly into Lorthas' eyes, saw flames burning deep within the twin, red orbs.

There was a blinding flash of light, and Jeran found himself lying in a grassy field. The sky above was blue, dotted with white, billowing clouds. Rolling hills of grass, spotted with thick stands of trees, surrounded him. It looked much like the Tribal Lands through which he was traveling.

He sat up, thinking he had awakened, but saw neither Tanar nor Mika. Nor any indication of anyone's passage. Taking slow, deep breaths, he allowed himself to calm, to regain his composure. Looking around, he almost jumped when he discovered he was not alone.

The dark-haired stranger, so familiar to him now, sat behind him, legs crossed, looking disappointed. "Only a fool would goad the Darklord," he said, admonishing Jeran.

"He said he couldn't harm me in the Twilight World," Jeran replied defensively. "He told me it was the truth, so it had to be true." He squeezed his eyes shut, and added a guilty, "I only wanted to break his reserve, to see behind the mask he wears."

"There are many layers of truth, Jeran," the stranger said, "and Lorthas knows how to bend truth to his will." He reached over and patted Jeran on the head fondly. "Your search for truth is admirable, my friend. I do not suggest you give it up, nor should you close your mind to the Darklord's words. Only by seeing all truths can real truth be known.

"And yet...." He paused, frowning, seeking the right words. "You take many risks. And you have no idea how much you risk." He clapped Jeran on the shoulder twice. "Be careful," he advised. "You still have a long path before you."

"Jeran?" asked another voice. "Is this the one taking up all your time?" Jeran turned his head, tensing, but a powerful hand grasped his shoulder, holding him still. "Stand up, child, so I can look at you."

Jeran did as he was told, inspecting the new stranger even as he was inspected. The man was a giant, tall and broad, thick with muscle. Brown hair hung loose and wild down his back; matching brown eyes, nestled between two prominent and angular cheekbones, studied him carefully.

"Kind of small," the man stated, his voice a low rumble.

"He is a giant in that which matters most," came the dark-haired stranger's reply.

"Why is he here?" the giant asked, his eyes still on Jeran.

"He...was meeting somebody."

The giant scoffed. "They still use the Twilight World to relay messages? One would think they'd have developed something better by now." His eyes finally left Jeran, returning to the stranger who was no longer a stranger. "Why do you spend so much time with him?"

"Do you ignore those you have an interest in?"

The giant blushed, and Jeran almost laughed at the sight. "No," he admitted. "You have a point. But if he is so–"

Cocking his head to the side, the giant broke off his speech. "Someone else is coming," he said. Jerking a thumb in Jeran's direction, he added, "I think he is following this one's thread."

The dark-haired man stood. "Best we be on our way, then."

The giant nodded. "And as for you," he said, snapping his fingers in front of Jeran. "Wake!"

Jeran sat bolt upright, momentarily disoriented. He lay on his bedroll, another clear, blue sky, dotted with clouds, above. Shaking his head, he tried to sort the dream from the reality.

Tanar sat beside him, his eyes closed, his expression one of concentration. Mika lay to the side of the camp, curled up tightly in his bedroll, sound asleep.

Tanar stirred; his eyes snapped open. "Who... Wha..." he stammered, unable to find words. "Where did you learn of the Twilight World?"

"Jes told me of it," he said, giving Tanar only half the truth.

The old Mage eyed him skeptically. "Jes may have told you of the Twilight World, but she didn't teach you how to access it. It was never a strength of hers. Did you discover it on your own? Is it yet another talent of yours?"

He waved away those questions. "No matter, we can discuss it at another time. Who was with you? I felt two other presences in your vicinity, but I didn't recognize them." He pursed his lips, his brow wrinkling in thought.

"I don't know who they are," Jeran said honestly. "The one was a stranger to me; I only met him a moment before they felt you coming and sent me away. The other one... He... He helps me sometimes. Keeps me from danger. Guides me. But I don't know who he is."

"There are many dangers in the Twilight World," Tanar warned. "I'm glad someone's keeping an eye on you." He paused long enough to scratch his beard. "You say they sent you away when they felt me coming?"

Jeran nodded, outlining his meeting with the two strangers. "If you insist on visiting the Twilight World, best you remain careful," Tanar warned. "You have little experience there. It wouldn't be hard for someone to harm you, if that were their intention."

"Harm me?" Jeran repeated. "Lorthas said nothing could harm me in the Twilight World. He said it was the truth."

He realized his mistake too late. Tanar's eyes were wide, his mouth hung open in disbelief. "What did you say?" the Mage whispered, his voice nearly lifeless.

Jeran swallowed, tried to work moisture back into a dry mouth. "Lorthas," he repeated in a whisper. "He told me nothing he could do could hurt me in the Twilight World."

Tanar's lips pressed together angrily. His face turned dark red; his eyes burned with a cold, blue flame, and he stared at Jeran with a mixture of scorn, disbelief, and disappointment. "How is it that you've come to speak with the Darklord?"

Jeran told Tanar of his meetings with the Darklord, and though he tried to keep to the barest details, Tanar pressed him for more information. In the end, he told the old man almost everything, keeping only two things secret: the frequency of the meetings and the fact that, despite his distrust and dislike of the Darklord, there were instances when he sympathized with Lorthas and the tragedies he had faced.

Finished, he licked dry lips and waited for the lecture. He did not wait long.

"Are you a fool?" Tanar demanded, his voice going up in volume, his hands tightening into fists. "What were you thinking? *Were* you thinking? He's the Darklord!" Jeran cringed away from the heat in Tanar's voice; the old Mage was nearly yelling.

Not waiting for Jeran's response, Tanar lifted his eyes to the heavens, and reached his arms up imploringly. "What have I done?" he demanded. "Is this a punishment for some crime I'm not aware of. Am I to be surrounded by ignorant, stubborn, willful children all of my life?"

"Tanar–" Jeran started, but the Mage did not let him speak.

His eyes returned to Jeran, his prayer cut short. "What could possibly possess you to listen to the lies of that monster?" he asked, sounding hurt and betrayed.

"You did."

The words stunned the old Mage. "I did?" he repeated, confused.

"A long time ago," Jeran smiled, almost enjoying turning the table on the old man, "you told me how time has a way of biasing history. You told me to listen to all sides of a story before passing judgment." Jeran shrugged. "What story could be more biased than that of the Darklord?"

"And do you... Do you believe his story?" Tanar asked nervously.

"Do I believe Lorthas is a misunderstood martyr, wrongfully imprisoned?" Jeran shook his head. "But I understand, or am beginning to understand, why he did what he did. There are times when I understand his motives, and even times when I sympathize with him.

"But I still don't believe he was justified," Jeran finished, offering a smile. "And, as Joam and Lord Iban always say, 'Knowing your enemy is the first step in defeating him.' "

Tanar let out a huge sigh. "*I* convinced him to listen to the Darklord!" he muttered, massaging his temples and again lifting his eyes toward the sky. "Why do my words always come back to haunt me?"

Jeran smiled. "They were good words," he said, trying to appease the Mage. "Very wise."

"Why do my *sagely* words," Tanar amended, "always come back to haunt me?" He looked at Jeran. "You will persist in this foolishness?"

Jeran frowned in thought. "Can he really harm me?"

"If he says he cannot, then he is bound by the rules. But there are many dangers in the Twilight World."

"If he can't hurt me," Jeran answered, "then I will continue meeting with him. I may learn something vital during our talks."

Mika stirred, stretched, and sat up. "Morning!" he called jovially. "Is it time to go, Lord Jeran?"

Jeran nodded, but it was Tanar who spoke. "After some breakfast, my boy!" His anger, fear, and anxiety disappeared, as if they never were, and he stood, grabbing Mika and hefting the boy from his blankets. "You're getting heavy!" he said, groaning. "Either that, or I'm getting old."

Mika laughed, and Jeran smiled, remembering his own mornings with Tanar. "Will you tell a story while we eat?" Mika asked, and the old man agreed, whisking the boy away to prepare the meal.

As Jeran watched them laughing and playing, he was suddenly transported to a time long past. A time when he, Aryn, and Tanar had spent long days at the farm in Keryn's Rest. His eyes filled with water; a tear threatened to fall. Steeling himself, he wiped a hand across his face, and hearing Mika's call, hurried to join the others.

The day passed as so many before it. They rode in relative silence, awed by the stark beauty of the Tribal Lands. At every turn, a new sight confronted them; the crest of every hill offered new wonders. The forests teemed with animals, some the likes of which Jeran had never before seen.

Tanar identified most of the things they saw, his knowledge almost limitless. He spent days pointing out plants and animals to Mika, instructing the child in their uses. In the evenings, he told story after story, and Mika was rapt, entranced by Tanar's skill at weaving words.

Despite the idyllic setting, Jeran was concerned. They had been long in the Tribal Lands and had yet to see any sign of the Garun'ah. Dahr was in danger, Aemon's letter had said as much, and yet he seemed no closer to finding the Tribesmen than when he stole through the gates of Lynnaei in the dead of night.

He had only Tanar's word to assure him that they were going in the right direction. "The Garun'ah are only seen when they want to be," the old man had told him. "They could be here, now, and you'd never know it."

Late one day, with the sun sinking in the western sky, Tanar grew troubled. Signaling a halt, he dropped into the waist-high grass and began to inspect the ground. "Something's wrong," he told them. "There's evidence of passage here. The passage of many people."

The Mage scanned the sky. "It's too early for the tribes to be moving to the winter lands." His eyes glazed over, and he sent out his perceptions.

Jeran dropped from his saddle and put a hand on his sword. He had not seen Tanar this disconcerted since the flight down the Anvil. Mika looked at him and started to climb from his saddle, but Jeran waved for him to stop. "If something goes wrong," he told the boy, "you are to return to Illendrylla. Let them know what happened."

Mika looked as if he wanted to protest, but held his tongue. Tanar shifted suddenly, blinking his eyes in surprise. "What is it?" Jeran asked.

"Trouble," came the response. "I think...." Taking a deep breath, he shook himself back to reality. "Quick! On your horse! We might still be able to elude–"

A rustling in the grass cut off his statement. Shadowy forms suddenly appeared all around them, encircling them, cutting off all escape. The Garun'ah were streaked with multi-colored paint, their chests bare, even the women wore only a minimum of clothing. Jeran's hand went to his sword, and Tanar waved frantically for him to stop.

A spear dug into the ground at his feet. "Keep hand from weapon, Human," said one Tribesman in a deep, bass voice. He turned to his companions and spoke in *Garu*.

Another Garun'ah, this one a woman, stepped forward, circling Jeran, drawing a hand around his body. "This one is solid, for child of Balan." Her gaze was appreciative. "I will take sword, Human."

As Jeran undid his sword belt, a third Tribesman blew a horn, long and low. They were led up the hillside, not treated as prisoners, but not treated as guests either.

On his horse, Mika was the first to see. His eyes widened and his mouth dropped open. A few steps later, Jeran saw, too, and his reaction was much the same.

Below, from east to west, thousands of Tribesmen filled the valley, traveling north. Wagons, laden with wares and grains, trundled north, pulled by slow moving oxen. Small bands, presumably scouts, broke off from the main body, disappearing into the wilds in search of game and enemies.

One small group was not going north. It headed south, toward them, at a slow walk. Jeran, Mika, and Tanar were brought to a stop before the small party of Garun'ah, and one, a barrel-chested man with raven black hair and dark eyes, stepped forward. He wore no shirt, despite the chill in the evening air. A scar, a series of claw marks, ran the length of his chest, disappearing into the hides around his waist.

He looked at the party of Humans, traveling north through lands not their own, and said. "I Sadarak *uvan* Zharik, *Kranor* of Afelda, called Cat's Claw among Humans. Who you, and what bring you to Tribal Lands?"

Tanar was the one to speak. He gave their names first, bowing formally. Sadarak's eyes shifted from one to the next as the Mage introduced them. "We are in search of the Tacha," Tanar explained.

"What business have you with Tacha?"

"We have friends among the Tribesmen," Jeran answered, "and carry a message of much urgency."

Sadarak's eyes took them all in. "Do you mean to harm Blood?" he asked, his expression grave.

"Ever have the children of the Twins been like brothers themselves," Tanar replied. "Should any of my party shed the Blood of Garun without cause, my blood will flow beside it."

Sadarak stared at Tanar with newfound respect. "You know the rite?" To his companions, he said, "The Humans have yet to forget old ways completely!" The statement earned smiles from the other Tribesmen.

"You in luck, children of Balan," Cat's Claw said. "Afelda go to *Cha'khun*. I give sanctuary. You travel with us to meet Tacha."

"May you spill the blood of your enemies," intoned Tanar formally, "and bring honor to the Great Hunter."

"May blood of Twins forever be one," Sadarak replied, bowing his head in completion of the ritual.

Chapter 31

"Kal!" Dahr yelled, jogging across the camp, and the *Kranach* of the Tacha looked over his shoulder. A broad smile split his face when he saw Dahr. "Kal! There's something I'd like to talk to you about."

"Greetings, little brother!" the Tribesman replied, waving Dahr over. Olin, bare-chested and sun-bronzed, stood with him, a spear in his hand. "I have good news! Olin asked me to be his *chanda*, and I have accepted."

"*Chanda*?" Dahr repeated, the word stirring memory. He scrunched up his face, puzzled. "It means brother, right? But not a brother. A friend so close he's like a brother."

Kal nodded, beaming from ear to ear. "You see, Olin. His *Garu* progresses. Dahr is a quick learner." The other Tribesman nodded, but remained silent.

"Didn't you have a *chanda*?" Dahr asked, and Kal's eyes dimmed.

"Calor," he answered sadly. "Calor *uvan* Renar."

"A fine warrior," Olin added.

"Calor and I were *chanda* since we were cubs," Kal explained. "Long before Garun led Olin back to the Blood. I owe him my life a hundred times." He shook himself, shrugging off his melancholy; his smile returned in full force. "I can never replace Calor," he admitted. "Nor would I want to. But while we should honor those who walk with the Gods, we should not bury ourselves with them.

"Every man should have a *chanda*," Kal continued, looking pointedly at Dahr. "One who knows his every secret. One he could never betray, or be betrayed by. I would have asked you, little brother, but I sensed your bond belongs to another."

Dahr smiled, his thoughts on Jeran. "Is there a ceremony? How do you become *chanda*?"

Olin laughed. "It is not a thing which must be witnessed by the tribe!" he said. "There is only the Asking, the Exchange, and the Oath."

"The exchange?" prompted Dahr.

"Once one is asked to be *chanda*," Kal explained, "the two exchange items of great personal value, a symbol of their shared soul."

"Then they share an oath of loyalty," Olin added, "and seal their pledge with blood."

"What did you exchange?" Dahr asked, then blushed. "I don't mean to pry."

The Tribesmen laughed warmly. "You redden like a maiden after her first courtship dance!" Olin said. "Are all Humans so easy to embarrass?"

"You do not ask a private question," Kal assured Dahr, "if that is what worries you. I gave Olin my spear, the one I used on my first hunt. It was fashioned by Hruta, my greatfather."

"And I gifted Kal a string of beads," Olin added, pointing at the multicolored string of beads around Kal's throat, "given to me in welcome when I rejoined the tribes."

Olin looked from Kal to Dahr and back again. "It is time I returned to the Hunt." He ran off, moving gracefully through the tent city, disappearing in the distance.

"It is well you are here," Kal said, turning to Dahr. "There is one who would see you." He started to walk away. "Come, Dahr!" he exclaimed, turning to look over his shoulder. "Time waits for none of us."

Dahr hurried to follow. When he was at Kal's side, the *Kranach* asked, "What is it you wish to discuss?"

"The other day...." Dahr paused, unsure of how to phrase his question. "Jakal said...things...after the Elves departed. About spiders and blood, and...and the *Cho Korahn Garun*. What did he mean?"

"Who can see into the mind of *Tsha'ma*?" Kal asked jovially. "None but the Wise Ones know why they do any of the things they do. Our place is not to debate their meaning, but to...." He trailed off, a smile spreading across his face. "You do not care what Jakal intended with his statement, do you, little brother? It is the words themselves you do not understand."

Dahr nodded and Kal tried, unsuccessfully, to suppress a laugh. "I forget you were not raised to our ways. You do not know of the *Prah'phetia*?"

"I have heard the word," he told the Tribesman, shaking his head, "but don't know its meaning." Around them, Kohr's Heart beat with activity. The Channa had erected their tents above the Tacha, forming a second ring around the lake, and a few of the smaller tribes had come since their arrival; all together, they half filled the valley with multi-colored tents. The only region uninhabited was along the stream that cut through the eastern wall of the depression and later joined the waters of the Danelle.

The Tacha, Channa, and smaller tribes had merged together seamlessly; to the untrained eye, they appeared as one large tribe. Hunters ranged across the plains and forests, the warriors of the tribes often intermingling, searching both for food and signs of enemies approaching the valley. Those who remained in the camp shared the chores: preparing the meals, mending and making garments, and caring for the young and old. Dahr doubted he would see such cooperation if a group of Alrendrians mixed with a group of Tachans. Or even with a group of Gileans.

"The *Prah'phetia* is the Word of Garun," Kal began, wending through the tents in the direction of the lake. "Given to us long before the time of the Darklord. It has been passed down from generation to generation, father to son, since the day it was first spoken."

The Tribesman stopped, and his eyes shot to the left. Dahr followed the gaze and spotted a large raven, roosting atop a tent. The bird stared at them with black, dead eyes. "A bad omen," Kal stated. "Ravens are carrion birds. Their presence presages death."

Dahr frowned and looked closely at the bird. "He's just hungry. Look how flayed his feathers are, how sunken his chest. Doubtless, he's hoping to find a scrap or two of food."

Kal looked at Dahr, grunted an unintelligible response, stooped, and picked up a rock. Casually, he flicked his arm, and the rock hit the raven square in the chest. It squawked and took to the air, leaving behind a trail of loose feathers. "One should never leave ill portents in his wake," the Tribesman explained, resuming his walk.

He continued the story. "The children of Garun strive to serve the Balance. It–"

"The Balance?" prompted Dahr.

Kal nodded. "The Balance. Nature." He swept his arm out, a gesture that encompassed the entire valley. "All of nature is in balance. The plants gain life from the sun and soil and are then eaten by the grass animals. These are eaten by the hunters, which, in turn, become prey to even larger hunters. When an animal dies, its spirit goes to the Heavens, but its flesh returns to the earth to feed the plants. And thus the cycle starts anew.

"But nature is a system made of countless parts, each part a system in itself, made of still smaller parts, and any change has untold effects on the whole. The larger the change, the more parts it encompasses, the greater the threat to the Balance.

"You must forgive me," Kal said, lowering his eyes in shame. "I do not mean to speak cryptically. The ideas are clear in my mind, but I find it hard to change my thoughts into the man-tongue. If my words are simple, it is my failing, not yours."

He took a deep breath, and his brow furrowed in concentration. "When we look at nature," he continued, "we can see the Balance. If you listen, you can hear its song. At times, the sound is beautiful, harmonious. Other times it is little more than noise.

"Of all the Races, the Garun'ah are most attuned to the Balance. We can see, almost feel, nature's pain when the Balance is disrupted. My father calls it the Voice of Madryn."

"I have heard him speak of it," Dahr replied. "But what has this to do with the *Prah'phetia*?"

"A moment, little brother," Kal said, turning aside. A Tribesman stepped from the shadow of a tent, calling out to Kal; a dog, teeth bared, eyes wide, stood at the Hunter's side.

Kal answered the Tribesman, then turned to Dahr. "Good news, Dahr. The Afelda have been spotted. They will arrive when the moon shines her full face upon us."

The Tribesman spoke again, and Kal frowned. He dropped to his knees and looked at the dog. "Dahr, Tupak says there is a problem with his hound. I see nothing wrong, but you have spent much more time around animals."

Dahr knelt beside Kal and put one hand on the dog's head; the other went under its chin. He looked the beast in the eye, and it whined, once, then calmed and allowed Dahr to stroke its head. Frowning, Dahr leaned in close, and opened the dog's mouth. Fearlessly, he reached inside, probing with his fingers, a grim look of determination on his face. Grating his teeth together, he closed his fingers around something and yanked.

The dog yelped, but instantly fell silent, and Dahr held up a jagged piece of bone. He looked at it for a moment, then offered it to the Tribesman. To the dog, he said, "Be more careful when you're eating."

He looked at Kal, who was staring at him consideringly. "Just a bone," Dahr told him. "Tell Tupak to find soft bark and scrub the inside of the dog's mouth gently each night for five days. There may be blood, but if it's more than a little, he's brushing too hard." As Kal relayed the message, Dahr stood and brushed his hands clean.

They continued walking. "When the Gods walked among us," Kal said, diving back into his story, "they instructed us to maintain the Balance. However," he added with a frown, "each race took their own view on how best to follow the Gods' decree.

"The Orog allowed the Balance to shift at will, fighting against only those changes so dire they threatened all of nature. The *Aelva* tried to force nature into their own view of the Balance, their own narrow interpretation of beauty." Kal's face grew stormy, and his eyes sought Dahr's. "Nature does not like to be forced. It struggles against all bonds.

"Humans," he added hastily, before he drifted further off subject, "all but ignored the Gods' command. As Balan instructed, they sought truth and knowledge, often without considering the effect their actions had on the Balance.

"Only we, the children of Garun, sought to preserve the Balance." His voice was full of pride. "Only we struggled against the threat to nature, fought to preserve the old ways."

"But what does this have to do with the *Prah'phetia*?" Dahr asked again.

"After the War of the Blood, what Human's call Aemon's Revolt, when the Drekka first strayed from the teachings of Garun and allied themselves with the Darklords, the *Tsha'ma* were visited by Garun. 'There will come a time when my Blood will turn from those in need," He told them. "They will forget the oaths made to their brother race and stray from the Balance. Darkness shall sweep the land, and a blight will befall the Races of Madryn. In the end, you will destroy the Balance, choosing between two great evils.'

" 'Surely, Master,' cried the *Tsha'ma*. 'It cannot be. Never would we turn from Your word.'

" 'It *will* be,' Garun answered. 'The seeds have already been sown. When the darkness comes, it falls to you, my Voice, to lead the Blood down the correct path.' "

Kal's face darkened. "And the God's words did come to pass. When Lorthas' icy touch first befell Madryn, the Tribes ignored the cries from their Human brothers. They refused to lend aid when the might of the tribes, combined with the armies of Alrendria, may have been enough to halt the Darklord.

"As Lorthas' power grew, as he gained allies from every land, still did the Garun'ah do nothing. My ancestors felt it was a Human problem, best solved by Humans. Even when the Drekka allied themselves with the Darklord, the tribes did nothing. 'If they raid against the lands of Man,' one *Kranor* was heard to say, 'they will leave us alone for a time.'

"It was not until Baele, daughter of Yatchak, was stolen from the Channa did the tribes come together. In their search for Baele, Jolam Strongarm and Batael *uvan* Yatchak learned of the Drekka's treachery and called *Cha'khun* to warn the Blood. If not for their sacrifice, the tribes would have been destroyed, and the Darklord's grasp on Madryn would have been all the stronger.

"In the end, we were forced to make a terrible choice, just as Garun had predicted. We could allow Lorthas dominion over Madryn, or we could raise the Boundary and trap the Darklord in *Ael Shataq*."

Kal looked ashamed, though not even his father's father had been alive at the time of the Raising. "We chose the Boundary. We desecrated nature. Destroyed the Balance. The world trembled for seasons after. Weather changed. Rivers flowed where, once, dry grassland grew. Old mountains crumbled, and new ones rose. In less than a four-season, we reshaped the face of Madryn."

They reached the edge of the tents, which came to an abrupt stop a thousand hands from the lake's edge. Garun'ah dotted the shore. Some fished, others washed clothes. In the shallows, a few children played, swimming through the crystal-clear waters like fish.

A quiet rumbling shook the ground, and as Dahr watched, the center of Kohr's Heart exploded in a fountain of water, spraying droplets across the lake. The children shrieked with joy as the water splattered around them, landing with the sound of raindrops.

Kal stopped walking and peered up into the slate grey sky. "But I still don't understand," Dahr stated. "This story has nothing to do with what Jakal said!"

"You have little patience," Kal commented, then shrugged. "Perhaps it is a Human trait. When one lives so few winters, time must be precious."

Kal dropped to one knee, stared at the lake, and pointed. "Look there, Dahr," the *Kranach* ordered. "By the young ones. There, by the shore, is a *bahver*, Garun's engineer, the one who builds bridges and dams. He is very near the children, and the *bahver* are known for having a short temper." He picked up a rock, testing its weight. "I will scare it away."

Dahr's hand restrained him. "She's only guarding her den," he said, taking the stone from Kal's hand. "Look at the way she keeps her eyes on the children, but makes no move to leave the edge of the lake. She won't bother them unless they come near her young ones."

Kal looked at Dahr, his face serious. "Perhaps you are right, little brother." He started toward the water, beckoning for Dahr to follow. "Come. We still have a little way to go."

Kal led him to the edge of the lake, where a raft of timbers, held together with vines, waited for them. A long paddle sat at the rear of the raft. Kal motioned for Dahr to climb aboard, then hopped onto the raft, which sank slightly under their combined weight. As a thin film of water rushed over the top of the timbers, Kal hefted a long, wooden pole and pressed it down against the lake's sandy bottom.

After stabilizing the craft, he set aside the pole and took up a paddle. As the Tribesman guided them out onto the lake, Dahr stared at the tranquil waters. Sighing deeply, he crouched in the rear of the raft and dipped his hand in the water. "It's warm!" he said in shock.

"And gets warmer near the center," Kal informed him. With slow, rhythmic strokes, he paddled toward the center of Kohr's Heart. Dahr lay back and relaxed, allowing the gentle sway of the raft to unknot the muscles in his shoulders. He waited patiently for Kal to continue.

"The tribes were punished for their failure to aid the Humans," Kal said, continuing his tale. "We were decimated in the MageWar. Of all the Hunters sent to battle Lorthas, only one in five returned. But the loss of our warriors was not the worst the punishment meted out by our God.

"Garun had the ability to see inside the minds of the lesser creatures," Kal explained. "He could hear their thoughts, commune with them as with men, understand their fears. Through their eyes, he saw the Balance, heard the Voice of Madryn clearer than any.

"When He left our world to walk the Heavens, Garun chose some of his favorite disciples and gifted them with the ability, that the Blood would always be able to preserve the Balance. The *Tier'sorahn*, Those Who Hear the Smaller Voices. As the *Tsha'ma* are the Voice of Garun, so are the *Tier'sorahn* the Voice of Nature.

"When the tribes turned against His teachings, Garun took away his gift." Kal sounded dispirited, as if the crime were not his ancestors', but his own. "Less than ten winters after the Raising, the last *Tier'sorahn* joined Garun in the Twilight World."

A small island appeared before them, rising from the center of the lake. Dahr frowned at Kal's words. "But Jakal said—"

"The story is not over, little brother," Kal chastised. "There is another part of the *Prah'phetia*. Garun prophesied that a time would come when darkness once again threatened the land. The tribes would be given a chance to atone for their sins, to right what they had wronged.

"It was said that *Cho Korahn Garun*, the Spear of Garun, would come before the darkness to lead the Blood." Kal closed his eyes, and his words took on a measured quality as he recited a portion of the *Prah'phetia*. "The *Korahn* will bind the tribes together, even as He tears the Blood apart. He will remove the veils from our eyes, the clouds from our minds, and make us see the truth. He will lead us into the darkness, a shining beacon of light, and we will follow blindly."

Dahr shook his head, his forehead creased in puzzlement. "But Jakal made it sound as if this *Korahn* would destroy you!"

A frown marred Kal's features. "Though the *Cho Korahn Garun* is the Hunter's messenger, he is yet a man. It is said that two paths lead through the darkness, one to salvation and the other to the Nothing. Which path the *Korahn* chooses is yet to be determined, but his fate will be the fate of all Garun'ah."

Dahr felt more confused than before he had asked his question. "How will you know when the *Korahn* has returned?"

"The *Prah'phetia* lists a thousand omens that signal the coming of the *Cho Korahn Garun*. The *Tsha'ma* watch for those signs, and have told the Blood that the *Korahn* will soon come.

"One of the most important signs of the *Korahn* is the return of *Tier'sorahn*." Kal cleared his throat and quoted, "Those Who Hear the Smaller Voices, Lost since the Balance was broken, shall come ere the darkness. The return of *Tier'sorahn* heralds the arrival of the *Cho Korahn Garun*. And He shall run from the Voice of Nature, though He denies his own blood in doing so.' "

The sandy island, with birds roosting on tufts of long, dark green scrub grass, loomed ahead of them. Small, dwarven trees with gnarled branches grew in the black and white-speckled dirt. Suddenly the birds took to the sky, and a low rumbling follows their flight.

"There is dissension among the *Tsha'ma* as to the meaning of the quote." Kal admitted, ignoring the rumble. "Some claim the *Korahn* will be *Tier'sorahn*, and will deny himself. Others claim he will denounce the *Tier'sorahn*, refusing his place as our savior."

The rumble built to a crescendo, and Kohr's Heart erupted, shooting a geyser of hot water hundreds of hands in the air. Dahr ducked reflexively, but could not dodge the shower of air-cooled water that rained upon him. When the waters settled, and the geyser was again quiet, he turned to Kal and asked, "Some of your people think *I* am the *Korahn*?" It was only half a question.

"Some," Kal admitted.

"Does Jakal think I am?"

"The words of Jakal were from the *Prah'phetia*. He believed the events of the other day satisfied a key passage of Garun's prophecy. As to whether or not he thinks you are the *Korahn*...." Kal refused to answer.

"Do you?" Dahr prompted.

The *Kranach* frowned. "It is hard to say, little brother. You fit much of what we know of the *Korahn*, and the signs all point to his return. Let us say that I am not yet convinced you are not."

Kal steered the raft through the shallows, and when the bottom bit into the bottom of the lake bed, the Tribesman pressed hard with the paddle, driving it a short distance onto the shore. Dahr looked at the barren little island. "I thought you said someone wanted to see me!"

"In a moment, little brother," Kal answered, starting toward the island's center at a fast walk.

Dahr followed, stopping at the edge of a small pool, dark and deep, nearly twenty hands across. Steam rose from the placid surface. "Do not stand too close," Kal warned. "More than one warrior has suffered burns from the blood pumped by Kohr's Heart."

Dahr dropped to one knee and touched his fingertip to the water. He retracted it quickly. "Aren't we in danger if the geyser erupts?"

"Only near its edge. If we stand on the edge of the island, we will only be showered with warm water."

"Why have you brought me here?" Dahr asked, looking at Kal suspiciously. The Tribesman ignored the question and turned his back, walking away, circling the island. Dahr hurried over and put a restraining hand on Kal's shoulder, but before he could pull the *Kranach* around and demand some answers, he saw a strange sight, and it left him speechless.

In unison, five birds landed on the speckled sand not more than twenty hands away. They stood in a line, each two hands distant from its neighbors. A golden eagle stood at each end of the line. Between them, from left to right, stood a hawk, an owl, and a raven. "That's strange," Dahr murmured, looking at the birds curiously.

"Tell me, little brother. Why do these creatures stand before us? What thoughts run through their minds?"

"How should I know?" Dahr laughed.

"Humor me," Kal said, his eyes boring deep into Dahr. "Take a good, long look and tell me what they think."

Dahr thought it a strange request, but he shrugged, dropped to his knees, and stared at the birds. He pointed to his left. "The eagle was hunting game," he said with a shrug, "and thought he saw something worth eating down here. The owl...."

He paused, gazing at the bird's snowy white feathers, and pursed his lips, surprised to see an owl about at this time of day. Dahr sighed, not enjoying the guessing game. "The owl is tired," he said at last, saying the first thing that popped into his head, "not sure why it has to be here while the sun is up.

"The raven," he continued, with a mocking smile at Kal, "is angry with you for throwing the stone." Dahr doubted that it was the same bird, but he could not resist the chance to poke fun at his Garun'ah friend.

"And the other two?" Kal prompted. "The hawk and second eagle?"

Dahr stared at them for another moment, then shook his head. "Why do birds do anything?" he asked. "They're probably here for the same reasons as the others."

"Hmm," grunted Kal. "But why do you *think* they are here?"

Dahr was silent for a moment. "They…needed…to be here. For something." He was confused as he brought his eyes back to Kal, not quite sure where the words had come from.

Kal stared at him for a long moment. "I am satisfied," he said at long last, turning to face the birds. "Are you?"

There was a shimmering in the air above the birds, and when the golden light faded, Jakal and Rannarik stood where the hawk and eagle had been. Jakal smiled at Dahr knowingly, and Rannarik stepped forward, extended an arm in greeting.

"Rannarik!" Dahr exclaimed. "It's good to see you again!" He started forward at a fast walk, but Kal's words brought him to a sudden stop.

"You may not be the *Korahn*," the *Kranach* told him. "But you are most certainly *Tier'sorahn*."

Chapter 32

"*Tier'sorahn*?" Dahr shook his head and laughed out loud. "No... No...That's silly, Kal. I've just spent a lot of time with animals. I know their moods." The birds took to the air in a wild flapping of wings; each flew in a different direction.

"Can you truly not see it, little brother?" Kal asked, his brow furrowed in confusion. "For quite a while I suspected that you heard the voices of Garun's first children, but the *Tier'sorahn* were gone long before my birth. I had only our legends and stories on which to guess.

"So I asked Rannarik," he added, pointing to the *Tsha'ma*, "who lived during the MageWar, who lived with *Tier'sorahn*. He and Jakal designed a test for you."

"Test?" Dahr repeated, dumbstruck.

Rannarik answered. "Jakal and I studied you closely these last few days. We observed you among the animals, watched you listened to them, heard how you spoke to them." He smiled broadly, exposing a set of white, slightly-pointed teeth. "You have Garun's blessing! You can hear the lesser voices!"

"And the creatures of Madryn can hear you too," Jakal added. "Your dogs, have you not noticed how they obey your every command, no matter how complicated?"

"They are well trained," Dahr replied, unwilling to believe.

"Perhaps," mused Jakal. "But training can only accomplish so much. Have you noticed how the dogs sense your mood, and respond to it, even when you are not near?"

"You have a gift," Rannarik added. "A skill which exceeds even the best trainers in the Human lands. You have said so yourself. Is it not possible that your skill stems from an ability to hear the thoughts of your lesser cousins? Can you not understand their fears?"

"Remember the stag?" Kal asked. "It knew you were watching even before you began the hunt." Dahr tried to turn away, but the *Kranach* grabbed his shoulders and held him steady. "The child's dog? You located its injury without examining the beast!"

"The test," Jakal stated, continuing the onslaught. "You knew the raven hungered."

"You sensed the problem with Tupak's hound!"

"You knew the *bahver* protected its young."

"And that it would not harm the children."

"The birds!" Jakal said finally. "You heard the birds; you knew why they had come. But you could not read a thought from Rannarik and I," he added, "even though we were in bird-form."

"You can speak with them too!" Dahr said, pointing an accusing finger at the *Tsha'ma*. "You called them here. You made them stand in line!"

The two Tribesmen shared a glance. "Rannarik and I wished to test you, true," Jakal admitted. "We had hoped to learn if you could tell the difference between a true animal and a *Tsha'ma* in animal form."

"The eagle, Varhatip, is a friend of mine," Rannarik said. "I spent many seasons training him, but I cannot read his moods, nor hear his thoughts. He came at my command, but not at my request."

"The raven and the owl came of their own accord," Jakal added. "As you said, they came at your call. You needed them to show you the way."

Rannarik smiled. "To prove you were *Tier'sorahn*."

"No!" Dahr snarled, clamping his hands over his ears. Cowering from the resolve, the conviction in the Tribesmen's faces, he dropped to his knees, trembling, and squeezed closed his eyes. "No... No... No...!" He repeated the word in a quiet murmur, a thousand images running through his head.

He remembered Aryn's farm, and the time he spent with the animals. He remembered how good he felt in the presence of the farm animals.

He remembered Thunder, the great bull. There were times when he had almost believed he could hear what the bull was thinking. Times when he was sure he saw curiosity, or humor, or anger in Thunder's dark eyes. *Was it my imagination? Or could it have been....*

He remembered Jedelle, Aryn's noble warhorse. Long evening walks, just he and the horse, talking to her, telling her of his day, and how happy he was to have finally found a home. It had seemed like she had almost understood his words.

The night she died, he remembered as well, and even after all these winters, it rent his heart. He heard her labored breathing, saw her tired, cloudy eyes. He had cried out that night, not wanting her to go, but Jedelle had nuzzled him gently, using the last of her strength. It was as if she were telling him she was ready, that he should not grieve for her.

Deer. He saw a herd of deer, saving him and Jeran from the Durange. *Did they happen upon the scene, or did they come at my call?*

His seasons in Kaper flashed by in an instant. His time spent in the stables, kennels, and aviary. The frightened animals that calmed at his approach; the wild stallions that ceased their struggles when he appeared.

A distant memory, a story he had once heard. An eagle, soaring above the an infant child. An eagle that led a lonely trapper to that child, saving it from it from certain death, and blessing the man and his barren wife with the son they always wanted.

A falcon attacking a slaver, protecting a frightened boy.

A mountain cat giving a young man the chance he needed to escape.

Dogs and horses and wolves and bears. *How much can be coincidence?*

"I don't want to be a monster!" Dahr wailed, hiding his face in shame.

Strange hands closed around his own, pulling them away from his face. "A monster?" Kal repeated, dropping to his knees at Dahr's side. "You are no more a monster now than this morning."

"You have had this gift all your life," Rannarik said. "You simply did not know it. You are the same man you have always been."

"This is a gift from Garun," Jakal added. "A blessing. The *Tier'sorahn* have returned! You are the first, but there will be others! Celebrate, Dahr, for this is a day to be remembered."

"I don't want to be different," Dahr lamented. "I want to be normal."

"What is normal?" Jakal asked, offering Dahr a weak smile. "You are different than Kal. Rannarik and I are different than both of you. No two creatures in this world are the same; each has his own strengths, his own weaknesses. Do not run from what makes you unique. Run toward it!"

"Come, little brother," Kal said with a look to the *Tsha'ma*. "I will take you to your tent. This has been hard on you. You need time to think." He pulled Dahr to his feet, took him by the arm, and started in the direction of the raft. Behind them, Kohr's Heart rumbled with pent up fury.

"We will speak later, Dahr," Rannarik said. "Remember, being *Tier'sorahn* is a part of who you are. Before you call it a curse, think on how your life would be without the animals."

Dahr felt numb. He moved slowly, finding it difficult to place one foot in front of the other. He could not speak, could not reply to Rannarik, could barely manage a glance over his shoulder. Behind him, a golden eagle and a speckled hawk took to the air.

Kal led him to the raft and sat him down upon the timbers. Returning to the shore, the *Kranach* pushed the raft, setting it adrift. Warm water lapped around Dahr's legs, but he did not notice, did not react.

Hopping aboard, Kal dipped the oar into the water. Behind him, Kohr's Heart exploded, shooting water high in the air. Dahr followed the water with his eyes, watching the hot droplets fall to earth. They splattered around him, on him, not quite hot enough to burn. He felt nothing.

They crossed the lake in silence broken only by Kal's attempts to wake Dahr from his stupor. Dahr did not answer, would not even acknowledge the Tribesman's question. His face remained a stony mask, and Kal, as he paddled the raft, prayed that he had not caused more harm than good.

When the raft grounded on the far shore, Dahr shook himself, turned, and stared at the grassy shoreline as if he did not understand what it was. Kal pulled him to his feet, put a hand around his shoulder, and led him to the Alrendrian tents.

The mood in the camp was quiet, reflecting Dahr's spirit. Most of the Hunters were gone, gathering food or patrolling the vicinity, ranging far afield to minimize the burden they placed on Kohr's Heart. They were gone most of each day, leaving the tent city with less than half its true population.

Those who remained were unusually quiet. Normally, the low buzz of conversation filled the camp as Tribeswomen and craftsmen bustled here and there, intent about some task. Today, no one was in sight. The camp seemed empty, deserted, as if only Dahr and Kal resided there.

Kal released Dahr only after depositing him in front of his tent. The Tribesman stood there for a long time, concern on his face. "I had thought to bring you peace, little brother," he said, sounding slightly ashamed. "The *Tsha'ma* say you search for yourself, and I thought learning what you were would help you."

"You don't understand," Dahr whispered hoarsely, forcing out the words. "I have been different my entire life. Different, in a land where too much difference is scorned."

"Your friend, Jeran, is different," Kal stated. "He is different from any Human I have ever met."

"He is not different enough!" Dahr snapped, then took a deep breath, calmed himself. "He looks normal, acts normal. Unlike me, he can hide the things which make him different." Tear-filled eyes stared up at the *Kranach*. "All I want is to be like everyone else."

Kal's eyes were sympathetic. "Just as soon ask the sun to be the moon, or one snowflake to look like another. We are all of us different, Dahr, but our differences do not make us better or worse people. That, our souls determine that."

He squeezed Dahr's shoulder reassuringly. "I will give you time to yourself, little brother. You need to seek the peace of Garun." Dipping his head in a parting bow, he turned and disappeared into the tents.

Full of nervous energy, Dahr began to pace. The dogs appeared, loping into the camp from every direction. They looked at him nervously, whined a couple of times, and circled the fire at his side. Fang came to him, pressing her head against his hand.

Dahr ignored her. He walked to the horses, to his massive warhorse, Jardelle. The great beast stomped at his approach, snorting hot gusts of air, and Dahr scratched him behind his ears, looking deep into the horse's eyes. "You don't understand me, do you?"

Jardelle cocked his head to the side, as if in answer, and Dahr froze in place. In the horse's gaze, he thought he saw something. Sympathy, perhaps, or maybe concern. The memory of his first meeting with Jardelle, when the King had gifted him the young horse, flashed into his mind.

Jardelle had struggled against his handler, not ready to be taken from its mother, but when he saw Dahr, he had calmed instantly. Dahr, still grieving over the loss of Jedelle, ran to the horse and stroked its flank, trying to soothe the frightened animal. There had been a moment of indecision, and then the horse had accepted him completely. And Dahr had known, without a doubt, that Jardelle would never fail him.

Dahr took a step back, suddenly wary, and Jardelle's eyes followed him. He retreated to the tents, sitting at the edge of the fire ring, where only blackened ash remained. Rubbing his hands against his temples, he tried to ward off the headache he knew was coming.

Fang approached, the other dogs several steps behind. Nuzzling Dahr's arm with her head, she stared at him with anxiously. Dahr sighed, reached out, and rubbed a hand along her head. "I'll be all right."

His words seemed to comfort the pack. Fang dropped to her haunches, her tongue lolling to the side, and the others crowded around. Dahr took a moment to pet them until, one by one, they laid themselves on the ground at his feet. Soon, only Fang remained sitting, staring at Dahr.

"You don't understand what I'm saying," Dahr told her. "You *can't* understand! You're an animal." He shook his head and laughed. "And I'm crazy! I doubt anyone else in the world is debating whether he's *Tier'sorahn* with a dog!" An image of their first meeting, in the camp of the slavers, came to him, and he laughed louder, trying to dispel his foul mood.

Fang started panting, as if she, too, were laughing. Dahr's own laughter cut off suddenly, and he looked at the animals warily. "You don't understand me," he repeated, more for his benefit than the dogs. This time, even he heard his doubt.

Without moving, he said, "Go to my tent." He did not point, nor gesture, nor even look in the direction of his tent. Nevertheless, Fang stood and loped over to the flap of Dahr's tent.

Dahr trembled, his mouth suddenly dry. "Go to *Wardel's* tent."

Fang sniffed the air, turned, and walked to the Guardsman's tent. She turned to face Dahr, a curious expression on her face.

"You can't understand me," he reminded her, looking around the Alrendrians' camp, a slight quaver in his voice. "Bring me Vyrina's bow, but don't bite too hard." Fang did not respond.

Dahr smiled, then a thought hit him. Closing his eyes, he imagined Vyrina's bow, imagined Fang bringing it to him, careful not to score the wood. He held the image for a moment, then opened his eyes.

Fang was standing before him, the bow held gently in her mouth.

"You can't hear me!" Dahr stated, this time more loudly. Fang titled her head to one side, looking at Dahr in confusion. He suddenly felt that the dog was concerned for his health.

"I can not hear you!" he said slowly, emphasizing each word. The other dogs shared a comical look, as if his statement only proved that he could hear their thoughts.

"I *can't* hear you," he insisted, leaning forward and staring directly into Fang's eyes. "It isn't possible for me to hear your thoughts. Humans can't communicate with–"

"I know I'm not Human," he interrupted himself. Shocked, he clapped a hand over his own mouth, and his eyes darted around the campsite. His breath came in short, ragged gasps; his heart pounded in his chest. "What's happening to me?"

Suddenly, a thought occurred to him. "It's the *Tsha'ma*! They're using their Gift on me, making me think I can hear animals. But I know the truth! They think they can–"

"It's not a ridiculous notion!" he said, jumping to his feet. Fixing Fang with an angry glare, he swung his fist in a vicious backhand. With a single, admonishing bark, Fang nimbly jumped away.

Dahr's anger turned to embarrassment even before he heard Katya call out. "What are you doing?" she demanded, running toward him. She was slick with sweat, fresh from the practice ring she and the Guardsmen had erected.

Dropping to his knees, Dahr beckoned to Fang, who approached without hesitation. "I was going to hit her," Dahr muttered, stroking her flank. "She's with child, and I was going to hit her."

He stopped, stunned, and looked at the dog. "You're going to have a litter?" he asked, leaning in. Fang licked his face in answer and dropped to her haunches.

"Dahr," Katya called. "What's wrong with you? What's happened?" She sounded concerned, a little frightened.

He stood, looked at her, really noticed her for the first time. "Katya," he exhaled, drawing her into a tight embrace. At their first touch, his anxiety melted away.

Katya held him tight, frightened by his behavior. "What's wrong?" she asked again, stroking his hair.

Pulling back just far enough to look her in the eyes, Dahr said, "They think I'm *Tier'sorahn*!"

"Who?" Frowning, she changed her question. "What's a *Tier'sorahn*?"

Dahr told her everything, starting with Kal's test and the tale he had told. He told her of the *Tsha'ma*, their prophecy, and *Cho Korahn Garun*. "They think I can talk to animals!" he concluded, ready for her to laugh off the statement.

"Hmm," she grunted. It was her only response.

"What's that supposed to mean?"

"It *would* explain a lot," she told him, and Dahr stared at her in disbelief. "Are you going to tell me you don't believe it? I've seen you!" She looked him in the eyes and pointed at the dogs. "How do *you* explain it? How do you explain them? You don't find it odd that they abandoned the slavers at your command, then followed you across the Tribal Lands?"

"I don't want this gift!" Dahr snapped, his anger resurfacing. "I don't want to be different!"

"Well, get used to it!" Katya returned, just as irritably. "You *are* different! Nothing you can do will ever change it. Stop acting like a child, and start acting like the man I love!"

She softened her voice, gentled her tone. "You're a good man, Dahr. Caring, loving, and tender. It doesn't matter that you're Garun'ah and not Human. It doesn't matter if you can talk with animals. It wouldn't matter if you could sprout wings and fly, or if you ate your evening meals in the company of the Darklord!"

Dahr winced at the last, but Katya seemed not to notice. "If you've been mistreated in your life, if others can't see past your Race, or your abilities, then they are the ones at fault, not you.

"You have a gift," she added. "But it's nothing new, nothing you haven't had before. You've been talking to animals all your life…Or at least since we met. It didn't bother you before. Don't let it trouble you now."

"How…." He stopped, unable to find the right words. "How can you make things seem so simple?" A smile spread across his face. "How can a handful of words bring me such peace?"

She smiled. "It's a gift."

He laughed, drew her to him, and kissed her passionately. "Come with me," he said, grabbing her arm. Confused, she followed as he half led, half pulled her through the tent city.

"Where are we going?" she laughed. A Tribeswoman looked up at their passage, frowned at them.

"I won't tell you!" Dahr replied, his expression one of nervous excitement. "Not yet at least. It's a surprise."

A yelp drew his attention. The pack was following him, Fang in the lead. They dodged nimbly through the tents of the Garun'ah, running around the busy Tribesmen. Dahr shook his head. "Not this time!" he said, almost pleading. "Just leave us in peace for a little while."

The dogs stopped, all but Fang. They looked at each other uncertainly, then turned and padded back toward the tents. Fang continued to follow, drawing closer, barking fast and loud to get Dahr's attention. She ran off to the left, reappeared a moment later, barked a second time, and ran off again.

Dahr stared after the dog. "Strange…." he said to himself, letting the word stretch out, then looked at Katya. "What do you think she's trying to say?"

Katya shrugged. "You're the one who can talk to animals, remember?" Her eyes flicked down, and a sly smirk touched the corners of her mouth. "Why don't you ask her?"

Fang was standing next to them, moving anxiously. She barked again, grabbed the leg of his breeches, and gave a sharp tug. Then she turned and ran away.

"I think she wants us to follow her." Dahr told Katya, and the Guardswoman tried to hide a smile.

"You really think so?" she mused sarcastically. "Does being *Tier'sorahn* mean you can speak with animals or state the obvious?" She asked the question without a hint of humor.

Dahr frowned, trying to look angry, but he could not maintain the expression. With a fond shake of his head, he changed directions, going in the direction Fang had chosen. He was not surprised when, only a moment later, the dog came back into view. She waited for them to draw near, then loped off again.

They played this game for some time, allowing the dog to lead them through the maze-like, almost deserted tents. With the Hunters gathering food and patrolling the countryside during the day, Kohr's Heart often seemed empty. Each evening, when the Hunters returned, the camp sprang to life, filled with music and songs and laughter.

Today's stillness, however, was not due to the Hunters' absence. Only a handful of women and children wandered the camp or worked in the shade of their tents. Most flaps were closed tight, though day had long since begun. As Dahr passed, one flap peeled back, and two small, almond-shaped eyes peered out. Seeing Dahr, they pulled the flap shut again.

A stiff breeze blew through the camp, rustling the tent flaps, and bringing the sound of heated voices to Dahr's ears. At the first angry words, Dahr hastened his steps, all but dragging Katya behind him.

They emerged in a clearing, a round opening in the forest of tents. Yarchik and Arik stood on one side, the hulking giant standing next to the withered, old Tribesman. Their faces were mirrors of stony resolution.

Across from them stood a group of young Hunters. Paint covered their faces, blood red on the cheeks with two lines of black, one from ear to ear, the other over the nose from brow to chin.

One of the Tribesmen stood in front the others, yelling at the *Kranora*, raving, flecks of spittle flying from his mouth. For the first time, Dahr wished he could understand the language of the Tribesmen.

The youth, finally finished, ducked his head and stared at the two chieftains defiantly. A tense silence followed while Yarchik looked at Arik. Quiet words were exchanged, then they nodded and turned to face the young warriors.

Arik stepped forward, reached over his shoulder, and drew his wickedly-curved, double-bladed axe. His expression tightened into an angry grimace, and he drew his hand along the length of the blade. A thin line of red ran down the silvery metal.

But it was Yarchik who spoke, his voice powerful, almost the antithesis of his appearance. The words were angry, and though unintelligible to Dahr and Katya, their meaning was clear. The Tribesmen were being told to leave.

Their leader, trembling with rage, lunged forward, stopping when the blade of Arik's axe landed in the loose soil at his feet, the shaft quivering with the force of the throw. Arik's voice rumbled like thunder, adding his opinion to Yarchik's. A hand dropped to his *dolchek*, and his eyes claimed that he would not aim for the ground if forced to use his second weapon.

The young Tribesman stepped back, his eyes on the axe. With a snarl, he turned. Seeing Dahr, his eyes narrowed, and his lips drew back in a scowl. Spitting on the ground, he fled the camp, his companions a few steps behind.

Arik walked forward to retrieve his axe. "I thought we had seen the last of those *Onahrre*," he said in *Huma*, spitting the last word.

Yarchik shook his head sadly. "There will always be children of chaos, my friend." His eyes grew distant, as if he were deep in thought. "It is the story of the tribe in the Anvil," he said at last. "They stand upon the edge of a sheer cliff. To one side winds a narrow path, slowly descending to the valley below. Most would follow the narrow path, difficult though it may be, so they could enjoy the reward at its end."

A sad smile ghosted across his face. "But some will always choose the quicker path, though it leads to destruction."

Arik nodded at Yarchik's sagely words. "Well come, Dahr. Well come, Katya," he said in greeting, turning to face the Alrendrians. "It shames me that you had to lay eyes on such creatures."

"Who were they?" Dahr asked.

"*Kohr'adjin*," sneered Yarchik, spitting on the ground.

"The Disciples of Kohr," translated Arik. "The Children of Chaos. They who have turned from the teachings of Garun and embraced the Father." His eyes glared hatefully at the tents behind which the Garun'ah had disappeared. "They refuse to listen to the Voice of Madryn. They are *Onahrre*. Without honor."

"What did they want?" inquired Katya, nervously watching the tents.

"They wished to join *Cha'khun*. To lend their voices to the Blood."

"Creatures such as they have no place among the Children of Garun!" Yarchik snapped.

"Are they Drekka?" asked Dahr, still not fully understanding.

Arik and Yarchik exchanged confused glances. "They are worse than Drekka," Yarchik answered, astounding Dahr with his vehemence. Tribesmen hated few things more than the Drekka, the tribe that had allied itself with the Darklord. Even the Elves were held in higher regard.

"The Drekka have turned from Garun's teachings too," Arik explained, "but they seek their own Balance. The *Kohr'adjin* seek glory for themselves, control over the other races. They seek to bring chaos to Madryn, and in doing so, they will destroy the Balance."

"The *Kohr'adjin* have followers among all the tribes," Yarchik said. "Though it shames me to admit it, even some of my own Hunters have been seduced by the words of their prophets." At the crippled man's admission, Arik nodded his own head.

"They are driven out when found, and many choose to leave rather than face the scorn of their brethren, but a few always remain in the tents, keeping their true selves hidden and poisoning the minds of the young." Yarchik's withered hands drew into fists. "Had I the strength, I would rid the world of such beasts myself."

"Let us talk of other things," Arik said, looking pointedly at Dahr. "I see the *Tsha'ma* have tested you."

Dahr felt his heart flutter. "Did Kal tell you."

The giant warrior shook his head. "My son respects your privacy, Dahr Odara. I know because I see it in your eyes. Often have I been tested by the *Tsha'ma*, and you look much as I feel after dealing with Garun's Voices."

Yarchik smiled, exposing a mouthful of sharp, yellowed teeth. "The methods of the *Tsha'ma* lack subtlety," he told Dahr. "Often their lessons are hard to swallow." His gaze hardened. "Did you pass their test?"

Dahr took a deep breath and nodded. "They think I'm *Tier'sorahn*," he said after a pause, bracing himself for the *Kranora's* ridicule.

Yarchik did laugh, loud and strong, but it was not at Dahr's expense. "You owe me a skin of your best *baqhat*," he said to Arik, then turned to Dahr. "It is the time of the *Prah'phetia*. Time for *Cho Korahn Garun* to come."

Dahr sighed. "That's what the *Tsha'ma* would have me believe."

Yarchik frowned. "You do not?"

Dahr shrugged, and Katya answered in his stead. "Dahr prefers to blend into the background. He doesn't like things that make him different. To speak with animals...."

"Being *Tier'sorahn* is more than hearing the Lesser Voices, the thoughts of Garun's first children," Arik explained in a calm and friendly voice. As always, hearing such gentle words from the mouth of such a giant surprised Dahr, but they also soothed him. "*Tier'sorahn* can hear the Voice of Madryn, can see through the eyes of nature itself. To restore the Balance, we need *Tier'sorahn* even more than the *Korahn*. They will lead the way." A serene smile covered the *Kranor's* face, and he looked up at the heavens.

"Do you think I'm... *Tier'sorahn*?" Dahr asked weakly, directing the question to the *Kranora*.

"Do I think the sun will rise in the east?" Yarchik asked, nodding. "Or that I am of Garun's blood? Yes, Dahr, I believe you are *Tier'sorahn*." In a lower voice, he whispered, "I believe you are much more."

Arik response was not a certain. "It may be," the giant said. "Far worse could have been chosen."

Dahr blushed at the praise, suddenly uncomfortable under the two inscrutable gazes. Grabbing Katya's arm, he pulled her away from the Tribesmen. "Come on," he said, bidding farewell Yarchik and Arik, "there's still something I want to show you."

Yarchik's voice came to him even as he led Katya away from the tents. "Do not fear your differences, Dahr. Savor them! Garun's greatest gift to his children was individuality."

Dahr led Katya through the tents, up the hillside, and out of the valley. He led her through the grasslands surrounding Kohr's Heart, ignoring her insistent questions, trying to change the subject with small talk about the Guardsmen and Garun'ah.

When he was sure no one was around, when the only sound was the beating of his heart and the quiet whispering of the breeze through the knee-high grass, he released her. She stopped immediately, put her hands on her hips, and pressed her lips together tightly. "Dahr Odara! I'm not taking another step until you tell me what this is all about!"

He smiled, nervously wiping a hand across his face, and stared at her, marveling at her beauty, still surprised that he had been lucky enough to find someone like her. "Well?" Katya prompted when no words were forthcoming. "Dahr! Wipe that silly expression off your face and tell me what this is about."

Dahr cleared his throat. "Katya...." He paused to clear his throat again. "I've been learning much about the Garun...my people. The other day I asked Kal... I wanted to know... I asked him...."

Katya's musical laughter brightened the day. "Spit it out, Hunter!"

Pausing again, Dahr took a deep, steadying breath, then removed the chain from around his neck. A ray of sunlight broke through the clouds, beaming down upon the silver figure of a mountain cat. "When I was... captured by the slavers, my mother gave me this chain. It was a wedding gift from my father, a token which has been in the family for hundreds of winters.

"My mother made me promise to keep it until I found someone to give it to." Sweat beaded his forehead, his breath came in short gasps, and his heart pounded so hard, that Dahr feared it might burst. "Kal tells me that when a Tribesman chooses a mate, he gives her something of himself. Something of great personal value. If she accepts, she keeps the object as a symbol of the heart she now possesses. If she refuses, she places the object in the fire, to symbolize the part of the Hunter which has died...."

Dahr's smile broadened, and he gazed lovingly into Katya's eyes. "You already have my heart," he told her. "You've had it since the night in the Dungeon, when you took a moment to talk to the King's Hound." He held out his hand, offering her the necklace.

"Oh, Dahr," Katya said, struggling to find the right words, "I–"

Dahr waved her to silence. "The Garun'ah mate for life," he said, quoting Kal's description word for word. "Once accepted, the pair is bonded for eternity. Their souls become one. Their hearts become one. They share each breath of the Waking World, and when their lives are finally ended, they walk arm in arm through the Twilight World."

A nervous, boyish grin stretched across Dahr's face. "Should you accept," he told her, his hands trembling in anticipation, "I'll be the happiest creature in all of Madryn. If I am *Tier'sorahn, Cho Korahn Garun*, or the Darklord's adopted son, it won't matter so long as you are by my side.

"But to me," he added, tears coming unbidden to his eyes, "your answer doesn't matter. My heart was yours long before today. Even if you refuse, there will be no other love for me." He licked his lips nervously. "My heart is yours, Katya."

"Oh, Dahr...." Dahr heard the uncertainty in her voice and hurried to reassure her.

"If you wish an Alrendrian ceremony, I won't object. I just thought, since we were with my people...."

Katya silenced him with a kiss, long and passionate. After a long while she pulled back to tie the necklace around her throat. "I will treasure it, Hunter," she said, one hand on the pendant. "As I treasure you."

He drew her to him. "My Kat!" he said. "My beautiful Kat!"

Much later, when the sun was sinking in the western sky, they stood, brushing the dirt from their clothes. "We should head back," Katya said, stretching an arm over her head and yawning.

Dahr nodded. He opened his mouth to speak, but the sudden cracking of a stick drew his attention. Alert, both he and Katya spun around, dropped to a crouch, and slowly made their way up the side of the small hollow in which they hid.

Not too far distant, a silhouetted figure crouched near a rock, fumbling with something. When Dahr and Katya appeared, he jumped and darted off, keeping his head tucked low, and disappeared into a nearby stand of trees.

"Was that Kraltir?" Katya asked, curious. "I thought he was banished." She began to pick a path through the high grass. "I wonder what he was doing by that boulder."

"He *was* banished," Dahr said, hurrying to gather their gear. By the time he reached the top of the hill, Katya was most of the way toward the boulder. Dahr swayed and put a hand to his head; a quiet buzz echoed in the back of his mind, sending waves of pain through him. He scanned the area, but saw no sign of Kraltir or any other Tribesman.

"I think he was banished for a full moon," Dahr called out, stumbling when the pain in his head flared anew. Again he tried to dismiss the angry hiss. "I'm not sure if they meant until the moon was full, which would be in a day or two, or when a full cycle of the moon had passed."

Katya neared the boulder and bent low to examine the ground. The buzzing in Dahr's mind grew more violent, and he pressed a hand to the back of his head, hoping the pressure would relieve the sensation.

All of a sudden, he heard it; a quiet, waspish voice whispering in the back of his mind. He focused on it, confused. Though the words were in his head, it sounded as if they were coming from the rock.

Understanding fell upon him like a hammer blow. "Katya, NO!" he shouted, dropping their things and running forward. He was too late.

"What's this?" she asked, reaching toward the multicolored object hidden in the shadows. She jerked her hand back when the snake sprung, but her well-honed reflexes were not quite quick enough. Letting out a squeal of pain, Katya fell back. The snake pushed itself further under the rock, seeking shelter.

Dahr was at Katya's side in an instant. He dropped to his knees, reached out with lightning-fast precision, and grabbed the snake. Squeezing forcefully, fueled by anger, he crushed it, and it flopped lifelessly in his hand. Fear quickly replaced his anger, and Dahr gaze anxiously at Katya.

"It's all right, Dahr," she assured him. "Just a little bite! Nothing to...." Her eyes rolled up into her head, showing nothing but white and she collapsed. Dahr barely had time to grab her and ease her fall.

"No," he said weakly, shaking his head. He felt for a pulse; it was fast, much too fast, and weak. Katya's breathing was shallow and erratic. "No," he repeated, trembling.

He shook her, hoping for some sign of consciousness. His eyes drifted toward the trees where Kraltir had disappeared, lifted toward the heavens. "NO!" This time he screamed it, and the Blood Rage consumed him. Anger flowed through him like a river, and he grasped his *dolchek* tightly, readied himself for the hunt.

"Dahr...." Katya gasped weakly. He looked down, the plea in her voice overcoming his Blood Rage. "Dahr...." she repeated, struggling for the words. "Love... Help...."

Tears streaming down his face, Dahr lifted Katya off the ground. As an afterthought, he stooped and grabbed the snake as well, draping its carcass across her chest. Anger filled him, rage consumed him, and he ran toward Kohr's Heart at full speed, screaming, "RANNARIK!" at the top of his lungs.

Chapter 33

Martyn tied the laces to his shirt, studying himself in the mirror. He wanted to look his best; tonight was the Emperor's farewell address to the Alrendrians. On the morrow, they would return to Kaper.

The farewell address was not a simple affair. For the last few days, *Ael Namisa* had scurried about the palace, cleaning the audience hall and dining chambers. The cooks had worked tirelessly, procuring the ingredients they would need for the feast. Cages of fowl were brought from outlying farms, herds of cattle were led to the back of the kitchens for slaughter, and wagonloads of bread were being baked in the palace's giant ovens.

Hundreds had been invited to dine with the Alrendrians on their final night in Illendrylla, and if Treloran's reports were correct, thousands planned to line the streets tomorrow to bid the Humans farewell.

Martyn, finished with his shirt, inspected himself in the mirror again. Lifting his chin, he ran a finger down the clean-shaven line of his jaw. A smile touched his lips.

"You look most regal, Prince Martyn," Kaeille said, entering the room behind him. She wore dark green leathers and had a bow slung over her shoulder. Her stance was strangely formal, her eyes distant.

Martyn was instantly wary. "What's wrong?" he asked in a whisper, hurrying toward her.

She swung the door closed, and her demeanor changed instantly. Her gaze softened, and her lips turned up in a smile. "There were Guardsmen in the hall," she told him. "I know you wish our...relationship...to remain discreet. I did not want to make them curious."

Martyn exhaled, not realizing that he had been holding his breath, and drew Kaeille into a tight embrace. She dropped her bow to the floor and returned the hug, her hands running playfully down the silky cloth of his shirt. They kissed, putting all the passion of their upcoming parting into it.

Martyn backed away, breathless, and Kaeille frowned. "I do not want you to leave," she said. "Lynnaei will seem empty without you."

"I don't want to go!" Martyn assured her. "I can't imagine returning to Kaper and not having you near."

Her eyes sparkled mischievously. "You will have your new wife to keep you company," she replied, pouting her lips. "It will not take you long to forget me."

"Kaeille! I would never...." Her laughter cut him off. Smiling, he pounced on her. With one hand he pinned her hands behind her back, with the other, he worked the ties on her armor.

"Martyn!" she laughed, throatily, "You are dressed for the feast!"

"I can dress again." He untied one knot, and the armor grew fractionally looser. Sliding a hand inside the leather, Martyn reached beneath the Elf's undershirt and ran his fingers along the smooth contours of her skin. Kaeille resisted at first, but gradually yielded to the prince's caresses and tender kisses.

Or so he thought. When he was certain she had the same idea as he did, he released the grip on her hands. Kaeille smiled, leaned in, and planted a light kiss on his cheek. Then she grabbed his arm, twisted, and sent him flying through the air.

He landed on the hard, stone floor with a thud. Kaeille fell atop him, pinning him with her legs. "I do not enjoy having such attention forced upon me," she told him, a haughty and aloof expression on her face. Her eyes, however, danced.

"Oh?" Martyn replied, looking guilty. "Well, *I* might like it! Why don't you force some attention on me!" Kaeille laughed musically, and reached for the laces of his shirt.

She jumped when a solid knock resounded on the door and was off him in an instant, her hands busily retying the clasps on her armor. "A moment!" Martyn called as he stood, his hands busily smoothing his shirt.

He opened the door to Jes, who wore a gown of blue and had her black hair piled atop her head, with matching curls twirling past her ears. "Lady Jessandra," Martyn stated, his eyes going wide. "You look most stunning."

A cool smile touched her lips. "Thank you, Prince Martyn," she replied, her eyes casually roaming his chamber. Kaeille stood at attention; one hand rested on the short blade at her side, the other held her bow. Upon seeing the Elf, the corners of Jes' mouth twisted up slightly, almost imperceptibly. "It was kind of the Emperor to provide you with a personal guard."

Martyn's cheeks reddened, but Jes pretended not to notice. "The Emperor is most generous."

Jes' eyes sparkled. "Is she satisfactory in performing her duties? If a full company of Alrendrian Guardsmen are not enough to guarantee your safety, perhaps you need more than one Aelvin guard. If I asked Charylla, I'm sure she'd assign a few more soldiers to your protection." Her eyes wandered back to Kaeille. "I could even make sure they were all female, if that's your preference."

Martyn swallowed, clearing his throat. "No, Lady Jessandra. That will not be necessary. Kaeille is more than adequate protection."

Jes stared into his eyes, making him uncomfortable. "Good. Caution is an admirable quality, but I'm sure your betrothed would not be pleased if you had too many guards on your person. Some wives desire a certain amount of privacy with their husbands."

Her eyes danced, but her expression remained cool, impassive. "Lord Iban wished for me to remind you that the feast will begin shortly. He wants you to be on time." She bowed her head, smirked to herself, and continued down the hallway.

Martyn closed the door. "I guess our farewells will have to wait," he lamented with a resigned sigh.

Kaeille gently caressed the back of Martyn's neck, sending shivers of pleasure down the prince's spine. "I will make it up to you this evening. We will have all night to say goodbye, and you have nothing to do tomorrow but sit a saddle." Her tone made it sound as if staying on his horse might be a problem.

Martyn pulled her to him again. "Will you not come with me?" he asked, perhaps for the hundredth time. "If I asked Treloran, I'm sure–"

She shook her head. "It would not be appropriate," she replied, the same answer she had given each time he asked. "When the Aelvin delegation is sent to Kaper, I will request to be among those warriors sent. If I am chosen, I will come to you. If not...." She let the statement trail off.

"Why wouldn't you be chosen?" Martyn asked, not eager to be separated from his Aelvin love.

"Long have I counted Astalian among my friends," she replied. "As *Hohe Chatorra*, he will choose who accompanies the embassies to Alrendria."

Martyn's eyes brightened. "Then we have nothing to worry about!" he exclaimed. "If you and Astalian are friends...."

Kaeille motioned for silence. "He may not include me among the delegation *because* we are friends. Like your Lord Iban, he sees only pain for us in this relationship." She looked at Martyn lovingly. "He would spare me that pain, if he thought he could."

They fell silent, lost in each other's eyes. After a while, Kaeille leaned forward and planted a kiss on Martyn's head. "Go to the feast," she told him, reaching for his cape, pure white with a yellow sun embroidered on the back. Tying it around his neck, she whispered. "I will be waiting when you return."

Martyn smiled as he left his chambers, and he strolled the halls casually, humming to himself. Guardsmen he passed saluted, fist-on-heart, and Martyn inclined his head to the warriors, calling them by name, offering warm greetings.

Bystral approached, wearing a dark coat over his leather armor. "My Prince," he said, bowing his head. "Has there been any word of Jeran?"

Martyn shook his head. "Guardsman, Jeran went off alone. Without permission. How would he get word to us without betraying his location?"

Bystral blushed, frowning. "You're right, my Prince. I wasn't thinking." He lowered his eyes to the floor. "I worry for his safety."

Martyn grasped the Guardsman's shoulder, and smiled in return. "As do I. As do I. But if anyone can survive out there alone, it's Jeran."

Bystral nodded. "You're right, of course, Prince Martyn. Sorry to have bothered you."

"Think nothing of it. It's always a pleasure to share time with the Alrendrian Guard."

Bystral saluted, then continued down the hall. Martyn frowned after the Guardsman, his thoughts on Jeran and Dahr. *Where are they? Are they well?* He hated that they could go off about their own adventures, while duty commanded him to remain with the delegation. He longed for their freedom, the ability to leave on a whim, to go where his heart desired, to love without caring about the consequences.

He continued down the hall, falling into a measured pace. His thoughts were so distant, he did not at first hear the accompanying footfalls behind him. When the click-clack of shoes on stone finally aroused his attention, he craned his neck around.

Utari Hahna walked behind him, wearing a dress of tan that contrasted her ebony skin. Her hair was piled atop her head in tiny curls, with golden rings interwoven between the strands. Golden bracelets adorned her wrist and two slender chains circled her throat. Her lips were painted maroon red; her dark eyes were locked on the prince.

Martyn slowed his gait, allowing her to join him. "Lady Utari," he said, greeting her. "You look most lovely."

"Thank you, Your Highness," came her cool reply as she fell in step at his side. The noblewoman towered over Martyn; she was more than a hand taller, but slender, with gracefully curving hips.

"We have had little opportunity to talk during our stay in Illendrylla," Martyn said, attempting to make conversation.

"With good reason, Highness," Utari stated. "I had nothing to say."

He suddenly found his interest piqued. "And you have something to say now, my Lady?"

She turned her head and looked at him, her stride not slowing. "I would offer you some advice." Martyn met her gaze, nodded for her to continue. "You play a dangerous game with Rafel," she told him. "Detestable as he may be, he has many friends among the nobility, and great wealth. Wealth can buy influence in times of need."

Martyn's gaze grew colder. "I acted hastily," he admitted. "I said as much to Rafel myself. But his behavior was unacceptable. I will not tolerate any man to treat another with such disrespect."

Utari pursed her lips, but Martyn did not let her speak. "You did not see him!" he snapped. "He acted as if the boy were less than a man. Had I not intervened...." He let his words fade, allowed Utari's imagination to describe the scene for him.

"I did not wish to arouse your anger, my Prince," she said, her voice still cool. "I see in you the compassion and concern of a great leader, else I would not be standing here now." She paused to look him over. "You are much different than the frivolous child who so haughtily strode aboard the River Falcon. Watching you grow has been quite an experience."

Ael Namisa scurried about the halls, carrying trays and platters, dusting, sweeping, polishing. They paused when Martyn walked by, staring at him with their haunting, slanted eyes. He chose not to respond to Utari's comment; instead, he allowed the silence to drag out until she spoke. "I have more advice for you, my Prince," she admitted, "though you will not wish to hear it. Nor will you listen to it."

Martyn looked at her again. "Advice?"

"The Elf girl who has captured your attention," Utari said, smirking as Martyn's eyes widened in astonishment. "You would be wise to forget each other, set aside your mutual desires, and return home with your memories unsullied."

"H...How?" Martyn stammered, trying to find his tongue. "How did you know?"

Utari laughed. It was a deep, throaty sound, and it echoed down the hall. "Your father did not choose fools to fill his delegation, my Prince. The way you look at each other when you think no one will notice. Your heroic attempts to ignore each other when someone will. Your feelings are so obvious, even the blind could see them!"

She laughed again, quieter. "I'm sure half the delegation knows of your tryst by now. Should your Elf come to Alrendria, there will be no way to keep your relationship secret."

Martyn's face turned red from both embarrassment and anger. "Who's to say I want to keep our love a secret!"

"Come, come, my Prince," she replied, tisking her tongue. "We both know you cannot flaunt your feelings for this Elf, even if what you feel is truly love. You have a kingdom to think of. A wife." Utari paused, and Martyn let his gaze roam down the hall. Everywhere he looked, couples walked side by side. Human and Human. Elf and Elf. Human and Elf. All around him were reminders of what he was denied, the freedom he could never have.

"Take your memories of the Elf," Utari repeated. "They'll give you more happiness than a lifetime with her by your side."

"Why do you tell me this?" Martyn asked, trying to control his ire.

"I will tell you a story," Utari said in way of answer. "Once, many winters ago, there was a girl. The Tachan War had destroyed her Family, cost them their status as a Great House, and she was the only surviving heir.

"Her parents, wishing to regain their former status, sent their daughter to the far off city of Vela, where she was to learn the ways of the court. Meanwhile, her parents plotted to marry her to a wealthy and powerful nobleman. Together, the two Families might have gathered enough support to form their own Great House.

"The girl however, had different plans. During her seasons in Vela, she fell in love with the son of a modest craftsman, a furniture maker. He was a simple man, far beneath her station, but caring and tender. She could not imagine loving anyone else.

"When her mother came and informed the girl of her impending marriage, she was furious. She swore she would not marry the man, knowing it was her duty to do so, and she plotted for the furniture maker's son to follow her after several seasons, so their affair could continue."

Utari paused and looked Martyn in the eye. "She was counseled by close friends to abandon her plan," the dark-skinned woman said, "much as I counsel you now, but she ignored their warnings.

"The girl left Vela and married the nobleman. He was older, severe and gruff, but he was also kind, and in time, she learned to care for him. But when her lover appeared, she forgot about her new husband and returned to his waiting arms.

"They were most discreet, careful not to arouse the suspicions of her husband and those around them. But even a castle can have only so much furniture. Eventually, her husband grew suspicious. One day, he returned to the castle early and caught them in each other's arms. In a fit of rage, he killed the simple craftsman. For, despite his brusque exterior, the nobleman had truly loved the woman, and her betrayal stung him deeply.

"As she lay there, in a growing pool of her lover's blood, her husband saw the pain in her eyes, and knew he had hurt her more than she had hurt him. Awash with guilt, he took his blade and drove it through his own heart. His last words were those of forgiveness and love."

Utari stopped before the door to the dining chamber and looked deep into Martyn's eyes. "Great care was taken to hide the truth behind the deaths. The woman escaped all blame, and both her husband and lover were given fitting burials. But the memory of their deaths, the consequences of her selfishness, remained with her for the rest of her life."

Martyn swallowed, clearing his throat. "Why do you think I won't listen to this advice?" he asked weakly.

Utari's eyes were sad. "Because I remember what it's like to be young, Prince Martyn. And I remember why I did not listen." She offered Martyn a smile, and he tried to respond but could not. Everyone except him, it seemed, thought his relationship with Kaeille was doomed.

Utari looked at the ornate doorway, the hand carved figures, the ornate craftsmanship. "Come," she said, smoothing the pain resurrected by her memories. "We have a feast to attend." She pushed the door, and it swung open noiselessly.

The banquet hall was set up much as before. To one side sat the Alrendrian servants, accompanied by *Ael Namisa;* on the other side, a row of *Ael Chatorra* shared their meal with the Alrendria Guard. At the far end of the chamber was the Emperor's Table. The imperial family sat in the center, flanked by prominent *Ael Maulle* and *Ael Pieroci.* Iban and the Alrendrian nobles sat opposite the Emperor's kin.

Unlike the first feast, there was much talking throughout the hall, and laughter reverberated from both sides of the room. Many were still wary of anyone not of their Race, but more than one friendship had been formed during the Humans' stay.

Elierian stood in the center of the room, his eyes everywhere at once. Quiet commands, spoken in Aelvin, flowed from his mouth, and servants scurried to carry out his orders. Seeing Martyn, he bowed deeply. "Prince Martyn. Lady Utari. Welcome. If I may show you to your seats."

They followed him to the head table. Martyn bid goodbye to Utari as she took her seat near Rafel. Elierian escorted Martyn to a seat opposite Treloran. Bowing, the *Hohe Namisa* departed.

As Martyn sat, he looked across the table at the Aelvin Prince. "Our last night," he said to Treloran. "You know, I think I'll miss you, Elf." He spoke the words coldly, but his eyes were full of friendship.

Treloran returned Martyn's gaze aloofly. "I must admit, Human, being forced to spend my time with you was only half as bad as I thought it would be." The hint of a smile touched Treloran's mouth.

"So glad you could join us," Iban said, turning to face the princes. "It's refreshing to see you could find the time for this simple banquet. I know how busy you've been these last few days, my Prince."

Martyn turned to Treloran. "Iban's upset because I cancelled our daily meeting. There were some people I wished to say goodbye to." Treloran nodded his head sagely, but Iban glowered at the calm dismissal. Martyn tried to smooth over his comment. "We will have plenty of time for talk during the journey home," he told Iban. "Without Jeran and Dahr around, you'll have my complete attention."

Iban grunted. "I suppose you're right," he said. "As it turns out, the Emperor desired an audience with me this morning, and I would have had to shorten our meeting anyway. I hope you spent your time wisely." He turned his back on Martyn to continue his conversation with Charylla.

Martyn shrugged, and the Emperor called for the feast to begin. Platters of food were brought, lightly spiced. The goblets were filled with deep, red wine. The aromas filled Martyn's nose and made the prince's mouth water in anticipation. Servants filled his plate as per his instructions, and he set to his food like a starving man.

"Ah, there he is!" called a voice across the table.

"We did not see you, Prince Martyn," said another. "With your head so close to the plate, you are easy to miss." Martyn looked up to see the elderly Aelvin twins, Nahrona and Nahrima, standing across from him. They wore the purple and gold robes of *Ael Maulle*.

Two sets of green eyes stared at him, full of life. Martyn shifted his gaze back and forth between them. "He looks confused, brother," said one, leaning forward to look Martyn in the eye. "I am Nahrona," he said, speaking slowly and clearly. "This is my brother, Nahrima."

Martyn bowed his head. "What can I do for you, honored *Ael Maulle*?"

"Nothing, child! Nothing," answered Nahrima. "We merely came to say goodbye."

"It was a pleasure having you in Illendrylla."

"Though we never had a chance to speak with you personally–"

"–your presence has caused quite a stir."

"Given us many amusing stories to listen to."

"There is one thing!" Nahrona said suddenly, as if just remembering. "If it would not be too much trouble. Perhaps you would deliver a message to Jeran Odara, when next you see him."

"We do not wish to be a burden," added Nahrima.

Martyn nodded his head, sipped his wine. "Of course. What's your message?"

"Tell him if he survives his test–"

"When, Brother. When!" corrected Nahrima, cutting off the other Elf.

"*When* he survives his test," Nahrona amended, "tell him to seek a place of solitude."

"Tell him to go to Aemon's Tomb."

"If he is ready, his teachers will come."

"We will be waiting for him."

Martyn's face grew puzzled. "Test?" he repeated. "Survive? Aemon's Tomb? But Aemon is alive!"

Nahrima smiled. "Jeran will understand." They bowed, turned, and walked away on silent feet.

Martyn watched them leave. "A strange pair." Treloran pursed his lips, swallowed a morsel of broiled beef, and nodded in solemn agreement.

The rest of the meal was eaten in relative silence. Course after course came, delicious meat platters, well-seasoned vegetables, fresh-baked breads, and desserts of the highest quality completed the dinner. All fed until stuffed, till none could cram another morsel into their mouths.

Finally, the Emperor stood, his plate barely touched, and addressed his guests. "I trust Our Human friends have enjoyed their meal, and their stay with Us. If it pleases you, let us adjourn to the audience hall, so we may say our farewells."

The Emperor's chair was pulled back, and a brown-robed servant offered the old Elf her arm. He took it slowly and hobbled toward the rear of the chamber, where a small door was opening. "The Guardsmen and servants may follow Elierian. My *Hohe Namisa* will show them to their seats." Tired, green eyes focused on Martyn, then shifted to Iban. "The Alrendrian delegates may follow me, if they wish. You will sit with me atop the platform, and there is a shorter way than through the halls."

They all stood to follow the Emperor, and Alynna wormed her way between Martyn and Treloran. "Greetings, my Prince," she said demurely, blinking her long lashes. The representative of House Morrena wore a gown of glittering red, which accented her golden blonde hair. Her eyes sparkled mischievously, and the tip of her tongue to played across her upper lip.

"Lady Alynna," Martyn said, bowing his head. When she took a step closer to him, he shook his head. "Do me a favor, my Lady," he said in a low voice, so only she could hear. "Please spare me your advances. I am flattered by the attention, but not interested."

His eyes twinkled merrily, but Alynna's face darkened. Hoping to distract the brazen noblewoman, he added in a slightly louder voice, "Perhaps Treloran would like to entertain you on our last night in Lynnaei. He has often lamented how little time he spent in your alluring presence."

Treloran started at the words, but could offer no response. Alynna turned her hawk-like, predatory gaze upon the Aelvin Prince. "Prince Treloran," she said sweetly, ducking her head shyly.

She stumbled over a step, and even Martyn could not tell if it were purposeful or accidental. The chivalrous Aelvin Prince offered her his arm, and Alynna took it gladly. She smiled, allowing him to lead her the rest of the way to the audience chamber.

The room was huge. The ceiling arched high above them, the top of the dome invisible in the light of the flickering lanterns. A large platform, with wide marble stairs rising up from the floor, stood at one end of the vast chamber. In the center of the platform sat a throne, flanked on either side by rows of chairs.

The Emperor stood before his throne, and at his gesture, the Alrendrian and Aelvin nobility took their places, intermingled on each side of the ancient Elf. Treloran and Martyn sat next to each other, just to the Emperor's right. Charylla and Iban had a similar place on his left.

The entire chamber, despite it size, was full. The Alrendrians sat to either side–the servants on the left, the Guard on the right–but Elves filled the remainder of the hall. The Emperor rarely held public audiences, and everyone able to attend had sought entrance to the palace. To be able to see the Humans one last time only added to their desire.

When everyone had taken their places, the Emperor raised his arms, and silence instantly fell over the chamber. Not a sound could be heard, not a single breath nor the clatter of jewelry. The Emperor smiled, his eyes full of love. "My People," he said in a low voice, though the words echoed through the chamber. "I welcome you."

The Emperor turned his calm, piercing gaze on the Alrendrians, and a warm smile reached his lips. "This has been a memorable season!" he said, turning to face his countrymen. A murmur of agreement went up among the Elves. "For the first time in centuries, Humans have walked our Sacred Forest. They came as strangers, as unsure of us as we were of them." He looked left, at the row of noblemen, Aelvin and Human. He looked right, allowing his eyes to scan those seats as well.

"They came as strangers," he repeated, "but they leave as friends! Our long silence is at an end. We Elves will once again embrace the world around us, share our place in its fate. We will stand by the sides of our Human cousins and help our newfound friendship blossom."

He reached out a hand to Martyn. "Prince Martyn of Alrendria," he called. "Please stand at my side." Martyn stood slowly and walked across the platform, trying to look more confident than he felt. He stopped beside the Emperor.

"In the last two seasons," the Emperor continued, "much has been learned by our Races. Where once existed mistrust and hatred, now blossoms of love grow. To symbolize this unity between Alrendria and Illendrylla, Prince Martyn has agreed to take an Elf as his *advoutre*." A gasp went up among the Elves. "His consort," the Emperor translated for the benefit of the Alrendrians.

With understanding, the gasp of surprise spread quickly among the Humans. "This cannot be!" Lord Iban said, rising to his feet. "Prince Martyn is promised to Miriam, Princess of Gilead. Their betrothal will take place soon after his return to Kaper! Their marriage not long after."

"This *WILL* be!" replied the Emperor, his voice thundering through the chamber, "else all we have wrought here will be for naught. Your land and ours will share this bond, tenuous as it may be. So long as Martyn has an Elf as consort, none will doubt his good will toward Illendrylla."

"But he is already to be married!" Iban insisted.

"Who speaks of marriage?" the Emperor asked. "An *advoutre* is an advisor, a confidante, a friend. Many Elves have an *advoutre* in their household. I myself had one, long ago. It is our way."

The Emperor turned to face Iban. "Prince Martyn may still marry this Princess of Gilead, but he will take an Aelvin woman as consort. She will join the delegation when it travels to Alrendria." To the assembly, he added, "I have anticipated *Ael Alluya*'s concerns. Prince Martyn will take as consort one of a low-born caste. Never shall a descendent of his be allowed to sit upon Valia's throne." He turned to the prince. "Is such an arrangement acceptable?"

Martyn swallowed, surprised by this turn of events. Slowly, he nodded his head, trying to look as if he were not pleased by the Emperor's announcement. "It is," he replied. "I will gladly accept one of your people as *advoutre*, if such is your desire."

The murmur spread throughout the hall, growing in volume. The Emperor used the distraction to lean in next to Martyn. "I doubt King Tarien of Gilean will retract the offer of his daughter," he whispered. "Just try not to look too happy with the prospect. Remember, you begrudgingly agreed to this only to appease the Aelvin Emperor, without whose support your trade negotiations would have been for naught."

Martyn swallowed again. "How can I ever thank you?" he asked, trying to fight back tears.

"No thanks, child," the Emperor said. "Likely as not I did you no favors. But once, a long, long time ago, I was forced to set aside love for country. I would not force such a decision on anyone else, no matter what my grandson might believe."

The Emperor turned back to the crowd and raised his hands for silence. This time, it took a little longer for the assemblage to still themselves. "The negotiations between our Races has been successful. *Ael Shenda Ruhl* will flow again! Our goods will travel throughout Madryn, and to us, exotic things will come from the far corners of the world!"

A cheer went up among the Elves. Martyn stood at the Emperor's side, looking out over the hall, and he saw Astalian, watching the Emperor with concern. Armed *Ael Chatorra* lined each wall, hands on their weapons. "At the end of winter, our two Races will exchange embassies. A party of Elves, under the leadership of Jaenaryn, will journey to Kaper, to be Our ears and voice to the King of Alrendria. Another delegation will travel to Grenz to secure the trade routes and prepare the way for the flood of wares which will travel *Ael Shende Ruhl.*"

Something flashed at the back of the room, drawing Martyn's attention. He searched for the source of the light, but could not identify it. "At the same time, a party from Kaper will travel to Lynnaei. Markets will be prepared for their use, and buildings grown for their comfort." Again the Emperor turned to Martyn. "Unless your father has a more suitable choice, I request that Lady Utari Hahna be your ambassador to my court."

Martyn bowed his head, but his eyes remained locked on the rear of the hall. "It will be as you wish, Emperor," he replied. There was another flash, to his right, far in the back of the chamber. He squinted, studying the crowd, trying to look disinterested in the proceedings.

The Emperor smiled. "We have a request to make of Alrendria. If you accept, We will be most pleased." His eyes shifted to the right, toward Treloran. "I have noticed a remarkable change upon my grandson since the Humans returned to Lynnaei. It has been a pleasure to watch him grow, mature into more than the angry youth he was two seasons ago.

"I would entrust him to you," the Emperor said, looking at Martyn, "send him to Kaper to learn your ways, as you were brought here to learn ours. If we Elves and you Humans are to forge a strong alliance, there must be understanding between our races."

A startled gasp escaped the assemblage again, though none seemed more surprised than Charylla. She looked at the Emperor in unhidden shock, and Treloran stared wide-eyed at his grandfather, his expression a mixture of surprise and excitement. "I will send no honor guard with my Grandson," the Emperor added.

He waved Astalian to silence before the *Hohe Chatorra* could voice a protest. "I know his safety will be of paramount importance to the Alrendrians. When Our people are sent to Alrendria, sufficient forces will accompany them to ensure his safe return."

For the third time, Martyn saw the flash. His eyes snapped to it this time, focusing. An *Ael Chatorra* stood in the corner of the room, bow in hand. He had an arrow notched, ready to draw. The light of a nearby lantern was flashing off the polished steel arrowhead.

Martyn exhaled, beginning to relax, when the Aelvin soldier hefted his bow, aiming it at the platform. He drew back the string, taking careful aim.

Martyn's eyes widened. He tracked the archer's angle.

"...certain both our Races will prosper from this exchange of–" The Emperor speech cut off as Martyn dove into him, shouting warning. He landed atop the Emperor with a bone-shattering crunch, and for a moment feared he had seriously injured the ancient Elf. Above him, a black-shafted arrow quivered in the wood of the throne.

There was a sudden commotion; shouts and screams filled the chamber. Astalian's voice could be heard over all. "Find the archer! Do not let him escape! Protect the Emperor!"

Iban was at Martyn's side in an instant, his eyes scanning the room for further danger. Astalian ran toward them, and a ring of Aelvin warriors had formed around the platform.

Martyn sat up, offering a hand to the Emperor. "I'm most sorry, Your Eminence," he said, slightly abashed. "I didn't have any other choice." Charylla knelt the Emperor's side silently, a look of worry on her face.

The Emperor waved off Martyn's apologies, groaning wearily as he pulled himself to a sitting position. A hand touched his aching hip. "Even a few winters ago I would have been most glad for your timely rescue, Prince Martyn. Now, I wonder if the arrow would be preferable. This bruise will last more than a season!"

Astalian appeared as if from nowhere to fuss over the Emperor. "I am fine, my friend," the Emperor assured him, rising to his feet. "Find the assassin. I am aware of the danger now. No attack will be able to reach me." Astalian frowned, then nodded. He disappeared into the crowd.

The Emperor rose so all could see him. He spoke in a loud and commanding voice, quieting the near-panicked crowd. "All is well, my children!" he told them. "My life has been saved by Prince Martyn of Alrendria. Already, We are indebted to Our new allies!"

His words calmed the frightened Elves. Iban approached, the arrow in hand. "*Noedra Synissti?*" he murmured, offering the shaft to Charylla.

The Aelvin Princess inspected the arrow, nodding her agreement. "Since their birth," the Emperor said, his words still carrying over the crowd, "the *Noedra Synissti* have never failed to kill their target. Now, not one, but two assassinations have been foiled, both by Humans! How can any doubt their friendship? How can any doubt their honor?"

A chorus of quiet agreements arose among the crowd. "It seems you have won us a few friends today," Iban said to Martyn.

Martyn smiled at the praise, but Charylla's comment quickly wiped it from his face. "If the Boundary is truly failing," she said, "we will need more than a few friends in the winters to come."

A stunned silence followed her statement. The Aelvin Princess turned to face Martyn; her eyes bored into him relentlessly. "You will protect my son," she said, and there was nothing of a request in her tone.

"With my life," he said, bowing.

"With your life," she agreed.

Chapter 34

"Everyone talks of danger in the Twilight World," Jeran said, interrupting Tanar, "but no one tells me what the dangers are!" He met the old man's gaze squarely. "Is it, or is it not, a dangerous place?"

Tanar exhaled sharply, his cheeks puffing out. "It is!" he said emphatically, then frowned. "But...." Lips pressed firmly together, Tanar fell silent.

"The threat of the Twilight World is not to the body," he said finally, choosing his words carefully. "It's to the mind. You have the ability to make things real there, just as you have the ability to unmake things there. What Lorthas says is true: he can do nothing to harm you. But at the same time, he may be able to convince you that he can, or has, done something that will harm you. If you believe it enough, it will become true.

"I can't cite specific dangers, because the danger varies from person to person. It is the conscious mind from which the threat emerges, and each mind is unique." Tanar took deep, resigned breaths; he had all but given up trying to convince Jeran of stopping his meetings. "I can only counsel caution. Remember two things at all times. One, only that which you believe can hurt you will."

"And the second thing?" Jeran prompted.

"There are thousand shades of truth, and the Twilight World does not distinguish between individual and absolute truth. So long as Lorthas believes what he says, it doesn't matter what the rest of the world believes."

Tanar's jaw clenched, and Jeran braced himself for another lecture on how foolish he was being. "Enough of this," Tanar said, waving his arms in dismissal, and Jeran sighed in relief. "Tell me how you're training is progressing. Are the exercises I recommended helping?"

Jeran shook his head. "I can seize magic at will," he told the older Mage, "but if I grasp more than the tiniest flow, everything unravels." His eyes grew irritated. "I know I can hold more magic!" he snapped. "I *have* held more."

Tanar's eyes were sympathetic. "This will be the toughest part of your training, my boy. Learning how to focus your Will is tough enough, but the feelings of helplessness that accompany learning how to maintain your focus are infinitely worse."

"Is there not a quicker way?"

Tanar shook his head. "Practice, Jeran. The only solution is practice. The quickest way would be to walk the world in a constant state of Focus, continually working your Gift. But the dangers along such a route are great. Eventually, you would fatigue, your magic would run wild."

Tanar's eyes grew distant as he pondered this dilemma. "If there were only some way to hold in check the flows of magic," he mused, "but still allow the apprentice the ability to focus." He reached over and patted Jeran's hand. "I wish you could control your Gift now, my boy. We will need every Mage in the winters to come."

A small frown marred the older man's features. "But, no matter how adept a pupil you are," he added, "it will be a decade before you have complete mastery over magic. I know of no way to hasten the process."

They rode in the center of the Afelda procession, heading northwest through the rolling grasslands. Small copses of thick-leaved trees dotted the hillsides. Above, the sky was an azure blue, with a few puffy, white clouds floating south. The late summer air was cool, though evening still lay some time off. Harvest was fast approaching.

Mika rode up to them, weaving his horse through the walking Tribesmen. During their travels, he had become an accomplished horseman. "Lord Jeran! Lord Jeran!" he called excitedly, waving for attention.

Jeran turned to look at the boy, and was surprised by how much Mika had grown during the last few seasons. His brown hair had grown out, curling at the edges, giving him a roguish look. Serious, intense, blue-green eyes stared at Jeran, and a broad smile was plastered across the boy's face.

"Lord Jeran!" he called again, slowing his horse alongside Jeran's. "Fox Eyes and Crying Wolf showed me how to use a spear! They said I'm old enough to join the hunt and want me to go with them! Can I?"

Two Garun'ah approached, but kept their distance. Fox Eyes was thin for a Garun'ah, with dark hair; narrow, probing eyes; and a sly expression on his face. Crying Wolf was lean and predatory, with lighter hair, bulging muscles, and two tear-shaped birthmarks beneath his left eye. They stood side by side, arms folded across their chests, awaiting Jeran's decision.

The three Humans had all but been adopted into the Afelda, especially Mika, who was fussed over by men and women alike. The men thought him a strapping young warrior; the women, an adorable little cub. Jeran and Tanar had seen little of the youth since the two parties had joined.

The Afelda had been more than generous. The Tribesmen eagerly shared their food and supplies, and they were willing to answer all of Jeran and Mika's questions. In exchange for the hospitality, the Humans were required to tell the Tribesmen about life in the Human lands.

This task primarily fell to Tanar, though Jeran did his fair share of storytelling, too. Each night, the Afelda crowded around a huge, central fire to listen to the Mage. Certain Tribesmen, those who spoke the Human tongue most fluently, translated the tales into Garu, repeating the tale for those too far from the fire. After the stories ended, the questions started. Jeran and Tanar struggled to answer them all; by the time the fire was extinguished and the Garun'ah made for their tents, the two were utterly exhausted.

Jeran looked at Mika and saw his exuberance, his barely contained eagerness. "Of course you can go," he said with a smile. "So long as you promise to heed their words and keep yourself from trouble." To the Tribesmen, he said, "If anything were to happen to the boy, his mother would be most displeased."

Fox Eyes smiled wryly. "Little more dangerous than angry woman," he replied, his words broken and choppy.

Crying Wolf chuckled. "Even Cat's Claw hide when Dancing Lily not happy." His hand touched the hilt of his *dolchek*. "Not worry, friend. We bring cub back unharmed."

"You not need horse, Little Tiger," Fox Eyes said to Mika. "It scare prey. Blood hunt on foot." Mika stopped his horse, dismounted, and stood holding the reins, not sure what to do.

Tanar laughed. "Hand her to me, Mika!" he said. "I'll watch her until you return." Mika ran forward to give the reins to Tanar, then he and the two Tribesmen disappeared into the crowd.

The Afelda marched resolutely, from sunup to sunset. The Tribesmen who did not hunt remained with the tribe, carrying baskets or drawing carts behind them, but those who walked in the procession–women and children, craftsmen and artisans–represented only a third of the tribe. The rest were Hunters. There were more Garun'ah than Jeran had expected, and the Afelda were small compared to some of the tribes.

Early each day, the tribal warriors formed small bands and disappeared, scouring the land for food and scouting the terrain for enemies. By spreading themselves out, Cat's Claw had explained, they minimized the stress they placed on the lands over which they walked.

"You leave your tribe undefended," Jeran once said to Sadarak, *Kranor* of the Afelda. "Don't you worry for their safety?"

The Tribesman's face had contorted in confusion. "What manner of creature would attack children? If there is battle, it be between Hunters. It Garun's way."

Amidst deep, resonating laughter, he added, "Besides, those foolish enough to attack Afelda would regret their dishonor. Our old ones can still throw spear. Our young have strong bite!"

Jeran had been even more surprised when he learned that the Hunters of the Afelda, the *Dar'Afelda*, were mostly women. While it was not uncommon to see women in the Alrendrian Guard, they were far outnumbered by men. The *Dar'Afelda* contained nearly four times more female warriors than male.

"It not so among all tribes," Cat's Claw had told them. "Most have equal number. A few, like Tacha, have more *Dahra* than *Dahrina*, but only Bahnje keep their women from Hunt."

One of the *Dahrina* approached Jeran now. She was of average height for a Garun'ah, slightly less than a hand shorter than Jeran. Her light brown hair, long and straight, came about as close to blonde as any Tribesman. Light brown, almond-shaped eyes, slightly twisted up at the corners, studied Jeran appreciatively. She was well curved, with long legs; a flat, muscular abdomen; and an ample bosom.

A skirt of hides wrapped around her waist, hanging to just below the knees, and a leather top covered her upper body, though it barely reached her midriff. Her skin was bronzed, smooth and unmarred, and she was unadorned except for a simple string of beads circling her throat and a feather running through her hair. In one hand she carried a long spear, and wore a *dolchek*, nearly two hands in length, hung at her right hip.

She walked alongside Jeran's horse, looking up into his eyes. "Little Tiger is your son?" she asked, with only the slightest hint of accent. When Jeran shook her head, she cocked a head to one side. "But he seeks your permission to join the hunt? Is his mother your mate?"

Jeran's eyes widened, and a smile touched Tanar's lips. "No," Jeran told her. "Mika is my friend, as is his mother."

"Then why...?" She did not finish the question.

"Mika is under my protection," Jeran answered, offering the Tribeswoman a smile. "If anything happens to him, it would be my fault. His mother is counting on me to protect him, and he seeks my permission because he knows we share the same fate, should trouble find him."

"Ahhh," she replied, nodding her head in understanding. "Among the Blood, a child answers only to his parents. If the parents are gone, the child assumes the role of adult, and is expected to behave accordingly."

It was Jeran's turn to look puzzled. "All children?" he asked incredulously. "What if the child's parents are killed?"

"If the cub is newborn," she answered, "he is given to a *Ga'dyian*, usually blood kin, who raise him as their own. But by eight winters, any child of Garun can care for himself, and should not be a burden to his tribe."

She looked up at him again, her eyes probing. "You are Jeran Odara?" Her eyes roamed over his body.

Jeran nodded, trying to hide a blush. "And you are?"

"I am Reanna, daughter of Isbek. Many call me Snow Rabbit. When the snows blanket the lands, none of the Blood can travel faster."

"What should I call you?" Jeran asked, not sure which name the *Dahrin* preferred.

The Tribeswoman's cheeks grew pink. "I would like for you to call me Reanna."

"Then that's what I'll call you," Jeran replied, a broad smile on his face. "Reanna," he said, testing the name. "It has a lovely sound." Behind him, Tanar's smile grew broader.

Reanna's cheeks turned bright crimson, and her eyes lowered to the ground. For a time she walked that way, eyes downcast. When she looked up, her earlier confidence had returned. "You are strong for a child of Balan," she said to him. "You would make a fine mate."

Jeran's eyes nearly popped out. "What?" he exclaimed, trying to keep his voice level. Tanar bit down on his lower lip.

Reanna's eyes sparkled. "You are strong and healthy," she told him. "You seem wise, and wisdom is as important as strength, though many do not believe so. Tanar says you are a mighty warrior." Her eyes roved unashamedly over his body. "And you are more than fair to look at. You will sire good children. You would make a good mate." She spoke the words matter-of-factly.

Tanar could no longer contain his laughter. Both Jeran and Reanna turned at the outburst, and the old man calmed himself. "Sorry," he said, "I just remembered something Limping Bear said." Jeran glowered at him.

Reanna turned her attention back to Jeran. "You are not interested?" she asked. "Have you a mate already? Is this why you hesitate?" She pursed her lips, looked him over again. "I would share you," she said finally. "But only with the right woman."

Jeran shook his head, waving his hands dramatically. "No. No! It's not that. It's just...." He trailed off, unable to finish.

Reanna laughed warmly. "You look like a mouse clutched in the talons of an eagle, Jeran. I do not wish for you to offer me a Heart Gift, nor name me your *bavahnda*. I only wanted to tell you of my interest. Should you wish to learn if we are...compatible...I would be...receptive."

Jeran's cheeks burned red. "You speak our tongue very well, Reanna," he said, hoping to change the subject.

She smiled at the praise. "My father, Isbek *uvan* Vureil, known as Frowning Squirrel, traded often with Humans. He even lived in Grenz for a time, until the walls of the city grew too oppressive. He respected Humans, especially Alrendrians, even after the slavers began raiding into the Tribal Lands, and he thought his daughter should learn your language, perhaps continue his trade." She shook her head. "I do not think he was happy when I chose the path of the Hunter."

Cat's Claw appeared, striding boldly toward them. "Good news, my friends," he called, raising his hand in greeting. "Kohr's Heart on horizon. By nightfall, we reach *Cha'khun!*"

He turned to Reanna. "Steel Fang return. She says Sahna half moon's travel west." A smile spread across his sun-darkened face. "Go greet our cousins, Snow Rabbit. Let see how fast you run when Kohr's icy breath not blanket world in white."

Reanna's eyes were all seriousness. "If I am not back in five days, then I walk the Twilight World with Garun!" She turned about, stopping only to look up at Jeran and smile, then ran west at a fast trot.

Sadarak watched her go, a thoughtful smile on his face. "Fine choice," he said to Jeran. "Snow Rabbit one my finest warriors." Tanar's laughter earned him another dirty look from Jeran.

Cat's Claw turned amused eyes on Tanar. "It said when man laughs for no reason, a God smiles on him."

"It may be so," Tanar mused. "But I have seen few signs of divine love during my life."

The *Kranor* of the Afelda walked to Tanar's horse, slapping it jovially on the rear. "My Hunters say many small tribes travel north. This be *Cha'khun* greater than even Garun has seen!"

He smiled, exposing white, slightly pointed teeth. "You walk with me," he told them, "to meet *Kranora*. Outsiders not come often to *Cha'khun*. I not want cousins to think I hide you."

He turned and started forward through the crowd. Jeran and Tanar followed, surprised at how fluidly the Garun'ah parted for their passage. In time, they reached the front of the procession, where two other Tribesmen waited. "You know Zyk *uvan* Linek," Cat's Claw reminded them, pointing to a broad, wide-mouthed Tribesman, "Called Thunder Runner." The Tribesman bowed, tapping his spear on the ground.

"This," he said, pointing to the other, a tall, olive-skinned woman with dark hair and eyes, "Eirha *uvan* Chizmit, Eirha Fleet-foot. She *Kranach* of Afelda." Twins scars ran down the length of Eirha's arms. She regarded the two Humans coolly.

"Us get...Us *reach* Kohr's Heart for twi...light," she said, struggling with the words, her voice heavily accented.

They continued in relative silence for the rest of the afternoon. Clouds drifted past, heading south, making it seem as if they traveled faster than they actually did. The hills, covered with green and golden grasses, flowed beneath them. Far distant, tiny forms could be seen standing on the hilltops, watching.

Eventually, the land began to rise, slowly at first, though the grade continued to increase. To the north, nothing could be seen but rising grassland, curving away to the east and west. Thunder Runner raised a bone horn to his lips and blew two long, low notes.

They continued on, climbing ever higher. When they were about halfway up the hillside, Cat's Claw signaled a stop. "Afelda wait here," he said in a voice that carried back over the plain. He nodded to Thunder Runner, who blew two more notes.

There was a sudden movement above, and a small group, silhouetted in the dying light of the sun, appeared at the top of the hill. One man, ancient and withered, rode on a palanquin carried by four Tribesmen. They set down their burden and disappeared. Two other Tribesmen stood side by side. One was a giant, so large in comparison to his companion that he made him seem a child.

Cat's Claw nodded again and started forward, Eirha Fleet Foot at his side. Jeran and Tanar started after, but Thunder Runner blocked their way. "You leave horse," he said slowly, gesturing at their mounts. "I care for."

Reluctantly, Jeran dropped from his saddle and handed the reins to the Tribesman. Tanar did the same, and they hurried to catch up to Cat's Claw, who was nearly to the top of the hill.

"I haven't been to a *Cha'khun* in a long, long time," Tanar mused, smiling at Jeran. "Do you remember your first view of the Anvil? The feeling of peace and awe in the Vale? This is another sight you will cherish for the rest of your life, Jeran."

They slowed their pace once they joined the *Kranor* of the Afelda. "We at Kohr's Heart," he said proudly, flashing a toothy grin. "Well come to *Cha'khun!*"

They crested the rise, and Jeran stopped, awestruck. Below, a vast valley filled his vision, descending gradually to the shores of a large, clear-watered lake. A thin stream wound through a narrow crevasse along the eastern wall of the depression. As if on cue, Kohr's Heart erupted, spraying water hundreds of hands in the air.

The stark beauty of nature was overpowering, but of equal effect were the incredible number of tents. Along the lakeshore, the ground remained barren, but it quickly gave way to the first of the Garun'ah's dwellings. The tent city reached more than halfway up the hill; with the addition of the Afelda, the valley would be filled to two-thirds its capacity.

Wagons, likely storing provisions, sat interspersed throughout the camp. Even now, small parties of Hunters returned from their daily foray, laden with the carcasses of giant herd animals. Other Tribesmen walked the tent city too, though the distance was too great for Jeran to tell what they were doing.

"*Jokalla, Yarchik uvan Greltar,*" Cat's Claw said, bowing to the ancient Tribesman. "*Jokalla, Arik uvan Hruta.*" The second greeting was to the giant, easily the largest man Jeran had even seen. Jeran recognized the third Tribesman even before Cat's Claw greeted him. "*Jokalla, Kal uvan Arik.*"

The three responded in unison. "*Jokalla, Sadarak uvan Zharik.*"

Cat's Claw smiled and pointed at Jeran and Tanar. "I know it unusual bring outsiders to *Cha'khun*, but *Tsha'ma* say Humans already here. They insist it Garun's will, allow these two as well."

Kal stepped forward and gripped Jeran's shoulders fondly. "*Jokalla, Jeran Odara!*" he said, squeezing tightly, then turning to address his father. "This Human helped free me from Soul Stealers. I owe him blood debt."

Arik smiled, the scar on his face pulling tight. "I am indebted to you, friend Human, for freeing my son's soul. The fires of the Tacha are open to you, always."

After exchanging pleasantries, Jeran looked around. "Where is Dahr?" he asked. "I thought he'd be here."

Kal's eyes darkened. "He is in the tents," came the sad reply. "There was an accident–"

Jeran's eyes widened. Afraid that he had arrived too late, afraid that Dahr had already been struck a mortal blow, he cut off Kal's explanation. "Take me to him!"

Kal nodded, bowed to his father, and started down the hill at a jog. Jeran followed, urging more speed from the Tribesman. They passed a line of children, hands tightly clenched on small knives, but Jeran hardly paid them any attention.

Kal wove through the tents, and Jeran followed blindly, barely seeing anything. They stopped before a large, green tent. Jasova and Wardel sat outside, and Wardel jumped up at their arrival, saluting fist-on-heart. "Lord Odara!" he cried. "Thank the Gods you've arrived."

Jasova stood as well. He saluted, but his eyes remained grim, sad. "How is he?" Jeran asked.

"As well as can be expected," Jasova replied. "He hasn't slept in two days."

Jeran pushed past Kal, between the two Guardsmen, and drew aside the tent flap. He stepped inside, surprised to find Dahr standing next to a cot. Two Tribesmen–one a stranger, short, with honey blonde hair; the other familiar to Jeran–flanked the bed. "Dahr?" Jeran called tentatively, and, hearing his name, his friend whirled around.

Dahr's face was haggard, his brown eyes sunken, ringed with deep lines; his shoulders were stooped; and tear tracks had dried on his cheek. His let out a shuddering breath when he saw Jeran and ran across the tent, enveloped his friend in a tight embrace. "She's dying, Jeran," he said. "She's dying."

Understanding dawned. "Oh, Dahr," Jeran replied, trying to console. Dahr buried his face in Jeran's shoulder; renewed sobbing echoed through the tent.

Jeran looked past Dahr. "Rannarik," he said in greeting, dipping his head slightly to the *Tsha'ma*. He looked at the bed, where Katya lay unmoving. "What happened?"

"She was bitten by *silbrahni*, the rainbow snake." Rannarik looked at Katya's ailing form sadly. "The poison is strong, quick. She would be dead already if Dahr had not been wise enough to bring the animal with him." The *Tsha'ma* lowered his head. "We have done what we can."

Jeran walked Dahr to the edge of the tent and sat him on a stool. Then he crossed the chamber to Rannarik, shaking his head. "You are *Tsha'ma*!" he reminded the Tribesman. "A Mage! You can heal her!"

"We are none of us skilled at Healing," replied the other Tribesman, who stood shorter than Jeran and stared at the new arrival with eyes uncommonly blue for a child of Garun. "What we can do has been done."

Jeran drew a deep breath, then jerked upright. "Tanar!" he exclaimed. He turned to Dahr. "Tanar is with me! He'll know what to do." He turned to the *Tsha'ma*. "The man I traveled with, he is a Mage."

Jakal looked at Rannarik. "He will be sent for," he said, leaving the tent at a run.

Rannarik gestured to Dahr. "He has not eaten, has not slept. It is best he go to his tent before we continue." He walked to Dahr, calling for Kal. The *Kranach* appeared, a worried look in his eyes. Rannarik lifted Dahr by the arm and led him to Kal. "Take him to his tent," the *Tsha'ma* ordered. "He is not to leave until morning."

Kal nodded, taking Dahr away, and Jakal returned. The two Tribesmen advanced on Jeran. "He will sleep," Rannarik said matter-of-factly. "By tomorrow, it will be decided. One way or another."

"It is better this way," Jakal added, a note of sadness in his voice.

"There has to be something we can do!" Jeran insisted.

Jakal shook his head. "We have done all we can." His eyes suddenly sparkled. "You can do something though, should you wish to."

"What do you mean?" Jeran asked suspiciously. "You're trained in your Gift; I can't hold the flows for more than an instant." At first, he did not realize that he had admitted to having the Gift. Once it dawned on him, he knew there was no way to take back the words. "What can I do that you cannot?"

"I have seen you in my dreams, little Human," Jakal replied. "You fight your Gift."

"Tell me, Jeran," Rannarik interjected. "Do the Magi still teach their apprentices to seize magic? To force the flows to them?" When Jeran nodded, Rannarik offered him a small smile. "It is as I thought."

"Seizing magic is one way," Jakal told him. "For some, that is the only way. But there is another method."

"Long ago," Rannarik explained, "Some Magi felt they had not achieved their greatest potential, and they came to the *Tsha'ma*, seeking training. We showed them our way, and for many, it opened a new world."

"Should you wish to learn this other way," Jakal added, "should you wish the training of the *Tsha'ma*, there is a chance we can save this girl child's life. But what you learn from us cannot be given to any save those with the ability. What you learn cannot be shared, not even with other Magi.

"It is why we need to speak with you now," Jakal continued, glancing toward the flap hesitantly, "before this other Mage arrives." He looked Jeran in the eyes. "Do you wish our training?"

Jeran nodded. "Anything!" he said, almost pleading. "Just hurry! Tell me what I must do."

Rannarik smiled. "For many with the Gift, the only way to touch magic is to force it to them, make it surrender to their demands. For a few, there is another way. If they open themselves to magic, if they surrender *themselves* to nature, it will come to them of its own accord.

"The advantages are many," Rannarik explained. "One who surrenders to Kohr's Gift can hold more flows than one who forces the magic to his will. Also can they follow the path of the warrior, while most Magi find themselves limited in their use of magic.

"The disadvantages are also many," Jakal added. "But we will discuss them at another time."

Jeran licked his lips nervously. "Surrender to my magic?" he repeated, slightly afraid. "I have done so before, though my teachers would not believe me." He shook his head. "I can't control so much magic. If I surrender to my Gift, it will run wild."

"If you draw the magic," Jakal said, "we can direct the flows. With the help of your Mage, we may be able to cleanse the poison from her blood."

The tent flap opened, and Tanar entered. He looked at the two Tribesmen, then at Jeran. "Are we agreed?" Jakal asked.

Jeran nodded. "Let's do it," came his stoic reply.

Chapter 35

Tanar's eyes flickered back and forth between the two *Tsha'ma*. "That large Tribesman said you needed me urgently" His forehead wrinkled in puzzlement.

Jeran pointed to the bed. "It's Katya!"

"Katya?" Tanar said.

Jeran nodded. "I forgot that you didn't know her," he replied, slightly embarrassed. "She's... She's Dahr's...."

"She is Dahr's *bavahnda*," supplied Rannarik.

"His wife?" Tanar said, translating the word. "Dahr's been busy since last I saw him."

"His wife!" Jeran repeated, his eyes going wide.

"She was bitten by the rainbow snake, Mage," Jakal said. "The poison has already worked through her body." He looked at Tanar appraisingly. "You are a Healer?"

Tanar returned the calculating gaze. "Not a Healer," he said, shaking his head, "though I do have some small talent in the area." He walked to the bed and turned the blankets down, exposing Katya's bare, sweat-covered flesh.

Jeran averted his eyes, his cheeks reddening. Tanar placed one hand on Katya's forehead, the other on her chest, just above the heart. He closed his eyes and took several slow, deep breaths. After a long moment, he shook his head. "There's nothing I can do," he admitted. "The poison has almost completed its task." His eyes were sympathetic. "I'm sorry, Jeran."

Turning to Rannarik, he asked. "You have no skilled Healers? Even in a camp this size?"

"The *Tsha'ma* do not restrict our powers, as do Humans," answered Rannarik. "We train every aspect of the Gift rather than focus on one strength. There are some among my brethren who have a natural talent for healing, but the best is less skilled than you."

Tanar sighed heavily. "Then there really is nothing to be done."

"We believe we have found a possibility," Jakal told him.

Tanar's eyes lit up. "Tell me!" he demanded.

"We will allow the young one to fill himself with magic," Jakal explained. "He has much strength, far greater than any one of us. Rannarik and I will control his flows, direct them to you, and you can use our strength to aid in the healing.

"I had thought to direct the magic myself," Jakal added. "But if you have even a little talent for healing, you are a far better choice than I." He looked at Jeran for a moment and smiled. "Besides, it may take both of us to control the young one's Gift. He shines so bright, my spirit eye is nearly blinded!"

Tanar cocked his head to the side. "You can transfer the flow of one person's Gift to another?"

Rannarik blinked in confusion. "Do you not do the same?"

"In training," Tanar explained, "the master often takes control of his apprentice's Gift, but only to dissipate the energy. No one has ever success-fully taken the Gift of one Mage and used the magic as his own." He eyed Rannarik askance. "It is something we have long thought impossible!"

Rannarik laughed, deep and resonant. "Perhaps it is impossible for Humans," he said wryly, looking at Jakal, "but it is not impossible." The blonde-haired Tribesman frowned, then nodded. "We will show you how," Rannarik added, turning back to Tanar, "in order to save the girl's life. But you must keep what you learn a secret."

"I give you my word," Tanar told them solemnly.

"Your oath is accepted," Jakal said with a bob of his head.

Jeran returned to the cot, where Katya twisted beneath her covers, sweat pouring from her body. Her lips were dry and cracked, her skin pal-lid. She moaned, but it sounded more a croak. A moist rag sat next to her, and Jeran grabbed it, daubing the Guardswoman's face. "Are we ready to begin?" he asked impatiently.

Three pairs of eyes turned toward him. "We must first explain to...." began Rannarik, but broke off abruptly and turned his gaze on Tanar.

"Tanar," supplied the white-bearded Mage.

"We must first explain the procedure to Tanar," Jakal repeated. "So he knows how to use our Gifts once we offer them. If he does not understand, if any of us make a mistake, we risk having all our magics run wild." He leaned forward, looking pointedly at Jeran. "I wish to see your friend recover, but I will not endanger the lives of my people."

While Jakal continued his explanation, Rannarik approached Jeran. "Peace, Jeran," the Tsha'ma said, his tone calmer. "A few more moments will make little difference if we are successful." He placed a calloused hand on Katya's brow. "You would best spend this time clearing your mind. Readying yourself."

Jeran nodded, touched Katya's cheek once more, then stepped a few paces back and sat cross-legged on the floor. He closed his eyes and slowed his breathing, starting the meditation Jes had first shown him on the way to Illendrylla, the meditation the Emperor had forced on him until it had become second nature.

He emptied his mind, taking slow, deep breaths to calm himself. He exhaled, forcing away unwanted thoughts. He inhaled peace. He exhaled emotion and doubt, inhaled confidence. Time and again he breathed, until his mind was blank, an empty canvas waiting for him to bring forth magic.

When he had first learned the meditation, it had taken him quite a while to reach this realm of complete calm. Now, it took but a moment. He could sense Rannarik approaching before the aged Tribesman placed a hand on his shoulder.

"We are ready, Jeran," the *Tsha'ma* said. Quietly, so only Jeran could hear, he whispered, "You are to embrace your Gift. Surrender yourself to it. Allow it to flow through you, even when it feels like you can hold no more.

"Jakal and I will be there. When you have filled yourself, we will take control. Do not fight us. Instead, surrender to us as you did to the magic. We will confine your magic, add it to our own, and send it to your friend, who will use it to heal Dahr's beloved."

The Tribesmen waited, giving his words ample time to sink in. "Are you ready, my friend?" he asked, and Jeran nodded. "Then open yourself to the magic."

Jeran imagined his source, a great cascading waterfall falling from the heavens into a deep, black pool. When Jes had taught him this meditation, she had insisted that he force the water to him, force it to do his bidding. It had been tough to make the water to come to him. At first it had refused, and for a while, Jeran had thought he would never be able to seize magic.

There were times though, even at the beginning, on the verge of giving up, when the waters had rushed toward him in a torrent. He had been frightened; the flood of magic had been more than he could control, more than Jes could control, more than even Emperor Alwellyn could control.

Since then, he had learned to seize magic. Now he could call it at will, though he could not hold the flows for more than a moment before they dissipated or ran wild. The magic did not rush toward him anymore, because he never gave up, never surrendered to it.

Now he was going to surrender to it purposefully, and the thought brought a spike of fear, threatened to break the meditation. Willing himself back to a state of complete calm, he ignored the memories of the near disasters that had accompanied his earlier attempts to surrender to his Gift.

In his mind, he saw himself walk into the pool of dark, cold water. The icy touch sent a shiver through his body. He waded toward the waterfall, nearly crushed by the torrent.

In reality, Jeran shuddered, and his body went rigid. The flows of magic poured into him, using him as a conduit. He was carried by those flows, helpless to resist them. And still he struggled to draw more magic, to fill every particle of his body with the life-giving energy.

Magic coursed through him, and he could hear every sound–the nervous breathing of the Guardsmen outside the tent, the fast–yet weak–beating of Katya's heart, the near thunderous booming as one of his three companions walked across the tent.

He opened his eyes slightly and quickly squeezed them shut again. There were millions of colors, each dazzling shade overpowering and yet beautiful to behold. He could not stand to look upon them.

More magic flowed into him, stifled him, threatened to drown him. He felt the power build to a crescendo, seeking a release, but he could not control it. He wanted to scream, but when he opened his mouth, only silence emerged.

Suddenly, he felt a second presence in his mind. Then a third. *Jeran,* said Rannarik's voice. *We are with you. Do not fear. Jakal and I will take your Gift and direct the flows to Tanar.*

Almost as a whisper, Jeran heard Jakal's voice. *So much power...!*

There was another moment of agony, and then the magic began to flow out of him. He felt it pulled away by the two *Tsha'ma.* Again he risked opening his eyes, and now the colors, though still more vibrant than he ever remembered colors being, were bearable. Two broad beams of white light radiated from his body, but he knew they were not really visible. He was seeing them with his mind's eye.

The beams of light diverged. They traveled to Jakal and Rannarik, who sat facing each other three paces away. The *Tsha'ma* had looks of intense concentration on their faces, and sweat beaded on their brows.

They had taken Jeran's magic, confined it, and amplified it with their own Gifts. Now they direct the flows to Tanar, who stood at Katya's side. The two beams of white light, interlaced with strands of yellow, gold, and blue, converged on the white-haired Mage.

Tanar glowed, appearing brighter than the sun, and again Jeran realized that only those with the Gift could see what he saw; those without, if they stood within the tent, would see nothing more than three people sitting on the ground and a fourth standing over Katya's prone form.

Tanar took a deep breath, then began to work the flows. He traced a hand along the outline of Katya's body. A sickly brown aura, muted and dull, surrounded the Guardsman. The lightest touch from the Mage was enough to make the brown swirl to color, revive some of Katya's vibrant life energy.

Tanar studied the Guardswoman, feeling for the source of her ailment. He took another breath, closed his eyes, then directed the magic into her.

At the first touch of magic, Katya's body jerked. Her eyes snapped open and she convulsed, nearly flopping off the cot. Jeran was so startled that he nearly lost his connection to his source. Lost his grip on the magic. Rannarik's voice was only mildly chiding. *Keep your focus, my friend. If we lose control, this will end in death for all of us. Perhaps others as well.*

Jeran nodded, calmed himself, and kept drawing magic. Tanar adjusted the flows and Katya relaxed. Her tensed and writhing muscles calmed, and she sank back into slumber, her eyes once again closing in sleep.

Tanar deftly wove magic through the Guardsman's body; tiny filaments of color wrapped around a core of pure white energy. Jeran stared in awe. Never in his life had he seen anything more beautiful than the dance of colors between Tanar and Katya.

The Mage moved to the head of the cot, and the beams from the *Tsha'ma* followed him. He placed a hand on either side of Katya's head, redirecting the flow of magic. Pulsations of white ran down the Guardswoman's body in waves, exiting through the toes. After a few moments, bits of the dull brown aura began to break away. They flowed with the white light, coalescing in a cloud around Katya's feet.

When the brown was gone, and Katya was surrounded by an aura of solid white, Tanar walked to the foot of the cot. He gathered the dirty brown energy in a tight ball, and with a flick of his wrist, sent it shooting toward the heavens.

The magic still flowed through Jeran in a river. It felt as if he were being pulled across the floor, the magic drawn through him, and he was not sure how much longer he could maintain his link. He prayed that Tanar finished quickly.

Tanar circled the cot, looking at Katya. All traces of brown were gone. In its place was a healthy violet color, interspersed with traces of black and gold. The colors were faint, but they pulsated with the beat of her heart.

Tanar looked at the *Tsha'ma*. "It is done," he said, smiling weakly. "We were almost too late. But we have cleansed the poison from her body and strengthened her spirit. She will live." He released his Focus, letting the magic return to its source.

Jeran felt the two Garun'ah in his mind again. Gently, they cut him off from his own source. The magic fought against them, struggled to continue flowing through him, but the *Tsha'ma* were relentless. Jeran felt the tide of magic pushed back, his tenuous connection to the flows dwindled, then released.

He collapsed onto his back, exhausted. Despite the chill to the air, sweat, unnoticed during the ordeal, soaked his shirt and ran off his body in rivulets. Quick, ragged breaths and the ferocious pounding of his heart accompanied Jeran to the ground.

After a long moment, he lifted his head slightly, opening his eyes to a squint, and saw that the others were not in much better condition. Rannarik and Jakal lay on their backs, breathing deeply. Tanar sat beside the cot, his head in his hands. His hair was matted to his head, and sweat dripped from his beard.

They stayed like that for quite some time, no one willing to break the silence. Tanar roused himself first. "Amazing," he stated, still breathing hard. "Never in my life have I had so much magic at my disposal." He looked at Rannarik. "The wonders which could be done with this knowledge! Think of what could be accomplished if the Gifts of all Magi were pooled!

"Why, even something as monumental as raising the Boundary would have been simple if we had used this technique rather than each using their own Gift individually." He looked at the *Tsha'ma* reproachfully. "How could you not tell us–"

He answered his own question before he even finished voicing it. "If miracles can be performed by using magic thus, then what of atrocities?"

Rannarik nodded. "Can you imagine such power in the hands of one like Lorthas? We *Tsha'ma* know this method, but use it only sparingly. Only when there are no other solutions. Those who misuse this knowledge, those who are even suspected of misusing it, forfeit their lives."

"Some have thought it worth the risk," Jakal admitted. "Every now and then, a few are foolish enough to combine their Gift, believing they can use their magic as a shield." He smiled, showing a toothy grin. "And they are right...for a time. But to break a chain, one must only break a single link." His smile grew wolfish. "In the end, all are given Garun's justice."

Jakal climbed to his feet, groaning as he stretched his neck and back. "You have great potential, young one," he said to Jeran. "Once you learn to tame the fires of your magic, you will be a force to reckon with." Jeran flushed at the praise, but was too tired to thank the Tribesman.

"And you," Jakal added, turning to face Tanar. "If you have 'some small talent' at healing, then those Magi who devote their lives to the study must be miracle-workers indeed! Never have I seen such a subtle inter-weaving."

Tanar returned the *Tsha'ma*'s smile. "I've had a few winters to prac-tice," he said humbly.

"Come," said Rannarik as he stood. "We have done what we can. We should leave Dahr's *bavahnda* in peace, so she can recover her strength." He started toward the tent flap. "We can continue our discussion at my fire," he suggested.

"Katya's not going to die?" Jeran asked, worry evident on his face.

"We all will die," Jakal replied, "but your young friend will have to wait for her chance to walk with the Gods."

Jeran released a breath he had not known he held. The muscles in his back unknotted, and he almost collapsed again, this time in relief. "Can I stay with her?"

Rannarik pursed his lips. "Briefly," he answered. "Assure yourself of her recovery, then join us at the fires of the *Tsha'ma*." He drew back the flap to the tent. "Do not stay long," he cautioned. "She needs much rest." He held the flap for Tanar and Jakal, closing it after he stepped through.

Jeran struggled to his feet, surprised at how little energy he had left. He stumbled to the cot and looked at Katya. Her color had improved; the white, pallid look was gone, and she was no longer drenched in sweat, though the blankets were soaked. For a time, Jeran watched the rise and fall of her chest, her breathing slow and regular.

Scanning the tent, Jeran found a second blanket folded on the ground. He grabbed it, shook it open, and draped it over Katya. Tucking it under her shoulders, he went to the foot of the bed and pulled the soiled blanket out from underneath. He did it carefully, so as not to expose the Guardswoman's naked flesh.

"How...chivalrous...." Katya said, forcing out each word. Jeran looked up as she spoke, a smile spreading across his face. He balled up the dirty blanket and threw it into the corner. "Afraid...you might...like...what you see?"

Jeran walked to the head of the cot and knelt at Katya's side. "Just trying to respect your privacy," he replied, forcing a light tone.

"Should have...taken advantage...might have been...last chance."

Jeran's smile broadened, and he put a finger to his lips. "Don't talk. You need to rest."

"Thirsty..." Katya croaked. "Water?"

Jeran looked around, found a pitcher and a small mug. "Can you raise your head?" With an expression of extreme concentration, Katya lifted her head a little more than a finger's width, then collapsed, shaking her head irritably. It seemed to take the rest of her strength. "No matter," Jeran told her, dipping a clean piece of rag into the pitcher. Wringing it out, he placed it in her mouth and allowed her to suck the moisture from it.

He had to repeat the process a score more times before Katya had enough. "What...happened?" she asked, her voice stronger, clearer. "How did you...get here?"

"You were bit by a snake," Jeran told her, shocked by the acidic glare he received. "Oh," he smirked, "you meant today." Briefly, he told her that he, Tanar, and the *Tsha'ma* had healed her, glossing over how it was done.

"And Dahr?"

"He is well," Jeran told her. "And will be even better once I tell him you're going to be fine." He shook his head, remembering Dahr's haggard appearance, his listless attitude. "He loves you very much," Jeran said, grinning evilly. "Just like a good husband should."

"I know he does," Katya answered, and there was a hint of something, almost sadness, in her voice. "I love him, too." She cast her eyes to the tent flap. "Can I see him?"

"Tomorrow," Jeran told her. "You need rest more than a reunion. In fact, I've already stayed longer than I should." He started for the door.

"Odara!" Katya snapped. Her voice was weak, but full of urgency. Jeran turned, a spike of fear passing through him; the Guardswoman's voice held within it a hint of urgency, of threat. "I owe you my life," she said, her green eyes boring into his.

He waved away her thanks. "We're friends, Katya," he answered. "You'd have done the same for me."

"Would I?" she mused. "I'm not so sure. Save you...certainly, but at the risk of my own life? No, don't try to deny it, I can see it in your eyes. Healing me put you in grave danger." She stared at him for a long time, her eyes calculating, weighing him. "We have to talk."

Jeran shook his head. "No," he said emphatically, "we don't. You need to rest."

"Jeran," she insisted. "You must listen–!"

"Katya!" Jeran snapped, a note of command in his voice. "You will shut your mouth and get some sleep! That's an order, Guardsman!" Winking, he added, "Besides, if Rannarik comes back and catches me here, I have a feeling *I'm* going to be the one in a sickbed tomorrow!" He started for the tent again.

"Jeran!" she called again, but her voice was weak, slurred. As the residual energy of the healing receded, sleep once again claimed Katya.

Jeran turned, one hand on the flap to the tent. "Believe me," he said, staring at her sympathetically. "Nothing you could say would surprise me. There'll be plenty of time to thank me tomorrow, once you've had some rest and are recovered." Without waiting for her response, he stepped through the flap and into the dark night.

Blinking in surprise, Jeran looked up at the stormy night. The sun had been well above the horizon when he had entered the tent, and no clouds had marred the perfect sky. Amazed that healing Katya had taken so long, Jeran released a deep sigh and looked around. Jasova still sat outside Katya's tent, but Vyrina, Lord Iban's niece, had replaced Wardel. "Lord Odara," she said in greeting.

"Jeran," he reminded her.

"Jeran," she amended. "How is she?"

"She'll be fine. She needs a great deal of rest, but the *Tsha'ma* purged the poison from her blood."

"Thank the Five Gods!" Vyrina said, casting her eyes toward the heavens. The stocky woman's eyes returned to Jeran. "My uncle?"

"He was well when we parted," Jeran told her, smirking. "Though I don't relish our reunion. I didn't exactly get his permission to leave Illendrylla."

"Then why...?"

Jeran shrugged. "Warning came from the Mage Assembly," he said, distorting the truth only a little. "I was told there would be grave trouble if I didn't set out immediately for the Tribal Lands." Craning his neck around to look at the tent, he said, "I guess they were right."

After a long, calculating silence, Jeran turned to Jasova. "I'd like a report, Subcommander, if you have the time."

"Nikki's replacing me shortly," Jasova replied. "I'd be happy to meet with you then."

"Perfect." Jeran turned to Vyrina. "Go to Dahr's tent," he ordered. "If he's still awake, let him know Katya is well, but that she cannot be disturbed tonight."

"And if he's sleeping?"

Jeran smiled. "Then let him have his rest. Either way, he won't get to see her till morning." Vyrina saluted and started for Dahr's tent at a run. Jeran bobbed his head to Jasova, then continued through the tent city, looking for Rannarik.

Instead, he nearly ran into Kal. The Tribesman stood more than a hand and a half taller than Jeran, but stepped back, as if he were the one about to be trampled. He looked down consideringly. "You have changed," he told Jeran. "Your eyes are older than when we parted."

"I have seen much these last few seasons," Jeran replied. "Done much."

Kal nodded. "Do you still believe the Dark Demon comes?"

Jeran nodded. "The Darklord has already begun to put his plans into motion."

"The Boundary will not hold?"

"The Boundary goes against nature," Jeran stated, paraphrasing the Emperor. "Nothing which defies nature can stand forever."

Kal smiled. "For a Human, you understand the Balance well."

Jeran's smile was a match for the Tribesman's. "What I know of the Balance, I learned from the Emperor of Illendrylla."

"An Elf?" Kal said incredulously. He paused, and his gaze turned inward. "An Elf...." he repeated, and this time, his tone was more thoughtful. "You are here to warn the Blood of this?" At Jeran's nod, he said stoically, "They will not like it."

"That's all right," Jeran replied. "I don't like it much either."

A long silence followed. "I owe you blood debt."

A flash of lightning accompanied the admission. "I haven't forgotten."

The two, Human and Garun'ah, stared deep into each other's eyes. "I will add my voice to yours," the *Kranach* said at last. "We will warn the Blood together. I know my father will listen to reason. I hope the other *Kranora* are as sensible."

Grasping Jeran's shoulder with his right hand, his face a mask of grim resolution, Kal added, "Even if all the tribes refuse to aid you, my *dolchek* will be at your side."

Jeran gripped the Tribesman's shoulder in response, mimicking the *Kranach's* gesture. "I welcome the blade," he told Kal, "but I welcome the hand that wields it more."

Chapter 36

The Garun'ah celebrated the arrival of the Afelda Tribe with a great feast. Jeran sat beside a roaring fire, his face red with the heat of the flames. Dahr was at his side, looking much refreshed after a night of sleep and his reunion with Katya. Jasova and Nykeal sat across the fire side by side, as did Vyrina and Frodel. Wardel and Elorn were nowhere to be seen.

Fires blazed throughout the camp, and Tribesmen danced around the flames. Music drifted on the night winds, the low bass beat of drums, the higher notes of pipes. Dahr turned to Jeran, smiling broadly. "When do you think we should talk to the *Kranora*?" he asked, nearly yelling to be heard over the din.

"Only one of the four largest tribes has yet to arrive," Jeran replied. "I think we should wait for them."

"I hope they don't take too long!" Dahr laughed. "It's getting crowded around here." Three more small tribes–the Bahnje, Jarturu, and Innesmok–each numbering a few hundred Tribesmen, had arrived during the day, and Kohr's Heart was now more than three-quarters full. The Hunters ranged ever farther afield, minimizing their impact on the area.

"A few more days!" Jeran told him, laughing. "We can wait a few more days." His eyes glinted mischievously. "Now tell me, old friend, when exactly did you and Katya wed?"

Dahr's cheeks flushed red, but his smile was broad and genuine. He told Jeran of the Garun'ah mating ritual and how he had asked Katya just prior to her getting bitten. "I couldn't be happier, Jeran," he said, grinning ear to ear. "She's wonderful!"

Jeran patted Dahr's shoulder reassuringly. "I'm happy for you!" he said, and turning to the Guardsmen, asked, "How have you enjoyed your time among the Tribesmen?" He and Jasova had stayed up late the night before, swapping stories. Jeran had been forced to repeat most of his tale to Dahr throughout the day, but had learned a few things about the Garun'ah that even the observant Jasova had not known.

Vyrina looked at Frodel, her eyes wide. "It's been a wonderful experience, Lor...Jeran," she said. At Jeran's sly smile, the Guardswoman's cheeks turned a bright shade of red.

"We've enjoyed ourselves as well," Nykeal agreed with a glance at Jasova. "The Garun'ah are a proud and honorable people. I've learned a great deal about them since our arrival." She looked at Jeran pointedly. "They'd make good allies." Jasova nodded his assent.

Jeran smiled at the thinly-veiled hint. "That's why I'm here, Nikki," he assured her. The evening passed, much of it in idle conversation–Jeran talking about his time in the Aelvin lands, the Guardsmen sharing their observations of the Garun'ah.

Kal appeared, with Mika not too far behind. "You did not tell me that you brought the little warrior!" the *Kranach* chided, feigning an angry expression. He looked at Mika fondly. "This cub has more spirit than a score of Humans!"

Mika ran up to Jeran. "Lord Jeran! I killed my first duck today! Fox Eyes said I'll make a good Hunter!" Suddenly, his cheeks flushed. "Once I learn to keep quiet and walk on clouds, that is." The boy's smile was broad, but his eyes drooped from fatigue.

"I think you've had enough excitement for today," Jeran said. "Remember, I need to return you to your mother more or less hale and healthy. Why don't you head for the tents." Mika's face fell, and his eyes grew sullen.

"His mother will never know!" Nykeal said, standing up for the boy. "Try to remember back to his age," she added, admonishing Jeran. "It couldn't have been *that* many winters ago. Would you have wanted to be sent to your tents?"

Jeran held up his hands in surrender. "Very well!" he said, laughing. "But I'm leaving him in your charge, Nikki. Good luck!" Beaming, Mika ran over and sat next to the blonde Guardswoman. She returned his smile, running a hand through his hair fondly.

"There you are!" said Rannarik, stepping out of the shadows, Tanar at his side. "I thought I would not have a chance to say goodbye!"

Jeran and Dahr were on their feet in an instant. "You're leaving?"

Rannarik nodded. "There are things I must do. Fear not. If Garun is with me, I will return before you leave the Tribal lands."

"I had hoped...." Jeran began. "That is, I thought you would stay to lend us your aid. You know the tidings we bear are not good."

Rannarik smiled knowingly. "Arik knows my mind, and he knows you have my support. My presence will not affect matters." He grasped Dahr's arm fondly, just above the elbow, and smiled into the younger man's eyes. "I regret that our reunion caused such sadness and pain. I pray to Garun, asking that you learn to accept what you are."

At Dahr's shy nod, the *Tsha'ma* laughed loudly. "Remember, my friend, you are no different now than before. Did you turn into an ogre the first time someone remarked upon your height?"

Turning to face Jeran, Rannarik repeated the gesture of parting. "You have some tasks before you," he said. "Once you complete them, return to us. We will continue that which we began last night." Inclining his head to the others, he departed.

Tanar followed the Tribesman with his eyes. "I think I'm going to miss him."

"There!" ordered a gravelly voice. "Set me down there! I wish to get a look at our new arrivals." All eyes swiveled at the sound. Yarchik approached, carried on his palanquin by four well-muscled Tribesman. The aged warrior's eyes were blurry, and his hands trembled in his lap.

They set him down in front of Jeran, and the old Garun'ah leaned forward, inspecting him closely. "I have seen you before," he stated. "In my dreams, you lead the Blood into a great storm, and I am not certain if we are strong enough to survive it.

"In my dreams, you are surrounded by crumbling walls, and you beat on them with a hammer of gold. 'Build! Build!' you shriek to those around you, even as you smash the walls asunder."

His eyes glazed over, and in a deeper tone, he recited. "One will come who will shatter all bonds, remove all allegiances, demolish all alliances. On the Anvil will he fall, to be molded by the Hammer of Kohr. Woe to the world should he break in the forge. Woe to the world should he survive his tempering. With the Elves in one hand and the Garun'ah in the other, he will run into the Darkness, to set right that which is wrong."

Jeran stared wide-eyed. "How do you... Are you *Tsha'ma*?"

"*Tsha'ma*?" repeated Yarchik. "Blessed Garun, I hope it is not so! I am just an old man. One who dreams too much and never learned to quiet his tongue."

"Then what...." Jeran started, again unable to complete his thought.

"My words?" supplied the Tribesman. "The first were my dreams. The rest, a passage from the *Prah'phetia*. Whether or not it applies to you...." Yarchik shrugged. "I felt the need to say it."

The old man looked at Tanar, then at Mika. A smile split his face. "Two strangers!" he said, somewhat joyfully. Mika recoiled a step at the elder Tribesman's tone, but Yarchik merely laughed. "Rare it is to find faces that have not already revealed themselves to me in the Twilight World."

"Enough of this!" he announced. "Tonight is a night of celebration! We should be dancing and drinking, not frightening each other!" The light in his eyes, which had flared so briefly to life, now died, and he looked down at his withered legs. "*My* dancing days, however, are long finished, and I find that strong drink no longer sits well on my stomach. Such things are the joys of the young.

"Should you wish it, I will tell a story. One of the Blood's many tales." Jeran looked at Dahr, who was staring eagerly at Yarchik. The Guardsmen all nodded in approval, and Frodel bowed his head solemnly, waving for those Tribesmen near enough to come listen to the words of the Great Yarchik. Of all those present, Mika was the most enthusiastic.

"Do you know the Story of the Gods?" Yarchik asked Dahr, who shook his head. Then he turned to Jeran. "And you, friend Human? Do you know the Story of the Gods?"

"I know *a* Story of the Gods?" Jeran replied cautiously.

"You do not believe my story will match the one you heard before?"

"In my experience," Jeran laughed, "the same story is rarely told twice, even when it's told by the same person."

"Wisely said," said Yarchik, gesturing to those around him. "Then gather round, my friends, and I will tell *my* Story of the Gods, the one passed down through generations of Blood." He laughed, loud and low. "You will forgive me if I fumble with the telling. Some words do not translate well to *Huma*.

"Long ago, before the Four Races walked this world, before this world was, there was the Nothing. The Nothing stretched from one side of creation to the other. It was barren, desolate; a vast, empty blackness.

"Then there was Kohr. The Father of Gods burst into being, stared at the Nothing, and thundered, 'I am!' Even the Nothing, whose own powers were infinite, shrank back from the power in the God's voice.

"Kohr traveled through the void, and wherever He went, the Nothingness fled. But the Infinite is lonely, and Kohr yearned for a companion, one to share his ideas of creation. 'I will create a companion,' said He. "One to wander the Infinite at my side.'

"There was a flash of light, and when it receded, Shael, the Mother, stood beside Kohr. Kohr had intended to create a submissive companion, one who would bow to his authority, but only a God can look into the Infinite without losing sanity. Only a God can face the Nothing and return unscathed.

"Shael looked around the Infinite and sighed. 'What a dismal place,' said She. 'I do not relish an infinity of boredom. I shall create a universe to amuse myself.' She studied Kohr intently, and offered the Elder God a small smile. "Would you care to join me?"

" 'I am partial to the emptiness,' Kohr told Her smugly."

A ring of Tribesmen formed around Yarchik; bodies pressed in on the Alrendrians from all sides. Yarchik continued, smiling at his people. " 'Then stay out here,' Shael said, and in a flash of light, She disappeared. Fuming, his rage barely contained, Kohr bellowed for Shael, but the Goddess ignored his cries and built the Heavens. Kohr watched Her from the shadows, and though He tried to pretend disinterest, He grew curious. Now eager to assist in creation, He joined the Goddess in the Heavens.

" 'What is this place?' He asked, looking around.

" 'These are the Heavens,' Shael replied. 'This is where I shall live.'

"Kohr studied it with a frown. 'I do not like it,' He told Her.

" 'Then leave,' Shael retorted, enraging Kohr, but the Goddess did not notice, so intent was She in creating the Twilight World.

" 'I would stay,' He stated boldly. 'But I would make some changes.'

"Shael stopped and looked at Kohr harshly. 'This is *my* universe you have entered,' She told Him. "I would share it, but there are rules.'

" 'Rules!!' thundered Kohr indignantly.

" 'Rules,' repeated Shael. "Conditions, if you prefer."

" 'I am the All!' Kohr shouted. 'The Father!'

" 'You have made that abundantly clear,' Shael replied. "Nevertheless, you will concede to my demands and share this universe with me, or leave here and create your own.'

" 'Name your conditions.'

"Shael offered her companion God a knowing smile. 'First, throughout this universe, from now until the Nothing returns to swallow Us, all that is made cannot be unmade. All creation must progress in its own way. I will not have you changing things every time your temper is aroused. Which, if your recent behavior is any indication, will be quite often.' "

Jakal appeared in the throng and used his Gift to give Yarchik's voice strength, so those far from the aged Tribesman could hear his story clearly. Using his magic, he translated the words of the story, making the image clear in the minds of all who heard the *Kranor*'s tale.

Yarchik smiled appreciatively at his *Tsha'ma*, then continued. " 'A reasonable request,' Kohr told Shael.

" 'You will take me as your wife,' Shael added. 'We will raise a family of Gods to rule the Heavens. The children you sire will be our equals in every way, allowed to follow whatever path they choose.'

"Kohr laughed; the idea of devoted Child-Gods appealed to him, and he nodded his assent. 'To symbolize our unity,' Shael continued, 'we will create a world together. We will share this world with our children and watch it grow.'

" 'A diverting pastime,' agreed Kohr. 'Have you any other...conditions...my Wife?' Shael considered his question for a moment, then shook Her head. 'Then let us create this world,' Kohr told Her, a smile spread across His godly face. 'First,' He said lasciviously, 'we shall satisfy your second condition.'

"The Goddess Valia, The Gardener, Daughter of the Gods, was created from their union. She grew while our world was created. Kohr created the sun and the fires which burn beneath the ground. Shael filled the seas with water and the skies with air. Kohr created storms, and Shael dug vast caverns to offer protection from them.

"When it was finished, the Gods looked upon their creation with pride. 'It is a wondrous thing, that which we have created,' Kohr said.

" 'Indeed it is, my Husband," Shael replied.

"The young Goddess looked around the desolate, barren world. 'It is colorless,' Valia told Her parents, closing her eyes. All across the world plants grew, covering the land with beauty and color, and when she was finished, Valia opened Her eyes and smiled. 'Much better,' She told Her parents.

"Shael smiled at Her daughter, but Kohr grew angry. 'You dare claim the work of your parents was not perfection?"

" 'Perhaps, Father,' Valia said, a twinkle in Her eyes, 'our definitions of perfection differ.' Kohr stared at His daughter in surprise, then filled the Heavens with laughter. With a flash of light, He departed the world.

" 'You have brought life to this world, Daughter,' Shael said, 'Where there is life, there must be death. Where there is life, there must be a balance.'

" 'She looked at the world and said, 'A caretaker must be found to tend this world.' At Shael's whim, the Orog were created. 'Greetings, my children,' she said, looking at them proudly. I created you to tend this world. Preserve the Balance.' They bowed to their Goddess and began to work.

" 'And what of these beings?' Valia asked. 'What will happen to them when they die?'

"Shael smiled beneficently. 'They will join us in the Heavens,' She told Her daughter.

" 'Only those who please us,' Kohr thundered down from above. 'Those who do not serve their Gods well will return to the Nothing!'

" 'As you wish, my Husband,' Shael replied, looking at Valia. 'So long as they serve one of us faithfully, they will be granted eternity in our presence.'

"Time passed, and Valia found herself displeased with the Orog. She believed they fell short in their attempts to maintain the vast garden She had planted across the world. The young Goddess wanted Her own Race to tend to the Balance. And so were born the Elves.

"Valia spent much time among her chosen people, instructing them in the proper care of Her other creations. A meticulous Goddess, She felt everything had a place. Orderly rows of flowers bloomed where She walked; wild growth drew back at Her approach. As the ages passed, She taught Her children how to force nature to their will.

"Kohr grew lonely in his daughter's absence, for Valia was often more agreeable than Shael. 'Wife,' he said, calling the Goddess. 'Surely one child is not enough for the Creators of this universe. Come to me, that we may make a son in our image.'

"Shael did as bid, for in Her heart, She had yearned for more children. In time, the Twin Gods, Balan and Garun, were born from the Elder Gods union, and Kohr stared at his sons in shock. 'Two!' he yelled. 'We meant to create only one!'

" 'And yet two we have,' Shael responded, stroking Her sons' cheeks fondly. 'Perhaps there is a purpose behind their birth. A power beyond us.'

" 'A power greater than the Gods?' scoffed Kohr. 'What foolishness do you speak?' He looked at the boys. 'One we wanted, one we shall have.'

" 'Might I point out, Father,' said little Balan, 'that you do not have the power to unmake us.'

"Kohr did not like His eldest son's tone. 'I have decided which of you will be unmade,' He growled.

" 'You're welcome to attempt it, Father,' Balan told him. 'But remember, you possess no powers that I do not also have.' Kohr seethed with anger at his son's indifference. He yelled at Balan, the first of many arguments.

"When we hear thunder," Yarchik said, digressing from the story, "it is Kohr yelling at Balan. Or so my father used to say."

With a smile directed at Mika, he continued. "To escape Kohr's anger, the Twins spent much time in the world below. They explored the world together, learned its many intricacies. 'There is not enough life down here,' Garun moaned one afternoon, as he and his brother lay in a grassy field. 'Not enough excitement.' He closed his eyes, and a shape materialized before him. It shook its head and stared at the world with innocent eyes.

" 'What is this?' Balan asked, picking up the creature. He looked at its long ears and wide, frightened eyes.

" 'I will call it rabbit,' Garun told him. Another appeared, this one a female. 'It is the first of my creations. Come, Brother, and play this game with me. We will fill this world with animals—the air with birds, the seas with fish, the plains with beasts of all shapes and sizes. This is the true balance! This is the real cycle of life!'

"Together, the Twins constructed all manner of creature, from the tiniest insect to the giant sea leviathan. After a time, their creatures worked their way into Valia's gardens, and She sought out Her brothers in anger, finding them relaxing in a narrow ravine. 'What is this...thing?' She asked, tossing a carcass at their feet.

" 'Do you like it?' Garun asked, looking at the animal. 'I want to call it dirt devil, but Balan thinks mole a better name. Which do you prefer, Sister?'

"Valia was not impressed," Yarchik said, laughing like he could see the expression on the Goddess' face. 'What was it doing in my garden?' She asked, ignoring Garun's question.

"Garun shrugged. 'One cannot tell nature where to go. I do not see you telling your trees not to grow up the sides of Mother's mountains. Nor do your Elves care where they settle, so long as there are trees nearby.'

" 'I shall instruct my people to catch your animals,' Valia told Her brother tartly. 'They will tame them, use them in their gardening. They will hunt them and kill them for sport. Best you tell your creations to stay away from me.' "

Yarchik chuckled at the Gods' argument. "Valia had inherited a short temper from Kohr," he explained. "But so had Garun. Feigning a calmness he did not feel, the Hunter looked his sister in the eye. 'As you will, Valia,' He told Her. 'But warn your Elves. Not all of my creations are like mole. Some come with defenses of their own.'

"After the Goddess left, Garun ranted to his brother. 'Why does she think she's better than us?' He strutted across the field in an imitation of the Goddess. 'Keep your animals from my gardens,' he mocked, imitating Valia. 'My Elves will take care of them!

" 'Why does *she* get a Race of her own?' Garun demanded, peering angrily across the field. A thought occurred to him, and he smiled. Taking a deep, steadying breath, he created the Garun'ah. 'That was fun, Brother!' the Hunter exclaimed, turning to face his creations. 'You are my Blood,' He said to them, 'My hands upon this world. You must struggle to maintain the Balance. To preserve nature.

'All life is sacred, my children. All of nature. You must listen to the Voice of Madryn, look for the tender threads of the Balance. You must–'

"Another group of beings appeared next to the Garun'ah, startling the giant God. The two Races stared at each other, still unused to their new bodies. 'I will call them Human,' Balan told His brother, smiling.

" 'They're not very big,' Garun pointed out, studying them carefully.

" 'It will force them to use their minds more than their bodies,' Balan explained, admiring His Humans. 'I hope.'

" 'And what task will you set your people on, my Brother?'

"Balan shook his head in answer. 'I will leave them to their own devices. Let them find their own path.' The Twin Gods suddenly found themselves in the Heavens, whisked away by Kohr.

" 'What have you done, my Son?' the God demanded.

" 'I have created a Race.'

" 'You do not guide them?' Kohr inquired. 'You give them free will?'

"Balan met His father's fiery gaze. 'That is my intention.'

" 'You will destroy all creation with this foolishness.' Kohr told His son. 'These creations of yours must be guided, shown the correct path, or they will not find it.'

" 'Perhaps I have more faith in them than you, Father.'

" 'Why have you never created a Race, Father?' Valia asked, trying to stop the argument from getting out of control.

"Kohr chuckled. 'You are all my creations, Daughter. Thus, your Races are mine."

"Shael's laughter filled the Heavens. 'Besides, would you really want a Race created by your father walking the world below?'

"Kohr grew indignant at the Goddess' words. 'To the wisest of each of your Races,' He told His children, 'I have given a gift. They will share in our power, the ability to create and destroy.' He looked at Shael scornfully. 'Since you insist on mocking me before our children, I have refused this Gift to your people.'

"The God's eyes danced with mirth. 'You will see how they abuse their powers,' He told His family. 'In time, you will come to understand what I already know.' His laughter followed the other Gods back to our world.

"For a long time, the Gods walked among the Four Races. Shael and the younger Gods spent much time with their Races, instructing them how best to maintain the Balance. Even more time was given to those 'gifted' by Kohr, who were taught not only how to use their powers, but also the responsibilities that came with their Gift. The Gifted were instructed to protect those born without the blessing of magic.

"Kohr appeared from time to time, inciting chaos, trying to subvert the Gifted. Balan once caught him in his machinations. 'You see, Father,' the young God smirked. 'They are more honorable than you give them credit.

" 'You cheat, my Son,' Kohr told Him flatly. 'The presence of the Gods prevents them from doing ill. Without your guidance, they would fall to temptation in seasons.'

" 'Then perhaps it is time we departed this world,' Balan said, issuing challenge.

"Kohr agreed, and the other Gods were told they would have to leave. 'I will not!' cried Valia, and for once, Garun agreed with his sister.

" 'You will do as I say, Children!' Kohr commanded, and with Balan offering his arguments, more logical and less emotional than Kohr's demands, the other Gods eventually agreed to withdraw from our world.

"They returned one last time, to say farewell to their Races. The Orog did not mourn Shael's departure, for they knew She would always be a part of them, but they honored Her memory as their creator.

"The Elves, however, grew frantic when Valia announced that She was leaving. They begged Her to stay, pleaded with Her, told Her they would not know how to tend the gardens without Her. 'You will know the way,' She told them, creating a beautiful garden in the heart of the greatest Aelvin city with the wave of a hand. 'This is my Garden. So long as you struggle to match its beauty, you work in my name.'

"She blessed them and prepared to depart. As an afterthought, She said, 'You are the eldest of the Races, save the Orog. My brothers' children are young, foolish, and prone to mischief. You must watch them carefully, keep them from harming the Balance. Save them from themselves, my children, and show them the proper path.' Her eyes took on a tired expression. 'You will need much patience,' She said knowingly.

"Garun had nearly as difficult a time leaving as His sister. The Blood demanded that He stay. 'We will not know how to serve the Balance. None can hear the Voice of Madryn as you.'

" 'My Blood!' the Hunter cried, beckoning his people close. 'All have the ability to hear the Voice of Madryn, you need only listen! Fear not, my children, for I will not be far. I will confer with the Tsha'ma across the Infinite. They will guide you.'

" 'But what of nature?' lamented one solitary warrior. 'Only You have the gift to commune with your creations!'

" 'Not so, my disciple!' Garun said, touching the warrior's head and the heads of several others. 'Now you will hear the Lesser Voices. You are Tier'sorahn.' Those blessed by the God stood back in awe, as a new world opened to them. Adoringly, they watched Garun return to the Heavens.

" 'What of us, Mighty Balan?' the Humans asked their God. 'What words have you for us?"

" 'Think with your head, decide with your heart,' the God told them. 'Your soul will always know right from wrong.' He pointed toward the Elves and Garun'ah, who stared at the Heavens. 'Do not seek for me among the stars. Forever will I be with you. If you need me, you need only look within.' In a flash of light, Balan, the last of the Gods to walk our world, vanished."

Yarchik looked around the circle. "And so goes the story of the Gods. It is said that, one day, they will return to take the righteous to the Heavens."

The crowd slowly broke up; casks of *baqhat* were opened, and the festivities were renewed. "Tell me, my young friend," Yarchik said to Jeran. "How does this story compare to the one you heard before?"

Jeran smiled. "There are many similarities,' he admitted. "But also many differences."

The old Tribesman nodded. "Such is often the case when one discusses Valia's and Garun's children. Do not look surprised! I know you Humans have little regard for religion. Your own God told you to seek within yourselves! And the Orog have long been lost. Since you came from the lands of the *Aelva*, I guessed it was their tale you had heard.

"You are both proud and honorable Races," Jeran told him. "How is it that you have so long been at war?"

"Wars rage between the children of Valia and Garun from time to time," Yarchik admitted. "But not as often as the Human histories would have one believe. Again you look surprised! I have been crippled for many winters. When one cannot travel the land, he must seek other diversions.

"There is still some bad blood between our Races," the *Kranor* admitted. "Some from as far back as the Great Rebellion. The Blood resents the enslavement the *Aelva* forced upon us, and they resent our breaking those bonds and killing their beloved Emperor.

"Another difficulty lies within our hearts," Yarchik added. "The *Aelva* believe that the Balance cannot exist without order, while the Blood believe that nature must run free of all bonds." He smiled. "I have often felt that both Races misinterpreted the Gods' meanings."

He broke out in hoarse laughter. "We must think on these things, Jeran. At all times must we think on these things. That is the problem with this world. There is far too much action, and not enough quiet reflection." His chuckling turned to a deep, hacking cough. "I never appreciated the wisdom in those words until I was incapable of action!"

Jeran smiled weakly. "I will think on your words,' he promised. "When I have the time."

"Time...." Yarchik said, his eyes growing distant. "Time you will have in abundance."

Chapter 37

"It's kind of like how King Mathis adopted me into the Odara Family," Dahr said, trying to explain the *chanda* ritual. "A *chanda* is a best friend… But it's more than a friend. It's almost like a brother. It's the one person you can always rely on, the one from whom you keep no secrets, and even if you tell them something horrible, they'll understand, because they're your *chanda*."

They sat on a hill about a league from Kohr's Heart; the open plains spread out around them all directions, and the sun shone brightly in a clear, blue sky. To the north, a large hunting party, nearly thirty warriors strong, returned to Kohr's Heart. "In that case," Jeran smiled, "it's already done! You've been a brother to me for ten winters, the only family I have!"

His smile grew broader. "I'll gladly be your *chanda*," he said, "if that's what you want. What do I have to do?"

Dahr outlined the procedure, telling Jeran about the three steps–the Asking, the Exchange, and the Oath. "I guess we just finished the Asking," he laughed, "so it's time for the Exchange. Kal says the object must be something of deep personal value, to symbolize the bond between the *chandas'* souls."

Dahr unhooked the *dolchek* sheath from his belt and handed the blade to Jeran. "Kal gave me this blade," he explained. "To me, it symbolizes my…reluctant…acceptance of being Garun'ah."

Jeran drew the curved blade and looked at the jagged, serrated edge. He smiled as he hooked it to his own belt, opposite his Aelvin longsword. "If I can get the warbow of an Orog," he mused, "I'll have a set!"

His smile turned into a frown while he decided what to give Dahr in exchange. Eventually, he thought of the perfect thing. Reaching behind his neck, he removed the golden chain on which hung the Wolf's-head medallion of House Odara, Aryn's parting gift to his nephew.

"I can't take that!" Dahr said when Jeran offered him the chain. "I know how much it means to you!"

"That's the whole point!" Jeran laughed. "Unless I misunderstood the whole purpose of this ritual."

Dahr shook his head. "No," he insisted. "Find something else."

Jeran's eyes gleamed dangerously. "You will take this," he said sternly, faking a severe expression, "or you can find yourself another *chanda*!"

Reluctantly, Dahr reached out and took the medallion from Jeran's hand. Swallowing reflexively, he laid the heavy chain around his throat. "Thank you," he said, his eyes tearing.

Jeran waved off the gratitude. "Now, what oath do we need to make?"

"Kal said there was no specific oath. We just have to promise to be loyal, honest, and honorable to each other, putting the needs and the life of the other before our own, until the day we die."

"Oh," laughed Jeran, "is that all?"

"Well," Dahr said guiltily, "we also have to seal the oath with blood."

Jeran smirked, drew his *dolchek*, and cut a narrow line across his palm. "I swear to you, Dahr Odara, that I will be loyal to you, that I will tell you no falsehood, nor keep any secrets from you. From now until the day I die, you will be my brother, as you have been since the day we first met." He handed the knife to Dahr. "My honor is yours."

Dahr took the blade, cut his own palm, and repeated the oath. They joined hands, and their blood mingled as one. "Does this mean I'm Garun'ah now?" Jeran asked, laughing.

Dahr's answering laughter thundered across the plains. "Actually, this was all a plan to finally make *me* Human!" he joked. "What do–" He broke off his statement, his eyes looking over Jeran's shoulder.

Jeran turned, not sure what to expect. Behind him, another large party of Garun'ah marched toward Kohr's Heart. Several hundred Tribesmen were visible, and more might be hidden on the far side of the hill. A few of the Garun'ah were laden with large packs, but most walked unburdened.

"That's too large to be a hunting party," Dahr mused.

"Maybe it's one of the smaller Tribes," Jeran suggested. "Since I arrived, two or three have joined the *Cha'khun* every day."

"Maybe...." Dahr stood, squinting to make out more detail. "But there don't seem to be any children with them, and only a few women and old ones." Dahr sniffed the air. "Something... I don't know. Something doesn't seem right." He shrugged, laughed. "I think I'm just paranoid!"

Jeran clapped him on the shoulder. "We'll ask about them when we return to camp. Surely Arik, Kal, or Yarchik will know who they are." Suddenly, he rubbed his hands together, a devious look in his eyes. "The ceremony's over, right?" When Dahr nodded, his smile broadened. "Then we're *chanda*! That means it's time for you to tell me all your secrets!"

Dahr's eyes grew instantly dark. "Come on, Dahr," Jeran urged. "You said this was part of being *chanda*! No secrets... You can trust me!"

Dahr tried to work some moisture into his mouth. "There is one thing...." he said, trying to find the right words. He fumbled, thinking, *How can you admit to anyone, even your blood brother, that you spend your nights in conversation with a demon?* "One thing that's troubled me a lot since you entered Illendrylla...."

A prolonged silence ensued. Jeran waited patiently for a moment, his good humor fading. Finally, he reached out a hand and placed it on Dahr's shoulder. "It's all right. You can tell me."

Dahr swallowed. "When I sleep...." he started, unsure which words to use. "When I dream... Sometimes my nightmares are interrupted by a different kind of nightmare. In it, I'm in a room. And there's somebody there with me. We... We talk about things.

"The room is barren," he said, digressing to delay the admission. "There's a fire on one side and a door on the other, but no matter how hard I try to get to the door, it's too far away." He paused, licking his lips nervously, and lowered his eyes to the ground. "In fact, I really don't even try to leave anymore. I sit and listen, even though I know I shouldn't... And... And...."

"And the wine never tastes that good," Jeran said. "No matter what Lorthas says."

Dahr nodded. "But that's not the worst part, Jeran. The person...the person I'm talking to... It's...." He stopped, looking up sharply. "What did you say?"

"I said the wine never tastes good," Jeran repeated, a small smile on his face. "No matter what Lorthas says."

Dahr's eyes went wide. His mouth opened, moved up and down, but no words came out. He finally found his voice. "How did you know that?" he asked, then understanding dawned. "You've seen him too!"

Jeran nodded. "In my dreams, just like you. And just like you, I sit and listen." He shrugged. "It's only fair, I suppose. Even Lorthas deserves a chance to tell his tale. History has a one-sided perspective on things.

"How far along are you in the story?" Jeran asked. Dahr told him, still surprised by the calm with which Jeran spoke of his meetings with the Darklord. "That far back?" Jeran said. "You must have let him rant on about his winters in the Arkam Imperium longer than I did."

"Jeran!" Dahr said incredulously. "This is the Darklord we're talking about, not the addle-brained old man who used to tell us stories while he curried the King's horses!"

"I know," Jeran replied. "Believe me, the fact that I speak with the Darklord is never far from my mind." He reached over and gripped Dahr's arm warmly. "But I know *he's* the evil one, Dahr. Not me. It was he who committed those atrocities, not me. It was even he who sought me out in the Twilight World." He paused long enough to offer a shrug. "Talking to him doesn't make me evil, too. And it doesn't make you evil, either."

Dahr's eyes had nearly bugged out of his head. "But he's the *Darklord!*"

"Well," Jeran admitted, "I don't exactly go around advertising my visits with Lorthas. But I figure it's a good opportunity. If we listen long enough, maybe we'll be able to figure out what he has planned!

"Still," he mused, running a hand along his chin, "it's probably best if we keep this a secret from him. I doubt he'd want us comparing notes."

They talked for a while about Lorthas' visits, sharing what they had learned, comparing the Darklord's words, searching for some clue to his intentions. Dahr shuddered at one point, still uncomfortable talking about his involuntary visits to the Twilight World. "The worst part isn't sitting in the room with Lorthas," he admitted. "The worst is that sometimes…sometimes I feel sorry for him. Sometimes, I agree with him."

Jeran nodded. "I know. But remember, bad things happen to a lot of people, and not all of them try to take over the world. What Lorthas experienced, the terrible events he witnessed, are enough to break even the hardest heart. But they do not excuse his actions! Other Magi witnessed those events without turning evil!"

"But he only wanted to protect his people," Dahr insisted. "He wanted to protect people like you, those with the Gift!"

"Perhaps," Jeran said with a shrug. "But if protection from the 'commons,' as he so benevolently refers to them, means the enslavement of all life on Madryn, I think I'd rather take my chances!" Dahr nodded in understanding, opened his mouth to speak, but remained silent when he heard someone approaching from the south.

Frodel crested the hill and looked around. Spotting them, he approached, stopping in front of them. He stood there, still, expressionless, his folded his arms across his chest, and looked at them through dark, serious eyes. Jeran and Dahr shared a curious look, then Jeran turned to the Tribesman. "Can I help you?"

The Garun'ah did not respond immediately. His eyes grew momentarily uncertain, though his features remained otherwise impassive. "I journey with you," he said at last. "Go Kaper when leave *Cha'khun*."

"You want to return with us to Alrendria?" Jeran asked, astonished.

The Tribesman nodded. "I go city. Live inside walls until Voice of Madryn call me home."

Jeran and Dahr exchanged another startled glance. "Why?" Dahr asked.

"I want ask Vyrina be *bavahnda*," Frodel told them. "I consult *Tsha'ma*, seek counsel from Garun. They commune with God and suggest I spend time among Humans. Be wise, they say, to learn her ways before offer soul. She will want live some time among her people.

"I go to Kaper," he explained. "Learn your ways. Learn if can live in stone prisons."

Jeran stood and grasped Frodel's arms just above the elbow. "We would welcome your company, Frodel *uvan* Merck. When we return to Kaper, you may ride with us."

Frodel nodded, as if this were the response he had expected. Dahr stood as well. "Vyrina will be glad to hear you're joining us," he said to the squat Tribesman. "I heard her tell Nykeal how much she'll miss you."

At Dahr's words, the Tribesman's face flushed red, and Dahr stepped back, surprised the by reaction of the stout Tribesman. He quickly changed the subject to lessen Frodel's embarrassment. "Did you pass a band of Garun'ah on your way here?"

Frodel nodded, regaining some of his composure. "Strange for large party to travel ahead of Tribe."

"Who were they?" Jeran asked.

"Sahna," Frodel told him. "I speak with Preltar *uvan* Syrip, leader of Hunt. They hunt for tribe, but reached Kohr's Heart early. Instead turn back, he decide wait at *Cha'khun*."

"The Sahna?" Jeran repeated, his brow wrinkling in confusion. He looked at Dahr. "Reanna returned this morning from her meeting with the Sahna. They're still ten days south of Kohr's Heart. Why would this band travel so far north of their Tribe?" He turned to Frodel. "And why would they pass Kohr's Heart and then double back?"

Frodel shook his head. "It seem odd," he admitted. "But it Preltar's band. He leads hunt, and Hunters follow him."

"We saw several hundred Tribesmen," Jeran continued, unwilling to accept Frodel's calm dismissal. "And it seemed like there might have been more." His eyes met the Tribesman's defiantly, begging him to argue. "I've never seen a hunting party of more than twenty-five."

"It seem odd," Frodel said again. "But who explain Sahna? They strange tribe. Live near Anvil. Spend too much time in mountains. Near Boundary. It bend souls."

A distant howl echoed from the south, and at the sound, Dahr sat up rigidly, sniffing the air. His eyes were distant, empty, and he sniffed the air again. "I remember!" he said, almost in a snarl. "I remember their smell." He stood, looking at Jeran and Frodel frantically. "We have to hurry!" he exclaimed, running in the direction of Kohr's Heart.

They followed after him. "How many Hunters are in the camp?" Dahr called back.

"I not know," the Tribesman replied, loping at Dahr's side. "Ten hundred, maybe more. Most hunt. Will return with dusk."

"Those in the camp," Dahr asked. "How long would it take for them to respond to an attack?"

"The Blood ready for battle, Dahr Odara," Frodel said, his brow furrowing. "But even the *Onatsal*...the *Aelva*," he corrected, "not attack camp of women and children."

"Unfortunately, it's not Elves approaching the camp," Dahr told him. "It's the *Kohr'adjin*."

"*Kohr'adjin!*" Frodel repeated, increasing his pace and drawing his double-bladed axe. With every stride, he growled, swinging the blade from side to side. Dahr ran easily, but Jeran had to sprint to keep up.

They crested the hill around Kohr's Heart, and knew they would not arrive early enough to give warning. The *Kohr'adjin* had fanned out below, forming a line nearly two hundred men across, several ranks deep. Around Kohr's Heart, several other lines of warriors marched steadily forward, forming rank at some unseen signal.

They had come in many small groups, so as not to arouse suspicion. Now, nearly two thousand warriors, armed and prepared for battle, walked down the hill calmly, in no apparent hurry, still pretending to be Sahna on their way to *Cha'khun*.

A line of young boys stood at the edge of the tents, watching the Tribesmen approach. They held small spears in their hands or clutched half-sized *dolchek*s in tiny, chubby fingers. Behind the boys stood another line of children, mostly girls and those boys too small to stand in the front rank. As tradition dictated, they stood in defense of the camp, reminding any who might consider attack of their dishonor.

At the top of the hill, Frodel paused for only an instant. The *Kohr'adjin* warriors were more than half the distance to the children. With a cry of despair, the Tribesman descended into the valley at a dead run, shouting '*Kohr'adjin!*' at the top of his lungs. Despite his short stature, his voice was a thunderous boom, echoing across the valley. Even from the top of the hill, they could see Garun'ah in the camp lift their heads at the Hunter's cry.

Dahr drew his greatsword from its sheath. The blade was nearly as tall as a man, but in Dahr's hand, it appeared little longer than a broadsword. He ran after Frodel, and added his voice to the Tribesman's warnings. Jeran drew the Aelvin blade, its polished steel flashing in the sunlight, and followed.

At Frodel's first yell, the *Kohr'adjin* drew their weapons and charged. Shrieking in rage, they descended upon the camp, upon the children who stood in their way. Jeran heard Dahr yell, "Get out of the way! You can't stand against them!"

But the children of the Garun'ah knew their duty, and though fear danced in their eyes, the young boys and girls tightened their grips on their weapons and prepared themselves to walk with Garun. The smallest of the children, those too tiny to hold weapons, ran into the camp, shouting warning.

Some Hunters, those closest to the edge of the camp, were running to aid the children. Others—men, women, young and old—gathered what weapons were at hand and started toward the *Kohr'adjin*. Jeran thought he saw a giant bear running toward the fray, but it was only Arik, his bearskin cloak wrapped around his shoulders, its head drawn over his own.

From every direction Tribesmen came, but none would arrive in time.

If I can seize my Gift, Jeran thought, *maybe I can do something. Slow them down a little.* He reached for the magic, tried to imagine his source, but the threads of energy slipped through his grasp. Desperately he clutched at them, begged them to heed his commands just this once, but every time he touched it, the energy dissipated.

Lightning flashed, appearing as if from nowhere, streaking across the clear blue sky and exploding the ground around the *Kohr'adjin*. Some of the attackers were thrown to the ground, as were some of the children, but the rest ran through heedlessly, continuing down the hill with a fanatic fervor in their eyes.

Jeran was surprised, mostly because he had not yet been able to grasp magic. Then he saw Tanar running toward the children, his dark brown robes flapping behind him. Another streak of lightning fell, this time behind the *Kohr'adjin*. They ignored it.

The attackers met the wall of children, scythed through them like wheat. The young ones fought furiously, and more than one battle-hardened Tribesman fell to their frantic attacks, but they were no match for their much larger competitors. Had the *Kohr'adjin* been interested in the murder of children, none would have stood a chance.

Luckily, the children of the tribes were not their objective. They pushed through, killing only those in their way. Then they were in the tents, slashing at everything that moved. Young and old, the blades of the *Kohr'adjin* sliced and hacked indiscriminately. Several carried torches, and with them, they set fire to the tents and grain wagons.

The *Kohr'adjin* searched for the Hunters of the Garun'ah. Still confused, disorganized, the few and scattered warriors were no match for the pairs of evil-looking Garun'ah who stumbled upon them, blades already swinging. And each warrior down meant one less to fight the enemy.

Frodel, Dahr, and Jeran finally reached the children. Some screamed, others cried, and still others stared lifelessly at the heavens. The younger children were doing their best to tend the wounded; the older ones were armed. They moved in groups of six, searching for *Kohr'adjin*.

The cries of the children rent Jeran's heart, but he dare not stop. The threat to the tribes must be dealt with first; only then could the wounded be cared for.

Frodel turned left; Dahr went right. "We should stay together!" Jeran called, to no avail. When the Blood Rage was upon them, the Garun'ah were not easy to reason with.

Jeran ran through the tents. He saw old women and children throwing water on the flaming wagons, quenching the fires as fast as they could. Turning around one wagon, he came face to face with a hawk-nosed *Kohr'adjin*. The Tribesman towered over him, and seeing a Human before him, he sneered with hate. Lifting his weapon, a giant spiked club, he swung it at Jeran's head.

Jeran stepped to the side, dodging the blow, and swung his sword in return. The magic-wrought Aelvin blade sliced through the thick, hard wood of the club with ease. Smiling, Jeran reversed his swing, cutting down the surprised Tribesman.

Pushing deeper into the tents, he looking for Tanar...Dahr...Kal...anyone he recognized. He saw Arik, bear cloak drawn over his head, double-bladed axe swinging back and forth, towering over three *Kohr'adjin*, all armed with spears, and he started toward them at a run, ready to help, but with two well-placed swings, the *Kranor* cut down all three opponents. Brown eyes met Jeran's blue, and Arik nodded his head before disappearing behind another tent.

Jeran turned around, running in the other direction, and he surprised two more *Kohr'adjin*. Before they could react, he cut one down. The other was faster; Jeran barely managed to catch his blow with the side of his sword. The Aelvin steel rang out loudly, and Jeran's hand went numb. He stumbled backward, and the dark-eyed Tribesman approached for the kill.

Backing up slowly, Jeran tried to get feeling to return to his hand. The Kohr'adjin advanced, murder in his eyes, swinging his axe back and forth. It was all Jeran could do to stop the hacks and slashes.

Suddenly, there was snarling and growling all around him. A dog flew in front of Jeran's vision, landing squarely on the *Kohr'adjin*'s chest, knocking the Tribesman to the ground. More dogs appeared, slavering and biting, tearing the *Kohr'adjin* apart. The Tribesman's dying scream cut off with a sickening gurgle. Then the dogs were gone, disappearing as quickly as they had come.

Jeran shook the sting from his hand and continued on. He saw Katya, Nykeal, and Jasova standing in a tight circle, blades at the ready. They looked relieved when he arrived. "Who do we attack?" Katya called, her eyes roving the tents.

"Anyone who attacks you!" Jeran replied, pivoting to parry the slash of a *Kohr'adjin* sneaking up behind him. He dispatched the Tribesman and turned around, but the Guardsmen were already heading into the fray.

He saw Dahr in the distance, battling two *Kohr'adjin*, and he ran to catch his friend. His opponents were skilled, but Dahr was Alrendrian trained, and feeling the Blood Rage as well. He easily held his opponents at bay, and it would not take long for his powerful strokes to defeat them.

Two more *Kohr'adjin* stumbled across him, but they were set upon by a pack of dogs. There seemed to be hundreds of dogs swarming the camp, hunting the *Kohr'adjin* as effectively as any warrior. Birds circled above, and one, a golden eagle, dove into the fray, shrieking as it dug its claws into the face of one of Dahr's opponents.

Another Tribesman approached Dahr from behind, walking proudly, his back straight and his eyes on the *Kohr'adjin*. At first, Jeran thought him an ally, but as he neared, he drew his *dolchek*, and a wicked smile spread across his face. The Tribesman was only a few paces behind Dahr, who remained unaware of the threat. Shouting warning, Jeran hurried to intercept the attack.

Dahr cut down one opponent and caught the other, still clawing at his ruined eyes, with the back swing. He turned in time to see Jeran tackle a Garun'ah warrior. They rolled across the ground, and Jeran lost his sword. After exchanging several hard blows, the Tribesman threw Jeran to the side with a mighty heave, and Dahr's eyes narrowed in recognition.

"Kraltir!" he growled, starting forward, hatred in his eyes. Three more *Kohr'adjin* appeared, and Dahr was forced to deal with them.

Jeran scrambled across the ground, and by the time he had recovered the sword, Kraltir was gone, hiding among the tents. Jeran ran to Dahr, and together, they dealt with the three attackers.

Breathing heavily, Jeran met Dahr's eyes. "From now on," he said, "let's stick together." Dahr nodded wordlessly, and they started through the tents. A couple of dogs followed.

A horn sounded far to the north, two long, low blasts. The Tribes were organizing. Hunters, those who had been in the camp, were running through the tents in small groups, trying to locate and dispatch the *Kohr'adjin*. The *Kohr'adjin* themselves were harder to find, and most of those Jeran and Dahr encountered were fleeing to the north.

They encountered a group of five, which rounded on them immediately, weapons raised. Jeran and Dahr lunged forward, and the dogs jumped to the attack as well.

The swinging blade of a *Kohr'adjin* cut down one of the animals, and Dahr went wild when the hound yelped in pain. His first violent swing shattered the axe of his opponent, his next sent the Tribesman's head sailing through the air. He leveled his blade at the *Kohr'adjin* who had killed the dog and stalked forward, death in his eyes.

Jeran fought the other three, but had difficulty making headway. None could land a blow, but neither could he break through their guards. Suddenly, a spear flashed past him, taking one of his opponents in the throat. Seizing the opportunity, Jeran rid himself of his other enemies, then turned to thank his unexpected ally.

Yarchik sat on his palanquin, another spear already hefted, his eyes scanning for the next best target. His litter-bearers battled twice their number of *Kohr'adjin*. All four were bloodied and wounded, but more than three times their number lay at their feet. Jeran ran to their aid, calling for Dahr. Together, they raced to the *Kranor's* aid, and with their help, the Garun'ah defeated the *Kohr'adjin* in a matter of moments.

The battle seemed to die with the last of Yarchik's attackers, and a strange quiet descended over the tent city. "Many thanks," Yarchik said in a rasping voice. "This late in life, I never thought to die in battle." He looked at the *Kohr'adjin* on the ground, spat at them in disgust.

Then the old Tribesman looked at all the bodies around him. "It is as if they hunted me. Strange...."

Dahr, still out of breath, raised his eyes to Yarchik. "Kraltir was among them," he said in a half-snarl. "Jeran stopped him from killing me."

Yarchik frowned. "You speak grave accusation against my son, Dahr Odara," the *Kranor* said. "Have you proof it was Kraltir?"

Dahr shook his head. Ripping a length of tattered hide from one of the *Kohr'adjin* at his feet, he wiped the blood from his blade. "Only my word."

Yarchik's eyes lowered to the ground. "If only your word were not proof enough," he said solemnly. A tear fell from the old man's eye. "My son has fallen from the path of Garun."

Tanar appeared, his eyes dark and withdrawn. "There you are, my boy," he said to Jeran. "Thank the Five Gods!" He stumbled over, laid a hand on Jeran's shoulder, and leaned in to whisper, "The *Tsha'ma* are healing the wounded as best they can, but there is much work left to be done. Jakal thinks we may need your strength if we are to save even a fraction of those who fell."

Jeran nodded, sheathed his sword, and followed Tanar into the tents.

Chapter 38

"Halt," Iban called, raising one hand. With the other, he scratched his beard, looking from left to right, surveying the countryside with his steely eyes. They had left the Aelvin lands several days past; the Great Trees and dense underbrush had since given way to thinner tracks of forest, broken by regions of rolling grasslands.

The column of Alrendrians had just reached the top of a long, broad hill, its sides dotted with thin trees. To the north and east grew forest, interrupted by the cracked and ruined remains of the Path of Riches. To the west, the old trade route continued through rolling grasslands. The mountains of Ahgar, the border between Gilead and the Tachan Lands, were silhouetted in purple on the southern horizon.

Frowning thoughtfully, Iban sniffed the air, looking up at the slate grey sky. The clouds threatened rain, as they had for the past three days. "Company, dismount!" Iban yelled. "We set up camp here."

Martyn urged his horse forward, and Treloran followed, seemingly uncomfortable on the back of his thin, white warhorse. "Stopping early today, Commander?" Martyn asked, squinting up at the heavens. "It's hard to locate the sun, but it can't be far past midday."

Iban turned cold eyes on the prince. "My gut tells me to stop," he said gruffly, and Martyn stiffened under the cold note of authority. "Over the winters, I've learned to trust my instincts."

Lifting his eyes from the prince, Iban cupped a hand to his mouth and shouted for Guardsman Willym. The veteran Guardsman, dressed in dark leathers, approached. "If you will excuse me," Iban said, addressing the prince, "there are things I wish to discuss with Willym."

Martyn bowed his head, dismounted, and led his horse to the tether lines being raised on the far side of the hill. Treloran dropped from his horse and followed, his eyes on Iban. "Your Guard Commander is a cautious man," he said after much consideration.

Handing his reins to a waiting Guardsman, Martyn defended the aging Guard Commander. "Lord Iban is an *experienced* man. If he thinks it wise to stop, then best you believe there's a reason."

Alynna, smiling broadly and wearing a light blue riding dress, approached the princes. Utari, dressed in a white blouse and shimmering black skirt, split up the side for riding, walked beside her. After a brief glance at Martyn, Alynna turned a predatory gaze on Treloran. "Prince Treloran," she purred, "we had little opportunity to speak this morning."

Treloran, now standing next to his white stallion, suddenly looked more uncomfortable than on horseback. "Lady Alynna," he said, bowing formally. "Prince Martyn and Lord Iban have kept me occupied. There is much I have to learn about Alrendria and its customs."

Alynna's eyes flashed conspiratorially. "There is much I could teach you...." she told him, reaching out to touch his arm, "about Alrendria." Treloran's cheeks turned bright red at the thinly-disguised advance, and it took all of Martyn's effort to keep from laughing out loud.

"Come, Utari," he said, offering his arm to the taller woman. "Perhaps we should leave these two to discuss... Alrendrian traditions... in private." Utari took the prince's arm, smiled thinly, and allowed him to lead her away.

As they passed, Treloran whispered, "I will not forget this, Human!" his voice a mixture of feigned anger and genuine anxiety. This time, Martyn did laugh, clapping the Elf on the shoulder fondly.

Utari and Martyn walked slowly through the camp, where Guardsmen and servants alike milled about aimlessly, confused by the early stop. Most stared at Iban blankly, watching the Guard Commander converse with a small party of Guardsmen at the summit of the hill. All huddled close, their words low and quiet.

The tents were unloaded from the wagons, but no one made an effort to erect them. They sat in a pile on the ground, surrounded by a ring of servants and soldiers. The supplies, save for those things necessary for immediate use, stayed in the wagons.

"It seems that I'm not the only one confused by Iban's order," Martyn said, gesturing to the Alrendrians. "No one seems to know what to do. They're waiting for his orders like children."

Utari's pressed her lips into a thin, tight line. "I have known Geffram most of my life," she told Martyn. "He is not a man given to rash action."

"He's also not a man given to stopping in the early afternoon," Martyn interjected. As he finished, the Guardsmen around Iban split apart and ran down the hillside, each in a different direction. As Willym jogged past, Martyn reached out to stop him. "What's going on, Willym?"

"Forgive me, Prince Martyn," Willym answered, bowing his head, "but I can't answer your question. More urgent matters require my attention." Before Martyn could stop him, the Guardsman was off again, grabbing the reins of a horse and disappearing into the thick grass to the north of camp.

Martyn turned back to Utari, his eyes wide with shock. "First Iban says he has a bad feeling about today, and now he sends our best trackers into the wood. I wonder if something's amiss."

Utari's dark eyes narrowed with worry, and she pressed her long fingers against her lips. "If Iban has a bad feeling," she told him in a calm, stately voice, "then trouble is on the horizon. In all the seasons of our acquaintance, I have never known his instincts to be wrong."

"Put those tents down!" thundered Iban, storming toward the Guardsmen who had finally decided to set up camp. "There'll be time for that later! Guardsmen, gather round! Servants too! Everyone, listen!"

All across the camp, conversations halted abruptly; all eyes swiveled to the Guard Commander. The Guardsmen fell in, forming rank, and the servants formed their own group off to the side. Martyn and Utari walked over, joining Treloran, Alynna, and Jes.

"Field exercise!" Iban yelled, and a quiet groan escaped from the Guardsmen. Even Martyn sighed angrily. "Silence!" Iban bellowed, and the assemblage instantly hushed. "This is no game," he told them sternly. "This is practice. Some day you may be called upon to defend Alrendria. When that day comes, I expect you to know what you're supposed to do."

He spun slowly, surveying the hilltop. Trees grew in isolated stands all around, and a small stream bubbled from beneath a large granite boulder. "I want a barricade ten hands high ringing the hilltop, four hundred hands in diameter with entrance ports to the north and south! Take the trees from the bottom of the hill! Leave those within our encampment for protection.

"I want watch towers there, there, and there," he added, pointing east, south, and west, "at least twenty hands tall, more if possible." He walked in a circle around the Guardsmen, surveying the area in more detail, calling out more specific orders.

"This area between the trees must be cleared for the tents!"

"I want a stack of firewood here... enough to last a score of days!"

"Harta! Jolina! Take a handful of Guardsmen and hunt some food! Bring as much as you can."

"Lady Liseyl, select a few of your charges and have them scour the vicinity for edible fruits and vegetables."

The commands came in rapid succession, one after the other, and Guardsmen hurried to obey. When he was finished, Iban raised his voice so the entire party could hear. He pointed to a tall, narrow tree growing alone on the peak of the hilltop. "I want that tree stripped of its branches and the Alrendrian banner hung from its top."

The Guard Commander's predatory blue eyes swept from person to person, cold and demanding. "These tasks will be done–and done to my satisfaction!–before nightfall. If not, I will double the requirements and none will rest until they are finished. I expect every man, woman, and child capable of lifting a tool to lend aid." He fell silent, and the Alrendrian's stared at him in wide-eyed shock. "Well," he barked, "get to it!"

The camp instantly roused to action; people hurried in every direction. Sighing resignedly, Martyn started toward the supply wagons. "Where are you going, Prince Martyn?" Alynna asked.

"To get an axe," Martyn replied, coming to a halt. "I'd rather be chopping down trees than building watch towers or fashioning bulwarks."

Alynna's eyes widened in disbelief. "You can't believe he means for *us* to help the Guardsmen set up the camp!"

Martyn smiled cruelly. "Feel free to discuss the matter with him, Lady Alynna. I, for one, wish to keep my pride intact." He continued toward the wagons, where Guardsmen were already lined up, passing out tools. Treloran, Jes, and Utari followed silently.

Iban's voice drifted over the din. "...n't care if you're King Mathis' most trusted advisor or the blessed disciple of Kohr! You'll grab a shovel and start digging, Rafel, or when trouble comes, you'll be waiting for it outside the walls!" With a squeal, Alynna hefted her dress and hurried after Martyn and the others.

When Martyn reached the cart, the Guardsmen stepped to the side, allowing him to move to the front. Flashing a showy smile, he looked at the Guardsman in the wagon, and said, "An axe, Farid." Winking at the other Guardsmen, who looked shocked, he laughed. "You don't expect me to let you have all the fun, do you?"

Quiet laughter spread among the Guard. Martyn took his axe and started down the hillside. Grabbing an axe of his own, Treloran followed the prince. They passed a handful of Guardsmen tracing a path in the dry grass of the hillside, marking where the battlement would be raised. Martyn nodded at them as he passed.

Once outside the encampment, Martyn turned to talk to Treloran, and to his surprise, nearly two score of the party stood behind him. With a smile, the prince pointed to the line of broken dirt that represented the wall. "If our barricade is to be raised there, then we need to clear all the trees from here to the bottom of the hill. Were an enemy to attack, they could use the trees as cover, protecting themselves from our arrows.

"Fan out and start chopping. Begin with the trees closest to the encampment and work your way down. Iban thinks we won't finish by dark. I say we show the Guard Commander what Alrendrians are made of! We'll have this fortification finished before the sun sinks beneath the western horizon!"

A cheer went up among the Guardsmen, and the sound of metal on wood soon echoed through the countryside. Hefting his axe, Martyn approached the nearest tree and swung, the sharpened steel biting deep into the trunk. He swung again, falling into a steady rhythm.

After a few moments, another axe attacked the tree from the other side. Martyn looked up, sweat cascading down his face in rivulets. "Lisandaer?" he said, greeting the bulky Guardsman. "You decided to join the forestry detail too?"

The broad, bull-necked Guardsman smiled. "To be honest, Prince Martyn," he said, "I'd rather be building watch towers, but Lord Iban told me I was to make sure no harm came to you."

Martyn scowled. "I don't need a nursemaid," he said flatly.

Lisandaer nodded. "Like as not, you don't," the burly soldier agreed. "But I just follow the orders I'm given, my Prince." His smiled broadened. "You shouldn't feel too bad," he added. "Three Guardsmen were assigned to watch the Elf."

Martyn turned to look at Treloran, and saw Bystral, Quellas, and Olivia standing near the Aelvin Prince. Bystral and Quellas were swinging viciously at the thick trunk of one tree, and Olivia used a hatchet to lop the branches off a smaller one that had already fallen. All three worked busily, but each kept a wary eye on the horizon.

Martyn turned back to Lisandaer. "I suppose you have a point, Guardsman," he said, trying to hide his smile. "I wonder what's going on."

Lisandaer shrugged. "We'll know when Lord Iban wants us to know." The tree groaned. "And not a moment before." Looking up at the swaying trunk, Lisandaer pursed his lips in concentration. Drawing back his axe, he said, "You might want to step back, my Prince."

Swinging with all his strength, he hit the center of their cut, and with a loud groan, the tree began to fall. Lisandaer yelled for the others to watch out, and stepped aside when the tree crashed to the ground. Once it had settled, he hopped onto the trunk and began to hack at the larger branches. "Leave those for the hatchets," Martyn said. "There are more trees to fell!"

The afternoon was a blur of activity. Tree after tree was brought down and chopped into usable pieces. Holes were dug and sections of the trees, ten to twelve hands high, were set and packed into the ground at regular intervals. Crossbeams, lashed in place with vines, were fastened between each of the braces. Gaps and holes were filled with jagged sticks.

The frames of three watch towers grew from the top of the hill. The one to the southern side rose forty hands; those to the east and west stood twenty-five. As soon as they were stable enough, Iban stationed sentries in the towers.

Jolina and the Guardsmen under her command returned to camp several times, burdened with the carcasses of deer and elk, goose and rabbit. Servants filled basket after basket with berries and fresh vegetables, until Liseyl finally ordered most of her women to stop foraging and prepare the meat brought by Jolina's hunters.

As twilight spread across the plains, Martyn supervised the placement of the southern gate. More a barricade than a gate, it consisted of a dense, tangled mass of branches and sharpened stakes. With the aid of several Guardsmen, the gate was pushed into place, blocking the only remaining gap in the newly-completed wall.

Martyn smiled with satisfaction as the last piece of the wall was set in place. The Alrendrians had worked tirelessly and had completed Iban's impossible demands in record time. Intent on earning his men some praise, Martyn started up the hill, Lisandaer a step behind.

At the hilltop, a small and wiry Guardsman shimmied down from the top of a now-branchless tree. When he hit the ground, he saluted Iban fist-on-heart and grabbed the rope dangling above his head. As he pulled the rope, the Rising Sun banner lifted into the air. Snapping crisply in the wind, the giant, golden sun caught the last glimmer of sunlight. For an instant, it seemed to burn with its own radiance.

Fires lit here and there cast their own warm glow on the encampment. Smiling proudly, Martyn jogged to the top of the hill to confront Iban. Exhausted, drenched in sweat, and smeared with muddy dirt, the Prince of Alrendria looked the Guard Commander squarely in the eye.

"I suppose you want praise?" Iban asked in a half question, his eyebrow arching comically. "Very well. You led your men well today, Prince Martyn. I set an arduous task, and it seems my training has not been completely ignored. You and the Guardsmen should be honored for your diligence and hard work." He trailed off, cocking his head to the side. "Is that enough," he asked wearily, "or do you want me to personally thank every Guardsman for following orders?"

Martyn was taken aback. Iban sounded angry, though it was often difficult to tell when the stoic Guard Commander was joking. "That won't be necessary," Martyn hastily said, just in case the old warrior was serious. "But perhaps you'd be willing to tell me why this was necessary. I–"

A cry from the south tower interrupted Martyn's response. "Rider approaching!" came the call. "It's a Guardsman!"

"Remove the gate!" Iban bellowed. "Let him in!" To Martyn, he added, "It looks like you won't have to wait long for your answers. Follow me."

The south gate was pulled aside, and the rider galloped into the camp at full speed. Skidding to a halt before Iban, Willym dropped from the saddle and stood shakily before the Guard Commander. His horse was lathered, its breathing labored. Liseyl rushed up with a flask of water, which she offered to the scout. Another servant led his exhausted horse away.

Willym took the water and downed it greedily, but his eyes remained locked on Iban's. "It's as you feared," he said solemnly.

Iban took a slow, deep breath. "How many?"

"Hard to say," Willym admitted. "About a thousand."

"By the Five Gods!" Iban swore, his face contorting in rage, his blue eyes cold and dark. "How long?"

"A day or two before they realize we've stopped, another day to mobilize and march here. Four days at most." His tone betrayed that he thought his estimate more than generous.

"Who?" demanded Martyn. "Who will be here in four days?"

"The Durange," spat Willym. "And an army of dark-armored monsters led by none other than Tylor the Bull."

Iban closed his eyes and pressed the heel of his hand against his forehead. He took a slow, deep breath and looked at Willym. "Assemble the men."

* *

Tylor raised his hand, signaling a halt. Before him, high on a barricaded hill, flapped the Sun Banner of Alrendria. A bonfire burned near the center of the camp, dispelling the dark of night. Watchtowers stared down at him, and Guardsmen lined the inside of the fortifications. He now knew for certain that Iban was aware of his approach.

"How!" he demanded of Halwer. "How could he have known? Our ambush was perfect. Perfect!"

Halwer, ever wary of his Lord's temper, spoke carefully. "Perhaps a scout chanced upon our encampment, or maybe the Alrendrians camped here for some other reason, and it only *seems* they knew of our trap."

Tylor grunted, dissatisfied with the answers. "He knew," the Bull insisted. "Somehow, the old fox knew I was waiting." His face contorted in an angry frown. "If ever I discover how we were betrayed...." He let the statement trail off unfinished.

Taking a slow, deep breath, Tylor turned to the right, staring toward the eastern horizon. The faintest hint of light was beginning to break the black sky. "How many men?" he asked, trying to school his tone.

"By all reports, they left Grenz with no more than five hundred Guardsmen," Halwer answered, "and maybe half as many servants. Some were killed in the attacks within Illendrylla. The *Kohrnodra* insist they removed threescore Alrendrians, but I feel this number is generous. Additionally, a small contingent was left within the Aelvin lands. I'd figure they number at most four hundred Guardsmen, with perhaps another two hundred servants."

"Had we taken them by surprise, this would have been an easy battle," Tylor mused. "Now that they've had time to prepare, it will be much more costly. Iban is a seasoned commander, and the Alrendrian Guard is not a force to be trifled with. Their fortifications are crude, but they will make our task much more difficult."

"Shall I order the men to stand down? Perhaps you wish to withdraw until you've had time to reassess the situation."

Tylor shook his head. "It's of no matter. Fortifications or no, we have two, maybe three times their numbers, and I, too, am a seasoned commander. A few more of our men may fall, but we will still be victorious."

He scanned the hill for a long time, and a tense silence fell between him and Halwer. "Get ten of our best men," Tylor said at last. "Tell them to circle the encampment and look for holes, weaknesses in the defenses. We'll attack before the sun clears the horizon."

"Are you sure this is wise, my Lord?"

Tylor spun around, and with his eye, he glared sharply at his aide. "I do not question you in your areas of expertise, Halwer! Extend to me the same courtesy. I will not delay here any longer than necessary, all the while giving Odara more time to escape. By nightfall I will have the heads of both princes, and that damned Elf will tell me where I can find Jeran Odara!"

* *

The camp was eerily quiet. Iban walked slowly, circumnavigating the wall. Whenever he passed a Guardsman, he offered either a word of comfort or a word of praise. One warrior, a child barely old enough to call a man, trembled as he looked over the top of the fortification. As he stared into the dark distance, seeking signs of Tylor's approach, his armor rattled noisily.

Iban hopped up onto the low platform constructed to allow the Guardsman to see over their wall. He reached out and patted the boy on the shoulder, but at his touch, the young Guardsman jumped as if struck. "Peace, Nystra!" Iban said, forcing a smile.

The boy, seeing his commander, relaxed. He saluted and tried unsuccessfully to still the quiet jingling of his armor. Iban laughed, and was proud when it sounded genuine. "You better watch out, Guardsman," he jested. "You'll give away our position with all that noise!"

"Yes, sir!" Nystra said, saluting again. He smiled weakly, but his eyes remained haunted and red-rimmed. "Lord Iban," he said, licking his lips nervously. "Do you think we have a chance?"

"There's a lot of them out there lad," Iban admitted. "But our defenses our strong, and the Alrendrian Guard is the best fighting force in Madryn." He patted the boy's shoulder again. "We can hold them off."

Nystra sighed in relief. "That's what I told Varten!" he said with some enthusiasm. "Excuse me, Lord Iban, but I should be keeping my watch." He turned around and stood up straight, peering bravely into the slowly-lightening darkness. Iban hopped down from the platform and continued his circuit of the camp. Behind him, Nystra's armor remained quiet.

As soon as he was out of earshot, he cursed himself. *By nightfall, we'll all be dead or enslaved to Tylor.* The Alrendrian Guard would fight bravely, of that Iban had no doubt, but Tylor outnumbered them greatly and Iban was not in the habit of deluding himself. He hated lying to his men, but he needed every bit of courage from them, if they were to have even the smallest chance of success.

He finished his patrol of the south side of camp, the side from which Tylor would most likely concentrate his attack. More Guardsmen lined this section of the wall than any other, their bows strung and sitting at their sides. Piles of arrows, as well as a spare bow in case their first was damaged, lay next to every Guardsman. All knew that, once Tylor breached the wall, they were as good as dead.

One servant walked along the wall, dragging a small cart laden with bowls and a cauldron of hot porridge. Stopping by every Guardsman, he ladled out a generous portion. Iban wished he could offer his men a better last meal than porridge.

Sighing, he walked to the south watchtower, which towered forty hands above the ground. Grabbing the sides of the ladder, he climbed to the platform, bowing his head to the Guardsman posted as sentry. "You're relieved, Guardsman. Get some breakfast. I'll take your watch."

The Guardsman saluted. "Thank you, Lord Iban," he said, hurrying down the ladder.

Iban looked around the platform. His men had been busy these last four days. The watchtower was big enough for a handful of men, and taller than he had expected. While they waited for Tylor, the Guardsmen had improved their defenses, going so far as to fashion simple walls and a roof to the three towers, giving them some small protection from the weather, which had been consistently stormy.

Iban walked to the south side of the tower and looked out over the countryside. The first hint of sunlight was brightening the eastern sky, sending fingers of purple and gold into the darkness. A large dark blotch marred the southern landscape, as if the thin groves of trees had grown into a forest overnight. Iban knew that Tylor and his troops waited there, waited for dawn to make their approach.

He watched for some time, until the first rays of sunlight broke the horizon. Shielding his eyes, he turned east, and was surprised to see a golden eagle perched on the wall of the tower.

Iban almost jumped, but quickly brought himself under control. "He said I would see you," Iban told the bird. "He told me I should stop my advance when I saw two eagles in the sky." Iban looked to his left and right. "Your friend didn't stay? Didn't want to watch the battle?" The eagle stared at him with piercing brown eyes.

"He told me I would see you, and he told me I should fortify my position when I did. As strongly as possible. I only half believed him, but for some strange reason, I felt that I should heed his words." Iban walked toward the eagle, stopping only a hand's length away. To his surprise, the bird did not take flight. Instead, it continued to stare at him, almost sadly.

"He told me what we would find. And what would happen. All of it." Iban wiped a hand across his face, scrubbing his beard to hide his weakness, his fear. "Then he asked me what I wanted to do! As if I had a choice!"

"There are always choices," said a voice behind him. "Some are just easier than others."

Iban whirled around, hand instinctively reaching for his sword. A Tribesman stood against the far wall, leaning back against the corner post so he could stand straight-legged without his head hitting the tower's roof. "You are well met, Geffram Iban of Alrendria. I am Rannarik *uvan* Gosha."

Iban released the hilt of his sword at the mention of the Tribesman's name. "He said you would be here too," Iban admitted with a grunt. "It was the first thing I thought he was wrong about."

Rannarik smiled. "You are having doubts?"

"I am in no hurry to die," Iban replied. "Nor do I relish the idea of sending my people to certain death. But as I said before, what choice do I have? We must do all we can to protect the princes."

Rannarik nodded. "As *I* said, there is always a choice. You could leave now. There is yet time. If you went alone you could be far from here before battle starts."

"But what of Martyn?" Iban asked hotly. "What of Treloran? Lady Alynna? Jes?" He looked down at his Guardsmen, valiantly manning their posts. "What of my men? What would be their fate?"

Rannarik shook his head. "If you took them all, the Dark Demon's soldiers would hunt you down. Your best chance is alone."

"Abandon my Guardsmen?" Iban asked incredulously. "How could you suggest such a thing?"

Rannarik frowned. "You could surrender. Throw yourself upon the mercy of the Bull."

Iban laughed harshly. "I am familiar with Tylor's mercy. Better I drive my own sword through the backs of my warriors. They'd die a better death." Iban met Rannarik's gaze squarely. "We can expect no aid from the Garun'ah?"

"My people are at *Cha'khun*. None are near enough to lend aid. I swear to you, Geffram Iban of Alrendria, were even a handful of the Blood within reach, they would be at your side."

Iban shook his head sadly. "Then we will do what we can, and pray to the Five Gods it's enough. I know what's at stake. I won't betray my king."

"Then it seems you have made your decision."

Iban smiled grimly. He gripped the hilt of his sword and rattled it in its sheath. "When Tylor and the Tachans destroyed my home and murdered my family, this became my life. I always knew it would one day be my death. Honor is a cruel master, but I know my duty to Alrendria. And to myself."

Rannarik stepped forward, reached up, and put a hand on Iban's shoulder. "The Orog had a saying which is still popular among both my people and the *Aelva*. 'In all the world, the only thing harder than living with honor is dying with honor.' "

He squeezed Iban's shoulder fondly. "We will sing songs of your bravery," he told the Guard Commander, "and of the bravery of those who die at your side. When Garun finally calls me to his side, we will hunt together in the Twilight World."

Iban grasped the *Tsha'ma*'s arm just below the elbow. A gesture of parting. "I look forward to that day," the Guard Commander said. "Tell me, Rannarik. He knows so much. Does he know if Martyn will survive this? Can you guarantee the prince's safety?"

Rannarik's eyes grew sad. "The fate of both princes hinges upon the actions of others. I am not even sure if Garun knows the outcome."

Iban bit his upper lip, nodded his head curtly. "I hope...." He cut himself off and turned to the south, to where Tylor's forces were now clearly visible, arrayed in a long line across the southern plains. They were approaching the Alrendrian fortification slowly, marching in rigid formation. "Peace and long life, Rannarik."

"Peace, Geffram Iban," came the Tribesman's quiet reply. When Iban turned around, Rannarik was already gone.

Chapter 39

"And that's all we know," Jeran concluded, looking over at the half circle of *Kranora* and *Kranacha*. He was still nervous, but not nearly as much as when first confronting this daunting group. "The Boundary is intact, but it grows weaker. For now, the Darklord is trapped, but how long he will remain imprisoned in *Ael Shataq* is a mystery. His servants already plague Madryn, and it's only a matter of time until another war begins."

Jeran paused, giving the meaning of his words time to sink in. He shared a quick, anxious glance with Dahr, who stood to his right. Dahr smiled weakly, then turned his golden-brown eyes back on the Garun'ah.

On Jeran's left stood Tanar, dressed in dark robes and carrying a long staff in one hand. He had not spoken during Jeran's speech, but had watched Jeran with interest the whole time. Noting Jeran's eyes on him, Tanar's cheeks flushed a light shade of red, and he leaned in close to whisper, "You did well. I hope it was enough."

Jeran addressed the Tribesmen again. "I come here to ask for your aid. Eight hundred winters ago, the Darklord was defeated because the Four Races stood united against him. Without the aid of the Garun'ah, I fear that Lorthas' touch will spread across Madryn like a pestilence.

"I have come to you from the lands of the Elves." A low mutter arose from some of the Tribesmen, and Jeran swallowed involuntarily. He had expected to meet with only the *Kranora* of the four largest tribes, but to his surprise, the leaders of every tribe, no matter how small, had been invited to attend, to learn 'what dire news the child of Balan thought would affect the Blood.'

Jeran raised his hands for silence. "I have come to you from the lands of the Elves," he repeated, "where I spent much time with the Emperor. He pledged the aid of his people. He said it was long past time we set aside our petty differences and embraced each other as friends again.

"You see, he remembers a time before the fighting. A time before the hatred and misunderstanding which have driven our Races apart. He wishes for all of us–Human, Elf, and Garun'ah–to live in harmony with each other and the world around us."

Jeran smiled and cast his eyes toward the heavens. Above, thousands of stars shone down in brilliant splendor, twinkling merrily. "The Emperor is very idealistic," he said quietly, almost reverently. "Far more idealistic than myself. I wish only to stop the Darklord. I want only to see our races unite against a common enemy. I wish only to restore the Balance, to finish what we started over a millennia ago."

He thanked Dahr silently for the last bit, the part about the Balance. Dahr had explained in detail how important the balance of nature was to the Garun'ah, and Jeran hoped that, if there were any doubt among the *Kranora*, this would be the thing that prodded them to action.

His speech finished, the silence rushed in and engulfed him. The *Kranora* sat in a large semicircle, their *Kranacha* standing behind them. The Tribesmen stared at Jeran mutely, each weighing the Human's words in his own way. Jeran's mouth grew dry under the intense scrutiny, and his hands trembled. A great deal hinged on the outcome of the next few moments. Nervously, he looked at the faces staring at him.

Directly across from him were Arik and Kal. Arik sat cross-legged, his bearskin cloak drawn up over his shoulders. Kal had spoken earlier, before taking his place behind his father, urging the Tribesmen to take Jeran's words to heart.

Yarchik sat to Arik's right, the only *Kranor* not sitting on the ground. He looked tired, older than when Jeran had first met him, though he had been less than twoscore days in the Garun'ah camp. Norvik, thin and wiry, stood behind the palanquin. His eyes were not on Jeran, but rested on the old man before him.

Sadarak Cat's Claw sat to Arik's left, scowling. Behind him stood a giant of a woman, taller than Katya, less than a hand shorter than Dahr. She had long, straight black hair and piercing dark eyes. Eirha Fleet-foot, *Kranach* of the Afelda. Her eyes were on Dahr, her gaze predatory.

To Cat's Claw's left was Bysk *uvan* Tohrpa, *Kranor* of the Sahna. He was short for a Tribesman but half again as broad and thickly muscled, with arms the size of Arik's. Behind him stood his *Kranach*, Uhte *uvan* Virat.

To either side sat the *Kranora* of the smaller tribes. There were more than a hundred small tribes, some numbering less than a score of Tribesmen, others over a thousand. Together, their numbers were as great or greater than any one of the four large tribes. Alone, or in small groups, their decisions would make little difference, but together, they would make a formidable addition to any army forces. Nevertheless, Jeran was most interested in the responses of the Tacha, Channa, Afelda, and Sahna Tribes.

Arik was the first to speak. "For more than a season," he said, breaking the silence, "have I listened to Rannarik lecture on the subject of unity. Since the arrival of Dahr Odara, he has insisted that I listen to the words of the Alrendrians and grant them aid."

Arik craned his neck first to the right, then to the left. "I believe the advice of the *Tsha'ma* is clear in this matter." There was a murmur of assent among the Tribesmen. The giant nodded to himself, then returned his gaze to Jeran.

"When Rannarik left on business of the *Tsha'ma*, I thought Garun had finally granted my prayers for peace." His eyes flicked upward, toward his son, then focused forward again. "But not long after, Kal began to speak much the same words."

Another silence ensued, this one even more ominous than the last. "It is foolish to ignore the advice of either my *Kranach* or Rannarik. It is doubly foolish to ignore them both." Standing, Arik drew his *dolchek* and slashed a thin line down his forearm, allowing his blood to flow across the blade.

"The Tacha will stand with you against the Darklord," he told Jeran. "Your enemies are our enemies. This blade, which tasted my blood, is proof of my oath. If the Tacha's pledge proves false, then by this blade my life will end." He smiled a broad, toothy smile.

Yarchik spoke next, though he was unable to rise. "I owe much to this Human and his companions," he said with a gesture to Jeran. "But I owe much more to Dahr. Without him I would not have learned of Kraltir's treachery, nor would I be alive to listen to these words." Slowly, he drew his own *dolchek* and repeated the oath of allegiance. "So long as I live," he said to Dahr once he had resheathed his blade, "the Channa will be your sword. You have but to call on us."

Cat's Claw stood next. "Afelda live close to lands of man. We learn much of their laws. Their wars. Their problems. I see with own eyes their sins, committed for sake of homeland." He stared at Jeran for a long time, appraising him. Finally, he shook his head. "I not pledge my people to any Human land," he said at last. "Not even Alrendria."

Jeran felt his heart sink. Without all four of the larger tribes, he was certain that the smaller ones would not offer their aid, and he had counted on the support of Cat's Claw and the Afelda. They had spent a great deal of time together since joining company, and Jeran considered the scarred Tribesman a friend.

"Yet," Cat's Claw added, drawing his *dolchek*, "though lands of man corrupt, with no concern for Balance, Humans themselves often have honor and pride to rival best of Blood. I not pledge Afelda to Alrendria, but we will follow you, Jeran Odara." He sliced his arm, wetting his blade with blood, then offered his own oath, pledging the aid of the Afelda to Jeran in his fight against the Darklord.

Bysk stood, looked at the three *Kranora* to his right, and frowned. He was little more than ten hands tall, shorter than an average-sized Human, and looked out of place surrounded by so many taller Tribesmen. His face was flat and broad, his legs as thick as tree trunks. "Mountains of Anvil dark place," he said in a deep, broken bass, his words heavily-accented, almost unintelligible. "Things...bad things...walk Boundary. Both side."

His eyes turned to Jeran, measured him. "Human speak truth. Seen creatures only live in Darklord's prison. Humans...*Aelva*...even Blood...crawl through mountains like timid mouse. Attack Sahna when discovered.

"Boundary grow weak. Sahna have vision of man in white. Hold staff of fire. All stand against destroyed." He paused again, turned to look at Uhte, his *Kranach*. The younger man shook his head slowly. "The Sahna offer no blood pact."

Uhte whispered something too low to be heard. Bysk nodded. "Sahna bind ourselves to no other. Not Blood. Not Human. Sahna been lone long time. We stay lone." Suddenly, Bysk's broad face split open in a wicked smile. "But when time come for killing, we kill with you." His eyes flashed with eagerness. "Sahna like kill things from cross Boundary."

Jeran let out a sigh of relief. It was not the strong alliance he had hoped for, but it was better than nothing. He smiled and turned toward Dahr, but a new voice interrupted him.

"Turape offer no blood pact!" Jeran faced the speaker, an older Tribesman, his hair all but white, his eyes beginning to dull. He glared at Jeran. "Humans bring trouble. We owe them nothing. Lorthas is their creation. I say, let them deal with him."

"They deal with the *Aelva*!" cried another voice, this one belonging to Gresh *uvan* Oeyt, *Kranor* of the Chahroke Tribe. "The *Aelva* talk peace, but their warriors raid across Danelle. Many Hunters fall to their arrows."

A murmur of agreement rose from the representatives of other smaller tribes, but Kal stepped forward to address the *Kranora*. "Have you seen these attacks with your own eyes, Gresh *uvan* Oeyt?"

"I have seen arrows," came the response. "Black, with marks of the *Aelva* all over them. I have seen bodies. Men and women, even cubs, cut down by the children of Valia."

"It is as I thought," Kal replied. He told the Tribes of Nebari and the captured Elves, the attacks on Aelvin soil by Garun'ah who raided villages and slaughtered innocents.

"No child of Garun would do such a thing!" exclaimed one *Kranor*, and several others shouted their agreement.

"No?" Kal replied, reminding them of the *Kohr'adjin* attack less than a score of days past. There was a quiet murmur among the *Kranora* as they discussed these new tidings.

Jeran listened to the words of all the *Kranora*, as they decided whether or not to add their strength against Lorthas. In the end, most of the smaller tribes followed the lead of the four larger ones, offering Jeran and Alrendria a bond of allegiance. But of those small tribes numbering more than a thousand Hunters, only the Bahnje sided with Alrendria.

Jeran was disheartened. "I was certain the smaller tribes would follow the larger ones," he said to Dahr. "A full fifth of the Garun'ah have turned against us."

"They are not against us," Dahr pointed out. "They're just not for us."

"The children of Garun are independent," Kal said, leaving his position behind Arik. "Each *Kranor* decided with his own heart, and did not allow the choices of others to sway him." He clapped Jeran on the arm fondly. "When the shadow of the Darklord spreads across Madryn, most will join our cause!"

Since the Tacha had summoned *Cha'khun*, Arik had assumed the role of leader. He raised his arms for silence and addressed the other Garun'ah. "We have heard the words of Jeran Odara, the warning from Alrendria, and have chosen with our hearts. This day, we rekindle our bond with the Humans. This day, we take the first steps toward righting the Balance."

Arik's voice echoed across Kohr's Heart. "Tonight, we discuss no more tribal matters. Tonight is a night for celebration. For those who have added their might to the might of Alrendria, return to your people. Tell them of our new allies, and prepare for a celebration the likes of which the Gods have never seen!

"For those who chose isolation over alliance," Arik added, turning a stony gaze on the *Kranor* of the Turape, "I ask you to join our celebration. Perhaps time will change your minds, and make our cause yours as well."

The *Kranora* stood and disappeared into the night, each returning to his tribe's location in Kohr's Heart. Tanar clapped Jeran on the shoulder. "You did well tonight, my boy," he said, smiling broadly. "I'm proud of you. Quite proud." He shook his head, staring at Jeran and Dahr. "I can't believe you're the same boys I found cowering in that trapper's cabin!"

The old Mage brushed the dirt from his robes and stretched. "Well," he said, "I can't begin to tell you how much fun this has been. It's been great to see you both again, but I must be going." He turned to walk away, but Jeran grabbed his arm, spinning the old man around.

"You're leaving?" he asked incredulously.

"Now?" Dahr added, looking up at the star-covered sky. "In the middle of the night?"

Tanar shrugged. "I've already stayed longer than I should have. The Mage Assembly told me to bring Jeran here. They didn't tell me I was supposed to stay until he left!" Smiling, he patted them both on the shoulder. "Besides, it looks like you two have things under control. I doubt you'll even notice I'm gone!"

"At least stay till morning!" Jeran pleaded. "Join us in celebration of our new alliance."

Tanar frowned, as if considering Jeran's offer. Finally, he shook his head. "I'd love to, my boy, but as I said, I've already stayed longer than I should. I'm just going to head back to our tents, say goodbye to Mika and the Guardsmen, grab my horse, and be on my way."

He laughed suddenly. "Don't look so glum, boys!" he laughed. "I've been to more than a few *Cha'khun* celebrations in my life. With a little luck, I'll still be around for the next one!" He put one arm around Jeran's shoulders, one around Dahr's. "Come on," he told them. "Walk an old man to his horse!"

They escorted Tanar to the Guardsmen's tents, where the Mage proceeded to gather his things. Mika came running up, having heard word of Tanar's imminent departure, and tried to convince the old man to stay. Tanar refused, using much the same words with Mika as he had with Jeran and Dahr. Finally, he hopped into his saddle, and with many goodbyes and promises of a quick reunion, he disappeared into the night.

With Tanar's departure, a grim silence descended upon the Alrendrians, broken by the distant sound of music–horns and pipes whistling a strange, exotic beat. Frodel appeared in the Alrendrian camp, looking for Vyrina. He looked at their sad, distant faces and frowned. "What wrong?" he asked. "You look as if final rites, not celebrate alliance!"

Vyrina forced a smile onto her face. "It's nothing," she said, shaking off her malaise and walking over to Frodel. "Come on!" she called, hooking an arm around the Tribesman's and waving for the others to follow. "There's no point standing here moping! We don't want to offend our hosts!"

Wardel was the next to recover, the mere mention of a party enough to bring a smile to his face. He started toward Vyrina and Frodel, who turned and walked off into the tents, heading in the direction of the music. Slowly, the others came around, and one by one, they followed the procession to the lake.

Thousands were already on the shores of the lake. Great bonfires flared intermittently along the banks, lighting the area nearly as bright as day and chasing away the late summer chill. Barges, heavily laden with wood and pitch, drifted toward the island, where it seemed an even greater fire would be built around the geyser.

Great casks of *baqhat* were opened and distributed among the Garun'ah. Tribesmen danced in circles around the fires, moving rhythmically to the beat of canvas drums. Pipes and horns played an exotic tune, accentuating the percussion. Even as the Alrendrians wove their way down to the festivities, Garun'ah filtered into the bowl of Kohr's Heart in ever increasing numbers.

"It's amazing!" Katya said to Jeran, pointing to the throng below. "I'd never have guessed there were half as many Garun'ah!"

Jeran nodded. "What surprises me is how peaceful they are. At least within the confines of the camp. Since arriving, I haven't witnessed a single fight, let alone an argument!"

Katya considered the statement. "Other than Kraltir, who doesn't seem to play by the rules, I'd have to agree with you." She scratched her chin. "It *is* amazing. You couldn't put this many Humans in one place and not expect trouble of some sort."

"Who's expecting trouble?" Dahr asked, approaching from the side, holding in his hands three large mugs, nearly overflowing with *baqhat*. He handed one to Jeran and a second to Katya.

"I am!" Katya replied with a smile. She lifted her wooden mug and drank deeply from the rich, pungent liquid. "I expect you'll be in a lot of trouble if you don't ask me to dance!"

Dahr's brow scrunched in confusion. "To this?" he asked incredulously, listening to the exotic beat of the music.

Katya nodded, drained her glass, and took Dahr's hand. "We'll improvise!" she informed him, dragging him toward the fires.

Jeran watched with amusement as Katya and Dahr tried to dance to the tribal music. He sipped his *baqhat*, not wanting the strong drink to go to his head. Wardel passed, a tall, buxom Tribeswoman on each arm, a mug of *baqhat* in each hand, and a skin filled to bursting with the drink strapped across his back.

The Guardsman bowed his head to Jeran as he walked by, but his attention quickly returned to his two friends. The three of them disappeared into the crowd.

Jeran wandered aimlessly through the valley, observing the interaction between the different tribes. Whenever possible, he watched how the Tribesmen reacted to his own people, and he was pleased with what he saw. Little remained of the animosity and fear that had plagued the Guardsmen before the start of this mission. They seemed comfortable around the Tribesmen, almost as comfortable as the Garun'ah seemed around them.

Jeran smiled to himself. Maybe Tanar and the Emperor were right. Perhaps it would simply take a shared goal and a little time to bring the three races back together.

He walked into the first row of tents, leaving the noise of the celebration behind. Turning a corner, he was surprised to come across Elorn. The dour Guardsmen was sitting on a stump, his back to Jeran, who approached cautiously.

"Is there a problem, Guardsman?" he asked, and Elorn whirled around, his eyes widening in shock, then quickly narrowing. Jeran chose to ignore the burning gaze. "Why aren't you out with the others?" he asked in a friendly manner. "We won't be staying much longer with the Garun'ah. I'd have thought you'd want to enjoy our last few nights with the Tribesmen."

Elorn pressed his lips into a thin line. For a moment, Jeran did not think he was going to answer. "The noise," Elorn said at last, almost reluctantly. "The noise was getting to me. I just came here to relax." Jeran nodded in understanding; he had entered the tents for much the same reason. "We will be returning to Alrendria soon?" Elorn prompted.

It was Jeran's turn to nod. "In a day or two," he answered. "As soon as I'm sure we have no further business with the Garun'ah."

"It will be nice to return to Alrendria," Elorn stated, but his tone carried a note of loss.

A sudden movement in front of Jeran interrupted his next question, and a figure stepped from the shadows, entering the dim light cast by the far away bonfires. A Tribeswoman, short for a Garun'ah, yet still more than eleven hands in height, strode forward boldly. She wore a leather top, pressed tight against her ample bosom, and a hide skirt that barely reached mid-thigh. Her skin was olive-colored and her hair raven black, a near match for her dark, depthless eyes.

Her eyes flickered momentarily to Jeran, then locked on Elorn. "I been look for you," she said in a lightly-accented voice. "I hear Humans leave soon. I promised mighty Garun I remove frown from your face before you return to the Human Lands." She took his arm, and Elorn followed meekly as the Tribeswoman led him away.

"Have fun, Guardsman!" Jeran called, earning himself yet another glare as the Guardsmen disappeared into the tents.

Jeran continued his solitary walk through the encampment. From time to time, he ventured into the bowl where the party raged. A huge fire burned in the center of the lake, ringing the geyser of Kohr's Heart. Each eruption sent thousands of glittering droplets soaring into the night sky, and each was followed by a loud hiss as the waters fell to the burning coals.

The night waxed and then began to wane, but the celebration showed little signs of slowing. If anything, it only grew more raucous as time passed. Jeran ran into his companions several times over the course of the night. Jasova and Nykeal were arm in arm, discussing life in the Alrendrian Guard with a circle of Hunters. Seeing Jeran, they insisted that he join them. As soon as Jeran sat, his *baqhat* was refilled and he was coerced into telling the Tribesmen some of his own adventures.

When he finally managed to escape the circle, he continued his wandering. He saw Vyrina and Frodel twice, each time talking with different Tribesmen. Jakal passed him once, a Tribeswoman on one arm. Kal and Arik sat together in the middle of a big cluster of Hunters, draining mug after mug of *baqhat*.

Suddenly, Jeran wondered what had happened to Mika. The boy was often in the company of Crying Wolf and Fox Eyes, but always made a point of seeking Jeran out to share his latest adventures. Realizing that he had not seen Mika since Tanar had left, Jeran's worry began to grow, and he began a frantic search of the camp.

He found Mika quickly, and without much searching. The boy lay curled in the lap of an old, white-haired Tribeswoman. She squinted up at Jeran's approach, and a smile spread across her face. "You Jeran?" she asked in a voice so accented it was virtually unintelligible. "Little Tiger speak good you. Good father, you."

Jeran flushed. "Mika's not my son."

The old woman nodded. "Better father be you then, when child own." She looked at the boy in her lap. "Little Tiger weigh more than ox. Sleep like dead. Perhaps take him now to tent."

Jeran nodded and lifted the boy into his arms. "Thank you," he said, and the woman offered a toothless smile. He carried Mika through the tents carefully and laid him on his bedroll. Leaving the tent, he was surprised to see Katya and Dahr approaching. The sounds of the party still roared in the distance.

He was about to call out to them when they embraced, and from the way Dahr stumbled, Jeran could tell that his friend was no longer sober. With a swift motion, Dahr scooped Katya up and carried her toward their tent. Jeran flushed when Katya said, "I bet if we try hard enough, they'll hear us at the lake!" Embarrassed, he fled deeper into the tents.

With the vast majority of Garun'ah at the celebration, the camp seemed deserted. He walked through the maze of canvas, then climbed the western slope of the valley. Alone, he sat on the lip of the bowl, looking down at the festivities until, without warning, a figure appeared at his side, materializing from the shadows.

"It is a beautiful sight," Reanna said, smiling at Jeran warmly.

He nodded. "I have learned much in my short time with your people. It saddens me that I must go so soon." They sat in silence, watching as the fires below slowly died. One by one, the revelers filtered back to their tents, until only the staunchest celebrants remained on the shores of the lake.

Reanna shivered, and Jeran put an arm around her for warmth. They watched the eastern sky brighten and the first rays of sunlight climb above the far side of the valley. Once the sun was full in the morning sky, they made their way back to the camp.

For two more days the party lasted. The *Kranora* met during the day, while the other Garun'ah slept. At night the feasting continued, in honor of the Humans and the new alliance. Finally, on the third morning, Jeran approached Arik. "It's time we returned to Alrendria," he told the giant warrior. "I must bring news of our success to the King."

Arik grasped Jeran's arm just above the elbow, and Jeran returned the gesture. "Whenever you need us, you have but to call. The Tacha will fight at your side." Jeran thanked him, but the Tribesmen waved off the gratitude. "We are brothers now, Jeran Odara. We fight the same fight. Go. Gather your people and your things. I will find those who will see you off."

Jeran returned to the Alrendrian tents, which were already disassembled and packed. The last of their gear was being tied to the pack animals, and a mount was being found for Frodel, who planned on accompanying them to Kaper. Jeran gave the signal, and the procession began the long march south.

Arik waited at the top of the hill with Yarchik, Cat's Claw, Kal, and a few others. Kal embraced Jeran and Dahr. "When *Cha'khun* is complete, I will come to Kaper," he told them. "Together, we will work out a plan for dealing with the Darklord."

Yarchik smiled at the Alrendrians. "Never did I think I would live to see the start of the *Prah'phetia*. Peace and long life, my young friends! With Garun's blessing, we will meet again."

Others arrived to say their farewells to the Guardsmen. While they were doing so, Jakal approached. "Trouble is in the air," he told them cryptically. "I wish I knew its source, but Garun is not always forthcoming. In my dreams, I hear the far off echoes of screams, and see blood smeared across the Tribal Lands. Be wary!"

Cat's Claw was last. He approached with a smile. "Good to meet Humans with honor again! Too long deal I with only slavers and thieves." He looked to the south and frowned. "With Blood all here, Tribal Lands dangerous place. Close to Drekka are we. You not travel alone." He clapped his hands and Reanna approached.

"Snow Rabbit escort you to Human Lands," Cat's Claw told them.

Jeran shook his head. "It's not necessary, my friend."

"Necessary?" Cat's Claw replied. "Perhaps no. But will happen. She requested duty." Reanna smiled mysteriously, and Jeran did not feel that he had any option.

Final farewells were made, and the party started out of Kohr's Heart. For days, Reanna led them southeast, turning south only when they reached the foothills of the Anvil, the mountains looming ominously in the west, all but impassable. Once there, they increased their pace, mostly because they were eager to return home, and the journey was uneventful, almost peaceful, until they ran across Rannarik.

The *Tsha'ma* lay on the ground in a pool of blood. An arrow had pierced his left side, just beneath the shoulder. At first, Jeran thought the old Tribesman dead, but to his great relief, he saw Rannarik draw a slow, ragged breath.

With Dahr and Katya's help, Jeran cut the arrow and removed it. Using the herbal knowledge learned from both Uncle Aryn and Tanar, he cleaned and dressed the wound as best he could, wishing all the time he could use his Gift to heal.

Even with his careful ministrations, he was not sure whether or not the *Tsha'ma* would pull through until the old man's eyes fluttered open, and he smiled in recognition. "Thank Garun I found you!" Rannarik whispered, ignoring Jeran's request that he remain quiet.

"What happened?" Katya asked. She had been on edge since discovering the Tribesman. She watched every direction, leery of attack.

"Durange...." came Rannarik's strangled reply. "Bull attacked Alrendrians...Princes fleeing north along... Anvil... Tried to keep sight... Bull spotted me... Not quick enough."

Jeran swallowed hard. "Martyn and Treloran...." he repeated. "We have to find them!" He looked to his horse, then back at Rannarik again, unsure of what he should do.

"Go!" the *Tsha'ma* said, his eyes drooping. "Will be fine... need... rest. Save princes! Much hinges on their... survival." Rannarik sagged in Jeran's hands, and for a moment, he again feared that the Tribesman had died. When Jeran saw the slow and shallow breathing, he laid Rannarik's head gently on the ground.

"Leave him food and supplies!" Jeran ordered. "Then mount up. We need to find Martyn and Treloran!"

"What about Rannarik?" Dahr asked.

"He said to leave him here!" Jeran snapped. "I don't want to, but I don't see any other choice. We have a duty to Alrendria! Martyn must be protected." Dahr frowned, but nodded reluctantly.

"Rannarik's a Mage," Katya reminded Dahr. "He just needs a little sleep. Once he wakes, his Gift will protect him."

"It didn't protect him very much from Tylor's arrow," Dahr pointed out.

"We don't have time to argue about this," Jeran said, turning to Reanna. "Can you find them?" he asked. "I don't know how large a party, but no more than six hundred, probably less. There'll be an Elf among them."

"I will find them," Reanna assured him. "Continue south along this path, and I will return when I have found them."

Jeran grabbed her before she could run away. "Be careful, Reanna," he warned. "They're being chased by Tylor Durange, one of the Darklord's allies. He'll have at least as many soldiers, probably more. No matter what happens, don't let them see you."

Reanna's face tightened. "You are concerned for the safety of your friend, so I will not take offense." Then she smiled warmly, and stroked Jeran's cheek in a tender caress. "No one sees Snow Rabbit unless she wants them to. I will return within five days time. Follow my trail south." She ran off, faster on foot than she would have been on horseback.

"Mount up!" Jeran said, a wave of panic nearly overwhelming him. "We have a hard ride ahead of us." He prayed to the Five Gods that they would not arrive too late.

Chapter 40

Martyn wiped away sweat with the back of his hand and looked at Treloran, who rode silently at his right. The Elf's clothes, once immaculate, were ripped and smeared with dirt; and his eyes, usually bright and alert, were dull, ringed with dark circles. A shallow gash ran down his left cheek.

"Gods!" Martyn said, trying to force a smile. "I hope I don't look as bad as you!"

Treloran did not quite manage to return the smile. "You look worse, Human," he said, with only a hint of joviality.

Martyn's grin faded when his horse stumbled. "We're going to have to rest soon," he told the others. "The horses are exhausted, and I'm about to fall from the saddle." He looked at each of his companions in turn and laughed. "None of you look too spry either!"

They all nodded in agreement, but only Lisandaer spoke. "There's a sheltered grove on the far side of that hill," he said, pointing to a dark copse of trees in the shadow of a sheer rock wall. "We can rest there with little chance of discovery."

"How can you say that?" Olivia countered, near panic. "Tylor has followed us every step of the way, discovered even our best-concealed camps! The Bull is relentless! There's no way we'll escape!"

"That's enough!" Martyn said harshly, nearly yelling. "The Bull hasn't caught us yet! We've managed to stay one step ahead of him for days."

He looked at the sun, which was beginning its descent in the western sky. Soon it would disappear behind the Anvil. "It will be nearly dark by the time we reach that clearing. We may not have lost Tylor, but I'm sure we've gained some ground on him. Enough to stop and rest the night."

"Half the night, at least," Treloran agreed, shaking the reins of his horse. At his command, the thin white stallion plodded through the thick grass. The others followed wearily, allowing the Aelvin Prince to choose their path. They had long since learned to appreciate the Elf's skill at hiding their trail.

They rode in muted silence, the whispering of the wind in the grass the only audible sound. When Treloran finally led them into the shelter of the trees, they were pleasantly surprised to find a small stream bubbling from beneath a boulder. "The horses need food and water," Martyn ordered, "and we need to gather what supplies we can while it's still light."

No one moved. Martyn stared at the worn and hopeless faces of his companions, wondering how he could inspire them. "Come on!" he urged, "We're not finished yet! I don't know about you Guardsmen, but I don't plan on giving up! You're the Alrendrian Guard! There's no fighting force in Madryn that can stand against you!"

His words did not have the rousing effect he had hoped for, but it did get the Guardsmen moving. Olivia and Bystral went to the horses, while Lisandaer and the others spread out in search of food. Martyn, alone, climbed the mountainside, hoping for a good view of the southern horizon. From there, he hoped to see how far away Tylor and his soldiers were.

When he returned to camp, he brought disheartening news. "Tylor is on the horizon. It looks like he's setting up camp for the night, but you can bet he's sent some scouts out looking for us. We'll be able to get half a night's sleep, but then we'll have to push north under cover of darkness."

A chorus of weary sighs rose around him. "Get some sleep," Martyn ordered. "I'll take the first watch." Lisandaer protested, but Martyn silenced him with a gesture. "Do what you're told, Guardsman! I promise, if any of Tylor's men come, I'll leave a few for you!"

Grudgingly, Lisandaer relented. One by one, he and the other Guardsmen retreated to their bedrolls, until only the two prince remained by the stream.

For a time, silence reigned. "Do you think they made it?"

Treloran shrugged. "There is no way to know for sure, but I doubt this Tylor Durange could have found us so quickly had he pursued Jes and the others."

A strained silence descended on them until Martyn clasped Treloran's shoulder fondly. "I'm sorry about this. We never should have taken you without an Aelvin escort."

"Even an honor guard would not have been enough to stop this man," Treloran said, laughing weakly. "Our fate is in the hands of the Goddess, Martyn. It is I who should feel sorrow for you. You have lost a friend."

"Iban...." Martyn whispered the word reverently, then met the Elf's eyes. "Sleep. It won't be too long before we have to ride again." The Aelvin Prince nodded wearily and went to his bedroll.

With Treloran gone, Martyn was left to his own dark thoughts. He wondered about Iban's fate. It was unlikely that the Guard Commander still lived. Tylor would have had to overrun the Alrendrian encampment before learning that the princes were no longer there. Had Lord Iban surived the attack, the Bull would almost certainly have killed him for the deception.

Martyn could not remember how many days ago they had parted. *Ten? Twenty? A thousand?* They ran together in a terrifying blur. He remembered arguing with Iban, insisting that their best chance was to stay together and fight from behind the walls of the fortification.

"To what end?" Iban had replied. "With our full strength we might be able to hold him off for a while, but Tylor is no fool. If he cannot breach our walls in one attack, he won't waste his men in futile sorties. He'll fashion siege weapons from the trees or call the ShadowMagi to his aid. If he doesn't already have some at his side."

Seeing the stubborn glint in Martyn's eyes, Iban reached out and gripped the prince's shoulder. "With all the Guardsmen here, we might be able to hold out a few days; but in the end, Tylor will win. All of us–every man, woman and child–will be killed, or at best enslaved. You will be executed, and Alrendria will be without an heir. Treloran... They will kill him too!"

With that, Iban had paused, allowing ample time for his words to sink in. "Can you not see what will happen if Treloran dies in our care? Luran and his supporters would use the Aelvin Prince's death to rally his people against us. The peace we've worked so hard for would be shattered before it was formed, and we'd find ourselves with another enemy instead of an ally!"

Finished, Iban's face had resumed its customary stoniness. "You and the others will head north!" he said, repeating his earlier order. "You'll have three, maybe four days before Tylor gets here, another day or two before he overruns our position. It isn't much, but it may be enough time for you to slip around him and get safely to Grenz.

"I'll keep a handful of Guardsmen with me, fifty at most! A couple of servants as well, if any are willing to stay. But I'll take only those willing to volunteer! Just enough to put up an adequate defense."

"Why leave anyone at all?" Martyn asked. "He'll come looking for us anyway? If he finds a deserted encampment, it'll still cost him time!"

"When we don't walk into his ambush, Tylor will send scouts. If they find an active encampment, the Bull will assume we're waiting inside. By the time he discovers the truth, you and the others will have slipped around him. But if his scouts find an empty encampment...."

"Then Tylor will start searching in every direction," Martyn finished. He looked at Iban pleadingly. "Come with us!" he all but begged.

Iban smiled, but shook his head. "How can I ask my men to face death if I'm not willing to stand at their side?" The Guard Commander squeezed Martyn's shoulder fondly, but spoke firmly. "This is not up for debate. The others are ready. Willym will lead you north under cover of darkness. Once clear of Tylor, you'll angle west until you reach the Anvil."

The salute that he offered Martyn had a certain finality to it. "Now go!" he had said, the hint of a tear in his eye. "You know your duty!"

Leaving Iban to his fate had been the toughest decision of Martyn's life. The second toughest came only a handful of days later, when Jolina had galloped into camp, her horse lathered in sweat and breathing furiously. "The Bull is on our trail!" the Guardswoman said breathlessly. "He's less than five days behind and approaching fast."

All eyes turned to Willym. "We split up!" he said after a long silence. "Parties of six, each moving in a different direction. The princes will travel with a score of Guardsmen and make a beeline toward the city. With luck, we'll all meep up again within the walls of Grenz."

"No," Martyn said authoritatively, bracing for the response.

"My liege," Willym started, "We have no other choice–"

"It's what Tylor will expect," Martyn said, thinking back to his many conversations with Iban. "We have to do the unexpected." Falling silent, he scratched his chin thoughtfully. "Treloran and I will go north. Alone. Jeran and the Garun'ah are up there somewhere. With luck, we'll find them before Tylor finds us. The rest of you will head toward Grenz with all possible haste."

"What makes you think Tylor will follow you two instead of our party?" Willym asked. "He'll assume you travel toward Grenz."

"Not if we make sure he knows we're the ones heading north!"

"And how do you propose we do that?" countered Jes, stepping up to voice her opinion. "Draw a sign in the dirt that says 'the princes went north'? I'm sure the Bull will believe such nonsense!"

Martyn frowned. "Someone will have to stay behind," he said at last. "Someone will have to volunteer to be captured."

"That's certain death," Jes pointed out, her voice calm, almost casual.

"Better one of us die than all, Lady Jessandra." he replied as he turned to face the Guardsmen. Scores of hard eyes stared back at him, but Martyn saw fear in most of them. "I won't order anyone to do this."

One of the older Guardsman, limping on an injured leg, stepped forward. "I'll stay, my Prince," he stated boldly, putting a hand on his sword. "Been slowing the rest of you down anyway, since my horse went lame."

"Are you sure, Harta?" Martyn asked.

A wry smile split his mouth. "It's okay if I kill a few before I surrender?"

"So long as you make sure they know I'm heading north before the end," Martyn laughed, gripping Harta's arm warmly. "You do Alrendria a great service this day, Guardsman. You will be remembered."

"A great service?" Harta repeated. "I'm going to betray the whereabouts of my prince to our worst enemy!"

"True," Martyn replied. "But with a little luck, you'll be sending that enemy into a horde of Garun'ah!"

When Martyn ordered Willym to take the others west he faced great resistance, but in the end they went, all but Lisandaer, Bystral, Quellas, and Olivia. "Iban's last orders to us were to ensure that you reached Grenz alive," Lisandaer told the prince, speaking for the group. "We won't let you go alone."

Seeing that his protests would have no effect, Martyn accepted their company. Bidding farewell to Harta, he led his party northwest, angling north after they reached the Anvil. The pace he set, from before dawn to well past midnight each day, was grueling, but it was not long before they discovered Tylor on their trail.

"It seems Harta did his job too well!" Quellas joked when they first saw the Bull's troops.

"Harta sacrificed himself that others might live," Martyn snapped in response. "I will not have you cheapen his memory with such comments." Chastened, Quellas had fallen silent, and the pursuit had begun in earnest.

The half moon set some time after midnight. Bleary-eyed, Martyn woke the others. "Saddle the horses," he ordered. "We'd best be on our way while we have darkness on our side."

"Shouldn't you rest, my Prince?" asked Bystral.

"I'll rest when we're in Grenz," Martyn replied sharply. "Or when I'm dead."

They stole down the back of the hill as quietly as possible, careful not to disturb the underbrush. Once on the grasslands, they quickened their pace. The Guardsmen spread out, each heading in a different direction and keeping a watchful eye out for Tylor's men.

The stark, grey rock of the Anvil slid past on their left; to the right, the first traces of light began to brighten the sky. With the approach of dawn, the princes urged their horses for more speed, knowing that they were exposed on the open grassland. Far ahead, on the edge of the horizon, the land grew forested, offering the promise of concealment.

Dawn broke just as they entered the trees. Quellas and Bystral joined them from the east, and Olivia and Lisandaer could be heard ahead, arguing. Concerned, Martyn signaled for Treloran to follow him, and he confronted the two bickering Guardsmen.

"–could not have gotten around us!" Lisandaer snapped.

"I know what I saw!" Olivia retorted.

"What's going on here?" Martyn demanded, riding up.

"There was someone at the edge of the forest when I approached," Olivia told him. "I didn't get a very good look, but there was someone there!"

"On horseback?" Lisandaer asked. When Olivia shook her head, the burly Guardsmen scoffed. "How could Tylor's soldiers get ahead of us without horses? I tell you there's no sign anyone's been here in seasons!"

"Nevertheless," Martyn interjected, "I think caution is in order. We'll continue on together. Keep your eyes open for anything out of the ordinary." He looked at Treloran, who silently grabbed his bow and pulled an arrow from the quiver at his back. "Not a bad idea," Martyn told him, reaching for his own weapon.

* * * * * * * * * * * * * * * * * * * *

"We don't have a lot of options," Jeran said to Katya. "We need to find Martyn and get him back to *Cha'khun*. The Tribesmen will be able to protect us from the Bull."

The Guardswoman nodded. "But we have to find them first!" she pointed out, wagging an admonishing finger in his face. "You shouldn't have sent Reanna to look for Tylor. She's more skilled at tracking than the rest of us."

"We need to know how far away Tylor is!" Jeran snapped, defending his decision. "Besides, Reanna said they were only a day or so south of last night's camp. Frodel and Dahr are looking for them. I promise you; we'll be heading north before sundown."

"I hope you're right," Katya said, a hint of fear in her voice.

"Something bothering you?" Jeran asked. "You've been on edge for the last few days."

Katya cleared her throat. "I think you need to–" Jeran raised his hand suddenly, interrupting her.

"Later!" he whispered. "Someone's coming!"

Frodel appeared at the edge of the clearing they had been using as a base camp. "Humans ahead," the Tribesman said. "Few. Five or six."

"Five or six?" Jeran repeated. "Is that all?" He swallowed hard, hoping they were not too late. "Let's move." He waved the Guardsmen forward, and they picked a path through the trees. Out of nowhere, Dahr appeared at Jeran's side, riding his giant warhorse.

Dawn had broken not long before, and the first rays of sun were peeking through the thick branches above. The forest offered few sounds, only the occasional rustle of leaves or agitated cry when the Alrendrians startled some animal from its home.

Rubbing sand from his eyes, Jeran urged his mount forward. They had slept little since encountering Rannarik, and the long days were beginning to show.

"How far ahead are they?" Katya asked before Jeran could.

"Not far," came Frodel's cryptic reply. "Other edge of wood. They move cautious, but straight toward." Looking embarrassed, the Tribesman added, "Think I one spot me."

Jeran laughed. "These are our friends, Frodel," he reminded the Garun'ah. "It's okay if they see us." But even with Jeran's reassurances, Frodel's expression did not improve. Vyrina moved her horse closer to him; their hushed voices carried softly through the darkened forest.

"Stop!" came a sudden cry, and up ahead, the bushes rattled. Jeran and his party came to an abrupt halt. "Keep your weapons lowered and you won't be hurt!" Jeran smiled at the familiar voice.

"From that distance, you're not likely to hit any of us, Martyn!" Jeran called back amicably. "I know how good you are with a bow!"

There was a short pause, then Martyn stepped out from concealment, Treloran at his side. "Is it really you, Jeran?" he asked, relieved. At his signal, a handful of Guardsman came into view.

It was a tense reunion, but Martyn and Jeran met halfway between their original positions, enveloping each other in a great bear hug. "I might not have hit you," Martyn admitted, "but Treloran could put an arrow through you blindfolded!" He stared at his friend and sighed in relief. "By the Five Gods, it's good to see you, Jeran! All of you!"

The prince next went to Dahr, all smiles and warm greetings. "We were beginning to think we'd never find you," Dahr told him.

"We would have made it easier if we'd known you were looking for us!" Martyn admitted with a broad smile.

Introductions were brief. Treloran and Frodel eyed each other warily, but otherwise the parties knew each other. Together, they started north, and Jeran pressed the prince for information. Martyn told them what had happened to the Alrendrian delegation, but he kept the details to a minimum.

"Poor Iban," Jeran said when Martyn told him of the Guard Commander's fate. "He was a good man."

"The best," Katya answered, her statement echoed by Dahr. At Dahr's side, Fang whined.

"We'll drink to him when we get back to Kaper!" Martyn said. "But right now we have more important things to worry about. Tylor and his soldiers are a day behind us, maybe less. We need to move! How far away are the Garun'ah? We'd hoped to use them as a shield."

When Jeran told him how many days it was to Kohr's Heart, Martyn's face fell. "I don't relish that many more long days and sleepless nights, but anything's better than being trapped by the Durange!"

"Then I have bad news," Reanna said, stepping from the shadows. Treloran had an arrow drawn in an instant, and it was only Jeran stepping between the two that prevented him from letting the shaft fly.

Reanna did not seem to notice her near brush with death. "The main body of warriors is to our south, advancing slowly. But last night, a group of riders a hundred strong were sent north at full speed. By now they are working their way down the Boundary."

"We're trapped!" Quellas moaned, his shoulders slumping.

"They sent riders north?" Katya asked nervously. "What of Mika?"

"Mika?" repeated Martyn.

"We sent him north to rejoin the Garun'ah," Jeran explained. "I didn't want him mixed up in this." The boy had resisted at first, relenting only at Jeran's insistence. "I made him believe that we were sending him north to rally the Tribesmen and bring them to our rescue."

An army of Garun'ah would have been an advantage, but it was unlikely that Mika would return in time. *At least he'll survive*, Jeran thought. *If he had made it past Tylor's soldiers.*

"We sent the boy north two days ago," Reanna reminded them, as if reading Jeran's thoughts, and some of the tension melted from his shoulders. "He will be far north of the riders. But it is unlikely he will return before we are forced to fight."

"What do we do now?" Martyn asked. He had not counted on being surrounded.

"Early this morning we passed a valley," Katya told them. "The bowl was open grassland, but the sides were steep and thickly forested. There was a rock ledge about a hundred hands above the valley floor. It's easily defensible and will offer us a good vantage point from which to watch Tylor's approach."

"Great," muttered Quellas. "I always wanted a good view of my own death."

"That's enough!" Jeran snapped, and the Guardsman immediately lowered his eyes to hide his embarrassment.

"There is one problem," Katya admitted. "The valley is nestled in the Anvil. I don't know if there's any other way out."

"We're already trapped," Martyn pointed out. "Might as well get ourselves trapped someplace where we can make a stand!"

The others agreed. Gathering what little gear they had, they followed Katya through the forest. It did not take her long to find the entrance to the valley, a narrow channel carved through the thick rock of the Boundary by a small, winding stream. Once through the opening, the passage widened into a lush, sheltered vale.

It was just as Katya had described, open on the bottom with steep sides and a rock ledge a hundred hands high, covered with trees. Near the entrance, the walls were too steep to climb; but farther back, the grade became more gradual, with numerous runoff trails providing access to the shelf above. The valley itself was long and narrow, five hundred hands across and nearly four times that in length.

"Let's get up to that ledge," Jeran told them. "We have a lot of work to do and not a lot of time to do it."

They scrambled up the slope, leading their mounts around the loose rocks. At the top, they found a sheltered alcove with a clearing large enough to accommodate the horses. "Tie them there," Jeran said to Dahr, who began to gather the reins.

Jeran took the lead, assigning duties to the others. "Reanna, scout the valley. Try to find another way out of here." With a nod, she trotted off, and Jeran turned to Jasova. "You too, Guardsman. We need to find another way out of here." Jasova departed in the direction opposite the Tribeswoman.

"Quellas, you and Frodel head to the mouth of the valley. See if there's anyway to start a rockslide. If we can trap ourselves in here, we might be able to hold out long enough for the Garun'ah to come." The Guardsmen saluted and took off at a run.

"The rest of you," Jeran called, waving them forward, "come here." They assembled around him. "We need to secure this valley. The rock ledge is our best defense. If we can keep Tylor trapped below, we'll have a better chance of staying alive. The first thing we need to do is limit the number of ways up here. Katya, pick out the trails we can best defend and mark them. The rest of you, follow behind and obstruct the others.

"I don't care how you do it," he told them. "Rock slides to remove the path or traps to catch Tylor's men unaware. But we need to make sure there are only a couple of ways to access this ledge, and we need to be sure we can defend them adequately." The Guardsmen saluted and turned to Katya; even Treloran waited patiently for his orders.

"All these can go," Katya said, waving to the four nearest trails. "In fact everything on this part of the slope can be removed. They're too straight. If Tylor rushes us, we won't be able to shoot down his men fast enough."

She surveyed the valley. "That side is steeper," she said, pointing southeast, "with more switchbacks. It'll give us more chances to pick off anyone foolish enough to approach." She waved for the Guardsmen to move closer, and when they did, she outlined her plan in the dirt.

"I'll start on the far side of the valley," she told them, pointing in the direction Reanna had disappeared. "If I want you to leave a path, I'll mark it by placing a large, white stone at the top. If you don't see a stone, destroy the path."

While Katya discussed her plan with the Guardsmen, Dahr approached Jeran. "What can I do?"

Jeran frowned in thought, but when he noticed the score of dogs that flanked Dahr, his frown turned into a broad smile. "We need to be sure that Tylor doesn't send any scouts in here. Is there any way you could...." Again, Jeran's eyes drifted to the dogs.

Dahr nodded in understanding. "Dogs," he said authoritatively. "Patrol." As one, the hounds loped off, scrambling down the hill at a run.

Standing, Katya dismissed her charges. "Be about it then!" The Guardsmen nodded and went immediately to work. After exchanging wry glacnes, the two princes followed. Without waiting to be told, Dahr trotted after them.

Katya turned to face Jeran, who was sitting himself on the grass. "And what are you going to do?" she asked smugly. "Take a nap?"

Jeran's smile did not reach his eyes. "I'm going to see if I can find out where Tylor is."

"Like before?" Katya prompted. "After the slavers?" When Jeran nodded, Katya's gaze grew apprehensive. "Do you need me to stay here to... to hit you again."

Laughing, Jeran shook his head. "I've gotten a little better at this since last time. I'll be fine."

"If you're sure," she said with a shrug. "I wouldn't mind hitting you if I had to."

"Get to work, Guardsman!" Jeran said, trying to sound authoritative. Katya forced a smile and disappeared into the trees.

The day passed quickly, and most of the news was good. Food was plentiful in the valley, as was water, so they would be able to survive until help arrived, provided they could hold Tylor at bay.

Jasova appeared at midday and told them that the north ridge was obstructed; there was no other passage out of the valley. The admission sucked much of the hope out of the Alrendrians, but Reanna renewed their spirits not long after, when she returned with better news.

"There is a small passage through the rock," she told them, "big enough to squeeze a horse through if you are careful. But it is in clear sight from the valley. Once this Bull is here, he will see us if we try to use it."

"Then we should use it now!" insisted Quellas.

Jeran had Reanna describe the location of the passage to him. He sat and extended his perceptions. After a few moments, he shook his head. "We have to wait for them to enter the valley before we use the passage," he said dejectedly.

"Why?" Quellas demanded.

"Because Tylor and his troops are camped on the other side!" Quellas seemed taken aback by the statement, but none dared contradict it. Jeran frowned, angered that he had had to reveal his secret to so many.

Despite their grim situation, only two bits of news truly worried Jeran. The first came when Quellas and Wardel had returned. "It's no use," Wardel had said. "We dropped some boulders into the mouth of the valley, but they didn't loosen enough rock. It might slow the Bull down, but it isn't going to stop him."

Jeran nodded knowingly. "It was worth a try," he told them. "Help the others block the trails, then have them start looking for provisions."

The second bit of bad news came near sunset. Returning his perceptions to his body, Jeran called for the Guardsmen to assemble. "Tylor's riders have rejoined his main forces, camped not far from here. Since neither found any trace of us, the Bull ordered his men to search the valleys along the Anvil. It's only a matter of time before he finds us."

"What do we do?" Vyrina asked.

Jeran shrugged. "Get some sleep. Tylor won't attack until morning, and I, for one, am exhausted." He yawned and stretched, peering toward the valley's mouth. "Two guards," he said, fighting a second yawn. "I'll take second watch."

It was a restless night for all. Tense with anticipation, the slightest sound had the Alrendrians reaching for their weapons; and the night was full of sounds, the forest restless. Wolves howled, their cries echoing through the canyon; the shrieks of night birds cut through the still, black night; and the deep bass lowing of moose and occasional roars of mountain cats punctuated the other, more common sounds.

Long before dawn arrived, the Alrendrians were awake, waiting nervously for Tylor to appear. They did not have to wait long. The first outriders entered the valley just after sunrise, and the main host was not far behind.

Jeran extended his perceptions, carefully surveying the countryside. "He's bringing everyone in," he told the others. "If we can get to the passage without being spotted, we'll be able to get away."

"And how are we going to do that?" Elorn demanded. "I was down in the valley. You can't tell the opening for what it is from down there, but you couldn't miss anyone approaching it. It's nothing but open rock for six hundred hands."

"We'll need a diversion," Jeran told them, returning Elorn's harsh gaze. "A way to distract Tylor long enough for the princes to slip through." He looked around hopefully. "I'm open to suggestions."

Elorn lowered his eyes to the ground. "You're wrong," Katya said, shaking her head slowly. "We only need to distract Tylor long enough for the princes to escape. The rest of us are expendable."

A tense silence descended upon them. "That's a last resort," Jeran announced, his expression grim. Above, hawks and other birds of prey circled the valley, floating on the warm updrafts rising from the mountains. They looked like carrion birds waiting for a meal.

To th east, Tylor's forces had just reached the obstructions at the mouth of the valley and were starting to work their way past. "We get ready to fight," Frodel said. "I not want be caught out of position."

"You know your places," Jeran told them, and they all turned to walk away. "Katya," Jeran called to the redheaded Guardswoman, "wait here. This is our best vantage point. I'd like to hear your suggestions on how to deal with the Bull." She nodded and dropped to the ground at Jeran's side. Together they wormed their way toward the edge.

While they waited, Jeran scanned the ridge. They had destroyed all but three paths: two were close together, allowing the groups stationed at the top to aid each other if the fighting grew too fierce. The third trail was toward the mouth of the valley, hard to spot; Katya had left it as an escape route. If all else failed, they would make a break for the plains from there.

Dahr, Frodel, Quellas, and Vyrina manned the farthest path; the two closer ones were guarded by the princes and the rest of the Guardsmen. Jeran and Katya would move wherever the fighting was fiercest, offering what aid they could.

The last of Tylor's troops passed the boulders, and the Bull ordered the advance. Over seven hundred men began the march to the valley's center; the Bull was holding nothing in reserve. "Iban made a good accounting of himself," he whispered. "Martyn says the Bull started with over a thousand."

Katya nodded. "Iban kept only fifty Guardsmen with him. He deserved the reputation he earned. His death is a great loss to Alrendria."

They fell silent, watching as Tylor stationed his troops. Standing in the center of the clearing, he turned slowly, surveying the countryside. Noting the debris-covered trails, a smile spread across his face. "I know you're in here!" he called out, and the valley echoed his words, sending them thundering into the heavens. "Surrender yourself to me, Prince Martyn, and I will spare you life!"

"Jeran," Katya whispered, "can you use your Gift? Is there anything you can do?"

He shook his head. "Not much, and certainly not from here. I can't hold magic for more than a moment without it running wild. Up here, I'd be more likely to kill us than him." He smiled in apology. "If I were in the middle of Tylor's camp I might be able to do something, but the Bull will kill me before I'm halfway down the hillside."

Katya frowned thoughtfully. "How important is saving Prince Martyn?"

Jeran squinted, measuring the Guardswoman with a probing gaze. "It's important."

"Is it worth your life?" she asked pointedly. "Both our lives? Is it worth everything that's important to us?"

After the briefest pause, Jeran nodded. "You know it is."

"Then I have a plan." She waited for Jeran's nod before continuing. "We should parley."

Jeran almost laughed aloud. "I told you, Tylor will have me dead before I reach the valley floor!"

"I can guarantee that you reach him alive." She closed her eyes, and her head dipped toward the ground. "Besides," she added, her voice sad, "if my plan works, we'll have a second distraction on top of your magic."

Jeran stared off into the distance consideringly. "Let's do it," he said, pushing himself back from the edge of the shelf. Keeping to the shadows, he dodged nimbly through the trees, Katya a step behind. Below, Tylor's deep voice thundered, "I have little patience, Prince of Alrendria! Surrender yourself to me now!"

Jeran reached the first path and signaled for those guarding the second to join him. Once they had clustered around, he told them what he and Katya planned. "We're going to parley with Tylor," he said, cutting off their stunned outcries with a sharp gesture. "After we're within the confines of the Bull's camp, I'm going to create a diversion.

"Don't ask me what it is," he quickly added, before anyone could ask. "You'll know it when it happens. As soon as Tylor's men are distracted, I want the princes taken through the passage. Jasova, you will protect them, along with Nykeal, Elorn, Bystral, Olivia, and Lisandaer. The rest of you will lay down cover fire until they're out of sight.

"Once they're safely gone, the rest of us will make our way to the mouth of the valley and try to affect our own escape. Under no circumstance should anyone follow the princes through the passageway. We need to keep its existence secret if we're to give them a chance at freedom."

He looked at the Guardsmen one by one. "Are we all agreed?" A chorus of subdued cheers met his question.

Smiling, Jeran signaled to Katya, and they started toward the trail. A hand grabbed his shoulder and whirled him around. "Jeran," Martyn said, a pained look on his face, "what are you doing? You know what Tylor will do if he recognizes you!"

Jeran's smile was sad. He gripped Martyn's arm fondly. "Sometimes, Martyn, the sword of honor cuts deeps. Duty compels me to do this for you. Duty compels you to let me do it." They locked gazes for a long moment, then Jeran winked. "But as my uncle used to say, we don't have to like it!" Martyn let go, and Jeran turned to Katya, signaling for her to continue.

"We wish a parley!" she shouted, but her voice did not carry well. She was forced to shout her request twice more before Tylor responded.

"How many?"

"Two," Katya called. "We will come with weapons sheathed. Do we have your promise of safety?"

The Bull did not hesitate long. "You will reach the bottom alive!"

Jeran and Katya exchanged nervous glances, then started down the trail. Soon they had left the shelter of the trees behind and found themselves facing a line of bowmen, all with weapons trained on them. Slowly, confidently, the pair continued down the hillside.

"You know," Katya said when they were halfway to the bottom. Her words were part statement, part question. Jeran nodded. "For how long?"

"Long enough," came Jeran's reply.

Another long pause followed. Above, everyone watched with baited breath as the two drew nearer to the enemy. "Then...why?" Katya finally stammered, unable to voice the question on the tip of her tongue.

"A person is the sum of his own actions," Jeran shrugged, "not the actions of others. I owe you my life several times over. You have proven yourself to me time and again. There are few in this world who I consider a truer friend." He paused, and after a moment, smiled broadly. "Dahr loves you," he added, as if that were reason enough.

"Not after today," Katya murmured. They had nearly reached Tylor. The Bull wore his spiked, ebony armor; the black metal shimmered in the morning sunlight. Recognizing Jeran, the Bull's gaze hardened, and his hand clenched around the hilt of his sword, but he held his temper and kept the blade in its scabbard.

Katya pulled Jeran to a stop in front of the Bull of Ra Tachan, her face set in a grimace of determination. Leaning in close, she quietly whispered, "I'm sorry," and cuffed him on the back of the head hard enough to knock him senseless to the ground.

Jeran landed in a heap, and Katya looked up at Tylor. "Hello, Uncle," she said, smiling at the Bull. Her words echoed up the sides of the valley. "I've brought you a present."

* * * * * * * * * * * * * * * * * * *

When Katya's words reached him, Dahr felt his heart break. A red mist clouded his eyes and he trembled uncontrollably. He saw Jeran fall to the ground, landing roughly on his hands and knees. Instinctively, Dahr reached for his sword, allowing his bow to fall unused to the forest floor. Around him, the dogs growled.

Frodel's hand restrained him. "Now not time for Blood Rage."

Dahr rounded on the Tribesman, ignoring the look of sympathy in the other man's eyes. "Too late." With a mighty shove, he pushed Frodel. The Tribesman flew backward, smashing into a nearby tree with bone-numbing force and dropping to the ground, dazed.

Turning before Frodel landed, Dahr ran for the hillside, his greatsword swinging free. He howled, a wail of pain and betrayal, and the sound echoed across the valley. The hounds howled too, adding their voices to Dahr's, and throughout the forest, others took up the cry. From all sides, from every direction, howls and shrieks and roars filled the morning air. The Guardsmen cringed at the haunting sound, and Tylor's soldiers scanned the treeline nervously.

Dahr's eyes flashed anew, and his pain turned to rage, fueled by fear for his friend's safety and his own inner pain. Inside, he felt a something break, and power surged through him.

He sprinted down the hill, desperate to save Jeran, eager to feed his sword on the bodies of Tylor's men. Clearing the trees, he howled again, and the pack echoed him.

Around him the forest burst to life; below, the valley exploded in flame.

* * * * * * * * * * * * * * * * * * *

Jeran groaned as his hands hit the ground. He coughed, the metallic taste of blood filling his mouth. He heard an angry howl echoing above, a cry of hatred from a creature he had never seen before.

Lifting his head, he struggled to clear his vision. Katya still stood at his side, her eyes on the hill, searching the ridge for the source of that terrifying sound, tears streaming down her face. Tylor's soldiers were anxious; they spun in tight circles, expecting attack from all directions. One man gurgled, clutching at his throat. He fell to the ground, the shaft of an Aelvin arrow pointing into the air.

Only Tylor seemed unaffected by the chaos. His eyes were focused on Jeran, as if nothing else existed in all the world. Jeran could see the Bull's good eye from deep within the dark helmet, and it burned into his soul with the heat of Tylor's hatred.

Drawing his sword, Tylor dropped from his horse and approached Jeran, his blade rising for the killing blow. *If I'm going to die,* Jeran thought, *I might as well make it a memorable death.*

He reached for his Gift, surrendered to it, and allowed the magic to flow into him. It flooded him, filled him in a raging torrent, until he thought he would explode. Knew he would explode. He screamed in pain, begging for an end, eager for Tylor's sword to drive through him.

The last thing he saw before blackness rolled over him was Dahr bursting from the cover of the trees, swinging his greatsword like a giant scythe. He descended the steep rocky slope at a run, surrounded by an army of animals.

* * * * * * * * * * * * * * * * * * *

The valley was chaos. Explosions rocked the ground, knocking stones loose from the rock wall and sending Tylor's men flying in every direction. Two great pillars of fire, nearly two hundred hands high, had risen from the ground, and Martyn stared in awe as they cut a swath of destruction through the Darklord's forces.

Katya's admission and betrayal. Jeran's fall and the terrific explosions that could only be the result of his magic. Dahr's wild charge, surrounded by bears, wolves, and all other manner of animal. Martyn could not believe it.

Jasova had to force the prince to move. He was stunned, both by the strange sights around him and by the selfless sacrifice of the two he considered his dearest friends. Prodded down the rock face by his Guardsmen, he allowed himself to be moved toward the shelter of the hidden passageway. Numbly, he kept an eye on the battle below, listening to the cries of men, watching through the ever-thickening smoke.

He and Treloran were surrounded by the Guardsmen Jeran had assigned to their protection. The others had followed Dahr into the fray, hoping to use surprise to their advantage. They would hit Tylor's troops with all they had, keep the fighting going until Martyn and the others were gone, then run for the mouth of the valley.

That thought brough Martyn back to reality. As long as he and Treloran were visible, the others would not try to save themselves. "Let's move it, Guardsmen!" he called sharply. "We have to get out of here!"

"Good to have you back, my Prince!" Jasova said dryly.

* * * * * * * * * * * * * * * * * * *

The world was chaos. All around him, his men were dying. Arrows rained down from every direction. Wolves, mountain cats, and bears charged his troops, gouging with fang and claw. Hawks and eagles, falcons and raptors dove from the sky, clawing at the eyes of his warriors, tearing their bows to shreds with their beaks. A herd of moose charged back and forth across the valley, trampling everyone in their path.

The ground still shook from the explosions that had shattered his army. One of the pillars of fire had died, but the other was climbing the far side of the valley, lighting trees and brush on fire. Two charred lines of destruction cut through the green grass around him. Bodies were everywhere, some lifeless, others crying in agony.

Through the thickening smoke, Tylor caught a glimpse of the giant. A titan, bleeding from a dozen gashes, wielding a sword over ten hands in length. He had eyes of golden fire, and his snarls blended in with the sounds of the other animals. The giant left death in his wake, death and the cries of the wounded, all whimpering the same word. Monster.

For a moment, the smoke cleared, and Tylor saw the one he sought. Trembling with rage, he approached at a run, his sword already poised to strike. It was *his* fault. *All* his fault.

Jeran lay on the ground unconscious, and Tylor, so intent on his target, did not see the body at his feet until it was too late. Stumbling, he twisted so he would land on the side of his armor with the fewest spikes and let his sword go, allowing the blade to fall free, minimizing the risk to himself.

The impact was jarring. With a groan, he pulled himself to a sitting position and went to kick the body out of his way, but stopped halfway through the motion. A gasp escaped the Bull's lips, and he leaned in close, pulling the helmet from his head.

"Grysbin!" he cried, looking at the body of his son. Squeezing his eye shut, he willed himself not to cry. When he opened it again, his rage returned, replacing his momentary weakness. Scrambling for his sword, he started for the Odara boy, ready to kill.

This time, a live body stood in his way. "Out of my way, Katya!" he snarled, trying to push past her.

"Uncle, NO!" she cried, keeping herself between Tylor and Jeran. "You know the Master's rule! All with the Gift must be brought to *Dranakohr*! No exceptions! Jeran has the Gift!"

"Two sons!" Tylor shrieked. "He's killed two of my sons!"

"The Master will kill the rest if you disobey his wishes!" Katya reminded him. "Think, Uncle, which is the better revenge? A swift death to an unconscious body, or a lifetime suffering in the mines?"

Ignoring his niece, Tylor tried to push past, but she would not allow it. Gripping him in a tight embrace, she refused to release him until he calmed.

Slowly, the Bull's breathing slowed, and he came to his senses. "Enough, Katya!" he said at last. "Enough! You win." Katya released him, and Tylor stepped back, surveying the scene. Around him his men were still disorganized, but it seemed like the worst of the fighting had passed.

He tried to walk, but something was pulling on his foot. Confused, he looked down, surprised to see a squirrel clamped to his leg, trying to gnaw through his armor. He kicked the thing away and called for Halwer.

His aide was at his side in a moment. "Tie up that body!" Tylor ordered, looking distastefully at Jeran. "He's a Mage, so keep him unconscious until we can drug him." Nodding, Halwer hurried to obey.

Tylor stopped him. "The Master would be displeased if the Odara died before we got him to *Dranakohr*, but if he offers any resistance...."

Halwer bowed. "He will regret it, my Lord."

Tylor turned to Katya. "Gather the men. However many remain. See if there are any other prisoners from your party. If so, keep them alive. For now."

"Where shall I tell the men we're going?" Katya asked.

"We return to *Dranakohr*."

* * * * * * * * * * * * * * * * * * * *

The valley floor was covered in thick, dark smoke. Martyn stared back from his position at the mouth of the narrow, rocky passageway. The others were already out of sight, and Martyn had promised that he would only be a moment, but he had to take one last look at the resting place of his friends.

Little could be seen of the once-green valley. An occasional shriek echoed up to the prince's ears, but for the most part, the sounds of fighting had ceased. Martyn's eyes burned, and as he squeezed them shut, two tears fell, landing on the stones at his feet.

He brushed his sleeve across his eyes and stared down at the valley floor murderously. "I told you once that I would make you pay if you ever hurt him," Martyn hissed. "I don't care if it takes the rest of my life, Katya Durange, you will suffer as no one has ever suffered before!"

Steeling himself, Martyn turned and hurried down the path, disappearing behind the thick rock walls. Jasova and the others were waiting for him, standing protectively around Treloran.

"Let's go," he ordered, pushing to the front. "It's time we returned to Kaper. I have a war to fight."

Afterthoughts

Tylor's troops marched east, and the valley slowly grew quiet. In the distance, a creature howled in anguish and loss, its mourning cries echoed by the wolves that ran in packs through the thick forest and broken rock.

Eventually, even those sounds faded, until there was nothing but the rustle of the wind and the crackle of the dying fires. The breezes strengthened, and the white smoke, which had blanketed the valley for most of the day, slowly dissipated.

Two figures emerged from the fog, standing on a lonely promontory that overlooked the valley. One was a raven-haired beauty, dressed in a gown of blue, the other an old man, his hair and beard completely white. Side by side, they stared silently at the ground below.

The woman sniffed, trying hard to keep the tears from her eyes. "Are you sure this was the right thing to do?" she asked, raising her head to look at the old man. Her question was half an accusation, half a plea for explanation. Her eyes demanded justification for what they had done.

An uncomfortable silence followed. "Right?" Aemon repeated, emotion straining his voice. "I don't know what's right anymore, Jes." Tears fell unashamedly down his cheeks, and Jes was surprised to see such emotion in her mentor. "What we did to those boys can't be right...It can't be!"

The great Mage's shoulders slumped, and he hung his head. "But what choice did we have?" Now his tone pleaded, begged, for understanding. "We knew what would happen if Dahr died at Kohr's Heart. We knew what would happen if Martyn and Treloran died returning to Alrendria. We know what will happen if Jeran can't learn control of his Gift faster than anyone in the history of Madryn!"

"Does that truly justify what you've done?" The pained expression on Aemon's face prompted her to amend her words. "What we've done?"

"Why do you two insist on personalizing these things?" asked a new voice. They turned, shocked to discover that they were not alone. Emperor Alwellyn stepped from the trees, green robes hanging loose on his gaunt frame.

"What are you doing here?" Aemon asked, surprised.

"Did you really expect me to stay away?" the Emperor laughed weakly. "I am just as responsible for this as you. Jeran may be your grandson, but he is my friend. The first friend I have made in a long, long time. I could not just abandon him to his fate."

"It is not as bad as it seems," Rannarik stated, stepping from the trees opposite the Emperor. A bandage was wrapped tightly around his arm and his face was pale, but other that that, the *Tsha'ma* looked healthy.

Aemon looked around suspiciously. "Is there anyone else out there?" he asked irritably.

Rannarik shook his head. "The others wait in the cottage. We should not keep them waiting long." The Tribesman looked around. "Any sign of Dahr?"

Aemon shook his head. "What do you mean," Jes asked, turning to Rannarik, "things are not as bad as they seem?"

"Few died today," Rannarik replied with a look into the valley. "At least, few on our side. The Dark One's forces, however, suffered great losses, considering how few they fought against. The princes live, and the bonds of friendship between the three Races are stronger than before. Stronger than they have been in a long time.

"Jeran was captured," Rannarik admitted with a sad nod, "along with a few others, but," here the Tribesman looked pointedly at Aemon, "I believe Jeran's capture was the reason this attack was orchestrated."

Jes turned an icy gaze on Aemon. The Mage's cheeks were red, and he refused to meet her eyes. "How could you!" she yelled, her temper flaring. "He's your grandson!" She lunged at him, her hand swinging back to slap. Rannarik restrained her, grunting from the stress put on his weakened arm. "He's your grandson!" Jes repeated, the strength fading from her voice.

"Later, Jes," Aemon answered, his voice strained. "I will explain later." Another tear threatened to fall down the old Mage's face. He wiped it away. "Come on," he said, opening a Gate. "There's nothing left for us to see here."

* * * * * * * * * * * * * * * * * * *

The tents were quiet. *Cha'khun* had ended, and the tribes were beginning their journeys to the Winter Lands. Most of the smaller tribes were days gone, and the Sahna had departed for their mountain homes at sunrise. The Afelda planned to leave before the next full moon, which was but a few days off.

A large party of Tachan Hunters even now rode south, following Kal and the child known among the Blood as Little Tiger. Kohr's Heart was emptying, and it brought a great sadness to Yarchik, who sat alone within his tent. In his dreams he spoke with Garun, and the God had told him that this *Cha'khun* would be his last.

But what a Cha'khun it was! he thought to himself. *One which will live in story until the world is consumed by the Nothing.* Once, as a small child many winters earlier, he had attended a *Cha'khun* with all of the tribes. Never had he believed he would see Kohr's Heart overflowing with the might of his people again.

Behind him, the flap of his tent pulled aside, and a figure entered, offering no greeting. Yarchik remained still until the figure was less than a pace behind him, then his voice cracked out in a harsh whisper. "Why have your returned, my son? Are you here to finish what your *Kohr'adjin* could not accomplish?"

Kraltir stepped back in surprise, his eyes widening warily. "You were never the target, father," he said defensively, but the lie sounded hollow on his lips.

"You dishonor yourself enough, Kraltir. Why waste what little remains on falsehood?"

"I have not come here to kill you," Kraltir insisted. "I come only to tell you that Norvik is dead. The Channa are without a *Kranach*."

Yarchik laughed, a dry, grating laugh. "Do you think this treachery will earn you his title? You will never be *Kranach*." Kraltir started to walk around his father's litter, but Yarchik snapped, "Do not step into the light! I will not poison my eyes with the sight of you."

A hand clamped down on Yarchik's shoulder, and Kraltir bent low. "It is not *Kranach* I wish to be!" he whispered, low and guttural.

"Then best you kill me now, Servant of Darkness!" Yarchik snarled, his heart breaking anew. "You will never have better opportunity."

"I will not kill you, Father!" Kraltir replied, his hand squeezing his father's shoulder painfully.

"But you will, my son," Yarchik replied coolly, ignoring the pain. "Blood will turn upon itself," he said, reciting from the *Prah'phetia*, "and evil will descend upon the Blood. The Channa will fall first, sundered by betrayal, scorched by ambition, burned by the fire of the sun."

Yarchik paused, trying to keep the tears from his eyes. "When servants of Kohr ravage the land, when the banished horde returns for vengeance, this will be the time of the Trial, when the Children of Garun can atone for their sins. Where is *Cho Korahn Garun*? Where is our Savior, who will lead us against the darkness? In the Anvil did His heart stop beating. His soul He chases through the icy mountains. Will the *Korahn* find life anew, or will He lead the Blood into the jaws of the Nothing?"

Kraltir's hand trembled against his father's shoulder. "Go!" Yarchik hissed. "Do not return until you are ready to kill me!"

Frightened, Kraltir let go his grip and ran.

* *

Ryan rode to the front of his army. The crown of Ra Tachan, still too large for his head, settled uncomfortably around his ears, and he pushed it back so that the golden circlet did not block his eyes. Before him, the army of Taren was arrayed against his own forces, and he reached for his sword, ready to lead the advance. He managed to bare half a finger's width of steel before a larger hand closed around his own.

"You aren't planning ta join the fight," Gral asked, "are you, cub?"

Ryan shivered at his commander's grim visage. Gral was scarred in a thousand places; some were old, never-healed wounds and others were fresh cuts, still-weeping blood. The left half of his face was a melted ruin of flesh, and his eyes–one dark blue and the other solid white, without even a pupil–were predatory and cruel.

Ryan steeled himself. "That is what kings do!" he said, a bit petulant-ly. "I will lead my men to victory." Glaring at Gral, he raised his chin proudly. "And you will call me King Ryan, not cub!"

"Don't be ridiculous, cub," Gral chuckled. "If you go riding down this hill, you'll be dead before the battle starts, even if you manage to stay in the saddle. Your place is here, serving as a beacon, reminding these upstarts who their true king is."

"But I want to fight in a real battle!" Ryan whined.

"Trust me, cub," Gral sneered, "you don't have the stomach for it." He grabbed the young man's reins and led him back to the men protecting the banner of Ra Tachan. "Guard your King!" he snarled at the soldiers.

Leaning over, he patted Ryan on the head. "Leave the fighting to the big boys, lad. Your uncles wouldn't like it if I let anything happen to you."

"How long will it take to conquer Taren?" Ryan asked, his lips half pouted.

"We'll have these traitors crushed in a few days," Gral told him. "Once we have things under control, we'll take the army to Feldar, just to remind them whose empire they belong to.

"And then we'll attack Gilead?" Ryan asked, almost eagerly.

"Patience, cub," Gral said with a smile, wondering if he'd ever make a real killer out of this feeble, womanly child. "It seems your cousin in Rachannon no longer considers his lands a part of Ra Tachan. We'll have to deal with them before Gilead."

Ryan pouted again. "When are my uncles coming?" he asked. He had always been eager to meet his uncles, the Bull and the Scorpion.

Gral laughed loudly. "Not for a while, cub. But I wouldn't be so eager for their arrival, were I you. I doubt you'll be king for long once Tylor returns to Ra Tachan!" With another laugh, he turned his horse and rode to the front of the Tachan army.

* * * * * * * * * * * * * * * * * * *

"How nice of you to meet with me," Salos said, accepting a glass of blood red wine from a waiting servant.

"Are you sure no one saw you enter?" Jysin asked, his eyes shifting from side to side nervously.

The dark-robed Mage chuckled, a low and rasping sound. "How little faith you have in my abilities! I assure you, once I am gone, not even this servant will remember my visit. You have nothing to fear."

The man visibly relaxed, drinking deeply from his own goblet. "I must admit," he said with a weak laugh, "I was worried when you first contacted me. But your offer was most…intriguing."

Salos smiled. "I had a feeling you would see the…advantages…in my proposal."

Jysin nodded, drained his wine, then folded his hands in his lap. Leaning forward, he stared at Salos eagerly. "Tell me more."

* * * * * * * * * * * * * * * * * * * *

There was a knock on the chamber door. "Enter, Astalian," the Emperor said, setting down the time-worn volume he was reading. The door opened slowly, and the *Hohe Chatorra* entered. The Emperor instantly saw the agitation on Astalian's face, the hesitation in his manner.

"Your Eminence," Astalian began, "I am sorry to bother you in your chambers, but there is a matter I felt needed your immediate attention."

The Emperor waved for him to enter. "Tell your friend to come in as well." Astalian's eyes widened, but he craned his neck to the side and spoke to his companion. Together, the two Elves entered the Emperor's private chambers.

"Sit," the Emperor told them, waving his guests to chairs opposite his own. He rang a tiny bell, and servants appeared, carrying three delicate glasses and a bottle of Aelvin wine. Astalian and the other Elf sat while the wine was poured. The Emperor used the silence to study his visitors.

Astalian appeared nervous, a trait uncommon in the loyal warrior. His companion, travel-stained and weary, as if he had spent many days on the road, looked worse. "Drink," the Emperor commanded when the Elves were handed their wine. "Your news cannot be that dire. A moment or two will make little difference."

Silently, the two sipped from their long-stemmed glasses. Once his guests had relaxed, the Emperor smiled. "Now tell me what is so important that you needed to bring this man to me before he could bathe."

The Elf's face turned bright red, and he cast his eyes to the floor. The Emperor waved dismissively. "Do not take offense. I am sure your need is great, else Astalian would not have allowed you here." The Emperor's eyes flashed. "He is *very* protective."

The Elf stood and bowed. "My name is Nebari el'e Salerian. I was in command of Your Holiness' Third Archer Regiment. I have much to tell you, my Emperor, concerning the 'war' we fought with the Garun'ah and my time spent among the Wildmen." The Elf swallowed. "I am afraid it is not a pleasant tale."

The Emperor remained silent for a long time. "You were captured by the Garun'ah?" he asked at last, tapping a withered finger against his lip. "The Tribesmen rarely take prisoners. When they do, even fewer are released."

"I owe two for my freedom," Nebari stated. "Kal *uvan* Arik, *Kranach* of the Tacha, and Dahr Odara, a Tribesman raised by Humans."

"I have heard of him," the Emperor replied, nodding sagely.

As Nebari told his story, the Emperor's face grew dark, and when he was done, the Emperor could not decide whether to be furious or sad. "Luran has ever been a troublesome child," he finally said, "but never did I suspect him of such treachery. Fabricating attacks by the Garun'ah. Inciting a war between our peoples."

"Certainly, he had help among the Tribesmen," Astalian stated, uncharacteristically defending the treasonous Aelvin Prince.

"Whether he acted alone in this madness is irrelevant. This time, his transgressions are unforgivable." The Emperor fell silent, considering his response. "Nebari, your service to the Empire is noted. I wish for you to return to the border as soon as you are ready. With Astalian's permission, I would put you in charge of Our border patrols." Astalian nodded his approval.

"I would ask that you seek out the Tribesmen," the Emperor added. "We have reopened relations with the Humans. Perhaps now is the time to approach our other cousins as well. I do not want this kind of foolishness to occur again." Nebari nodded, bowed to the Emperor, and asked for permission to depart.

Once he was gone, the Emperor turned to Astalian. "Tell *Ael Chatorra* to find Luran," he ordered sadly. "He is to be brought to me. Alive if possible, but if he puts up any resistance…" The Emperor could not finish the statement.

"It will be as you say, my Emperor."

* * * * * * * * * * * * * * * * * * *

The ShadowMage materialized in the center of the room, startling its two occupants. "I apologize for my tardiness," the Mage said slowly. "I had other duties to attend to."

"Where is Salos?" demanded Murdir, King of Corsa.

"The High Inquisitor," the Mage replied politely, "regrets that he cannot attend this meeting himself. He sent me in his stead. I assure you, I have the High Inquisitor's full confidence. Any arrangements we make today will be fully binding."

The second man frowned. "I am having doubts."

"Doubts you are allowed," the Mage replied, smiling wickedly. "You may even have reservations. But you have made a deal with the Master, and the Darklord does not take kindly to those who betray him. Bear that in mind, should you wish to renege on your part of our bargain."

"What of New Arkam?" the man demanded. "What if Chovra decides to take advantage of the situation?"

"King Chovra will be dealt with in time," the Mage replied. "For now, it's more important that we keep Mathis distracted from events in the east. The two of you must begin raiding Alrendria." The Mage's smile returned. "Without Geffram Iban to aid them, you'll likely fare better than before."

The second man did not look convinced. "Calm yourself, Hasna," Murdir said, struggling to hide his utter contempt for the man. "If it eases your mind, I will have my raiders attack New Arkam's coastal towns. It should be sufficient distraction for you to pull your troops north to aid in our assault."

"Excellent." The Mage offered them both a slight, cold smile. "Now perhaps we can move on to other matters...."

* * * * * * * * * * * * * * * * * * * *

They reached the top of the hill, and the towers of Grenz appeared in the distance. Martyn gasped, and his shock was echoed by those around him. His surprise was not directed at the city, for they had fully expected to reach Grenz by afternoon, but at the vast warhost that approached.

More than two thousand mounted warriors walked in their direction, under the banner of Alrendria. At its front rode a familiar, blonde-bearded figure.

With a smile, Martyn heeled his horse to a gallop, urging his horse for even greater speed. The Guardsmen followed, crying out joyously at the sight of their countrymen. Even the Garun'ah seemed elated. They followed the Alrendrians at a run, almost keeping up with the horses.

"Father!" Martyn cried as he neared the King, pulling his horse to a stop and jumping from the saddle. Mathis was already on the ground, running toward the prince. They met in the middle of the field, clasping each other in a tight bear hug. "Father!" Martyn repeated.

"Martyn!" The relief in Mathis' voice was pronounced. "I never thought to see you again, boy! Lady Jessandra sent word to Kaper as quickly as she could. We sailed immediately, but I fully expected to have to scour the Tribal Lands for you."

Eventually Mathis released his son, though his instincts told him to keep the boy close. He looked at the approaching mass of Garun'ah. "What is this?" he asked curiously.

"Our allies!" Martyn answered. "The ones we've been hoping for."

A third horse pulled up next to them, and Treloran dismounted, bowing deeply to the King. Martyn made a grandiose gesture. "Father, may I present Treloran el'e Kelemeilion, grandson of Emperor Alwellyn, and His representative in Alrendria until the embassy arrives."

King Mathis bowed and offered his hand. "Well met, Prince Treloran," he said with a pleasant smile. "Though I would have preferred a more suitable location for our introduction."

Treloran's answering smile was equally warm. "I am glad to be able to meet you at all, King Mathis."

Mathis's eyes were drawn back to the Garun'ah. "But what of them? Surely they were not part of your bargain with the Emperor!"

Martyn smiled. "It was Jeran," he explained. "Jeran and Dahr. Between the two of them, they've secured us alliances with both the Elves and the Garun'ah!" Suddenly, Martyn's smile faded.

"Where are they?" Mathis asked, scanning the crowd. He regretted his question instantly; the look on Martyn's face was answer enough. "Gods!" Mathis said with a violent exhale of breath. "Oh Gods, no!"

He wanted to cry out, the news was almost more than he could bear, but instead steeled his expression; he preferred to grieve in private. Raising his head, he met the eyes of the Garun'ah. "For returning my son to me, I owe you much," he said in welcome. "Come! Let us celebrate our new alliance with a feast in your honor."

"I have much to tell you, Father," Martyn whispered.

"Later," Mathis replied. "Tonight, let us celebrate our reunion. There will be time enough tomorrow to mourn."

* * * * * * * * * * * * * * * * * * * *

Jeran was pushed through a dark passage. His head spun from the drug they fed him day and night; his muscles were stiff from long days tied in the back of a wagon. A wave of dizziness passed over him, and he stumbled, squeezing his eyes shut in anticipation of the lash he knew he would receive.

To his surprise, no blow fell. Warily, he opened one eye, then the other. Another hand pushed him from behind, urging him forward. Not wishing to press his luck, Jeran followed.

Tylor, still wearing his black armor, though the helmet had been discarded, led the way. "Where are the others?" Jeran asked, the words slurring in his mouth. He remembered there being others in the wagon, others captured at the time of the battle; though at the moment, he could not have named them if his life depended on it.

Tylor ignored him, and Jeran stopped walking. His guard shoved him, but he refused to move. Summoning his courage, he called out more loudly, "Where are the others?"

Tylor stopped in mid-stride. He turned toward Jeran slowly, his good eye seething with anger. "They are being cared for," he replied, and his tone suggested that their care was not something he relished. "The Master wishes to add them to his work force." A smile touched the Bull's face. "Better for them if the Darklord had allowed them a quick and painless death at my hands."

Tylor continued down the hall, and the guard pushed Jeran again. He resisted at first, but Tylor called back, "Don't hurt him any more than you have to, but if he refuses to walk, carry him."

Reluctantly, Jeran moved forward, noting a mild buzzing in his head. With every step through the dark, twisting passageway, the buzzing worsened, growing in volume, pounding against the inside of his skull until he could no longer stand the pain. He dropped to his knees in anguish.

A dark figure was at his side instantly. "You feel the Boundary already?" asked a sibilant voice. "You must be very strong indeed. The Master will be pleased." Hands drew him to his feet, and the voice spoke again. "Focus your gift, child, but do not try to handle the flows. I won't like it if you try to use your magic on me."

"More importantly," added a voice from Jeran's other side, and a second ShadowMage stepped into position, "the Boundary won't like it if you try to use magic this close. And the Boundary is far crueler than we."

"We're trying though," the first ShadowMage assured Jeran with a smile.

"Enough!" snarled Tylor. "Let's get this over with."

Jeran was led from the passage into a lighted chamber. The room was spartan, with no decoration or ornamentation, and only two entrances: the one through which Jeran was pushed and an identical one across the way.

The effort of holding his focus nauseated Jeran, and he was surprised that his magic had not yet run wild. He wondered absently, between waves of dizziness, whether it was the ShadowMagi or some effect of the Boundary that held his Gift in check.

From out of the shadows emerged a frightening figure, a legend made flesh. Long, white robes glided silently across the floor, but they stopped only a few paces inside the hall. "Bring him closer," whispered a familiar voice.

Jeran resisted, but was drawn forward against his will. Blood red eyes stared at him as he approached. Pale lips compressed in a thin line. A bony hand reached up to push back a stray strand of curly, white hair.

"Jeran," the Darklord said in a sibilant whisper, shaking his head sadly, almost compassionately. "I wish we had been able to meet under more amicable circumstances. Truly I do. I have come to enjoy our little chats, despite the consternation you sometimes cause."

Lorthas smiled and made a tisking sound with his tongue. "You have put me in quite a spot though, my little friend," he chided, wagging a finger admonishingly. "I wasn't ready for you to join us yet. I don't even have suitable accommodations prepared.

"Perhaps it's for the best, though," the Darklord added with a shrug. "You have the nasty habit of interfering with my plans. It will be easier to keep you out of trouble while you're here in *Dranakohr*."

Jeran blanched, and an icy smile split the Darklord's face. "I do have a proposition that may interest you, if you'd care to hear it. You've had the chance to listen to my story; you know I fight for the good of those with the Gift. Our goals are the same, Jeran! We both want to end the suffering that plagues Madryn. We both seek peace among the Races. With you at my side, our goal could be reached ever so much faster.

"You will have whatever you need. Troops… time… the ability to train your Gift… anything! Whatever you desire will be yours, Jeran. All you have to do is swear yourself to me." Tylor stiffened, and the gaze he fixed on Lorthas could have melted stone. He opened his mouth, but Lorthas silenced him with a gesture.

Jeran shook off the ShadowMagi's hands and approached the Darklord. "Not too close," Lorthas warned, raising a hand in warning. Tiny blue sparks began to dance in the air.

With a tight grimace, Lorthas pressed his palm flat, and the sparks intensified; tiny bolts of lightning jumped up and down the Darklord's arm. "You're standing close to the Boundary. In your weakened state, touching it might not be the best idea."

Jeran squared his shoulders and met the Darklord's gaze. He wondered if he would be so brave without the Boundary separating between him and Lorthas. "I will never serve you, Darklord," he said defiantly, speaking each word slowly and clearly, his icy blue eyes flashing.

Lorthas took a slow breath. "I'm sorry to hear you say that, Jeran." Closing his eyes, he lowered his head and shook it sadly. "You have no idea how much it hurts to hear you say that."

His eyes snapped open, and the Darklord's fixed a fiery, confidant gaze on Jeran. "But I have faith. In time you will come to share my vision."

He turned to walk away, but paused. When he spoke, his words sounded sincerely regretful. "Until then, you leave me no choice, I'm afraid." To the ShadowMagi, he said, "Collar him!"

Hands grabbed Jeran from behind. He struggled, but was pulled away from the Boundary, toward the dark passages of the caves below. "You may work him with the others," Jeran heard Lorthas say to Tylor, "but I don't want him or his companions seriously harmed. And Tylor, I will not stand for any of your foolishness. Set your childish feud aside! Jeran is to be our ally, not our enemy. I expect you to treat him accordingly."

Tylor's response was drowned out by one of the ShadowMagi. "You should have sworn yourself to him," the Mage told Jeran. "There's no punishment worse than the collar."

"It's just like the Boundary," the other Mage added. "You'll be able to focus your Gift, you can even hold the flows if you have a mind to, but you won't be able to use magic. Won't be able to feel the power!" The Mage shivered. "How anyone who's tasted magic can willingly give it up…?"

Jeran did not hear the rest. His mind was whirling. Able to focus magic but not use it. The words of his teachers came back to him. "The hardest part of training is learning how to hold the flows for extended periods without the magic running wild," Jes had told him. "This is why an experienced Mage must accompany his apprentice for the first five to ten winters of training."

Emperor Alwellyn: "It will be seasons before you can hold magic for more than a moment. If you try, it will run wild, releasing itself with unpredictable results. For some, it takes decades of diligent training before they master magic. But the more you seize it, the longer you hold your focus, the greater strength and control you will acquire. Repetition is the key."

Tanar: "Be careful when focusing your will. Holding the flows too long can be dangerous—not just for yourself, but for those around you. Until you have mastered magic, there's no point in teaching you how to use it. But no matter how adept a pupil you are, it will be a long time before you have complete mastery over your Gift."

"The collar won't let me use magic?" Jeran asked.

The ShadowMage misinterpreted the anticipation in Jeran's voice for fear. "Forever will the sweetness of magic be beyond your grasp. You will be forced to live your life as a common, never able to realize your full potential."

Realization and understanding came with the ShadowMage's statement, and Jeran laughed. It was a mad laughter, almost a cackle, and he shook with the force of it. It echoed through the halls of *Dranakohr*, and wherever it was heard, conversations stopped, heads were lifted, and curious stares were cast into darkened passageways.

The laughter even reached the Darklord. He paused in the middle of issuing orders to Tylor, and his eyes moved slowly toward the passage down which Jeran had been taken.

As he listened to the laughter, a small frown spread across the Darklord's face.

The Lands of Madryn

Ael Shataq: Created at the end of the MageWar (0 A.R.), when the Alliance of the Four Races raised the Boundary to imprison the Darklord Lorthas and the bulk of his ShadowMagi. For the last eight hundred winters, Madryn's most vile criminals have been banished to *Ael Shataq*, but little is known of the lands behind the Boundary; none of the explorers who ventured in have ever returned.

Alrendria: The first land ruled by man, ceded to Humans at the conclusion of the Great Rebellion (5152 B.B.). Alrendria is a confederation of Families organized into Minor and Great Houses, all under the authority of a common king. Originally called *Ael Ehrandrylla* (the Land of Freedom), Alrendria once spanned half of Madryn, and its Great Houses numbered in the hundreds, but wars and rebellion have greatly reduced its size and influence. Today, only six Great Houses remain: Batai, Morrena, Velan, Odara, Menglor, and Aurelle.

Corsa: Once part of Alrendria, present day Corsa was annexed by House Arkam during the Alrendrian Secession (1257-1255 B.B.). Following the MageWar, Corsa separated from the Arkam Imperium, but many of the Imperium's prejudices and hatreds remain intact.

Feldar: Once of the Tachan Lands, Feldar did not become a nation of its own until the end of the Tachan War (754 A.R.). It is an unremarkable land, isolated from the majority of Madryn, and most remembered for being the center of the Purge, a dark period in Madryn's history in which Tachan Inquisitors sought to free mankind from the 'curse' of magic.

Gilead: Originally part of the Tribal Lands, the Garun'ah gave Gilead to Humans for their aid in defeating the Drekka during Aemon's Revolt (4208 B.B.). Located in the center of Madryn, it quickly became the center of trade between Alrendria and the Garun'ah. With the founding of the Tachan Empire, Gilead was caught between two strong opposing powers, a fact that has made the nation increasingly isolationistic in recent winters.

Illendrylla: Located deep within the Great Forest of the north, Illendrylla is all that remains of the Aelvin Empire, which once spanned the breadth of Madryn. The current emperor, Alwellyn the Eternal, has ruled since the end of the Great Rebellion (5152 B.B.), when the Humans and Garun'ah overthrew their Aelvin oppressors.

The Lands of Madryn

Midlyn: Prior to the Alrendrian Succession (1257-1255 B.B.), Midlyn was part of Alrendria, and its capital city of Jule was perhaps the most prestigious of the Mage Academies. The city was annexed at the beginning of the Succession, and the Academy destroyed, but it took half a century for King Peitr to quell the resistance. Midlyn was separated from the Arkam Imperium at the conclusion of the MageWar (0 A.R.). It is now a prosperous trade nation, the only land route between New Arkam and the rest of Madryn.

New Arkam: Originally part of Alrendria and the center of House Arkam, the nation of New Arkam has a tragic history. Upon learning that his son Roya would not assume the Alrendrian throne, Lord Peitr Arkam declared war on the other Great Houses. The Alrendrian Succession lasted three winters and resulted in the creation of the Arkam Imperium, an oppressive empire remembered for its harsh treatment of those born with the gift of magic. During the MageWar, the Imperium was one of the Darklord's most fervent allies, a union of opposing ideologies that has perplexed scholars for nearly a millennium. The Imperium was dissolved in the winters following the MageWar, after a successful coup led by the crown prince, and New Arkam was returned to him for his service. New Arkam is now a small nation, isolated from the majority of Madryn.

Ra Tachan: Located in southeastern Madryn, Ra Tachan once belonged to the Garun'ah. Following the end of the MageWar (0 A.R.) a long running rift between the King of Alrendria and the High Seat of House Torvein resulted in Lord Torvein and his people leaving Alrendria and resettling in the Tribal Lands southeast of Gilead. Refugees from the war flooded to this new land, which quickly expanded, displacing the tribes of Garun'ah. In less than a century, the Tachan Empire became a nation to rival Alrendria, encompassing all of present Ra Tachan, Taren, Feldar, and Rachannon. A tyrannical society, the Empire encouraged hatred of both the Magi and Madryn's other races. The Tachan War (754 A.R.) brought an end to the empire. With its King dead and Crown Prince exiled through the Boundary, a regency was established to govern Ra Tachan until its heir came of age.

Rachannon: Originally part of the Tribal Lands, Rachannon was later conquered by the Tachan Empire, and only became its own soveriegn nation at the conclusion of the Tachan War. Rachannen are a rough and rugged people, and their land has become the center of Madryn's slave trade.

The Lands of Madryn

Roya: A large, mountainous island off the southern coast of Alrendria, Roya was mostly uninhabited until the winters following the Alrendrian Succession (1257-1255 B.B.). Roya Arkam was the son of Lord Peitr Arkam, but he did not share his father's hatreds. When the Succession began, Roya gathered those loyal to Alrendria and led them to Kaper. During the war, he commanded the Alrendrian forces and was instrumental in reclaiming much of the land annexed by his father's forces, but his service went unrewarded; in 1255 B.B. he was banished from Alrendria by King Norin. After Norin's death, the banishment was rescinded, but Roya had already established a new nation. The alliance he formed with Alrendria has survived undiminished for two millennia.

Taren: Originally part of the Tribal Lands, Taren was annexed by the Tachan Empire in the years following the MageWar. Located at the southern end of the Tachan peninsula, the Tarens have a long history of resisting their conquerors. Taren became its own nation following the Tachan War (754 A.R.).

Tribal Lands: At the end of the Great Rebellion (5152 B.B.), the Tribal Lands stretched from the river Celaan to the Eastern Ocean (excepting the Great Forest of the Elves) but its size has been greatly reduced over the intervening winters. Following Aemon's Revolt (4207-4208 B.B.) the lands of the Drekka tribe were given to the Humans as a gesture of gratitude for their help in the war (see Gilead), and after the MageWar, the Tachan Empire conquered much of the remaining Tribal Lands, forcing thousands upon thousands of Garun'ah to leave their ancestral homes. Today, the Tribal Lands form a region bounded by the Anvil in the west, Illendrylla in the east, and the nations of Gilead and Rachannon in the south. Though once common visitors to the lands of man, the Garun'ah have grown wary around Humans and now rarely venture out of their own territory. As a consequence, few alive can recognize a Tribesman on sight, and much of what is 'known' about the tribes is a mixture of myth, rumor, and falsehood.

B.B. - Before Boundary
A.R. - After Raising

About the Author

Bret Funk was born in New Jersey, but relocated to New Orleans, Louisiana in 1994 to attend Tulane University. After six years and two degrees, he decided to shift his focus to writing. In addition to the Boundary's Fall series, he is the author of numerous short stories and articles.

Bret_Funk@TyrannosaurusPress.com

We hope you enjoyed *Sword of Honor*

To order this and other Tyrannosaurus Press titles,
Check your local bookstore, or order an autographed copy from us!

Tyrannosaurus Press Quick Order Form

Path of Glory (ISBN 0-9718819-1-X)   Trade Paperback   **$19.95**

_____ copies   _____ Autographed   _____ Not Autographed

Sword of Honor (ISBN: 0-9718819-0-1) Trade Paperback   **$19.99**

_____ copies   _____ Autographed   _____ Not Autographed

Check our website regularly for promotions and new title information.

For shipping and handling, (USPS Priority Mail) please enclose an additional $3.95 for the first book and $1.95 for each additional book; for USPS Media Mail, rates are $2.00 for the first book and $1.00 for each additional book. Other shipping arrangements available upon request.

Residents of Louisiana, please include appropriate sales tax. (4% state / 9% Orleans Parish).

Payment must accompany order. Allow three weeks for delivery.

My check or money order for $_____ is enclosed.
Credit Card orders are accepted at our online bookstore!
(Our secure server uses Paypal, an online transaction service)

Name: _____

Organization: _____

Address: _____

City/State/Zip: _____

Phone: _____ E-Mail: _____

Make your check payable and return to:

Tyrannosaurus Press
PO Box 15061
New Orleans, LA 70175-5061
Phone (504) 284-3313 • **Fax** (206) 984-0448
E-mail: Info@TyrannosaurusPress.com
Web Address: www.TyrannosaurusPress.com